# MR. MOTO

## FOUR COMPLETE NOVELS

## ABOUT THE AUTHOR

JOHN P. MARQUAND was born in 1893 in Wilmington, Delaware. Marquand graduated from Harvard in 1915, and settled in Newbury, Massachusetts. He worked as a reporter for the *Boston Transcript* and the *New York Herald Tribune* and served as a lieutenant in the army during World War I.

An extremely popular writer, Marquand was noted for his novels of manners, which earned him the title of "martini-aged Victorian." In 1938 he won the Pulitzer Prize for his novel *The Late George Apley.*

His character Mr. Moto, a Japanese agent, was a highly successful creation, both in the book and in the movie version, in which Peter Lorre played Mr. Moto.

Marquand died in 1960 in Newbury, Massachusetts.

# MR. MOTO

## FOUR COMPLETE NOVELS

By John P. Marquand

YOUR TURN, MR. MOTO

THINK FAST, MR. MOTO

MR. MOTO IS SO SORRY

RIGHT YOU ARE, MR. MOTO

Avenel Books • New York

This Omnibus edition was previously published in separate volumes under the titles:

*Your Turn, Mr. Moto* (originally published as *No Hero*) copyright MCMXXXV by John P. Marquand. Copyright renewed © MCMLXIII by John P. Marquand and Christina M. Welch.
*Think Fast, Mr. Moto* copyright MCMXXVIII by John P. Marquand. Copyright © renewed MCMLXV by John P. Marquand, Jr., and Christina M. Welch.
*Mr. Moto Is So Sorry* copyright MCMXXXVIII by John P. Marquand. Copyright © renewed MCMLXVI by John P. Marquand, Jr., and Christina M. Welch.
*Right You Are, Mr. Moto* (originally published as *Stopover Tokyo*) copyright © MCMLVII by John P. Marquand.

This 1983 edition is published by Avenel Books, distributed by Crown Publishers, Inc., by arrangement with Little, Brown & Company, Inc.

Manufactured in the United States of America

**Library of Congress Cataloging in Publication Data**
Marquand, John P. (John Phillips), 1893–1960.
Mr. Moto : four complete novels.
Contents: Your turn, Mr. Moto—Think fast, Mr. Moto—Mr. Moto is so sorry—Right you are, Mr. Moto.
1. Detective and mystery stories, American. I. Title.
PS3525.A6695A6 1983 813'.52 83-12269

ISBN: 0-517-421844

h g f e d c b a

# CONTENTS

# YOUR TURN, MR. MOTO

# 1

COMMANDER JAMES DRISCOLL, attached to the Intelligence branch of the United States Navy, has asked me to write this, in order that my version may be placed in the files with his own account of certain peculiar transactions which took place in Japan and China some months ago. My immediate reaction, when Driscoll made the request, was the same as it is now. I had a vision of certain executives in the service reading this sort of thing. I told Driscoll that no one would believe it, and his answer, if not a compliment to me, was partially reassuring.

"Maybe," he said, "but I have a hunch they will. You'll probably write it so badly that they'll know it is the truth."

"But it's preposterous," I said. "It's melodrama. Honest to goodness—no one in his right mind, Driscoll, if he isn't in the scenario department of some movie outfit, writes this sort of stuff."

Driscoll thought a moment. The idea appeared to interest him so much that I believe he has really thought of writing fiction in his softer moods.

"Don't let that worry you," he said finally. "It wouldn't go. Any sort of narrative has to have a hero in it to get over with the public, and, believe me, you weren't any hero. Oh, no, you don't need to be self-conscious for once in your life. Just snap into it. It won't take you long. Besides, there's another angle to this sort of thing. Probably no one will ever read it, anyway."

"Then why do I write it?" I inquired. Curiously enough, this question seemed ridiculous to Driscoll. He reminded me that I had been in the service myself at the time of the World War and that I should understand about army and navy paper work.

"You can just go right ahead," he said comfortably, "with the almost complete assurance that the whole thing will be stored away somewhere in a room in Washington. Why, if I can possibly avoid it, I won't read it myself."

"Thanks," I said, "but how do I begin?"

His answer, though practical, has proved of no great help.

"You sit down with a pen and ink and paper, and you write it. You can still form your letters, can't you? You tell what happened, Lee."

So that's what I am doing. I'm using Driscoll's time-worn phrase of snapping into it. I am trying to cast back into this series of incidents which occurred on the other side of the Pacific Ocean, but although the pieces have all been fitted quite completely together, when I try to start, the elements of this artificial beginning are as mysterious as the beginning was in fact. My mind lingers on certain incidents. I think of a suave scion of the Japanese nobility named Mr. Moto, if that is his real name. I think of a dead man in the cabin of a ship; the roaring of a plane's motor comes drumming across my memory, and I hear voices speaking in Oriental tongues. The past of an ancient race mixes peculiarly with the present. And in back of it all I see a girl,—one of those amazing wanderers in our modern world, disinherited and alone. International espionage moves in a world of its own, and its characters must always be lonely.

"Under-cover work is always like that," Driscoll said to me once. "The people one encounters are much the same. They may be shady and raffish, but don't forget they're all of them brave. They do their work like pieces on a chess-board and nothing stops them from moving along their diagonals. You mustn't feel animosity toward them, Lee, for they feel none toward you. They're working for their respective countries and that's more than a lot of people do."

Perhaps what is still the most interesting part of this adventure is its complete impersonality, its lack of rancor. I believe honestly that if Mr. Moto, a most accomplished gentleman, and I were to meet today that we might enjoy each other's company; and I should be glad to drink with him in one of his minute wine cups to the future of Japan. I have an idea that he would agree with me heartily in wishing for perpetual amity between Japan and the United States, as long as that amity did not interfere with what he and his own political faction conceive to be his nation's divine mission to establish a hegemony in the East. Distance sometimes makes it difficult to remember that Japan is a very great country and that the

Japanese are capable people, sensitive and intelligent. Still, although it sometimes seems incredible that our two nations should ever go to war, there is always the thought of war behind the scenes in every nation. Given a shift in the balance of power, men like Moto must start working, I suppose.

But I am getting away from my beginning.

Probably I had better start in the Imperial Hotel at Tokyo one afternoon in spring about a year ago. Out of some confused notes which I made at the time I have been able to rescue the essential dates and scenes. With their help and my memory, I'll do the best I can.

In the first place, I suppose I must tell who I am and what I was doing in Tokyo one spring afternoon. Though time moves fast and characters appear and disappear in a hasty procession before the public eye, the readers of the newspapers for the past decade may be vaguely familiar with my name. I am the "Casey" Lee whom various publicity directors have touted as a war ace. My first name incidentally is not "Casey" but Kenneth C. Lee—K.C.—not that it makes much difference. I am the Casey Lee who flew the Atlantic at a time when previous flyers had rather taken the first bloom off that feat. My reputation and my personality used to be as carefully built up in those days as a pugilist's or a motion-picture star's, for my personality meant money. In short, I was one of that rather unfortunate group of almost professional heroes who sprang up in the boom days after the war and whose exploits diverted a jaded and somewhat disillusioned nation. I was a stunt flyer, having been a Chasse pilot in the war, a transcontinental flyer and a transatlantic flyer with a row of American and Italian war medals besides. My picture looked well in the rotogravure sections. My testimonial looked well in the advertisements of clothing and lubricants and nourishing foods, but when the cloud of depression grew blacker, people quite reasonably seemed to grow tired of heroes. I was pushed more and more into the background with others of my kind. Thus, it was not strange that when money was running very short and a large tobacco company offered me the chance of making a flight from Japan to the United States, I should have welcomed the opportunity. I welcomed it even though I had no great conviction that I was any longer in a suitable condition to go through with such a business. I was only glad to attempt it because I was rather tired of life. That was why I was in Tokyo, in a country which was entirely strange to me, waiting for a plane to be shipped from the States and for the usual publicity to start.

I can still see the yellow stonework and the curious floor levels and galleries in the Imperial Hotel and their strange sculptured decorations, half modernistic and half Oriental. I can see the intelligent, concentrated faces of the waiter boys and the outlandish mixture of guests,—Europeans from the embassies, tourists from a cruise ship, Japanese in European clothes, Japanese girls in flowered kimonos, Japanese men in their native *hakimas.* That background of costume is startling when one stops to think of it. It is like the East and West meeting in two waves of unrelated cultures which swirl about Tokyo's streets.

It was a fine sunny day outside, I can remember. It occurred to me that I had been drinking heavily since early in the morning, but this state was not unusual with me. At the time of the war we pilots had drunk in the evening to forget the imminence of death, and after that most of us had continued, to forget the imminence of boredom. I think we had a reasonable semblance of an excuse. When one starts air fighting at the age of eighteen the values of life are apt to become distorted. One craves for the thrill of excitement as the nerves of an addict clamor for his favorite drug. I cannot feel so badly about the drinking of those days.

It was the drinking that I had done to drown the depression that inevitably follows a man unlucky enough to become a publicized hero of which I cannot boast. Liquor had become a problem to me, when, after weeks and months of every sort of adulation for having made a transatlantic flight, I was dropped as suddenly as if a wing had come off my plane. The depression which follows the excitement is the worst of it. In those moments of let-down I could sometimes see myself as I must have appeared to others,—not Casey Lee, one-time war ace, who had fought in Poland and Spain against the Riffs, nor Lee the ocean pilot, but only a shell of that Casey Lee.

I remember that I was talking. There was a crowd around me as usual, of people who had nothing better to do than listen to me talk, and who enjoyed the association with a celebrity even if he might have been a trifle seedy.

"The plane's being shipped next week, a new type Willis Jones AB-3," I was telling them. "Give me another week to tune her up and I'm ready for it. I'll take her across alone, straight on the shipping lane, with one stop at Honolulu. The Pacific isn't any worse than the Atlantic, if you fly high, I guess."

"Will you have another drink, Mr. Lee?" someone said.

"Yes," I answered. "I will have another drink. I'm perfectly glad to have several more. Does anybody here think I can't fly the Pacific?"

"Oh, no, Mr. Lee," came a voice from the crowd; "of course not."

"There's only one thing that can stop me," I said, "and that's money, and I've got the financial backing this time. Give me a crate to fly and refueling planes and I'll fly a non-stop around the world."

"Why not make it twice around the world, Mr. Lee?" another voice said.

With a little difficulty I focused my attention on the speaker. He was a pale pimply youth whom I had never seen before, obviously an American. "Listen, baby," I said to him. "You're the only product that America's turned out since 1918. When I see you, I know the United States is going to hell. I don't have to listen to your lip. Everybody knows who I am."

"Of course they do, Mr. Lee," said someone. "Won't you have another drink?"

"Yes," I said, "I don't mind if I do. Always glad to have another drink, always glad to try anything once or twice—that's me."

"Tell us," said someone respectfully, "who is backing you this time?"

"It's a cigarette company," I said. "They're using a part of their advertising appropriation for a transpacific flight. Believe me, it's the first break I've had in a long time. The Mayor of Tokyo gives me a couple of packages of their cigarettes, or somebody in Tokyo, I don't remember who. And I deliver one pack to the Governor of Hawaii and another to the Mayor of New York City. I'm going to be a good-will ambassador between Japan and the United States. But I don't care so long as I have a crate to fly. The good old American game of nonsense doesn't bother me."

"You needn't yell about it so," a voice objected. "You're an American, aren't you?"

"That is where I was born," I answered, "but I'm broadminded enough to have my own ideas. I've fought for the Spaniards and the Poles. There are other nations besides the United States—in case you don't know—several others."

"All right, Lee," said someone, "but here you are in a public place. Keep your voice down. A lot of these Japanese are looking at you."

"Let 'em look," I said. "Why should I care if they look? And I'll say anything I damn well please any time at all."

As I spoke, I became aware that my voice must have been louder than I had intended. I saw individuals staring at me curiously and I set down my glass. I was reaching a stage, which I had known before, when I became sorry for myself. And I had a sufficiently good reason to be sorry for myself half a minute later. One of the hotel boys, bowing and drawing in his breath noisily between his teeth, presented me with a cable. The words were slightly blurred and I had to concentrate to make them clear, before I could understand their meaning. The cable was signed by the codeword of the cigarette company. "Plans for flight off," it said. "Bank will pay your passage home."

My first thought was one of sickening hopelessness, for I had not realized until I saw that cablegram how much I had counted on this opportunity. It had raised me in my own estimation above other flying men I knew, and it offered me a prospect of redeeming myself in the eyes of others. I knew well enough why I had been selected,—on account of my name and my past reputation, not because of any present ability or future promise. I even had a sufficiently uncomplimentary idea of myself to suspect why the plan had been vetoed. I could hear them in New York saying that Casey was through. It seemed to me that everything was over then; I could see myself returning to the rôle I had played for several years, living on an out-worn reputation. I suppose whoever we are, we try to rationalize all our failures. We push away our own faults and try to blame them on someone else. That is exactly what I did then. In some irrational way, I attributed my own failure directly to my country and to my country's eccentricities. The group around my table was looking at me curiously as I stared up from that cable. I tried to return casually to the subject where we had left off, a difficult matter when the words of that cable were ringing, with the drinks I had taken, through my thoughts.

"Since when was it a sin to criticize one's country?" I inquired. "I'm tired of having everyone wince and look scared, if a word is said in public against the present Administration. If it represents the will of America, it is not the country that I used to know. The United States are in the hands of a lot of communized visionaries, if you want my idea. I'm not afraid to say I'm ashamed of certain aspects of my country. I could tell you a thing or two about what's happened to commercial aviation. Can you sit here and admit that my country has not repudiated its just obligations to its citizens by juggling with its currency? The word of the United States isn't what it used to be, and the sooner we all know it the better. The national character isn't what it used to be, and I can prove it by this cable in my hand. Now that our government can repudiate its obligations, any citizen seems to feel free to break an agreement any time—as long as the man he breaks it with can't get at him."

"What's the trouble, Lee?" someone asked. Even in my stimulated state, I felt that I had become involved beyond my depth, and that I had made a statement which I could not back by intelligent argument. I was no expert on the problems of currency and I realized that the economic woes of the world were as insoluble as my own.

"Those double-crossers back home," I said. "They've turned me down."

"Maybe they heard something," a voice suggested. "You've been raising a good deal of hell, Lee."

There was no doubt that the remark was true, but its implication was enough to make me lose my temper in a way I never had done before. I could see myself going straight down the ladder without friends and without respect. I whirled upon the man who spoke and I shouted at him. In my total lack of self-control I did not care for consequences. I did not care where I was or who heard me.

"Some damn sneak like you has been telling stories on me!" I shouted. "By God, do Americans have to have Boy Scout masters and Sunday-school teachers to fly for them? To hell with you! To hell with the whole bunch of you! And particularly my fellow citizens."

I could see that my last remark shocked them, and now I can understand why. National solidarity becomes important in direct ratio to the distance we are away from home.

"Be quiet, Lee!" one of the group said.

"Who for? You?" I answered.

"No, for yourself. You shouldn't slam your country in a foreign place."

"And who's going to stop me?" I shouted back.

That was when I saw an American naval officer had joined us, a former friend of mine. He must have heard me talking. I had not seen Jim Driscoll for years, but we had served together in the war as naval aviators on the Italian front. I knew him right away when he walked up to my table,—a trim stocky man in a white uniform, with commander's stripes and a heavy determined face. "So you're drunk again, are you, Casey Lee?" Jim Driscoll said.

As I say, I remembered Driscoll well enough. To see him appear just then out of nowhere was like a final blow by destiny to my own self-esteem. We had started even once. I had been a better man than Driscoll back in the war, and now we stood there, both changed by the pitiless marks of time,—Driscoll a commander in the navy, and myself an arrant failure.

"Not too drunk to know you, Jim," I answered.

Jim Driscoll had put on weight since I had seen him last, and was too heavy for flying now. He had assumed an expression that I had seen others of my own friends wear of late. In it there was a hint of pity, and it annoyed me that Driscoll should pity me or should be in a position to administer reproof.

"Casey," Jim Driscoll said, "I used to think you were the bravest man in the world. You'd better sleep it off. You wore the uniform once."

"The luckiest thing I ever did was to get out of it," I told him. "It gives me a chance to say what I think. It's more than you can do, Driscoll, and you can remember that I'm not one of your enlisted men. You heard me; what are you going to do about it? I don't like my country."

"I can tell you what I think of you," Driscoll answered. "You're making yourself into a public disgrace as well as a nuisance. If I weren't leaving for Shanghai tonight, I'd see if your passport couldn't be revoked."

I took my passport out of my pocket, tore it straight across and tossed it on the floor.

"And that's what I care for my passport," I said. "There are plenty of other countries. Take Japan—Japan's a nice country."

But Jim Driscoll paid no more attention to me. He had turned a stiff back and was walking steadily away. Then I saw that I was alone at the table where I had been sitting, deserted by everyone I knew.

It dawned on me that I had gone much further than I had intended, beyond the bounds of reason or decorum, in my criticism. I had spoken in a maudlin way, when I would much better have kept my ill-regulated thoughts to myself. Now that the damage had been done, I was too proud to retract a single word, if my life had depended on it. If they wanted to judge me by what I said in my cups, I would let them judge me.

Two Japanese army officers were staring at me fixedly. Also a short dark man with his hair cut after the Prussian fashion—a habit which so many Japanese have adopted—was seated at a table near me, regarding me with curiosity. He was dressed in a cutaway coat and wore tiny patent-leather shoes. There was a signet ring on his left hand. I saw him look down at this ring and back at me again. I remember thinking that he seemed like a Japanese trying to masquerade as a continental European and not succeeding very well. He raised his hand as I watched and beckoned to one of the clerks behind the desk. The clerk hurried to him and bowed. Then the clerk turned to me.

"Perhaps you are tired, Mr. Lee?" the clerk said. "Will you have someone conduct you to your room?"

Then I found myself being helped to my room, whether I liked it or not, by the clerk and the small man in the frock coat, one on each side of me.

"It is too bad," the small man said. "I am very, very sorry."

I did not know until later that it was Mr. Moto who was speaking to me. I still do not know his exact rank, but he was a gentleman, no matter what his race might be.

"I am sorry," said Mr. Moto again, "very, very sorry. You will be better after a little sleep, perhaps."

He spoke sharply to the hotel clerk and the man bowed in a way that made me realize even in my condition that Mr. Moto was a man of importance.

"You may go now," he said to the clerk, "and understand, this gentleman is to have anything he may want."

The door closed softly behind him and I found myself sitting on the edge of the bed, with little Mr. Moto standing attentively before me. I have never felt so much an alien, for the conviction was growing upon me that I was cut off from everything I had ever known before. I, a man without a country, was closed into one of the curiously furnished rooms of the Imperial Hotel with that Japanese who exactly fitted into the surroundings.

I looked up to find him still gazing at me thoughtfully. I wondered what he wanted. I wished, with a sudden intensity, that he would go away.

The furniture was of some light-colored unvarnished hard

wood. There was a built-in dresser, showing an odd unsymmetrical arrangement of cubbyholes for clothing. There were several chairs with legs short enough to accommodate a low-statured race. A writing table was covered with hotel notices in both English and Japanese. Beside the bed was a pair of hotel slippers, reminding me that the Japanese spent a large portion of their life in changing from one set of footwear to another. I looked at the man again. I still wished he would go away.

"May I help you to bed, perhaps?" he asked.

"No," I answered. "What's your name?"

He smiled deprecatingly. "Moto," he replied. "That is my name, please, and I should be glad to assist you. I was once a valet to several American gentlemen in New York." He knelt down and began to unlace my shoes.

"Please," he said, "thank you. America is a magnificent country."

"Maybe," I said. "But it's thrown me over flat, Mr. What's-your-name."

"Moto," he repeated patiently.

"Well," I said, "you're not a valet here in Japan."

"No," said Mr. Moto, "but Americans always interest me. I saw that you were not well and that your friends had left you."

"Listen, Mr. Moto," I said, "when they can't get anything more out of you, Americans always go away."

"It was not kind of them," Mr. Moto said. "I am sorry."

"Mr. Moto," I told him, "suppose you stop saying you're sorry. What do you want with me?"

"Only to assist you," he explained. "You are a foreigner, a guest, in my country, who has met with misfortune. Everyone knows who you are, of course. We have a great respect for American aviators." He drew in his breath with a peculiar little hiss. Even though he was dressed as a European and acted like one, he could not avoid some of the involuntary courtesies of his race. "I have seen you before. I think last night, in fact. I saw you dancing with a girl—a very beautiful girl with yellow hair. Was she not a Russian?"

I cast back into my mind with difficulty, trying to remember the hazy events of the night before. For a longer while than I cared to remember days and nights were hazy. They were made up of afternoons of drinking at some bar, cocktails before dinner somewhere, and more drinks, and then oblivion. Then I remembered that there had been a girl, a nice girl. My embarrassment, as I recalled what had happened, made me speak of her casually, as though she belonged to a lower class, but I knew better, nevertheless.

"Yellow hair?" I said. "Oh, yes, I met her somewhere. Yes, her name was Sonya. I don't know her last name—one of those Russian names. We got on very well until—well, I wasn't myself last night. She tossed me over when I made a pass at her. All right—what do I care? She might have known I didn't mean anything by it. Everybody's tossed me over!"

"Please," Mr. Moto said, inhaling through his teeth, "here are your pajamas. . . . You made a pass at her—I do not understand the phrase. Will you explain it, please?"

"Haven't you ever made a pass at anyone?" I inquired. "You might have, Mr. Moto. Since you're so curious, I don't mind telling you that I tried to kiss her in a taxicab. That's making a pass. She made the driver stop and got out and left me flat. I'm sorry about it, if you care to know."

"How do you mean?" said Mr. Moto. "She left you flat?"

"The way you see me now, Moto," I said. "I'm much obliged to you, but I wish you'd go. I want to go to sleep. I want to forget I was ever born."

I must have been half asleep then, but it seemed to me I could remember Mr. Moto moving carefully about my room. I was in a stupor, I suppose, somewhere between sleep and waking, with the fumes of Japanese-made whisky curling like mist through my consciousness. I seemed to be in an airdrome, in the cockpit of a fighting plane, ready to take off over the Austrian lines. Then, for no good reason, I seemed to be sitting on the lowered top of an automobile, riding along Broadway with the air full of ticker tape and torn-up telephone directories. I could hear the crowd shouting and a man in a cutaway coat like Mr. Moto's was making a speech. "America is very proud of you, Casey Lee," he was saying. Plenty of people were proud of me in those days. They were proud to have me at Newport and Southampton. They were proud to have me examine new trimotor planes. They were proud to have me autograph books. It only came to me later that they were proud to take my money. I wondered what had happened to those days. They had moved away from me into a series of speak-easies and club barrooms, leaving me finally—there was no use mincing matters—a broken-down adventurer. For no reason, I suppose, except because Mr. Moto's question had made me remember her, I thought of that girl of the other night. She had been the best-looking girl in the room, and the best-looking girl had never been any too good for me. And who was this girl? A Russian *émigrée,* a spy perhaps; Japan was full of spies. At some time while these thoughts raced, I must have gone to sleep. Sleep was the closest thing to being dead, and I wished that I were dead.

## 2

I WAS awakened at 12:30 the next afternoon. I remember the time because I looked at my wrist watch. Someone was knocking on my door and the sound waked me. My door must have been unlocked, because one of the hotel boys was standing beside my bed when I opened my eyes. I had all the usual physical feelings of having been drunk the night before. My head was aching and my hands were shaking.

"If you please, sir," the boy was crying.

I pointed a quivering finger toward my bureau, and observed, to my surprise, that my room was in perfect order, my clothes neatly folded instead of being strewn, as they customarily were, in every direction. Then I remembered Mr. Moto, who said he had been a valet in America.

"Wait a minute, boy," I said. "Do you see that flask on the bureau?" It was an old leather-covered flask which I had carried ever since the war. "Pour me out a half tumbler of that quick!"

"Please, sir—" said the boy again.

"Do what I tell you!" I interrupted him. My nerves were jangling like discordant bells. "Pour it out and hand it here! Never mind a tumbler. Take the cup off the bottom and fill it up!"

I had to take the little cup in both hands when he handed it to me, but once the liquor was inside me it steadied me. My head cleared, my hands quieted, my muscles were again in some sort of coordination. Then I recalled the last afternoon, and that my backers had left me flat. For a moment I had the impossible hope that they had reconsidered, that the boy was bringing me a cable, but his next words removed such illusions.

"A lady is waiting for you, please," the boy said. "She sent you this, please." And he handed me a note.

I tore open the envelope and read it. I remember the writing still, large, bold, and foreign.

"Where are you? Don't you remember you asked me for lunch? I am waiting. I am not used to be kept waiting. If you ever want to see me again, you had better hurry."

It was signed "Sonya." I had not the slightest recollection of having asked her or anyone else to lunch, but I had enough pride not to wish her to think I had forgotten.

"Run me a cold bath," I said, "and tell the lady I'll be out directly."

The cold bath did me good. When I stepped out of it, I felt better and younger, for the cold water seemed to have washed out some of the lines around my eyes. In fact, I was surprised how well I looked, considering the life I had been leading. There were signs of that life in my face, but my body had resisted most of it, and my muscles were still hard. I looked at the scar on my left shoulder where an Austrian machine-gun bullet had shattered my collarbone, and at the long gash in my right calf which had been torn by a splinter when I had crashed behind the lines—but that was long ago.

A girl was waiting for me outside—a pretty girl—which made me remember that I must still possess some attraction. I dressed carefully in a blue serge suit. I said to myself, "After all, Casey Lee, you're still a man," and I walked out into the lobby, cheerfully, because I knew that soon I could have another drink. I even recall humming that song we used to sing in the evenings when flying men gathered.

"I'm Going to a Happy Land Where Everything is Bright. Where the Hangouts Grow on Bushes and We Stay Out Every Night."

The yellow stone had been transformed overnight, evidently for the arrival of some important guest. The pillars were decorated with artificial peach blossoms and crossed banners,—one the rising sun of Nippon and the other a flag which I did not know. There was a bustle of preparation in the lobby, engineered by khaki-clad army officers with boots and sabers, and men in cutaway coats holding silk hats, evidently from the government offices. All of them wore the same intent, worried expression which I had observed often among the Japanese, as though they were conscientiously determined that everything should be done with absolute correctness in the face of a critical world audience.

I did not notice the excitement much, however, but looked instead for the girl whom I had forgotten that I had asked to lunch. As I sought her out among the Japanese and foreigners sitting at the little tables, I discovered I did not remember what she looked like very well. I could only remember that she was really beautiful and that she had yellow hair. I moved at once toward the only girl I could see who answered that description and I knew she was the one because she was looking at me. She was a tall girl, almost lanky. Her hair was reddish gold. Her eyes, dark blue, gave the combined impression of being both shrewd and seductive. Her lips were painted a deep red, and her hands were very long and slender. She was dressed in a white tailored suit. Although there was nothing specific in her appearance to betray it, I knew she was not American. She had the social poise and the adamantine quality of a more sophisticated world. I knew that girl had been about and had seen strange sights—many of them not pleasant—and she could take care of herself, probably, in any situation. I knew that she was a Russian, because I had seen her type often enough during my short stay in the Orient. I had seen her sort at fine dinners and in cheap dance halls but there was a similarity to all nationals of her sort. They were all aloof, but all charming companions, able to be agreeable in any mood, able to give an adventurous sense of competence, and displaying at the same time their own sadness, for they were sad people who wandered without a country. I took her hand and bent over it, clicking my heels together, a trick I'd learned in Rome, and she smiled at me.

"You are late," she said. Except for a throaty catch in her voice, her English was perfect, and I imagine she would have done as well in half a dozen other languages. "Did you not remember you asked me for lunch?" She was looking half reproachful, half amused, but she patted the chair beside her and I sat down.

"Will you forgive me if I tell you something?" I asked her. "I was under the impression, the only time we met, that you did not like me."

"But you would not care if I liked you or not?" she inquired. "Would you, Mr. Lee?"

I looked at her thoughtfully and told the truth. "I'm not sure," I said. "Mademoiselle—?" I stopped, because I could not remember her name.

"Have you forgotten my name already?" she asked. "Karaloff. But you called me Sonya the other night."

"Perhaps," I suggested, "it will be just as well if we forget the other night. Where would you care to go to lunch? And will you have a cocktail, Mademoiselle?"

She smiled, white teeth, crimson lips, slightly slanting eyes. "Sonya," she said.

"You are very kind to me," I answered, "—Sonya."

"Perhaps," she said, "I wonder . . . I like you, Mr. Lee. I like brave men."

It seemed to me that there was a tinge of sarcasm in that last remark. The boy came, and she gave her order for a glass of sherry and I ordered a double Scotch. "Sonya," I suggested, "suppose we leave out the brave stuff. I'd rather be a coward today, and I'm afraid of you, if you want the truth."

She laughed softly and leaned toward me, so near that I could catch the scent of gardenia in her hair. "Why," she asked, "are you afraid?"

"Just a peculiar intuition," I said, and I meant it. "I shouldn't like to be in love with you."

She laughed again. She had that way of making one seem scintillating even when one said nothing amusing. "You're a funny man," she said. "Why?"

I finished my drink and watched her before I answered. It seemed to me that I had never seen such a mobile face as hers, and I suspected its mobility. First, she had been watchful and her eyes had been hard and shrewd. Now she seemed to have tossed away that watchfulness. "Because you'd make a fool out of me," I said bluntly. "It's been done before."

"Perhaps," she said. She smiled at me and I could see gold lights dance behind the blue of her eyes. "Brave men are so apt to be children."

I cannot describe the way I felt. I seemed to be lost in the personality of that Russian girl, in spite of common sense and instinctive caution. "That doesn't flatter me," I said. "You probably come from a sophisticated world where people live on logic. You can't help being beautiful, can you?"

"Do you think I do?" she asked me "—Casey?"

"Yes," I said. "I wonder who you are, and I know that you won't tell me."

Her eyes grew hard for a moment and again she had that look of someone who could go through anything untouched. She seemed about to make an indiscreet remark and then checked herself.

"Perhaps I'm not what you think I am, altogether," she said. "Are you what I think you are, I wonder?"

"Does it make any difference?" I asked her. It amused me to observe how deliberately she brought the curve of the conversation back to me.

"Your country's done a great deal for you," she said. "You must love it very much."

I rose to her suggestion almost without thinking. "My country took me when I was a kid of eighteen," I said. "I wasn't a bad kid, either, Sonya. It jammed me into naval aviation and put me in a plane that wasn't fit to fly. They killed a lot of my friends, those planes that shouldn't have left the ground at flying school. Then my country sent me to the Italian Front, and when it unsettled me for any sort of useful living, it closed the door of the navy to me because I was just a kid without real officer's training. And now it's left me flat in Tokyo; that's all my country's done for me. I'd give up my nationality any time."

She opened her handbag and drew out one of those long Russian cigarettes. "You're joking, aren't you?" she asked.

"No," I said, "I was never more serious in my life."

When I leaned forward to light her cigarette, she bent over the match and rested her fingers on mine, it seemed to me longer than was necessary, but I did not mind the touch of her fingers. "A man without a country," she said. Her voice was genuine and sad. "I'm sorry."

"Well," I said, "I can take what's coming to me."

"Casey," she asked, "do you like Japan?"

"Yes," I said. "Japan's a country that deals with facts sensibly. By the way—" My attention was caught again by the artificial peach blooms and the flags in the lobby. "What's all the excitement here today?"

"Don't you read the papers?" She laughed. "It's the delegation from Manchukuo come to call on the Emperor. Do you feel as the American State Department does about Japan's adventure in Manchukuo?" That husky voice of hers was softly, playfully caressing, but her eyes were not.

"No," I answered promptly, and I meant it. "If you knew my country better, you would understand that it's characteristic of it to take a holier-than-thou-attitude. Before 1906 your people held Manchuria virtually as a colony, didn't they? You're Russian, aren't you?"

Her eyes clouded and she nodded with a hopeless, sad look

which I had seen on the faces of other *émigrés* when their lost country was mentioned. "I thought so," I continued. "Well, no one objected when your Czar controlled Manchuria; why should we object when Japan does? It's against the laws of fact to keep eighty million Japanese on a few small islands. If Japan is strong enough to run it, why shouldn't she run Manchuria?"

She nodded and it seemed to me that my answer relieved some doubt in her. "You know a great deal of history," she remarked, "don't you, Casey Lee?"

I finished my third drink before I answered, and my answer made me pleased with my own astuteness. "I know enough about history," I said, "to understand that God and justice are on the side of the heaviest artillery." And then I stopped. "Hello," I said, "what's that?"

But I knew what the sound was. I was only asking the significance of the sound at that particular time and place. I had heard it on the Piave and in the Balkans and in Africa—the sudden thumping of a drum and the cadence of feet on a pavement—hundreds and hundreds of feet moving in unison of infantry—well-disciplined, sedulously drilled infantry. Outside of the hotel I knew that there must be at least two companies of Japanese soldiers,—short, muscular boys with conscientious, half-worried faces, in neatly fitting khaki uniforms with rifles and shining bayonets. The beat of a drum and marching feet was a common sound in Tokyo.

She understood my question. "The Manchukuo envoys are coming back from their audience," she said, and then she rose. "Have you had enough to drink before lunch?" she inquired politely. "It seems to me you have. Perhaps we'd better go."

Once I was on my feet, I felt the effect of my three double whiskies. I felt comfortable and nonchalant and friendly with the world, aware that people were looking at me, aware that I was walking beside the best-looking girl in the hotel.

"Wait!" I heard Sonya say beside me. "The party is coming in."

The steps to the hotel door were lined with officers and government officials, each one of whom seemed to know his place. I was tall enough to look over their heads. An old Chinese gentleman was walking up the steps, straight and active, though he must have been well in his seventies. He wore the long black gown of China with a blue vest over it. His face was a scholar's, benign and calm.

"It is Premier Cheng of Manchukuo," I heard Sonya say. "He has followed the Emperor Pu Yi through his exile."

The old man, rising tall and a little bent above his escort of

Japanese, seemed to me to have more dignity than anyone in that gathering. His native dress stood out, simple and suitable among the Europeanized uniforms and the cutaway coats and silk hats. He was the only one who seemed genuine—a man with an ideal who looked a trifle sad. I moved toward the door again.

"Wait," said Sonya, "you cannot go out now."

"Why not?" I asked and began to push my way through the crowd.

"Wait!" said Sonya again more sharply.

But before I heard her, I had shoved against a man in khaki uniform who turned around quickly. I saw by his insignia that he was a captain of cavalry. A short man, with a square copper-colored face.

"No, no!" he said and pushed me on the chest.

Before I thought of the consequences, I took him by the shoulders and spun him out of the way. I must have been rougher than I intended, for he gave an indignant cry, and his voice caused half a dozen other officers to gather angrily around me. "Get out of the way!" I said. "I'm going out this door." Then I saw that Sonya was beside me, speaking quickly to one of the officers in Japanese.

She had opened her handbag and was holding a signet ring in her hand which I thought I had seen somewhere before. It came over me abruptly where I had seen it: it had been on Mr. Moto's finger that other afternoon. Either the ring or her explanation had an immediate effect. The officer whom I had treated rudely bowed to me jerkily and Sonya and I walked calmly out the door of the hotel. As we stood in the cool spring air, a motor moved through the porte-cochere, obviously not one of the usual public cabs, but a more expensive car driven by a man in dark livery.

"Get in," said Sonya. "I know a perfect place to go to lunch." And I climbed in beside her. She was speaking in Japanese to the chauffeur, in sharp staccato phrases. Then she leaned back contentedly and I could smell again the perfume of gardenias. She seemed perfectly at home in that car. "We will go to a teahouse," she said, "and have lunch, just you and me."

"Sonya," I said, "you're a very remarkable girl."

"Oh, no," she said, "but I like you, Casey. I think you're very nice."

I did not answer. Whether it was true or not, I was pleased that she liked me, but I still had sense enough to know what she was by then. The ring had told me. It revealed, among other things, that I had never asked her to lunch and that she was a Japanese spy. Not that the idea shocked me. Instead, it pleased me. She was a Japanese spy and I was no one—footloose and entirely on my own, being speeded through Tokyo in a limousine.

"Sonya," I said, "I don't care where we're going as long as you come along."

She laughed and touched my hand for a moment. "It's beautiful," she said. "Isn't Tokyo beautiful in spring?"

I did not answer. As a matter of fact, I did not think that Tokyo was wholly beautiful. The new Tokyo of the earthquake was entirely European. We were passing the marble façades of buildings which seemed to have been reared yesterday and which might have been part of Europe—as alien to that land as I was. It was a confusing, dreamlike place and the people on the streets seemed to share that confusion in their mixture of Japanese and European clothes. The motors and the tramcars and the bicycles shared it. The people of Tokyo seemed trying hard to be something which they were not; and everything was change and chaos—everything except the green parks on the right and the ancient black wall and moat of another age which surrounded the mystery of the Imperial Palace Grounds, where roofs and rock pines jutted out unobtainably against the sky.

"It's beautiful," I said, "as long as you're here, Sonya."

## 3

THE DRIVE was a long one, through streets of factories and through densely populated sections of crowded wooden bungalows, lightly, impermanently constructed, as though solider homes were not worth building in the face of the earthquakes that so frequently visit those islands. More recent experiments with steel and concrete, such as had risen in that part of Tokyo which had been destroyed in the earthquake disaster of 1923, might mean a general rebuilding of Japanese cities; but until this slow process was completed, I could understand Japan's sensitiveness to any enemy threat from the air. A sight of those unpainted matchboxes of dwellings, with hardly air space between them—and our motor moved through street after street—explained why Japan watched with unconcealed misgivings the construction of our airplane carriers and the development of Chinese and Russian aviation. A few incendiary bombs were all that would be needed to bring about almost unimaginable disaster, and I had been told that the inflammability of Osaka and other great industrial nerve centers of the Empire was even more pronounced.

Sonya has told the driver where to go and finally, after perhaps twenty minutes, the car stopped at the entrance to one of those narrow alleys where the Japan of the Shoguns meets the life of a modern aspiring nation.

"We must walk here," she said, as we got out. The alley was a twisting, flagged street which wound between the low façades of shops and houses.

I think those small streets will always be fascinating to a foreigner. They seem perfect and yet so fragile that a gust of wind might blow them out to sea: tiny, sliding, latticed paper windows, balconies with potted dwarf trees standing on them; minute provision and hardware shops, the flash of flowered kimonos and the clatter of wooden shoes. The alley which we traversed seemed as harmless as an illustration in a tale for children. I remember thinking that it had the same naïve quality of Germany before the war—of something not to be taken wholly seriously.

"Where are we going?" I asked.

Sonya smiled. "Are you impatient walking?" she asked. "It's so pleasant here. You and I seem like something in the book of the English writer named Swift. 'Gulliver's Travels', isn't it? We are going to a teahouse where we can have *sukiaki.* The management is expecting us."

As she finished speaking, she pointed to an unpainted wooden wall of a building larger than the others. "It's here," she said, and she pushed open a gate. Once inside the wall we were in one of those miniature gardens which represent an art so completely mastered by Japan.

Sonya and I were standing, two giants in a countryside where ponds and streams and plains and mountains rose in contours around us hardly ever above the knee. We looked upon dwarfed fir trees, the tallest not above two feet, with green lawns beneath them. Among the mosses by the pools all sorts of small flowering plants were bending over the water, and goldfish were swimming beneath the surface, peculiar breeds of goldfish whose propagation had been carried on through centuries. That small yard gave us all the perspective and vista of a huge garden, all condensed into the space of a European room. A door at the end of the walk had opened already, and three women in kimonos came out, smiling and bowing. Being familiar with the habits of such places, I sat down on the step leading to the house and took off my shoes and thrust my toes into a pair of slippers which one of the girls handed me, while Sonya did the same.

"It's like playing dolls," she said. "Did you ever play dolls, Casey? I used to at Odessa, long ago."

"No," I answered, "only soldiers, Sonya."

"Dolls are better," she said. "We might put on kimonos, do you think?" She spoke to the eldest of the three women, and the two girls brought out kimonos.

I took off my coat and put one on. Then one of the women pattered before us, leading the way along a matting-covered corridor and pushed aside a sliding door, smiling. We both of us kicked off our slippers and entered a private room which was already arranged for us. The furnishings were as simple as a room in ancient Sparta and as fragile as a painting on a fan. A table not more than two feet high was in the center of the room, with a cushion on the floor on either side of it. A charcoal brazier was burning at one end of the table and saucers of meat and chopped green vegetables and soybean oil were standing near it,—the component parts of that informal Japanese dish, as delicious as anything I have ever eaten, called *sukiaki.* At one end of the table, sliding paper windows opened on a balcony that looked out on a similar small garden. Opposite the balcony at the other end of the room there was a recess in the wall that held the only decorations,—a single porcelain figure of a god standing in a teakwood holder with a scroll painting of cherry blossoms behind him. At a lower level in the niche was a vase of flowers meticulously and perfectly arranged according to the careful dictates of the flower art in Japan. That was all; otherwise the room was bare.

I sat on the floor at one side of the table and Sonya sat on the other side. One of the serving girls in her flowered kimono, with her hair done like a Japanese doll's, knelt at the doorway, then bowed and entered and took her place at the charcoal brazier, filling the cooking utensil with the ingredients of the meal. It all made a pleasant sizzling sound of cooking and there was a smell of things to eat above the acrid smell of charcoal. A second girl, kneeling at the foot of the table, placed two tiny cups before us and filled them with hot *sake* wine.

"Here's looking at you, Sonya," I said and tossed off my cup, which the girl refilled immediately. There was a heady quality about that heated wine of Japan. Though it is taken in minute quantities, the cup is always full and one is apt to forget the amount one consumes.

"I hope you like it here," said Sonya.

I told her that I liked it, and I did. Her watchfulness and preoccupation seemed to have left her as she sat there on the floor by the little table. She seemed to have thrown off care with that volatile habit of Russians. She was a hostess who had brought me to a quiet place to be shared by herself and me. Her long lashes half drooped over her violet eyes and her red lips twisted in playful interrogation.

"Why don't you sit here beside me?" I asked.

"Oh, no," she said. "It isn't proper now. Later, perhaps, when the servants leave." We were each handed a green bowl with the yolk of a raw egg in the bottom and then the meal was ready. We reached toward the brazier with chopsticks for bits of the meat and vegetables.

I was aware that a certain pretense between us had been dropped. We had both of us accepted the fact that I had not asked Sonya to lunch but that Sonya had asked me, and she must have understood that I knew well enough that she had asked me for some definite reasons. I was perfectly content to watch her and to drink cup after cup of the *sake* wine while I waited for her to lead the conversation. Her first remark was almost banal.

"Here we are," she said, "you and I."

I nodded and answered, "That's my good luck, I think, and I haven't had much luck for quite a while." I saw that she was watching me, but not suspiciously; rather as any woman might watch a man in whom she took an interest.

"It seems strange, doesn't it," she remarked, "that you and I, Casey Lee, should be in this foreign room so far from any place that either of us knows? It's such a small inoffensive room—don't you think? And yet it represents the culture of two thousand years. It is a part of the beliefs and life of one of the most powerful nations in the world."

"Yes," I said, "go on—if you don't mind my staring at you, Sonya."

"No, I don't mind," she said. "Your eyes are kind. The eyes of most Americans are kind. Your life has been so secure—is that the reason? But there is no security here. Have you felt it? It's a nervous place—Japan.

Her words did not interest me as much as the huskiness in her voice and the lights that kept dancing in her eyes. Her eyes seemed to be asking me wordless questions. Probably we were each wondering about the other as we talked.

"Yes," I said, "Japan is very nervous. Well?"

"Perhaps she has a right to be nervous," she said. "Perhaps it is a state of mind. I wonder. Japan is very proud."

"I don't see what there is to be nervous about," I said.

She laughed.

"Haven't you ever felt that fate, that everything, was conspiring against you? I've felt that way sometimes."

"I wonder if you feel that way now?" I asked her.

Her eyes grew hard for a moment. "Never mind about me," she said. "Japan feels that the world is conspiring against her. It makes no difference whether she is right or wrong if she has that conviction, and she may be right. On one side, of her is the United States—"

"I know," I interrupted. That talk had always made me impatient. "What has the United States ever done to Japan except to pass the Exclusion Act?"

"There are your interests in the Orient," she said.

I had heard enough diplomatic talk in my occasional visits to Washington to be familiar with phases of our Pacific relations.

"I know," I answered. "That is a vague term and I've never heard it specified."

"Think of it this way," she said; "think of a great country which is always moving forward—taking. The United States is moving toward Asia—her hand has reached out over Hawaii, over Guam, over the Philippines. Where is she going to stop?"

"I don't know and I don't care," I said. Grotesque as it seemed to be talking to a pretty girl about the affairs of nations, I was curious to see where the conversation would lead us.

"Then on the other side," her voice went on, "on the other side of these little islands is Russia." She was speaking with a feeling that showed me that these matters were real to her. I could not understand why she was concerned when they meant so little to me. "Russia also is always reaching out; Russia was driven from Manchuria at the time of the Czar, but perhaps she is moving back again. They are double-tracking the Trans-Siberian Railway. Vladivostok is a fortress. There are great military bases along the frontier. Russia has stretched out her hand until she holds Outer Mongolia as a buffer State. Where will she go next?—That's what they're wondering in Japan. If you were a Japanese—" She looked at me and stopped.

"I'd be upset," I said. "Is that what you want me to say?"

"I don't want you say anything," she answered. "I want you to see how certain people feel. The world, through the League of Nations, has repudiated certain political bets of Japan. She has suffered, like all the other nations, from the economic depression. It is not hard to see why a Japanese must feel surrounded. China dislikes and fears Japan. China is building an air force and Japan is vulnerable from the air. Do you blame the average Japanese if he feels hemmed in?"

"No," I answered, "I don't blame him."

"Neither do I." Sonya's voice grew softer. "He looks to the east and seems to see the gray wall of the American battle fleet. He looks to the west and seems to see the Russian army and the Russian air force. And China. Mongolia is full of agents, Harbin is full of spies. He is unhappy—he is restless. The thing which makes him unhappiest is that he has not the understanding and the approval of other nations. I'm sorry for Japan."

"Perhaps they've got themselves too much on their own minds," I said.

"Perhaps," she answered. "But so have you. I seem to have known you for a long while, Casey Lee."

"That's nice," I said.

I had a sudden desire to end this general conversation, though I knew it would have been wiser to have waited. "Have you seen my *dossier?*" I asked.

"Your *dossier?*" She smiled again. "How should I see that?"

And I smiled back. "Because Japan is a suspicious country," I explained. "Every foreigner is thoroughly investigated by the secret police. I can imagine what my *dossier* says, Sonya. 'Casey Lee, a former American naval aviator, and a freelance air fighter in little wars, who publicly expressed his discontent with his own country. A drunkard, discredited.' . . . Why don't we get down to business, Sonya?" She did not smile when I had finished.

"Business," she said. "All right. May I ask you a question, Casey Lee? You have fought under other flags, your nationality does not tie you particularly. Am I right?"

"Dead right," I said, and drank another cup of *sake.* "So you were sent to sound me out?"

She nodded simply.

"Because I would talk more freely to a pretty girl?" I suggested. She nodded again.

"It's true," she agreed. "The word has come that the people in America will not pay for your transpacific flight. There are certain persons here—never mind who—who wish to ask you a question. Would you fly the Pacific in a Japanese plane—and let Japan have the credit?"

She must have known before I spoke what my answer would be. It seemed to me like the chance of a lifetime. I would have my own revenge if I succeeded.

"Sonya," I said, "for the last hour I've wanted to kiss you, but even if I hadn't, I'd want to now. If you can get me a plane, if you can give me this chance, I'll do anything in the world for you—anything at all." I could see her looking at me with the same expression of pleasure that I have seen a player wear when he has finished a game successfully.

She knew she had me then. We were no longer people but abstractions. Her voice was cool, almost businesslike, as though she said, "Very well, I do not have to bother you any more." But instead she said:

"Will you please wait here," and she rose from her cushion on the floor, tall, lithe and straight, and moved toward the sliding door.

I also rose from my cushion beside the little table, becoming aware as I did so that a foreigner was not fitted for dining in the Japanese manner. The joints of my knees and ankles were stiff from my unaccustomed posture, so that I was glad to stretch myself. It could not have been more than three minutes later when the door slid open. I was not greatly surprised to see my friend Mr. Moto exactly as I had remembered him, with his Prussian-cut hair, cutaway coat and somber studious eyes.

Sonya had evidently given him back the ring, for it was again on his finger just as it had been the previous afternoon. He smiled, bowed and drew in his breath between his teeth. I wished that I could imitate the perfection of the Japanese bow where the head drops forward suddenly as though a knife had severed the spinal cord and then snaps back upright.

"Mr. Moto," I said.

"You remember me, then?" said Mr. Moto. "That is kind of you, when I thought you might have forgotten. I am so glad to see you here."

My gaze seemed to glance off the smoothness of the little man's determined courtesy. "The pleasure is all mine," I said.

"I can well understand," he answered. "Miss Sonya is so charming. I am pleased that you have both come to understand each other. A very remarkable girl."

"Where is she now?" I asked.

Mr. Moto smiled again. "She will be back," he replied; "have no fear. But first I wish to speak to you alone. I represent a group, if you understand me, that has been seeking for someone to fly the Pacific in a Japanese-made plane. You would not object, I hope, to taking our side in a friendly rivalry between Japan and the United States."

"You show me the plane," I said, "and I'll thank you to the end of my days. I'm a good pilot, Mr. Moto."

"There is no need to discuss your qualifications," he said. "I know very well you are."

"I thought you did," I answered.

"If you had been born in Nippon," Mr. Moto's voice was slow and careful, "I think you might have had more consideration. America is so large and powerful that she forgets more easily than we do, I think."

I knew that he was referring to my wild talk at the hotel. I shrugged my shoulders.

"Without discussing my feelings," I told him, "I can tell you frankly that my nationalistic sentiments will not interfere with my flying a Japanese plane, or even working in some other way. I cannot see how there is anything more than friendly rivalry between Japan and America."

Mr. Moto looked at me enigmatically. There is a nameless something in a man, whether he is Asiatic or European, which raises him above the average and I knew that Mr. Moto had that attribute. Neither of us had committed ourselves in a single detail and yet Mr. Moto seemed satisfied with my answers. He even seemed entirely familiar with my thoughts and sympathetic with my situation. "You interest me," he said softly. "Would you mind explaining yourself?"

"What I mean," I replied, "is the event of war. Both our countries have discussed it, but I do not see the possibility of war between us. I think that possibility was over when the United States gave up using the Philippines as a large naval base. The United States has no means of attacking you. While the Hawaiian Islands are under the American flag, it is nearly impossible for you to reach the coast of North America. With the Japan sea, a Japanese lake, and with your present naval building program, I see no chance for an American fleet to approach Japan. Sensible men discount war talk, I think, Mr. Moto."

My speech appeared to please him. "I am so glad," he said. "I can only say that I agree with you heartily. You are a sensible man, Mr. Lee. Shall we have a drink together? Whiskysoda, eh? American whiskysoda for good Japanese and good Americans."

He walked to the door in his stocking feet and called out an order to a servant and a minute later we were sitting down at the small table with our drinks.

I drank mine quickly and filled my glass again, but Mr. Moto consumed his in small careful sips, like a man who had no faith in his alcoholic capacity. I felt the time had come for us to be frank with each other.

"Mr. Moto," I said, "you have found me at a time of great misfortune. I am under no illusions why you are interested in me. You probably heard something I said yesterday at the hotel. I am not prepared to retract any of my remarks. If the opportunity you offer me is genuine, I shall do a great deal to earn it. I imagine I'm close to being an internationalist, Mr. Moto. I know that you don't offer that opportunity for nothing. What is it that you want?"

He did not reply for a while. Instead he looked at the vase of flowers in the niche along the other wall.

"I am very glad to be direct," he said. "I do want something—nothing that will hurt your conscience, I think. You know a good many naval men in your country's fleet. They're friends of yours. You can meet—" he looked at my half-empty glass thoughtfully—"and drink with them, Mr. Lee. They might talk more freely with you than with one of my own countrymen. You follow me?"

"Yes," I said, and I had a curious sensation in my spine as the end of our conversation became more obvious. The little room with its flowers and porcelain figure had assumed in my imagination an ominous aspect. I had a very definite though indefinable sense of personal danger. It was not attributable to Mr. Moto, who sat there in a conscientious parody of a European negotiator. It seemed rather to lie in the bare paperlike walls of that room. There was no disturbing sound, nothing; and yet I was willing to wager that had I started up to leave that room just then I should not have been allowed beyond the door.

"I follow you so far," I said, "but you'll have to go farther, Mr. Moto."

"Gladly," he replied, "as long as you're thoroughly willing."

I knew that he was conveying half a warning, half a threat, but I was willing.

"I understand you, I think," I said.

"Yes," Mr. Moto nodded, "yes, I think you do, so I may be correspondingly frank. A paper, a plan, to be exact, has been abstracted from our naval archives. It is probably now in the hands of some power. My government is simply anxious to learn what power. If you can find out for me that the United States navy is familiar with the plans of a certain new type of Japanese battleship, that is all I wish of you. Do you understand?"

"Yes," I said, and I felt relieved. "I see no real harm in that. You'd find out sooner or later."

"Exactly so." Mr. Moto also looked relieved. "It is a harmless commission. I should not strain your loyalty by giving you a greater one. As a matter of fact, we shall be pleased if your government has this. We fear other powers more. I am being quite open with you. I hope that you agree."

"Very well," I said, "I'll do anything I can." The request seemed harmless enough, but I had an idea that it would have been dangerous if I had refused, and Mr. Moto's next words, distinct and devoid of tone or emphasis, convinced me I was right.

"I am very glad," he said. "You will obey orders then?"

"Yes," I said, "I can mind orders."

"I am very glad," Mr. Moto said again. "I am afraid, Mr. Lee, you must obey them, now that we've gone as far as this. No one would be greatly surprised if you were to disappear—would they, Mr. Lee?"

"Is that a threat or a promise?" I asked.

He paused a moment before he replied.

"I will leave the answer to your own intelligence. When you get back to the hotel you will find a ticket in your room for the *Imoto Maru,* which sails from Yokohama to Shanghai tomorrow night. You will be given ample money for expenses. You will simply mix with the colony of your countrymen in Shanghai—particularly naval officers. There will be further instructions for you later. You understand, I hope."

"Yes," I said, "I understand. And it's understood I have a plane to fly the Pacific when this job is over."

Mr. Moto nodded and held out his hand. "That is entirely understood, and now, I am so glad to have met you. Miss Sonya will see you back to your hotel. There must be no mistakes." There was something in Mr. Moto's manner that showed me there must be no mistakes.

My opinion was confirmed when he slid open the door and I saw several men lounging in the narrow hall outside. A minute later Sonya and I were walking up the narrow street and at its end the same car was waiting for us. Though she was beside me, I had never felt so completely friendless or so cut off from everything I had known. The business I had accepted, though not wholly creditable, seemed harmless enough, particularly when the reward was considered; yet I wondered—was it harmless? Sonya walked beside me, humming a little tune, strange and wild—some Russian peasant song.

"There is one thing," she said, when we were seated together in the automobile. "You must recognize no one on the boat."

"Very well," I answered. Her eyes were on me curiously. She was looking at me soberly and somehow she seemed dangerous, competent. I could imagine that she had an automatic pistol in the white handbag on her lap.

"Any other orders?" I asked.

"No," she said, "not now. So you are one of us, Casey Lee. We are both without a country now." Her words were like the slamming of a door. All my past seemed to be definitely closed and definitely behind me.

I was aware in some way that I had sold part of my soul. I did not mind just then, so long as I was getting value for it. "It is flattering that they have set you to watch me, Sonya," I said. "You're a pretty nurse. Shall I call you nurse?"

"You're right," she answered. "I'm watching you."

"Sonya," I asked her suddenly, almost involuntarily, "what are you getting out of this?"

"Never mind." Her eyes were hard. "I'm being paid a price. You'll do well not to ask questions after this. Simply obey orders, Casey Lee."

I looked at her. Her figure beneath her tailored dress was lithe and strong. Her long fingers were strong and capable. "You're a pretty nurse," I said, "but I'm sorry you're a nurse."

"Let that be as it may." Her throaty voice tinkled like ice in a glass. "We're only even. I'm sorry you're what you are."

"We've got that much in common," I answered cheerfully. "I guess we neither of us have much to boast about, but we're professionals, Sonya. We can earn our pay."

I have tried to set down an accurate and unbiased record of these scenes, without a single effort to put myself or my motives in a favorable light. I wish emphatically to affirm that I meant every word which I said to Moto, that I entered in good faith into a contract which doubtless would seem shocking to many of my fellow citizens. The only reason I can conscientiously offer for my conduct is a humble one, not valid in any court of law—that I did not understand. I did not understand, until subsequent events forced the comprehension upon me, how strong the ties of nationality and race become, when they are presented clearly. There is no quibbling with those ties; there is no way of rationalizing them, when events force one to make an actual decision. I was faced with that decision sooner than I expected—on the very night, in fact, when I boarded the *Imoto Maru,* which reminds me that I am writing a record that has no room in it for moralization. I had better get on with my report, only pausing for one addition. Men die for their faith who have never been inside a church, and men die for their country, although they may have spent their lives criticizing all its works. The amazing thing about it is that they are probably surprised by their irrational willingness to die.

# 4

HALF AN hour after I was aboard, the *Imoto Maru* had moved from the dock in Yokohama and was slipping past the harbor lights of that great port into the Pacific, on her way along the Japan coast to China. She was taking me on a trail which was entirely new to me, for aside from those useless weeks of waiting in Tokyo I had never seen the Orient. I had a comfortable sensation of excitement such as one has nearly always when a ship carries one into the dark. There is always a sense of the unknown in the darkness which may be inherited from the dread of ancient mariners who thought their ship might slip off the end of the world into space. From my point of view the simile was almost true. The *Imoto Maru* had carried me off the edge of my world, it seemed to me beyond hope of returning. I did not mind it very much.

First I took a turn around the first-class quarters of the ship. The *Imoto* was small, as liners go nowadays. Except for her swarthy, stocky-looking crew, she reminded me of the transport which had carried me to France in another incarnation. Companion steps led from the promenade deck down to the bow and the cargo hatches and I climbed down, as there seemed to be no restriction, and walked past the battened hatches and hoisting gear out toward the bow itself. Everything ahead was black except the water beside our hull, which was so brilliantly phosphorescent that evening that it glowed and flashed into flame.

Suddenly it came over me, without my being able to analyze the reason, that I had been followed ever since I had been on that boat. I turned and stared into the dark shadows of derricks and ventilators but I could see no one. Then I felt in the side pocket of my coat for my leather-covered flask and took a drink. It occurred to me that the time had come to do some serious thinking, but the drink from the flask make me delay it, and instead, I thought of Sonya. I wondered if I would ever see her again. Probably not, I decided, for one who has led my sort of life becomes used to inconsequent shifts of personalities. Still, I was sorry that she had left me, and the poignancy of my sorrow surprised me and filled me with a desire to see lights and people, a desire which led me aft to the smoking room.

The *Imoto*, as I have said, was a small ship and the smoking room was a small cabin done in the dull, dark wood decorations of smoking rooms the world over. Japanese and Chinese business men were seated about the little tables, reminding me that the Orient was fast becoming like the rest of the world and that manners and customs were superficially, at any rate, becoming nearly the same in every part of it. At first I thought I was the only European there until I heard someone calling me. A small, hard-bitten, sandy-haired man was waving a glass at me from the other end of the room.

"Has the liquor got me at last," he whooped, "or is that you, Casey Lee."

Then I knew how small the world was and how strangely paths become crossed. A picture of the sandy hair, and the sandpaper-like features flashed across my mind, though I had not seen them for a long while. The man was one of those wanderers like myself;

Sam Bloom, an old pilot from one of the army squadrons who had come into my life during the war and who had disappeared almost as casually. At another time I should have been glad to have seen him, for there is a companionship among flying men which time does not efface, but just then I was almost embarrassed. How was I to explain to Sam Bloom exactly what I was doing? Far from feeling my embarrassment, Sam gave another whoop of delight.

"Come on, Casey!" he shouted. "Come over here and we'll drink out the bar!"

"Sam," I said, "let's get out of here," and I took him by the scruff of the neck and yanked him out the door onto the deck.

"Hey," said Sam Bloom.

I got a firmer grip on his coat collar. "Come down to my cabin," I said. "We can talk better down there."

Bloom's topaz-colored eyes grew alert. "Anything the matter, Casey? What are you doing here?"

I did not answer him until we were in the cabin, an outside room on B deck, on an aisle amidship. The cabin was big enough to show that Mr. Moto had done me well. A large bed, two upholstered armchairs, a wardrobe closet.

"Say," Bloom said, "you're living in style, aren't you, Casey? Well, you're in the big money now."

"I'm not," I said. "The Pacific flight's all off. I'm going to Shanghai."

"Is that so?" said Sam Bloom, and for the first time in our conversation, his voice had turned cautious. "If you're looking for a job—" He eyed me and tapped a cigarette against the back of his hand. "You're able to take a job, aren't you, Casey?"

"What makes you think I'm not?" I asked.

"You're looking seedy," he said. "Your fingers shake. Listen, Lee, it wouldn't make me popular if I said it out loud here on a Japanese boat, but I'm a flying instructor for the Chinese army. Say the word and I'll get you in."

I was embarrassed as to how to answer.

"Maybe—I don't know," I said.

We must have talked there about old times for an hour, and when he left me I felt bitterer than usual. Bitterer because Sam Bloom also had pitied me, and out of the kindness of his heart had offered me the only opportunity he could think of, the chance of teaching young Chinese soldiers how to fly. I almost wished that he had offered me that chance a day before, because I think I would have taken it gladly, but it was too late now. Then another thought struck me.

No one had asked me for my tickets or my passport—a strange omission for a passenger vessel—and how was I to land in China?

It had not occurred to me until that moment that I had torn my passport in two and had thrown it on the floor of the Imperial Hotel in Tokyo. I reached automatically for my inside pocket that contained the envelope with my steamship tickets. I had not examined them carefully before, but now that I did so, I was confronted by an astonishing sight. In the envelope beside the tickets was my passport, so perfectly mended that I could hardly detect a break in its pages. The sight of it reminded me that Mr. Moto had thought of everything.

The engines of that ship were pulsing beneath me, sending a steady throbbing tremor up and down my spine. That restless feeling of vibration reminded me again that I was being carried to an unknown place on an incomprehensible errand. The knowledge made me feel distinctly ill at ease and the uncertainty made me restless. My wrist watch told me that it was late, already close to midnight, but I had no desire to sleep. Instead, I walked back through the companionways and up the stairs to the smoking room. That was when I had my first shock of surprise, just as I stood on the threshold of that small and rather ugly room.

The passengers had cleared out by then, except for a Japanese in a cutaway coat and a woman with reddish-gold hair, who was seated with him at one of the round tables. At first I thought that I was dreaming, but there was no mistake as to who those two were. Mr. Moto and Sonya Karaloff, whom I had believed I had left permanently in Tokyo, were there in the smoking room, talking in low voices. In my astonishment I found it difficult to analyze my feelings, but I experienced something like a twinge of jealousy when I saw the girl with Moto at the table.

"Why, hello," I said. "I thought I was here alone."

It was a silly enough remark, as I knew I had not really been alone since Moto had clapped eyes on me at the Imperial Hotel. I knew that I had been watched carefully ever since. But their reaction was amazing.

Mr. Moto turned toward me politely and raised his delicate eyebrows so that his forehead puckered in wrinkles up to the shoebrush cut of his black hair.

"Excuse me," he said, "there must be some mistake."

"What?" I asked him. "What mistake?"

He smiled apologetically. "It is so easy for a foreigner to mistake one of my people for someone else," he said. "I am so very sorry. I have never had the pleasure—of meeting you before."

Sonya was looking at me also, blankly, half amused. "Nor I either," she said. "There must be some mistake."

I gazed at them stupidly before I remembered Sonya's cautioning me that I was not to recognize anyone on the boat.

"I beg your pardon," I said then. "This was careless of me."

Mr. Moto smiled tranquilly and answered, "It is quite all right, but it is better to be careful."

That was all there was to the scene. We did not say another word and perhaps there should have been no need for anything further to convince me that I was in the midst of something that was dark and devious, almost sinister—not after seeing those two there.

I sat in the corner of the smoking room for a little while as though I were a stranger, watching Sonya and Moto from the corner of my eye. I did not like it. I did not like to see her sitting with Moto, though it was none of my business. I felt that she did not belong in such a rôle. Finally I rose and went on deck. There was nothing but a warm breeze and a dark sea on deck, but, all the same, although the promenade seemed deserted, I had that same feeling of being watched. I could have sworn there were footsteps behind me as I walked by the rail. Once I was so sure of it that I spun around sharply on my heel, only to discover that there was no one visible—only the bare promenade behind me with a row of electric lights above it. Finally I went to my stateroom again, not because I wished to sleep, but because the place, on account of my baggage, was familiar and reassuring.

The cabin was just as I had left it, with my bags in exactly the places I remembered, but in some way I knew that someone had been there in my absence. Perhaps everyone, some time in his life, has had a similar experience of awareness—nothing else. As soon as I turned to bolt my door, I knew that my intuition was right, for the bolt had been removed. I could see the holes where the screws had been driven into the white woodwork of the door, but there was no bolt, and the sight gave me a second idea. I reached for my large leather suitcase and began fumbling with the straps, hastily and rather clumsily. If there was no bolt on the door, at least I wanted to be armed.

I had traveled in Japan with a thirty-eight automatic. I cannot remember exactly why I had taken this precaution, except that the Orient had always seemed a distant and peculiar place. I had carried it in my pocket through the customs and then had deposited it in the bottom of my bag. When I looked for it that night, however, it was not there. For a moment I stood with my hand close to the steward's call button before common sense came back to me. They might not have wished me to lock myself in and they might have abstracted my automatic, but this was probably a part of the meticulous caution of a suspicious race which, I decided, probably meant no harm. Half an hour later I was in bed and had turned out the light. The porthole was open and a breeze blew across the cabin and I lay for a while listening to the swish of water and the throbbing of the engines before I went to sleep.

I have never been sure of the time when I woke up. It must have been in the dark of the small hours of the morning when something caused me to open my eyes, only to find myself staring into the black; but a flyer's life makes the senses quick to perceive changes of atmosphere which may not dawn on others who have passed quieter days. As soon as I opened my eyes, I knew there was something wrong in spite of the same steady pulsing of the engines, and the same sound of water. Yet there was some change in the darkness which I could not describe. I knew I was not alone in my cabin. The knowledge did not frighten me as much as it annoyed me, for I was growing tired of constant espionage.

"Who's there?" I said.

A voice answered, so close to my ear that I gave a start. Though I could not see a thing, I knew that whoever was there must be kneeling beside my bed.

"Hush!" It was a man's voice, speaking very softly. "Please do not speak loud. I am a friend, Mr. Gentleman! I do not hurt."

"Who are you?" I asked. Something in his voice made me careful not to raise my own. "What are you doing in here?"

"Please—" the voice was nearer to me—"don't turn on the light! I do not wish them to see light. It is very dangerous, so many watch."

I reached down and grasped an arm of the man beside me. "Who are you?" I demanded again. "What do you want?"

"Only to speak to you." The answer came again, so softly that I had difficulty in catching the words. The arm did not move away. The impassiveness of that arm more than the voice made me listen. “Please do not speak loud or turn on the light. I’m in very great danger, Mr. Gentleman. I come and no one see, I think. I go and no one must see. I have something which they want. You are an American—you know American navy men.”

“Well,” I said, “what of it?”

“You know an American navy gentleman they call Commander Driscoll? You see him. You tell him I come to you. You tell him Ma come. I am in great danger, Mr. Gentleman. I think they know who I am. Mr. Moto, he know, I think. Will you tell Commander Driscoll, please—”

“Tell him what?” I whispered, and I knew that the man beside me was afraid of something—deathly afraid.

“I leave you note,” he said, “tomorrow, not now. I see you again tomorrow night because you are American. If I die, you tell Mr. Wu Lai-fu in Shanghai, if you please. You give note to him, if Commander Driscoll is not there.”

“What are you taking about?” I whispered.

“Please,” the voice was trembling in a strange appeal, “I have no time to say. Great danger. If I give you note, you take it, please.”

“Why?” I asked.

“Because,” the voice seemed closer to me, “because you are American gentleman. Americans all very good people. You see when you get note. You give Driscoll. You tell Wu Lai-fu. Please, I’m going now.”

For a moment I lay there, wondering if I were asleep or awake, wondering if I were going mad; then I moved quickly and switched on the light. My cabin door was just closing very softly and there was no one in the cabin.

I could have believed that I had been asleep if it had not been for the sight of that softly closing door. Those whispered words in my ear were exactly like the words spoken by some agency in the subconscious mind which ring in one’s memory sometimes when one awakes suddenly and inexplicably in the middle of the night. That closing door was all which proved to me that I had not been asleep. I had been wide awake, listening to mysterious, dreamlike words spoken by a man whom I had not seen. Even though I could not understand those words, I had sense enough to see that they were ominous. They and my nerves conveyed to me the impression that a drama on that Japanese ship was moving silently around me and that I was being drawn into it whether I wished it or not. It was the first time, I think, that I had any definite idea of the seriousness of my own position.

As I tried to set my mind in motion to recall what I had heard, I grew uncomfortably aware that I could not be sure of myself, that my recollection and logic were blurred by alcohol and sleep. I was ashamed to admit to myself that my condition made me unfit to play a definite part in a crisis. Nevertheless, I did the best I could by trying to recall just what had passed. An unseen man, an Oriental, by his voice, who said his name was Ma, had been kneeling by my bed. He had spoken like a man who had been followed and watched; like a man laboring under fear. He had alluded to his imminent danger and to some message which he wished me to convey to Commander Driscoll. He had mentioned the name of a Chinese in Shanghai, and for some reason that name stuck peculiarly in my memory, perhaps because of its phonetic quality—Wu Lai-fu. But what was it about? What business was developing on that ship? What was Moto doing there, or Sonya? Why had the lock been removed from my door and my baggage searched? It was all entirely beyond me, but I felt that my heart was beating fast. I felt that I needed a drink and reached toward my old leather-covered flask which stood on the washstand. I reached for it and then I stopped. For the first time in years my own caution stopped me, for something warned me that my mind needed to be steady—steady without the relaxing effect of alcohol. So, though my nerves were jangling, I did not touch the flask. As I look back, I can always believe that night was a turning point in my career. My life had made me used to excitement and it had also made me reasonable. I was fully aware that it would have been useless and even dangerous to have raised an alarm. Instead of calling, I switched out the light then and got back into bed, not that I could have slept if I'd tried. Nor did I have the slightest desire to sleep, for I had an idea that the invisible stranger might be back again.

If so, I wished to be ready, therefore I half sat up, waiting in the dark, listening to the waves and wind outside my porthole singing that ceaseless song of the sea. There was no way of telling the time, but I must have been there for quite a while before I knew that I was right. Someone was entering my cabin again.

There was no sound of footsteps to warn me, but simply the noiseless opening of the unbolted door, showing first a crack of light from the alleyway outside, a crack which grew appreciably wider. Then, as I saw the light blotted out by a shadow, I slipped noiselessly off my bed. I was able to cross the cabin almost at a single leap and an instant later I was grappling with that shadow. Physical contact gave me a sense of reality. There was a moment's noiseless struggle but whoever I had my hands on was not so strong as I. I could feel heavy woolen cloth and hear a sharp hissing breath. It is hard, at such a time as that, to remember just what happened, but suddenly the cabin light went on without my being able to recall which of us touched the switch. I could only recall that suddenly the light was on and that I was standing in the middle of the cabin, holding a Japanese ship's officer by the throat and shaking him so that he choked.

"Please," the man was saying, "excuse—"

And then I let him go. I let him go but I placed myself between him and the door and slammed it shut, while he stood in the center of the cabin feeling his windpipe.

"Excuse," he said. "Excuse."

I examined him for a moment before I answered. He was a small man with a face which reminded me of toy breeds of bulldogs which I'd seen at home. Even in that instant, however, there was one thing I was certain of intuitively. He was not the man who had been kneeling beside my bed, because he was not frightened. This little bulldog man had the assurance of a hunter and a bravery incommensurate with his size.

"Excuse," he said again.

"Next time you come in here, knock!" I said. "What's the big idea?"

He began to bow, bobbing his head like a character in Gilbert and Sullivan and raising his hand politely in front of his lips. "It was a mistake," he said. "I am so very, very sorry."

"You're all of you so very, very sorry," I said. "Suppose you answer my question. What brought you inside my cabin?"

He was looking carefully about the room with his square jaw thrust forward, but finally he smiled at me in a bland mirthless way. "There is some mistake," he explained. But obviously something puzzled him. "I thought there was someone else here. Excuse—was there not someone else?"

Some instinct prompted me to lie before I had a definite reason for my motive. It had something to do with the other's face which, in spite of the worry and embarrassment on it, looked relentless.

"What do you mean?" I asked. "Why should anyone else be here? I have this cabin to myself."

Then he straightened himself officially. "I must explain," he answered. "It was my duty. I found myself called away. My duty was to watch your door. I have done very badly. If no one was here, I am very glad."

"No one was here," I said. His narrow eyes bored sharply into mine. Then he glanced about the cabin again.

"You are sure no one has been here and left something? It is important, please."

"No," I said again, "no one has been here."

His eyes concentrated on me keenly, as if something in my manner did not entirely satisfy him.

"Why were you watching my cabin?" I asked.

"Please," he answered, "for your own safety. If no one was here, I am very glad." He bowed again and started toward the door, and I opened the door and let him out.

"Don't come in here again," I said.

"No," he answered, "no, I will not come in again. Please excuse. Good night."

When he was gone, I pushed an armchair against the door. I knew there would have been no use in asking further questions. Nevertheless, one thing was very clear: he had not been there to watch me but to watch someone else. He had not watched sharply enough, and in the space of time when his vigilance had relaxed, someone had entered my cabin. It was as though my room were a trap and as though I were a bait for someone. I knew that the bolt had been removed from my door so that someone could enter my cabin.—Why? I could not answer.

Curiously, however, none of these speculations or events impressed me as much as another matter. A single detail had moved me strangely—irrationally, I could almost think. It had to do with the appeal of that invisible stranger who had whispered in my ear. He had appealed to me because, by accident of birth, I was an American, and something inside me which had lain dormant for a long while was struggling to answer that appeal, strongly, mutely, against my reason, my cynicism and self-interest. My nationality had become so important to me, a matter of such deep significance, that I was startled. I had never realized that a place of birth could mean so much, but it was true. My entire point of view was changing, because I had been called an American.

# 5

I AM TRYING to set down the events as they occurred. It is not my fault if they sound fantastic. As I look back, the strangest part of that adventure was the impervious tranquillity of the life aboard that ship which moved on with no reference to myself. When I sat with Sam Bloom in the dining saloon at breakfast the next morning, we seemed so like tourists on a pleasant outing that I could almost forget everything which had occurred. The sun shone through the portholes of the dining saloon upon neat white tablecloths and white-coated efficient stewards.

"Did you sleep all right?" Sam Bloom asked.

"Like a top," I said.

"You don't look it," he answered. "Shall we go up topside and have a drink?"

"No, thanks," I said, though I wanted a drink very badly.

Then he made a remark which sounded like a tourist's.

"The Japanese are an amazing people."

I nodded.

"But dangerous," he added. "They're always watching us, they suspect us all the time." He stopped, looking over my shoulder in such a startled way that I followed his glance, to find that the head steward was standing behind my chair.

"Please," he said, "if you are finished, there is a gentleman who wishes to see you."

"Who?" I asked.

"Please," the steward said, "if you have finished."

I rose and followed him out of the dining room, while Sam Bloom watched us curiously. The steward guided me to one of the *de luxe* staterooms on the upper deck.

"Who wants to see me?" I asked again.

The steward did not answer, but tapped softly on the door until a voice answered in Japanese. Then I was in a private sitting room with the door closed behind me, facing my old friend Mr. Moto, who sat behind a little table, sipping a cup of tea.

Mr. Moto, in his cutaway coat, looked immaculate and composed, and I was glad to see him, for I fear that Mr. Moto owed me an explanation. He waved me to a chair, smiling as he offered me a cigarette.

"Good morning, Mr. Lee," he said. "We may recognize each

other in private. Are you quite comfortable? I am so sorry that you did not sleep well last night."

"Thanks," I said, "I didn't. Do you mind if I make a further remark?"

"No," he answered. "Please what remark?"

"I'd like to say," I replied, "that I'm confused."

"Life," Mr. Moto answered, "is often confusing; do you not think?"

I dropped my cigarette into an ash tray, the bottom of which was filled with water.

"Will you have a drink?" Mr. Moto asked. "What? Not drinking? Something must have disturbed you last night."

"One of your officers disturbed me," I said. "I found the bolt was off my door and one of your officers put his head in. Would you care to tell me why?"

It was plain he did not care to tell me why. Instead, he wriggled his shoulders apologetically.

"I have heard," he answered. "Excuse. It was so very careless of the man. His duty was to see that you were not disturbed. He was not true to his duty. Was that the only thing that disturbed you, Mr. Lee? I shall like it if you will tell me."

"Yes," I answered, and I still don't know what induced me to prevaricate except that new national sense of mine. "Only the officer bothered me. Suppose we be frank, Mr. Moto," I added.

"Why not," he answered. "That is what I am here for, yes? You are sure there was no one else in your cabin? It is very important—and so I ask."

"I was drunk last night," I said. The answer must have satisfied him, for I could feel a certain tension relaxing in the room and Mr. Moto sank back in his chair and lighted a cigarette. In the silence that followed, the turgidness of everything began to strain my patience.

"Perhaps," I suggested, "you were expecting someone else to come into my cabin?"

His expression changed at that. To my surprise, I found him looking at me almost with respect. "So. That is so. Yes," he answered. "That is why I wish to speak with you. You can be of very great use to us, Mr. Lee, if you do exactly what I say. I do expect someone to come to your cabin, and if he does, I hope you will ask no questions, no matter what may happen. It is very important—do you understand?"

"Why is it important?" I asked.

Mr. Moto stared thoughtfully at me for a while before replying, his opaque brown eyes devoid of meaning.

"I cannot tell you why it is important," he answered. "I only ask you to do exactly what I say, please. There is someone on this ship whom we desire very much to interrogate. Unfortunately, we have no exact description and do not know who he is. We—ah—guess he is on this vessel, and I hope so much we guess right. We hope that he comes to your cabin. Then, you see, we will know him."

"Why should he come to my cabin?" I asked.

Mr. Moto paused a minute. He gazed at me as if I were a figure in a column of addition, not a person of flesh and blood. "I will be frank," he answered finally; "because you were once an American naval officer he will come. It is nothing that concerns you, if you please. You need not be disturbed. You are not disturbed, are you?"

Though I tried to keep my expression blank, I was very much disturbed. "Any other orders?" I said.

"No," he replied, "not now. Simply amuse yourself, Mr. Lee, and—yes, this: Do not think too much of anything that has happened. There is very good brandy in the smoking room and it is a very nice morning. You must not worry. You do so well and everything goes so nicely." He rose and bowed. "Good morning, Mr. Lee."

I bowed also, and then I found myself outside the door, unpleasantly aware that I was a pawn on Mr. Moto's chess-board, which did not please my egotism, because I have never liked to be a pawn. I had not told Mr. Moto of the visitor to my cabin, and now I knew that nothing would induce me to tell him.

I shall never forget the rest of that day, if only because of its utter lack of incident, for nothing happened, absolutely nothing. The life on that *Maru* steamer simply lowered itself to the routine boredom of shipboard, leaving a passenger like me to his own limited devices. At such a time, to anyone of my temperament, the lack of definite outlet of action was peculiarly appalling. On another occasion I would have relieved the suspense by drink, as I was tempted to do more than once that day. But that desire to keep my mind clear was still uppermost in my thoughts. I paced the deck for a while, looking out to starboard at the blue mountainous coast line of Japan and watching the occasional slatted sails of fishing fleets. I could not blame the Japanese very much for desiring more land; for the islands of the Empire seemed, as one viewed them from the sea, almost entirely composed of jagged mountain slopes which offered little opportunity in the way of life or husbandry. Behind the pastel purples and blues and greens of distant mountain ranges, which seemed to conceal the secrets of Nippon, I could think of a teeming population longing to leave that unstable volcanic coast. The fishing fleet was like a part of that desire pushing out from the mountains to the horizon. Our own ship, with its squat capable sailors, was a part of it. The red-and-white flag of Nippon was pushing out to sea, to end no one knew just where.

As I walked forward and glanced toward the line where the horizon met the sky in soft gray clouds, I saw another sight which made me halt at the rail and stare—an apparition that was half beautiful, half sinister. Out of the cloud bank by the horizon appeared the masts of ships that seemed to have, at that distance, almost the impalpable qualities of clouds. A division of a battle fleet was out on one of its perpetual maneuvers—gray Japanese cruisers moving behind a formation of submarines and destroyers. There was a foreboding quality to that half-visible sight, because I understood, as everyone who has walked a deck of an American warship understands, that Japan's naval strength might some day be directed at my country; that it was reaching out like an arm across the Pacific toward our coasts where our own fleet was watching. There was destiny in the sight, which was a part of the obscure irrational destiny of peoples never to be wholly clarified by reason. It was solitary being on a Japanese ship, the only representative of my country except that casual aviator, Sam Bloom. That situation made me feel very keenly the differences of race, and more aware than I think I ever have been, even in the distant days of the World War, that I was an integral part of my country. Then I heard Sam Bloom speaking to me and I was glad that he had come to stand beside me. I had never been so much drawn to that little sandy-haired friend of mine as I was at that moment, simply because we were strangers among a strange people. I had an impulse to tell him everything which had happened to me, I think I should have, if I had not felt suddenly ashamed of my position and of myself.

"Nice-looking lot of boats, aren't they?" he remarked.

"Yes," I said.

"I wonder if we'll ever fight 'em?" remarked Sam Bloom.

"A lot of people wonder that," I found myself answering, glad to speak to someone who had an intonation like my own. "I hope to heaven we don't. In spite of the arguments about the Japanese never having encountered a first-rate power, I'm afraid they'd make a lot of trouble, Sam."

Sam Bloom squinted his eyes out toward the horizon and drummed his stubby fingers on the rail. "Last time I was in Shanghai, there were a lot of rumors," he said. "The word is, those boys are up to something; that they've hit on some new naval secret. They're clever and persistent. That's the word—persistent. They're getting so that they can beat us at all our manufacturing trade. But we can't stop them, can we? How about a drink?"

"No thanks," I said. "I'm on the wagon."

I did not blame Sam Bloom for being incredulous.

"Say, Casey, is anything on your mind?" he asked.

"Only myself," I answered, "and that doesn't amount to much."

"Say," said Sam. "There's a pretty girl around here. Did you see her? Reddish-yellow hair. Russian, I suppose. Shanghai is full of white Russians—not that any Europeans meet them socially. Let's go and talk to her. She doesn't look as if she'd mind."

"Try it," I said. "I tried last night." I saw that Sonya was walking toward us down the deck.

"You watch me," said Sam and took off his hat and smiled. "Hello. It's a nice morning!" But Sonya walked by like an alluring figure of the imagination, nothing more.

Those violet eyes of hers stared straight through us. There was a whiff of gardenia scent and she was gone.

"Well," said Sam Bloom. "My mistake. We're not popular on this boat, Casey. How about a drink?"

"You have one," I said.

There is no need to describe any further the events of that day. They rolled by as easily as the ship rolled through an oily sea. A stop at the docks of Kobe. A game of cards, lunch in the small dining saloon, where Japanese passengers ate with chopsticks and made strange noises over their food. Another game of cards in the smoking room, where I watched Sonya and Moto talking at a table near the door.

"So that's the answer," Sam Bloom said. "She's that little swell's mistress—that's the answer."

"That isn't so," I answered, before I thought.

"Say—" Sam Bloom looked at me—"how do you know?"

"I don't believe she is—that's all," I said.

Yes, the day dragged on, a horrible, eventless day. Dinner in the dining saloon and back in the smoking room again, an interminable walk along the deck and back to the smoking room again. I was waiting for something to happen, but nothing happened. Finally, when Bloom and I were left alone in the smoking room except for two sleepy stewards, I believed that nothing would happen. My lack of sleep the night before began to make me very drowsy and finally I said good night to him. I hope he had a good one.

## 6

IN SOME curious way my mood must have been changed by the dullness of the day until I was lulled by its dullness into bored security. I had no real suspicion that anything would be wrong when I opened my cabin door. First, when I opened the door, I recall having the distinct impression that I had made a mistake and that the quarters were not mine. Of course, such a sensation as this was only a matter of an instant, which I mention simply to bring out the complete unexpectedness of what I encountered. Subconsciously I knew all the time it was my cabin, although my common sense told me that it could not be because there on the floor a man was lying face upward—a moon-faced Asiatic man whom I had never seen, dressed in a shoddy suit of European clothes.

He lay on the floor like a drunkard, sprawled out in an attitude of complete abandon and carelessness of convention, shaven-headed, open-eyed, and open-mouthed. For another split second I had a sensation of outrage because I could not understand what he was doing in my cabin overcome by liquor, but the truth manifested itself in an instant. That Asiatic man in the shoddy European clothes was offering his own mute apology for lying face upward on the carpet. A stream of blood, that was making a puddle behind his shoulders, was excuse enough for his seeming rudeness. The man had been stabbed in the back, and not long ago either. But that was not all of the picture. A sound of an indrawn breath made my glance dart from that sight on the floor to the recess near my porthole. Standing there, her face as white as paper except for the paint on her lips, was Sonya Karaloff, holding a knife in her hand.

Anyone who has been through the war is inured to the sight of death. I have seen it, in scores of forms, strike out of nowhere. I have seen dead men mangled by shellfire and dead men lying pallid like men asleep. I have seen the unbelievable liberties which war has taken with the bodies of men, but this present spectacle was different. It was the first time in my life that I had witnessed the scene of cold, premeditated murder, and for a moment it made me sick; and for a moment I felt a wave of nausea rise in me and with the nausea faintness. Then I pulled myself together because, I suppose, my reflexes are unusually quick. Those reflexes were making me move so accurately that they surprised me; even before my mind began to function, I found myself closing the cabin door behind me, not carelessly but very carefully, so that the latch clicked gently. And then, with my eyes on Sonya, I began to speak, without giving way to the horror that was in me. I believe I spoke quite calmly, fortified after the shock was over by my intimate acquaintance with dead men.

"I am sorry," I said. "I'm afraid perhaps I have intruded."

She stared at me, speechless, still holding that knife in her hand, and I noticed that the blade was wet.

"But after all," I said, "this is my room, you know."

And still she did not answer.

Then I found myself making an inane remark. "I didn't know you were that kind of girl," I said. "You must be very muscular or surgically inclined. They tell me it isn't easy to stab a man in the back so that he drops right down like this one here."

She opened her lips and closed them—wordlessly.

"It's curious," I said, "the element of time." I found myself continuing simply to steady my own nerves. "If I had been sleepy five minutes sooner, this moon-faced man might still be alive, perhaps. If I had been sleepy five minutes later, I doubt if I should have had the pleasure of having a delightful golden-headed girl like you in my cabin. Which would have been better, I wonder?"

Then, for the first time, she spoke. "It's Ma," she said. "It's Ma—"

Initially the name meant nothing, but then the truth dawned on me. The man I had not seen the night before, the man who had wished to give me something because I was an American, the man who had told me that his name was Ma, was now lying beside my bed, and he would not whisper any more.

"I believe you're right," I said; "it must be Ma."

"You—" she said. She stared; a trace of color came into her cheeks; and I saw the pupils in her violet eyes widen. It was not pleasant to see her there in an evening wrap, with a knife in her hand.

"How did you know that?" she asked.

I leaned against the closed door of the cabin but I did not take my eyes off her.

"I think," I suggested, "I should feel more comfortable if you put down that knife. I don't think I've ever struck or mishandled a woman, but believe me I will, if you don't set it down. I don't want my throat cut too."

She looked blankly at the knife she was holding and then she dropped it on the floor. "I did not know I'd picked it up," she said.

"That was very absent-minded," I answered, "don't you think?" Then she moved a step towards me and came near to stumbling over that figure on the floor.

"Please," she said, "please, won't you help me?"

Her suggestion seemed to me grimly amusing—so amusing that I wanted to laugh out loud.

"Don't you think you're very well able to help yourself?" I suggested. "You've done an efficient job—not exactly neat, but efficient. Do you always stab them in the back?"

I do not believe that she heard me. At any rate, she disregarded my question.

Her hand went up to her bare throat, a slim, white trembling hand.

"I—" she stopped and seemed to choke upon her words. "I came here to see you." Again I had an almost uncontrollable desire to break out into laughter.

"That was thoughtful of you," I answered, "but selfishly, perhaps, I am just as glad that I was out." She did not seem to hear me.

"It's Ma—" Her voice was choked. "Don't you see it's Ma?"

"You mistake your tenses," I suggested. "You mean it was Ma, don't you? You Russians are so linguistic that you've conjugated him from the present to the past."

"Don't!" she whispered. "Don't!"

"Oh?" I said. "Perhaps you're sorry, now?"

"Don't!" she whispered again. "Please, please—I didn't kill him! I came to see you. And I found him lying here. It's Ma—"

"So you've said several times," I answered. "Who is Ma?"

By that time she had regained her self-possession. In spite of her delicacy and beauty she always, as I have said, gave one the sense of competence to encounter any situation.

"You don't understand," she said. "I didn't know he was here. Why didn't he speak to me? I suppose he didn't dare."

"Perhaps you didn't give him a chance," I suggested.

"Don't!" She did not raise her voice, but its intensity made me stop. "Don't speak like that! I swear I didn't kill him. You don't understand. He was my father's old interpreter and servant."

Though my intellect told me she would naturally be lying, something made me believe her, for no one could have simulated her look of pain. I thought for a second that she would lose control of herself and weep. Her face became convulsed. She raised a handkerchief to her lips.

"Don't!" I said sharply. "Who killed him then?"

"They—" she whispered. "He must have had a message. They suspected something. Why didn't he tell me?" Then she was completely calm again. Whatever she might have been and whatever she meant, that girl was brave.

If I could not understand what part she was playing in that drama, at least I could admire her bravery. She must have lived a life where one made accurate decisions, without time for much mental debate.

"We must leave here at once," she said. "If he knew I had come here, I don't know what would happen. Please—" she touched my arm and nodded to the door. "Quickly, quickly, please!" Her urgency and the swiftness of her decision made me respond instantly.

I whipped open the door and then we were out in the corridor and her hand on my arm was trembling. There was no one in the passageway.

"This way," she whispered and pulled me around a corner. "Listen! Here they come."

She was right. At the end of the passage we had left I heard soft steps and low voices. If she had not been decisive, they would have seen us in another instant. She snatched at the handle of the cabin door beside us, but even in her haste she was adroit and quick, and fortunately the door was not locked. A second later we were in the dark of a vacant cabin, listening to footsteps and the voices through a crack of the door. Then she closed it noiselessly and we were plunged into pitch blackness, standing close together—so close that I felt her breath on my cheek. She still held my arm and her fingers tightened on my sleeve. I felt her lips brush my cheek as she whispered so faintly that I could hardly hear her.

"I don't think they saw us. You must never say that you came down to your cabin—never! You must wait here for just a moment, not too long. When I open the door, move to the right and go straight up to the deck. Someone will speak to you there, of course. They will say they've changed your cabin."

I whispered back to her and I felt my forehead touch that soft gold hair. "What did you want to see me for? What was it?"

"Because I was a fool," she whispered. "Because I grew to like you. I wanted to tell you something—about this rotten business. I wanted you to be sure you knew what you were doing . . . sure you knew what he was using you for. I can't tell you now because you must go . . . but when you get to Shanghai, go home to America! Go anywhere. Don't trust them! No one should like anyone in this business. I know I've been a fool. Now go quickly up on deck."

"What about you?" I whispered.

"Never mind about me. I know how to look out for myself. Good-by."

But I did not move. I did not want to go away. "I rather like you too," I said. "Will I ever see you again?"

"Probably not," she whispered, and suddenly she threw her arms around me. She held me close to her for an instant. "Good-by—now go!" she said.

I crept through the half-open door and turned to the right as she directed. Except for the vibration of the ship, everything was very quiet. I did exactly what she told me, because I knew she meant every word she said. I hurried up on deck. I could not have been there more than a minute, looking over the rail, when that toy bulldog of an officer came up to me.

"I have been looking for you," he said. "Something has occurred. I am so sorry, if for a few minutes you cannot go to bed."

"Why not?" I asked him. "What's the matter?" And when I asked, I could not help wondering if he was the man who had driven home the knife.

"So sorry," he said apologetically, "so very sorry. The water pipe in your cabin has been leaking. We are removing you to a better one, a *de luxe* cabin on this deck. It will not take long."

"All right," I said. "I never liked that cabin."

"No," he agreed, "it was uncomfortable. A very nice night, is it not?"

They were doing everything very smoothly. Clearly, as a part of the plan, the little officer was there to watch me safe to bed. "It is a nice night," he said again, "is it not?"

"Fine," I answered. "I've been up in the bow. I hope you weren't looking for me long."

"In the bow," he answered; "that is very nice. No, I was not looking for you long."

Five minutes later a steward spoke to the officer softly in Japanese.

"We can go now. Your room is ready," my bulldog said.

He was right that my quarters were improved. I was shown to a fine cabin with a large square port. My pajamas were laid out, and my slippers and my bags were all in place, in the same order that they had been in the stateroom below. Even my leather-covered pocket flask was standing by the washbowl. Further, to my relief, my cabin door had a bolt on it, which I drew noiselessly as soon as I was alone. Then I looked carefully at my bags and saw that the clothes in them had been moved, although they were folded neatly. My baggage had been searched again. Every one of my pockets had been searched. Every inch of my baggage had been gone over by deft-fingered experts. They had been looking for something in my old cabin. They had been searching for something with a tireless zeal. It was because that dead Chinese had left something there,—some note, some message for me before he had died, a note which he hoped I would give to Commander Driscoll because I had been in the American navy. It must have been an important message, important enough, at any rate, to cost a man his life. I wondered if they had found it. As I wondered, I looked at my pocket flask longingly, for after the excitement, the desire for a drink was very strong in me. I even picked it up and had my fingers on the silver cup that formed the bottom of the flask before I checked myself. I knew more than ever that it would be wise to be cold sober, and I set the flask back in its place.

Then I thought of Sonya Karaloff. I could still feel the touch of her hair against my forehead and the pressure of her arms as she held me close. Had she been sincere at that moment, I wondered?

Or was it simply a part of seduction, because she thought I was a broken drunkard who might be used? I could not tell, but I hoped that she had meant it, I was surprised how much I hoped. . . .

I examined the bolt on my door carefully before I undressed for bed, but the bolt was firmly set and I was not disturbed that night. The lock on the inside was perfect, but when I moved back the bolt and endeavored to open the door, I found it had been fastened on the outside also. I was a prisoner in the cabin.

I have never been under any illusion that I'm intellectually brilliant beyond the average. Yet it is true that the shock of such a sequence of events and the realization of imminent danger are calculated either to cause panic or to set the mind at work. They had on me a beneficial effect which was close to a sort of regeneration. They gave me a new perspective on myself.

I knew something which Mr. Moto did not. He was looking for a message and he had not found it, or else he would not have locked my door. Since he had locked me in, he clearly thought that I had found it.

"Let him think," I whispered to myself. "He won't get any change from me."

For I was sure of one thing by then. I was through with Mr. Moto and through with the whole lying devious affair in which he had involved me, and through with all the motives which had drawn me into it. I was myself again. I was Casey Lee. It was a long while since I had been myself.

## 7

I DID what I thought was best under the circumstances. I went quietly to bed, confident that I would not remain locked in my room indefinitely; nor was I mistaken. At eight o'clock in the morning there was a tapping on my door, which grew increasingly persistent until I arose and drew back the bolt. It was a room steward carrying a tray with fruit and coffee, and he drew in his breath politely.

"So sorry," he said, "so very sorry. Somehow the door was locked. Please, there is a gentleman to see you." He set the tray on a chair beside my bed.

"Where is he?" I asked.

"Please," the steward said, "if you are ready, he will come right in." He must have taken it for granted that I was ready, because an instant later Mr. Moto appeared in his morning coat.

We must have looked strange, me in my pajamas, and Mr. Moto in his morning coat, but neither of us forgot the formalities. I bowed and Mr. Moto bowed and the steward departed.

"Moto," I asked, "why was I locked in here last night?"

Mr. Moto raised his eyebrows. "I do not understand," he said. "Some mistake, I think." He sat down in a little straight-backed chair near the washstand and lighted a cigarette, and then he said what all his people say continuously: "I am so very sorry. Now I must ask a question. I hope you do not mind."

"Does it make any difference if I mind?" I inquired.

He appeared to consider his answer carefully. "No," he admitted, "perhaps not. What I wish to ask is this—did you visit your cabin last night after dinner?"

"No," I said. "What of it?"

Mr. Moto blew a cloud of cigarette smoke and smiled apologetically. "There is no use lying, Mr. Lee. Please excuse the word."

"Moto," I said, "you shock me."

"I am sorry," Mr. Moto answered, "but were you not in your cabin?"

"You heard me," I said promptly. "I said no."

I wondered if he would speak of what had happened in the cabin and I did not have long to wonder. His opaque brown eyes studied me cryptically for a moment and then he said:

"The knife was moved."

It reminded me of the old days when we sat about a table playing poker, with a heavy pile of chips in the center. I had an idea that Mr. Moto was bluffing, that he was not entirely sure of my movements for about five minutes the night before.

"What knife?" I asked.

Again Mr. Moto considered his answer carefully. "Well," he said, "it makes no difference. You remember our conversation yesterday, Mr. Lee? I have come to get the message."

Then I knew that I had guessed right; they had not found what they had been looking for.

"What message?" I asked.

"There was a message in your cabin," repeated Mr. Moto politely. "It is very important that it should go no further. You have that message, I think."

"Do you?" I asked.

"Yes," said Mr. Moto; "will you give it to me, please?" His tone was considerate. Mr. Moto always was a gentleman.

"I told you," I repeated, "that I haven't got a message."

"I'm so sorry," said Mr. Moto. "If you do not give it to me I shall have men in here to search you, Mr. Lee. It will be an indignity that I shall be sorry for. A very careful search of your body. Come—will you give me the message?"

I took a step toward Mr. Moto's straight-backed chair. "Moto," I said, "if you call anyone in here to search me, I'm going to break your neck."

Mr. Moto dropped his cigarette into one of those water-filled ash receivers and reached thoughtfully into his pocket, I believed for his cigarette case, but instead his hand whisked out with a compact little automatic pistol.

"I am so very sorry," he said. "You will stay where you are, Mr. Lee." And he called out in his native tongue. At that exact instant that he called, the door shot open and three stewards filed in silently.

"I am so sorry," Mr. Moto said again, "but you must submit to have them search you. Please."

A single glance at the stewards and at Mr. Moto convinced me that any further argument was useless, for the men all had an air of complete efficiency written on them which displayed a familiarity with forms of business not usually practised by steamship employees.

"Very well," I said to Mr. Moto. "You have entirely convinced me."

He did not answer but he smiled most agreeably and put his automatic back into his inside pocket.

If I had not been so personally involved in this search to the extent of losing a good deal of my own dignity, I should have found their procedure interesting. I never really knew until then what was meant by thoroughness. First they went through my bags again, even going so far as to pull out the linings. Then they examined all my clothing and my shoes, shaking, exploring, touching every seam with their fingers. While this was going on, two stewards had the cabin carpets up and the mattress and bedding ripped off to be examined. I will say that they were neat about it. Once they finished, every article was put carefully back in its place. The top of my flask was unscrewed and one of the men probed its contents with a long wire. For easily half an hour the cabin was a vortex of silent, lubricated activity. Each of the men knew exactly what to do, and in case they did not, Mr. Moto made occasional gentle suggestions. Once they had finished with the room, two of them turned to me.

"So sorry," Mr. Moto said, and they stripped off my pajamas, leaving me in a state of nature.

"Like a diamond miner in Kimberly, eh—Mr. Moto?" I suggested.

"Believe me," said Mr. Moto seriously, "what we are looking for is worth more than the Kohinoor, Mr. Lee."

I tried to be indifferent under their prodding fingers and I was somewhat cheered by Mr. Moto's growing air of surprise and discouragement.

"So it is not there," Mr. Moto said. "I am sorry."

"I told you it wasn't there," I answered, "and now do you mind if I put on some clothes?"

"No, indeed." Mr. Moto rose and regarded me seriously. "I am very much afraid that what I am looking for has been destroyed. Can you tell me, Mr. Lee?"

"I can't tell you anything," I answered.

The stewards filed out but Moto paused beside the door. "I am very much afraid," he said, "that what I want rests inside you there." He tapped his wrinkled forehead. "If that is so, you must tell me. You really must. We cannot be good fellows about this matter."

"Why not?" I asked.

"Because what I'm looking for," said Mr. Moto softly, "must not go any further. Will you think this over carefully, please, and someone will be in to talk to you later? I dislike certain parts of my profession very much. Now you must stay here while you think, please." Then Mr. Moto was gone and I heard the lock on the cabin door click softly.

I do not recollect that I was as much alarmed as I was puzzled, not having the slightest idea of exactly what Mr. Moto was looking for. I could not entirely understand why he was so serious, nor did the implications of his remarks immediately dawn upon me. It only seemed to me incredible that a comparatively harmless person like myself, who, a few days ago, had nothing but self to think of, should be caught up in the edges of a completely fantastic snarl. The only thing I could think of by the time I had finished dressing was that I must remain composed.

Now that the door was locked, the air in the cabin seemed still and oppressive and the walls seemed closer together. I walked over to the square porthole and looked out on the shining waters of the ocean, perhaps twenty feet below, but there was no consolation at the sight of that blank sea. Then I tried to open the port, only to discover that it was one of those sliding windows which one screwed down with a cranklike implement which fitted into the sill. That appliance was not there, however. It must have been intentionally removed and there was no way for me to leave that cabin by door or port. It is curious what eccentric matters may disturb one's calm. Nothing upset me as much as that discovery that I could not open my port, that I could not feel the air on my face. It gave me an unreasoning sense of suffocation and panic, which aroused in me a desire to cry out for help, although I knew there was no help and that I must take my medicine. If I had told Moto frankly everything I knew, I might not have been locked inside, but I would be hanged before I would tell him.

It must have been an hour later that I heard the lock of my door snap back with a sound which made my nerves leap strangely. It was not my actual situation but the complete uncertainty of what might happen next that was making me unstrung. Actually the thing that occurred was the last that I expected. The door snapped open and instead of a man that Russian girl came in. She wore a blue dress and a sable scarf hung around her neck. The wind outside had ruffled her hair, making it look as warm and chaotic as fire.

She closed the door carefully before she spoke and stood for a moment watching me with that worldly glance of hers, and I could not tell what she was—a friend or an enemy—from that glance.

"Good morning," she said. "Good morning, Casey Lee."

"I begin to think, Sonya," I said, "that I should be happier if I had never met you. What are you after now?"

"You," she said, but she did not smile.

"How do you mean, me?" I asked.

Sonya shrugged her shoulders. "You ought to understand," she said. "If you can't, please try to think. Why should I be introduced in here? I'm not bad-looking, am I?" Her throaty voice was like her looks—mysterious, alluring. In fact, I had never seen anyone easier to look at and I told her so.

"Well," she said, "don't you see? That's why I'm here. Mr. Moto thought you might be more likely to tell me about what happened to a certain message than anyone else. I think it was rather kind of Mr. Moto, don't you? He's not a brutal man."

"You mean you're here to seduce me?" I inquired.

"You'll be reasonable, now, won't you, Casey dear? It will be so much better. We don't want to be unpleasant. Oh, Casey, please, please, tell me everything you know—" It seemed to me that her voice was unnecessarily loud, before I guessed the reason. She was speaking so that someone outside the door might hear, and her actions were different from her voice, for while she spoke she drew me down beside her on the edge of the bed. "Casey," she whispered, "did they hurt you?"

I shook my head.

"I am thankful," she whispered. "They didn't see me last night. And you didn't tell them. Thank you, Casey."

I did not answer because her actions were entirely beyond me. I did not know whether to suspect her or to trust her. I put my hands on her shoulders and looked hard into her eyes. She returned my glance without faltering.

"What are you here for, Sonya?" I asked.

"The message," she whispered. "There must be some message! I didn't find it. They didn't find it. They think you were down there. Did you find anything, Casey?"

I smiled at her, and my thoughts were very bitter, now that it seemed perfectly clear that she was there to worm something out of me. "You tell Mr. Moto to be damned," I said. "I didn't tell him about you—and I won't tell anything."

"But do you know," she whispered "—do you know anything? You must."

"I guess I'm stubborn!" I said. "I'm not talking, Sonya."

"Casey," she whispered, "please, it isn't that. He thinks you've memorized the message and destroyed it. If that is so, the message can't go any further. That's why they murdered Ma." She paused and looked at me somberly. "That's why they're not going to let you off this boat alive, because this message can't go any further." Her eyes held my glance, but her eyes revealed nothing. I could not tell whether she was telling the truth nor could I entirely catch her meaning.

"You mean," I inquired, "that I'm going to be locked in here indefinitely?"

She shook her head and the gold in her hair danced in curious rays of light.

"No," she said very softly, "you won't stay on the boat. Your body will be thrown overboard. You will have drowned yourself."

I recoiled from her, edged myself away, and I felt my hands grow cold and my tongue grow thick. There was no use in deceiving myself that I was receiving a hollow threat when I looked at that Russian girl's eyes. There was no use in trying to believe that she was incapable of playing such a part, now that she had spoken. I remembered her in the cabin with the knife, and the memory of that, as much as my own danger, made me sick and dizzy. I was afraid because I was facing the prospect of dying in cold blood, but I was more afraid of her. Pride—for I suppose synthetic heroes are always proud—made me struggle to conceal that fear, made me prefer to die then and there rather than have her know the way I felt and I was determined to tell them nothing.

"So it's murder, is it?" I inquired.

She nodded, as though she found it hard to speak, and I saw her slim white hands clasp and unclasp in her lap.

"Casey dear," she whispered, "you could call it that. I should rather call it a secret agent's life. If you had lived in my country you would know. It's part of the profession. You must not blame them. Don't you see, it's the only thing they can do?"

I cleared my throat because her nearness seemed to choke me.

"Casey," she whispered, "there must be some message. Will you let me read it, please?"

I grinned back at her, or tried to grin, but my lips were stiff and cold and my facial muscles seemed cramped by the effort.

"Sonya," I said. "This business has taught me a good deal. It's taught me that there is still something worth dying for. Go back to your gang and tell them anything you like. Then perhaps you'd like to come back and see that I can die decently. In the meanwhile, if you have any decency, you'd better go away."

I had intended to continue further in saying what I thought of her, but her expression made me stop. She had grown deathly white. She was staring at me as though I had slapped her face.

"Casey," she whispered, "I came here to help you."

"My dear," I answered, "I don't want your help. It's time I learned to help myself. I had nearly forgotten how."

"No," she whispered, "no!" She had pulled the sables from her neck and she was ripping at the lining. "Listen to me! Please, please listen. I have nothing to do with this. I *am* trying to help you. Please, I don't want to see you killed."

"Would it make you any calmer," I inquired, "if I told you I don't believe a word you say?"

She had pulled something from her furs and was holding it in her hand. A metal crank for the port window.

"Don't you believe me now?" she whispered. "This will turn your window down. Hide it in your bag. They won't search again. They sent me here, but I'm trying to help you, Casey."

I felt the cold metal in my fingers.

"You don't understand," she whispered. "I want that message as much as you. I did not know about it until I saw that it was Ma. I don't want them to have it. They mustn't have it!"

I passed my hand across my forehead and my face was wet and clammy. "What's all this nonsense about?" I demanded. "What is this message?"

She was silent for a moment. "You won't believe me, I suppose," she said finally. "The word is from my father. Don't ask me any more. We can't talk here. They're only keeping him alive until they get his papers."

"That's interesting," I said. "Why don't you tell the truth?"

She raised her hands helplessly. "It is the truth—it is, if you only understood the situation." She rose. "This is too dangerous. I must be going now. They are listening at the door. Won't you trust me? Won't you believe me? They're going to kill you. I swear they are. You're caught in something that's desperate. They would have killed you already if it weren't for that American friend of yours—that Mr. Bloom on this ship. They don't want him to suspect anything. You'll be safe until he leaves at Shanghai tomorrow. Casey, will you listen to me, please? When this ship comes into the river opposite the city, as it will early tomorrow morning, open that porthole, jump out and swim ashore. Throw the crank out when you go, or they'll know I brought it to you. If you have trouble, ask for a man named Wu Lai-fu and tell him what has happened. Say the name to anyone along the shore, and then go away and never come back! Ask Wu Lai-fu to help you. He's the only one who will.

I shan't see you again, I think. Good-by—" She looked younger when she said it. Her eyes were begging me to believe her. She looked unhappy—close to tears.

"Thanks for that window crank," I whispered. "I'll throw it out."

"And one thing more," her voice was strained. "Don't eat anything they give you, Casey Lee. Hide some of it, as though you had. Don't touch anything—do you hear?"

"Thanks," I answered. Now that she was leaving, I was grateful and I wanted to show her that I was grateful. I took her hand, a small cold hand. "You weren't meant for this, Sonya," I said.

"No," she answered. "Neither were you. God help you, Casey Lee."

I wanted to speak to her again, but she shook her head and opened the door. I heard it locked behind her, but she still seemed to be there in the cabin. There was a suspicion of that gardenia perfume and the window crank was in my hand. . . . Who was she? I did not know. What was she? I did not know. But at last I was sure that she had meant kindly by me, that she had risked more than I cared to consider by telling me what she had. What did she mean by her allusion to her father and his papers? It was more than I could tell. Nevertheless, it added to the sum of knowledge in my possession to an extent that made me aware that somehow my country was involved, and this suspicion made me stubborn. The dead man Ma had asked me to communicate with Jim Driscoll and I was determined to do it, if I lived.

There is no need to describe the day of waiting, shut in that cabin, or the night either. The steward brought my luncheon in and I tucked part of it away in my suitcase as Sonya had suggested. At seven in the evening there was another tap on the door, and in came dinner with a bottle of champagne. A visiting card was tied around the bottle, bearing Mr. Moto's name and four words were scrawled beneath it. "With my sincerest compliments." I left the bottle untouched, but stored away some more of the food. No one came to take the tray away. I was not disturbed again. They may have had their reasons for believing that I could make no trouble after the evening meal. I lay for a long while on my bed, listening to the noise of the ship. I must have dozed off in spite of myself, for my next recollection was one of smoothness, and my cabin window was dusky with early dawn. I stared out for a while upon a strange world that was different from Japan, teeming with a patient vitality, serene, in spite of poverty, famine and war—the world of China. The ship was running at half speed up a broad river called the Whangpoo, as I found out later, one of those tributaries on the watery delta of the great Yellow River, connecting the city of Shanghai with the sea. The water flowing past our ship was colored a thick sedimentary yellow which reminded me of the muddy rivulets one made in the country as a child, when the frost has left the ground in spring. The current, I saw, was swift and the distance from shore was wide enough to make me doubt my ability to swim it. The shore itself was low, with green fields which I learned later were rice fields squared off by dykes and ditches. The life on the river was amazing to a stranger who had never seen the East. Besides occasional launches and tugs which might have plied a waterway at home, there were Chinese junks under sail, moving ponderously under great banks of brown canvas slatted with bamboo, looking like an illustration from a book—the relics of another age. They seemed to be as high in the bow and poop as the vessels of Columbus, and at the bow of each a pair of painted eyes made the hulls look like living monsters. Aboard one of them that passed near us a crew stripped to the waist was pulling her mainsail halyard, singing a rhythmic chanty that might have risen from the capstan of a clipper ship. I wished I might have been with them there aboard that junk. Then, in addition to these sailing vessels, the river was filled with smaller craft which were propelled by men with huge sculling oars, and which had deckhouses of matting in their bows. Now and then one of these boats moved hopefully toward the *Imoto Maru*, and once I saw the owner picking up refuse with a net. I only knew later that I was having a glimpse of a strange side of Chinese life—the river life of China, and of a river fleet on which men lived and died without hardly ever stepping onto land. But that first glance gave the impression of a land so teeming with humanity that part of that humanity was pushed into the water.

Even in that gray of early morning I could tell that we were coming to a country where life was cheap because of its abundance. A short time later I saw buildings and wharfs along the shore. From the size of the place, this could be nothing but Shanghai and if Sonya was right, it was time for me to go, provided I wished to live.

I made my preparations quickly, since they were completely simple. First I shot the bolt on my door, then I kicked off my shoes, took off my coat, and wrapped my scanty supply of money with my passport inside my oilskin tobacco pouch. As I did so, my glance fell on my flask and I jammed it into my hip pocket also, in the belief that I might need a drink if I should be cold and tired. Then, as quietly as I could, I began opening the port. Something—I have never known what—must have made some watcher outside my door suspicious, for just as the window was halfway down, I heard the doorknob turn and then there was a knocking. I did not answer that knock. No cabin window ever went down as fast as mine, and a moment later I had wriggled my shoulders through it and stared into a surge of yellow water. There was no chance to dive. A straight fall of easily twenty feet out of the ship was all that I could achieve. Even that fall was not too soon, for when I was in mid-air I heard a shout which warned me that someone had seen me go. I struck the water flat with a force that shook me badly, without shaking my sense entirely away. Once under water, I stayed until my lungs were nearly bursting. Then, when I came to the surface for breath, I had a glimpse of the ship behind me. They had seen me. I heard shouts and saw men leaning over the rail. Someone had whipped out a pistol and I dived for a second time. When I rose again, the force of the current had driven me away from the ship—perhaps for a hundred yards. I was gasping for breath and struggling with that current when I saw one of those small boats beside me. Just as I saw it, I knew that I would never have the strength to reach the shore, so I struck out toward it and snatched upward at its side. Then a wiry muscular arm reached out and seized my collar, and then another arm. I found myself being lifted bodily out of the water, choking.

There was an excited chattering of voices around me. Shrieks of children, squawks of chickens, and a grunting of pigs. I was on one of those vessels which I had seen following the ship, lying on my back in a cargo space, looking forward at the entrance of a matting-covered cabin. I was surprised at the number of persons on that small craft. There must have been three generations, all family, there, staring at me. An old man with a drooping wisp of gray mustache, bare to the waist, with ragged trousers, was asking me some question. Women were staring at me from under the matting cabin. Three younger men had dropped the sculling oar and were shouting excitedly at their elder; and children, boys and girls in ragged cotton clothes, round-faced, with dark slits of eyes, seemed to be crawling from every crack. The old man was pointing over the side, shouting at me, and I could gather what he meant by his gestures. He was preparing to take me back to the *Imoto Maru*. I shook my head.

"No, no!" I shouted, but it did no good. And then I remembered the name—the name which both Ma and Sonya had mentioned. I pulled myself up to a sitting posture, choking a cough.

"No, no!" I shouted at them. "Wu Lai-fu!"

I have never known three syllables to have such a definite result. The old man looked startled. The younger ones stopped their talking, and taking advantage of the pause, I reached in my hip pocket and drew out a handful of money and pointed to the land.

"Wu Lai-fu," I said again.

No masonic symbol could have been more useful. The old man bowed and took the money. The younger ones leaped to the sculling oar and began working toward the shore. I staggered to my feet and looked across the water at the black hull of the *Imoto Maru*. They had seen what had happened; an officer on her bridge was shouting at us through a megaphone, and to my surprise the crew was lowering a boat. I cupped my hands and shouted over the water.

"Good-by, Mr. Moto," I shouted. "Excuse me, please. I am so very, very sorry."

# 8

NO REMARK I had made in a long while seemed to me so laden with wit or gave me greater pleasure. It was so scintillating from my own viewpoint that I began to laugh, and to my surprise, that boat-load of strangers began to laugh too, either out of politeness, or because they had some intuitive idea of what was happening. At any rate, their interest in working in toward shore was most intense and gratifying. The men at the scull were bending at their work, grunting sharply as their bodies moved back and forth, while the old man stood beside me, staring at the ship. Finally he nudged me with his elbow, pointed and displayed a row of toothless gums. The lifeboat was being raised again; with good reason, I think, for we were in the middle of other small craft by then, all of such conventional pattern that it would have been hard to have picked us from the rest. Then the reaction came over me and my teeth began to chatter, but in spite of my physical wretchedness, I shall never forget the sights of that early morning, because they were as unfamiliar to me as though I had arrived upon the moon. The boat was being worked into a bay or inlet below a great modern city whose tall buildings were rising out of the morning mist. The body of water was jammed so thickly with boats and small craft that one could walk to shore by stepping from boat to boat, for almost half a mile, so that the cove had been transformed into a floating city, where every craft seemed to have a definite place. The laundry was hanging out to dry and women were scolding and food was cooking and babies were squealing wherever one cared to look. Our boat ran up alongside some others near the shore and our men made it fast. Then one of the young men started to go ashore and I had leisure to look at the people about me. We all had an excellent chance to examine each other, due to an almost complete lack of privacy and inhibition. The crews from the other junks and their women and children began to gather around us until, as I stood there in the hold, I seemed to be in an amphitheater, surrounded by curious chattering people, yet I always remember they were friendly enough and even merry. One of the old women, who handed me a cup of tea, motioned me inside the matting cabin to sit down. Tea never tasted better than the cup I drank there, enthroned on a pile of rags which were probably filthy with vermin; but I was in no condition to worry about cleanliness. The old man was repeating "Wu Lai-fu" and motioning me to be patient.

I can still see that crowd in my imagination gathered about me in a gradually contracting semicircle, staring. Whenever my mind brings back their faces and rags, an impression of China comes with them which has never been erased. Paradoxically, perhaps, in spite of their poverty and evidences of disease and of grinding labor, that impression has always been one of peace. It was a peace born of a knowledge of life and of human relationships. I could understand why China had absorbed her conquerors when I watched that ring of faces. Their bland patience was impervious to any fortune. They stood there staring at me, speaking softly, laughing now and then. . . .

There I was, soaking wet, without other clothes, almost without money, waiting for something or nothing. Now that I come to think of it, I did not have so long to wait, three quarters of an hour perhaps, before there was a stir in the crowd around me and a young man in a long gray Chinese gown, wearing a European felt hat, stepped over the side of the boat.

"You wish to see Wu Lai-fu?" he asked. His face was lean and intelligent; he spoke in very good English, with an enunciation better than my own. He did not seem in the least surprised to see me sitting there, dripping wet out of the river.

"Who told you," he asked, "to see Wu Lai-fu?"

"A Chinese named Ma," I said, "on the Japanese boat. They killed him."

He betrayed no surprise, if he felt any, but my explanation must have satisfied him. He waved a hand toward me, a thin hand that emerged gracefully from the loose gray sleeve of his gown.

"You come with me," he said, and that was all. We walked from boat to boat until we reached the shore, without any further explanation.

Once we were ashore there were two other Chinese waiting for us, dressed, like my companion, in long gray gowns. One of them moved to one side of me and the other walked behind us.

"It is all right," the first man said. "Do not be alarmed. We will take you in an automobile. Here it is."

My next memory was being shown into the interior of a large American limousine, where I was placed between two Chinese and was looking at the backs of two others in the driver's seat. The swiftness of the whole procedure struck me as disturbing. Although the car was parked in a narrow street of shops with Chinese signs, something in the appearance of my companions gave me an impression of the Chicago underworld—and a suspicion that I was going for a ride. No American chauffeur ever drove faster or more recklessly than that Chinese driver. We were off a second later with our horn blowing steadily, twisting through a labyrinth of streets which might have been in the moon, for anything I could tell. The man beside me spoke again, politely:

"You know Shanghai?"

"No," I said.

"You know China?"

"No," I said.

"Shanghai is a very nice city," he remarked.

As though directly to contradict his statement, something went slap against the window of the limousine with a sound that made me duck my head. The men on either side of me looked interested but not disturbed.

"Do not be afraid," my companion said. "The glass is bullet-proof. Someone, I think, does not like you very much."

We must have ridden for fifteen minutes, perhaps longer, through very crowded streets, when the car drew up before an unprepossessing gate in a high gray wall. They must have been expecting us because the gate opened at the sound of the motor horn and six or seven large-boned, slant-eyed men stepped out and gazed searchingly up and down.

"What's the matter?" I asked. "Is there going to be a war?"

My sallow-faced companion smiled slightly. "There is always something of a war. Come, please. Walk quickly in!" A second later we were in a courtyard with low tile-roofed buildings about it that gave one the idea of an entrance to a prison. The Chinese who were standing there had a semi-official, military manner; all of them were large men, impressively so, after my experiences in Japan.

"What is this place?" I asked.

"You are coming to the home of Wu Lai-fu," my guide answered. "Will you please to step this way?" We walked across the court into a smaller one and then along a covered gallery into a building on the right.

I was surprised, when we were inside the building, to find that the interior was comfortable according to foreign standards. We were in a bedroom with teakwood chairs and scroll pictures on the wall, where two men in white gowns, evidently servants, were waiting. My guide spoke to them rapidly.

"You are to bathe and change your clothes," he said. "There is a hot bath running for you and they will bring you eggs and fruit and coffee. We have only Chinese clothes. You do not mind?"

I was too confused to be surprised or to thank him. All these impressions, which had come so suddenly upon me, have made my recollections of the entrance into that place vague, and nothing seemed to me strange by then, not the pillars in the courtyards or curving tiled roofs or marble dragons by the gates. I only recollect that no English valets could have waited on me more conscientiously or correctly than those men. They helped me into a tiled bathroom and into a tub of steaming hot water. Next I was in a silk suit of pajamas, with a robe buttoned over it, eating an excellent breakfast with a knife and fork. I ate in a sort of daze and went through all the motions of dressing without asking any questions, while the servants stood attentively by me. I had just finished my coffee and one of them had offered me a cigarette from a silver box when my guide returned.

"Wu Lai-fu will see you now," he said.

I have no coherent idea of the establishment of Wu Lai-fu, but only the recollection of walking through buildings and through courtyards until we came to a large room which was part Oriental and part European. A blue carpet with yellow dragons was on the floor. The furniture was black lacquer. There were two paintings on silk of old landscapes on the wall, and a large commercial map of China. At the end of the room there was an office desk with two telephones upon it, and a typewriter stood upon the table beside it. A middle-aged man sat behind the desk, with his hands folded in front of him, a Chinese in a plain black robe. His closely shaved head was partly gray and his face had an ageless, reposed expression, as though all emotion had evaporated. The man might have been forty or sixty—a slim man who looked at me through a pair of horn-rimmed spectacles like a school-teacher or a scholar. He nodded to my guide, who left the room at his nod, closing the door and leaving me standing before the desk. This man was not like Mr. Moto. He showed no anxiety or nervousness, but only a placid calmness.

"I am Wu Lai-fu," the man behind the desk said. "What is your name, please?"

"My name is K. C. Lee," I answered.

He did not answer for a moment, but sat with his hands clasped on the desk.

"I suppose," he said—his English was flawless— "you do not know who I am?"

"No," I answered.

He smiled, and his whole face broke into arid wrinkles. "Then I will tell you," he said. "Your countrymen say I am the wickedest man in China. They say I control various guilds in this city, including the thieves and prostitutes. As a matter of fact, I am a merchant, whose business has connections. I hope you will tell me the truth, because if I have the slightest doubt that you do not—and I understand the faces of you foreigners—if I find that you are lying, I can make you tell the truth."

His manner was contemptuous, as though he were speaking to a barbarian; it was the first time that I had the feeling that I was a savage. I can never explain, but in some way I had the sense that his race was vastly older than mine and older even than Mr. Moto's.

I could believe that the thin ascetic man in his black robe was living in another world of intellect.

"Are you threatening me, Mr. Wu?" I asked.

"Exactly," the other said. "I am asking you to tell the truth. Tell it quickly, please."

"You have the advantage of me, Mr. Wu," I said.

His hands on the desk moved, but his face did not. "Yes," he answered. "So much so that it is my pleasure to be frank. Some day I hope to see you and all of your kind driven into the sea."

I felt my face growing red. "No one asked me here," I answered. "I came here as a stranger. I have always heard of your courtesy, but now I know that you have bad manners."

Mr. Wu shook his head but he did not smile. "It seems to me you've been treated with courtesy," he said. "You were picked out of the river like a half-drowned rat. You were brought to my house. You were bathed and fed. You are standing before me in my clothes. The lowest Chinese coolie would have bowed to me and thanked me. You have not thanked me, Mr. Lee. What do you know of manners?"

"I know enough," I said, "not to threaten a guest beneath my roof. If I picked you up like a rat, Mr. Wu, I should have treated you better."

"Ah, but you have not a roof," he answered. "You have nothing. What is the English phrase? You must sing for your supper, Mr. Lee. Please sing, because I am busy. Why did you jump off a comfortable steamer into our Whangpoo River?"

"Because they were going to murder me," I said.

"Who were?" he asked.

"A Japanese named Moto," I answered.

The thin hands on the desk closed together tighter, but Mr. Wu's composure was not altered. "Why?" he asked.

"They thought I had a message from one of your countrymen," I said. "His name was Ma, and that's all I know about it, Mr. Wu."

Mr. Wu sat for a moment, watching me coolly. "Where is Ma?" he asked.

"Dead," I answered. "They killed him in my cabin."

Mr. Wu's lips moved but everything else about him was motionless. "There are many Chinese lives," he said. "Where is the message? I wish you to tell me promptly—and truthfully—or I shall call on men who can make you."

I looked at the dragons on the carpet. The dragons seemed to be writhing toward me slowly, as it came over me that Mr. Wu wanted the message too, as poignantly as Mr. Moto wanted it. I wondered if he would believe me. I hoped he would, because he was not bluffing.

"Mr. Wu," I answered, "I have not got that message."

"Ah," said Mr. Wu; "they found it then?"

"No," I answered, "they did not find it. They thought I had read it and destroyed it."

Mr. Wu unclasped his hands and tapped a bell beside the desk, and then the thing that happened has always been hard to believe. I had to tell myself that I was Casey Lee, and yet I might have been in the Middle Ages that next moment. A door opened behind me at the sound of that bell and four men walked through it. Two of them seized my arms, while two others stood beside them, holding ropes and wooden and iron instruments.

"And now," said Mr. Wu, "you will tell me what the message is—sooner or later."

I tried to keep my voice steady. "I told you," I answered, "I have never seen the message." And then I had another thought. "Before Ma died—the night before—he spoke to me. He told me to deliver that message if he should give it to me, to a commander in our navy. If I had it, he should have it—not you, Mr. Wu. And if I knew that message, which I don't, you could cut me to pieces before I said a word."

"I wonder," said Mr. Wu softly, "I wonder—"

"You needn't wonder," I answered. "Go ahead and try!"

"You are brave," said Mr. Wu softly. "Savages are always brave." Then he spoke to the men and they dropped my arms. "I think you had better tell me everything, Mr. Lee—everything from the beginning." He spoke again and one of the men moved up a chair. I dropped into it, because my knees were weak.

"I will if you give me a drink," I said.

"Drink—" Mr. Wu smiled slightly. "So you have a drunkard's courage? Very well, you shall have your drink."

I gripped the arms of the lacquer chair. That taunt of Mr. Wu's stung more than the remark of any prohibitionist. "Never mind the drink then," I said. "I don't need it to talk to you! Furthermore, I've been in worse spots than this. I'm not afraid."

Mr. Wu smiled again. "Oh, yes," he said; "oh, yes, you are. . . . " He was speaking the truth and he knew I knew it.

"Perhaps," I said, "I am, but it doesn't make any difference, because I haven't anything to tell you."

Mr. Wu leaned back in his chair and folded his arms in his sleeves. "Now," he said, "you're speaking the truth, and that's what I want—the truth, and nothing more. And then we will have no trouble, Mr. Lee."

"As a matter of fact, I should rather like to know the truth myself," I said. "I don't understand what's happened, Mr. Wu."

Mr. Wu smiled again. "And you probably never will know," he answered. "Why should you? I am not depending upon your rather turgid intellect. Who paid you to come here?"

"A Japanese," I answered, "named Moto."

"Ah," said Mr. Wu, "so you've been hired by them, have you?"

The unbiased accuracy of his words made me more keenly aware of what I had done than I had ever been before. "I'm not proud of it," I explained. "I rather think that's over, since Mr. Moto tried to murder me."

Mr. Wu leaned further forward across the desk. "I think you'd better tell me the circumstances," he said softly. "How did you meet this countryman of mine named Ma? And what was it that Mr. Moto wanted you to do?"

I could never in my life have believed that anyone like Mr. Wu existed, but he was completely believable then. Although I disliked him, I found myself telling him frankly, with hardly a reservation, what had happened. I told him about the visitor in my stateroom. I quoted our conversation word for word, while Mr. Wu sat there listening to me, never moving a muscle of his face or hands.

"So you were in the American navy," he remarked, "and an aviator. We are interested in aviation here. It is one hope for a weak, disorganized nation. You are not, by any chance, interested in naval design, Mr. Lee?"

"No," I said, "not in the least."

"You have never been a naval architect?" Mr. Wu asked softly. "Or studied fuel combustion?"

"No," I said.

Although he did not move, I could see that he was taking all my words, weighing them, polishing them in his mind and working them into a pattern. "That is very curious," he said. "There was a message. Now there is no message. Ma was a very capable man. He had a sense of habit and behavior. I have dealt with Ma."

I sat in front of the desk, and the room was very still while I looked curiously at the man who sat there thinking.

"You spoke of a Russian," he said finally. "A woman or a girl? Tell me what she looks like, that is, if you possess sufficient powers of observation."

I described Sonya to him as carefully as I could and for the first time his placidity left him. His eyes sharpened and he rubbed his hands together.

"So she was there," he said, "and she found nothing, also. That is interesting, Mr. Lee." He tapped the bell on his desk again. I am free to confess that the sound sent a shiver down my spine, but only a servant entered at the signal. Mr. Wu spoke to him in his elusive language, evidently a question, and then he smiled at me when he got his answer. His entire manner changed with his smile. There was no cruelty left in him, but instead, the sympathy and anxiety of a host.

"I am asking the man to bring me whisky," he said. "And I beg of you to take it. The trouble is over now. Sit down, Mr. Lee, and be as comfortable as you can in your strange clothes. Some others have been ordered for you already—the impractical useless garments of the foreigners, if you will excuse my saying so. I am intensely nationalistic, Mr. Lee; intensely racial might be a better expression. I am proud of my own people and I have seen many of them. They are superior to other people. Do not disturb yourself. The trouble is over now—because I have found you have told the truth."

"What are you going to do with me?" I asked.

Mr. Wu raised his thin hand. "I do not blame you," he remarked, "for being worried about yourself. Your face tells me that you have thought only of self for many, many years. There is nothing in this world more unfortunate. What am I going to do with you? You must wait and see." Just as he finished speaking, the servant came back, stepping noiselessly across the heavy carpet. The servant said something and Mr. Wu rubbed his hands again. His expression had become almost benign and kind when the servant had finished speaking.

"Do not speak, please, Mr. Lee," he said. "You must excuse me. I have important matters on my mind. I congratulate you that you have told the truth. This girl you speak of—I wish that she were here."

I thanked heaven that Sonya was not there. "She doesn't know anything," I said.

"Perhaps I can find out." Mr. Wu's voice was calm. He had picked up one of his telephones and was evidently calling for some number. He listened attentively, then he spoke in a singsong cadence, set down the instrument and rang the bell and gave another order to the servant.

"I will not keep you much longer, Mr. Lee," he said; "only a moment, please." His dark narrow eyes were intent, but, as he continued speaking, I think his mind was somewhere else and he was only speaking to pass the time. "You do not know China? It is a sad country," he said; "the most exploited country in the world. The barbarians are snatching at her again. The Japanese are barbarians and the Russians— But we may perfect our own methods some day."

"If the Chinese are all like you, I am sure they will," I said.

"Thank you," said Mr. Wu. "Unfortunately, they are not all like me."

I heard the door open behind me and then I heard a voice which made me start—the throaty voice of the Russian girl named Sonya. There she was, walking across the dragon carpet, in white with her sables around her shoulders, a white suede bag clasped under her arm. I felt those violet eyes of hers upon me for a moment in a cool guileless glance.

"So he came here safely," she said.

"Yes," said Mr. Wu, "you did very well to send him here."

I found my voice with difficulty.

"Sonya—" I began.

"This was better for you than being killed, Casey," she said simply.

My voice grew sharper as I answered. "Where do you fit into this picture, Sonya?"

"Does it make any difference?" she asked me, and there was a mockery in the way she spoke. "Haven't you had nearly enough trouble?"

Mr. Wu was smiling. He was standing up straight behind his desk, his hands folded beneath his sleeves.

"Yes," he said, "I think you have had enough, Mr. Lee, and I am obliged to you. Your clothing will be waiting for you and a sum of money for your pocket. You will be taken to your foreign quarter, where no doubt you can go and drink yourself into a stupor. If you do not move out of it, except to take the first boat to your native land, perhaps you will be safe. Good-by, Mr. Lee."

"Sonya—" I said again. I tried to frame some question but hesitated and stopped.

"Yes, Casey," she said, "now that this is over, I think you had better take the next boat home. You were not meant for this. It is not your fault."

Even then it amazed me that in my position I should feel angry and hurt. It seemed to me that Sonya's manner had something of the superciliousness of Mr. Wu's. The door had opened and a white-robed servant was standing in the doorway.

"Sonya," I said—I spoke to her instead of to Wu— "you think I'm a fool, don't you? I don't understand a single thing that's happening here but I don't like it. You're not finished with me yet."

Mr. Wu nodded as though my speech had confirmed some thought in his own mind.

"Foreigners always boast," he said. "Foreigners always grow angry. You have no idea how much you are to be congratulated, Mr. Lee, that you are leaving in such a pleasant manner. Now I advise you to leave at once before you are made to leave more quickly."

I looked at Sonya again. "Good-by," I said.

I walked out of the doorway with the man in white at my elbow, assiduous and polite. I was so much disturbed by the whole affair that I paid no attention to where we were going. I felt a deep humiliation at everything which had happened. The thinly veiled sarcasm of Mr. Wu had not been lost upon me. He thought that I was an irresponsible drunkard, who had been tossed up by the sea. There had been a moment—I could not tell just when—in which his interest in me had suddenly vanished. Something inexplicable had happened which had made me as useless to him as a sucked orange. He had extracted something from me without my being able to tell what. He had been anxious about that message to the point of trying to extort it and then his anxiety had waned. It had waned before Sonya had appeared seemingly out of nowhere.

That whole scene and that whole place has always been to me like a page of an Oriental romance, with no bearing on the actual life I have known. Perhaps the Orient is all like that. There may be in every Oriental a love of involved dramatics and fantasy that is expressed to us by the pages of the "Arabian Nights." I do not know about this and I do not care, because I am only trying to state the actual facts as they occurred.

Once I was back in the room where I had been dressed, I had a proof of Mr. Wu's prosperity. A new and very good European suit, with shoes and linen, was waiting for me, and even a suitcase with a change of clothing. One of the servants explained the appearance of these articles in English, the first time I knew that he was familiar with the language.

"You take," he said, "compliments of Mr. Wu. Mr. Wu he say the motor wagon waits for you."

Fifteen minutes later I found myself dressed in a gray flannel suit which did not fit me badly. One of the men had lifted my bag and I had turned to leave the room, when one of the servants spoke.

"Please," he said, "the master has forgotten. His money and his flask." And he handed me my tobacco pouch, containing my Japanese notes and my passport and my leather-covered flask with the metal cup in place at the bottom. I was glad to have my flask, for it seemed like an old friend, the only link that connected me with a previous incarnation—a doubtful one perhaps, but one in which I possessed my own integrity.

I set my hat on the back of my head and tossed a ten-yen note to the servants.

"All right, boys," I said, "let's go!"

Then there was a walk through that labyrinth of courtyards and I was out of the gate where that same motor which had conveyed me there was waiting. I was inside it with my bag and the gate had closed behind me. The car started with no directions of mine, evidently because the driver had already received his orders. While I leaned back in the seat, without interest in the sights I saw, absorbed in my own thoughts, for the first time in many years I was thinking consecutively and fast; not of myself, for the first time in years, but of something more important then myself. If Driscoll were in this city, and I recalled that he had spoken of coming here, I knew that I must find him. Something was going on of actual importance. Men did not act as Moto and Wu Lai-fu had acted without grave cause. I did not have the message, but I had sense enough to know that there might be significant details in my adventure which a man in Driscoll's position could understand. Clearly, in some way beyond my knowledge, the interests of my country were at stake. It seemed strange to me that I must see Driscoll.

I had another impression besides these thoughts which I have not forgotten; that impression came upon me suddenly with the motion of the motor car, without the interposition of any specific sight or sound. I was aware that I was in a strange place where anything might happen, and believe me, I was right. I doubt if any city in the world is more amazing than Shanghai, where the culture of the East and West has met to turn curiously into something different from East and West; where the silver and riches of China are hoarded for safety; where *opéra-bouffe* Oriental millionaires drive their limousines along the Bund; where the interests of Europe meet the Orient and clash in a sparkle of uniforms and jewels; where the practical realities of Western industrialism meet the fatality of the East. I say I could feel this thing, and now I only state it as an explanation of Mr. Wu and of the events which follow. Believe me, I repeat, anything can happen in Shanghai, from a sordid European intrigue to a meeting with a prince.

## 9

THE AUTOMOBILE took me out of China into a city which might have been planted there from Europe or America, except for the rickshaw boys and the Chinese faces on the street. There were skyscrapers and stone buildings with all the tradition of the Renaissance, which looked upon warships from Europe and liners and junks floating on the muddy yellow waters of the Whangpoo. I could feel an excitement in the air, as though history were in the making, as though I were present at the changing of a world, and I have never forgotten that excitement. The car stopped at the door of an excellent hotel, where a doorman in livery took my bag. At the sight of my own people, seated drinking at little tables in the lounge, at the sight of its calm and order (I remembered that there was even a notice of the meeting of the Rotary Club posted in white letters on a bulletin board), I felt the security of things I knew. Once again I could almost believe that everything which had happened to me had been a dream. As I walked up to the hotel desk, I could hardly conceive that I was the man who had jumped through the port of a vessel to avoid death, or the man who had been picked up like a drowned rat, as Mr. Wu had said, from the waters of the Whangpoo. The clerk at the desk was handing me a registry card, after the custom of the best hotels at home.

"Can you tell me," I asked him, "where I can find a naval officer named Commander Driscoll?" In the light of everything which I had gone through, the casualness of his answer did not seem logical.

"Certainly, sir," he answered. "Commander Driscoll is staying at this hotel—Room 507. Do you wish to see him, sir?" He reached toward a telephone. "May I ask the name?"

"Tell him Lee," I answered. "K. C. Lee, and have my bag sent to my room." I heard him speak into the telephone. The Chinese boy in the smart uniform of a bellhop bowed to me and pointed to a lift. I had not recovered from the unreality of returning to my own world before we were standing before a room door where the clerk had told me Driscoll lived. I knocked and the door opened. The door opened and seemed to admit me back again to my own people, for there was Jim Driscoll, heavy and stocky, standing on the threshold staring at me, and as I glanced across his shoulder, I saw May Driscoll, Jim's wife. It seemed a thousand years ago, before the fall of Babylon, that I had known such people.

"How did you get here?" Jim Driscoll asked. "And what do you want here?" His manner was neither friendly nor approving. He was no longer looking at me as a friend or as a member of his own caste, but as an unsavory stranger.

"Jim," I said, "I want to talk to you. Something important, or I wouldn't be here now."

Driscoll turned toward his wife. "May," he said, "you'd better go into the bedroom and close the door."

I heard May laugh. "Why, Jim," she said, "it's Casey. Hello, Casey darling—Can't I talk to Casey, Jim?"

"No," Jim Driscoll said. "You heard me, May. Please go in there and close the door." And Jim Driscoll and I stood facing each other in the parlor of a hotel suite decorated with all the curious lack of taste which is common to any hotel suite.

"All right," Jim Driscoll said; "what do you want? Are you drunk or sober, Lee?"

"Sober, Jim," I said. "Cold sober."

He laughed shortly. "Are you? With a flask sticking out of your pocket?"

"That doesn't mean—" I began.

"Doesn't it?" Jim Driscoll inquired. "Not that it makes any difference, after Tokyo."

I tried to keep my temper. "I want to tell you something," I said. "Are you in the Naval Intelligence?"

He nodded shortly. "All right," I continued, "a Chinese told me to give you a message. His name was Ma. He was murdered on the *Imoto Maru*."

As I was speaking, Driscoll had been pacing in front of me, a habit which he probably acquired from shipboard; but at the name of Ma he stopped dead in his tracks. He stopped and spun on his heel and puckered up his eyes.

"Ma," he said, as though I were not there. "That's old Karaloff's man!" He closed his hands and opened them and took a step toward me. "Where did you pick up this bit?" he inquired. "Are you serious?"

"Yes," I said. "I'm telling you the sober truth. I ought to know, because that man Ma was murdered in my cabin on the *Imoto Maru*."

Jim Driscoll snorted contemptuously. "The sober truth," he said. "It's been quite a while since you told that. How did you get on the *Imoto Maru*? The last time I saw you, you were pickled in Tokyo. What got you aboard that ship?"

It was difficult for me to remember that I had come with information that was more important than my own feelings, because Driscoll's manner was not conciliating, and I have never been good at restraining my temper.

"Jim," I said, "I'm taking this from you because this may be more important than you or I. You remember there in the hotel, the way I was talking? Well, someone heard me. A man named Moto."

Jim Driscoll swore. "So that's the play, is it?" he said. "And what did this man Moto look like?"

"What do any Japanese look like?" I inquired. "He was small, almost delicate. He wore a morning coat, little feet, little hands—intelligent, polite. He could speak English as well as you can. Patent-leather shoes, a green ring on his finger. He kept saying he was so very, very sorry."

Jim Driscoll exhaled a deep breath and moved a step nearer to me. I might have been a prisoner being interrogated by the military police.

"By God," said Driscoll, "that's the baby! Lee, what is your relationship with that man? How did he get hold of you?"

"He offered to supply a plane so that I could fly across the

Pacific," I answered, "for certain considerations. My tobacco company welched on me. There I was."

Jim Driscoll turned his back on me, paced across the room and back. "You might be a little steadier if you had a drink," he suggested. "Eh, what, Lee? Your mind might move along a more even groove. It probably takes a drink to give you guts. All right—" He opened a closet door and pulled out a bottle of Scotch and a glass.

"Thanks," I said. "Are you joining me?"

Jim Driscoll snorted through his nose. "It isn't my business to drink with everyone," he said. "I'm giving you a drink for medicinal reasons, Lee. Help yourself."

I pushed away the bottle. "When I'm through here," I said, "I promise you I won't trouble you again."

Jim Driscoll laughed. "That's mutual," he answered. "And now, so we can reach that point, perhaps you'll tell me exactly what happened to you."

I told him; for the second time that night, I told the truth. And as I did so, I could not help comparing Driscoll unfavorably with the black-robed Wu Lai-fu. Against that other man Driscoll seemed blunt and stupid and incapable of any act of brilliance. Although he listened to me carefully, I wondered if he caught any real significance in what I said. I did not believe that anything much registered with him, to judge from the opinion which he rendered after he listened to me. He paced up and down the room again and halted in front of me.

"There's one thing obvious," he remarked; "you can't be trusted."

I felt my self-control leaving me. "That is hardly fair," I said.

Driscoll smiled with an elephantine sort of politeness. "Please excuse me," he answered. "I didn't mean to hurt your feelings. Have you got any feelings left, Lee? I gather you're a spy in the pay of Japan. You can't blame me for wondering exactly what your position is. So you haven't got the message? Is that all you came to tell me?"

"I thought maybe you could do something," I answered. "But, of course, I was mistaken in that. You always were a dumbbell, Jim—just one of the routine people who gets ahead in the Service." It pleased me to perceive that my remark nettled him.

"Thanks," he answered, and walked to the room telephone, and called out a number in the same way he might have signalled the engine room from the bridge. "So Wu Lai-fu's in it, is he? You've got yourself into pretty company. All right, I want to see Wu—" His voice trailed off and changed into Chinese, as someone answered from the other end of the wire, reminding me that Driscoll had been a language officer in Peking. He talked for nearly a minute, unintelligibly, finally turning to me again when he had finished.

"We'll get this straightened out here and now," he said. "Wu's coming here himself. There must be something in the air to make that fellow call. This is serious and we've got to get on with it. . . . Now this Russian girl—what did you say her name was?"

"You heard me," I answered. "Sonya."

Driscoll gazed at me pityingly. "Who in hell cares about first names?" he inquired. "Are you sure you don't need a drink to pull your wits together? Use your mind. What was her last name?"

I tried to think, but my indignation made thinking difficult. "I'm trying to think," I replied. "She told me once—yes, I've got it now—she told me her last name was Karaloff."

Driscoll's manner changed. His mouth dropped open and he stood stock-still. Whatever the name might have meant to him, I knew it was important.

"That tears it," he said softly, seemingly to himself. "It doesn't seem possible, but I believe it's right," and he began to grin. "Lee, you've earned a drink. By God, that will be Karaloff's daughter! That's important! Help yourself! There's the bottle, Lee."

I pushed the bottle away. "Not your whisky," I said. "Who's the old man?"

Driscoll laughed again. "If you don't know, it won't hurt you," he answered. "I'd sooner tell a secret to a microphone than talk to you. But listen Lee, I want to ask you a favor."

"Can you advance any reason why I should do you a favor under the circumstances?" I asked him.

Driscoll answered earnestly. "Not for me," he said. "I'm asking you in behalf of the land where you were born. In the hope that you have a drop of patriotism left. That girl must like you, Casey, if she tried to save your life. If she likes you, that's something we can use." And he began to pace the floor again.

"What?" I asked.

"We want this message," Driscoll said. "It's strange, the agencies which shape events. It just happens that you have blundered into something through the elements of chance. It may interest you to know that a phase of this business may concern the entire balance of power on the Pacific. Or does it interest you to know?"

"Isn't that your occupation?" I inquired. "Isn't that why you get a cut out of our income taxes? Aren't you a public servant?"

Driscoll ignored my remark.

"Casey," he said, "that girl knows something. We don't know what. We have no real way of reaching her, but you can." He looked toward the closed door of his bedroom, where he had sent his wife. "You have a way with the ladies. They all love aviators. I ought to know. Now listen to me, Lee. A woman is always the weak link in such an affair as this. She can pry the secrets from the diplomat, and the gigolos can get the secrets from the ladies. You get my idea, Casey?"

"No," I said.

Driscoll became patronizingly patient. "Excuse me for being subtle," he apologized. "Let us come down to words of one syllable. Sex appeal, Casey. It's clear the girl likes you. Well, cultivate her acquaintaince. Gain her confidence. You know her. There's an easy and elemental way to do it with which you are familiar. And when," Driscoll smiled, "when you've gained her confidence, when she can't bear to exist without you, ask her about her dear old father. Find out what she knows about the message and work fast, Casey." He looked at the bedroom door again. "I know you're a fast worker."

"And then what do you want?" I asked.

"I want you to trot around here and tell me what you've found. Do you want money for entertainment? I can help you out."

First it had been Moto, then Sonya, then Wu Lai-fu, and now Driscoll, all asking for that message. I still could only half believe what I had heard. I could only half believe that this man was the same Driscoll I had known in the old days. It was not conceivable that he could think me capable of such an action.

"Jim," I said, "you don't mean that, do you?"

Driscoll looked puzzled. "Don't be a damn fool," he said. "I may have ridden you, Casey, but you deserve to be ridden. This is serious, and I want you to believe it is serious. Go out and get that information from that girl!"

I was still incredulous. "Jim," I asked him, "do you honestly think I will?"

But he was in deadly earnest. He reached out a hand and took me by the shoulder.

"We're not talking about honor, Casey," he said. "There's no honor in this business. This isn't Lady Vere de Vere's drawing room. We're dealing with realities and not with any code of chivalry. That belongs in another incarnation, but not in the Intelligence Service; that's a fact which is recognized by everyone in the game. Now, Casey, this business has been worrying us for months. We've heard rumors of it through our own sources of information. We must get this straight, if we can, no matter what it costs, and you look like our one white hope. I'd go to Wu Lai-fu, but he may swing away from me if he knows too much. You've got to get that girl and bring her into camp."

I struggled with my thoughts again and asked him:

"Is that message so important?"

He moved impatiently. "It's damned important, more important than you or me or any neurotic little Russian skirt." He drew a wallet from his pocket and tossed five hundred dollars in Chinese bills on the table. "There you are. That'll pay your expenses. Get going, Don Juan!"

I looked at the money on the table and back to Driscoll, who waited expectantly, his face molded into the familiar lines of service and duty; and that face was like a mirror, because his opinion of me was reflected in his eyes. His expression resembled the revelation which had come over me that night aboard the boat. I knew that I had come on a long rough road, but I had never completely visualized the end of it until then. That he should think me capable of such a combination was what hurt me most; and yet he must have had his reasons; and Driscoll was no fool. He had made his request after observing my appearance and my conduct, obviously thinking that the matter would be simple and that I would willingly agree. I can remember every detail of that tawdry sitting room—the label on the whisky bottle, the empty glass, the cigarette butts in the ash tray, a lace shawl on an untidy sofa, Driscoll's white-visored cap tossed upon the table.

"All right," I said, "I'll try to get your message."

I saw Driscoll smile with artificial heartiness. "That's the boy," he said. And then his expression changed. I moved closer to him and he must have seen something in my face.

"But not that way," I said. "Listen to me, Driscoll. I'm talking to you now. I came here of my own free will to tell you something, and in return you've made a proposal which I do not like. You don't know this girl."

I did not know why I was so angry until I made that speech. It was not on account of myself, but because of her.

"Wait a minute!" Jim Driscoll's face grew red. "You don't understand this game."

"No," I said, "and I don't want to understand it. You may be an officer, but you're only a gentleman by act of Congress. If that message is in existence, I'm willing to try to get it my own way, and when I get it, Driscoll, you can have it—and to hell with the whole lot of you! I'm not a gigolo—not yet."

Driscoll opened his mouth and closed it. "Don't be a damn fool," he said. "What are you going to do—make a noble speech?"

Then something snapped, and I lost my self-control.

"I'll show you what I'm going to do," I answered. "That girl's worth any ten of you, Driscoll. At any rate, she saved my life, and you can keep your hands off her."

I drew back my own hand almost without consciousness and brought my palm across his face.

It is amazing sometimes how an act like that will clear the air. I had never intended to take such an action; and the thing which impelled me was entirely beyond my own control. Now that it was over, I think that I was more surprised than Jim Driscoll. His lips, by some sort of reflex, drew back in a stupid grin.

"You don't think I'm going to stand here and take that?" he said.

"Have it your own way," I answered. "You got what was coming to you, and you know what to do if you want some more."

Driscoll rubbed his hand across his cheek. It was interesting to see the effort he made to control his anger.

"We can't go on with this here," he said, "and you probably know it. We'll have to wait till this is over, Casey. I told you—you and I don't matter in this business and maybe this will prove it to you."

It did prove it in a way. I even found myself admiring Driscoll for his self-control.

"Just the same," I answered, "what I said goes and you'd better know it."

"You've been damned obvious," said Driscoll.

"I hope so," I answered. It is useless to speculate where this might have led us, since, fortunately perhaps, a tap on the door interrupted us and Driscoll's anger left him.

"That's Wu," he whispered. "Straighten yourself out and snap into it!" And he opened the hall door.

It was Mr. Wu, right enough. He still wore his black silk gown and he was holding a brown felt hat in his hands, bowing humbly.

"The honor is so great that it makes me afraid," he said. "You have summoned me, Commander Driscoll?"

Driscoll nodded. "Do you mind if we don't go through all the courtesies?" he inquired. "And come straight to the point?"

Mr. Wu set his hat down on the table, thrust his hands inside his sleeves and nodded.

"If you do not care for the amenities, we need not have them," he said. "I can be as direct as you. So you've seen this countryman of yours." His eyes moved toward me thoughtfully. "That is very good. It was my belief that he would come here."

"Was it?" said Driscoll. "You were very astute, Mr. Wu."

"Oh, no," said Mr. Wu and shook his head. "It is only that my people are an old people living in a land so crowded that it has made us familiar with personal relationships. I guess that you are bothered about a certain message. This man has naturally told you of it. Do you think it perhaps has to do with the matter we have spoken of?"

Driscoll looked at him earnestly. "I know it has, Wu," he said, "and I know that you can help me if you want. You came to me a while ago to open negotiations, so I hope we are still working together. What do you know about this message?"

Mr. Wu's expression was studiously blank, but there was a sardonic glint in his eye; and then his lips twisted superciliously. "Yes," he said, "it is true that I did come to you, a while ago—but only as an agent. I am sorry that I cannot help you any longer, Commander Driscoll. I have myself to think of, and now I have decided to take the matter into my own hands. There are so many others interested who may pay better. England perhaps, or Russia perhaps."

"Look here," Driscoll's face grew red, "you came around to me."

Mr. Wu's hands moved out of his sleeves, thin placating hands.

"I did," he answered, "but if you have thought that I was exclusively your servant in this, that was a misunderstanding. I find it better to be by myself just now."

For a second time Driscoll seemed to find it difficult to keep his temper. "By God," he said, "you've double-crossed me, Wu!"

Mr. Wu looked amused. "You put it very crudely," he said. "I simply approached you some time ago. I have given you my word about nothing."

Then I began to laugh. Without knowing exactly what was passing, it was clear enough that Mr. Wu had been a match for Jim Driscoll, and in some way he had extracted something from him and then had left him flat.

"I was afraid you wouldn't be any good, Jim," I told him, "and now I know it. Mr. Wu has got you in a hole, hasn't he? Good-by, Jim. You must excuse him, Mr. Wu. He isn't very bright." I clapped on my hat and had started for the door before I had another thought. "I don't know China or the Chinese, Mr. Wu," I added, "but I know one thing that probably works here the same as it does anywhere. You're too pleased with yourself. Even if you are, it never pays to show it." It seemed to me that Mr. Wu's expression grew sharper, and he might have replied if I had given him a chance to answer, but I did not. Instead, I walked into the hall, leaving Mr. Wu and Driscoll to talk as they pleased.

In spite of Mr. Wu's skill at dissembling, I was more sure than ever that there had been a change in him. That change had occurred when I was talking to him at his house. Mr. Wu knew something which none of us knew and he was very much pleased by his knowledge.

# 10

I WENT and sat a while in my own hotel room because I wished to be alone and to think. The room, completely European in its furnishings, looked over the tramcars and automobiles and crowds and turbaned policemen of Nanking Road. But all those foreign sights and sounds are blurred in my memory, only forming a hazy disturbing background which simply served to make my thoughts unpleasant. In my heart, I knew that the words I used to Driscoll could not be backed up by any action of mine. On the contrary, everything which Driscoll had said of me was true. What was going to happen to me when my money ran out, I wondered. Now that I had broken with Mr. Moto, there would be no Pacific flight, if he ever really meant it. There was some hope that Sam Bloom might find me something on some flying field, but this hope was vague enough. As far as finding anything about the message, it was entirely beyond me. I knew I was as close to being finished as I had ever been in my life. I knew it better when I went up to the dining room for lunch. It was a large ambitious dining room with snow-white tables and crystal chandeliers and an orchestra.

There was a superficial gaiety in that place which had a feverish quality of unreality. All the Europeans in Shanghai seemed to be gathered at lunch, each trying to forget something—thick-set businessmen from their offices and banks, a majority with the heavy faces of confirmed drinkers; naval officers and businessmen's wives and officers' wives, who all probably knew too much about the private lives of everyone else. There was a furtive undercurrent of gossip and intrigue, combined with an exiled loneliness, resulting from a thousand longing thoughts of home. I could believe that no one there was happy, that no one was entirely at ease. At any rate, the atmosphere served to intensify my own restlessness. I was glad to go back to my own room again, in spite of my having no real reason to go there. I had no reason to do anything, and it occurred to me that I had never had much for anything I did.

This mood of mine probably intensified the surprise I felt to find that a letter for me had been pushed under my door during the interval I had been away. It was a square blue envelope, which carried my name in a bold, woman's handwriting. There was a scent of gardenia from the page when I opened it that seemed to me needlessly strong. The note read:

> Casey dear, I cannot leave you the way we left. I am so worried as to what may happen to you because I think you know my deep interest. I must see you—I must—about something which will help you very much. Something about you and me. Will you come please to the Gaiety Club tonight? At half-past nine o'clock? Ask the manager to show you to my table. I need you, Casey dear. You mustn't fail me—please. And bring your flask. The liquor is not good there. That's a darling.
>
> SONYA.

I put the note down and lighted a cigarette. My first impression was that its contents were too tawdry and banal to be in keeping with what I had understood of Sonya's character. It was more like a streetwalker's effusion than a note which she might have written. There was no subtlety or restraint in its appeal. It was the sort of note—I paused and extinguished my cigarette—exactly the sort which might have been written to bait a trap. It was no compliment to me that she should have paid so little respect to my intelligence; or Mr. Moto, for I suspected that Mr. Moto's hand was in it. The whole composition exhibited the clumsiness of someone trying to appeal to the psychology of another race.

It made me ashamed that I had stood up for Sonya, because the writing was an indication that Driscoll had been right; that chivalry did not count. Mr. Moto must still believe that I knew something, and Driscoll believed that Sonya knew something.

It may have been a strange occasion on which to have felt grateful, but nevertheless my sensation was one of deep gratitude, because I had been given a chance, at last, a definite chance for positive action. Slender as that chance might be, and I was under no illusions on that score, now that I had the invitation, I was in a position to make a decison of my own, instead of following, as I had until then, the drift of events. If I answered that invitation, I had the possibility of finding what lay at the bottom of this business. It was my only opportunity. If I could once reach Sonya, I would not leave her until I knew. What? I could not guess what. I could not even decide upon a course of action, but I did not have much to live for.

I had my hands on something tangible at last, something which could be played to the limit. I would show them that I was better than they thought I was. I had been in tight places before that. If it cost me my life, as it probably would, I was determined to go to the Gaiety Club, wherever it might be, and see the game out to the finish. I did not care if I was completely alone; I had been alone before.

For a little while I played with the idea of telling Driscoll, but I did not tell him. In some way, I knew that my vindication lay in doing this alone.

It was half-past two in the afternoon by then. In seven hours I would be in a place called the Gaiety Club. In eight hours I might be dead. In the meanwhile I needed rest, so I took off my coat and lay down and tried to sleep.

At about five o'clock my room telephone rang. There was a Mr. Bloom, I was told, who wished to see me and I said to send him up. I was glad to see Sam Bloom, simply from a desire to see a friendly face, but I had no wish to have Sam Bloom know or become involved in anything I proposed.

"Listen, boy," said Sam Bloom, "what happened to you today? What happened on that ship? You needn't tell me—there was something wrong, I've been looking for you everywhere. Say, I began to think—what happened? You can tell me."

"Never mind," I said.

Sam Bloom sat down heavily and scowled. "I'm a friend of yours," he told me, "and I know more about this place than you do. I know you're mixed up in something. You'd better tell me what's the matter."

But I told him that I couldn't.

"None of my business, what?" said Sam. "Is it as bad as that? You don't want any help?"

I thanked him and told him I didn't and Sam Bloom flicked a card over to me.

"I'm not butting in," he said, "but in case you want anything, here's where I'm staying. All right, I'm not inquisitive; but is there anything you want to know? I know this town."

"Do you know a place called the Gaiety Club?" I asked.

Sam Bloom whistled. "A tough joint," he said, "in the Chinese City; a dancing place. You don't want to go there, Casey."

"Thanks," I said. "Do you know a man named Wu Lai-fu?"

Sam Bloom whistled again. "Are you mixed up with that baby? Everyone knows Wu. He wouldn't seem real anywhere else in the world. He's in secret brotherhoods. He's got a finger in politics. He's mixed up in everything. I don't believe any white man alive can make him out. He started out as a boy on a junk and then he was a houseboy in a missionary family. And then some Chinese official became interested in him. Don't you have anything to do with that baby! You don't think I'm butting in, do you?"

"No," I said. "I'm obliged. Have you got a gun you could give me?"

He reached inside his coat and unstrapped a shoulder holster. "It's a nice gun," he said. "If you use it remember it throws a little high." He looked at me and held out his hand. "You and I have been around. You know your business, Casey. If you don't want to tell anything more, don't. If you want me later, there I am. Good luck!"

"Thanks, Sam," I said again. I was more moved by his impersonality than I could have been by any warmer interest. Sam and I had been too long in a world where anything might happen.

"Maybe it wouldn't be healthy for you if I were hanging around," he suggested.

"Same to you," I answered.

"I'm not backing down," said Sam. "Do you want company at the Gaiety Club? I'm pretty good at dancing."

"No, thanks, Sam," I said.

"Well," he said, "so long!"

"So long, Sam," I said. I think both of us were quite sure that we would not meet again.

A Chinese city even as Europeanized as Shanghai is a peculiar place at night. It is filled wth sounds strange to a foreigner—of street crowds, falsetto voices, and of high stringed music that strikes a rhythm different from our own. Even above the blowing of the motor horns—and every Chinese driver seems to keep his hand on the horn unceasingly—there is the padding of feet of rickshaw runners. This background of sound confuses itself with my recollection of the Gaiety Club. I think of running slippered feet and of unfamiliar enunciation; of lights and banners before shops which display unfamiliar wares—the goods of old China mingling with Japanese and English and American novelties. I think of a China meeting the impact of the West and somehow absorbing and changing the West to conform to its ancient culture. At any rate, until the hired motor set me down in front of the Gaiety Club, everything was unfamiliar.

It was left for the Gaiety Club to demonstrate how amazingly American taste and culture have penetrated the East. The club was on the second floor of a semi-Europeanized building, and, in spite of its distance from its prototypes, it might have been a second-rate Sixth Avenue cabaret, except for the Asiatic faces of the dancers. There was the same dance floor in the center of a dimly lighted room. There were the same circles of tables about it, clustered too closely together for comfort. In the same mingled auras of perfume, liquor and cigarettes the orchestra was playing the same jazz music. A crooner, even, was rendering through a megaphone a ridiculous imitation of a negro voice. The men, nearly all of them Orientals, were in European clothes. The Chinese girls wore beautiful long gowns which fitted their figures closely and seductively. A Chinese boy took my hat, and a man, evidently the manager, a fat heavy Chinese, met me at the head of the stairs, bowing and smiling as though he were on the lookout for me.

"Miss Sonya's table," I said.

"Yes, please," he answered courteously. "Miss Sonya, oh, yes, she is waiting."

I stood a second on the threshold of the room, pulling at my tie, in order that my hand might be near the shoulder holster, for I suspected that anything could happen at any time. The music continued, waiters moved from table to table with drinks.

"This way, please," said the fat Chinese, and we walked into the vitiated air of the Gaiety Club, threading our way between the tables.

Then I saw Sonya seated by the edge of the dance floor at a small round table for two. I had never seen her looking so beautiful. Her evening dress was violet, like her eyes. Her bag lay on the table before her. She looked surprisingly young. Her figure beneath the festoons of paper flowers was that of a girl in her teens. When she saw me, she waved and smiled.

"Casey dear," she said. "How prompt you are!"

"Always prompt for you, Sonya," I said.

"Come," she said, "come sit close beside me. That is, unless you want to dance."

The orchestra was playing "The Last Roundup," old, to be sure, to anyone from the States, but perhaps still a novelty in Shanghai. I listened to the artificial syncopation and thought how far a roundup was from there.

"I'm going to my last roundup," the Chinese singer said through his megaphone, "my last roundup" . . . and I held Sonya in my arms. There never was a more perfect dancer. Her hair was brushing my cheek. Her lips were close to my ear.

"Whose roundup?" I asked her. "I got your note. Do they mean mine?"

She laughed as though I had said something casual and amusing and then I heard her whispering in my ear.

"You fool—what brought you here? I tried to make my note show that you shouldn't come. Casey, I thought you'd understand!"

"I understood," I whispered back and held her closer. "And that's exactly why I'm here. You're going to see a lot of me tonight."

"Casey," she whispered, "they're going to kill you."

"I thought so," I whispered back. "And you're putting the finger on me, aren't you Sonya? Well, try—but you won't get away from me."

"Casey," she answered, "I can't—I can't let them kill you."

"Then what did you get me here for?" I asked. "You sent that note, didn't you?"

"Be careful," she whispered. "They're watching us. Try to laugh—try to smile. You might—even try to kiss me, Casey."

The idea amused me. I tried and she drew her head away. I've never heard anything more genuine than her laughter.

"I'm going to my last roundup," the Chinese was shouting again, "roundup."

"Casey," she whispered, "please, I had to send that note, but I made it obvious enough. He thinks—he thinks you have it on you, Casey—that message."

"Who thinks?" I asked.

"Moto," she whispered. "Casey, I ought not to tell you but I can't help it. Why were you dull enough to come? I shall have to help you now. Casey, we're going back to the table. Then I've been told to leave you. As soon as I do, a fight is going to start. The lights are going out. What are you going to do?"

"Find out what this is about," I answered. "It was the only way I could think of to see you again."

Now that the program was laid before me, I was not particularly alarmed, because the unknown is what is most alarming. "You'd better understand me. I thought this was set for a killing, but I came to see you. I came to find out what all this is about and you're not going to get away from me this time, Sonya."

She laughed again, that ingenuous careless laugh, and moved closer into my arms. "We haven't time to argue," she whispered. "But I'll promise you this—I'll swear that I'll be waiting for you in an automobile in the street. Don't try to leave by a door. Go out a window; don't go down the stairs. Remember, nothing has happened. Look as though you loved me, Casey."

I tried to laugh. I tried to talk about something else and then the music stopped.

"I'll see you later, Sonya," I whispered. "I give you my word for it." And we walked back to the table. "Sonya," I said, "you're beautiful." And we sat down beside the dance floor.

I believed what she had told me—that she would help me. She kept talking to me gaily. I never could remember about just what, but once she said beneath her breath:

"You'd better look around you, Casey. I'm going in a minute." She did not need to tell me.

There was a waiter standing near us who looked as heavy as a wrestler. His face was dull and claylike and his hands were not made to handle trays of dishes. On either side of us and just behind us were three tables where only men were seated. All of them were Japanese.

"Waiter," I said, and he moved toward me, "get me a bottle of champagne." I felt better when the bottle was on the table. I raised my glass and smiled at Sonya.

"Happy landings," I said, and added softly, "I believe you'll be waiting for me. I want to see you, if I get out of this."

She rose and said, "Will you excuse me for a moment?"

And I rose also and bowed. Then I sat down again, alone at my table, the fingers of my left hand playing with the bottle, my right hand moving up and down over my necktie. I tried to look deeply interested in the dancers. The music had started up again as I sat there waiting. Seconds and minutes drag at such a time, but, after all, I did not have so long to wait.

Voices in one corner of the club were growing louder, like sounds offstage. It flashed across my mind that the plan for my elimination, as Sonya had outlined it, was not a bad one; indeed it would cause scarcely a ripple of excitement if it were handled right. It would simply appear the next day that K. C. Lee, once a well-known airman, who had fallen on hard times, had been killed in a nightclub brawl. It would be a natural comprehensible epitaph to nearly everyone who knew me. I had been mixed up in enough free-for-all fights before to have some idea of looking out for myself, and this was my only hope, combined with my knowlege of what was due to happen.

The noise from the far corner of the Gaiety Club grew louder. There was a shout and a table crashed. Since I fully understood that there would be no use fighting my way toward the stairs because they would expect me there, I was trying to get the plan of the Gaiety Club and the disposition of its patrons clearly in my mind.

I was hemmed in by men on three sides, by tables. A glance over my shoulder showed me that the heavy waiter was just behind my chair, probably waiting to fall on me or to knock me over from behind. He was by far the most dangerous element in the picture. For the rest, it seemed to me they had made a tactical mistake in seating me next to the dance floor, because my way across this floor was clear to a row of tall shuttered windows just to the right of the orchestra. I gauged the distance carefully, for by that time there was no doubt that Sonya was correct. Pandemonium was breaking loose in the Gaiety Club. I gathered my feet under my chair, waiting, and then the lights went out.

I do not believe they knew I was ready, and this, combined with the quickness of my reflexes, probably saved my life. At the instant the lights went, I did three things: I kicked my own table hard in the direction of one of the tables near me, I threw the champagne bottle straight at where the faces had been at the table to my left, and hurtled backward with all my weight, chair and all, into the Chinese waiter's stomach. I must have hurt him, because I heard him scream as we went down, but I managed to roll free of him just as we touched the floor, and I had out Sam Bloom's gun by the time I had gathered my knees beneath me. Then I fired three shots fast and bounded to one side. There is nothing worse than staying in the same place when you are shooting in the dark. Then, as I started to run, they must have guessed where I was going. I heard a voice rising above the others, shouting out some order, but I maintained my sense of direction and kept my wits about me so completely that the whole affair, in spite of its tumult and darkness, remains with me in a sort of geometric exactitude. I made a dive across the dance floor, bending low, slithered against a table and plop! into someone's arms.

An arm went behind my back and a hand clamped on my throat. There was no time for amenities just then, because it was my life or the man's who held me. I presented my automatic at his middle and pulled the trigger. He dropped free of me and I plowed on through a clatter of glass and dishes, and just then the lights went up, giving me a momentary picture of the Gaiety Club which looked as though a tornado had struck it.

I was just beside one of the windows. Two men across the dance hall were swinging automatics in my direction and in another split second they would probably have got me as easily as I might have hit a pipe in a shooting gallery. There was only one thing left for me, as there had been all along—to hope that the window was flimsy and that there was a street outside not too far below. I took a shot across the dance hall. Then I dove into the window, straight through it, frame and all. I could see the dusky blackness of the street just as I lost my balance and went pitching out the window. I was very lucky in my landing in that I struck the street on all fours. Though the impact was bad enough to make me groggy, my instinct made me run for the shelter of the side of the building.

"Casey!" I heard Sonya's voice call me. "This way, Casey!" I saw a closed motor with its door open. I heard the engine running as I staggered toward it. I think Sonya must have pulled me inside, because I have not much recollection of getting there. The automobile was tearing very fast along the street. Sonya's arm was around me, her hand moved gently across my face.

"Casey," she was asking, "are you hurt? You must be hurt."

I tried to answer conscientiously, but I was in no condition to take stock of myself.

"Sonya," I said, "they didn't do that very well. They thought I'd be too easy. And now I think we're going to have a little talk. That's what I came for, Sonya."

"Casey," she was touching my right shoulder—"you're bleeding! They've shot you!"

I had felt nothing, because one feels little at such moments.

"All right," I said, "they had a damn good chance"—and Sonya seemed used to such matters.

"Quickly!" she said. "Take off your coat!" The car was still going at high speed through dim streets, but there was enough light to see that my left arm was bleeding badly. Sonya ripped back the sleeve of my shirt, which was soaked with blood.

"There," she said, and I said:

"Thanks. Tear off a piece of my shirt and tie it tight. That's a good girl, Sonya." I must have been in pretty bad condition, but she acted like a nurse in an emergency ward. The bleeding stopped when she tied my arm up tight. She leaned forward and spoke to the driver.

"Well," I said, "what next?"

"I'm stopping to buy you an overcoat and a new hat," she explained. "People mustn't see you this way, Casey." The car had stopped before a half-Chinese, half-European clothing store.

"Stay here," said Sonya. "I won't leave you, Casey."

I did not notice very much what happened for the next few minutes. Then she came back with a hat and cheap overcoat and bundled it around me.

"Where are we going now?" I asked. I trusted her absolutely then, if for no other reason than because there was nothing else to do.

"We're going to your hotel," she said. "It's nearly the only place where we can be safe, I think." Her voice caught in half a sigh and half a laugh. "I've burnt my bridges, Casey. They'll know I got you away. They'll know I warned you. You and I are outlaws, now."

"Are we?" I asked her.

"Yes," she said, and I took her hand.

"All right," I said, "as long as you're one too. Will it be possible at the hotel?"

My question made her laugh again. "You have American ideas. I don't think they'll bother much. You can say that I'm your wife. Let me wipe your face clean. And put that pistol in your pocket."

I had forgotten the pistol, but there it was, still grasped in my right hand.

## 11

I SUPPOSE they thought at the hotel that I was drunk. I might have been, for all that I remember. Sonya steadied me like a capable nurse and locked the door. I put the automatic on the bureau and wriggled out of my overcoat and found myself staring at my image in the mirror. There was no doubt that I had been through the mill. There was a gash on my scalp that was still bleeding. My shirt had been stripped off me. A sleeve of my coat was torn and bloody. My trousers were ripped at the knees.

"Casey," Sonya said, "you look dreadful."

"You're right," I answered, "but you don't, Sonya." My hand touched something in the side pocket of my coat. I pulled it out with my flask. "I'll feel better, maybe," I said vaguely, "if I have a drink."

"You'll feel better," Sonya said, "if you let me wash you, Casey," and turned me gently around. She was looking at me respectfully. "There are not so many people who could have left the Gaiety Club tonight," she said. "And I know what I'm talking about."

"Yes," I said soberly. She was standing beside me, as untouched and unmoved by what had happened as though it were all a part of her life. "I'm afraid you know too much," I said, and ended with an inconsequent question:

"Are you glad they didn't get me, Sonya?"

Her answer was simple, entirely devoid of emotion.

"Do you think I'd be here, if I weren't? I never thought that I should allow sentiment to mix itself with this. I shouldn't have. It may be the end, perhaps, but I don't seem to mind. I've seen members of my own family shot like dogs, but I couldn't let them kill you, Casey. It was too ugly, I think, with me a part of it. You'd better lie down, Casey. I'm going to fix your arm."

There comes a time when events are moving so fast that one's mind becomes immune to new impressions, which I suppose is the reason that everything seemed natural. I could not think it was odd that Sonya and I should be there alone. It was what I had wanted. It seemed inevitable that we must reach some final understanding. Who was she? What was she? I knew that I would find out that night.

I stood there, holding my old flask. The leather case was as battered as myself.

"If you'll excuse me," I said, "I think I'll have a drink. Perhaps you'll have one too?"

Then I saw that something about her had changed indefinably. I noticed, as I tugged at the cup on the bottom of the flask, that her glance seemed sharper, suddenly anxious.

"No," she said. "First you let me fix your arm. Casey, please put down the flask."

Her voice was sharper, like her eyes.

"Why?" I asked. There was something different between us.

"Your arm," she said, "it may be bad for you."

She was not telling the truth and I knew it.

"What's the matter with you, Sonya?" I said. "This won't hurt my arm."

I yanked off the bottom of my flask as I said it but I did not take a drink. Instead, I stared at the bottom of the cup—at a bit of rice paper in the bottom about the size of a paper for rolling cigarettes, with writing upon it in Oriental characters. I saw Sonya's hand move toward it and I drew the cup away. I was learning what she wanted faster than I thought I would.

"No, you don't," I said. "So that's your little game! No, Sonya, you're a nice girl, but you don't get it now." I picked up the automatic from the bureau. "Drop your handbag, Sonya!" I said. "We don't want any more trouble. We're going to get the truth right now."

A part of the truth had already come over me, stunning me

completely. I knew what that paper was in the bottom of my flask. I had never put it there.

"Drop your handbag, Sonya!" I said again. "You've done a good job but you haven't done it quite well enough. It looks as though I have the message now. Not that I can read it," I added, "but perhaps before we're through you'll read it for me; and Commander Driscoll can check you up. He's here in the hotel. Do you hear me? Drop that handbag, Sonya! I don't want you reaching in it for a powder puff. I'm going to call Commander Driscoll now."

"No," she said, "no! Don't do that. You mustn't!" and her handbag dropped out of her fingers to her feet.

The nervous stimulation which had buoyed me until then had not left me. I could see Sonya with part of my mind but the rest of me was back in the cabin on the *Imoto Maru.* I had to admire the astuteness of that man named Ma, who had thought of the cup on the bottom of my flask. Where would have been a better place to have left a message to a man like me than where he must have chosen before he had been discovered? Where would there have been a place where others would have been less likely to have discovered it? It was Ma's bad luck that I had never used the bottom of my flask until that moment. He had not counted on my unnatural abstemiousness. That was all.

"No," said Sonya again. "Casey, please, you mustn't. That was why they wanted to kill you. They wanted that flask, Casey. I had to ask you to bring it—Do you remember?"

I nodded to her agreeably. "And that's why you wanted to save my life, I suppose," I said. "I'm grateful to you, Sonya."

"No," she said. "It wasn't entirely that. Casey, we must think. Let me see that paper."

I put the paper back in the cup again, snapped the cup back on the bottom of my flask and put the whole in my hip pocket. Then, bending quickly, I recovered Sonya's white handbag from the floor. I found, as I expected, a small pearl-handled automatic in the middle compartment of her bag.

"You won't need that tonight," I said "and we're going to talk about this paper; but you won't need to see it."

She did not seem surprised by my answer, not offended. "Casey," she said, "don't you think I'd better fix your arm now? It's beginning to bleed again."

"Stay where you are," I told her. "Right in that corner of the room. I'm not going to give you the chance to knock me over the head, Sonya."

She stood watching me irresolutely. "Don't you trust me, Casey? Wouldn't you, if I promised you?"

"No," I said. "I don't see why I should. Do you?"

She moved her white hands in a sort of hopeless gesture. "Casey, someone's got to help you. Someone's got to wash your head. Someone must bind your arm. I—I want to, Casey."

"You're a beautiful emotional actress," I said. "Don't act any more. Sit down!"

She began to cry, and I knew she was not acting then. "Casey," she said, "Casey, please, I swear I only want to help you."

I felt my resolve slipping, moved by that appeal. There was no doubt that I needed someone to help me.

"Very well," I said. "But mind, I'm watching you, Sonya."

As a matter of fact, she did it very well. She took me into the bathroom and stripped me to the waist. She washed out the wound with hot water—a flesh wound, I found it was, hardly more than a graze, which would probably make my arm stiff and wretchedly sore by morning, and might also give me a degree of fever; but I doubted if it would be much worse. Then she washed my head and fetched me a clean shirt from my bag.

"You feel better now?" she asked.

I felt a great deal better and I told her so. "If you'd be straight with me," I ended, "I'd like you, Sonya."

We had seated ourselves facing each other and the room was very quiet. We seemed like old friends, and perhaps we were old friends, for nearly every semblance of pretense was gone from us.

"I'll have to tell someone," she said finally. "I'm going to tell you, Casey, because I'm all alone. I'm going to tell you and beg that you may help me."

"Is that straight?" I said. "Because that's what I've been waiting for."

She answered directly. "Yes, that's straight. I swear it. You see," she sighed, "I don't suppose that my mind is as quick as some people's. I'm rather new to this, Casey. I wasn't really brought up to it. You see, Mr. Moto guessed this noon that there was something in the bottom of that flask. I was there when he guessed it."

I forgot the throbbing pain of my arm and the dull ache of my head. "But how did he guess it?" I asked. "Have the Japanese got second sight?"

Sonya smiled, and her eyes, as they met mine, were no longer hard. "Oh, no, not that, but Mr. Moto is clever, very clever, Casey, in some ways. He has to be, in work like his. This morning I was with him as he sat thinking, and he told me what he thought. I think he rather likes me, Casey."

"Oh," I said, "does he?"

She continued, ignoring my remark: "You mustn't blame Mr. Moto. He has a very difficult time, and sometimes he seems such a little man to do everything and arrange everything. When the ship came in, he went to the Japanese Consulate and began pacing up and down a little office, trying to reconstruct what might have happened. He began with the belief that you had not seen a message or destroyed it; then he reviewed the entire search of your things. He was completely satisfied that every inch of your cabin, bags and clothing had been searched. He was sure of that because, when you left the boat, he went through everything a second time. He was sure the clothing you wore had been searched thoroughly. There was only one thing left—your flask. They had opened the top of the flask. They had seen it was full of whisky. A message inserted in a pellet might have been dropped into the whisky, but they had shaken the flask and nothing had rattled. It was only this morning that it occurred to Mr. Moto that there might be a cup fitted onto the bottom of the flask. By what you might term the process of elimination, that cup was the only place left where a message might be left. You had taken the flask with you when you jumped overboard, but he was quite certain you did not suspect the existence of a message. He had watched you carefully when your cabin was being searched. You had given no sign of interest—not the flicker of an eyelid—when they lifted up the flask. That's about all, Casey. He was right, wasn't he? You must admit that he was clever."

I could not help but admire the astuteness of Mr. Moto—an alarming astuteness—and the complete logic of what she said convinced me that she was telling the truth; but I needed more facts than that. I had reached the end of my patience, and for once in all that transaction I had something which was close to being the upper hand.

"That's good as far as it goes," I said. "Mr. Moto was a brighter man than I am. Do you know Driscoll, of our Naval Intelligence, Sonya? I had a quarrel with him this morning, but I'll go to the telephone and call him unless you'll tell me what this message is about."

Sonya leaned back in her chair, watching me almost sleepily while her hands rested limply in her lap. "Very well," she said, "I'll tell you," and then she laughed in that light way of hers, as though she could detach herself from the seriousness of the moment and be genuinely amused.

"What are you laughing at?" I asked.

"You," she said. "Excuse me, Casey. You may not understand why it strikes me as funny that anyone like you should be involved in this, and that I should be here compromised with a strange American. You are so different from what you ought to be, to appear in such a situation. You aren't devious. You're honest, Casey. You have no real awareness of the intrigue around us. Don't be angry with me. I'll tell you. I don't suppose you even remember my last name."

"Karaloff," I said.

"But it doesn't mean anything to you, does it, Casey?"

I shook my head. "Only that it's your name, Sonya."

"And the name Alexis Karaloff? Think—have you ever heard that name?"

I shook my head again and she shook hers back at me mockingly. "You never heard of Alexis Karaloff? Or of his work with crude petroleum? Or of his improvements on the Burgeius formula? Yet here you are. Even Wu Lai-fu thought you must have some idea. He told me that he asked you."

"I'm glad you think it's funny. Just who is Alexis Karaloff?" I asked.

Her expression grew set. "Your tenses are wrong. He was my father, Casey—a kind father. I heard he was dead today." She paused a moment and caught her breath. She was tragic, sitting there, but not intentionally tragic.

I said, "I'm sorry, Sonya," and put my hand over one of hers.

"Thank you," she answered. "We're used to death in Russia, Casey. I have suspected he was dead for quite a little while. But now I know, it's worse than I thought. It leaves me all alone except perhaps—"

"Perhaps what?" I asked her.

"Except perhaps for you. I'm not lying, Casey. You and I are both alone. I hope you'll understand what I tell you. You would, if you knew Russia; but you don't. I hope you'll not think it is too fantastic. You've probably heard so many Russians telling tales of greatness. The illusion of old grandeur grows on one, when one has not got it left. But this is true, Casey. The Czar was my father's patron. My father was a naval inventor. He was interested above everything else in oil as a fuel for naval vessels. He was very loyal to the Czar. I was a little girl then—too little to remember much. At the time of the Revolution he left Russia. My mother was murdered in the streets. He took me to Harbin after the Kolchak fighting. He was too much involved in the White Russian army ever to cross the border again. . . . Have you ever seen Harbin?"

"No," I said. "I had hardly heard it spoken of until I came to the Orient, Sonya."

She sighed and closed her eyes and then opened them. "Harbin," she said softly. "I wish you could have seen it when things were going well. It's my city, where I spent my childhood, Casey—a strange city of exiles; but it was gay. We Russians were always gay even when we were sad and beyond all hope. If Harbin were what it used to be, it would be the place for you and me. You should have seen the cafés and heard the singing. You should have seen the hospitality. No one thought of tomorrow in Harbin except to think of Old Russia coming back. Everyone was an aristocrat." She smiled slightly. "Whether he was or not, you understand. Harbin—the boats on the Sungari River—you should have seen the boats. You should have seen the lumber and the grain. We lived in Harbin, you see." She paused and, as her voice stopped, illusion stopped with it. I had been able to understand vaguely something of the life she was trying to tell me, when it was expressed in the soft modulation of her voice; but when she stopped, we were back in the hotel bedroom, no longer in Harbin.

"Go on," I said, "if we're getting anywhere."

"Harbin," she said; her voice was softer. "Have you ever heard it called the Paris of the Orient? It is the last city of my people, the *émigrés* from Russia. You see the rest of us scattered here in China—Russian policemen, Russian women in Chinese clothes begging on the street, Russians dressed like coolies working with the coolies on the docks—but it was gayer in Harbin. There was quality and rank. Old generals, admirals, scholars, ladies and gentlemen from the old nobility. Why, our merchants could even compete with the Chinese store-keepers in Harbin. You should have heard us talk, Casey. There was great talk in our parlors because there was always hope, you see. Red Russia could not last. It was incredible that it could last. We were always plotting for a *coup,* building castles in the air. We were always thinking of how to seize some part of Siberia. Old officers would talk of smuggled arms and of ways to set up a Russian kingdom in Mongolia or around Bakal. We are fine people for theories, Casey. We can make them logical through self-hypnotism. You should have heard all the names that were mentioned—secret correspondence with this one and that one. I suppose it was the same in France when the old régime fell down. They would whisper about Horvath and Kolchak and Semenov. They would be buoyed up by hope. There would be talk of some mythical help from Chang Tso-lin, the old marshal, you remember, and, later, the young marshal. Chinese are like us in that way. They all of them love to talk. Then later there were dealings with 'little' Hsü, who was darting over Mongolia in his motor cars. And then there was that impresario, the Buddhist Baron Ungern Sternberg. Oh, I can give you lists of names. That was the atmosphere I was brought up in, Casey—sitting in my father's house, listening to him talking as he pored over maps and figures with strangers late at night. I have never known half of the logic of his theories. Perhaps they made no difference. Perhaps—I wonder, Casey—perhaps my father did not believe them. After all, he was a scientist who spent most of his day with his drawings in his laboratory, for he had brought some money out of Russia. I am not sure. Perhaps he did believe them. If we are unhappy, we always try to imagine something different, don't we?"

"Yes," I said, "I've imagined a lot in the last few years. Do you mind my saying this doesn't sound practical, Sonya?"

She smiled inquiringly, as though she did not understand. "Practical?" she said. "Of course, we are not practical. Have you read our literature; have you heard our music, Casey? Not much of it is practical but some of it is beautiful. We are creative artists, Casey, but my father did one thing that was practical back there in Harbin. He invented a process of treating crude petroleum, and an especial burner, which would make one gallon of oil do the work two gallons had done before. You see the implication, Casey? Japan did, when he took that invention to Japan. It meant that a warship would have twice the cruising radius that it ever had before. Can you wonder that Japan was interested? Can you wonder, Casey? My father did that—Alexis Karaloff did that. He may have been a visionary but he was a scientist. I think his name will be remembered for a long while after you and I are dead."

I tried to get my thoughts together. At last the light was dawning on me. "Do you mean that the Japanese navy is going to have a cruising radius twice as great as ours?" I said. "Why, that's going to eliminate coaling stations. It's going to change every base. If there should be a war—" I stopped.

At last I understood why Driscoll told me the matter was important. It still seemed hardly credible that such an invention should not have come from our own laboratories instead of from a city called Harbin. If she was telling the truth, and I believed she was, any nation in the world would have struggled for such a discovery.

"Has Japan got his plans?" I asked. "Tell me what happened, Sonya?"

"I'm going to tell you, Casey," she answered. "I'm going to tell you, because it seems the only thing left to do, and because my father would have agreed with me, I think. He did not care very much about himself. Do you think many people do, who live in a world of intellect? He really cared for only two things—the abstract complications of ideas and the Russia of the old régime."

"Didn't he care for you?" I asked.

She considered a moment before she answered. "As much as he could for any human being, I think, but his opinion of the human race was not very high, Casey. Never mind about that. He appreciated the value of that invention and its significance and implications as keenly as any industrialist, without ever wishing that value for himself. He wished it to further his fixed idea. You guess the idea, perhaps? I am sorry that I have no particular knowledge of its details, but at any rate, they do not matter. It was another one of those whispering plots of my people, but this time I think it had some basis, slight as it might be. For once, they were not pinning all their faith on the dreams of some adventurer. Yes, there was a semblance of reality this time. It had to do with the concentration of Red Russian troops on the Manchurian border, when Japan became interested in the adventure of the State of Manchukuo. It seemed to my father and his friends that Japan might welcome and even might help White intervention along the border by supplying arms and money. There was one of those usual plans, perfectly logical down to the last detail. As I say, I do not know it. I only know that my father brought me with him down to Tokyo and that he was greatly excited. He offered his formula and his drawings to the Japanese Government in return for their support of a White adventure, and they accepted. They had reason to accept. He was very happy until he found out that the political balance had been changed. First the Japanese hesitated to supply arms and then they entirely refused. My father felt that he had been betrayed. He left Tokyo and started for Harbin, as though Japanese troops and spies were not everywhere in Manchuria. He was allowed to leave Tokyo readily enough, because he had already handed over his drawings. It was some days later before they understood the plans were not complete. My father had taken the page of the chemical process back with him to Harbin and nothing was of any use without it. He was planning to sell it elsewhere, of course. He even began starting negotiations with America through the agency of the man you've seen—Wu Lai-fu. But you can guess the rest of it. This may not be the sort of life you're used to in America, but believe me, there is plenty of it here, where all life is unsettled, where there may be an explosion at any time. That is a period which develops men like Mr. Moto and Wu Lai-fu, but you can understand what happened."

"Perhaps," I said; "but you'd better tell me, Sonya."

She leaned back wearily and closed her eyes. "The Japanese were not going to let such a secret as that go, and I don't blame them much, do you? They caught my father in Harbin. They made him a political prisoner in the new capitol of Manchukuo—high-handedly perhaps, but they had reason to be high-handed. They held him while they searched for papers in his house, but they could not find what they wanted. Then they approached me. I had received my education in Tokyo, you understand, and I have many friends among the Japanese. I was approached and asked politely if I could not help in this hunt for the paper, and there was a hint that my father might not live if it were not found. I wanted him to live because I loved him, but perhaps you can imagine now why they did not find the paper. I had no intimation of it until we were together on that ship and there was a dead man in your cabin."

"Perhaps I could guess," I answered, "but you'd better tell me, Sonya."

"It was Ma," she said. "Ma was my father's old interpreter and servant, a very faithful, absolutely reliable man devoted to my father, as Chinese occasionally become devoted to their masters. I have known him ever since I was a little girl, and he would have died for us any time. As a matter of fact, he did die, didn't he? . . . What happened is clear enough now. My father, when he knew he was going to be taken, gave Ma that formula and I rather think told him to try to sell it to America. Ma escaped with it but was afraid to have such a thing on his person. He left it somewhere in Manchuria. The message, I think, was to tell us where that paper is." She paused as though she expected some response from me, but I did not answer her. "Then I heard the rest of the news today. It came from Wu Lai-fu. He has all sorts of devious connections. I think he is one of the Chinese who is secretly financing bandits in Manchuria. There is no penny-dreadful novel more lurid than parts of China and Manchuria these days. He had word, and he tells the truth, that my father was shot, trying to escape. I've been telling you the truth too, Casey. And that's about all there is. I have told you because I want you to help me. I owe nothing further to Mr. Moto. . . . Will you show me what is written on that paper in your flask?"

I paused awhile before I answered, trying to make up my mind. I paused, but I believed every word she said, however incredible it may sound as I have set it down on paper. Words in black and white about such matters as I have tried to describe do not convey any great basis of credibility, because the time and place do not go with those words or the personality which spoke them. There is no way which I know for me to convey the impression of her voice, or for me to describe the restlessness of Asia, since both of these are wholly indescribable to anyone who has not known them. I can only say again that I knew she told the truth. I knew it, if only from the way her story fitted with the small details I had seen. Her rôle was clear at last and Mr. Moto and Driscoll and even Wu Lai-fu came into place, cleverly and perfectly. More than anything else I knew that she was telling the truth because I liked her, and I have found it pays to trust quite implicitly to one's instinctive likings.

"Sonya," I said, "I think you're being straight with me."

"I am," she said. "I am." And her fingers gripped my hand. The pressure of her fingers reminded me that I had been holding her hand all the while she was speaking.

"If you see this message," I asked her, "what are you going to do?"

"I'm going to find that paper, if you'll help me, Casey."

"If you find it," I asked, "what will you do then?" She was no longer candid. She did not meet my glance.

"We'll talk about that later," she said. "The point is, we both want to find it, don't we? Will you take out your flask?"

"Yes," I said, "I'll trust you, Sonya. Can you read Chinese?"

She nodded, and I drew the flask from my hip pocket. I snapped the cup off the bottom and handed it to her.

"With my compliments," I said.

She took the cup and lifted out the paper very carefully between her thumb and finger and bent over it, first thoughtfully, then incredulously.

"Why," she exclaimed suddenly, "why—"

"What's the matter, Sonya?" I asked her.

Her eyes were fixed on mine—bewildered candid eyes. "Ma never wrote this," she said. "I know Ma's grass characters. He taught me when I was a little girl. Someone else wrote this—not Ma!"

There was a silence while I tried to think. Again I knew that she was telling the truth, though the whole matter was becoming too complicated for me to understand.

"Are you sure?" I said.

"Yes," she answered, "I'm sure."

"But who else could have written it?"

"I don't know," she said. "Let me try to think." She sighed and frowned in her perplexity and said again, "Let me try to think."

It seemed to me that it would do no good for me to help her because I was entirely beyond my depth.

"If you don't mind," I said, "I'll take a drink while you're thinking," and I reached and took the cup away. Then I unscrewed the top of the flask. I was just about to pour a drink into the cup when my glance fell on the gold-washed bottom.

"Sonya," I said. "Look! There was another paper here. Look down at the bottom of this cup. You can see where it was lying. A corner of it's been stuck to the bottom. Look!"

She reached for the cup and drew in her breath sharply. She was bending over it, staring. Dimly, yet clearly enough to see, there was the outline of where a similar bit of paper had been lying. The presence of a little moisture had caused its edges to adhere slightly to the bottom of the cup. Someone had pulled it out hastily, a little carelessly. It was different from the paper in her hand. Her eyes were wide, her lips were in a thin straight line.

"Casey," she asked, "did you do that?"

"No," I said, "I didn't."

"Then," her voice dropped unconsciously to a half-whisper, "take that cup and wash it very carefully. Dry it with a towel. Don't let your fingerprints stay on it. Someone has taken that message and left this one, and no one else must know."

"But who?" I asked. "I wonder who."

"We'll have to find out, Casey," Sonya said. "We'll have to try to—you and I tonight. After all, who would have done it, Casey? Not Mr. Moto. He only guessed this morning what was in there. Who else was there? You took that flask with you when you jumped into the river."

I had never tried to play the rôle of Sherlock Holmes before. "Well," I said, "let's try to think. Suppose you read me that message, Sonya."

She looked at it again. "Why, that's very queer," she said.

"What's queer?" I asked. "You'd better read the message."

"It doesn't say much," she answered, "but it's enough to understand. It says 'The house of Ma Fu'Shan at Fuyu.' That's what the message says, of course, but that isn't what is queer. Ma Fu'Shan was our man Ma's elder brother, Casey. I've seen him often enough. His house is not at Fuyu. Ma has often told me where he lives—at a farm village near the hills, a few miles outside of Chinchow. Casey, that message has been changed."

"Let's forget about that for a minute," I said, for I had a flash of intuition. "Whether it's been changed or not, I know where the thing is, Sonya. It's at Ma's brother's house. Ma left it there."

"But who changed the message?" she asked me. "Why?"

And then I had another thought. My mind had leapt dazzlingly from inconsequence to fact. In my excitement, I put my hand on her shoulder.

"Listen," I said, "have you thought of Wu Lai-fu? Listen, Sonya, he's as clever as Mr. Moto, isn't he? Why shouldn't he want this for himself? Listen, Sonya. I think I can tell you what's happened."

She looked incredulous but I knew that I was right. I had remembered something which had happened back in that room of Wu Lai-fu's.

"I remember how his manner changed toward me when he was talking to me," I said. "He had someone look inside the cup of this flask, Sonya, as sure as I'm alive. When he was talking to me. I know he did. Can't you see? It was his idea to have that message changed. He knew that Moto would be after me. He knew that sooner or later Moto's mind would come to that flask. He wants Moto out of the way, Sonya, because he wants this for himself. He's probably sent someone off already."

Sonya looked thoughtful and then the lights were dancing in her eyes. "Casey," she said, "that's clever of you. I never thought it possible that you could think like that."

"Thanks," I said. "I didn't either—if you want to know."

Sonya moved, and I felt her shoulder tremble. "You're right," she said; "you're absolutely right. It's Mr. Wu. He's sent someone there already, probably by train this noon. It's too late for us now."

"Wait a minute," I broke in, for I had another idea. "I don't know anything about this country. How long does it take to reach this place, wherever it is, by train?"

Sonya frowned again. "Quite a time, I think. You would have to go by way of Tientsin and through Shan-hai-kwan."

"That means nothing to me," I said. "Would anyone starting this morning reach there by tomorrow noon?"

Sonya laughed. "Your ideas of rail travel in China are too American, Casey. It would take him another day, at least. But he's ahead. We can't catch up to him now."

"Can't we?" I said. "Have you forgotten what I am?"

"No," she said seriously. "I think you're splendid, Casey."

"Not that," I answered. "I'm an air pilot, Sonya. I doubt if Mr. Wu has thought of sending a man by plane."

She leaped quickly to her feet. "Casey," she whispered, "Casey, do you know where to get a plane?"

I nodded. "I know where I can try. And if you know where this village is on the map, I can set you down there tomorrow morning. How far away is it, do you think?"

"Five hundred miles," she said.

"All right," I said. "There's no use starting now. We can't make it in the dark."

Then her excitement left her. "Casey," she said, "Casey dear, there's no use talking this way. We can't do it at all. Moto's men are watching this hotel. We're cornered in here like two little rats."

"Oh, no, we're not," I said.

Now that I had thought of the plane, my mind was running smoothly. Now that there was no longer mystery, I could deal with actual facts. "If you do what I tell you, Mr. Moto will lose all further interest in us tonight. Sonya, are you listening to me? Get Mr. Moto on the telephone. Tell him to come up here. Tell him you've got the message. It was in the flask. Tell him I'm glad to give it to him. It's no affair of mine. There's the telephone. You go and tell him, Sonya."

Sonya stood an instant thinking and then she said, "Casey, I think you're very clever. I mean it. You're brave, you're quick. I should be glad to go anywhere with you, Casey, anywhere on earth."

"Thanks," I answered. Her words had made my own words unsteady. She had not been acting when she said them. We were friends. "The same goes with me, Sonya."

And she walked to the telephone and lifted off the receiver.

"Remember," she said quickly, "clean out the inside of the cup, Casey dear. And you'd better show it to me when you've finished."

Not being able to understand Japanese, I have never known what Sonya said. As a matter of fact, I did not mind any longer, because I trusted her. We were like very old friends as we waited for Mr. Moto.

"You must put on a tie, Casey dear," she said, "and put the flask back in your pocket. I want you to look nice when Mr. Moto comes. Perhaps it would be just as well to put those pistols in the bureau drawer."

"You're sure we won't need them?" I said.

"Why, Casey," she looked shocked; "that isn't kind of you. Why should there be, when Mr. Moto is getting what he wants? He's not a villain, Casey. He is a very considerate man."

Her remark struck me as amusing, now that I had encountered several examples of Mr. Moto's consideration, including a bad arm and a lacerated scalp.

"No," she said, "Mr. Moto will treat you very nicely now."

I was curious to see. Sonya was picking up the room and making it presentable. From melodrama the situation seemed to turn into something almost resembling a tea party.

"Casey," Sonya said again, "since when have you had a drink?"

I tried to think back. "I have not had a drink for hours, not since at Mr. Wu's," I said. "I don't believe I need to drink, if there's anything that interests me."

"Do I interest you?" she asked.

I told her that she did and she looked pleased. The Gaiety Club and sudden death and White Russian plots of Harbin had dropped away from her.

Mr. Moto would appear with an armed bodyguard, I thought, since he would be suspicious of some trap, but I did not give his perspicacity sufficient credit. Mr. Moto came alone, without a suspicious glance. He was dressed for the evening, carefully, in what is known as a dinner coat in America, and what the French call a *smoking*, an inoffensive man bowing, smiling, and holding an opera hat. He displayed his relief and pleasure by grinning so disarmingly that I very nearly liked him. There was a row of pearls on his pleated shirt front; a handkerchief was sticking neatly from his pocket; his small feet glittered in their patent-leather pumps.

"Hello, Moto," I said.

"Hello, Lee," he answered. His smile could not have been anything but genuine. "I am so glad," Mr. Moto said, "so very, very glad, but I'm so sorry for what happened tonight. I hope you have not been hurt? If we could only have reached this conclusion before—but it was my fault, not your fault."

I stood up and shook hands with him. The situation was curious and Mr. Moto's wish to be friendly was nearly moving.

"That's all right, Moto," I said. "I only wish you'd thought of the flask sooner. I didn't, Moto."

Mr. Moto laughed and even his laughter was relieved, not the studious social laughter which one hears so often in Japan. "My dear fellow," said Mr. Moto, "I am so very glad that nothing happened to you. It would have been such a mistake. And you have been so very useful. Suppose now we have a drink. Good whisky for good Japanese and good Americans."

"Out of the flask?" I asked him.

Mr. Moto laughed gaily. "That is very good," he said. "You are a good companion, Mr. Lee."

Then Sonya interrupted. "No," she said, "Mr. Lee is not drinking."

It was the first time that I had known I was not drinking.

A shadow flitted across Mr. Moto's smiling countenance and after it a light of comprehension.

"Ah," said Mr. Moto, "so that is it. You have not been drinking? I remember now. How much more fortunate it would have been if you had been drinking," and he laughed again, so infectiously that I joined him as I handed him my flask.

"There is good whisky inside that for a good Japanese, Mr. Moto," I told him. "And there is one thing which perhaps you have not noticed. There is a cup on the bottom of the flask."

Mr. Moto was being a very good fellow. He patted my arm gently.

"You are very funny, Mr. Lee," he said. "I like men who are funny. We understand jokes in Japan. We love American jokes. Will you permit me?" He took the flask and his eyes became narrowly intent. He pulled the cup off quickly. "Ah—" he said, and he had the bit of paper in his hand.

"Mr. Moto," I said, "I want you to understand something."

"What?" he asked.

"I want you to understand that I am very glad you have this paper," I told him. "I want you to know that I bear you no ill will for anything that has happened—not even for your talk of a flight across the Pacific. I have had a very interesting time."

Mr. Moto's face looked genuinely troubled. "Perhaps we will talk about the Pacific flight later," he said. "But now I wish not to inconvenience you. The belongings you left aboard the ship will be sent to you at once, and in the meanwhile you have been subjected to great unpleasantness through my fault, and I am very, very sorry. I understand that you are a gentleman, Mr. Lee, and I am giving this to you, entirely with that understanding. You are alone here without money. You will not mistake my motive, I ask you, please." He drew in his breath between his teeth with a sharp little hiss, pulled a wallet from his inside pocket and extracted two large notes, each for five thousand yen.

"Please," he said.

I hesitated, because I did not wish to touch his money under such circumstances. Sonya's glance stopped my refusal. "Thank you, Mr. Moto," I said. "This is too much."

"No," said Mr. Moto, "no." And he made one of his curious bobbing bows. "It is nothing for the pain you have suffered. You must not think badly of Japan. Will you take it, please?"

"Thanks," I said again.

Mr. Moto was relieved. He picked up the cup again and poured himself a drink. He raised the cup, smiling at me in a most friendly way. "Good whisky," he said, "for a good Japanese. *Banzai!* And your very good health too, Miss Sonya. You have been very, very kind. I know you have had sad news today. You will not blame me for what happened, will you, Miss Sonya? Because I am very, very sorry and I like you very much."

Sonya's gesture surprised me, but it was genuine. She put her hands on Mr. Moto's shoulders. "And I like you very much, Mr. Moto," she said.

Mr. Moto tossed off his cup of whisky with a slight tremor, since the drink was probably distasteful to him, but he tossed it off because of manners.

"Moto," I said, "I take it I may come and go as I please now? You've got what you wanted, haven't you? You won't mind my saying that you make me a trifle nervous?"

"My dear fellow!" Mr. Moto answered. "This is all over between us. If there is any help you need, call, please, at the Japanese Consulate. Mention my name, please, because I am a friend. And if you come back to Tokyo, ask for me, also. I wish you to like Japan. We are a small people to have come to so much, but we are a good people, Mr. Lee."

I thanked him and I meant it.

"And we will talk about flying the Pacific later," Mr. Moto said, "but—" His glance traveled from Sonya to me, "but perhaps now I interrupt?"

"No," said Sonya. "I'm going now. I've done everything, I think."

"Yes," said Moto. "You have done very, very well. May I offer to take you where you are going?" Then he turned his attention to me again. "You have been hurt, Mr. Lee," he said. "You are wounded in the head. It is nothing much, I hope. You haven't been hurt elsewhere?"

"A flesh wound in the shoulder," I answered. "It is nothing much."

"I am so sorry," said Mr. Moto. "So very sorry. May I send a physician?"

"No, thanks," I said. "Sonya's fixed me up. Good night, Sonya."

"I'll call to see you in the morning," Sonya said, "that is, if Mr. Moto does not mind."

"Mind?" said Mr. Moto. "I am delighted. You are free, as free—what is the English expression? I am ashamed I do not know. Oh, yes, as free as the air!"

I wonder if Mr. Moto ever thought again of that phrase he used— "as free as the air."

"You will not think too hardly of us?" Mr. Moto said.

"Good night, Casey," said Sonya. "I'll call to see how you are in the morning."

"Moto," I said, "if I've killed anyone tonight, I am very, very sorry."

"Please," said Mr. Moto, "you must not bother. It was duty for our Emperor, Mr. Lee, and we are all very pleased to die for him. Good night and rest comfortably, will you, please?"

"Good night," I said, and then Mr. Moto and Sonya were gone.

I stood for a moment listening, and then I looked at my watch. A year had passed, for all I could estimate, since I had thought of time, and the shortness of the actual lapse was incredible. The hands of my watch indicated only five minutes to twelve. In less than two and a half hours I had been through events which might have filled ten years of an ordinary span. I was living fast. Sonya was right. I did not need a drink. I found the card which Sam Bloom had given me and asked for his number over the telephone. I knew what Sam Bloom had said was true, that he would stand by me for anything I wanted.

"Come up here, Sam," I said. "As soon as you can, please."

"Okay," said Sam. "I'm coming."

He was there in a quarter of an hour, with his hat tilted on the back of his head, asking, "What's the matter, Casey?"

"I want a two-seater plane," I said, "first thing tomorrow morning. I'm flying to a village six miles outside of Chinchow."

"Chinchow," said Sam Bloom. His intonation proved that he had the map of China on his fingertips, as any good aviator must know the country where he flies. "That's between six-fifty and seven hundred miles and the Japanese will spot you when you get across the line. They'll probably shoot at you. We'd better talk about this, Casey. Why do you want to see Chinchow? It's a walled town on a plain. I can show you plenty of 'em."

I knew that I must tell him the truth, but I did not mind, because I knew that Sam Bloom would stand by me if he could. "Sam," I said, "you're an American and I'm an American. Listen to this, Sam." As Bloom listened, I remember thinking how calmly he took it, as though he understood a part already.

"Well," was his only comment. "Why don't you tell Jim Driscoll? He's in the Intelligence."

"I've told him," I explained. "I've quarreled with Jim Driscoll; and now I'm going to do the rest of this myself. If anyone is going to get these figures, or whatever they are, I think I'm in the positon to do it. All I want is a two-seater plane, Sam. Are you going to come across or not? That's all I want to know."

Bloom moved his felt hat restlessly between his fingers. "You're asking more than you think," he said.

"Probably," I answered. "I want a plane and maps."

"You'll have to refuel," he objected, "before you get back home. How are you going to do that, Casey?"

"I don't care," I answered, "as long as I get there."

Bloom rubbed his hand along the back of his head. "There's an observation plane up at the airport," he said, "that has been assigned to me. You can have it, Casey."

"What time?" I asked.

"Eight o'clock tomorrow morning." Bloom pulled a map from

his pocket and handed it to me. "It may be that I'll lose my job, but you can have it, Casey. I'll see you in the morning. There's the mark where you're going. I'll tell you more tomorrow. And now you'd better get some sleep. Good night!"

## 12

EXCELLENT AS his suggestion may have been, like so many of one's friends' suggestions, it was hard to follow. It took me a long time to get to sleep. I was under no illusions about the next morning. From the things Sam Bloom had left unsaid, together with the gossip to which anyone in the Orient must listen, I was certainly off on a harebrained errand. Nevertheless, I had gained a composure which arises from a definite knowledge of a mission, combined with a certain faith in one's ability. I could get a plane from one point on the map to another, even an unknown map, as successfully as any other pilot. I knew that Sam Bloom would secure me a plane, because he said he would. What reasons he might give to his superiors were up to his own invention, not to mine, but my reputation as a flyer would probably be a help. In my time I had been given the courtesy of plenty of airports.

For a while I pored over the small-scale pocket map of China which Sam Bloom had left me. It is strange how casual one's knowledge of a country is until one is actually in it. I had never been personally cognizant before of the immense area of China. A map could speak to me more eloquently than the pages of a book, as it will to any experienced air pilot. The point which I proposed to reach, fortunately for me, lay close to the seacoast, along the line of the Mukden-Tientsin Railroad, where level land dwindles to a narrow strip between the sea and a rough mountainous country. Not so far from my proposed destination was the symbol of the Great Wall of China, winding down a mountain range to Shan-hai-kwan, the frontier town between China and the new Manchukuo State. Given the proper air conditions, the flying problem would be principally a matter of following the seacoast, then across the promontory of Shantung, then over the Po-Hai Gulf, keeping land on the left, then bearing easterly along the gulf of Liao-Tung. The political implications were what bothered me most. At the time there were Japanese forces in Shan-hai-kwan, and beyond the Great Wall there were further concentrations of Japanese troops. I was fully aware that a Chinese plane would not be well received, that it might create an incident which would involve the occupants of such a plane in very real danger, if they were taken. It was my hope to keep sufficiently high and out to sea, so that we could not be observed until the last possible moment. In the end, the whole matter would come down to the question perhaps of minutes. If we could get what we wanted quickly enough, there was a chance that we could return to the plane and take off before troops should intervene; but this was a matter which lay in the future. I believed that there would be petrol enough, if we could get back to the plane, to take us to Tientsin. If I could once arrive at the airport there—and I knew there was an airport in the line of the Peiping-Shanghai air route—my intention was to leave the plane and to go fast as I could to the American Consulate. Aside from such rough conjectures, there was obviously nothing more that I could do about the matter. It was not even worth while to weigh my chances, but there was one thing in my favor. I was definitely convinced that Mr. Moto was off the track and that I could reach the airport without interference and perhaps without suspicion. As far as everything else went, there was nothing to do except to dismiss the matter temporarily, and this was not so difficult for me as it may sound, because the life of a flyer is made up of a series of shifting crises.

I did dismiss the matter from my mind, only to have something take its place which was of greater significance—the story which Sonya had told me. I had a smattering of engineering such as anyone may gather from a study of airplane engines. I had read about the breaking down of the atom, and understood that only a fraction of the energy of fuel was expended in either a steam or internal-combustion engine; that, in spite of all engineers could do, their contrivances for propelling us on water or in air were wretchedly inefficient. If it was true that this man Karaloff had perfected, let us say, some catalytic agent which might be added to fuel oil, it was quite easily within the realm of possibility that its efficiency as an energy-producing force might be doubled. Granting this accomplishment, even a tyro like myself could gather the immensity of its implication. On the water or in the air everyone was struggling to increase the cruising radius of vessels or of planes. Given an oil fuel of double its present power, a Japanese cruiser division could raid the Pacific Coast in the event of war and return without refueling. Nor was that all. If such a discovery should be known to all the world, it was incredible what might happen. Spheres of influence might be doubled and there would be any number of possible clashes before new spheres of influence could be established. The possibilities and complexities were too many to be grasped. There was only one thing I was sure of: with Japan the sole possessor of this secret, the influence of my country in the Pacific would be gone, and my country itself might be in danger. The idea was so apparent that I was tempted to go to the telephone and call up Driscoll, yet on second thought this seemed to me to be of no great use. If anyone could get this paper composed by this scientist who was Sonya's father, I stood as good a chance as any of my countrymen, particularly as I knew that we did not have a very closely knit Secret Service in the Orient. I may have been mistaken, but at any rate I made the decision to keep the matter to myself, and lay on my bed fully dressed.

In spite of the throbbing of my arm and the pain of my head, I went into a deep sleep and that was something I can be grateful for; if anyone needed sleep, I did that night. I was better when I was awakened in the morning at seven o'clock by the hotel porter who brought me my bags from the Japanese ship, exactly as Mr. Moto had promised. I was glad to get into my own clothes again. Although my arm and head were aching, I felt better. I put on a good heavy winter suit and a sweater. I looked over my maps also, which I had purchased for that Pacific flight—it seemed a thousand years ago—and found a larger-scale one among them of the China Coast. Then I took Sam Bloom's automatic and put it back in the shoulder holster.

At a quarter before eight the telephone rang and Sonya's voice answered to say that she was waiting downstairs. Five minutes later, just as I finished my last preparations (I had taken out a leather coat and my own goggles and helmet from my baggage), Sam Bloom called up to say that he was waiting too. Everything was going very smoothly, but I was not surprised, for life is much like that, like a gambler's run of luck—first a number of ill chances and then everything's smooth.

Bloom was waiting at the hotel desk and Sonya was seated near him, but he did not see Sonya's connection with the business until I told her to come ahead.

"Say," said Sam, "that's the girl on the boat."

"Never mind," I told him. "Sonya's coming with me. She'll want some leather clothes. Hers don't look very warm." Sonya looked more ready for a walk along the Bund than for a seven-hundred-mile trip in a plane. There was an automobile waiting for us, and again everything went easily. Once the surprise of seeing Sonya was over, Bloom began talking to me, giving me technical directions.

"She's an observation plane," Sam said. "A Davis M type; you'll like her, Casey. Any fool can handle her. She has extra fuel tanks installed. She's good for seven hundred miles. And maybe two hundred more. I'm not asking a single question because I don't want to know what you're doing. They're glad to let you use her to try her out, because you're a well-known flyer. I don't know where you're going. It isn't my fault what may happen."

"Thanks, Sam," I said.

"You'll find maps," Sam went on, "and thermos bottles and sandwiches. Keep her up around eight thousand feet, and when you get to the gulf get twelve thousand altitude and keep as far from land as you can. Don't swing over the railroad until you have to. There are troops at every station, but I don't have to tell you about flying, Casey."

"Thanks, Sam," I said.

"That's all right," said Sam. "She's warmed up now. You can go as soon as we get there."

We were getting clear of the traffic by then. "Sam," I said, "is anybody following us?"

Bloom looked out the back window of the car. The corners of his eyes wrinkled and he shook his head.

"No," he answered, "I don't think so, and if they are, believe me you're going just the same."

There is a similarity about all airports and this one at Shanghai was no exception to the general rule. Our car drove into a dusty open space. A single-motor plane was being warmed up in front of a hangar and the motor sounded well. I was pleased to see that the ship was a model which I had flown before. She should be good for a hundred and fifty miles an hour, crusing speed, once I got her in the air. Sam Bloom was bringing out a coat and helmet for Sonya. The noise of the engine was deafening. I took Sonya by the arm and shouted in her ear.

"Are you all right?"

She smiled at me and nodded, as though we were not going anywhere.

"All right," I said, "let's go!" She climbed into the cockpit behind me and I turned around and spoke to her again. "If you want anything, write me a note," I shouted. "You think we can get what we want in twenty minutes after we land?" She nodded, smiled and patted my shoulder; then I sat down at the controls. Sam Bloom and I shook hands.

"Good luck!" he shouted. "I'll take care of things this end. Take her back into Tientsin."

"Tell Driscoll if I don't get back," I called back.

I had turned back to the controls by then, but just as I did so, I saw a man running toward us across the field—a Chinese in a long gray gown which was flapping in the wind, and I knew who he was. He was the man who had taken me to Mr. Wu's after I had been picked up from the river. I did not care to speak to him. I gave my engine gas and pointed my ship into the wind. When we were off the ground, I circled for altitude up and up, until the tall buildings of Shanghai and the canals and rice fields of the Yangtse delta all came into a curious order, as events in a life do when one is far enough away from life. Then China was like a map such as I had seen the night before. We were circling up into a fine clear morning sky. When my altimeter read eight thousand feet, I flattened out and took my bearings; then we were going seemingly slowly, though the speed was a hundred and fifty miles an hour.

Sonya tapped my shoulder and handed me a note. "Casey," it read, "you're very nice."

There is no need to describe that flight. I have not the literary gift to convey the sensations of flying. The visibility was good and the air was clear, and there is nothing like the air at such altitudes as that. All the trappings of the world are out and one is close to the infinite in such air. The throb of the motor has always seemed to me like the drumming in one's ears when one takes ether. A flight is a sort of oblivion. I am happier in a plane than I ever am on land, I suppose because I was born for it. I am capable in the air and more alive than I am on earth. When we die, I hope our souls go to the air out of the world, up above the cloudbanks where the sun streaks down on oceans of pink and gold. There is a beauty in it which is greater than the beauty of the sea, but I am not here to write an esthetic essay. I am here to stick to facts. Sam Bloom's maps were excellent. With my mapboard and my instruments, I should have been incompetent, if I had not reached my destination, particularly given good weather. The clock on the instrument board pointed somewhere before the hour of two when I knew we were getting near.

We were swinging in toward the land over curious muddy water—water that held the silt of eroded Chinese hills and fields. We were down to five thousand feet by then and out ahead I could see the ribbon of the railroad track and the orderly outlines of a great walled town near it. Beyond, inland, at the base of bare brown hills, there was a smaller village which appeared to be built entirely out of earth, so that it looked like something from the insect kingdom. I saw the glint of running water near it. I turned and looked at Sonya and pointed.

She nodded but I did not need any confirmation. My map told the story, and my instinct backed it up. There was the village we wanted.

I wrote another note. "We're coming down. Soldiers will see us by the railroad. We must hurry, Sonya." Then we were coming down fast, in a sideslip. The wind had tossed up clouds of dust which gave me its direction. The earth was coming up to meet us, growing clearer, clearer. We were coming down to realities again. We were coming to a land that was brown, still untouched by the softness of spring, down toward bare flat fields where men were moving like pygmies, down to that town of earth. It was a fine place for a landing. I had shut off the motor as the land was coming up. The wind was singing through the struts wildly in the most beautiful tune I know. The land was coming up with the speed of an express train. We landed well, almost without a bump. We were taxiing across a plowed field straight toward the wall of mud surrounding low mud houses, with willow trees jutting up above their roofs, and with a rising tier of bare hills beyond them. A lonely place, a cold country that reminded me of parts of our own West. I had done what I set out to do. We had come to the town where the brother of Sonya's father's man Ma had his dwelling place.

The strange thing was how easily the matter went, although I have observed that an anticipation of difficulty sometimes makes difficulty vanish. Again, perhaps the actuality seemed simple because of my interest in everything I saw, for it was the first time I had ever seen a Chinese village with habits, architecture and customs that might easily have dated to the Stone Age. I crawled out of the cockpit and helped Sonya down to the yellowish-brown earth. We both of us were tired and stiff and deafened by the drumming of the motors and by the change of altitude. The sight of both of us appearing so suddenly from the sky had drawn the village out, gaping, large-boned men and women in coarse blue clothing that was stained from their labors. They were the servants of the soil, the peasantry whose prototype exists in every country in the world where man gains his sustenance from the earth.

"Sonya," I asked her, and I steadied her for a moment until she was used to the solidness of the ground, "can you talk to them? We'll have to hurry, Sonya."

"Yes," she answered. She smiled at the crowd reassuringly and used her gift of tongue. Whatever she said appeared to please them, because they smiled a little stupidly, still half comprehending perhaps, and pointed to the wall. An old man moved toward me deferentially and felt timidly of my leather jacket. The children were staring at my goggles; when I pulled them up from my eyes to my forehead they gave a sigh of wonder.

"Come," said Sonya. "It's all right, Casey. Ma's brother is here in the village. We must go and find him. No, we don't have to! Here he's coming now!"

A tall Chinese in a long blue gown was walking toward us in swift easy strides. His skin was swarthy and coarsened from the weather, but I could distinguish the resemblance between him and the dead man on the boat, and plainly he and Sonya knew each other. He placed his palms together and smiled and bowed, and the red button of his skull-cap moved in an arc with the nodding of his head. After they had spoken for a moment Sonya said to me:

"Come, Casey, he will take us to his house."

We hurried, stumbling across the plowed field to a little path winding toward the gate, with half the village trotting behind us, making low polite remarks. There was a God above the gate and a little mud shrine stood just inside, with another God in the niche.

"He is the God of Learning," Sonya said. "The scholars burned prayers before him in the old days when they studied for the government examinations. Have you never seen a Chinese village?"

"No," I said.

"I'm sorry," Sonya answered, "that we haven't got more time. They are pretty places, Chinese villages, and the people need so little to be happy."

We were walking along the main street, and it was like looking at some picture I had seen before, but had never believed till then.

The combination of complete simplicity and of a sort of airy beauty with it fitted with that interval in the sky, and the place was unrelated to anything which I had ever seen. The walls, the houses, even the roofs were made of beaten earth, but the proportion of the houses was wholly perfect. The roofs had fanciful curves, the lattices of the paper-covered windows each different from the other, and nearly every house had its own wall enclosing a courtyard. A man was drawing water from a well beside the street, and there was a small temple near the well.

"The God of Health is there," said Sonya. "And probably the God of weather."

It was a place of strange gods, and simple suspicions hovered over it. Ma's brother walked before us and I saw that he was very worried. He obviously wanted us to get away, and I could not blame him. There would be ugly questions from the authorities about a plane which had landed.

"He tells us to be quick," said Sonya.

"That goes for me," I said. "We can't be quick enough."

The man had stopped at the gateway leading to one of those mud courtyards and was gesturing to us to enter. It was a homely place, reminiscent of a peasant's yard in northern France. Two bullocks were tethered beneath a mud-roofed shed. An old dog chained near them rose stiffly and began to bark. Some hens ran away from us, cackling. A woman was turning a stone handmill. Ma's brother walked straight across the court and opened the door of a low building and ushered us into an empty room, evidently the family living quarters. There was a stove made out of mud bricks, with a copper teakettle boiling on the top of it. The flue from the stove buried itself in a raised platform, covered untidily with bedding. There was a crude wooden dresser with utensils on it, a wooden cupboard, probably for clothing, and that was all. I had never seen such complete stark poverty or such grim efficiency. It would have been hard to have found a better place to have left that paper, for no one would have thought of looking there for anything of value.

Sonya must have understood my thought because she said:

"Ma's brother is a rich man, but he keeps his money hidden somewhere underground. There is probably a little hoard somewhere beneath the floor of nearly every house here. One must be careful not to look rich in unsettled times."

Sonya was talking, but her mind was not on what she was saying

. . . unsettled times. Sonya had seen enough of those to be completely familiar with their developments. She was at home in that place, at home, but her mind was on something else. Her glance was strained, expectant. She was watching Ma's brother move over to that raised platform. He was lifting a corner of the matting which covered it. He was drawing out a sheet of paper about the size of ordinary foolscap. He handed it to Sonya with a bow. Her hand trembled as she took it. She bent over it attentively. Then she turned to Ma's brother and smiled. She had opened her purse. She was giving him money.

I did not have to ask her if she had found what she wanted.

Ma's brother was expostulating and his voice and Sonya's answered each other for almost a minute, in a half-comprehensible dialogue, while I stood watching. I could half imagine what they were saying, because Ma's brother pushed away the money. He was saying he did not wish it because he was an honorable man.

Sonya's voice became more insistent. She was saying something which was important, as I could gather by the attention with which the tall Chinese countryman listened. She must have alluded to me at some point, because he turned and looked at me thoughtfully and impersonally. Then he took the money, bowed himself to the door, leaving Sonya and me standing there alone.

She had changed, now that she had the paper in her hand, displaying a new sort of gravity, a new sort of decisiveness. The paper had come between us, making us both a little different.

"So that's it?" I asked. "That's the thing you wanted?"

Sonya signed. "Yes, Casey," she said slowly; "that's what we wanted."

I reached toward the paper, but she drew it away from me.

"No," she said, "please, Casey dear. If I could, I'd let you see it."

"What do you mean?" I asked. "Sonya, what's changed you?"

She sighed again and her voice was gentle.

"Casey dear," she said, "I want you to understand. If it were only you or me, you know I'd do anything—anything. I want you to know that. I wanted to be alone with you for a minute, and that is why I sent the man away."

I did not follow her. "What do you mean?" I asked. "We've got what we wanted, Sonya. We'd better get out of here. We'll have to leave right off."

Sonya shook her head and her lips trembled. "No," she said; "please, Casey, you don't understand. You must go, but I'm not going."

That speech jolted me into stupidity. "You're not going with me?" I said. "Why, what's the matter, Sonya? Aren't we friends?"

"Casey"—her voice was imploring—"Casey dear, I like you better than anyone I know; that's what I want you to understand. I'd do anything for you if it were only me; but in a matter like this, please, don't you see that friendship doesn't count? Casey, I want you to see. I'll tell you something else to make you understand. I think I love you, Casey. I've never loved anyone before as much as I love you, but it would make no difference, Casey. You see I'm going to take this paper, because it is not mine. I know what my father would wish. He would wish me to take it to friends of his in Harbin. He would want them to use it to help what he was planning. It was a cause he was thinking of. There's something here which will help, Casey. Don't worry about me. Ma's brother will take care of me. I'm used to being alone."

Everything she said was so unexpected that I could not get my thoughts straight. Yet I should have known long ago that Sonya would have such an idea. I thought of what use she had made of me, but I could not be angry. Instead, I felt kindly toward her. Instead, I was deeply moved.

"So that's your game," I said. "I should have known it, Sonya."

"Casey," she answered, "Casey, please—"

"Sonya"—I tried to control my voice—"I don't believe you understand. I've come to get that thing you're holding, and I'm going to get it. Do you think I'm going to risk my neck and then let you take it away, so that you can sell it to someone else? Sonya, listen, please. I can understand you, but your ideas are wrong. Who are your people? What can they do? I heard you talk of them last night. You love them but you know that anything they try hasn't much validity."

"Perhaps," she said; "but that makes no difference, Casey."

"I'm sorry, Sonya," I said, "but it does to me. Think of yourself. You're alone in the world. I'd be glad to look after you. I can do it, Sonya. I don't want to talk about patriotism, but I'm going to have that paper. You and I are here alone. I'm stronger than you are. Will you give it to me, please? I don't want to take it from you, Sonya."

She appeared surprised when I had finished. "Casey," she asked me, "do you really think it is as easy as that? Do you really think—"

"Sonya," I said, "if you think I'm going to let you take this away, you're mistaken."

Sonya's voice grew calmer. "Don't think that I have not a respect for your ability," she said. "I'm sure you'll do anything you can, but you can't do much. You see, Ma's brother understands. Casey, why do you think I talked to him so long? They will stop you if I tell them to. They will come in if I call."

"Try and call," I said; "and I'll drive everyone out of this village."

"Don't," said Sonya sharply. "Please wait a minute, Casey. You mustn't! You don't see! One of the things they'll do is to smash your plane. There are men out there ready to break it if they hear a single shot—and where will you be then? Where will you go? What can you do? They'll call for the soldiers, Casey. There's no place for you to hide."

There was truth in what she said, but truth and logic did not matter to me. There are times when it does no good to weigh the pros and cons of a situation. I was convinced that this was one of those times. There was only one reason why I hesitated—because I was sorry. I knew that I would not see Sonya again.

"Sonya," I said, "I'm sorry."

"So am I," she answered. "If you're going now, I'll go to see you off, but you mustn't wait any longer."

"Sonya," I said, "it seems to me you're fixing it so that we both have to give up everything for nothing. I don't want you to think I'm not fond of you, because I am. I don't like to think how different things might be."

"Please," she said, "please don't say that."

"All right," I answered. "Have it your own way, Sonya."

She must have been taken off her guard. If she was, it was exactly what I intended, much as I hated what I was prepared to do. She may have forgotten momentarily that she was still holding that sheet of paper.

I half turned, reluctantly, as though I were going to go. Her hand and the paper were out of my line of vision for a moment but I knew exactly where it was. I darted sideways. My fingers reached the corner of the paper and I snatched. If I had thought I could be too quick for her, if I had thought that I could snatch the paper out of her hand, I was mistaken. Her hand drew back the instant mine caught the corner of the page. There was a tearing sound and Sonya had stepped away from me. We each were holding a half of that foolscap and staring at each other stupidly. I think she was going to cry out but I stopped her. If I did not have the whole paper, at least I had half.

"Be careful, Sonya," I said. "There's one thing I can do now—I can destroy this if you call."

She understood me. At any rate, she did not cry out and I looked at my half of the torn page. There were words on it in fine penmanship in a language I did not understand, and formulas of what I knew to be organic chemistry from the groups of symbols that were bound together in valences.

Sonya was speaking gently. "That wasn't fair of you," she said.

"My dear," I answered, "do you think you've been entirely fair? Are you going to give me that other half?"

"No," she said, "not as long as I live. And you won't get it, Casey."

We stood there facing each other. That short interval of time is the oddest which I have ever experienced. The surroundings made it stranger—that wretched mud hovel, the kettle steaming on the small brick stove, the tamped earthen floor, the faint light through the paper windows. I shall never live through a moment like that again, or, if I do, it will be no more credible to me than the scene through which I lived. I do not believe I exaggerate as I think of the importance attached to this paper which we sought. It may be that I am mistaken, but in my heart I am close to being sure that I held half the future of the Pacific basin in my hand as I stood in that Manchurian farmhouse, and that the girl opposite me was holding the other half. I had never realized the complete seriousness of my position until I held that paper. It was a responsibility about which I could not be entirely certain, but it was one which I had to take. My mind seemed to go in a circle, futilely seeking for another step, when Sonya interrupted me.

She was calling out for help.

I realize now that Sonya's call lifted all decision from my hands. I shifted my paper from my right hand to my left and got out my automatic just as the door burst open.

"Wait," I said. "Sonya, tell those fools to wait a minute!"

I knew already that there was only one thing left for me to do. I was even relieved by the thought and I still believe that I did what was best, and all that was possible.

Ma's brother, with a group of men behind him (all of them big Chinese) stood irresolutely in the doorway. Some of them were holding hoes and mattocks. One of them held an antiquated rifle.

"Tell them to wait a minute, Sonya," I said.

Sonya called to them sharply. I had to make my next move quickly and accurately, before anyone could guess what I intended. There was a glow of embers in the draft in the mud-brick stove. I bent quickly, still watching Ma's brother and the men.

"Casey!" Sonya cried. "You can't do that!"

I thrust the paper into the embers of the stove while the echo of her voice still rang. A bit of flame licked up at it. The paper was on fire and I straightened up, holding the burning half sheet.

"I think that's the only answer, Sonya," I said. "I think we both did our best." The flames burnt my fingers and I dropped the charred fragments on the floor. Then I moved toward her, and I was glad, now that it was over. "I guess that's the end, Sonya. You'd better burn up your half of that. It won't do you any good, I think, but it might be dangerous. Burn it up, Sonya. I'm going to take you home."

She swayed toward me, and then she was sobbing on my shoulder. "You're not angry," she was sobbing, "are you, Casey?"

"Yes," I said, "don't you see, everything's all even, Sonya." And a sound made her straighten.

We both knew what the sound meant. It came from the sky, reverberating between the roofs and the smoky rafters above our heads—a droning sound which grew louder, louder and then stopped. It was another plane. Its pilot was cutting off the engine, landing. Voices outside were rising in a torrent of sound.

"That will probably by the Japanese police," I said. "Give me that paper, Sonya." And I put it in the fire. "I'm sorry," I said to Sonya again and I took her hand.

"Don't be sorry," she answered. She looked happier, younger, the way she should always have looked. Her lips curled up into a smile. "Don't be sorry," she said, "because I think the police will be"—and she mimicked the English of Japanese—"very, very sorry."

"And on the whole, I'm pleased," I said; "very, very pleased. What do you think they'll do to us? Shoot us or put us into jail?"

There were no sounds from the street any longer. The villagers must have gone away and we found ourselves a minute later, staring at an old friend of ours. Mr. Moto, out of breath, was standing in the door of Ma's brother's house. Mr. Moto's composure was ruffled from his haste and he no longer wore his morning coat. Instead, his clothing was more incongruous—a tweed golf suit and a brown tweed cap. I knew enough not to laugh because Mr. Moto was serious.

"So you have not gone," he said. "You are clever, Mr. Lee. As long as you have not gone, I am very, very pleased."

"I like it here," I answered. "Why should I go away?"

"Do not joke, please," Mr. Moto said. "You cannot get away from here. We have you, Mr. Lee. And you too, Miss Sonya, and we want what you have come to find—right away, please. Do not joke!"

"The fuel-oil formula?" I said.

"Yes, please," said Mr. Moto. "Thank you so much. I am so glad you know what I mean. This is serious. I must have it, please."

"No, Mr. Moto," I answered, "I'm afraid you can't."

"Please," said Mr. Moto, "do not be funny, Mr. Lee."

I found myself close to laughter again, but I did not laugh. It would have been discourteous to laugh, when Mr. Moto was laboring under such excitement.

"The trouble was," I said, "you have wanted this and I have wanted it, and so has Sonya here. When people like the three of us want something, what happens, Mr. Moto?"

"I am being very patient, Mr. Lee," Mr. Moto said.

"The trouble was this," I explained to him. "Miss Sonya had that paper. I snatched for it and it tore in two. There seemed to be only one thing to do with that difference of opinion." I pointed to the fire. "I burned my half. Then the thing was useless. Then Miss Sonya burned her half. You can see the charred fragments on the floor. There is the story, Mr. Moto, and I am very much afraid that Japanese and American battleships will continue to burn oil in the same old wasteful way. And perhaps it's just as well. What do you think, Mr. Moto? I ask you because you're a sensible man."

I thought he would be angry, but he was not. He grew grave, as he stared at the charred fragments on the beaten earth floor. Then he looked up at me.

"Sometimes," said Mr. Moto, "I do not think, in spite of my study and my admiration for your people, that I understand them very well. But please, Mr. Lee, you are a man of honor, I think. We have tricked each other and I am very, very sorry. I do not wish to cause you further pain. Will you give me your word of honor that a single large page of paper containing chemical symbols was what you have burned?"

"I swear it, Mr. Moto," I said. "You can throw me into jail, you can strangle me, but there isn't anything left—anything at all."

Mr. Moto's forehead wrinkled. "But why should I strangle you, please," he said, "when it would do no possible good? When this is burned, we cannot help it, can we? This must conclude the matter. As long as I am sure, and I *am* sure. A little while ago I should have been relieved to know that this was not in existence. . . . Yes, perhaps you are right. You have not got it and I have not got it; our nations have not got it. In one way I am very very sorry; at the same time I think I am very, very pleased. We can be friends now, I think. There is nothing more to fight about, I believe."

He had swallowed his disappointment. He no longer seemed a comical figure in his tweed suit.

"Moto," I said, "if I have tricked you any way, forgive me. I am sure Miss Sonya means the same."

Mr. Moto removed his cap and bowed. "I have always liked Miss Sonya," he said. "Miss Sonya is very nice."

"I think so too," I answered. "I am going to marry Miss Sonya."

"Please," said Mr. Moto, "would you object if I should shake hands with her and offer her my congratulations?"

Sonya began to laugh. "Excuse me," she said, as Mr. Moto looked hurt and puzzled, "I'm not laughing at you, Mr. Moto. I'm laughing at all three of us—that we should be in a place like this."

"Oh, yes," said Mr. Moto. "Ha-ha, that is funny. Life is so very strange."

"Moto," I asked him, "would you mind telling me something? How did you get here so soon?"

Mr. Moto was still smiling. "My dear fellow," he said, "it was difficult. I understand that you know Mr. Wu Lai-fu. He saw you leaving in the plane. He had not thought of that, so of course he came to me in order to save something for himself. He told me where you were going, for a price, and I came very quickly. Mr. Wu is a clever man."

"Yes," I said. "Mr. Wu is clever."

"But then," said Mr. Moto, "perhaps we are all—you and Miss Sonya and me."

Sonya laughed again. "Too clever to be comfortable," she said. "What are you going to do with us now?"

"We will go to the military barracks," said Mr. Moto, "if you please."

"Oh," I said, "we're prisoners, are we, Moto?"

"Please," said Mr. Moto, "you must not say that. We go to the barracks to be warm and comfortable. The officers, they are good fellows, and I shall get you fuel for your plane. There is no sense in prisons. And Mr. Lee, we shall have some whisky, perhaps."

"No," said Sonya, "Casey isn't drinking."

"Oh," said Mr. Moto, "I am very, very sorry."

"So am I, Moto," I told him, "very sorry and surprised."

I believe I have reached the end of what I set out to write, unless Commander Driscoll has some further suggestion. Now that I have reached the end, it comes over me suddenly; it seems as difficult as the beginning. After all, exactly what did I do, I wonder? Jim Driscoll was the one who helped me out with this question. Naturally I saw Driscoll when I came back to Shanghai, and I brought Sonya with me.

"What you don't know won't hurt you," Driscoll said. "The Orient is different from America. I shall want you to lunch with the Admiral tomorrow, and then you will probably have to write this out, because it is important. When you write it, you can say anything about me you like, but I should like to have you make one addition. I might have treated you better, Casey. We were both of us excited that other day, and let's forget it. And there's another thing—you might go and call on Wu Lai-fu. I think he'd like to see you."

So this is as far as I am going to go and further, perhaps, than I had anticipated. I have finished a narrative which is difficult to believe, now that I am away from the place where it occurred and may never see that place again.

"Don't worry," Driscoll said, "anyone who has been out here can understand that anything can happen. You ought to be grateful to the Orient."

Perhaps I am—at any rate when I think of Sonya.

# THINK FAST, MR. MOTO

# 1

IT HAD not taken Wilson Hitchings long to realize that the firm of Hitchings Brothers had its definite place in the commercial aristocracy of the East, and that China had retained a respect for mercantile tradition which had disappeared from the Occidental world. There were still traditions of sailing days and of the pre-treaty days in the transactions of the Shanghai branch of Hitchings Brothers. The position of its office upon the Bund was enough to show it. The brass plate of HITCHINGS BROTHERS was polished each morning by the office coolies so that it glittered golden against the gray stone facade. Nearby were the venerable plates of JARDIN MATHESON and of the HONG KONG AND SHANGHAI BANK. The plate of HITCHINGS BROTHERS had the same remote dignity, the same integrity, the same imperviousness to time—which was not unnatural. That plate had been made when a branch of Hitchings Brothers, under the control of Wilson's great-grandfather from Salem, had moved up to Shanghai from the factories of Canton during the epoch when the place was little more than a swampy China-coast fishing town.

Reluctantly, but accurately, Wilson Hitchings could feel the venerable weight of that tradition. The involuntary respect which the tradition had engendered in the narrow European world that maintained its precarious foothold in the Orient was accorded to Wilson Hitchings himself, in spite of youth and inexperience, simply because he bore the name. Old white-suited gentlemen whom he never recalled meeting previously would suddenly slap him on the back as though he were an Old China Hand. Leather-faced matrons from British compounds would smile at him archly. Sometimes even an unknown, fat Chinese gentleman calling in the outer office would look at him and smile.

"Mr. Hitchings," the old gentleman would say, "so nice you have come here."

"Gentlemen," someone would say, toward evening at the bar, "this is young Hitchings, just out from America. He doesn't know me but I know him. He looks the way old Will did when he came out. . . . Boy, give Mr. Hitchings a drink. . . . We have to stick together these days. Anything I can tell you, Mr. Hitchings, simply let me know."

It had not taken Wilson Hitchings long to realize that he was a public character by right of birth. He grew to understand that the small shopkeeper and the lowest inhabitants of the International Settlement all knew him and that there is no such thing as privacy in the East. Sometimes late at night strange, ragged ricksha boys would speak to him, in the limpid pidgin English of the place.

"Marster Hitchings," a strange boy would shout. "Please, I take you home. I know where Marster Hitchings lives."

And sometimes at the street intersections where the pedestrians and the carts and the motors went by in an unending ribbon, the bearded Sikh policeman would bare his white teeth in an unexpected smile.

"All right," the man would say. "All right now, Hitchings Sahib."

He had begun to realize that a part of Shanghai belonged to him, a part of that rich, monstrous, restive, sinful city where so many races dwelt noisily. It belonged to him because a Hitchings had been there ever since foreigners had come. A Hitchings had seen the city grow out of the East, where China, with that adaptability peculiar alone to itself, had absorbed the conveniences of the West and had made them into something genial and mystic and peculiar. The firm of Hitchings Brothers, on the spot it occupied along the Bund, had become a part of the life. The windows of the firm, never entirely clean in spite of diligent washing, looked out like the eyes of cynical old men upon one of the strangest sights in the world. Beside the Bund flowed the yellow treacherous currents of the Whangpoo River; warships and huge liners were moored in the river, the last word of Occidental ingenuity, and past them always drifted brown-sailed junks, almost unchanged since the oldest Chinese paintings. Sampans, propelled by a single sculling oar, plied their ways across the river. Scavengers, in the sampans, fought raucously over ships' garbage; and down on the street beneath, men stripped to the waist struggled like beasts, pulling burdens while limousines passed by. Out of the firm windows one could see all the comedy and tragedy of China struggling in a world of change, all the unbelievable inequality of wealth, ranging from the affluence of fortunate war-lords to a poverty reduced to a limit of existence which no stranger could envisage. It was all beneath the windows, restive and fascinating, something much better accepted than studied.

Wilson Hitchings reluctantly admired his uncle for his cold acceptance of the enigmas which moved about them. Uncle Will Hitchings had grown to accept street riots and homicide as easily as he accepted his whisky-and-soda at the Club, provided dinner was properly and efficiently served as soon as he shouted "Boy!"

"My boy," Uncle Will used to say, "there's one thing for you to get in your mind—the firm of Hitchings Brothers is an honest firm. It has an excellent reputation upriver. Every Chinese merchant knows us. We seldom lose our customers; you must learn who these customers are; but don't worry much about the rest. Treat our customers politely, but don't mix with the natives. It's confusing to you now. It used to be confusing to me at first, but you'll get used to it. Don't try to speak their language. You can't learn it and it will only make you queer to try. I've seen a lot of nice young fellows who have got queer trying to learn Chinese. Just remember our family has got along on pidgin English. The main thing is to be seen with the right people. I don't care how much you drink if you do it with the right people and in the right place; and don't worry too much about wars and revolutions. Everything is always upset here. All we need is to be sure we get our money, and there's just one thing more—about women. Be sure you don't marry a Russian girl. And get as much exercise as you can, and remember I am broad-minded. Come to see me when you're in trouble, remember that nothing will shock me—nothing; and don't forget you have the firm name. I'll see you before dinner at the Club."

It was a strange life, an easy life, and altogether pleasant. In spite of the size of the city, the city was like a country club where everyone of the right sort knew everyone else, where everyone moved in a small busy orbit, surrounded by the unknown, and where everyone was friendly. It did not take him long to realize that it was a responsibility to bear the family name.

"You see," his uncle told him, "we are one of the oldest firms in China and age and name mean a great deal here. I want you to come to dinner to-night. My new cook is very good. I want you to change your cook, he is squeezing you too much. I want you to be sure to be at the Club every afternoon, and I want you to use my tailor. His father and his grandfather have always dressed the Hitchingses."

"Do you think there is going to be trouble up North, sir?" Wilson Hitchings asked.

His Uncle Will looked at him urbanely. His broad, red face reminded Wilson of the setting sun.

"There is always trouble up North," Uncle William said. "I want you to get yourself a new mess jacket. The one you wore last night didn't fit, and that's more important than political speculation. You had better go to your desk now. I shall have to read the mail. Well, what is it?"

The man who sat in front of the door of William Hitchings' private office—a gray-haired Chinese in a gray cotton gown—entered.

"Please, sir," he said, "a Japanese gentleman to see you—the one who came yesterday." Uncle William's face grew redder.

"My boy," he said to Wilson, "these Japanese are always making trouble lately. They're underselling us all along the line. You may as well sit and listen. How long have you been here now?"

"Six months, sir," Wilson Hitchings said.

"Well," his uncle said, "we have important interests in Japan. You had better begin to get used to the Japanese. Yes, sit here and listen." He waved a heavy hand to the office attendant.

"Show the man in," he said.

Red-faced, white-haired, and growing heavy, William Hitchings sat behind his mahogany table with the propeller-like blades of the electric fan on the ceiling turning lazily above his head. Short as the time had been since he had been sent to China, Wilson could understand that much of his uncle's attitude was a façade behind which he concealed a shrewd and accurate knowledge. He sat there looking about his room with a heavy placid stupidity which Wilson could suspect was part of his uncle's stock in trade. Even his bland assumption of ignorance of Chinese was valuable. His uncle had once admitted, perhaps rightly, that it gave a sense of confidence, a sense of old-fashioned stability.

It had been a long while since the firm had started dealing in cargoes of assorted merchandise; and now its business, largely banking, was varied and extensive. The firm was prepared to sell anything up-country through native merchants who had been connected with it for generations, and the firm was the private banker for many important individuals. Wilson could guess that his uncle knew a great deal about the finances and the intrigues of the Nanking Government, although his conversation was mostly of bridge and dinner.

While they waited Uncle William began opening the pile of letters before him with a green jade paper-cutter. Once he glanced at the clock, then at the door and then at his nephew. It was three in the afternoon.

"My boy," said Uncle William. "I want you to listen to this conversation carefully and I want you to tell me what you think of it afterward. I want you to consider one thing which is very important. You must learn to cultivate a cheerful poker face. That is what you are here for, and it will take you years before you can do it."

"You have one, sir," said Wilson.

"Yes, my boy," said Uncle William, "I rather think I have." He laid down his paper-cutter and raised his voice a trifle.

There were footsteps outside the office door. Uncle William looked at the wall opposite him, which was adorned with an oil painting of the first Hitchings factory at Canton, beside which was a Chinese portrait of a stout gentleman in a purple robe seated with a thin hand resting on either knee. It was the portrait of old Wei Qua, the first hong merchant with whom the Hitchingses had dealt. Wei Qua's face was enigmatic, untroubled and serene.

"Now in the races tomorrow," Uncle William said distinctly, "I like Resolution in the third. There are going to be long odds on him tomorrow and he is always good in mud. Yes, I think I shall play Resolution."

The office door was opening and Uncle William pushed back his chair. A Japanese was entering, walking across the room in front of the corpulent Chinese clerk with swift birdlike steps.

"Mr. Moto, if you please," the Chinese clerk was saying.

Mr. Moto was a small man, delicate, almost fragile. His patent leather shoes squeaked lightly as he walked. He was dressed formally in a morning coat and striped trousers. His black hair was carefully brushed in the Prussian style. He was smiling, showing a row of shiny goldfilled teeth, and as he smiled he drew in his breath with a polite, soft sibilant sound.

"It is so kind of you to receive me," he said. "So very, very kind, since I sent my letter such a short time ago. Thank you very, very much."

"The pleasure is all mine," Uncle William said. "Thank you, Mr. Moto."

Mr. Moto had handed him a card which William Hitchings took carefully, almost gingerly.

Wilson had already grown to understand that manners in the Orient demanded that a visting card must be treated with studied respect.

"This is my nephew," Uncle William said. "Mr. Wilson Hitchings, Mr. Moto." Mr. Moto turned toward Wilson swiftly; his eyes and his teeth sparkled.

"Oh," said Mr. Moto "—Oh, your nephew? I am so pleased to meet you sir, very, very pleased." His English was perfect, his voice was soft and modulated with little of the monotonous, singsong articulation of so many of his race. Mr. Moto's eyes met Wilson's studiedly.

"You have not been here long, I think, sir," he said. "I hope you like it very much. It is so nice to see you. I hope you like Shanghai. It is such a very nice city, is it not?"

"Yes," said Wilson. "I like it very much."

"I am so glad," said Mr. Moto, "so very, very glad."

"Please," said Uncle William. "Won't you sit down, Mr. Moto?"

"Thank you," said Mr. Moto. "Thank you, so very much."

"Wilson," said Uncle William, "pass Mr. Moto the cigarettes. Will you have tea or whisky, Mr. Moto?"

Mr. Moto laughed genially.

"Ha, ha," said Mr. Moto. "Whisky soda, if you please, because it is an American drink. I have resided in your country. I like it so very, very much."

"Boy!" called Uncle William. "Whisky soda. . . . Here's to you, Mr. Moto." Mr. Moto laughed again.

"Here is looking to you, gentlemen," he said. "That is the American expression, is it not? What beautiful weather we are having!"

"Yes," said Uncle William. "We were speaking about the races. What do you like in the third race, Mr. Moto?"

"What do I like?" inquired Mr. Moto, a shade of bewilderment crossing his face. Then he smiled again. "Excuse," he said. "Now I understand. I do not like any horse in the third race very much." He turned to Wilson still smiling and sipped a little of his whisky. "We are so fond of American sports in Japan," he said. "Ha, ha, we have great sports there. We have tennis and golf and skiing and baseball—such a great deal of baseball. Sports are very, very nice, I like them very, very much. Do you like sports?"

"Yes," said Wilson. "I like them very much."

"I am so glad," said Mr. Moto, "So very, very glad. We shall see you in Japan, I hope."

"Yes," said Uncle William. "I am planning to send him to Tokyo for a while next year. We are breaking him in here now."

"Breaking him in?" said Mr. Moto. "Oh, yes, I understand. That is very nice. You mean he will be a member of the firm—that will be very nice. We admire this firm so very much."

"Thank you, Mr. Moto," Uncle William said. "It is kind of you to say so."

"Thank you," said Mr. Moto, "very, very much." And he took another drink from his glass.

"Wilson," said Uncle William, "give Mr. Moto a light for his cigarette."

And they began to talk again about nothing. The atmosphere was formal, but neither Mr. Moto nor Uncle William seemed to be oppressed by any sense of time. Wilson had been told to listen carefully, but his mind could hit on nothing important. Mr. Moto sat there nervously, politely, chatting about nothing. And then at last he asked a question. He asked it casually, but Wilson could guess what he had come for was to ask that single question.

"I have been looking for a Chinese gentleman," Mr. Moto said. "A gentleman named Chang Lo-Shih, such a very nice gentleman. He is buying some of our bicycles. You remember him, perhaps?"

Uncle William looked at the ceiling.

"Chang Lo-Shih," he said. "No, I am sorry, at the moment I do not remember."

"He had business in Manchuria," Mr. Moto said. "At the time of the old Marshal."

"I am sorry," said Uncle William, "I still do not remember. That is getting to be a long while ago. Like so many other American firms, we have closed our offices in Mukden, Mr. Moto. But if you are interested I can look through our files."

"Oh, no," said Mr. Moto. "Please, please no! It is nothing, really nothing."

"Have you been in Manchukuo lately?" Uncle William asked.

"Yes," said Mr. Moto. "It is very, very nice."

"Yes," said Uncle William. "It is a beautiful country."

Mr. Moto took another sip of his whisky.

"But the bandits," said Mr. Moto. "They still make trouble. You read of them in the papers, do you not? I myself had trouble with the bandits."

"I hope it was not serious," Uncle William said.

"Oh, no," said Mr. Moto. "It was nothing. Only a very little trouble." Mr. Moto rose. "You have been so very, very kind to receive me," he said. "Thank you so very, very much."

"It has been thoughtful of you to call," said Uncle William. "Give my regards to the head of your firm when you get home and please come in again, any time at all. It has been a great pleasure to see you, Mr. Moto."

"Thank you," said Mr. Moto, "very, very much." He set down his whisky glass carefully. It was still three quarters full. He bowed and smiled and shook hands.

"Wilson," said Uncle William, "see Mr. Moto to the door."

"Shanghai is a beautiful city," Mr. Moto said. "So very, very many different people."

"They call it the Paris of the East, don't they?" Wilson asked.

"Ha, ha," said Mr. Moto. "That is very good—the Paris of the East! I am so very glad to have met you, Mr. Hitchings. I hope so very much that we may meet again."

Back in his private room, Uncle William was busy opening his letters.

"Well," he asked, "what did you think of Mr. Moto?"

Wilson smiled.

"I thought he was very, very nice," he said.

Uncle William looked at the portrait of Wei Qua. The fan above his head moved its mahogany wings slowly, noiselessly.

"What did you think of the talk?" he asked.

"Nobody said anything," Wilson said.

Uncle William slit another envelope with his green jade cutter, pulled the letter out and unfolded it.

"That's exactly why I wanted you to listen," he said. "You may not know it, but that was a highly important call. Mr. Moto and I knew it. And now I'll tell what I think. You heard him mention Chang Lo-Shih? Let me tell you something—that means that old Chang is meddling in Manchukuo. I said I didn't know him, but I do. It's as good as a warning not to do business with Chang, and I'll tell you something else—Mr. Moto isn't a businessman. Can you guess what he is?"

"No, sir," Wilson said.

"Well, I'll tell you what I guess I think he is," Uncle William said, "and I'll know tomorrow if I'm right. Mr. Moto is a Government agent, and he's after my old acquaintance Chang Lo-Shih; and just you remember this, Wilson: Be careful of Mr. Moto. I'll bet you run into him again and when you do, don't tell him any of the firm's secrets—not that you know any—and don't drink any more whisky than he does, Wilson. Now if you'll wait for five minutes we'll go over to the Club."

"Yes, sir," said Wilson. He sat quietly watching his uncle, aware of his own complete uselessness to cope with such situations. He sat there wondering, not for the first time, whether he would ever understand the complications of the new life he had started. He even wished vaguely that he was back at home and he felt a growing respect for the abilities of his family. The Hitchingses had coped with China for a hundred years and they could still cope with China. Then a sound from his uncle startled him.

His Uncle William had slammed a paper on the desk.

"By God!" said Uncle William, "that woman still has our name on that gambling house in Honolulu!"

"What woman?" asked Wilson.

"Cancel any engagement you may have," said Uncle William. "You are to dine with me alone tonight." Uncle William mopped his forehead. It occurred to his nephew that he had never seen his uncle look so disturbed, and he knew why—the name of Hitchings was something to be taken very seriously out there in the East.

"Read that letter," said Uncle William, "and then put it in your pocket. I want you to think about it. I'll talk to you about it seriously after dinner."

Wilson examined the letter carefully, because he had learned that the external appearance of a letter often told more about the writer than the contents. It was written on several large sheets of paper, of a good quality, evidently intended for a typewriter, although his uncle's correspondent had written it by hand with a stub pen and blue-black ink. The writing at first glance seemed scrawling and careless but the whole was perfectly legible and each letter was incisive and distinct. He would have known it was a woman's writing even if his uncle had not indicated it. Then it had the lack of discipline of penmanship peculiar to his own generation. The sender's address was embossed on the top of each page by a well-cut die.

"HITCHINGS PLANTATION," the letterhead read, "HONOLULU, T.H."

He remembered afterward that the letterhead surprised him, since he had never heard there was a plantation anywhere in the world bearing the family name. He mentally contrasted it with the heavily engraved letterhead of the Hitchings firm: "HITCHINGS BROTHERS, BANKERS AND COMMISSION MERCHANT, HONOLULU, SHANGHAI, CANTON." To anyone familiar with the American vicissitudes of mercantile ventures, during the past century, those words were illuminating enough. They indicated that the Hitchings family had built up and maintained a commercial position which was still strong after nearly all the houses that had started with them had disappeared. The firm letterhead told of the northwest trade and the China trade. It indicated more than clever management. It indicated complete mercantile and banking integrity. Even then Wilson had an intuition that the letter headed "Hitchings Plantation," which he was holding, indicated something entirely different. He felt an instinctive cautious resentment that the family name should be embossed upon it—a resentment which extended to the writer. The letter read:—

> Dear Mr. Hitchings,—
>
> I suppose you are a distant relative of mine, since my father sometimes spoke of you when he was alive, but I don't know how we are related. Frankly, I don't much care. Mr. Wilkie, your Branch Manager in Honolulu, advised me to write you personally. That is my only reason for doing it.
>
> Mr. Wilkie has forwarded me several times your offers to buy the house which my father left me and which has always been called "Hitchings Plantation," with exactly as much right as you call your own firm "Hitchings Brothers." He has explained your anxiety to purchase the property from me on the grounds that it is a gambling establishment and that its name is hurting the fine old traditions of your own business. From what I know of your business pursuits, I don't believe that a roulette table can hurt them very much. You have been so anxious to buy me out that I wonder if you have not some other reason. Bankers so seldom tell the real truth.

At any rate, whatever your reason is, this letter is to tell you that you are wasting your time in making me offers. "Hitchings Plantation" is going to remain open as long as I have anything to do with it. There is no reason why I should have any sympathy for your delicacy about the family name. As a matter of fact, I feel that my particular way of earning my living is about as honorable as yours, even if it doesn't pay so well.

I wonder if you remember what happened when my father had financial reverses a few years ago. When he went to his rich relatives and asked for help, he did not even get sympathy. That is why we began having card tables in the house: because we had to do something to get along. People like to come out to the Plantation. There has never been enough disturbance to make the authorities object. When my father died, I put in a roulette table and frankly made it a gambling casino because I had to earn my living. A good many people here sympathize with me, which perhaps you know. You could have helped us once and you didn't. There is no reason why I should help you now—and I won't. I haven't any more use for you than you have for me. You can try to bring legal pressure to bear, if you want to, but I don't think you will. You don't want publicity any more than I do, so I should let the matter drop and let the black sheep of the family alone.

Very truly yours,—

EVA HITCHINGS.

Wilson laid the letter back on his uncle's desk and his uncle did not speak. There was a quality in his silence which told Wilson that it would be just as well not to appear amused, although the letter did amuse him. It referred to circumstances of which he had known absolutely nothing, so that he could think quite freely of the person who wrote it. Evidently, a girl who was angry—yet the anger seemed to him harmless. A gambling house bearing the family name was a circumstance which the older generation might consider more important than did his own. He could even wonder what the place was like and what the girl was like who ran it. He had never realized that there was any branch of the Hitchings family on an island in the middle of the Pacific, and the idea interested him.

His uncle looked at him over the papers on his desk.

"Well, what do you think of it?" his uncle asked.

"I wonder what we did to her father?" Wilson answered. "Who is she? I don't see that it is very important."

His uncle placed the point of his paper knife on the palm of his heavy hand. His face seemed more vacant than usual.

"You must learn not to make snap judgments," his uncle said. "Out here nothing that is important ever seems important, Wilson. I don't like that letter and I don't know exactly why. There has been too much talk about that gambling house. It's getting too well known. People are beginning to associate it with the Bank, but that isn't why I don't like the letter. There is some sort of situation behind it. . . . There is something wrong in Honolulu. . . . You asked me who the girl is. Well, you are having dinner with me. We'll talk about that tonight."

His uncle moved his hands through his letters, quickly, almost carelessly, and his momentary annoyance was gone; but Wilson knew that something was disturbing him—some unexplained suspicion was disturbing his uncle. The Hitchingses were always a cautious and suspicious family.

## 2

IT HAD been his uncle's habit to dine with him quietly, at least three evenings a week, and talk after dinner of certain aspects of the business. Wilson would sit at such times and listen, fascinated, wondering if he would ever learn it all. Uncle William lived in the family house that had been built in the seventies in a garden behind high compound walls. The house, entirely European, always reminded him of a Chinese copy of a European picture, for in some way China had crept into the architectural plan. Yet there was nothing definite about the house which indicated it. It may have been only the sights and sounds around it. The house was of gray stone, with a gray mansard roof. Inside the furniture was mid-Victorian, and except for the servants there was nothing Oriental in the house.

First there was whisky-and-soda on the back porch overlooking the garden; then, after dinner, they sat on the back porch again, smoking cigars.

"Wilson," Uncle William said, "I think I ought to tell you something."

"What is it, sir?" asked Wilson.

"Frankly," said Uncle William, "when you first came out here I was disappointed in you. You seemed to me shy. You did not seem to be able to mix or to have the human touch; but you're improving, Wilson."

"Thank you, sir," said Wilson. And then he added something which had been on his mind for some time. "It's not easy to be natural when you are a part of an institution."

"No," said Uncle William, "but you are doing better, Wilson. A number of the women at the Country Club have spoken of you in very high terms. There is something about you that women like. I am very glad of that. Do you think you are going to like it here?"

"Yes, sir," said Wilson. "I think I will, when I understand it."

"Boy!" called Uncle William. "Whisky soda." He flicked the ash from his cigar and looked across the garden. It was almost dark by then and the noise from the city all around them was mysterious in the dark.

"I am glad to hear that you are going to like it," Uncle William said, "and I am particularly glad that you have reached no conclusions yet. When you stay out here as long as I have, you will find that it is better to make up your mind about only a very few things. You drink very well, Wilson, and you do not talk too much. I believe that you have got brains. I believe eventually that you can take control of this Branch of Hitchings Brothers."

"Thank you, sir," said Wilson. He knew that it was a great deal for his uncle to say.

"Of course," said his Uncle William, "you have done nothing as yet. You have simply met a few people. I have not bothered you with office routine. I have only tried to help you a little with social values and position. Now I am going to give you something to do. It will be your first job, Wilson. Did you read that letter?"

"Yes, sir," Wilson said.

"Well," said Uncle William, "you are going to call on that cousin of ours in Honolulu. I want you to close that matter up. I haven't time to do it." He looked through the door leading to the main part of the house as though something troubled him. "Boy," he said, "bring me a cigar."

Wilson Hitchings sat up straight. It was not the first time that his uncle had startled him.

"But how do you want me to settle it?" he asked.

Uncle William's voice was bland.

"By using your own judgment," he said. "It's time you had a chance to use it. You can draw on the firm for any amount. I'll leave that up to you."

"But I don't know anything about this," Wilson said.

His uncle flicked the ash from his cigar and stared thoughtfully at the evenly glowing end. "Your remark reminds me that I know very little myself," he answered. "When you have been out here as long as I have, you will find that intuition counts as much as knowledge. The family has always had intuition. Frankly, it's a rather difficult gift to define. I think perhaps you have that gift. A connoisseur can look at a picture which seems correct to a layman, but a connoisseur may have an indefinable sense that something is wrong with its values. Without really knowing anything, it has been dawning on me for the last short while that something is wrong with the values of our Honolulu Branch, although I can give no explicit reason. Business is quiet enough there. The Branch is more of an ornament inherited from the past than a paying proposition. Now, if you will listen to me carefully, I will try to give you a few details. They may explain my unrest when you put them together. Have you ever been to Honolulu, Wilson?"

"No, sir," Wilson said. "I came out here by way of Europe, you remember."

"Of course," said his uncle. "Then you have never seen the Islands. Well, you have something still to see. They are rather close to being South Sea Islands, and for once the travel circulars are right. It is hard to exaggerate their beauty and their climate. The only trouble is that the externals of life are too easy. Men are apt to grow a little soft when life is too easy. I sometimes think that is what is happening to Wilkie."

"You mean our Branch Manager out there?" Wilson asked.

His uncle's talk seemed discursive, almost rambling, but he knew it would pay to listen carefully.

"Yes," his uncle said. "Joe Wilkie. He's been the Branch Manager out there for thirty years now. . . . He's had an easy life; the last time I was there, he had enough leisure for yachting. He has bought one of those Japanese power boats that are used for fishing and has had her made all over as a cruiser. That sort of thing is all right within limits, but outside activities seem to have taken his mind off work. He has been careless in this business about Ned Hitchings' daughter. I wonder; I sometimes think he may have been deliberately careless—not that I have ever seen the girl, and I hadn't seen Ned Hitchings for years before he died. I should like you to watch Wilkie, Wilson, I don't think he has the capacity to be actively dishonest; but watch him, please."

Wilson nodded in obedient agreement.

"I always try to watch," he said. "Who was Ned Hitchings?"

At first Wilson thought his uncle had not heard his question. His uncle was watching him obtusely and carelessly.

"I have seen you watching people," Uncle William said. "It is a habit you mustn't lose, and I hear you can move quickly when it is necessary. They told me there was a fight at Joe's Place last night. A drunken sailor bumped into you."

Wilson could not guess how his uncle had ever heard except that any event, however small, seemed to be public in Shanghai.

"It wasn't anything—" he said. "I suppose I look quieter to people than I really am. There wasn't really much trouble. I rather like Joe's Place."

His uncle appeared to have forgotten the subject at hand but Wilson knew that it was a habit. He knew that his relative was worried.

"Have you ever tried the wheel upstairs?" Uncle William asked. "Joe knows all the gambling tricks from Monte Carlo to Canton. Well—you were asking me about Ned Hitchings. I guess he knew them, too. Ned was a wild boy back at home."

"I never heard of him, sir," Wilson Hitchings said.

His uncle pursed his lips.

"When the Hitchings family drums anyone out of camp," Uncle William answered, "they don't speak of them to the rising generation. Ned Hitchings is your father's and my third cousin. He had a share in your great-grandfather's trust estate. Your grandfather was executor. When the estate was settled, your grandfather took him into the New York office. Ned and your father and I were younger then. That was before I came out here. Ned used to shock me then. He wouldn't shock me now."

"No," said Wilson. "I don't suppose he would."

"You see," Uncle William explained, "one grows tolerant as one grows older. Even in the Hitchings family. Yes, Ned was quite a boy. He didn't fit well in the office. That money he inherited didn't fit well with him. He married a dancing girl out of one of those Broadway extravaganzas. It rather shocked me then. It wouldn't shock me now. Come to think of it, she was a rather pleasant girl, but it finished Ned. You couldn't have a man like that active in the business. Be careful whom you marry, Wilson, please. Be careful."

"Yes, I will," Wilson answered.

His uncle flicked the ash from his cigar.

"Well," he said. "Ned drifted out to Honolulu and put all his money into a house that he called 'Hitchings Plantation.' Ned always spent his money freely. They had a daughter; then his wife died; then he lost his money. He mortgaged his place. He wrote your father and me asking us to help him out. We didn't. Maybe we were wrong. . . . That's all. I never thought about the girl until she turned the place into a gambling establishment. Have you never heard of it?"

"No, sir," Wilson said.

"Then I would find out about it, if I were you," said Uncle William. "It seems they want to keep the tourists entertained in Honolulu. The place is called 'Hitchings Plantation' and the authorities are rather partial toward it. Every tourist with sporting proclivities goes straight there from the boat. It's the talk of the world cruises. They are joking about it out here now. They are saying it is part of Hitchings Brothers. It isn't good for business, Wilson. We have been trying for the last six months to buy Ned's daughter out and close the place."

"And she won't sell," said Wilson.

Uncle William shrugged his shoulders.

"You saw the letter," he answered. He glanced over his shoulder toward the open door behind him as though he were listening for some sound.

"Are you expecting a caller, sir?" Wilson asked.

"You are rather quick, aren't you?" his uncle answered. "As a matter of fact, I am; a rather secret caller, and I am not going to do business with him either. . . . Well, you know as much as I do about Hitchings Plantation. I want you to see what is the matter, Wilson. I want you to buy it and get it closed, and you had better rely on intuition. The only thing that has kept our heads above water here is intuition. Don't ask me any more. I have got other things on my mind tonight."

The door behind them creaked. There was a soft pad of slippers on the veranda and William Hitchings' servant, a white-robed figure in the dark, was whispering something softly.

"He is waiting now?" asked Uncle William.

"Yes, marster," the servant said.

Uncle William rose and lighted a fresh cigar.

"Anything else you want to know?" he asked.

"No, sir," Wilson said. "Perhaps I had better find out someone who knows about Hitchings Plantation before I go to bed. It is time I began to put things together."

"Yes, it is time," said Uncle William. "I wish I might help you, but there is a gentleman here to see me. I wonder if you could guess who he is."

"How can I guess, sir?" Wilson asked.

"Think," said Uncle William. "Try to think carefully about what happened this afternoon."

"Do you mean that Mr. Moto is calling?" Wilson asked. He could not see his uncle's face, but he guessed that his uncle was smiling.

"No," his uncle said; "not exactly, but Mr. Moto probably has someone waiting in the street outside. No, Wilson, not Mr. Moto. Mr. Chang is calling—the gentleman who once had business interests in Manchuria. And I can guess what he wants. He wants me to help him with some more business. Well, I won't. There's a point where one must stop. I'll see you in the morning, Wilson."

As Wilson Hitchings walked down the hallway to the front of his uncle's house, he did not realize that his uncle was not behind him until he was close to the front door. Near it on the left, the door to his uncle's study was ajar and only a dim light was burning in the hallway. As Wilson passed the study, the door opened wider and a voice spoke softly.

"Mr. Hitchings." The voice was so quiet and assured that Wilson was neither startled nor surprised.

"Yes?" he said, and turned to the study door, to find he was facing a man whom he had never seen. The man was a broad-shouldered Chinese, past middle age, dressed in gray, European clothes. He had close-cropped iron-gray hair. Wilson had been in the Orient long enough by then to realize that all Chinese did not look alike. He was even able to identify certain types. The man, he concluded, because of his delicate, rather nervous features, was from the South rather than from the North of China. His dress and his manner showed that he was a man of ability. Just at that moment, the Chinese gentleman looked very much surprised. He was staring at Wilson, unblinking, almost suspiciously, and he had forgotten to be polite.

"Excuse me," he said. "I thought you were Mr. Hitchings, sir."

Wilson smiled.

"You mistook me for my uncle, sir," he said. "But I am Mr. Hitchings, too." Wilson was astute enough to perceive that the man was very much relieved. He smiled also and held out his hand, a slender, delicate hand.

"I am so glad," he began. "I thought you were a stranger." And then Wilson heard his uncle's heavy step.

"Yes, it's my nephew, Mr. Chang," his uncle was saying, "and you need not worry. My nephew knows how to keep his mouth shut. Our family has always been tight-lipped with customers."

Mr. Chang's smile grew broader, and he bobbed his head in a quick, nervous bow.

"Yes, indeed, I know," he said. "That is why I have come to you tonight, and why I hope so much that I may interest you."

His uncle's car was waiting outside the wall and Wilson Hitchings told the driver to take him home. He sat looking through the window at the city streets which for the most part in that quarter were like the streets of a Continental European city. But there was an intangible addition, something exotic that made him ill at ease. The shops and the faces on the streets were like that day: superficially correct but inwardly bewildering.

"There was something wrong about today," Wilson Hitchings said to himself, yet he could not have told exactly what was wrong. It was only the inherited intuitive sense which had kept his family afloat for several generations that told him things were not exactly right. And there had been a curious inflection in his uncle's voice, when he had spoken of Mr. Chang, which had been sharper than amusement. What disturbed Wilson Hitchings most was his utter lack of knowledge and his consequent complete inability to give a reason for his uneasiness. That unrest of his was as enigmatic as the tension which surrounded the city of Shanghai. He had felt that disquiet more than once when he had been by himself doing nothing. In the back of his mind there was always the impression of mysterious things happening inland that came out in garbled accounts in the local press. Shanghai had seemed more than once, as it seemed to him tonight, an impermanent safety square in some enormous game—a city which might disappear overnight. The clubs, the offices, all the people of his race, were only there on sufferance. They were probably doing nothing permanent, but that impermanence made it interesting. His family had ridden successfully on the turbulence of China. He wondered if he could do it. He wondered if his life would be a series of errands such as the one his uncle had assigned to him that night. His uncle had thought nothing of sending him on a six weeks' journey and, curiously, the implications of that journey did not worry him as much as the unknown implications around him. At least there was something definite in what he was going to do.

His rooms had the austere simplicity of his family's house at home. He had not taken many things with him when he had been sent to the East, although he knew that he would be there for a long while, perhaps indefinitely. He had brought perhaps a hundred volumes which now stood on plain white shelves. There was a family Bible and some old books on travel and navigation. There were some pictures on the wall, all of which had to do with the family—one was a faded photograph of the old square Hitchings house in Salem which had been torn down fifty years ago. There were framed photographs of the Hitchings family portraits, whose faces were like reflections of his own face in an oddly distorted mirror. On the whole, they were soothing faces, both intellectual and strong. And he was proud of them; the family had always been proud of its ancestry. He had been used to a simple life at home, and he had not yet overcome a sense of surprise to find his Chinese servant ready and waiting when he came home at night.

"Zsze," he said to his servant, "you must get your accounts ready. In a few days I am going on a journey."

"Yes, marster," the servant said. "Upcountry, marster?"

"No," Wilson told him. "I am going to Honolulu just for a while."

"Oh, yes, marster," the man said; and then he turned to the table and picked up a card. "A gentleman—he came to call on you this evening."

"What sort of a gentleman?" Wilson asked.

"A Japanese gentleman," the man said. "He was very sorry you were out. He left his card."

Wilson took the card, read it and placed it in his wallet. It was one of those business cards to which he had already grown accustomed. On one side were characters, on the other was a European name.

"I. A. MOTO" the printing read, and beneath was written in pencil: *"So sorry you were out. I hope to see you soon."*

The inscription on the card amused him, but what impressed

Wilson most was the accuracy of his Uncle William's prophecy. He recalled that his uncle had said that Mr. Moto would probably try to meet him. Although he had the gift of an orderly mind which could set aside a train of thought and turn readily to another, and though he understood that Mr. Moto was no affair of his, he did not feel like sleep. Intuitively he had the sense that something was happening in Hitchings Brothers. Both Mr. Chang and his uncle had been obviously ill at ease.

When his servant had gone, he picked up a book to read;—a translation by Gilbert Murray of Euripides' "Medea." He began reading the play, purely for conscientious reasons, and because he had brought the volume with him, hoping sometime to read it; but when he reached Medea's first speech to the women of Corinth, the words began to hold him. The bitterness and the anger of that woman, whom he had always considered a pleasant girl in Hawthorne's "Tanglewood Tales," and Euripides' own knowledge of the depth of a woman's mind, filled him with reluctant wonder. There was the conviction of universal tragedy in the bitterness of Medea. Was it possible, he wondered, that all women possessed this latent bitterness? It had certainly not been manifest in his own relations with the girls he had met at home. They had been nice girls, happy girls, and their mothers had been contented and poised. Then, much as he deplored the conduct of Jason, in that it differed rather strongly from his own personal standards, it occurred to him that there was much in Jason which was universal also, and there was too much of Jason's psychology which he could understand. The Hitchingses had always been looking for the Golden Fleece. There was something of the spirit of Jason in all the Hitchingses—the same restiveness—the same relentlessness.

Vaguely, and inaccurately, he could identify himself with those pages of Euripides. Somewhere in the night sounds outside his room, the Greek chorus was singing a noiseless, mysterious song that was ringing in the background of his thoughts. He, himself, had been selected to deal with a bitter and a probably unscrupulous woman who was using the family name despitefully, because of resentment. Wilson sighed and turned a page of his book. He was logical enough and frank enough with himself to understand that he was not well equipped to cope with such a problem. He had never been successful with the sort of woman whom he visualized—the adventurous type; and undoubtedly, the proprietress of a gambling house would be exactly that. On the whole, he could not understand why his uncle had said that he was the sort that women liked.

"Unless I am perfectly safe," he said to himself. "That is probably the reason."

The evening was still young and it did no good to read. He could not compose himself for reading because of his own uneasiness. He called for his servant to get him a motor and a driver and walked out into the warm, noisy street.

"Joe's Place," he said to the driver. He wanted to find out more about Hitchings Plantation before he went to sleep and he knew that Joe Stanley was probably the one to tell him. The car moved into the dark city, through streets of twinkling electric signs, more effective than any he had ever seen, perhaps because of the Chinese characters depicted on them in red and green and blue. Joe's Place was in the French concession, on a noisy street, lined with restaurants and cabarets. There was an American bar on the lower floor, with tables and music. There were gambling rooms upstairs. Joe Stanley, himself, was standing near the bar and Wilson wondered, as he often had before, what had brought Joe Stanley to Shanghai to end his days. It was a story which Mr. Stanley never told.

Although he must have been in his middle sixties, he was remarkably well preserved, a soft-spoken courteous American, like a character in a Bret Harte novel. Wilson had seen him more than once, and each time he had learned something new but vague about Mr. Stanley's past.

Mr. Stanley took a cigar from the corner of his mouth and gave Wilson a friendly nod.

"Going upstairs to play?" he asked.

"No, thanks," said Wilson. "Not tonight."

"Well, I'd go upstairs, if I were you," said Mr. Stanley.

But Wilson sat down at a small table near the bar.

"I am just going to stay long enough to have a glass of beer," he said. He had to speak loudly to be heard above the noise of drinkers at other tables and of patrons by the bar. "Won't you join me, Mr. Stanley?"

Mr. Stanley sat down next to the table and pulled his yellow vest straight.

"You know I never drink," he said. "I wish you wouldn't sit down here tonight. There's too many rough boys here."

"I won't be here more than a minute," Wilson said. "Have you ever heard of Hitchings Plantation in Honolulu, Mr. Stanley?"

"Yes, son," Mr. Stanley said. "I've heard of it. Why do you ask me?"

"The name," said Wilson. "I was interested. That's all."

"That's funny," Mr. Stanley said. "There was a party in here talking of it, this afternoon. That isn't why you are asking, is it?"

"How do you mean?" Wilson asked him.

"Nothing," said Mr. Stanley. "Nothing. A Russian named Sergi was talking of it this afternoon too. Does that mean anything to you, son? He was in here with a Chinese businessman named Chang Lo-Shih. They tell me they play for high stakes there. There is a croupier named Pierre—but maybe you know it already, don't you, son?"

Wilson sipped his beer carefully and tried to think, but he could not understand Mr. Stanley's attitude. It presupposed a knowledge which he did not possess. Mr. Stanley's eyes had grown narrow, and he was smiling faintly, mockingly.

"Why do you think I should know?" Wilson asked. "I have never been to Honolulu."

"No?" said Mr. Stanley. "But your name is Hitchings, isn't it? I don't know what you are aiming at, Mr. Hitchings, but you don't get me dragged in. I'm too wise and I'll keep still—so don't you worry. There is Sergi sitting over there." He nodded across the room, and Wilson followed the direction of his glance. A man with a pale, waxen face was sitting alone at the table, staring at an empty glass. A cigarette drooped listlessly from between his lips. "You know Sergi, don't you, Mr. Hitchings?"

"No," said Wilson. "I don't. I came here to ask you a simple question and I don't know what you are driving at."

"No?" said Mr. Stanley. "Listen, son, it's getting late and it's time you was in bed. If you want to know about Hitchings Plantation, ask Mr. Chang, not me. I'm not taking a hand in this. Do you get me, son?"

"No," said Wilson. "I don't."

Mr. Stanley rose.

"It don't matter if you don't," he said. "I know when to keep my mouth shut. No one will get anything out of me. What I know won't hurt a soul. Are you glad of that, son?"

"I still don't know what you mean," Wilson said.

Mr. Stanley held out his hand.

"Put it there, son," Mr. Stanley said. "You haven't been out here long, but if I was running a big enough show, I'd have you in it.

You're right to be looking out, but I'm not going to blab what I know to any Japanese. Understand me, son?"

"No," said Wilson patiently; "but I don't suppose you'll explain."

"That's what I'm telling you, son," Mr. Stanley answered. "You can sleep easy and not worry about me. That Jap has been here asking about Hitchings Plantation, not an hour ago."

"What Jap?" asked Wilson.

"You know it already, son," said Mr. Stanley, gently. "A guy named Mr. Moto, and he didn't get a damn word out of me. It's all right, son, go home and go to sleep. I'm not talking, understand? Good night."

"Good night," said Wilson, and he walked out to the street. Mr. Stanley's manner, the whole conversation, puzzled him; but one thing had stopped him asking more. There was only one thing he understood—that Mr. Moto had been very busy, and he could not tell why. He decided to keep the matter to himself until he found out why. He decided not to tell his uncle. He had been told to do the job himself. There was one implication that had been clear enough. For some reason that he did not know as yet, Mr. Stanley had thought he was completely conversant with a situation which he had only heard of that evening. His Uncle William had been right again. There was something wrong with Honolulu. He was sure of it that night. . . .

## 3

SINCE WILSON HITCHINGS had been taught to be methodical in dress and in thought and in action, he approached the problem before him methodically. The first thing he did the morning he landed in Honolulu was to call on Mr. Joseph Wilkie, the Manager of the Hitchings Brothers Branch. He walked up a broad street slowly, dressed in tailored white, like a traveler accustomed to the tropics, but he looked around him curiously because it was the first time that he had seen these Islands. They had seemed from the ship like a background of a stage. Even when he was safe on land, walking through the warm bright sunlight, the place did not seem any more real than his errand. He still carried in his mind his first view of the city, from the water, with the serrated ridges of volcanic mountains behind it. He could remember the soft fresh springlike tones of green, the blueness of the water, the bronze bodies of boys swimming beside the slowly moving ship, the giant pineapple rising above a canning factory on the waterfront, and the civic tower with the word "Aloha" written on it and the notes of the band playing Hawiian music. The docking of the ship had been arranged with a theatrical skill which was characteristically American, but there was more than that. There had been something of the old spirit of the Islands in that landing. When the first ships had entered the harbor natives must have been swimming beside them, and there must have been music; there must have been flowers. He could never forget that impression of flowers which stout Hawaiian women in gingham dresses were holding out for sale. A trade wind was blowing, moving through coconut palms, and the waterfront was clean and beautiful.

The offices of Hitchings Brothers were in a new yellow stucco building, with palm trees growing in a plot of strange stiff grass beside the door. Inside, the offices were cool and airy and no one seemed in a hurry, not even when Wilson Hitchings handed his card to a man of his own age, also dressed in white.

"Does Mr. Wilkie expect you?" the man asked.

"No," said Wilson. "I don't think he knows I'm coming."

The manager's room was comfortable, like the managers' rooms in all the Hitchings' branches. There was a homelike familiarity in the decoration as far as Wilson Hitchings was concerned that made him feel pleasantly sure of himself; but the assurance left him when he examined the man who was waiting for him there. On the trip out, with the meager information at his disposal, Wilson had tried to construct an imaginary Mr. Wilkie—a bad practice, he learned in later times, since imagination hardly ever coincided with fact. His uncle had told him to watch Mr. Wilkie, and he watched; but his first glance showed that Mr. Wilkie was different from anything he anticipated. Wilson could perceive no sinister traits in the man before him—in fact nothing to attract his attention. There was only one thing which particularly impressed him. It had been his uncle's idea that Mr. Wilkie should receive no warning of his visit, and it was clear that Mr. Wilkie was surprised and upset, almost unduly upset for such a circumstance, although his lack of composure seemed due largely to hurt pride.

"Good morning, sir," said Wilson. "My uncle said there was no need to cable."

Mr. Wilkie was standing up in the cool shady room. He was a thin iron-gray-haired man, dressed in tropical white. His face was deeply tanned; his eyes were brown. Something about him indicated an emphasis on dress that came of a preoccupation with personal appearance. There seemed to be a fussiness in his manner, the rather provincial fussiness of a man conscious of his position. There was an effort at façade that went with his clothes and with William Hitchings' account of Mr. Wilkie's cruising boat. It seemed to Wilson that the older man was making a distinct effort to conceal an emotion of annoyance, but annoyance was written in the curve of his close-cut gray mustache. He seemed to be saying silently: "I'm an important man, in an important position. You had no right to come here without telling me. This upsets me very much."

It was largely that annoyance which Wilson noticed, combined with surprise, but there might have been something else.

"It's a great pleasure to see you, of course," Mr. Wilkie said, "the very greatest pleasure. There's nothing like a surprise, is there? A pleasant surprise? How are your uncle and your father? You look like them, Mr. Hitchings. If I had known that you were coming, I should have arranged to have you stay at my house, of course. You'll excuse my not asking you now, won't you? I can't imagine why no one sent me word."

"They thought it wasn't necessary," said Wilson smoothly, and he saw Mr. Wilkie raise his eyebrows. "My uncle asked me to give you this letter. He said it would explain everything."

Mr. Wilkie read the letter attentively, holding it between his carefully tended fingers, while Wilson sat and watched him. As Mr. Wilkie read, his lips tightened, as though repressing an exclamation, and Wilson heard him catch his breath. Then Mr. Wilkie glanced at him curiously and smiled.

"So they're still worried about poor Eva's plantation," he remarked. "I hoped I had made my position clear about it, but I'm afraid I didn't. This has been embarrassing for me, Mr. Hitchings. I can hardly tell you how embarrassing. It hurts to be considered so inefficient in a negotiation that a younger man is sent out; but perhaps it's the best way. I'm very glad to wash my hands of it, Mr. Hitchings, and leave it all to you."

"I'm sure no one meant to offend you," Wilson said. He was thinking even as he spoke that there was something devious in Mr. Wilkie's glance. His intuition was telling him something. It was like his uncle's thought that something was not right. "I didn't ask for this job myself. The whole thing is new to me."

"Yes," said Mr. Wilkie, "I suppose it is. I'll be glad to discuss your plans with you. I'm here to do anything I can to help. I suppose you'll want to see Eva this afternoon."

Wilson sat impassively while Mr. Wilkie spoke. When he answered, he was still trying to read what was in Mr. Wilkie's mind. Although he could put his finger on nothing definite, there was something strange in the air. It occurred to him that no one was natural when Hitchings Plantation was mentioned. Mr. Wilkie was smiling faintly.

"You'll know her better when you're through," he added.

"I'm sure I will," said Wilson slowly.

"Yes," said Mr. Wilkie with the same faint smile, "I'm sure you will."

There was a pause, and then Wilson spoke deliberately.

"It sounds as though you'd like a ringside seat when I see her. Would you, Mr. Wilkie?"

"Yes," said Mr. Wilkie. "You'll excuse me. It's not personal; but, frankly, I should rather enjoy it."

Wilson sat impassively, because he found that impassiveness helped in any interview, and he watched Mr. Wilkie carefully.

"I think I should rather see the Plantation first," he said. "I suppose it will be running tonight? Could you arrange that I get a card? I should rather go there without anyone's knowing who I am."

Mr. Wilkie smiled again, and his smile was polite but not reassuring.

"Nothing is easier than a card, Mr. Wilson," he said, "though I am afraid that Eva will know exactly who you are."

"Why?" asked Wilson. "Unless someone tells her?"

"No one will need to tell her," Mr. Wilkie said. "She will only need to look at you. You are the image of her own father when he first came to the Islands. You have the same narrow face, the same eyes, the same build, the same hands. Anyone would know you for a Hitchings."

"Thanks," said Wilson. He kept his glance concentrated steadily, rather disconcertingly, on Mr. Wilkie's face. "Now you'd better tell me something else."

"Certainly," said Mr. Wilkie, "anything I can."

Wilson leaned forward in his chair. His Uncle William had been a good teacher and he endeavored to imitate his Uncle William's urbanity.

"Mr. Wilkie," he said, "since I have been here you have made me feel conscious of a certain reserve on your part. It surprises me a little. Your manner is not entirely friendly. I think you had better tell me why."

Mr. Wilkie's face grew red; for a moment he looked almost astonished.

"You are speaking rather frankly, aren't you?" he said. "I haven't the slightest intention to offend you."

Wilson paused a moment before he answered, and he had the satisfaction of believing that Mr. Wilkie no longer looked upon him as wholly incompetent.

"I did not say you offended me," he answered. "I said it seemed to me that your manner was unfriendly and then I asked you why. It still seems to me a fair question. We are both employed by Hitchings Brothers, Mr. Wilkie."

Mr. Wilkie's face grew redder.

"You Hitchingses think you own the earth, don't you?" he inquired. The irritability was surprising to Wilson, but it told him what he wished to know—that Mr. Wilkie did not like the family. He felt himself growing cooler in the face of Mr. Wilkie's anger.

"Not the earth, Mr. Wilkie," he said, "but we do control the stock of Hitchings Brothers. That's why you can't blame me for being somewhat surprised."

Mr. Wilkie shrugged his shoulders. Now that he no longer had to conceal his animosity, Mr. Wilkie seemed almost relieved. The lines in his tanned face relaxed as he leaned across the desk.

"You've never been here before, have you?" he asked. "Or you wouldn't be surprised. I've lived here for thirty years, and Ned Hitchings was one of my best friends. I've always known Eva Hitchings, everyone has always known her, and everyone knows what his family did when Ned Hitchings lost his money. He was a fine man—everyone loved Ned; and you can get me fired if you want for saying it."

Wilson Hitchings rose. "If you'd told me that in the first place, I wouldn't have taken so much of your time," he said. "You have a perfect right to your own views, Mr. Wilkie. If you had told my father he would not have held it up against you. But, under the circumstances, I think it would be better if I arranged matters by myself." Mr. Wilkie arose also and his manner had changed.

"That's very fair of you," he said.

"Thank you," said Wilson. "I hope you have always found us fair; at any rate that's all I mean to be here. I mean to be fair to Eva Hitchings, too. You can tell her so if you want to."

Mr. Wilkie cleared his throat.

"There's one thing that you ought to know," he said. "We've a rather small society here, and being so far away, we are a rather close corporation. Ned Hitchings was very popular. You'll find that everyone takes his side here, and his daughter's side. You will find the Hitchings Plantation is rather universally accepted if only because everyone feels that your family has been unfair."

"I am glad to have you tell me so," said Wilson. "You mean I won't be very welcome?"

"I'm afraid not," said Mr. Wilkie, "and Eva won't close the Plantation because the Hitchingses want her to."

"Well," said Wilson, "don't think of it further, Mr. Wilkie, and I'll say nothing about it."

Mr. Wilkie looked incredulous.

"You won't?" he said.

"No," said Wilson, "why should I? You have a perfect right to your own opinion."

Mr. Wilkie looked at him hard.

"I guess," he said, "they've sent a clever man out."

"Don't say that, Mr. Wilkie," Wilson answered. "I only say what I think, that's all."

"Wait!" said Mr. Wilkie. "Don't go. Won't you stay for lunch at the Club?" Wilson Hitchings shook his head.

"No," he answered, "thank you just as much. I'd better stand by my side of the family. That's all that is worrying us—the family. I'll settle this without troubling you again. Good-by, Mr. Wilkie."

Wilson walked out into the bright street, but the sun no longer seemed warm or pleasant. He was not angry, but he was surprised—surprised because he was used to being treated cordially, yet here in one of the branches of the family's office he had met with a curious reception. He had been told that he would not be liked because his family had been unkind to a girl named Eva Hitchings, and he, as a symbol of the family, was to take the blame for this unkindness. He walked back toward the pier where he had left his bags—solitary, puzzled. The sights on the street registered on his mind half mechanically; the faces he saw bespoke of a mixture of races from all sides of the Pacific Ocean; the flowers in the park by the waterfront, like the people on the streets, had been gathered from the ends of the earth to bask in that springlike air. There was nothing which he saw that was not pleasant. Another time he might have enjoyed it more, but just then there seemed to be something sinister in the brilliance of the flowering trees, in the softness of the wind, in the scent even there in the city, of sea spray and of flowers.

"There is something that isn't right," Wilson was saying to himself. He was not thinking of the city, because the city was beautiful; he was thinking rather of something in his own mind. There was an intuitive uneasiness in his thought, a sense not exactly of danger, but of impending difficulties.

Nevertheless he always remembered a good deal of that day with pleasure, although his thoughts kept obtruding themselves on what he saw. There was an automobile at the pier waiting to be hired, and he selected it because it was an open car. It was driven by a coffee-colored boy in his shirt sleeves, who wore a wreath of flowers around the band of his felt hat.

"I want to hire you for the day," Wilson said. "I shall want to see the Island, but first I'll go to the hotel."

He went to one of the largest hotels on Waikiki Beach, whose name he had often heard travelers mention—a huge building, in a grove of ancient coconut palms, whose leaves rattled hollowly in the trade breeze. The clerk read his name carefully while he registered but he made no comment. It occured to Wilson that after all the name of Hitchings was not necessarily peculiar.

"If there is anything we can do to help you enoy yourself, sir," the clerk said, "be sure to let us know, because that's a part of our business. There's the beach, of course, outside, and we can arrange to get you a car from the Golf Club. If there is anything else you want to do be sure to let us know."

Wilson hesitated, looked at the clerk and smiled.

"I've heard there is another club, here," he said, "called 'Hitchings Plantation.' If it isn't asking too much, could you get me a card for that this evening?"

The clerk smiled back at him. "Certainly," he said. "There will be a card waiting for you by dinnertime. Don't mention it, the pleasure is all ours."

Wilson motored through the city that afternoon and out into the hills, as thousands of other tourists have done before him. He was familiar enough with the Hitchings Brother's history to know something of the history of the city, and he had enough imagination to see the past as it mingled with the present. It amused him as it had in Shanghai to realize that a Hitchings had been there in the beginning even before the wooden mission house had been set up on the spot where it still stood, close to the old coral stone church. That white clapboarded prim New England house had been carried in sections around Cape Horn in the hold of a sailing vessel. It had been, to all intents and purposes, the first house on the Islands, standing among the thatched huts of the natives. The huts were gone, but the mission house still stood and the palace of the Hawaiian kings faced it across the street, and there was the courthouse and the statue of King Kamehameha, with his spear and his feathered cloak, and then the buildings of a modern city with shaded streets of bungalows beyond them. The city was like its history, partly peaceful, partly exotic, partly tolerant, partly strange.

Wilson leaned forward and touched the driver on the shoulder.

"I should like to see Hitchings Plantation," he said. "Will you drive past it, please?" The boy nodded and smiled. He had been talking, describing the sights as they moved by them, and Wilson listened idly to his words.

"King Street. . . . Post Office. . . . Library. . . . Chinese temple. . . . Alexandra Park. . . . Banyan trees. . . . Monkey-pod trees. . . . Shinto Temple. . . . Punch Bowl. . . . High School. . . . King's graveyard. Kukui trees. . . . "

The words moved by dreamily like the sights of the city. The road was leading into the hills and then into a valley bordered by high mountain peaks where rich green vegetation grew on black lava cliffs and ended above them in a mist of low hanging clouds. The valley itself was as rich and green as the Elysian Fields. The driver turned to him and smiled.

"Lovely place," he said.

"Yes," said Wilson, "lovely place."

They were evidently passing through a rich residential section where houses stood on wide lawns behind hibiscus hedges. The car turned to the right down a narrow road and then the sun was gone. There was a light sprinkle of rain.

"Liquid sunshine," the driver said. "We call it liquid sunshine. You see it stops so soon." The car was slowing down. They had reached the end of the branch of the road and he was pointing straight ahead.

"Hitchings Plantation," the driver said.

It was late afternoon by then, an hour which was very close to sunset. The driver was right for the flurry of rain in the valley had been over in a moment leaving the air moist, soft and clean and full of the scent of flowers. Now that the car had slowed down, he was aware of a sense of solitude such as he had not felt all day. They had left the complexities of the city which formed one of the crossroads of the world and were stopping in a cleft between high, dark, green hills whose peaks rose mistily into a sky that was growing reddish with the sunset. Except for the house which was standing where the road ended he could believe that this part of the valley had hardly ever changed. The wildness and isolation of older days hung over it mistily. Wilson Hitchings remembered feeling cold, not entirely because the sun was going down or because of that touch of rain. The Island had changed from a distant, pagan paradise of gods and drums to an outpost of a nation that was half a fortress, half a garden. The missionaries had come to bring the word of God to a childlike trusting people, and the traders had come, and the whaling fleet and the French, and the Russians and the English. The fields had been planted with sugar cane, riches such as no one had ever dreamed of had flowed in. The beaches had become a playground. The city had become a carpet of twinkling lights, but the valley had not changed. It was growing sad and shadowy, a tropical island valley brooding over a simple past. The steep hills seemed to Wilson Hitchings to be waiting, waiting for a time when the vanity of man was gone and when the strong trees and vines would march from down the mountains again into the clearings.

"Hitchings Plantation," the driver said politely, "a lovely place."

"Yes," Wilson said, "a lovely place." He was thinking of the ironies of life. He had reached the spot toward which he had traveled a good many thousand miles and now he gazed at it somberly. The road had ended in a valley stopping at a driveway, flanked by two tall posts that bore the name newly painted, "Hitchings Plantation." The house stood on a lawn that was dotted with fantastic branching trees—a rambling wooden house that had been built in the style of the South at home. He could understand its name as soon as he saw the house—there was a high pillared portico, there were wings and verandas. When he saw it he could understand what Ned Hitchings had done with his money. He had sunk it all prodigally into one estate; it was simple enough to see what had happened afterward, because the house and the grounds above it gave an impression of desuetude and of disrepair. Ned Hitchings' money had gone into the house and now there was no more money. A building could not last long in that genial climate without upkeep. The grass about it was unkempt, shrubbery was growing wildly against the white wall, the paint was growing dingy, the shutters were sagging.

"They play roulette every night," the driver said. "You want to go inside?"

"No," said Wilson, "not now. I'll go back to the hotel."

He did not say what was in his thoughts, that the loneliness of the hills was in that house and vanished hopes. Something caught in his throat, because it must have been a gallant place once. Then another thought was running through his mind.

"Anything might happen there," Wilson said to himself, "anything might happen."

Then they were going through the outskirts of the city back to the hotel on the beach where music was playing. They were passing along a street which might have been in the Orient. There were open-front Chinese shops where dried fish and parasols and cloth were out for sale. There was a rich smell of cooking and of bean oil—there were rice cakes on the counters, the streets echoed with the notes of Oriental voices, and someone was singing in high falsetto notes. The dark was coming down quickly like a curtain, blotting out the contradictions of that city that was neither East nor West.

"All kinds of people here," the driver said. "Japanese, Chinese, Filipinos, all kinds of people."

"Yes," said Wilson, "all kinds of people." The darkness made the place mysterious and he stood for a while on the hotel lawn beneath the palm trees looking at the sea. It occurred to him that he had never felt so lonely. He was thinking of the valley and of the house.

The clerk gave him his card to the Hitchings Plantation Club and he put it in his pocket and then he went up to his room, a large room overlooking the sea. He unlocked the door and turned on the light and then he noticed a piece of paper lying on the carpet. Wilson picked it up and bent over it frowning.

It was a plain slip of paper with a single line of typewriting upon it. It had evidently been pushed beneath the crack of his bedroom door.

*"You look healthy,"* the paper said; *"if you want to keep healthy, keep away from Hitchings Plantation."*

He could hear the soft noise of the surf outside and he could smell that strange sweet smell of sea spray and flowers—all these made the note in his hand utterly incongruous. For the first time in a long while he felt his heart beat fast. There was no doubt that the message was intended for him. There was no doubt that the message was a threat. He folded the paper carefully, opened one of his bags and took out his evening clothes. He moved deliberately and thoughtfully, but his mind was filled with an incredulous sort of wonder. For the first time in his life he was entirely alone at the mercy of his own resources with no one to lean upon for advice or help. For once in his life he was aware that his family name and his connection was something on which he could not lean. He was surrounded by ill-wishers. The note had taught that much, and more than that it had made him understand that this ill will was not entirely passive.

He tried to keep his thoughts calm. The family had always been logical. The significance of the message puzzled him. If it had been intended to frighten him its psychology was very poor, because the note had aroused in him a streak of stubbornness of which he had never dreamed. He was amazed at his own anxiety to get to Hitchings Plantation now that he had received the message. As he stood before the mirror arranging his tie he noticed that his face looked pale and that his eyes were unusually bright. He was wondering where the message had come from. Then he remembered that Honolulu was only a small town as far as his own race was concerned. His name had been on the ship's list and anyone might know him. Mr. Wilkie himself had intimated that anyone might recognize him who was familiar with the Hitchingses—he had the same long nose, the same narrow forehead, the same deep-set eyes, the same large tranquil mouth. Wilson Hitchings stared at himself thoughtfully in the mirror. On the whole the sensation that he was entirely alone was not wholly unpleasant.

"I can probably take care of myself," his mind was saying. "The family always have." The idea of the family was reassuring—it had always reassured him when he thought of his family.

The orchestra in the hotel dining room was playing Hawaiian music, the waiters were Japanese in trim white uniforms. The diners as far as he could gather were all strangers like himself, pleased with the music and with the sea outside. It was like a tranquil June night at home. Against the background of the sea and palms there was a new significance in the music. There was a lingering sadness in it—the echo of old days—the echo of the voices of a dying race. A large man in evening clothes stopped by Wilson's table. Even before he spoke, Wilson guessed who he was.

"Good evening, Mr. Hitchings," the man said. "I am the manager. We are all pleased to have you here. Hitchings is an old name on the Islands."

"And I am new on them," Wilson said. "Won't you sit down for a moment, sir? You have a name for people like me, haven't you—a native name?" The manager seated himself and smiled, the patient smile of one who has answered the questions of a thousand inquisitive guests.

"The name is *malihini.* It's the old Hawiian word for 'stranger.' I am the exact opposite—a *kamaaina.* I have been born and brought up on the Islands. I've played with the natives here ever since I could walk. But what are you doing to amuse yourself tonight?"

"I am going to the Hitchings Plantation," said Wilson. He looked carefully at the man opposite him and realized that the manager had known it all the while. "I wonder if you'd tell me something I am curious about," Wilson continued. "If you've been here always, you must have known a distant cousin of mine—of my father's: Ned Hitchings."

"Ned Hitchings?" the other said, and his formality left him when he said it as though something in the name made him warm and friendly. "Yes, I knew Ned. There aren't many left like him. You should have seen the Plantation in the old days when Ned was playing host. It was a grand place then—music all the time, and all the champagne you could drink. Everybody in the world was there. Nearly any night. Ned was the greatest host in the world. You should have heard his stories! The Hawaiians loved him, everyone in the world loved Ned. There was a time when the old Queen wanted him in her court, but that was long ago."

Wilson was thinking of the former owner when he saw Hitchings Plantation again that night. That mysterious soft darkness of the tropics, which had fallen so suddenly like the dropping of a curtain, had shut out the loneliness of the valley, leaving only the brightness of the house lights shining through the dark. Looking backward far below him, Wilson Hitchings could see the lights of the city like the embers of a huge campfire in the night. The lights of the house where he was going looked like the sparks which had been blown from the edges of that fire.

Now that it was dark an electric light burned above the sign at the gatepost showing the name Hitchings Plantation with a clarity that made him wince; but even so, even as his car moved up the drive, he seemed to feel something of the personality of the man who had made the place. He recalled the words he had heard earlier that evening: "You should have seen the Plantation in the old days when Ned was playing host." There was still an air of genial expansiveness now that it was dark. Although the place was being run for money now, and filled with paying guests, there was still an atmosphere of hospitality, almost of careless generosity, as though money did not matter. The great veranda and the columns spoke of it and so did the wide hall inside. There was no doubt that Ned Hitchings had once lived high. As Wilson walked up the steps he could hear music and laughter and through the window he had a glimpse of people dancing in the hall. There was a man at the door, enormously muscular, a Polynesian with grizzled hair, dressed in white trousers and a white silk shirt, a wreath of flowers around his neck. His features in the glow of light were regular and almost imposing, and Wilson could imagine that he had been with the Plantation for a long while.

"Your card, please, sir," the doorman said, and he read the card carefully, and then he smiled benignly.

"Good evening, sir," he said. "Miss Eva said you might be coming."

"She knew I was coming?" Wilson asked.

"Oh, yes," the doorman smiled again. "Oh, yes, she knew." Wilson smiled back at him as they stood there in the doorway. The hall was brilliantly lighted. There were chairs and tables around the walls such as might have belonged in a gentleman's drawing room, and been moved aside for an informal party. There was a white-shirted orchestra playing stringed instruments in the corner, just as though they had been called in only for the evening, and almost opposite him, in direct line with the door, was an open fireplace, a needless addition to a house in such a climate. Above it was a portrait, three-quarters length, of an elderly man in white, a pleasure-loving man, whose face in the bright light stared out genially over the strangers in the hall. There was no doubt at whom Wilson was looking, for it was a family face, although the countenance was less practical and less austere than the Hitchings faces which Wilson had known. Ned Hitchings in his portrait was looking over his domain, much as he must have done in life. You could see that he would have loved the music and the dancing and the general disorder of the place. Wilson Hitchings smiled at the huge doorman.

"It's a nice house," he said, and the doorman smiled back.

"Yes," he said, "it's a nice house. Everybody has a good time here." He paused and looked about the hall. "Everybody has always had a good time here." Wilson could agree with him. There was something indefinable about the place—an ineradicable sense of happy days and happy nights. Wilson, himself, could feel it.

"Have you got time to show me around?" he asked.

"Oh, yes," the doorman said. "Miss Eva, she wants to see you. Give that boy your hat and come this way."

"Have you been here long?" Wilson asked.

"Oh, yes," the doorman said. "I have worked for Mr. Hitchings always. My family, they have lived here always. They have lived here when Mr. Hitchings bought the land." In a certain way his voice seemed like the Hawaiian music—it had the same sad gaiety.

"Yes, the house is very fine. Miss Eva, she keeps it very well. There is always dancing in the hall and refreshments in the dining room and tables on the great *lanai,* and lights in the garden. Then here are the card rooms and the fan-tan room, and in back the roulette room. Miss Eva will be there."

The music followed them as they walked through room after room on the lower floor of that large house. Except for certain people in the rooms, they might have been in a gentleman's house at an evening party. The house was furnished in excellent taste; the bridge room had been the library and the books were still along the wall. There was a studious concentration in the room, although it did not come from the volumes. The dining room and the great terrace beyond it were set and ready for an evening party.

"You may help yourself to anything you want," the Hawaiian said. "Miss Eva, she won't take no money. The entertainment is on the house. Will you have a glass of wine before you go to the roulette room?"

"Thank you, no," Wilson said.

Wilson was listening to the music and looking at the people. The house was full of people, and he doubted if there would have been such a wholly democratic company in old Ned Hitchings' time. There was one thing they had in common—the guests seemed well-to-do. But beyond this all resemblance ended, because Hitchings Plantation appeared to be open to every type and to every race. There were tourists easily distinguished from the rest, there were adventurers and adventuresses such as he had seen in other seaports, there were steamship officers, businessmen, and army men in civilian clothing, there were Portuguese, and dusky-skinned part Hawaiians in whose blood ran either white or Chinese strain. It seemed to Wilson that all the visitors who had ever touched the shores had sent some representatives to the racial congress moving through the rooms of Hitchings Plantation. There were Japanese businessmen and bland Chinese and there was a Hindu with his turban—taken altogether they made a mysterious and diverting sight and one which appealed to the imagination. He had read of the varied races on the Hawaiian Islands and of the experiments in Democracy and now he could see it working beneath the protection of the outlawed democracy of chance. There was no apparent prejudice in that mingling of the races. There was nothing but good humor and an order which was almost decorous. It amazed Wilson to find himself thinking that representatives of his own race seemed the least attractive of any in that room, but this may have been because he understood them better. He had seen enough of the world to recognize the political, professional gambler type among his own people and he observed that several men of this sort were watching him curiously and he could imagine what they were thinking. They were thinking of how to reach him and of how to get his money. Still smiling, Wilson turned toward the huge Hawaiian who stood beside him.

"This is all new to me," Wilson said. "Are there always so many different sorts of people here?"

The man's teeth flashed again as he answered.

"Oh, yes, we have all sorts of people on the Island. All people get on very well together on the Island, they have always. So many strangers are surprised like you. Anyone can come here as long as he behaves."

"What if he doesn't behave?" Wilson asked.

The large dark man frowned thoughtfully.

"He is sent away," he said. "There are men to take care of every room. There is never any trouble." The music was playing again, one of those gay sad tunes, and the room was sweet and fresh from the warm air which came through the open doors and windows. He could see lights from the exotic trees on the terrace.

"Miss Hitchings runs this very well," he said. "She must be very capable."

"Oh, yes," the man said. "Miss Eva, she is a fine lady, everybody likes her very much."

"Yes," said Wilson, "so I've heard."

He was glancing toward the door which led to the entrance hall as he said it and he remembered afterward that he was thinking of the strangeness of the place. He was thinking as he had at first that it had an air of kindly, tolerant hospitality more than any atmosphere of vice or folly. The rooms with their white woodwork were fine and well-proportioned—in spite of everything it was a gentleman's house.

"Well," he said, "shall we go to the roulette room? I mustn't take too much of your time." And then he stopped—a figure in the dining room stopped him, and he felt the same surprise as though someone had called his name. A small man in impeccable evening clothes was standing in the doorway, glancing about the dining room, holding an ivory cigarette holder between two slender delicate fingers. He was examining the room thoughtfully and the light fell on his face.

For an instant Wilson was looking at him straight in the face; for an instant Wilson could not believe it was so, but he had an accurate memory for faces and he knew that face. It was that of the Mr. Moto he had seen in Shanghai, and though it seemed contrary to every possibility, he could have sworn it was Mr. Moto in the doorway.

"Wait a minute, please," said Wilson, and he took a step forward, but as he did so, the small man in the dinner coat turned and walked away and Wilson did not follow him. He suddenly realized that he was being foolish, that there must be a large number of other members of the Japanese race who might resemble Mr. Moto. It occurred to him that he was a long way from any place where Mr. Moto could possibly be.

"Excuse me," Wilson said, "I thought I saw a man I knew, a Japanese I met once in Shanghai, but I must have been mistaken. But Japanese look so much alike."

He was surprised to find the heavy man beside him looking at him curiously. And there was something in the glance which Wilson could not understand. There was no subtlety in that broad dark face. The doorkeeper of Hitchings Plantation looked troubled.

"Yes," the big man said, "Japanese do look very much alike. I think we had better go to find Miss Eva now."

## 4

THE ROULETTE ROOM was in what had probably been the owner's study. Like all the other rooms in that strange house it was large and well-proportioned and retained a certain dignity. It was finished in some dark wood—from the Island *ohia* tree, Wilson found out later—with cupboards in the paneling and with high windows opening on another terrace. At one end of the room was a closed door bearing a legend on a brass plaque: DIRECTORS' ROOM, PRIVATE.

The table with its wheel in the middle of that room was a new and an expensive specimen. It gave the place the same atmosphere which a gaming table gives any room no matter on what end of the earth one may find it. Wilson had been in Monte Carlo once. He remembered the faces of the people who had sat or stood about the green baize tables there. They had represented nearly all the nations of Europe or the Near East, from blue-eyed blondes of Scandinavia to olive-tinted Levantines. The tables at Monte Carlo had each reminded him of an amusing parody of the League of Nations, and the table there at Hitchings Plantation was much the same. The cashier, a pale, sharp-eyed man, sat behind the desk near the door through which he entered. There must have been fifteen persons in the room putting counters on the number and watching the turning of the wheel. A third of them were women and the rest were men, again a congress of nations. Some Europeans, some Eurasians, two Chinese in evening clothes, two Japanese, a young American army or navy officer, a red-fisted Norwegian sea captain, a Russian, and again some tourists, those representatives of some world cruise who crop up perpetually in every Pacific port. The croupier was spinning the wheel as Wilson entered, and oddly enough he was speaking in French—the French of Indochina.

*"Faites vos jeux, messieurs, 'dames . . . Rien ne va plus."* The words

sounded strangely above the whir and the rattle of the ball in the otherwise silent room—so strangely that the croupier caught Wilson's attention first, making him wonder what strange chance had brought him to the Islands, for like all croupiers he was an interesting man. He seemed to be part French and part Malay, exotic, muscular and adroit; the swiftness and the accuracy of his eyes were in his fingers. His jaw was square, almost pugnacious; his manners, like all men in his profession, were impeccable. Another man sat beside him whom Wilson imagined was also an employee of the house—a thin, pale man, with an Adam's apple and watery, sleepy eyes that were riveted on the patrons at the table. He looked up as Wilson entered. Their glances met and immediately he looked away, but in that second there was something startling in those watery eyes, yes something that was icily cold, unhealthy and deliberate, something which told Wilson instinctively that the man was not good company.

The wheel had stopped and the croupier was speaking. "Rouge impair," he said.

There was a decorous clattering of chips and low even voices. A girl in a red silk dress with a pattern of white flowers on it who was seated near the head of the table rose and walked toward them, a tall girl with dark eyes, short wavy auburn hair, and a mouth that was bent upward in a fixed sort of expression of cynical amusement. There was the same amusement in her eyes and an odd sort of nervous vitality which was close to laughter. Her face and her bare arms were brown, she walked toward Wilson with the careless, athletic grace of a dancer, and looked at him squarely.

"Good evening," she was saying.

There was no doubt who she was—she was the head of the house. She had the air of being able to cope with any situation.

"Miss Eva," Wilson's guide said, "this is Mr. Hitchings." Wilson bowed and she nodded to him curtly, but did not hold out her hand.

"Yes," she said: "of course, I've been expecting you. Moku, you may go back to the door now. I'll look after Mr. Hitchings."

Wilson bowed again.

"I'm sure you will," he said, and she nodded in cool agreement.

"Yes," she said, "I'm sure I will. Uncle Joe Wilkie said you were coming. He said you wanted to come incognito, but that was rather silly, wasn't it?"

"Yes," agreed Wilson, "very silly."

"You see," she said, "the Hitchingses are such an important family that everybody knows the name. That's why it's such a help to have it on the house. Shall we go into the directors' room? It will be more quiet there. I suppose you want to talk."

"Thanks," said Wilson, "it might be better. I don't want to disturb your guests."

"I wonder—" she said. "Are you always as considerate as that? This way, please." He followed her toward the door marked PRIVATE, and the croupier was saying, *"Messieurs et mesdames–faites vos jeux!"*—and when the door closed behind them, they were in a smaller room, with bare walls and an oval mahogany table, with Chippendale chairs around it, and windows that looked out into breezy, rustling darkness.

Wilson looked about the room courteously and noticed that there was a second door marked OFFICE. That distant relative of his seated herself at the head of the table.

"Well," she said, "sit down, Mr. Wilson Hitchings, anywhere at all. And if I don't seem polite, it's only because I'm surprised. Few of the family have ever called on us; none, as far as I remember."

"I'm sorry for that," said Wilson, and he sat down in the chair beside her. Her lips curled up but her eyes were cool and unfriendly.

"Well," she said, "on the whole I don't think I'm sorry, because I dislike you all very much." They looked at each other for a moment without speaking, and Wilson tried to imagine what sort of girl she was, and he found it difficult because he had never seen anyone just like her. There was only one thing that he was sure of in that silence which fell between them, and that was that she did not like the Hitchingses. There was something deep, almost venomous in her dislike.

"Would you mind telling me why you don't like us?" he inquired.

"Not in the least," she said; "but there's something I must ask you first. . . . We've always been hospitable to strangers in this house. My father taught me that. Let me order you something to drink, Mr. Hitchings."

Still looking at her, Wilson shook his head.

"No," he said, "thank you just as much."

"I suppose," she replied, and her tone was acidly polite, "that you don't want anything to disturb your logic. The Hitchings were always so cold-blooded."

"No," said Wilson, "it isn't that. I've always made it a rule only to drink with friends, that's all. Why is it you don't like us, Miss Hitchings? It might help if I could find that out."

Her hands were lying on the table and they closed and opened as he spoke and her lips were pressed together more tightly. For the first time it occurred to Wilson that the girl beside him had a temper and that she was having difficulty in maintaining her cool poise. He could see a glint of anger in her eyes which made him add another statement quite deliberately.

"When I am sitting with a pretty girl," he said, "I don't need to drink. You are fortunate that you don't resemble the Hitchingses. You don't resemble us at all."

She leaned toward him and there was a catch in her voice as she answered.

"That's the nicest thing you could possibly say. It makes me feel better than I have for a long while. Thank Heaven! I don't resemble them at all."

"Yes, it is a relief," said Wilson easily. "I was afraid you would have our nose, and that's a drawback. You have got our jaw, though, and that is your very worst feature—a stubborn jaw. Do you mind if I smoke?"

"Don't be foolish," she said, "I don't mind anything you do."

"That makes everything easier," said Wilson, and he took out a cigarette case and laid it on the table. "And, of course, you won't mind anything I say, either?"

"No," she answered, "not a bit. Why should I?" Wilson pushed the cigarette case toward her and she shook her head.

"Then you won't mind if I say that I like you," he said. "I like you so much that I haven't the slightest intention of saying or doing anything that may offend you. You know why I am here, I suppose? I may as well come to the point." He smiled and lighted his cigarette. "I like this place so much that I'd like to buy it. Can you think of me as a stranger who is making you a business proposal? That might be the easiest way for everyone."

She raised her head a trifle and that flicker of amusement which he had observed the first moment that he saw her came over her face again reminding him of wind rippling over placid water. He could believe that she was pleased that he asked the question and that the whole moment pleased her. Her smile grew more pronounced as she sat there considering his suggestion and the smile took away some of the hardness from her face, making her look younger and less experienced. It made Wilson realize that she was younger than he was. It made him think for the first time that she might be an agreeable person under agreeable circumstances. For the first time he realized that there was a warmth and charm in Eva Hitchings. In some way, without his being able to explain why, she had ceased to be an abstraction, a purely business problem, and had become an attractive girl who did not belong in that environment. She even appealed to his protective instinct, although he put the thought away from him at once. He examined her more attentively; she had none of the attributes of a hostess at a gambling house, her red and white dress was simple and in perfect taste, and her color was natural and she wore no jewelry. Her hands, as they lay before her on the table, were beautiful. They were a lady's hands, sensitive, indicative of breeding. He suddenly suspected that her hardness and her control were purely make-believe. More the product of a strong will than character.

"Well," she asked him, "suppose you begin by telling me why do you want to buy my house? Do you want to run it, Mr. Hitchings?"

"I wonder why you ask me," Wilson inquired, "when you know the reasons very well already."

"Because I want to hear you give those reasons," she answered. "You can, can't you?"

If Wilson had never believed that there was something in inheritance he would have believed it then, because he was almost surprised at the clarity and the order of his thoughts. Now that he sat there at the table he knew that he had the family ability for negotiations and for estimating a situation. All the details, all the things that he had seen and heard, came accurately together in his mind by a curious sort of instinct. His mind moved easily toward a number of truths, even while he was speaking.

"Please don't forget that I'm not here for myself," he said. "I was sent here by the family. I rather like this place. Personally I rather admire you for running it, because it can't be such a pleasant thing for you to do. It must take a great deal of experience and a great deal of ability. And I don't believe you like it very much, do you, Miss Hitchings? I don't believe you like being cordial to all the riffraff I've seen in this house tonight. It can't be pleasant to combine hospitality with business. It made me think you'd be a different sort of person, and I see you're not. You can't like that croupier of yours, and that man behind him, very much."

Eva Hitchings shrugged her shoulders.

"Don't preach," she said. "I asked you why you wanted to buy this place."

"I'm not preaching," Wilson answered. "As a matter of fact I think you're a rather brave girl to be doing this. I wish you could think I was speaking to you as a member of your family, however distant. I don't like to think of any of our family having to be in your position. I really think, although no one has said so, that this is what disturbs my father and my uncle more than anything else."

"Oh," said Eva Hitchings. "You mean it rather shocks you?"

"No," said Wilson, "I know you'd like to have it shock me, but it doesn't. Nothing shocks me very much, because we're living in a rather shock-proof time. I know plenty of girls at home running teashops and working in department stores. There's nothing you could do that could shock me because you're not the kind."

"Really?" said Eva Hitchings. "You might be very much surprised."

"I doubt it," said Wilson. "I doubt it very much. But of course there's another aspect which you know as well as I do. Our name on your house is not good for a banking business. Then there's a second reason why I'm here to buy your house. It's a beautiful place, and of course you must be fond of it. I don't want to speak too much about money because you're in the family, but I'd like to have you live in this house as you'd like to live. How would it be if you still owned it and took the sign off the gate? And had it as a place for your own friends the way it used to be? Would you like that, Miss Hitchings?"

"Well," she said, "go on, what else?"

"If you agree," Wilson added, "we will talk about a sum in trust, the income of which will keep you comfortably. Things can't go on like this, you must see that."

Eva Hitchings leaned toward him. "Why not?" she asked.

Wilson lowered his voice and spoke more slowly.

"Because sooner or later you'll get into trouble," he said. "As a matter of fact, I think you're in trouble now."

He could tell that she was startled when he said it, more from instinct than from any change in her. She was smiling but her eyes were wider.

"Why do you think that?" she asked. Although her voice was level and pleasant he knew that she was startled. He could feel it in the room and in the rustling of the wind outside.

"Do you really want me to tell you why?" he asked.

"Yes," she said. Her voice was too casual, too easy. "I shall be delighted, Mr. Hitchings." Wilson took a paper from his pocket—it was the typewritten sheet which he had found in the room of his hotel.

"Read it," he said. "I wonder who sent me this? I don't think you are the kind of person who would do it. You're not so stupid as all that."

He watched her as she read the paper and he had to admire her composure. She read it and she laughed. It was the first time he had heard her laugh—her laughter was easy and pleasant and there was a ring of intimacy in it which seemed to bring them nearer together.

"You're right," she said. "I'm not such a fool as that."

"And now," said Wilson, "I'll tell you what I think. You needn't tell me if I'm right or wrong. You're not running this place all yourself, Miss Hitchings! You're not the kind to do it. You have some people running it for you. I have watched everything outside; everything is smooth and very professional, as professional as a New York night club. You're the front, Miss Hitchings, but there is someone else behind you. Whoever that may be, and I don't care who it is, because it's none of my business, is afraid that you may sell out. Whoever it may be is trying to stop you; that's why I got this note. And that's exactly why I think you'd better sell out. There's nothing for you to gain by not selling." There was a silence when he had finished. He could hear the sound of music and the sound of the trade wind, and she was looking at him as other people had looked at him sometimes—half surprised, almost with respect.

"You're rather clever, aren't you, Mr. Hitchings?" she said. "I didn't know you could be so clever with your environment and background!"

Wilson nodded. Her eyes and her voice were almost friendly, and it was as though they were playing some sort of a game, and he rather enjoyed the game because there were so many imponderables in it and because he and she were alone together. Some barrier between them had dropped down after he had spoken and he found himself telling her exactly what he thought.

"You know I'm a little surprised at myself," he said; "because all this is new to me; this is the first time I've ever been entirely on my own. I suppose I may be clever, as you say. I never thought of it exactly that way before, but it suddenly came over me, now that I have seen you and now that I have talked to you, that you are in trouble. After all, we're both in the family. I hope that you'll remember that. I have come here for a definite purpose, but I really hope you'll believe that I want to help you. I thought you'd be quite a different person. I don't like seeing you here alone." She did not answer for a moment. She only sat looking at him, puzzled and seemingly undecided what to say.

"You're different than you look," she said. "You're different than I thought you would be, too. I wonder if you're frank or if this is just an act. I suppose it's just an act."

"No," said Wilson. "I'm being frank. I've only said exactly what I think. I'm not tricky; actually I'm rather a guileless person."

She sat up straighter, still looking at him, and then she spoke carefully as though she had made up her mind exactly what to say, and he knew that she was saying something which had been on her mind for a long while.

"You'd make a very good gambler, Mr. Hitchings," she said. "I ought to know because I've seen plenty of them in the last few years. I never knew it until just this moment. You have a gambler's face, you have a gambler's coolness; you've played your cards exactly like a professional. I don't believe you are guileless because everything you have said has been so perfectly balanced. You have appealed to me in every possible way and you've really done it very well—so much better than I thought you would. You've been frank, and now it's my turn. And now I'll say my little piece."

"I wish you would," said Wilson.

"You've only made one mistake," she answered. "Your mistake is in talking to me about the family—that was exactly the wrong card to play, because I hate the family. I wonder if I can make you understand how much I hate them. Your family turned on my father because he didn't have your cool face, Mr. Hitchings—and didn't have ice water in his blood; because he wasn't correct and poised like you; because he didn't do the right thing. He made the great mistake of marrying my mother—I'm very glad he did, because that's why I'm not like you, that's why I haven't got your self-importance and your manners, and your easy condescension. That's why I'm a plebeian, Mr. Hitchings. And why I associate with these low people. And I'll tell you something more—Father was not a businessman. When he lost his money, when his back was to the wall, when you could have helped him easily, as you are offering to help me now, not a member of your family raised its hand. You're only doing it now, and you know it, because I'm interfering with your business interests. If you want to know the truth, I had made up my mind to interfere with them, after Father died."

"Simply out of spite?" said Wilson.

"Yes," she answered, "simply out of spite. I am paying you back by running this place. I know I am. And one of the pleasantest moments I have had is to be able to sit here and to tell you so. To see you come here, and to hear you try to buy me out. This place is going to be run as long as I can run it and as long as it can hurt the Hitchingses. You couldn't buy it for a million dollars! Is that quite clear?"

"Yes," said Wilson, "it's very clear; but it's rather foolish, don't you think?"

"No," she answered, "not if you knew what I've been through on account of the Hitchings family; it's not foolish to me at any rate. I hate every one of you—I hate your sanctimonious pretense."

"Do you hate me?" Wilson asked.

"Yes," she said, "of course I hate you. And I have sat here long enough, listening to your patronage. I'd like to see you try to close this place! I'd like to see any of you try."

"Well," said Wilson, "I'm sorry. At any rate, I don't want to see it closed tonight; I rather like it."

"Then go out and enjoy yourself," Miss Hitchings said, "we've been here long enough." Wilson rose.

"It's been good of you to give me so much time," he said. "I think I'll try roulette."

"Don't mention it," said Miss Hitchings, "the pleasure has been all mine. I hope you will have a pleasant evening."

"You are sure you don't want to be friends?" said Wilson.

"No," said Miss Hitchings, "I'm sure I don't."

There was a discreet tapping on the door and a Japanese servant entered. "A gentleman wants to see you, Miss," he said.

"Very well," said Miss Hitchings. "Show him into the office." And she turned to Wilson, smiling. "I'm sorry that I am busy now," she said.

"So am I," said Wilson. "Good evening, Miss Hitchings!" Then, just as he turned away, he found that the other gentleman was entering—Mr. Moto was standing in the doorway, bowing, smiling.

"Excuse me," he was saying, "do I interrupt?"

There was no doubt in Wilson now that it was Mr. Moto.

"No," Miss Hitchings said, "this gentleman is just leaving."

"Yes," said Wilson, "I'm leaving." He hoped that he showed no surprise, he hoped that he was smiling as cordially as Mr. Moto.

"Good evening, Mr. Moto," he said, "I thought I saw you a while ago. I did not think I'd see you here."

"Oh, yes," said Mr. Moto, "isn't it very nice? Such a nice place, so beautiful. How nice to see you, Mr. Hitchings." And Mr. Moto drew in his breath through his shining gold teeth.

It sometimes seemed strange to Wilson how small half-forgotten details returned to him later when he reconstructed that scene. All sorts of things registered in his memory—the black rectangles of the open windows, the sound of the wind outside as it rustled through large unfamiliar leaves, the scratches on that bare oval table where the light struck it, the shine of the light in Eva Hitchings' close-cropped hair, that half malicious, half mischievous smile of hers because she was composed again, completely herself. There had been a moment in that outburst of her anger when she had revealed a new side of her personality. He had been able to understand her loyalty and her bitterness, not so much by what she had said as by its implication. There must have been some prepossessing quality about Ned Hitchings, for his daughter had loved him as everyone else seemed to have who had known him, in spite of all his faults.

But what surprised Wilson most was the unexpected interest which she had aroused in him, which was more than curiosity. She had not spoken of her loneliness but he had seen it. She was not a person who was meant to be alone. Suddenly he realized that he was thinking of her emotionally, not logically; that she was appealing indirectly to his sense of chivalry, and he knew that this was foolish. Then he heard Mr. Moto speak again.

"Please," Mr. Moto was saying, "I'm afraid I interrupt."

That close-clipped voice of Mr. Moto's brought him to himself and made him realize that both of those persons in the room were waiting for him to go and that he had been standing almost stupidly with his hand on the knob of the door looking at Eva Hitchings.

"I'm sorry," he said. "Good night."

"Good night," said Eva Hitchings.

He remembered that Mr. Moto had been glancing at the open window as he spoke.

"Good night," said Mr. Moto. "I shall see you soon again, I hope. It will be so very nice."

Eva Hitchings was standing motionless waiting for him to go and Mr. Moto was glancing back at the windows. Wilson's back was half turned, he was reaching for the doorknob, when a sound like the snap of a whip made him whirl about. Even with his back to the room, he knew that the sound had come from the night outside. It was its sharpness more than its loudness which startled him. His first thought as he was turning was that a motor had back-fired in the driveway, and in the same second he was ashamed that he had started.

"I am sorry," he began, "I didn't mean to jump." And then he stopped. He found himself looking at Mr. Moto. Something had happened in that instant which was very odd. Mr. Moto was crouching, staring out of an open window. He was holding a small automatic pistol, he was absolutely motionless, evidently listening. In that first second of amazement Wilson did not move. He remembered that he glanced almost stupidly about the room wondering what had happened, for nothing in the room had changed. Eva Hitchings was standing just as he had seen her last but she was no longer smiling. She was holding tight to the back of the chair, also staring at the open window.

"What's the matter?" said Wilson. "What was that?"

No one answered for the moment. Mr. Moto still peered into the darkness and Eva Hitchings gave no sign of hearing. Then, still holding his pistol, Mr. Moto straightened himself and turned away from the window. It seemed to Wilson that his color was lighter, but Mr. Moto was smiling. And his eyes were dark and placid.

"Excuse me," he said, "I think perhaps you know. It was a pistol shot—the bullets will be in the wall somewhere behind me. The man was a very bad marksman, Miss Hitchings. You should get one who is more steady. Yes, he was very bad and I was very very foolish. I did not think that such a thing would happen. Yes, I was very foolish, but I do not think that he will try again to-night because he moved away. The next time that you and Mr. Hitchings try to kill me, will you do it better, please, I hope you will. Thank you very, very much. And now, Mr. Hitchings, please stand away from the door. I think I shall be going now. Good evening, Miss Hitchings! Thank you very very much."

There had not been much excitement in Wilson Hitchings' life and the idea of such a piece of melodrama was more than he could grasp at once. The thing had happened so suddenly, and yet so casually, that it became ordinary and matter of fact. The ordinary quality of such an episode seemed reflected in Mr. Moto's manner, and judging from appearances such an event had happened often in Mr. Moto's life.

"What do you mean?" said Wilson, and he still stood in front of the door. His sense of law and order was so outraged that his mind moved dully trying to reconcile what had happened with ordinary fact. "What are you talking about, Mr. Moto?"

He had thought of Mr. Moto in the past as an insignificant man but now he looked as compact and as nerveless and as efficient as the pistol he was carrying. Mr. Moto's dinner coat was double-breasted and cut in extreme lines; his round head and his black hair arranged in a shoebrush pattern was almost grotesque, but there was nothing grotesque about Mr. Moto's answer.

"Excuse me, please, if I did not make myself clear," he said, "perhaps I was excited. Please, I am not excited now." Mr. Moto's eyes were bright and steady, he was breathing fast through his closed teeth. "A shot was fired at me through the open window. I'm very very sorry—I did not expect one so soon. Attempts have been made to liquidate me before, Mr. Hitchings. Enough of them so that I should have been more careful. I had not thought I had been asked to this room to be murdered. I am very very much surprised. Please, I shall be going now." And he took a step toward Wilson, who stood with his back to the door.

Wilson glanced at Eva Hitchings. The girl looked pale and frightened but she did not speak, and the absurdity of the situation began to dawn on him. Mr. Moto and his automatic looked absurd, so amusing all at once that he almost smiled.

"Well," said Wilson, "I've always heard you Japanese were egotists. Do you really think I paid a man to stand outside to murder you, Mr. Moto?"

Mr. Moto smiled.

"Excuse me," he said, "I'm so very very sorry. It is not nice to say so, but I think that is what you and Miss Hitchings did. Excuse me, I must be careful. Please do not move your hands."

"And what do you propose to do about it?" Wilson asked. He found the matter increasingly amusing. The idea of his being connected with Eva Hitchings in any capacity amused him.

"I propose to do nothing about it," said Mr. Moto. And he said it genially, like someone anxious to be kind and forgiving. "These matters happen, do they not? Let us say no more about it, please. It would be very very much better, don't you think? Please, it does not make me angry. It was so very badly done."

"Perhaps you won't mind then," suggested Wilson, "if I tell you what I think."

"Oh, no," said Mr. Moto, "except I am in a hurry to be going, please."

Wilson moved a step nearer to him and looked down at Mr. Moto.

"Please," said Mr. Moto again, "do not move your hands."

Then Wilson heard Eva Hitchings speak and her voice sounded frightened.

"Don't," she said softly, "don't move."

Wilson thrust his hands deliberately into the side pockets of his coat.

"That will do for your giving me orders, Mr. Moto," he said pleasantly. "Personally I think you are rather too high-strung, and that you have a powerful imagination. I don't know much about these things but I don't believe anybody fired at you, Mr. Moto. Try to think of it calmly; a car made a noise outside probably. Or else a window shade snapped up. Now, if I were you I'd put that pistol in your pocket where it won't do any harm. I don't know what manners are in Japan but I don't think you have been very polite to Miss Hitchings, Mr. Moto, and you have startled her a good deal. Personally, I don't mind; in fact, I rather enjoy it, but I think it would be very very nice if you said 'good night' to Miss Hitchings and begged her pardon."

Mr. Moto's expression had changed since Wilson had spoken; his forehead had wrinkled into little creases; he looked puzzled, almost hurt.

"Excuse me," he said, "I do not understand. Please, do you think this is funny, Mr. Hitchings?"

"Yes," said Wilson, "mildly funny. Now don't you think you'd better put that gun away? And tell Miss Hitchings you are sorry? I won't hurt you, Mr. Moto, really I won't."

Mr. Moto put his pistol in his pocket and his breath hissed through his teeth, then his tenseness and his watchfulness entirely disappeared, and he bowed his head to Eva Hitchings. There was a strange, submissive dignity in his bow.

"Excuse me, please," he said, "if I have done anything to be rude. I am so very very sorry, and I am so very very sorry if I have been funny. Excuse me, please. Good evening, please."

Wilson opened the door to the roulette room and when he closed it he began to laugh.

"Excuse me, please," said he to Eva Hitchings. "I am very very sorry." Then something on the dark polished floor, near the wall, caught his attention, he never knew just why. Close by the door he had just shut were a few grains of new white plaster. Something made him look upward to the wall. There was a small hole where something had struck and had knocked the plaster down. He looked from the dent in the wall toward Eva Hitchings, curiously. She was no longer the same person he had seen before—she had regained her poise, but she was no longer as she had been before Moto had come in. Somehow as she stood there, resting her hands on the back of the chair, she looked enigmatic and extremely capable.

There was a mysterious quality about that dent in the wall which had changed the point of view. Wilson could feel a number of illusions leaving him and the sensation was almost physical. For one thing he felt as cold as though he had lost a comfortable covering; for another his visual faculties seemed entirely different. Eva Hitchings was no longer a lonely girl, no longer a flower on a midden, not to be associated with such a place as Hitchings Plantation. She was looking at him coolly, almost contemptuously, he thought, and in a way which made his next remark seem immature and stupid.

"So it was a shot?" he said.

Her shining reddish head moved in a brief sarcastic nod.

"What did you think it was?" she inquired, "a bean from a blower? This isn't exactly a Sunday School, Mr. Hitchings."

Wilson leaned against the wall with his hands in his pockets watching her. He did not know what attracted him, certainly nothing which was right. He knew that he was close to something which was dangerous and he had never known that danger would carry with it an intriguing fascination. He was aware of a strange exaltation beneath his training of habit and formality.

"You're quite right," he agreed. "This isn't like any Sunday School that I remember. And you're not like a Sunday School teacher, either."

"No, but I could teach you a good deal," she said. "I could teach you enough so that your family wouldn't know you, Mr. Hitchings! Perhaps you have learned already that this isn't the place for you. The name of Hitchings is being dragged in the mud, isn't it?" She paused and laughed and seated herself on the edge of the table, and Wilson noticed mechanically that she wore gold slippers, and that her legs were bare. "I hoped for a minute that you were going to be dragged in the mud, too. It did look as though you were going to get into a brawl with Mr. Moto—that wouldn't have looked well, would it? A Hitchings shot at Hitchings Plantation? That would have made the family jump."

He could not understand why the remark annoyed him as much as it did.

"I should have been careful of him," he said. "I don't want to hurt any of your friends." She laughed again and swung her slippers slowly back and forth, tossing her head back a little, and holding to the edge of the table.

"Don't be so naïve," she said, "and don't worry. I'll see you won't get hurt."

"Thank you," said Wilson. "I suppose you know who fired that shot?"

Her face had grown hard again; she looked at him without speaking for a moment.

"If I were you," she said, "I'd keep my lily white hands out of this, because it's none of your business, Mr. Hitchings."

"I wonder," said Wilson. "It might be my business if that shot were meant for me; perhaps you know whom it was meant for—me or Mr. Moto. Would it be too forward of me if I asked you?"

The gold slippers were motionless; she leaned toward him and her eyes grew narrow.

"What do you mean by that?" she asked.

"I mean," said Wilson, "that you are not exactly a Sunday School teacher, Cousin Eva. You can't help my having vague ideas."

Her voice changed; it was low and urgent.

"Stop! Be quiet," she said.

Wilson Hitchings smiled at her; he could not understand why he felt so tolerant or so kindly toward her unless it was because of a sense of his own superiority. He thought his remark had frightened and shocked her; certainly she looked frightened.

"Why should I be quiet, Cousin Eva?" he asked. "Have you got a sense of free guilt, as the psychologists put it?" Then her expression told him that she was not listening, at least not to him. He saw that she was tense and motionless, staring at something beyond his right shoulder and he turned and followed her glance. The door to the roulette room was opening very slowly.

"What is it?" asked Eva Hitchings. "Who is that?"

It was the man with the watery eyes, the watcher at the roulette table. Now that Wilson saw him standing up, the man's awkwardness was gone. The man was thin with a whiplike thinness and his voice showed he was a long way from home. It was a New York City voice.

"It's me, ain't it," he said. He spoke slowly, huskily, as he closed the door behind him and walked almost noiselessly to the center of the room. "I thought maybe there might be a little argument in here." He looked Wilson slowly up and down. "Who's the guy, Miss Eva?"

Miss Eva slid down from the table.

"Have I, or have I not told you not to interrupt me, Paul?" she asked. "You might frighten someone sneaking in that way."

"Nuts!" the thin man said softly. "Who's the guy?"

"This is Mr. Hitchings," Miss Eva said. "This is Mr. Maddock," Miss Eva said.

Mr. Maddock's pale eyes turned upon Wilson unblinkingly; his Adam's apple moved languidly.

"Oh, it's you, is it?" he said. "How are you, pal?"

Wilson Hitchings stared back at him. There had been a sneering lightness in his speech which was entirely new to him, and Mr. Maddock represented a world he had never known, but Wilson knew enough to know it was not a congenial world.

"Quite well," he said, "under the circumstances."

"Oh, yeah!" said Mr. Maddock. "Well, this is a funny place, pal."

"Yes," said Wilson, "and there are lots of funny people in it."

Mr. Maddock's thin lips formed themselves into a smile.

"You got that wrong," he said softly. "I'm not so funny, pal. Has this boy been getting fresh, Miss Eva? I thought there was some trouble here."

"I wish you'd mind your own business," said Eva Hitchings shortly. "Mr. Hitchings and I have been talking—why should you think there has been any trouble?" A lump in Mr. Maddock's throat moved slowly and he glanced casually toward the open window.

"I'm funny that way," he said in that soft voice of his. "I always did have a sense for trouble, see? That's what makes me useful, see? I seen that Japanese come out of here and I did not like his looks. He looked like someone had tried to run him out and then when no one else came after him—" Mr. Maddock paused and shrugged his shoulders. "You know how things happen among customers; we've got to watch everything, Miss Eva."

"Well, nothing happened," Miss Eva said.

Mr. Maddock walked toward her softly; his pale face looked cynical and kindly.

"Listen, girlie," he said, "it couldn't be that Hitchings came here to make you a proposition? You wouldn't be holding out on me, would you?"

"No," said Eva Hitchings promptly, "of course I wouldn't, Paul. Mr. Hitchings has come here to buy me out and I've turned him down."

Mr. Maddock took a long thin cigar from his inside pocket and lighted it very carefully.

"That's the little lady," he said softly, then he turned to Wilson and exhaled a cloud of smoke. "Tough luck," he said, "but she knows who her friends are, pal."

"Yes," said Wilson, "I'm sure she does." Mr. Maddock removed his cigar from the corner of his mouth.

"It's getting kind of late, pal," he suggested. "Maybe you had better be going home."

"Why," asked Wilson, "do you own this place? I'm not in any hurry to go." Then he heard Eva Hitchings laugh, and she spoke before Mr. Maddock could answer.

"Paul," she said, "will you send someone to bring around my car? Mr. Hitchings was just leaving. I am going to drive him home."

"Drive me home?" echoed Wilson, and he tried not to show his surprise. "You don't have to—but it's very kind."

"It will be better for you if I did, I think," Eva Hitchings answered, and Mr. Maddock raised his eyebrows.

"What's the big idea?" Mr. Maddock asked. "Some of the boys can take him."

Eva Hitchings shook her head. "No," she said, "I'd like the ride." Mr. Maddock frowned thoughtfully.

"You're lucky, pal," he said, "it isn't everybody who gets a ride with her."

"Yes," said Wilson politely, "I'm sure I'm very lucky."

"Well," said Mr. Maddock, "I'll be seeing you."

## 5

WILSON FOLLOWED Eva into the dark-paneled room where the roulette game was going decorously forward beneath that indefinable shadow of concentration which always hovers above a well-conducted gaming table. There was no sound but the whirring of the wheel and the rattle of the ball moving distractedly in its first burst of speed. No one looked up as they entered. They might have been walking into a laboratory where scientists were gathered to watch a final, critical experiment, and yet Wilson Hitchings had never felt so strangely, so mysteriously alive. All his senses seemed to have awakened into a peculiar stimulated watchfulness. He had never felt so much like an actor in a play. He was aware almost unconsciously of mysterious, possibly of dangerous matters, all around him. He was aware that anything might happen. But he was surprised to find that the knowledge stimulated rather than disturbed him.

Miss Eva Hitchings walked in front of him carelessly, gracefully; and he remembered thinking that everything tended to make her desirably beautiful, just as though he and she were characters in a romantic story. Mr. Maddock was walking just behind him. He could feel Mr. Maddock's presence and he knew that it was dangerous. Even so, the sight of the table interested him. The imponderables of the laws of chance were calling to something in his blood. It may have been that those imponderables were a good deal like the unknown factors around him, and a good deal like life. He knew that you could not beat life any more than you could beat the house, and it struck him that the thought was interesting, although he knew that it was rather cheap and trite. He could not beat life any more than Eva Hitchings or Mr. Moto, or the slender Mr. Maddock. They were all together in some pattern, according to some logic of chance, like the numbers in the squares. The lights and the green of the table were making him speak almost before he thought. They almost made him forget his immediate problems.

"Do you mind if I play for a few moments?" he asked. "I should like to leave some money with the house."

Eva Hitchings looked at him over her bare, brown shoulder.

"That's what the tables are intended for," she said. "That is, if you are sure it won't hurt your morals."

"Mr. Maddock will watch my morals," said Wilson. "Won't you, Mr. Maddock?"

"Yes," said Mr. Maddock, softly. "I'll watch your morals, pal. The cashier's desk is over there. The numbers have been running odd tonight around the second dozen, in case you want to know."

"Thank you," said Wilson. "Thank you very much." And he spoke to Eva Hitchings again. "Don't go away. You might bring me luck."

"I am very much in doubt if I'll do that," she said.

"After all," said Wilson, "you never can tell, can you?"

He bought fifty dollars' worth of chips and stood by the table for a minute or two watching. He saw that the play was heavy. A Chinese in evening clothes with a large heap of chips in front of him was playing the numbers covering an area with his bets. Wilson watched him lose once and watched him lose again; all the while his mind was working along channels which were new to him. It was probably the Hitchings' instinct to be careful of money which made him wait patiently until he could form some definite plan of action. He watched the imperturbable croupier and the masklike man at the wheel. Judging from the personnel, he believed that the game was probably a crooked one. He could understand that the house at that hour of the evening might be coveting the winnings of its Chinese guest.

Thus logically he knew that it was better to confine his activities to some other section of the board. He had seen the game before and he understood enough of the combinations not to play entirely like a beginner. He bet on *manque* and doubled his stake. He placed it on red and lost. He made a play *à cheval* and lost again. And then he won on a *transversale pleine*. He was playing idly, carelessly, without any thought except to keep away from the region of heavy betting. Then suddenly he had a streak of luck. He played *en carré* and won, increasing his take eight times. Taking out half of his money, he placed the remainder on the cross between twenty-eight, twenty-nine, thirty-one and thirty-two; and thirty-one came up. His luck was causing a ripple of interest, but the Chinese player across the table from him played placidly, still losing. Then a few seconds after the wheel was placed in motion, Wilson placed a stake where the zero and three joined *manque*, and won again. He pulled his chips into a pile without bothering to count them, and put the total on black. He was neither surprised nor elated when he won, because he had the sense that winning was the result of some vague sort of justice.

"Well," said Eva Hitchings, "what next?"

"No next," said Wilson and he scooped the chips into his pocket. "Not tonight."

"The Hitchingses are always careful, aren't they?" Eva Hitchings said.

"No," said Wilson, "but sometimes they know when to stop." He did not realize until he had cashed the counters that he had won five hundred dollars. The looks of the croupiers made it very plain that not many guests left the table with such heavy winnings in their pockets, and that he had done a good deal to cut the profits of the evening. He handed a hundred dollars to the two croupiers by the wheel and another hundred to Mr. Maddock.

"Something to remember me by, in case I come back again," he said.

"Thanks," said Mr. Maddock, sourly. "We'll remember you all right."

"I'm sure you will," said Wilson, and then Eva Hitchings was saying, "My car is outside, if you don't want to stay."

They walked together through the innocent-looking front rooms where the only amusements were bridge and supper and dancing. There was a runabout by the front steps, and the doorman, in his white clothes, was standing by the running board, Wilson handed him two bills.

"Excuse me, sir," the man said, "there must be some mistake. You've given me two hundred dollars."

"No," said Wilson. "No mistake at all."

The car jumped forward viciously as Eva Hitchings stamped her foot on the accelerator.

"Why did you throw the money away?" she asked. "On account of religious scruples?"

Wilson Hitchings laughed. He felt extraordinarily gay, irrationally elated, although something told him that he should be careful. Something told him that he knew nothing about the girl beside him; but he did not mind. What interested him more was that she was quite different from anyone he had ever known. As he sat beside her, with his shoulder touching hers, he felt kindly toward her, almost sympathetic.

"I don't want to take your money," he said.

"Thank you," she answered. "It was a pretty, if a rather vulgar gesture. You can't buy Moku for two hundred dollars. He was on the place before I was born."

"Honestly," said Wilson, "I didn't want to buy him."

"Didn't you?" she answered. "I thought perhaps you did."

"I wish you wouldn't be so suspicious," Wilson said. "I don't mean you any harm."

"Really?" she answered. "Perhaps I am franker than you are. I mean you a good deal of harm. You might as well know it, Mr. Hitchings."

Wilson did not answer for a moment. They were moving down a

dark valley through warm, heavy, mysterious darkness which seemed to shut them away from any particular reality. The headlights of the automobile made dancing circles along the edge of the road revealing strange trees and flowers that flashed up exotically from the black and disappeared as the car moved on.

"I have an idea that you saved me a good deal of trouble by taking me home," he said. "I'm grateful to you for that."

"Don't be grateful," she answered. "I've an idea that you can look out for yourself very well, Mr. Hitchings."

"Then you have a higher opinion of me than I have," he said.

"I hope not," she answered, "because I have a rather low opinion."

"Then why are you taking me home?" he asked. He could not see her face in the dark, but her voice sounded amused and almost friendly.

"Because I have never seen anyone like you."

"Well," said Wilson, "I've never seen anyone like you. Have you always lived here, Miss Hitchings?"

"Yes, Mr. Hitchings," she said. "Always."

"Then you must know the place rather well," said Wilson. "It all seems rather strange to me. How are you able to run the Plantation? It must be against the law."

"It's a private club," she said. "It's quiet. Why do you ask me? You know how such things are done."

Wilson looked at the road ahead of him. They were moving toward the lights of the city and he could see the sea in front of them, dark against the lighter horizon.

"You shouldn't be doing it," he said. "It's a rotten sort of business." She moved impatiently, and her voice was sharp.

"No rottener than yours," she answered. "You needn't preach to me."

"Would you mind telling me," Wilson asked her, "what you mean by that?"

"That's what I'm here for," she said. "That—and curiosity. I think you might as well know exactly where I stand. I think it would make things much simpler. When we get to your hotel, if you'll walk with me up the beach, I'll tell you. I'm not afraid of you, Mr. Hitchings."

"I'm glad of that," said Wilson. "There's no need for you to be."

"Isn't there?" she asked him. "Excuse me, if I don't agree with you. I've watched you tonight. I know a good deal about people and I think that you're a very able and a very unscrupulous and a very dangerous sort of person. I used to think that Paul Maddock and some of the other boys were dangerous, but they take second place when it comes to you. They haven't got your coolness. They haven't got your poise. They haven't got your personality."

Wilson Hitchings wanted to laugh but he did not. The whole affair was as unreal as the place around him.

"Are you serious?" he asked.

"Do you really think I am joking?" she inquired. "There is only one thing that puzzles me. I admire you, in a way. I suppose it is because I have always admired people who do things well and who can take a chance without being nervous. I admired you with Mr. Moto, tonight. I liked the way you placed your bets at the table. You did it in such a well-bred way. I think you would shoot anyone very nicely. You must dance very nicely. You must make love very nicely; but you had better not try with me."

Wilson Hitchings drew in his breath. He was glad that she could not see the astonishment that he must have shown.

"You make me rather surprised about myself," he said. "Now shall I tell you what I think of you?"

"I wish you would," she answered.

"All right," said Wilson. "It's a little difficult, because I'm rather confused. Everything that has happened tonight has rather confused me. I got off the boat this morning, in my opinion, a rather ineffective person. Now I'm a dangerous man. I think you have a very vivid imagination. Now, personally, I've been thinking that you're a dangerous girl, exactly the sort that I've been warned against. The sort of girl who might turn my head and make me forget the serious purposes in life. But perhaps we both are wrong. Shall we let it go at that?"

He heard a laugh in the dark beside him.

"No one could turn your head," she answered, "or else, perhaps, I'd try." She stopped the car. "Here's the beach," she said. "We might walk on it for a while. I can always talk better when I am not driving."

"I'm surprised," said Wilson, "that you're not afraid to be alone with me."

"Yes," she answered. "So am I."

What surprised him most was that her voice was neither entirely sarcastic nor unfriendly. Instead she seemed to have a rather reluctant admiration for him, as though she actually believed what she was saying. Although not a word of it was true, although he had no great vanity, that admiration was curiously comforting. Oddly enough it made him see himself in a different light. It made him come close to believing that he might have certain unsuspected capabilities. At any rate that inaccurate picture which Eva Hitchings had of him was not entirely unpleasant to his imagination. Indeed he often thought afterward that it had something to do with his subsequent actions, simply because of a desire to make her see that she was not entirely wrong. In some ways that picture of himself blended perfectly with the setting. He had never felt more like an adventurer. He had never before felt carried so far beyond the limits of reason.

The windows of the hotel where he was staying were rectangles of yellow light. The outlines of the building itself were vague against the stars in the sky. They were walking down a path toward the beach through a grove of tall coconut palms. The fronds of the palms clattered in the steady trade wind above their heads like the flapping wings of unseen birds. They made a mild sound when one heard them above the beating of the waves on the coral reef, perhaps a half-mile offshore. And, with that elemental music, there came snatches of a tune from a stringed orchestra which told him that the guests in the hotel were dancing.

"Those trees are very old," Eva Hitchings said. She was as shadowy as the trees, as she walked beside him. "Some of them are well over a hundred years. Palms stop growing after a certain time. They say King Kamehameha landed near this grove. I remember it before the hotel was built. I liked it better then."

"It's all strange enough to me," Wilson Hitchings said. "Everything here is a little bit beyond me, if you want to know the truth. I don't know what is natural or what is artificial. I don't know what is spontaneous or what is forced. I really don't know anything."

"Don't you?" she said, and her voice was mocking. "I wonder if all deep people are as open and as frank as you are. It is becoming in a way and it's convincing. I could almost believe you, if I didn't know a great deal better."

They were by then on a cloudy, white, deserted stretch of sand, with the palm trees just behind them. She had stopped walking and was looking up at him. The wind was blowing her short, auburn hair and blowing at her dress, making her look restless and unsubstantial, although she was standing still.

"What do you know?" Wilson asked.

"Come nearer to me," Eva Hitchings said, "so I won't have to shout. That's better. Now no one else will hear." She was leaning toward him, almost touching him and her words came to him very clearly, so that there could be no doubt what he was hearing.

"I know you had a man outside in the shrubbery," she said, "who tried to shoot that poor Japanese man, Mr. Moto. I know why you want to get rid of Mr. Moto; but I don't think it's very nice, do you? At least not for a well-bred member of the Hitchings family. I am still a little surprised, but not very much, to know that Hitchings Brothers go in for murder. But I suppose financial competition is very keen these days. Don't start, Mr. Hitchings. No one can prove anything, of course, and I won't tell anybody, yet."

If Wilson Hitchings started, he steadied himself immediately, and he was surprised at his own control; but it was probably astonishment more than will power which kept him standing, looking at her as casually as though they were speaking of the sky and sea.

"Please don't think I am shocked," Eva Hitchings was saying. "I'm quite used to the gang you have working for you at the Plantation. You did everything very nicely, except for the man you hired for murder. I can't see why you didn't do that better."

Wilson Hitchings cleared his throat.

"Now that you've been so frank," he suggested, "you'd better tell me what else you know."

"Very well," said Eva Hitchings. "You see, I'm not afraid of you, Mr. Hitchings, not one bit afraid. I know exactly why you're so anxious to buy me out, and why you want to get rid of me. Your talk about the family name is silly and we might as well both admit it. You want to buy me out so that I won't be around to find out what you are doing. Well, I won't be put out as easily as that, not until I'm ready, and I think you may as well understand it."

Wilson Hitchings felt that his heart was beating faster than it should and that his mind was moving vaguely in a cloud of stupefaction.

"Exactly what do you think I'm doing?" he asked.

"I don't mean entirely you," said Eva Hitchings. "I mean your whole family, its banking house and all its rotten connections. Do I really have to tell you anything more?"

"I think perhaps you'd better," Wilson Hitchings said, "now that you've gone as far as this."

"All right," said Eva Hitchings. "I don't mind. It isn't any news to you, is it, that Hitchings Brothers is arranging to smuggle money into Manchuria for Chinese clients? Don't worry, I haven't told another living soul—not yet. I'm waiting until I find out a little more, and when I do, I wonder what is going to happen to the general reputation of Hitchings Brothers. It's a little late to stop me now, unless you want to kill me too. It's a little late to be sanctimonious. You're nothing but crooks, Mr. Hitchings, like a good many other business people. Do you think I have said enough?"

"Yes," said Wilson Hitchings, "almost enough. I just want to understand you clearly. What makes you think that Hitchings Brothers is doing any such thing as that?"

There must have been anger in his voice, because he felt himself growing angry, and his astonishment was leaving him, now that the first shock of incredulity was gone. He was angry, not on account of himself but on account of the aspersions which had been cast upon the family, and he knew that he was the only member of the family there to face them.

"Don't be silly," Eva Hitchings said. "Don't be honestly indignant. I know too much of the game that Hitchings Brothers is playing, and Mr. Moto knows it too. It isn't a very high-minded piece of finance; but then finance is never high-minded, if Hitchings Brothers and your father and your uncle and you are good examples."

Wilson Hitchings did not answer for a moment and he knew what she was thinking. She was thinking that his silence was a tacit acknowledgment of everything she had said; and yet in his blank surprise, he did not know what to answer. He had never realized until then that the family firm and the family were so much a part of himself that every one of her words played on his emotions. Nevertheless, he had the sense to know that an indignant denial would do no good and that she would not believe it.

She was looking at him, expecting exactly such a denial. He knew it was time for him to do something but he did not know what to do. He was trying to recall everything she had said, and to make it logical; but he could not find any definite line of logic, except that the girl was carried away by some hysterical sense of antipathy.

"Well," Eva Hitchings was saying, "I've told you where I stand. What are you going to do about it?"

Wilson Hitchings did not answer, but it was clear that he had to do something. For once in his life, circumstances were compelling him to take a definite course of action, and he found himself completely at sea, influenced more by anger than by logic. In spite of his irritation he could admire the courage of Eva Hitchings and he was ashamed to feel that he was inadequate to meet that courage. Then he remembered a piece of advice which his father had given him once—advice as conservative as the Hitchings Brothers policy. He even remembered his father as he had given it, seated behind his desk five thousand miles away, with the tips of his fingers placed gently together.

"Sit quietly," his father had said. "Never do anthing unless you know exactly what it is you are going to do."

He had always admired his father's composure and imperturbability, without realizing that they might both be family traits. It might have been that old advice or instinct actuating him. He was never exactly sure. He stood there trying to piece unrelated facts together, trying to recall what his uncle had said of Mr. Moto in Shanghai.

"So Mr. Moto knows about this?" he asked. "Are you absolutely sure?"

"You know he does, as well as I do," Eva Hitchings answered. "Well, we've had our talk and I think I'll be going now."

He knew it was time for him to do something, even if he did not know what. She was just turning away, when he reached forward and grasped her wrist. He must have been rougher than he intended because he heard her give a cry, half of surprise and half of pain. Nevertheless, that action and the feel of Eva Hitchings' wrist inside his hand, held tightly enough so that she could not get away, made all these motives clear to him.

"Oh, no, you're not going yet," he said.

"What do you mean?" she asked, sharply. "Let go of my wrist, let it go, or else—!" She made a swift, lithe motion. She moved so suddenly that he nearly lost his grip. He had not realized that she would be so strong but he did not let her go.

"Oh, no, you don't," he said. "We're going to get to the bottom of this before I let you go. You've made a number of accusations. I'm not thinking of myself. I am thinking of the family."

"Oh, are you?" said Eva Hitchings. "Well, you'd do a whole lot better to think about yourself. You don't know how ridiculous you sound."

"It may sound ridiculous to you," said Wilson, "but it doesn't to me. I've listened to your insinuations and every one of them is untrue and you're going to admit it before you go back to your crooked gambling house."

"Crooked?" said Eva Hitchings. "What do you mean by that?"

"Exactly what I say," Wilson answered. "If all the Hitchingses are crooked, you've inherited the trait. That wheel of yours is wired. Any sensible amateur could see it. You were fleecing one of your Chinese customers just when we were leaving. It was so crude that it was almost amusing. And we'll find out some more amusing things before we're through."

"So the pot is calling the kettle black," said Eva Hitchings; and she laughed, but her laugh was not convincing.

"If you want to deal in metaphors," Wilson told her, "the pot and the kettle are going to get shined clean. I'm going to find out exactly what you mean—and it won't do any good to wriggle."

"Then why don't you search in your own conscience?" Eva Hitchings asked— "Provided you've got a conscience. But then, all the Hitchingses are always conscientious, aren't they?"

"Yes," Wilson answered. "We're always conscientious, and I am going to do this conscientiously."

"Do what?" asked Eva Hitchings.

"I am going to call on Mr. Moto," Wilson Hitchings told her. "I am going to take you, right now, tonight, and I am going to tell him everything that you have told me, and then we'll see exactly where we stand. That's fair, isn't it?"

Eva Hitchings looked at him incredulously. "You wouldn't dare do that," she said. "You couldn't."

"You're going to find out," said Wilson, "that it's exactly what I intend to do. We're going back to your car and we're going to look for Mr. Moto. I imagine you know where he lives, as long as he came to call on you tonight."

"Suppose I don't go?" Eva Hitchings said. "Why should I?"

"If you don't," Wilson told her, "I'll know that you're afraid to back up anything you have said. And I can probably find Mr. Moto by myself."

"You've got a good deal of impudence," Eva Hitchings said. "As a matter of fact, I wouldn't miss this for anything. You can let me go. I won't try and get away. As a matter of fact, I know exactly where Mr. Moto lives. He's staying in one of the cottages by the Seaside Hotel. It isn't far from here. We could walk, if you like."

"Very well," said Wilson. "But I hope you don't mind if I take your arm. You're a palpable fact, Miss Hitchings, and I have always been told to stick close to palpable facts."

"Very well," said Eva Hitchings, "but you're too subtle to be palpable. I suppose that makes you interesting."

"Thanks," said Wilson Hitchings. "You're rather interesting yourself. I don't know when I have had such a pleasant evening."

"Before you say that," said Eva Hitchings, "I'd wait until the evening is over."

# 6

THEY WALKED UP from the beach and turned to the right on a broad avenue, the name of which Wilson Hitchings had learned from his guide, that afternoon—Kalakaua Boulevard. His wrist watch showed him that the hour was 12:15, but the street was still wide awake. In the warm darkness, it reminded Wilson almost of a street in a suburban town at home. The dark had blotted out the background and left only the doubtful imprint of America. He saw that institution, the filling station, with its pumps all lighted, exactly as they were at home, and an all night lunchroom and a drugstore. America had come to those Islands, leaving as definite an impression of ideas of living as England invariably left on the outposts of the British Empire. It amused Wilson to think that the lighter ideals of his own country were stronger and more in tune with the present than those of the older nation. He recalled the jazz orchestras in the Orient, each a conscientious imitation of Broadway; and the Wild West motion pictures in Tokyo, and the baseball in Japan, and the amusement parks of Shanghai. The genius of his own nation was in them all—tawdry, superficial, but somehow strong and appealing. That genius of his country made him feel at home that night and Wilson was grateful for it, because it was something he could understand.

For the rest, he was surrounded by imponderables. The only thing he knew quite definitely was that Eva Hitchings was walking beside him. They had been thrown together involuntarily by forces which he could not understand. They were walking down the street as though they were deeply interested in each other. In a sense, perhaps, they were. She was walking quickly, without speaking, and he tried to put her from his mind as much as possible. He tried to forget the warmth and the languor of the evening. She had spoken of Manchuria and he was recalling, as clearly as he could what his uncle had said in Shanghai. That seemed a long while ago, on the first afternoon he had met Mr. Moto.

"You may not know it," he remembered his uncle had said, "but that was a highly important call. Mr. Moto and I knew it. You heard him mention Chang Lo-Shih—that means that old Chang is meddling in Manchukuo."

He knew that Manchukuo was the new state at Manchuria but aside from that he knew nothing very definite. There was only one other thing he was sure of. No matter who else might be meddling in Manchuria, no matter what anyone else might be doing there, he knew that his own family were well out of it. His uncle had told him as much. He knew that Hitchings Brothers was not an adventurous firm. It might have been a hundred years ago, but not at present.

"What are you thinking about?" Eva Hitchings asked him.

"About what's brought us here," he said.

"Then you'd better think hard and fast," Eva Hitchings answered.

He did not reply. Although he knew that her advice was good, he was not particularly well able to follow it. He was thinking of the destiny which drew lives together. He and Eva Hitchings and Mr. Moto and the Chinese gentleman named Chang Lo-Shih whom he had seen only for a fleeting moment back in Shanghai, and the croupier and Mr. Maddock—all were drawn together in some curious, temporary relationship.

By now they had turned into a dimly lighted side street and now they were walking up a driveway.

"This is the Seaside Hotel," said Eva Hitchings, and she stopped walking. "There is the main building and there are the cottages connected with it. This isn't one of our best hotels. The place is managed by Japanese. Mr. Moto told me in his note that he is staying in Cottage 2A. Have you thought it might be dangerous to call on Mr. Moto?"

"No," said Wilson, "I hadn't. Why?"

"Well, you know best," Eva Hitchings said. "I should be if I were you."

"We're going just the same," said Wilson. "Where is the cottage?"

The main building and some of the cottages were still lit up.

There were electric lights on the driveway and along the garden paths where the cottages stood, enough to show Wilson that he was in a world strange enough to him. The street outside had been primarily American but the Seaside Hotel bore the traces of Japan. There were sliding windows entirely Japanese and a pool and a Japanese garden. A girl was singing somewhere in a high falsetto voice.

"They have *sukiyaki* dinners," Eva Hitchings said. "Mostly for tourists who are interested in Japan, but a great many of the Japanese in town stay here too. We go down this walk here. . . . There's Cottage Number 2A, with the royal palm in front of it. Now what are you going to do?"

"I am going to knock on the door," Wilson Hitchings said. "I told you we were going to speak to Mr. Moto."

There was a small detached cottage in front of them. Two steps led up to a covered porch where an electric light was burning, but the windows in the cottage itself were blank and dark.

"Come on," said Wilson Hitchings. "What's the matter, are you afraid?"

"No," said Eva Hitchings. "I'm not. Are you?"

Wilson did not stop to analyze his emotions. He walked up the steps noisily and pounded on the cottage door.

"Mr. Moto," he called. "Are you in there, Mr. Moto?"

He listened, but there was no sound inside and for just a moment the silence startled him. Then he heard a voice behind him.

"Excuse me, please," the voice was saying, and Wilson Hitchings turned to the path by the cottage. Mr. Moto was standing on that path, just behind them. The light from the porch was full on his face. He was still in his evening clothes and he was bowing and smiling.

"Excuse me, please," said Mr. Moto again. "I was waiting for someone else. This is very, very nice but I am very, very much surprised." Mr. Moto moved forward quickly. "How nice of you both to come," he added. He brushed by Wilson, drawing in his breath, politely, and opened the door of his cottage, switched on a light and bowed again. "Please, do come in," he said. "This is so very, very nice. Will you allow me to go in first?"

They followed Mr. Moto into a little sitting room, furnished with a table, a couch and two chairs—a bare, plain enough room.

"This is so simple," said Mr. Moto. "I am so very, very sorry, but there is whisky in the bedroom."

"Never mind the whisky," Wilson Hitchings said. "What were you waiting outside for, Mr. Moto?" Mr. Moto's eyes were dark and expressionless. The gold fillings in his teeth glittered as he smiled mechanically.

"Please," he said. "I wish to see you come in to my poor house, before I come in too. Sometimes it is so very, very necessary."

"Do you do that sort of thing often?" Wilson asked.

"No," said Mr. Moto. "But sometimes it is a very useful thing to do. Several times it has saved my life. Please to sit down, Miss Hitchings. The room is poor but the weather is so pleasant. Such a lovely night. Yes, such a lovely night." Mr. Moto drew his breath through his teeth.

Eva Hitchings sat down on the couch and Wilson sat down beside her. The whole scene was becoming almost ridiculous. Now that Mr. Moto was chatting about the weather, there seemed to be no logic in it. Wilson looked at Mr. Moto and Mr. Moto looked back, bland and imperturbable.

"Well," said Wilson, "I am glad to see you, Mr. Moto." Mr. Moto drew in his breath again, sibilantly, politely.

"And I am glad to see you," Mr. Moto said, "so very very glad." Wilson leaned forward, trying to set his thoughts in order, but his thoughts seemed to break against the enigma of Mr. Moto, like waves against a rock.

"I suppose this is a little unusual," said Wilson. "I haven't seen much of you before. As a matter of fact, I don't exactly know who you are and I don't know what you are doing, but Miss Hitchings said a rather curious thing tonight. She intimated that it was I who had tried to kill you, Mr. Moto."

Mr. Moto moved his slender hands in a quick, disparaging gesture.

"Please," he said, "it makes so very, very little difference. So many people have tried to kill me. Please, we must all die sometime." Wilson moved impatiently, and his voice was harsher.

"But I didn't try to kill you," he said, "and I would like to know why you think I should? Why should I, Mr. Moto?"

"Please," said Mr. Moto, "there is nothing personal, of course."

"Well, there is to me," said Wilson. "Frankly, I don't like it. Back in Shanghai, my uncle told me you were a Japanese agent; is that true?"

Mr. Moto regarded him unblinkingly, with the same, fixed nervous smile, and Eva Hitchings shrugged her shoulders, impatiently.

"Don't be so naïve," she said. "You're only making yourself ridiculous."

Wilson kept his glance on Mr. Moto. He tried to master his sense of exasperation. Of the three, he was the only one who knew nothing of what was happening and he was determined not to leave that room until he found out something. But he had not realized the difficulty of enlisting information from a man like Mr. Moto. He could not gather from any past experience what sort of person Mr. Moto was. He could not tell whether Mr. Moto was ill at ease or not, or whether Mr. Moto's jerky, birdlike manner was natural or assumed.

"I suppose I am making myself ridiculous," Wilson Hitchings admitted, "because I know nothing, absolutely nothing. I don't understand what you are talking about, Mr. Moto, or you either, Miss Hitchings."

Eva Hitchings smiled at him through narrowing eyes. Mr. Moto rose and rubbed his hands softly together.

"It is so nice of you to say that, Mr. Hitchings," he said, "so very, very nice. It means we will have a pleasant talk. I shall be so very glad to talk; but first please, I must be hospitable. I have some whisky in my bedroom. We shall talk over a glass of whisky. Please, do not say no. It will be so much more friendly, I think. Besides, all Americans talk business over whisky." Mr. Moto's voice broke into a sharp, artificial laugh. "Please, it would be no trouble. Please, I must insist."

Mr. Moto opened a door which apparently led to an adjoining bedroom and he was back in another moment, carrying a tray on which was a whisky bottle, a soda bottle and two glasses. Mr. Moto's personality seemed to have changed now that he was holding a tray. He set it down on the little table with an adroit flourish that made him seem like a Japanese valet and he was quick enough to read Wilson's thoughts.

"I've served whisky so often for gentlemen in America," Mr. Moto said. "I am so very, very sorry there is no ice. Please, Miss Hitchings, you'll excuse Mr. Hitchings and me. Will you have some soda? I know so very few American ladies drink whisky."

"No," said Eva Hitchings. "Nothing for me, thanks."

"But you will excuse us, please," Mr. Moto begged. "And I am so very, very sorry there is no ice, but there is whisky, ha-ha, there is whisky, and that is the main thing, is it not? Will you say how much, Mr. Hitchings, and how much soda? Up to there? Just so? And now excuse me, I shall pour a little for myself." Mr. Moto's hands moved swiftly and accurately from bottle to glass and then he handed a glass to Wilson, bowing. It was a beautiful bow, better than a Frenchman's, Wilson thought. Mr. Moto lowered his head, slowly. His whole body seemed to droop in a gesture of complete, assumed submission and then his head and shoulders snapped up straight.

"Please," said Mr. Moto. "Thank you very, very much." Wilson took the glass and nodded back. Mr. Moto was holding a glass also. He raised it and bowed again.

"To your very good health," Mr. Moto said, and Wilson was aware of a note of music in his voice, as though he were intoning a religious response. "Please, I really mean it, Mr. Hitchings." Mr. Moto's studied courtesy was amusing. In spite of himself, Wilson Hitchings smiled and did his best to respond. "Here's looking at you, Mr. Moto," he said, and he raised his glass to his lips.

The rim of the glass was just touching his lips, when something occurred so unexpectedly that he could never reconstruct it. He remembered the feel of the glass on his lips and the next instant, the glass was at his feet. The glass was lying broken, its contents were running over a woven palm-leaf mat. Mr. Moto had leapt forward and struck the glass out of Wilson's hand.

"Please," Mr. Moto was saying. "Please excuse. I am so very sorry."

"Here—" Wilson began stupidly. "What's the matter, Mr. Moto?"

Mr. Moto's indrawn breath hissed obsequiously between his gold-filled teeth.

"Please," said Mr. Moto, "I hope you will forgive me. Everything is so very, very clear now. I could not believe that you would mean to drink. Please, I believe you now. I believe that you know nothing, Mr. Hitchings. You are very, very honest. Yes, excuse me, please."

Wilson Hitchings was still seated on the couch.

"Of course, I meant to drink it," he said. "Why shouldn't I?"

"Please," said Mr. Moto again. "Excuse me, I have been so very, very stupid. Please, let me explain. That whisky, I left it on my bureau. I nearly always take a little before my bedtime. Excuse me; this evening, I came home to find that the whisky was poisoned with cyanide of potassium. Please, you may smell a little, if you like. The odor is so very distinctive; one has to be so careful, always. Now, I know that you know nothing, Mr. Hitchings—and I must apologize to you very, very much. Now, I can believe anything you say."

Wilson Hitchings felt that his forehead was growing moist.

"You mean," he said "—you mean, you thought that I had done *that*?"

"Please," said Mr. Moto. "Not you, but I thought, perhaps, you knew who did. Please, Mr. Hitchings, I am so very, very sorry."

Then Eva Hitchings was speaking to him and he saw that her face was pale.

"You were going to drink it," she said, almost mechanically. "You were really going to drink it. I didn't know about it, I swear I didn't know." She reached out her hand and placed it gently on his knee. "I'm awfully sorry for anything I have said," she added. "I guess I have been an awful fool. Will you forgive me? I'd have believed anything out of a Hitchings."

Wilson Hitchings smiled but he felt very cold inside. The significance of everything was dawning on him, slowly.

"So you take back what you said?" he asked her.

"Yes," she answered steadily, "I take back everything."

Wilson Hitchings sat up straighter.

"Well," he said stiffly, "I'm glad you do. And now I'll tell you something, and you too, Mr. Moto. The Hitchingses mean what they say. We're pretty honest on the whole. I should have been glad to have swallowed that whole glass, if it could have helped the family."

Mr. Moto rubbed his hands. "That is very nice," he said. "It is so very Japanese. It is very, very nice."

Eva Hitchings drew her hand away.

"Can't you ever get away from your family, even for a minute?" she asked. "Don't be such a prig! Who cares about your family?"

Mr. Moto was on his knee picking up the bits of broken glass.

"I do," said Wilson. "I care."

"Well, I don't," said Eva Hitchings. "I don't care a button. I only know you nearly killed yourself."

"Oh, no," said Mr. Moto. "Please. I was watching carefully. I was watching all the time. Poison is so common sometimes, that one must be very, very careful. Now I think we had better talk quite quickly, if you please, because I think whoever fixed that whisky will be coming here and I want to know who it is so very, very much. That was why I was waiting outside when you came in to call."

"Are you going to tell me what this is all about, or aren't you?" Wilson asked. "You excuse me, Mr. Moto, but I'm getting very much confused."

Mr. Moto was pouring some soda water over his fingers and was rubbing them dry with his handkerchief. "Yes," said Mr. Moto, "I should be so pleased to tell you everything, now that everything is so very nice. You're quite right, Mr. Hitchings, I have come here to do a little work for my country. I shall be so very pleased to tell you but I must think a moment. Someone will be coming here, coming very soon, I think. There must not be too much noise. I must speak very softly, so that I can listen. Let me listen, please."

Wilson Hitchings could hear nothing but the sound of the wind outside and if Mr. Moto heard more than that, it could have been nothing to disturb him.

"I think," said Mr. Moto, softly, "it would be well to keep our voices down, for things are a little bit mixed up. Just answer me softly if you do not mind. Please tell me why you came to Honolulu when I did, Mr. Hitchings? That is what made me think wrong things. Did you know that I was coming?"

Wilson Hitchings shook his head.

"I hadn't the least idea," he answered; "and I don't mind telling you my reason. I was sent here because Miss Hitchings was running Hitchings Plantation. Its name, being the same name as Hitchings Brothers, was interfering with the reputation of the firm. I was sent to try to buy Miss Hitchings out, and to have the establishment closed."

Mr. Moto raised his eyebrows slightly and his forehead wrinkled.

"You actually wish the place closed?" he repeated. "You had no other reason to come here?"

"Absolutely none," said Wilson. "Don't you believe me, Mr. Moto?"

Mr. Moto rubbed his hands together and the wrinkles in his forehead deepened.

"Then there must be someone else," he said. "Yes, there must be someone else. I thought it might be Miss Hitchings, but since she is here with you, I do not think so. It did not seem right from the first. I should have known Hitchings Brothers was too old a house, that it could not afford to take such a risk, that it would not. I am very, very sorry."

Wilson Hitchings leaned forward, impatiently.

"It seems to me," he said, "that you are either very glad or sorry about something, all the time. Is it possible for you to be direct? I don't know who you are, Mr. Moto, and I don't much care, but I would like to know what you are sorry about."

The wrinkles left Mr. Moto's forehead and his cheeks creased in another smile.

"I am beginning to be very, very sorry for you, Mr. Hitchings. They would be anxious to liquidate me, of course, under the circumstances; and now, if you wish to buy the place they may wish to kill you also. It is very, very funny how things sometimes grow confused."

It seemed to Wilson Hitchings that the room had grown hot and close. He took a handkerchief from his pocket and mopped his forehead. He was surprised that Mr. Moto's remark had no great effect on him, rather it confirmed something which he had been suspecting.

"Who are they?" he asked.

Mr. Moto looked at him rather sharply and shrugged his shoulders.

"Certain persons who are not very nice, I'm afraid," he said. "Excuse me; when I saw you first, I could not believe that you knew so litle. You are, without knowing it, in a situation which is not very nice. I do not mind telling you frankly, and perhaps you will understand. I speak for my country, Mr. Hitchings, and I am here for it. You know of the new nation of Manchukuo, in which my own country has been so much interested?"

"Yes," said Wilson, "everyone knows that; but it seems to me you are getting a little far away."

"That is just it." Mr. Moto rubbed his hands again. "This is so far away that one might not connect the two. Manchukuo is a nice country. It is very, very beautiful and I have had many pleasant times there. It is too bad that there is so much trouble in it. There are still a good many bandits in the mountains. Certain persons have been causing factions to make trouble lately. Certain Chinese and certain persons of another power. Am I being too vague, Mr. Hitchings?"

"Yes," said Wilson. "You certainly are, Mr. Moto."

"Please," said Mr. Moto. "I shall try to be more clear. It has been known for some time that large amounts of money are being passed from China to certain insurgent leaders in the mountains. It has been my duty for some months now to try to trace the paths through which that money goes. It has been my duty to try to block those paths. It has been very, very hard. Do you understand me better, Mr. Hitchings?"

"No, I don't," Wilson Hitchings told him.

"Please," said Mr. Moto, "I hope that you will in just a moment. The channel through which the money first passed was stopped six months ago. I do not think it will be reopened again." Mr. Moto paused and smiled. "At least not by the same person. Fortunately such matters can be arranged very easily over there. Here it is so much more difficult. When that channel was stopped, I and my associates were much surprised to find that sums of money were still coming in. This time American dollars were appearing. We did not know from where. Then I began looking into the affairs of a Chinese gentleman, named Chang Lo-Shih. Do you remember that I mentioned him, Mr. Hitchings, in Shanghai?"

"Yes," said Wilson. "I remember."

"He is not a very nice gentleman," Mr. Moto said. "He does not appreciate my country or understand its aims. He has been handling a great deal of that money." Mr. Moto paused and sighed. "Just a little while ago, I found that this Mr. Chang has been sending large sums of money to an account in the Hitchings office here."

"If you'll excuse me," said Wilson. "I don't quite see the connection."

Mr. Moto bobbed his shining black head in a polite gesture of assent.

"Please," he said, "that is what I am looking for. That is what I am hoping to find: the exact connection. Perhaps you do not understand. These matters are so misleading, so intricate, so very, very difficult. In your own great country, Mr. Hitchings, perhaps you have read of the investigations into the bank accounts of gangsters and unworthy politicians. It it is so very, very interesting the way a clever man can cover the trail of money. Sometimes it seems to be thrown like water upon the desert sand. It evaporates and yet somewhere it condenses back again into money. As I say, I am looking for the connection. I and my associates have been looking for it very, very hard. Now here is one thing we have noticed. We have noticed American dollars in many sections of the nation of Manchukuo. They drift into the banks for exchange, a little here and there. This has struck us as being a little odd. There is no reason, of course, why a Chinese in Shanghai should not have banking connections here. Mr. Chang is a businessman and there are many Chinese businessmen in Honolulu. It is such an interesting city. Now, let me tell you something else."

"I wish you would," said Wilson.

"We have found," said Mr. Moto, slowly and softly, "that this money which Mr. Chang is sending here is being employed for a purpose which is a little unusual. It represents the capital of a gambling syndicate. A representative of this gambling syndicate has been drawing upon it for gambling purposes at Hitchings Plantation. I hope I am being clearer now, Mr. Hitchings. We know through our sources of information that American money comes to Manchuria through Japan from vessels which have touched at this port. I do not need to go into the details or the methods. They would not be very interesting. But what is very interesting to me is that Mr. Chang has been sending money here. It goes to Hitchings Plantation. Where does it go from there? That is what I should like so very much to know?"

"If that's all you know," Wilson Hitchings said, "it seems to me you're only guessing, Mr. Moto. It seems to me you're only shooting in the dark."

Mr. Moto bobbed his head and smiled.

"Ha-ha," he said. "That is a very nice joke, shooting in the dark. So much has to be done by guessing, Mr. Hitchings, the way things are today. I guess and guess and then sometimes I guess right, and can you think how I know?"

"How?" asked Wilson. "By your native intuition?"

"Please," said Mr. Moto. "There is something more than that. I am sure that I am right; very, very sure, when someone starts shooting at me in the dark. Please, do you remember? Someone did tonight when I called at Miss Hitchings' lovely place. Did someone, Miss Hitchings?"

Eva Hitchings did not answer but she nodded. Mr. Moto's expressionless eyes were on her and Wilson watched their glances meet and saw her look away.

"Don't you think that is a rather dangerous way of finding out things?" Wilson Hitchings inquired.

"Please," said Mr. Moto. "So many things I do are dangerous. Besides, if I found out what I wish, I should be very, very pleased to die. If I do not find out, I am afraid that I must kill myself, so that all is very much the same."

"You don't look like a fanatic," Wilson Hitchings said.

"I am not," said Mr. Moto. "The day before you arrived, Mr. Hitchings, for I traveled very fast to get here, I called on the lady who is with you. She asked me to come back tonight. She said that she would tell me something that would interest me. She said that she did not like your family, Mr. Hitchings."

"That's true, I don't," Eva Hitchings said.

"You were present at the interview tonight," Mr. Moto continued, "and now I think you can understand my line of thought. You arrived quite suddenly, Mr. Hitchings. Mr. Chang had an account at Hitchings Brothers here. His money was used at that very nice gambling table and I was shot at in the dark. Please excuse me for suspecting you, Mr. Hitchings. Perhaps you will agree that it was natural. Hitchings Brothers and Hitchings Plantation seemed quite the same to me and very, very clever. Now I know that I was wrong. Nevertheless, the only thing I need to know now, I am very, very sure, is how Mr. Chang's money disappears at Hitchings Plantation and appears in Manchukuo.

"It has been a very clever and a very unusual device, that way of passing money, and a difficult method to trace. That is its great advantage. Please, may I make myself clearer? Usually in such cases, a sum of money is passed from one person to another. The person who receives it may be identified eventually by suitable police methods, but here it is like water thrown on sand. These funds disappear across the table to a number of different persons or to the house. I do not quite know how the method is worked. It is not perhaps important, but there is one thing of which I am now very sure. The money which is lost from Mr. Chang's account is collected all together and is given to a single individual who comes here at intervals and takes it away. I believe he is coming quite soon. When I find who that person is, the whole plan will break down. A few simple words over the cable to suitable authorities will make it possible to have him stopped. The person who finally takes the money—his identity is all that I wish to know."

Mr. Moto paused and rubbed his hands.

"Please," he said, "Miss Hitchings, will you tell me now what you were going to say tonight?"

Eva Hitchings clasped her hands together in her lap and sat up straight, then she shook her head.

"I think you know enough already, Mr. Moto," she answered. Her voice was cool and hard. "And I think you're so clever that I don't need to tell you anything. I was almost taken in by your trick about the whisky. I think you'll be able to manage Mr. Hitchings very well by yourself and perhaps I had better leave you, so that you won't be embarrassed. I think I'll be going now."

For a moment Wilson Hitchings found it difficult to speak.

"Don't you believe me?" he said. "Don't you believe me at all?"

Eva Hitchings' glance was cold and self-possessed. She pushed a strand of hair from her forehead, folded her hands again.

"If you really want to know what I think," she said, "I think you're the smoothest liar since Ananias. I think you can tell Mr. Moto exactly what's happening to that money, and I rather think that Mr. Moto knows that you can tell him. I still believe what I told you on the beach, Mr. Hitchings. You never meant to touch that drink on the table—did you?"

For the first time that day Wilson Hitchings realized that he was very tired. He felt a weariness which numbed his ability to reason and it placed him beyond surprise and beyond incredulity.

"I don't exactly understand you," he said.

Eva Hitchings shrugged her bare, brown shoulders.

"I've noticed that you don't understand anything," she remarked. "You're quite attractive when you are naïve. I imagine Mr. Moto understands you. I don't think you've fooled either of us."

"Yes," said Mr. Moto. "Thank you very much." He seemed about to continue, and then he stopped and lowered his voice to a whisper.

"Be quiet, please," he whispered. "Do not say a word, please. Sit just as you are. Someone is coming up the path."

Then Wilson knew that Mr. Moto must have been listening all the time and that his ears were very keen. For several seconds Wilson could hear nothing except that soft, ceaseless, tropical trade wind which seemed to form a background to all life, and then he heard a footstep; a quick, decisive footstep. The sound made him move uneasily.

"Quiet," hissed Mr. Moto. "Quiet, please!" There was an insistence in Mr. Moto's whisper which made him absolutely still and Eva Hitchings' face made him even quieter. Her face was a little pale. Her lips were half-parted and her self-confidence and irony were gone with the sound of the footsteps. They were coming nearer. They stopped and Wilson knew that someone was pausing before the window of the cottage. Then there was another sound. Whoever it was outside was walking up the porch steps directly to the door.

The back of Wilson's neck was cold and his mouth was dry, and if he had tried, he could not have moved just then. Mr. Moto was standing on the palm mat in the center of the room, still with a faint mechanical smile. Softly but deliberately, Mr. Moto thrust his right hand into the side pocket of his coat. The steps had stopped by the door and again there was not a sound except for the wind. Then there was a rapping on the door. The sound seemed very loud in the stillness of the room but Mr. Moto did not move or speak. Then the knob of the door turned and the door was opened briskly.

Wilson could not have said what he expected to see, but the actual sight was a complete anticlimax. A man stood in the doorway, dressed in a light linen suit and wearing a panama hat that had a band of feathers round it, a peculiar product of the Islands which Wilson had already noticed. A thin, oldish man, with a close-cropped mustache and a lean, tan face. . . . Wilson remembered the droop of the mouth, half good-natured, half querulous, and the benign, rather lazy cast of the eyes. It was Mr. Wilkie, the Office Manager of Hitchings Brothers, standing in the door. Mr. Wilkie stood for a moment, quite motionless, as though the light confused him.

"Excuse me," he said quickly. "I was looking for—" and then he saw Eva Hitchings. It was plain that he had not noticed her at first, because his voice changed.

"Why, Eva," said Mr. Wilkie "—so there you are, you little hide-and-seek. I've been looking for you everywhere!"

Eva Hitchings stood up and she laughed a quick, nervous laugh of complete relief.

"Why, Uncle Joe," she said, "you didn't need to look. I don't need a caretaker!" She rose and walked toward him, still laughing, and Mr. Wilkie placed his arm around her shoulders.

"Oh, yes, you do," he said. "At least I think you do. Good evening, Mr. Hitchings. Eva always seems like a little girl to me, like my own little girl. I still get worried when she's out alone at night. They told me that she'd taken you home, Mr. Hitchings, and when she did not come back, well, I thought that I might as well go and find her. Of course nothing can happen to anyone on these Islands, not since King Kamehameha laid down the law that women and children were safe wherever they went; but there is a time for girls to go to bed, even nowadays. I saw Eva's car by the hotel and walked over to the beach, then one of the boys over at the filling station told me that they had seen Eva coming here, and one of the boys at the Seaside had seen her walk this way. And I knew that Eva was at her old tricks again, forgetting what time it was, forgetting that it was after one o'clock; so the old man has come to take her home. I am sure that Mr. Hitchings understands."

"Certainly," said Wilson. "I was just about to take her back myself, Mr. Wilkie. We just stopped in to call on Mr. Moto. My uncle introduced me to him in Shanghai."

"Yes," said Mr. Moto. "It has been so very nice and it is so nice of you to come, sir. May I not offer you a glass of whisky, Mr.—Mr. . . . ?"

"Mr. Wilkie," said Wilson. "Excuse me; this is Mr. Wilkie, Mr. Moto, the Manager of Hitchings Brothers' Branch."

Mr. Moto bowed.

"I am so honored," he said, "so very, very honored. I have been to call on Mr. Wilkie, but twice he was out. Please, will you not have some whisky, Mr. Wilkie?"

"No, thank you," Mr. Wilkie said. "Some other time, but not tonight. I've just come to take my little girl away. If you are ready, Eva?"

"All right, Uncle Joe," said Eva. "Good night, Mr. Moto. Good night, Mr. Hitchings."

Mr. Moto stood at his doorway, watching the two walk down the path—for a longer time, it seemed to Wilson, than was necessary. Then Mr. Moto closed the door gently and looked at Wilson Hitchings. His face was tranquil and passive, and he was not smiling. He had withdrawn his right hand from his pocket and was rubbing both his hands together gently, in a curious half-submissive gesture.

Wilson walked to the tray with the whisky bottle.

"Well," he said, "I'll have a drink now, if you don't mind?"

Mr. Moto did not move but he spoke very gently.

"First," he said, "I think you had better smell that whisky carefully, Mr. Hitchings, and then if you are tired of life, pour yourself a little in the glass. Everything will be over reasonably quickly, although the effect of cyanide is not as rapid as is usually supposed. It depends on the condition of the individual and when he has eaten. Nevertheless it is a very, very deadly poison—but you are an educated man; I do not need to tell you that."

"Then you weren't fooling me?" Wilson Hitchings asked "—the way she said?"

"No," said Mr. Moto. "That would be what you call in your country a cheap trick. I am not cheap, Mr. Hitchings, at least not very often, I hope.

"No. Mr. Hitchings, please, I have meant what I said to you and I have believed exactly what you said. You know nothing about this matter and I am very, very glad that it is so. Will you permit me, if I give you now my humble but best advice?"

Mr. Moto walked closer to Wilson Hitchings.

"I have believed you, Mr. Hitchings," he said, "but I am very, very sorry that I do not believe the young lady. I am so sorry to say that I do not think she is very nice. I should be very careful of her, Mr. Hitchings. I should not see her again."

Wilson Hitchings was surprised at his own answer. He was indignant without knowing that he would be.

"You're wrong there," he said, earnestly. "I'll guarantee you that Miss Hitchings has nothing to do with this, absolutely nothing. There's no doubt there is a bad element in that place of hers, because I have seen some of them myself. I suppose a bad crowd gets into every such establishment; but it isn't Miss Hitchings' fault. She accused me of being mixed up in this. She would hardly do that, if she were involved."

"Why not?" said Mr. Moto gently. "Please, will you answer me why not?"

Wilson scowled and was surprised. He found Mr. Moto's question hard to answer.

"Well, she wouldn't," he said. "She's honest, Mr. Moto."

Mr. Moto blinked and for the first time it seemed to Wilson Hitchings that there was genuine amusement in Mr. Moto's smile.

"Excuse me," he said, "please, excuse me, Mr. Hitchings, if I say something which is not very, very nice. Please, I have been to very many places in both Europe and America during the course of my work and my education. I have seen many types of people and there is one thing I have observed about your great country, Mr. Hitchings. You do not treat women very realistically. You think they are all very nice, because they are women. You think Miss Hitchings is very nice. Why? Because you think she is beautiful. You like her wide violet eyes. You enjoy the flame color in her hair and no doubt the way she swings herself when she walks. Excuse me, please. I come from a race with a tradition which is very, very different. Excuse me, I do not think Miss Hitchings is beautiful at all. Please, that is why I can see her more clearly than you do, Mr. Hitchings. A beautiful woman is so very, very confusing to a man. He desires her. Excuse me for my rudeness, but you desire Miss Hitchings."

"I don't," said Wilson Hitchings, quickly. "I don't, at all. I am only trying to be fair."

"I hope so much that you will excuse me, please, when I make myself so very rude as to contradict, because I do it to be nice. She interests you, Mr. Hitchings, very, very much; and she knows it—women always know. She is playing with you, Mr. Hitchings. She is clever to put the blame on you because she thinks I may be deceived by it. Believe me, I am not deceived. She is in company which is not very nice. No one in that company can be nice."

"Now, wait a minute," Wilson interrupted. "Miss Hitchings is a distant relative of mine. She's had a hard time. Her father lost his money."

Mr. Moto shrugged his shoulders.

"Please," he said. "Please, stop, Mr. Hitchings. All such persons have an interesting history which is very, very sad. The life of everyone, I think, is very, very sad; but misfortune must not interfere with logic. It is fortunate for you, I think, that she came here with you tonight, because I can help you very much. You have come only to close the Hitchings Plantation. Honolulu is so very, very beautiful. There are so very many things to do. Amuse yourself, please, after this. Bathe in the warm seas. See the other pretty girls. Listen to the lovely music. Sit in the sun and think, but not about this affair, Mr. Hitchings. You are out of it, now. I think, when I am through, that Miss Hitchings will be very, very glad to close her establishment. And now that matters have gone as far as this, they will move very, very quickly. Please, you need not give it another thought. You only have to wait."

Mr. Moto lighted a cigarette.

"Yes," he said. "This is my business. You only have to wait."

In spite of his small size, Mr. Moto looked grimly adequate and Wilson Hitchings could understand his logic. What he could not understand was his own reluctance to agree. Although he knew that Mr. Moto was right, he knew that he could not leave things as they were. He tried to think it was a sense of responsibility which prompted him, but he knew it was not that. It had something to do with the grim finality of Mr. Moto's voice. He did not want to leave Eva Hitchings to Mr. Moto. He wanted to attend to Eva Hitchings himself. He wanted to see her again. He wanted to speak to her again, and it was utterly unthinkable that he should not be allowed to do it.

"You're wrong, Mr. Moto," he said. "I'm in this as much as you."

"Please," said Mr. Moto. "I do not understand."

"I am out here to represent my family," Wilson said. "I was sent here to deal with Miss Hitchings, and I am going to."

"Please," said Mr. Moto. "It is dangerous. There is no need."

"Never mind," said Wilson Hitchings. "I am going to. You needn't worry about me, Mr. Moto."

"I shall be sorry for you," said Mr. Moto. "Very, very sorry. What are you going to do?"

"Tomorrow morning," Wilson said, "I am going to speak to Mr. Wilkie."

"I should not do that," said Mr. Moto. "It will do no good."

"Well, I am going to," Wilson Hitchings said.

"Please, may I give you a present? You will need it very much, I think." Mr. Moto's hand moved to his pocket. He was holding out an automatic pistol.

"Nonsense," said Wilson. "I won't need that. No, thank you. Good night, Mr. Moto."

"You are sure you will not take it?" Mr. Moto said. "You may need it even before you get to your hotel. Good night, Mr. Hitchings. I am so very, very sorry."

It was after two in the morning when Wilson Hitchings reached his room in his hotel and locked the door very carefully behind him. Once he was inside his room, where all his personal belongings lay methodically and neatly according to his habit, nearly everything which had happened that day assumed grotesque proportions. The wind and the sound of the surf on the reef had dropped to a lazy reassuring murmur and he could feel around him nothing but security. It was the old security in which he had been bred and reared, where nothing happened which was unusual—nothing which was not the result of balanced thought and plan. Viewed in that perspective, the entire day and night seemed to move beyond his mental grasp as something to be discounted, as something which had not actually occurred; and now his mind was busy proving that many things meant nothing. The impressions which were crowded on him were too numerous to be assimilated and his mind was tossing half of those impressions into discard. The internal struggles in the former province of Manchuria were too far beyond him to disturb him any more than the threats that Mr. Moto made of personal danger. He could believe it was complete exaggeration now that he was alone. The faces and the voices which he had heard, now that he was trying to get to sleep, had become as unconvincing as those of actors in a badly directed play. There was only one face of the entire gallery which remained with him as evidence of actual experience.

He could not, although he tried deliberately, push Eva Hitchings from his mind. She was so entirely different from anything he imagined that his thoughts dwelt on her speculatively. He could still hear the irony of her voice. He could recall the way the light glittered in her hair. He could remember a dozen half-graceful, half-careless gestures; the way she had pulled petulantly at the shoulder strap of that red dress with white flowers, the contemptuous ease with which she had driven her car, the way her eyes had met his squarely, more like a man's eyes than a woman's. Hers was the only face in that gallery which stood out distinctly and which had nothing furtive about it, nothing deceitful and nothing ugly. And he knew why she was distinct to him and he knew that his conviction was not induced by sentiment as Mr. Moto had said. It was because she did not belong with those others, because she had an integrity which all those others lacked. She had been completely frank with him on her likes and dislikes. She did not belong there. She was entirely alone. There had been moments, too, when he believed she was afraid; and in a sense he felt responsible for that isolation of hers because, in a way, it was the fault of his own family. He knew that he could not leave her and keep his conscience clear, without giving her another chance to get away from the situation in which she was placed. He was convinced that his intuition was right, that she was in some sort of trouble.

He closed his eyes and he could hear the music at Hitchings Plantation. Then the music died out and he seemed to be back in that dark-paneled room with the green rays of the gaming table beneath its hard white light. He could hear the clinking of the counters and the soft whirr of the wheel and the oily-faced croupier was saying: "*Rien ne va plus.*"

He knew that the wheel was crooked. There was not much doubt that one of the men beside it could manipulate it, so that the house could either win or lose. That was the last thing he remembered thinking before he fell asleep.

# 7

HE WAS awakened by the ringing of his telephone. His sleep must have been very light, because the sound of the jangling bell ran through him like a shock of electricity that aroused him to complete and instant consciousness. Yet, in spite of his awareness of everything around him, he had that sensation, that everyone must have experienced at some time or other, of a temporary lack of memory, of not knowing exactly where he was. The room was full of sunlight, the breeze was blowing the curtain of his open window and he heard that restless perpetual sound of the sea. He almost believed that he was at home on a June morning until he saw his dressing-case on his bureau and heard the sea. He was still trying to gather his thoughts together when he picked up the telephone. A girl's voice was speaking in a mechanical, impersonal way—peculiar to the switchboard operator of a large office or hotel.

"Mr. Hitchings," the operator was saying, "there's a man downstairs who wants to see you. His name is Mr. Maddock."

"Mr.—who?" said Wilson.

"Mr. Maddock," the operator said. "Shall I tell him to go up?"

Then everything came back to Wilson Hitchings. The telephone had awakened his body and now the name had awakened everything in his mind. He remembered Mr. Maddock very clearly and not very pleasantly. He looked at his watch and found it was after ten o'clock.

"Send him up," said Wilson, "and send up a waiter, please. I want some breakfast." He shoved his bare feet into his slippers and put on a silk dressing-gown and looked at himself carefully in the mirror, as he brushed his straight, brown hair. He was pleased to see that his face looked serene, although he felt very much disturbed. He sat down with his back to the open window, with an empty chair opposite him, waiting.

"You must be very careful," he said to himself. "You must try to use your mind." He tried to use his mind while he waited. He tried to recall everything he had observed about Mr. Maddock, none of which was particularly reassuring, but he did not have long to wait. Mr. Maddock rapped on the door. When Wilson told him to come in, his visitor edged himself sideways through the half-open door and closed it softly behind him. There was a smoothness and a caution about Mr. Maddock's entrance which made Wilson wonder whether the action was instinctive or assumed. Mr. Maddock's yellowish eyes focused themselves studiously upon the details of the room before he spoke.

"Hi," said Mr. Maddock and he waved a skinny arm in a genial, loose-jointed gesture. His Adam's apple moved convulsively and he smiled, a swift, confidential smile.

"Hi," said Wilson Hitchings, and examined Mr. Maddock, as Mr. Maddock continued to examine the room. Mr. Maddock looked as stringy as ever, but he was beautifully turned out in a fresh light-tan Palm Beach suit which fitted closely around his narrow waist. His shoes were white buckskin, his tie was a salmon-colored foulard, his black hair was glossed to a patent-leather finish.

"Nice rooms they have here," Mr. Maddock said.

Wilson pointed to the empty chair.

"You can sit down there, if you want to," Wilson told him, "and a waiter will be up in just a minute to take my order for breakfast. I thought perhaps you'd like to know."

Mr. Maddock sat down and adjusted the creases of his trousers and stared at Wilson, unblinkingly.

"Wise guy, ain't you?" Mr. Maddock said, "and I suppose you're going to write on the order blank to have the house dick waiting in the corridor. Yea, I spotted you for a wise guy. Skip it, pal. There's no rough stuff. This is a purely social, confidential call, and I think you'll like it, pal, really I do."

Wilson smiled brightly at Mr. Maddock.

"No poison in the whisky, Mr. Maddock?" he inquired. It was a shot in the dark and he knew it, but his question did not appear to surprise Mr. Maddock in the least. He raised his dark eyebrows slightly and his long fingers hung limply on the arms of his chair.

"You go around nights, don't you, pal?" said Mr. Maddock, softly.

"Sometimes," Wilson said.

Mr. Maddock leaned his head against the chair back and half-closed his yellow eyes.

"Listen, pal," he said. "I'm a guy who's got to be careful. I am always careful, that's why I'm here on the damn Island with the ukuleles and the grass skirts and not back home where I belong. I got too much on my own mind for rough stuff. Besides, I don't like it on an island, wise guy. Guess why if you want to." Mr. Maddock made his fingers move in an engaging wavelike gesture. "Too much water. It's too damn hard to get off an island, and there's one island I don't want to try getting off of—Alcatraz Island, San Francisco Bay. . . . Snow, pal, if you don't get my drift."

"I suppose you mean to imply that you have a criminal record, Mr. Maddock," said Wilson, and he felt more at ease than he had, because Mr. Maddock's cool indolence was reassuring. He even found himself growing interested in Mr. Maddock, and aware that he was faced with an unusual opportunity to study an unknown world. "You really didn't need to tell me, Mr. Maddock," Wilson continued. I guessed as soon as I saw you that you were on the Public Enemy list."

"Okay, pal," said Mr. Maddock, softly. "All this is just a big vacation. This racket is small-time. . . . Snow, if you don't get my drift."

"Very well," said Wilson. "I'll snow if I don't. Please go on, Mr. Maddock."

Mr. Maddock opened his eyes dreamily and half-closed them again.

"The spot is getting hot," said Mr. Maddock gently. "I don't want no steam room. I want ear muffs. . . . Snow, if you don't get my drift."

"You are fond of that expression, aren't you, Mr. Maddock?"

Mr. Maddock closed his eyes.

"Yes," he said; "but I don't use snow, pal, and I don't drink or smoke and I don't step out with any finger molls. I am always God-damn careful."

"It's nice of you to be so frank," Wilson said. "You make me feel so much easier. Do you live at the Y.M.C.A., Mr. Maddock?"

Mr. Maddock's lips curled upward and his shoulders shook but he made no sound of merriment.

"Funny guy, pal, aren't you?" he said. "And you got a damn dead-pan. It's comical, you're kind of new to me."

"You're new to me too, Mr. Maddock," Wilson Hitchings said. "But snow, if you don't get my drift."

"I've never snowed yet," Mr. Maddock said. "I've never snowed on anybody, pal. You're a wise guy. You and me can play."

"Play what?" asked Wilson Hitchings.

"Ball," said Mr. Maddock. "Ball, pal." Mr. Maddock half-closed his eyes again and sighed and Wilson Hitchings could feel his own interest growing. At any rate, he was playing a word game with Mr. Maddock and experimenting purely with an unknown quantity and beginning to delve incredulously into Mr. Maddock's past.

"Do I understand that you are making me a proposition?" he inquired.

Mr. Maddock gazed at the fingers on his right hand, blew softly on his fingernails and polished them on his coat sleeve.

"Pierre and I were talking about you last night," he said. "You'd really like Pierre."

"I'm afraid I don't know him," Wilson said.

"The guy who speaks French," Mr. Maddock explained. "The croupier at the table last night. He's a pal of mine. You'd really like Pierre."

There was a knock on the door. It was the waiter with the menu card.

"Will you join me?" Wilson asked.

"Sure," said Mr. Maddock. "A glass of hot milk, please." Mr. Maddock closed his eyes and sighed, but when the waiter was gone, he opened them again.

"First Pierre and me placed you for a college boy," said Mr. Maddock, and his voice was more incisive; "then we didn't, when you played the wheel."

"It's a crooked wheel, isn't it?" said Wilson.

Mr. Maddock signed again. "Yes," he said, "it's crooked, pal. Don't act dumb, pal. It's so crooked that it's hot. It's too damn hot and I don't like the crowd. When they propositioned me, I fell for it as a straight gambling proposition, when it ain't. Them Russians and them Chinks—they're too damn jumpy, pal. I'm used to big shots who keep cool. They got the jitters and they tried to kill the Jap last night. You know, you're wise. Well, an island ain't no place. First that Jap guy comes. Then you come, and now the little lady is getting wise. There isn't anybody out there at the dump with a business head. They haven't been in the wars, like I've been, pal. They got the jitters and they're going to blow wide open. There's no executive ability. Pierre and me, we're going to lam. Snow, if you don't get my drift."

Wilson Hitchings watched Mr. Maddock's unblinking yellowish eyes.

"You're being rather frank, aren't you?" he inquired.

"Yes," said Mr. Maddock. "Because I'm too hot for trouble, pal. I'm just looking for the angle where I can cash and lam."

The waiter came with the breakfast tray and Mr. Maddock closed his eyes again. Then he sipped his hot milk, daintily, and drew a purple handkerchief from his breast pocket and wiped his lips.

"And you've come to me for cash?" Wilson Hitchings suggested.

Mr. Maddock set down his glass of milk.

"Yes; you or the Jap, pal," he said, "and when I cross I'd rather cross to a white man. I set you down for a right guy, pal. Here's the picture. Snow, if you don't get my drift."

"Go ahead," said Wilson. "Don't let me stop you, Mr. Maddock."

Mr. Maddock sat up straighter and his fingers closed gently around the arms of his chair.

"Last night you propositioned the little lady," Mr. Maddock said, "because the name of her house hurts your business. You propositioned her to buy for a hundred grand and close it out. The little lady turned you down."

"You think so?" said Wilson, carefully. "How do you know that?"

"Don't worry, pal," said Mr. Maddock. "The crowd's got ways of knowing. They don't want the house closed just yet, but I can tell you something that can close it, pal. The authorities"—Mr. Maddock drew out his handkerchief and wiped his lips—"won't stand for the racket unless it is quiet and refined. They've said as much. Well, here's the proposition, pal. I know something that will close that house so tight it will never open. No one would dare to open it and it won't cost you a hundred grand either to know it, pal. Five grand is my price and you can pay either by personal check or cash. You can close the little lady out for five grand and she's through. She's only the front, pal. She's not worth a hundred grand and I'm putting it to you straight. If you don't think what I tell you is worth the money, you tell me. How about it, pal? Snow, if you get my drift."

"You mean you're going to squeal?" Wilson Hitchings asked.

"Yes," said Mr. Maddock. "I mean I am going to squeal."

Wilson Hitchings lighted a cigarette and thought carefully what he would say next.

"I suppose," he spoke slowly, watching Mr. Maddock, "you're going to tell me that money is being sent to Manchuria. It isn't worth the price. I know it already, Mr. Maddock."

The Adam's apple moved in Mr. Maddock's throat. He opened his eyes and half-closed them.

"Wise guy," he said, "ain't you, pal?"

"Do you think so?" Wilson Hitchings asked. "It never occurred to me until I came here that I was particularly wise."

Mr. Maddock nodded dreamily.

"Yea, I think you are," he said. "I think you're a damn wise guy. Any time you want a job back home in a real organization, I might put in a word for you. You've told me all I need to know. I'm picking up the marbles, pal, and calling it a day. They got a Hawaiian word for it out here. I'm *pau.* That means I'm washing up. Kind of tough on the little lady, too. She had a nice layout before we muscled in, but I guess she's *pau.* Thanks for the information."

"You're very welcome," Wilson Hitchings said. He could guess without exactly knowing what Mr. Maddock was thanking him for. He could believe that Mr. Maddock was speaking the exact truth, and that someone knew too much. Already someone knew too much about money going into Manchuria and Wilson could guess who it was. He was very sure that the work in which Mr. Maddock was engaged was genuinely distasteful to him.

Mr. Maddock half-reclined in his chair and gave no sign of leaving.

"Well"—he said—"There's five grand gone; not that I was betting on it, pal. I wonder if you would tell me something, just idle curiosity." Mr. Maddock's eyes opened wider. "Will that Jap G-man come in when the pay-off comes tonight? It's a nice-sized roll that's going."

Wilson Hitchings tried to copy Mr. Maddock's languor. He tried to show no more interest than Mr. Maddock showed.

"I don't know what you are talking about," he said, "but go ahead. I am interested."

Mr. Maddock rubbed his fingers on his coat sleeve.

"Nuts," he said. "One of the carrier pigeons is going out tonight, but then I guess you're wise. Well, I think I'll be moving. Thank you for the hot milk, pal." Mr. Maddock drew his feet from beneath the chair, and prepared to rise.

"Just a minute," Wilson said. "Just a minute before you go. What was your idea in coming here, Mr. Maddock? Do you want to tell me, or shall I guess?"

Mr. Maddock rose and brushed his coat.

"You don't have to guess," he said. "I've told you, pal, and you're not snowing, because you got my drift. I came here to see how much you knew and you know plenty. Not as much as I thought you did—but plenty. You know enough so that the spiggety crowd I'm in won't sit still and be reasonable. I told you, I won't be mixed up in a killing on an island. For you, you can suit yourself, but for me, I know when it's time to lam. I'm telling you the truth and you're wise enough to know it. Take care of yourself. I'll be seeing you sometime, pal." Mr. Maddock nodded, waved his right hand genially, and opened the door with his left and moved out sideways, while Wilson Hitchings stood in his dressing-gown, staring after him.

Even when Mr. Maddock was gone, the echo of his homely phrases seemed to remain in the room. Wilson Hitchings drew his hand across his forehead. He had never realized before that the world was made up of so many divergent personalities. He had never seen anyone less trustworthy than Mr. Maddock. Nevertheless, he was almost sure that Mr. Maddock had been telling him the truth, that there was something weighing heavily on Mr. Maddock's mind. There was no longer any doubt, also, that Mr. Moto had been telling him the truth. The Hitchings Plantation was only a façade and Eva Hitchings was only a part of that façade.

"I've got to get her out of this," Wilson Hitchings spoke out loud. "She doesn't understand them. She can't understand."

Then it occurred to him that it would do no good for him to reason with her. He must speak to someone whose judgment she would respect. His mind turned logically to Mr. Wilkie, the Manager of Hitchings Brothers. He remembered Mr. Wilkie had said that Eva Hitchings was like his own little girl, and Mr. Wilkie was an honest man. He would talk to him that morning and Mr. Wilkie would talk to Eva Hitchings.

He was pleased with his decision, because he knew it was just the sort of thing the family would have applauded. Mr. Wilkie had been employed by Hitchings Brothers for a long while—too long, Wilson thought, for there to be the slightest doubt as to his personal integrity. No matter what his feelings toward Hitchings Plantation might have been, now that there was a possibility of the Hitchings Banking House becoming involved in an unsavory matter Mr. Wilkie would undoubtedly be loyal. Besides, he certainly did not know that Eva Hitchings might be in definite danger.

## 8

THERE WAS not the slightest doubt in Wilson Hitchings' mind that he was doing the proper thing that morning. The day was enough to confirm his opinion; the air was neither hot nor cold, the sun was out, and white clouds moved slowly across the sky keeping pace with the gentle breeze. All along the road to the city there were hedges of oleander and hibiscus, and the sea was a fine dark blue; the soft greens of the Island and the cloud haze over the tops of the mountains made a contrast against that level blueness of the sea which was restful and reassuring. The city itself had that same reassuring quality of solidity and ease. Wilson Hitchings could believe that nothing out of the ordinary could possibly happen here, in a day that was too clear and in a life that was too pleasant for undue exertion.

The offices of Hitchings Brothers had that same sort of solidity and ease. There was no undue hurry in the high, cool outer rooms, but Wilson Hitchings was pleased to see that he was known already, and he was shown at once to Mr. Wilkie's office, without any questions being asked.

Mr. Wilkie's manner was different, also. He rose and hurried around the corner of his desk, hospitably.

"Now this is a coincidence," Mr. Wilkie said. "You've been on my mind all morning, a clear case of guilty conscience. I'm afraid I wasn't—well—not very hospitable yesterday. It was the surprise of your arrival, and it was a busy day."

"Please don't be worried," Wilson said. "I imagine you have been worried, Mr. Wilkie."

"Only worried because I may have appeared casual," Mr. Wilkie said. "But I made a plan this morning. I hope you will fall in with it. I was just going to telephone you. I was about to send you a cordial invitation." Mr. Wilkie paused and smiled. "Perhaps your uncle told you that I had a sea-going boat?"

"Why yes, he did," said Wilson. He spoke politely, although it made him impatient that Mr. Wilkie's mind should have turned to yachting at such a time.

"It's a hobby of mine," said Mr. Wilkie. "I suppose a rather expensive hobby, but you might take advantage of it on a day like this. I was going to ask if you wouldn't like to take my sampan for a turn outside the harbor, and I've asked—a friend—to go with you. I've ordered lunch put aboard, in case you'd like to go. I hope you will because it will combine business and pleasure, in a way."

Some time later in trying to recall the circumstances which surrounded that offer of Mr. Wilkie's, Wilson Hitchings could only remember with surprise the simplicity of his own reaction when he received it. He remembered that his uncle had implied that boating was an outside pleasure which perhaps took Mr. Wilkie's attention away too much from business. Mr. Wilkie's appearance that morning was too good natured, too much like a man of leisure . . . and yet he might have been wrong. The entire atmosphere of the Island was so genial that morning that perhaps Mr. Wilkie represented something that Hitchings Brothers needed there in the way of friendliness and good will.

"Exactly what is a sampan?" Wilson asked.

Mr. Wilkie's laugh was enough to show that any pique he may have felt toward Wilson the day before had entirely evaporated.

"I forgot you were a *malihini,*" Mr. Wilkie said. "That means a newcomer to the Island, in case you don't know the word. We all get to using a bit of the Polynesian language out here. You will too, if you stay long enough, and I keep forgetting that a Hitchings doesn't know the Island as well as I do. I was worried yesterday and you must forgive me for it. I might have known that you would be absolutely fair in dealing with Eva. But to get back to what I was saying. You don't know what a sampan is, then. It is a vessel designed by the Japanese fishing fleet here. You may have seen some on your way from the hotel. They are about as seaworthy a craft as you can find anywhere. They are used by the tuna fishers, for expeditions sometimes a thousand miles offshore. They are a sturdy type of Diesel motor craft, built along Japanese lines, with modern Diesel engines. Mine has a cruising radius of more than two thousand miles. I use my sampan for fishing and cruises about the Islands, and for moonlight picnics. I always offer visitors a trip aboard her. I hope you will say you will go." Mr. Wilkie paused. His mild brown eyes were kindly. "I hope you'll say you'll go, because I asked Eva to go with you."

Wilson Hitchings laid down his hat on the corner of Mr. Wilkie's desk at the same time he tried to lay aside any expression of doubt or astonishment.

"I can't imagine that she accepted," he said, "but I am glad you brought her name up. I came here to talk to you about her. Do you mind if I close the door?"

Mr. Wilkie closed the door himself and sat down behind his desk.

"I am very glad of that," he said, seriously, "because I wanted to do the same thing, Hitchings. I talked to Eva seriously last night and I have been thinking of her a good deal this morning. She told me about the offer you made. I had never believed that you would make her an offer so fair and generous. Frankly, I wanted her to accept that offer and I wanted her to forget all her pique. You probably feel as I do that a gambling house is no place for Eva. It's a gesture on her part that has gone far enough. I think if she can get to know you better, if she can understand that you are perfectly sincere, she will agree to everything. That is why I suggest a few hours at lunch today. I know as well as you do that we must clear this matter up."

Wilson remembered something which his uncle had said in Shanghai, while Mr. Wilkie was speaking. His uncle had spoken of a connoisseur's ability to judge a picture. His uncle had said that an amateur might see nothing wrong but to an experienced observer the values might not be right. There was something wrong in the picture now. There was something wrong about Mr. Wilkie. He was betraying an excitement which was not natural. His eyes were too bright. He was laboring under some excitement beyond Wilson's knowledge but there was one thing of which Wilson was sure. For some reason of his own, Mr. Wilkie wanted him out of the way. He wanted him aboard that boat. He remembered that his uncle had spoken of Mr. Wilkie's sampan. He could not help remembering that only yesterday Mr. Wilkie had been almost hostile. He presented his last thought to Mr. Wilkie in a question which was almost blunt. As he did so, he looked at Mr. Wilkie again. There was no doubt that Mr. Wilkie was agitated—in spite of all his efforts to be casual.

"You didn't feel this way yesterday. What has made you change?" he asked.

Mr. Wilkie's face grew serious.

"Sober afterthought, if you want the truth," he said. "Eva is like my own little girl, Mr. Hitchings. I have felt her wrongs very keenly and I have felt the anomalous position in which she has been put through no fault of her own. When you came here yeterday, your assurance annoyed me; but I am over all that now. The best thing for Eva and the best thing for the firm is to have her take your offer. Eva understands it now, I think. She'll be down at the sampan in half an hour."

Wilson Hitchings listened carefully; his opinion of Mr. Wilkie was falling as he listened. It seemed to him that Mr. Wilkie was not the man to be head of the Hitchings office; that he was weak and full of contradictions.

"I am wondering," Wilson said, "just what you heard about

Hitchings Plantation to make you change your mind. Have you heard anything, Mr. Wilkie?"

Mr. Wilkie opened his mouth and closed it.

"Heard about Hitchings Plantation?" he answered. "Why, what is there to hear? It's a trifle illegal, but it's conducted by the authorities, and it's very well conducted. I never go there, myself, except to see Eva now and then. I don't understand you, Hitchings. What could I have heard?"

The very vagueness of Mr. Wilkie's answer made Wilson believe him. It was the answer of a man who had allowed himself to fall into a languid rut until he had become oblivious to everything, except what went on immediately around him.

"Then you don't know who runs the gambling end of the establishment for her?" Wilson inquired.

"Why yes," Mr. Wilkie answered. "Of course I know. Eva has hired some professionals, of course. A Mr. Maddock and some others. Rather unusual types, but they are honest. What do you mean to imply, Hitchings?"

"Would it surprise you," Wilson Hitchings asked, "if I told you that I had a talk with Mr. Maddock this morning in which he told me that something so serious is going on there that he is planning to leave?"

Mr. Wilkie raised his hands and dropped them softly in front of him on the desk. "Good God!" he said. "What has been going on?"

There was such astonishment in Mr. Wilkie's voice that Wilson was almost sorry for him. There was not much further doubt in his mind that Mr. Wilkie had been very careless of the interests of the firm. There would be trouble for Wilkie when they heard of it at home.

"That's just what I am going to find out," answered Wilson Hitchings, slowly. "I'll tell you what I know. I am sure no one suspected anything like this, when my uncle sent me here. A Japanese secret service agent is watching the Plantation, Mr. Wilkie. He is watching it because there is a gang there which is using the establishment as a means of transferring money from China to revolutionaries in Manchuria. The funds are first deposited in this Branch of Hitchings Brothers, Mr. Wilkie."

Mr. Wilkie rose and leaned against the desk.

"You are not serious," he said. His speech was hoarse and uncertain. "It—it isn't possible."

"I'm afraid it is," Wilson answered steadily. He was sorry for Mr. Wilkie, but he blamed him also, for his complete carelessness and lack of observation. "I'm afraid that you and Miss Eva have been used by some rather unscrupulous persons. A Chinese, named Chang Lo-Shih, has been forwarding money here. It has been taken to Hitchings Plantation and distributed. I think I can find out exactly how, tonight, but in the meanwhile, you had better get Miss Eva out of there because it is dangerous. Also we must get the Bank cleared of all this. I hope you understand."

There was no doubt any longer that Mr. Wilkie understood, and also that it was a blow to Mr. Wilkie. The color had drained from his face, making him look old and uncertain.

"We had better call for the police," he said, hoarsely. "This must be stopped at once—at once."

"No," said Wilson, quickly. "That's exactly what we mustn't do. We mustn't get the Bank involved in any such publicity. I want to get to the bottom of this myself, because I represent the family. There mustn't be any talk until we find out how the transfer is made. I think I can find out tonight. In the meanwhile I am going to send a cable to Shanghai. Miss Hitchings must be kept out of it. I'll leave that part to you."

Mr. Wilkie squared his shoulders.

"You must talk to Eva yourself," he said. "I could swear that Eva doesn't know a thing about this. Yes, I can see. We must go on as though we know nothing. I shall go over the Chang account. I am right behind you, Hitchings."

He held out his hand and Wilson took it. "I did not think about this when I suggested the sampan, but now I think it is the very thing. If anyone is watching you, it will throw them off the track. I shall be busy here with the Chang account. Someone must find out just what Eva knows. You must do that, Mr. Hitchings, and then come back here. I will take you down to the boat myself. I am right behind you, understand? You will do that, won't you?"

Wilson Hitchings hesitated, because something in Mr. Wilkie's manner confused him even then, and it half-aroused in him an inherited sense of caution. It occurred to him again that Mr. Wilkie seemed disproportionately anxious to get him on board that sampan. It occurred to him again that Mr. Wilkie was anxious to be rid of him, although he could not tell just why. The best way of finding out why might be to go aboard that boat. Mr. Wilkie seemed to read his thoughts.

"We must get things straight with Eva," Mr. Wilkie said. "That's the most important thing just now. She must not be involved in this, as you said. If she is, it will hurt the name of the firm more than anything else. I am aroused now, Hitchings, very much aroused. You must see Eva and arrange to close up Hitchings Plantation, and the sampan is the very place. No one will overhear you. There'll be lunch aboard for you and you will be back by two o'clock. Then we will attend to the rest of it and we will move fast."

Mr. Wilkie's idea was plausible. Wilson realized that he could not have made a better opportunity to make Eva Hitchings see reason if he had tried. A good many things could be cleared up by seeing Eva Hitchings. If he could convince her of the seriousness of the situation, a great deal might be done; and now he had his chance. More than anything else, however, he realized that he wanted to see Eva Hitchings. He wanted her to see him in a proper light. He wanted to help her in spite of her coldness to him and in spite of her disbelief in him. It did not take much intelligence to realize that matters in some way were coming to a head. Mr. Moto's manner had indicated that, and so had Mr. Maddock's. Wilson knew that the Plantation was no place for Eva Hitchings any longer.

"Are you absolutely sure that we will be back by two?" he asked.

"Absolutely," Mr. Wilkie's voice was emphatic. "There's too much to be done to have you delay any longer. I'll give all the orders."

"Are you coming too?" Wilson asked.

Mr. Wilkie shook his head.

"No," he said. "It would only complicate matters, having me along, and there is a good deal for me to do here. I must go over the Chang account. You will excuse me, won't you?"

Wilson felt relieved to hear that Mr. Wilkie was not going—without knowing exactly why, except that he preferred to see Eva Hitchings alone.

"All right," he said. "I'll go."

"Good," said Mr. Wilkie, and he took down his Panama hat from a peg. "Then we had better start at once. Come along, Eva will be waiting."

They had nearly reached the door when the telephone rang on Mr. Wilkie's desk. He turned impatiently and picked up the receiver.

"Hello," he said. "Who?"

From where he was standing, Wilson could hear the telephone

making a tinny, singsong sound and he saw that Mr. Wilkie was watching him as he listened.

"Yes," Mr. Wilkie was saying. "Yes, I understand. I'll see you in a quarter of an hour. Yes, certainly, in a quarter of an hour." And he set the telephone down, slowly, and there was a tremor of excitement in his voice.

"Do you know who that was?" he said. "I couldn't have believed it; it's the very man we were speaking of. It's Mr. Chang Lo-Shih. He must have come on the same boat with you. He wants to see me right away. Don't worry. I'll see that he won't suspect anything."

"I would like to see him myself," said Wilson.

"You shall," said Mr. Wilkie. "You shall, this afternoon." And they walked through the office in the bright sun of the street. Mr. Wilkie was walking swiftly toward the waterfront. "This is serious," he said.

"Yes," said Wilson. "I think it is." And he wondered if Mr. Moto knew that Mr. Chang was there.

Mr. Wilkie rested his hand on Wilson's shoulder.

"Don't you worry," Mr. Wilkie said. "I've lived in the Orient. I can attend to Chang. We will have to close out his account, right away. We've got to get clear of this. I'll close up with Chang and you manage Eva. Don't be worried, Hitchings. You will find these troubles come up every now and then. Everything will be all right."

"Yes," said Wilson. "I am sure it will." But he was not sure. In spite of Mr. Wilkie's sudden burst of energy, he felt entirely alone. He wished that his Uncle William were there, because he felt so alone.

"There is just one thing," he said. "Will you cable Shanghai, Mr. Wilkie, and tell them to close out Chang's account there?"

"Of course," said Mr. Wilkie. "Don't you worry. We have had undesirable clients before. We will have a confirmation, by the time you are back. Well, here we are."

Wilson had been so busy with his own thoughts that he had not noticed where they were going, except in a half-conscious way, until Mr. Wilkie spoke. They were standing on an open pier, looking down at the deck of a boat that was moored beside it. She was a heavily built, wide-beamed motor craft, painted blue, with an awning over the afterdeck. There was a deck cabin and an open hatch leading from the engine room, forward. The lines of the vessel were new to Wilson Hitchings. They were blunt and heavy and foreign, but she was a capable-looking craft. On the forward deck, two of the crew were standing—squat, barefoot men, with dungarees and white shirts, with bronze skins and uncertain racial traits. Eva Hitchings was seated in a canvas chair beneath the awning. When she saw them, she waved her hand.

"George," called Mr. Wilkie. "George." A snub-nosed man in a greasy hat climbed up the ladder in the hatch. He was a European and a sailor, the sort that one might see in any seaport, with strong forearms and a heavy face. He looked like a piece of driftwood that had been banged about by the sea, with scars of experience printed on his skin.

"George," said Mr. Wilkie, "this is Mr. Hitchings."

George grinned slowly and rubbed his hands on his dungarees.

"Pleased to meet you, Mister," he said. His movements were slow and his face was dull and heavy. There were deep creases about his eyes and his teeth were very bad.

"George," said Mr. Wilkie, "Mr. Hitchings must be back by two o'clock. Be sure to get him back."

"Yes," said George. "Sure."

"Well," said Mr. Wilkie, "that's all. Have a good time, both of you."

Eva Hitchings stood up. "Aren't you coming with us, Uncle Joe?" she asked.

"No, my dear," said Mr. Wilkie. "Not today. We are very busy at the office. But George will look after you, and Kito is in the cabin to get you lunch."

Eva Hitchings frowned. "I thought you said—" she began.

But Mr. Wilkie interrupted her.

"Please, Eva," he said. "I had no idea I would be so busy this morning."

"Well, I don't like it," Eva Hitchings answered, and she gazed at Wilson coldly. "I didn't ask for this."

Wilson Hitchings was standing by the steps of the stone pier which led down to the deck. But, before he walked down them, he hesitated.

"Perhaps Miss Hitchings would like it better if I didn't go," he said.

"Nonsense," Mr. Wilkie said quickly, his lowered voice urgent. "Get aboard, this is important. You can cast off, George, but remember what I told you."

"Sure," said George. "Cast off, you!" And he disappeared down the forward hatch.

There was a sound of the starting engine, powerful and steady. One of the crew was casting off the lines. The other walked to the wheel at the stern. Their casually quick motions showed that the two hands knew their business. The sampan was moving from the dock and Mr. Wilkie waved his hat.

"Good-by," he called, and Wilson waved back, but Eva Hitchings did not move. She was standing on the deck beneath the awning, the wind was whipping her light silk skirt. Her legs were brown and bare. She was wearing a blue sweater and it seemed to Wilson that her whole dress was as casual as her manner.

"Well," she said, "now that you are here, you may as well sit down. Kito, bring a chair for Mr. Hitchings."

A Japanese boy in a white steward's uniform came out of the cabin, bringing another canvas folding armchair.

"I did not arrange this," Eva Hitchings said. "Uncle Joe asked me to have lunch with him. I hadn't the least idea that you would be connected with it."

Wilson Hitchings looked at the dock where Mr. Wilkie still stood watching. He was still puzzled by something in Mr. Wilkie's manner. The older man had been very anxious to see him safe aboard and out into the harbor. There was no doubt of that. Now that the sampan was moving out to sea, it occurred to him that Mr. Wilkie had been almost too anxious. He looked at Eva Hitchings curiously.

"Don't apologize," he said.

"I am not apologizing," she answered.

"All right," Wilson told her. "I am glad you are not. Then I won't apologize either. May I make a suggestion, now that we are here?"

"What suggestion?" Eva Hitchings asked. "Are you always so cool and calm? Do you always act as though you were addressing a directors' meeting? Doesn't anything ever stop your being so complacent?"

"As a matter of fact, I am not cool or calm at all," Wilson answered slowly. He wanted her to like him. Although he knew that his desire was unreasonable, he wished that they could be friends. "I was only going to suggest," he explained, "that we might stop quarreling for a little while. I did not plan this either, but Mr. Wilkie wanted me to talk to you."

"Don't you think you have talked to me enough? I know almost everything that is in your mind."

"Don't you think you could just treat me as a poor *malihini?*"

Wilson answered. "That's the name you have for it, isn't it? I've always heard that the natives here were supposed to be hospitable. This is your boat more than mine. Couldn't we get along without quarreling?"

She smiled at him and when she smiled he knew that there was something between them, whether they admitted it or not.

"Do you think we could ever stop quarreling?" she asked.

"We might," said Wilson. "You never can tell until you try."

"I am afraid not," Eva said. "You and I are both rather determined people and we don't want the same thing."

"I only want to help you," Wilson said. "I have told you that."

Eva Hitchings looked at the water and back at him.

"Why?" she asked.

"Because I like you," Wilson said. "Haven't I told you that?"

"No," she said. "You haven't."

"Well," he said, "I have told you now. . . . Mr. Maddock called to see me this morning."

Her eyes grew darker and he knew that she was startled.

"He did?" she replied carelessly. "And what did Mr. Maddock want?"

"He wanted to tell me something," Wilson said. "Mr. Maddock is very much disturbed by something which he thinks may happen. He says he doesn't want to get mixed up in a killing on an island. Do you know what he means?"

Eva Hitchings shrugged her shoulders, and then her voice was appealing. "Can't we forget all this for a little while? Can't we—can't we, please? I am tired of thinking—thinking all the time. I am sick and tired of everything. I should rather like you, too, if I had met you somewhere casually, particularly if your name were not Hitchings. Kito, will you bring us some cocktails, please?"

When he tasted the cocktails, Wilson realized that Mr. Wilkie had done things very well. And everything had changed now that Eva Hitchings had spoken. They began to talk of ships and sailing. He had always been fond of the sea, as the sea had been in his blood. He felt better when they were through the opening in the reef and heading straight out over the blue water. The color of the sea inside the waves, and the fresh breeze on his face, made him forget a good deal. What interested him most was that an attractive girl was with him and that he was having a pleasant time. He never remembered exactly what they had talked about, but he knew her a good deal better before they were through.

# 9

KITO, THE Japanese, brought them sandwiches from the cabin, then afterward they went forward and sat near the bow. Nothing disturbed Wilson for a long while until he looked at his watch. Their course had been straight from land and they had been going at a good rate of speed, until the Island had grown hazy and everything upon it indistinct except for the tones of the browns and greens in the mountains.

"I never knew it was as late as this," Wilson said. "We are going to be late getting back. We ought to turn around."

Eva Hitchings looked back at the Island and nodded. Wilson walked to the open hatch of the engine room. The white man, George, was leaning over a piece of machinery. The noise was loud enough so that he did not notice Wilson looking down. The man's heavy back was bent forward. There was an indistinct bulge in his hip pocket but its outlines were plain enough for Wilson to see that George was carrying a gun. It was the first thing since they had left the dock which disturbed him, the first thing which made him suspicious and alert. Wilson raised his voice above the smooth sound of the engine.

"You, down there!" he called.

George straightened up quickly at the sound of his voice and rubbed his heavy forearm across his forehead and scowled into the sunlight.

"You had better turn," Wilson called to him. "It is late."

George climbed up the ladder to the deck. Wilson did not realize how heavy and powerful the man was until he stood beside him. George was greasy and perspiring freely.

"All right, Mister," he said. "You can tell the boy at the wheel to turn her. You and the lady had better stay aft. The bow will get wet when he turns."

"Thanks," said Wilson. "I am sorry I have to go back so soon, but we are going to be late, anyway. We must be a good ten miles offshore."

"Yes," said George slowly. "About ten miles, Mister, but I will get you back all right."

The smile lingered about George's heavy lips as though something amused him.

"Yes," he repeated, slowly. "I'll get you home, Mister."

"Thank you," said Wilson. "I am sure you will." He called Eva Hitchings and they walked aft past the cabin into the cockpit beneath the awning.

"I suppose Mr. Wilkie has had George for a long time?" Wilson said.

"Yes," Eva Hitchings answered. "What makes you ask?"

"Only idle curiosity," Wilson said. But he was no longer idly curious, because certain elements of the morning were growing picturesquely and startlingly together. Mr. Wilkie's anxiety to get him aboard that boat and even Eva Hitchings' efforts to be agreeable came logically together when he thought of the man in the engine room. He moved over toward the coffee-colored, barefoot sailor by the wheel.

"You can turn now," he said. "We're going back."

The man looked at him vacantly and grinned.

"Do you want to go back now?" he asked.

"Yes," said Wilson, sharply. "George told me to tell you."

"All right," the man said. "Oh, yes, we go back." And he began to move the wheel.

As the sampan responded, they felt the full force of the rolling sea and the trade wind. The motion changed so that he had to brace himself, and then the pulsing of the engine stopped. Wilson looked at Eva Hitchings, questioningly.

"I wonder what is the matter now?" he said.

"I suppose there is something wrong with the motor," she answered.

Wilson nodded and climbed out of the cockpit.

"Where are you going?" she asked. It might have been his imagination, but it seemed to him that there was a new edge to her voice and he did not answer her. Instead, without speaking, he walked around the cabin and paused by the engine-room hatch. The second member of the crew was sitting near the bow, staring into space. The sampan had lost her way already and was rolling idly in the sea. Then Wilson climbed down the ladder quickly. The engineer was seated, doing nothing, but he rose when Wilson stepped off the ladder, and grinned.

"What is wrong?" Wilson asked. "Why have we stopped?"

The grin on George's face grew broader.

"Something wrong with the pump, Mister," George said. "It looks like we're busted down."

Wilson Hitchings tried to make his face show nothing, but his heart was beating fast. There was a rack of wrenches beside him and, as the ship rolled, he lost his balance and regained it by leaning his hand against the rack.

"Will it take a long while to fix?" he asked.

George grinned at him more openly than he had before.

"Yes," he said. "It's a tough job, Mister. I'll get you in all right, but you might as well be patient. We ain't gonna tie up to any dock until mighty late tonight."

Wilson stared at the machinery with all the stupidity of a landsman, and allowed his voice to rise.

"But I've got to get back; it's important I get back," he said.

His anxiety seemed to afford George a certain amount of quiet amusement.

"Well, you ain't going to, Mister," George said. "The engine is busted and we're going to stay right here."

Wilson stared at the machinery again.

"That's funny," he said, slowly. "Everything looks all right to me, except I saw you fiddling with that pump when I called you five minutes ago. Who told you to fiddle with it? Was it Mr. Wilkie, George?"

It was clear that deception was not in George's line. His face was enough to show Wilson that he was absolutely right. The answer was written in the flicker of George's eyelids. A good two seconds before he spoke Wilson knew as sure as fate that it was Mr. Wilkie who had put him on that boat and it was Mr. Wilkie's intention that he should stay there. As he watched George struggling with the mental problem which confronted him, Wilson knew that he must do something very quickly, before George thought ahead too far.

It was amazing how quickly and eccentrically his mind ran in that brief lapse of time, before that slow-witted man could speak. He felt, with all the sharp shock of surprise, incredulity that Mr. Wilkie should be playing any part in such an affair as that. But it all was perfectly clear as he stood in the oily engine room. He tried to restrain his anger and think. The man in front of him was more than a match for him physically, and Wilson knew that George knew it, and was ready to use his strength. Wilson knew that he must do something very quickly, something which he had never done in his life before; but he had already pictured the whole act in his mind. His hand was resting on a wrench. It was loose beneath his hand in the rack and George was speaking.

"What if he did?" George said. "It ain't my business, Mister."

"No," said Wilson, slowly. "It's not your business, George."

He intended his next move to be unexpected, and it was. He had pulled the wrench gently out of the rack as he was speaking, and he swung it in a sharp sidewise blow that caught George behind the ear. The result was more than he had anticipated, although he had been careful not to strike too hard. The sailor's mouth sagged. His eyes glazed and his knees buckled. He sank in a heap at Wilson's feet and sprawled on the grating beside the engine, while Wilson stood looking at him, half amazed, half shocked at himself, still holding the wrench in his right hand. At first he had a sickening thought that he had killed the man, but he saw it was not so a moment later when he stooped and felt behind the greasy hair where he had struck. He had not broken the skull, but the man was knocked out cold. What surprised Wilson most was that he felt no perturbation or panic after that first sickening moment. Instead he could almost have believed that he had been used to such actions all his life.

He seemed to know exactly what to do. First he reached into the hip pocket of the figure that lay sprawled before him, then drew out a gunmetal revolver and placed it in his own pocket. Then he felt in the side pocket and pulled out a knife. There was a coil of light rope lying by the ladder. He cut two lengths of it quickly, and tied the man's hands and feet. Then he took the rest of the coil and climbed out of the engine room to the deck. Everything was exactly as he had left it. The ship still rolled in the trough of the sea. He could see the helmsman gazing at him over the top of the cabin. The second man still sat in the bow. Wilson called to him.

"You there," he called, "George wants you."

The man moved toward him slowly, without the least suspicion that anything was wrong. He did not notice that anything was amiss until he was down the ladder and in the engine room, and then he had no chance to make a sound, because Wilson told him not to, with a revolver in his hand, just as though he had done such things always.

"You don't want to get sick like George, do you?" he said. "Then lie down on your face and don't make any noise. I am going to tie you up, boy."

Three minutes later, Wilson walked aft, still holding the revolver.

"Stand still, you," he said to the man at the wheel. "Stand exactly where you are!"

Eva Hitchings was staring at him, open-mouthed.

"What is it?" she cried. "Have you gone crazy?"

Wilson Hitchings shook his head.

"There seems to be a little trouble here," he answered. "You said I was a cool customer and I begin to believe you are right. I have tied two men up and now I am going to tie up this one. Will you go into the cabin, please, and stay there until I call you?"

"No," she said. "I won't."

"I am afraid you will," Wilson answered, "unless you want me to pick you up and toss you in there. Go into the cabin and stay with the steward."

He did not think she would do what he ordered, but she did. She turned away without a word, and he slammed the cabin door behind her.

Ten minutes later, Wilson Hitchings pulled out the piece of iron which he had inserted in the hasp of the cabin door. He had removed his coat and rolled up his sleeves, for he was hot from unaccustomed exertion.

"Kito," he said, "you come out here!"

The Japanese steward came out slowly, holding his hands above his head.

"Please sir?" he began. "Please?"

"Put down your hands!" Wilson told him. "Are you going to be a good boy, Kito?"

"Yes," said Kito. "Oh, yes. I do not understand."

"There is only one thing you need to understand," said Wilson. "I am in charge of this boat now, Kito. You behave, and I won't hurt you. Stay in the cabin, unless I call you. If you try to sneak forward, I will wring your neck."

"Yes," said Kito. "Oh, yes, sir."

"And now," Wilson said, "you tell the missy, I want her to come out and talk to me. You tell her to come out quick."

Wilson stood with his feet apart and his hands on his hips, swaying with the rhythm of the drifting sampan. He could not believe he was the same person he had known all his life: a quiet, well-mannered, conventional person, both repressed and shy. He was still half-stunned by his own capacities, which had been revealed by what he had done in those last few minutes. He wondered if a criminal felt as he did on achieving his first deed of violence; whether his surprise was the same. He had heard of the subconscious mind and of the unexpected capabilities of persons laboring under great excitement. He could almost believe that he was a psychological case, a dual personality. He still could not exactly believe all he had done and yet some voice inside him prompted him to go ahead. He felt a curious mixture of disillusion and of anger. It seemed to him that he had never known, until then, any real emotion, hot and strong, that could galvanize the nerves into sudden action and could tear away inhibitions and manners.

When he saw Eva Hitchings walking toward him, everything that he had thought about her, and every wishful illusion that had warped his opinion of her from reality to some sort of mawkish romance, was gone into ashes like a sheet of paper that strikes a bed of white-hot coals. It seemed to him that he saw her at last entirely accurately, just as Mr. Moto saw her. He could hear Mr. Moto saying, "I am afraid she is not nice. I am very, very sorry."

Eva Hitchings must have seen what he was thinking, because her face was assuming a startled look. First she had looked as though she were about to demand an explanation but now she was obviously startled.

"What is it?" she asked. Her voice was timid. "What has come over you, Wilson Hitchings?"

She was acting still, and he wanted her to know that he knew it.

"I guess it's common sense, Eva," he told her; "common sense has come over me for the first time in my life. I should have known what you are and what your friend Mr. Wilkie is, if you had not been so pretty, Eva Hitchings. You are both of you a pair of crooks, using the Hitchings Bank in your schemes. But when you thought I knew too much, you thought you could get me out here, while you cleaned up your game. You wanted me out of the way and you thought I would believe some story about a broken engine, while your Uncle Joe—isn't that what you call him?—cleaned up his business with Mr. Chang from Shanghai. Didn't you, Eva Hitchings? Well, you made just one mistake. I happen to know a good deal about boats and Diesel power. There is nothing wrong with that engine that I can't fix up in five minutes. I saw your seagoing friend George throwing it out of whack."

"But what did you do?" she asked. "I don't see how you could have . . . "

Wilson laughed at her and she did not finish her question.

"It surprises you, does it?" he inquired. "Well, I guess that Hitchingses are a tough lot, Eva. It probably runs in the family. I was a little surprised myself, but I am getting used to it now. I will tell you something else, Eva, that perhaps you did not know. I am perfectly able to start that engine and to bring this boat in by myself and I am going to do it. Now I think you had better go into the cabin again, unless there is something you want particularly to say."

Eva Hitchings did not move. Her eyes met his and the trade wind blew her hair across her forehead.

"I don't believe a word of it, not a single word."

Wilson shrugged his shoulders.

"It doesn't really make much difference what you believe," he said. "The Hawaiians have a word for it. Your friend, Mr. Maddock told it to me, this morning. You are through, Eva Hitchings, and the word for it is *pau.* I like that word. You and your gang of crooks are very nearly *pau.* I offered to buy your place last night, but now I am going to save the money. You are going to be put out with your gunmen, Eva."

Eva Hitchings moved convulsively, as though something invisible were clutching at her throat.

"It isn't so!" she cried. Her voice was strained and discordant. "It isn't so!"

"It won't do any good to act that way," Wilson told her. "If you are going to have hysterics, have them in the cabin."

Eva Hitchings pushed her hair back from her forehead.

"I won't have any," she said. "I would not give you the satisfaction; but I repeat, it isn't so."

In spite of himself, Wilson looked at her admiringly.

"No, Eva, it won't do," he said. "Who came last night to see if Mr. Moto had taken his drink of whisky? Your friend, Mr. Wilkie, came. I thought it was coincidence, until he got me aboard this boat."

Eva Hitchings opened her lips and closed them, as though something stopped her from speaking.

"I don't believe it. I can't believe it."

"Well," said Wilson, "that's your own affair."

"I don't care about myself," she continued, as though she had not heard him. "They—they bought me out six months ago, with an agreement that I should stay on for a year, so that no one should know about it. Uncle Joe arranged it, but he wouldn't do a thing like that."

"Wouldn't he?" Wilson asked politely. He was interested in spite of himself, although he was not entirely sure that he believed her. "So you don't own Hitchings Plantation?"

Eva Hitchings shook her head.

"No, I don't," she repeated. "But I was glad to pretend I did. I told you last night that I wanted to find out what they were doing. I thought, of course, that your family was in it. Uncle Joe as good as told me they were in it. I wanted to find out exactly what they were doing. I have never liked your family."

"And you thought I was in it?" Wilson Hitchings asked.

"Yes, of course, I did," Eva Hitchings answered. "But I don't think so now."

"Would you mind telling me why you don't?" Wilson asked her. And her answer was logical enough.

"Because you wouldn't do what you have done," she said. "You wouldn't start tearing this boat apart." She looked at him steadily. "I still don't see how you did it. You haven't killed anybody, Wilson Hitchings?"

"I haven't yet," Wilson told her. "I think you tend to overestimate my capacities. I have thought so, all along."

Then he began to believe that he should never have allowed her to talk, because the ideas which he had formed about her and which he thought he had entirely eliminated were returning to him again, making his judgment fallible. When she turned her head, the curve of her neck interested him—and her change of expression when she spoke, making him forget the actual elements of the problem.

"No, I don't think I overestimated you," she answered. "I said that you were capable and I certainly think you are, but you have overestimated me. I haven't enough capacity to be a good adventuress. Sometimes I've wished I had, but I haven't. I have just been caught in something which I haven't been able to control. I imagine you have been caught in the same thing. We are really babes in the wood and we think that we are tigers. I guess we are both wrong."

Wilson found himself repressing a strong desire to laugh.

"Are you trying to convey the idea," he inquired, "that you are a nice girl that has been led into bad company and is still at heart a thoroughly nice girl?"

Eva Hitchings nodded.

"Yes, that is roughly what I am trying to convey," she said; "but I don't suppose you believe me."

"No," said Wilson. "I don't suppose I do."

"Then, what are you going to do about it?" Eva Hitchings asked.

"I am going to put you back in the cabin," Wilson answered, "and then I am going to get the engine started. If you are so anxious to keep me out here, it must be interesting on shore."

"And you still think I had something to do with it?" Eva Hitchings asked.

"Yes," said Wilson. "Of course I do."

She gave no sign of being hurt by his disbelief, instead she seemed almost pleased.

"You were right about what you said when I first met you," she told him. "You told me you were a guileless person. I really think you are. Hasn't it ever occurred to you that I might be here for just the same reason you are—because I know too much? I hadn't thought of it that way until a few minutes ago; but it is the reason. We are both of us here because we know too much."

The drifting boat and the sounds of the sea made her words surprisingly simple. If he could believe her, everything seemed clear, and he could very nearly believe her.

"Then what are you going to do about it?" Wilson asked.

Eva Hitchings shrugged her shoulder.

"I don't know," she said, "unless you have some suggestion."

He did not understand her. He could only wonder where her thoughts might lead him next.

"Well," he replied, "I haven't any suggestion."

She looked back at him steadily.

"You don't seem to do much about using your opportunity," she said. "You said you liked me a little while ago."

"Yes," Wilson nodded, "a little while ago."

"And you don't now," Eva Hitchings asked him. "That's the way things go, isn't it? You don't like me anymore. I don't suppose you trust me and now I have just begun to like you. I like you better than anyone I know."

"I am sorry I don't follow you," Wilson Hitchings said. His voice was cool enough but his thoughts were not. He was standing closer to her than he thought. She was looking up at him, brushing her hair from her forehead, and she seemed very young just then, transparently a young person.

"I don't exactly follow myself," he heard her say. And then she smiled. "I suppose it's because I am thinking about the Hitchings family."

He must have been more interested in her than he believed because he heard no sound behind him until he heard a voice and he saw Eva Hitchings start and saw her eyes grow wide and incredulous.

"Excuse me," someone said behind him. "I'm sorry that I interrupt, so very, very sorry."

Wilson Hitchings had turned as quickly as though someone had touched his back. The door of the cabin was open and Mr. Moto, blinking in the sunlight, was looking through the opening.

# 10

WILSON HITCHINGS rubbed the back of his hand across his eyes. Mr. Moto was still standing looking through the cabin door. There was no mistaking the shoebrush cut of his hair and the gold fillings in his teeth or the delicate hands or the nervous determined smile. Mr. Moto was dressed in a dark alpaca suit that was somewhat wrinkled and there were smudges of dust on his coat which he was brushing off carefully when he stepped into the cockpit.

"Excuse me," Mr. Moto said again. "I could not help but overhear. It was so very, very interesting what Miss Hitchings said, that you are both here because you know too much. And so very, very true. It is also a very good joke. That is why we are all here—because all of us know too much. Excuse me, I did not mean to startle you. Have I startled you, Mr. Hitchings?"

Wilson sat down at the edge of the cockpit.

"You did in a way," he said. "I suppose you could imagine my next question. Did Mr. Wilkie ask you to come with us, Mr. Moto?"

Mr. Moto smiled patiently but his smile appeared to be more genuine, and Wilson thought he could detect a gleam of amusement in Mr. Moto's dark birdlike eyes.

"No, he did not ask me," Mr. Moto said. "This was purely my own idea. Please, do not look so nervous, Mr. Hitchings. I do not wish to have you nervous, because that might be very bad for me. Please, I did not know you could be so violent, Mr. Hitchings."

Then Eva Hitchings spoke.

"But where have you been?" she asked. "How did you get here? I didn't see you in the cabin, Mr. Moto."

Mr. Moto laughed. It was apparent that he was pleased and

amused by the entire episode, with an almost childlike amusement.

"I will tell you," said Mr. Moto, rubbing his hands and smiling. "There is a passage forward, connecting with the engine and the crew's quarters. There is a small corridor leading from the passage. It was confined in there and not very nice. Your steward, Kito, introduced me to it. Please," Mr. Moto raised his hands decoratively, "do not interrupt me, Mr. Hitchings. I should be very, very frank. The cabin boy, Kito, is very nice. I have known his family in Japan. Please, it is this way, Mr. Hitchings. This vessel has interested me very much for several days. It is such a well-found vessel and so very, very seaworthy. It has interested me why Mr. Wilkie should desire such a vessel for ocean trips. There is a certain cargo steamer which touches here and then makes for Fusan in Korea. Do you understand me, Mr. Hitchings?"

"No," said Wilson, "but I am trying to, Mr. Moto."

"Ha-ha," said Mr. Moto. "That is very good. You are going to understand. Everything will be very nice, I think. The name of the steamer is the *Eastern Light,* carrying lumber from your West Coast, Mr. Hitchings. Several hours after she leaves harbor, I found this sampan leaves also. She meets the *Eastern Light* out of sight of land. Now what do you think of that?"

"I think it is very, very interesting," Wilson said.

"Thank you," said Mr. Moto. "I am very glad you think so. There is a passenger on the sampan who boards the *Eastern Light.* I have been very interested to find out just why. It must be because he does not wish to be seen walking up the gangplank. Do you not think so, Mr. Hitchings? Now there is something else which is very, very interesting. The *Eastern Light* is sailing this afternoon." Mr. Moto rubbed his hands. "This morning the sampan filled her fuel tank. I was very, very interested and then this morning Kito told me something else. It was so very, very nice that I should know him, don't you think?"

"Yes," said Wilson Hitchings. "Very, very nice."

Mr. Moto cocked his head to one side.

"Please," he continued, "would you like to guess what Kito told me? Your mind is so very, very quick that possibly you could guess."

"Possibly," Wilson agreed, "but I'd rather you told me, Mr. Moto, and if you don't mind, tell me quickly! I want to get the engine going."

"Yes," said Mr. Moto. "That will be very, very nice. I should be so glad to help you, Mr. Hitchings. This morning Mr. Wilkie hurried to the dock and gave orders that you and Miss Hitchings were going out for a little sail. He asked especially for the engine to break down so that you would not get ashore until twelve o'clock tonight, after which he wished everything ready to put to sea again. Please, when I heard of this, it made me think of several things. It made me think that I would be very much safer with you and Miss Hitchings on the sampan than any place on shore. I want to be safe, very much indeed, until tonight. Also I was worried about you, Mr. Hitchings. When I heard you in the engine-room I nearly interfered. I did not think that you would do everything so very, very nicely."

"Thank you for saying so," Wilson Hitchings said.

"You are so very welcome," answered Mr. Moto. "Please, I did not know that you understood the small boats."

"Do you?" Wilson asked.

"Oh, yes," said Mr. Moto. "Please. I was in the Navy once."

"Well then, let's get the engine going," Wilson said. "I want to get ashore."

"Please," Mr. Moto raised his hands. "If I may make a suggestion . . . If I may be so very rude . . . The engine will start very easily, but I do not think it will be nice to go ashore until the sun goes down. Please, do you understand me? Someone is surely watching us from shore, right now. They will be so very, very glad to see us rolling here. I think it would be very nice if no one should know exactly when we land. There will be time after dark, I think. I hope you understand me, Mr. Hitchings."

"Yes," said Wilson, "I think I understand you."

"Then please," said Mr. Moto, "I think it would be very nice to go forward and see that everything is secure in the crew's quarters, and then perhaps it would be very nice if Kito were to give us a little refreshment. I am so glad that everything is going so beautifully. There is only one thing more."

"What's that?" Wilson asked him. But it seemed to him that there were a good many other things more.

Mr. Moto bowed toward Eva Hitchings.

"It is about Miss Hitchings," he replied. "I said some things about her which were not very nice and I am afraid that you believed them, Mr. Hitchings. Excuse me. I was very, very wrong. You must believe what she tells you, because I think she will be very nice now. I think we will all be very nice and now perhaps we had better go forward, Mr. Hitchings. There is a question I should like to ask the crew."

Little as Wilson Hitchings understood the Oriental mind, it was evident that something had happened which gave Mr. Moto both relief and pleasure. For a while at any rate, a proportion of his tenseness and his eagerness had left him. He hummed a tune softly, as he examined the engines.

"You are pleased," said Wilson, "aren't you, Mr. Moto?"

"Yes," said Mr. Moto. "Very, very pleased. I have learned several things. Matters will go nicely now, I think. I simply need to set eyes on several persons. I simply need to make an observation. Then, everything will be arranged."

Mr. Moto paused and began to laugh again.

"Excuse me," he said. "I was simply thinking of certain persons who would be very, very sorry not to see me back on shore. They will be looking for me so very hard. They will be so very anxious to have me put out of the way, I think. Yes, I should like to see their faces. They will be so much annoyed. And now, please, shall we see the fellows you have tied? I wish to ask a question."

There were four bunks in the crew's quarters in the bow. George and his two helpers lay bound in the bunks where Wilson Hitchings had tossed them, and their positions indicated that they had all been struggling with their ropes. The engineer raised his head and scowled.

"Say," he said, "what the hell is the big idea? I'll get you for this, Mister." His glance moved to Mr. Moto ominously. "And that little monkey with you too. You can't get away with this, Mister."

For almost the first time that Wilson had known him, Mr. Moto looked annoyed.

"Please," he said, "what did you call me, please?"

"A monkey," said George. "I seen you snooping on the dock and I say you can't get away with this."

"Excuse me," said Mr. Moto. "I should look at the knots, I think. I mean no criticism, Mr. Hitchings, but it takes training to tie a man securely. I may be more expert, please."

Wilson was almost inclined to take the criticism to heart, for he felt that he had done his tying rather well. The only light in the small sleeping space came from a skylight on the deck and the light fell dimly on the heavy recumbent figure of the engineer as he lay on his side in the lower bunk. Mr. Moto was bending over him and Wilson was watching almost idly, when he saw something suspiciously intent in the large man's glance. He was looking over Mr. Moto's shoulder, directly into Wilson's face, and his eyes were growing narrow.

"Ah," Mr. Moto was saying. "Exactly as I feared. The arms are very greasy and the rope—"

"Look out!" said Wilson suddenly. But Mr. Moto was not quick enough. In the half-light Wilson saw that something was very wrong. George was free of his ropes.

"Look out!" Wilson called. But Mr. Moto was not quick enough. From the semi-obscurity of the bunk George delivered a sharp, decisive blow on Mr. Moto's jaw, and Mr. Moto staggered backward and sat down. In the same instant, George had rolled out of his bunk, landing on his feet on the deck.

"Pile on him, boys," he shouted. "We've been waiting for you, Mister."

Wilson sprang backward instinctively, and as he did so, the man who was lying on the upper bunk hurled himself on his back. The impact threw Wilson forward and nearly made him lose his balance. He always said the thing that happened next was luck. The deck hand who leaped for his back slid over him and sprawled into George's stomach and the two landed in a heap. The next instant was like the click of a camera shot. The two men were in a heap trying to get up. Mr. Moto was already on his feet, the third man was half out of his bunk.

"Get back in there!" said Wilson and, still half doubled over, he whirled on his heels and struck the man on the face. As he did so, he heard a scream of agony. George was sitting on the deck holding his left arm. The other man was struggling to his feet, standing undecided, and Wilson moved toward him; but as he did so, he saw that the trouble was over.

"All right, sir," the man said. "I won't make no trouble, sir."

"Then get up there and lie down," Wilson Hitchings told him.

"Please," Mr. Moto was saying. "Fetch some more rope, Mr. Hitchings. I can handle everything very nicely, please."

There was no doubt that Mr. Moto was amazingly adroit. Wilson watched him with deep interest as he worked and Mr. Moto conversed quite cheerfully.

"Please, Mr. Hitchings," he said. "It was my fault as much as yours not to think of this before. I should have known they might work loose. They were waiting, of course, for you to come here. They did not wish to show themselves because you had a weapon. I am sorry that I broke the man's arm but he was not very nice. Please, Mr. Hitchings, it only shows how careful one must be. But all this is really nothing." Mr. Moto leaned over George again and felt his arm.

"Now," he said, "perhaps you will answer a question, please. It is what I came for, in the first place, please. I am sorry I shall hurt you if you do not answer. You were to bring out a passenger, a man, to the *Eastern Light* this evening. What does he look like, please?"

George groaned but did not answer.

"Quickly, please," said Mr. Moto. "I do not wish to hurt you."

"Take him away from me," George shouted. "Please, Mister, take him away."

"What does the man look like?" Mr. Moto repeated softly. He was holding a small photograph before the sailor's face. "Please—is that the man?"

"I don't know," George gasped. "I ain't never seen his face. He keeps it hid. I tell you that's the truth. He comes on with money from the Hitchings' gambling house and we put him aboard the hooker, but I ain't seen his face."

"Thank you," said Mr. Moto. "Are you sure? I am very, very sorry. Answer me another question, please. I do not wish to hurt you. This man, are you going to take him out tonight?"

"Yes," said George. "He's going out tonight. Now will you take your hands off me? I don't know any more. I'm just obeying orders."

"Thank you," said Mr. Moto. "And the money comes from the gambling house? I thought so. Thank you very much."

"Wait a minute," said Wilson. "I've got a question too. Does Mr. Wilkie bring this man down to his boat?"

George looked sick and pale. He looked so bad that Wilson was very sorry for him.

"You had better tell me, George," he said, "and I'll give you a shot of whisky. I don't like this business any more than you." George's heavy eyes moved toward him.

"I wish I had set you down for a tough guy—when I seen you," George said. "Sure Mr. Wilkie takes him down. It's his boat, ain't it? Me—I'm just obeying orders." Mr. Moto straightened up, drew a handkerchief from his pocket, and wiped his hands.

"I am so very, very sorry," he said. "I do not like putting subjects to the question. It is a method with which I know you do not sympathize but in this case it is important. It is so very, very kind of you to be so broad-minded, Mr. Hitchings. I think now we can leave this place. They will not make more trouble. I very seldom drink but I think we might all have something now. It will be so very, very nice. I shall find who the man is when we get ashore. If you will excuse me, I shall join you in a few moments. I wish to look at the engines again. One must be so very, very careful."

## 11

Eva Hitchings was sitting aft by the wheel looking across the sparkling, restless water across the sea toward the Island. It was late afternoon and clear and beautiful, but the clouds of the mountains in the distance and the moisture in the air cast a faint enigmatic haze over the Island and passing clouds darkened the mountain slopes with shifting shadows. Even then Wilson had time to think that the Island was beautiful, although its soft coloring and its partial absence of definition were as disturbing as his thoughts. No matter what Mr. Moto might do, Wilson was thinking that he must deal with his own affairs.

There was no doubt any longer that Mr. Wilkie had been using his connection with the House of Hitchings in such a way that the Hitchings' reputation was in danger. Wilson had been taught that the reputation of their house was something to be guarded even more carefully than individual honor. A breath of scandal might blight it. No matter what happened the family bank must not be involved. And yet, he could think of no way to stop it. There would be an open scandal, if Mr. Moto were to expose half of what he knew and Mr. Moto would surely do it, if it were to help his interests, and Wilson could not blame him.

There must have been such thoughts which had been in the back of his mind all the while and now they were bearing on him heavily in his reaction from excitement. He had forgotten that he was not a free agent and now he remembered that he was not free—that he was tied hard and fast to family. For the moment he almost hated his family with all its pedantic ramifications; but even so, he knew he was a part of it, a part of it through the simplest laws of inheritance. What was worse, no one to whom he could appeal would understand his position.

Surely, Eva Hitchings would not understand it, and if she did she would only be amused, simply because she had reason to dislike the family, rather cogent reason. She turned when she heard his step and her eyes gave him the startling idea that she had been crying, although he was not entirely sure.

"Where is Mr. Moto?" she asked. "Has anything gone wrong?"

Wilson shook his head.

"Mr. Moto is examining the engine," he answered. "There was trouble with the crew."

"You don't look very happy," Eva Hitchings said.

"Neither do you," Wilson told her. Her face looked drawn and tired.

"Why should I be?" she asked. "It isn't nice to be disillusioned. It isn't pleasant to know that someone who has been kind to you is entirely different from what you thought he was. I am feeling rather sick if you want to know, sick and tired of everything. I know what you must think of me and I can't blame you much. I know what everyone will think by the time this thing is finished. I used to think that I could be independent, and now I am a part of a rotten world. It didn't used to be rotten when Father was alive. I don't suppose you believe me, do you?"

Although he did not answer, he was surprised that he did believe her, because she was not asking anything of him and because her loneliness appealed to his own loneliness.

"So you agree with me about Mr. Wilkie now?" he said. "I know the way you feel. It isn't very nice."

"No," she answered, "it isn't very nice. You are probably right about what you said a while ago. I won't have much reputation in a day or two. I'll be out in the streets with the gunmen, I suppose."

There seemed to be no reason not to be frank, since she probably understood the situation just as well as he.

"There is one thing that may console you," Wilson said. "The family won't have much reputation either. This business is too ugly for pieces of it not to come out. If the name of our firm is mentioned in it, it will be almost enough to spoil us. It doesn't take much to hurt a bank. You will probably only have to say a few words, Eva, and you will have your wish. You will get back at the family for everything they've done to you and more. That ought to console you, don't you think?"

Eva Hitchings looked surprised—genuinely surprised.

"You think I would be such a cad as that?" she said.

"Why not?" said Wilson. "You told me yesterday that was what you proposed to do. I thought that I might stop you but I don't think so now. If I did, I wouldn't be speaking as I am."

Eva Hitchings was looking at him incredulously.

"You really think I am such a cad as that?" she repeated. "Yesterday I thought your precious family was engaged in this whole business, because Mr. Wilkie told me so, and now I know they are not. I don't tell lies. The Hitchingses are decent people even if I don't like them. I am afraid I don't know many decent people."

Wilson moved toward her, surprised that all his resentment was gone.

"Do you mean that?" he asked her, quickly. "Do you mean that about the family?"

"Yes," she said. "You are part of it, aren't you? You are the only part I have ever seen. Except my father."

There was no doubt that she was telling the truth then—that she had always told the truth; and vaguely she was part of the family. Without actually knowing that he was going to do it, Wilson took her hand.

"It might be better if you told me what you know," he said.

"Yes," she said. "I'll tell you."

"Thanks," said Wilson, quickly. "Now quickly, before Mr. Moto gets here,—I don't know what's keeping him, but thank Heaven he is taking his time,—tell me what you know about this. The money is deposited in the Hitchings Bank. It is drawn out and brought to Hitchings Plantation. Then someone gets on his sampan and catches a vessel out at sea. What happens at the Plantation, Eva?"

Her fingers closed on his more tightly.

"You almost guessed," she said. "You would have guessed in a little while. They bring the money up a little at a time. It is lost across the table to certain persons or the house. You guessed it was a crooked wheel and I have guessed it too. Three or four win the money but it never goes out of the house. It's put in the safe. Then once in so often the same man comes, a dark man, a Russian, I think, and he wins more one night. Then he takes all the money in the safe and goes away. I never knew about the boat. I just knew about the crooked wheel and the money being lost."

Wilson thought for a moment and everything was very clear.

"That ties it," he said. "We've got the story now. Is a lot of money lost, Eva?"

"Yes," she said. "A lot over a period of weeks, but gradually. I didn't notice it at first because the house gets a profit just the same. The house is paid, whether it wins or loses. That's what I noticed first."

"And the money goes out tonight?" Wilson said.

"Yes," said Eva Hitchings. "It seems that way. A lot of money."

"All right," said Wilson. "That's the story. I wish I had known it sooner. Listen to me, Eva. The money must go out tonight. There mustn't be any trouble. Mr. Moto mustn't make any trouble. Do you understand?"

"No," she said. "I don't. I thought you wanted to stop it. Of course, I don't understand."

"Don't you see?" Wilson's voice was urgent because he saw it perfectly. "The money must go out and there will be no trouble. Everything can be arranged quietly once the money is out. If there is no hitch, there will be no scandal—nothing. I can arrange with Mr. Wilkie after that. I wish to Heaven they had told me, but I suppose they didn't think I knew so much. It's the Bank I am thinking about—the family. I don't care a tinker's damn about their money. Let the bandits have it in Manchuria as long as no one hears about it. It isn't a matter for the police, you understand. If Mr. Moto learns any more, he can say enough to ruin the Bank and I don't trust him, Eva. And you come in it too. No one will know that you are involved in this, if the money goes out tonight. Don't you see? Do you know what I am going to do?"

"No," she answered. "What?"

Wilson Hitchings drew in his breath.

"I don't like it, but I am going to do it. As soon as we get ashore, we are going to the Plantation. I am going to see Mr. Wilkie, or whoever is running this and I think I know who it is. At any rate, I am going to warn them how much Mr. Moto knows. I don't like it because Mr. Moto has taken me into his confidence. At the same time, it might very well save his life. They tried to shoot him last night and then they tried to poison him. They'll leave him alone now. They'll be too anxious to get that money away before they catch him. Mr. Moto is not going to get hurt. No one will get hurt. When it is all over, Mr. Moto can stop the money from going into Manchuria. I can save Mr. Moto's face, as they say in China. Do you see what I mean?"

"You mean you are not going to hurt anybody?" Eva Hitchings said.

"Yes, that's just what I mean," Wilson Hitchings told her. "Not

Moto—I like Moto; not even Mr. Wilkie—as long as the Bank is out of this. It's the only possible thing I can do and the best for everybody. I am thinking of the family."

"Are you always thinking of the family?" Eva Hitchings asked.

"Almost always," Wilson said. "But I am thinking of you too."

Eva Hitchings smiled faintly. "But not too anxiously," she said, "I'm not as delicate as a bank."

"Yes," said Wilson Hitchings. "I suppose that is true."

The smile on her lips grew broader and her eyes were mocking.

"You are not very gallant, are you?" she said. "When it comes to Hitchings Brothers, you haven't got much sense of humor."

At first Wilson did not understand why she had taken his statement personally. The family banking house was too nearly a part of himself for him to be patient when it was treated lightly. He wanted to explain to her that a bank's reputation was at the present day, at any rate, more fragile than a woman's. In the disastrous years of the depression, he had seen how rumor could destroy faith. If a rumor should gain credence that Hitchings Brothers, even indirectly, had been engaged in financing dubious political groups, the whole credit of the firm would fall into disrepute, particularly when financial competition was growing heavy in the East.

"You arc right," he admitted. "I have no sense of humor when it comes to Hitchings Brothers. I don't suppose I have much, at any rate. But when you are brought up in a certain mold, you can't laugh about that mold. I wish you could understand how serious this is. Japan is gaining a very strong commercial hold in the East. Japanese financiers who are competing against us would give a good deal to hear how Hitchings Brothers is involved. Mr. Moto is a Japanese. We can't hope that he'll be quiet—"

She must have been impressed by something he had said, for she was entirely serious again.

"You mean you would allow yourself to be implicated in this mess, to help the family?" she asked.

Wilson Hitchings sighed and nodded.

"I hate it worse than poison," he agreed. "I hate being in this thing. I hate having you in it. The only thing that anyone can do is to rely on his best judgment. This seems to me the very best way out, that's all."

"You don't think much about yourself, do you?" she asked.

"No," Wilson Hitchings said. "I haven't had much time."

Eva Hitchings moved her shoulders impatiently. Her eyes as she looked at him were wide and dark.

"I wonder if you will ever have time to think about yourself," she said. "I wonder if you will ever have the time really to be yourself. You're not so attractive when you are part of a machine. I wish I could get you away from it. I like you when you forget. What would you do right now, if you and I were ordinary people? If we were just out here looking at the sea? If there wasn't any family?"

Wilson Hitchings looked back at her, and in spite of himself the idea amused him.

"If there wasn't any family," he said, "if you weren't the hostess at the Hitchings Plantation. I'd tell you that you are one of the prettiest girls I had ever seen. I might even go so far as to say, probably incorrectly, that you are one of the nicest girls that I have ever known. I'd probably be quite foolish about you because I wouldn't have to think. I'd ask you to give me as much time as possible while I was staying here. I should ask you to have dinner with me tonight. I might even ask you to come back to Shanghai. I should tell you quite irrationally that you are the sort of person I have always been looking for. You are in a way, although I don't know exactly why."

"I should certainly change you," Eva Hitchings said. "You wouldn't know yourself when I got through with you. You wouldn't know yourself even in the mirror."

"Well, I don't suppose I should mind very much," Wilson Hitchings said. "Naturally I would try to change you too."

"I shouldn't mind either," Eva Hitchings answered, "but what would your family say?" Wilson Hitchings began to laugh and the shadows left his mind.

"I imagine they would say a good deal," he answered. The idea was new and it interested him. "I imagine they would be very much surprised." Then Eva Hitchings was laughing too.

"You're nicer now," she said.

"Be careful!" Wilson told her. "Here comes Mr. Moto. Eva, you won't let me down?" Her hand closed over his.

"No," she whispered. "I won't let you down. . . . Why, Mr. Moto, where have you been?"

Mr. Moto rubbed his hands together.

"I have been telling the boy to bring us some whisky and soda," he said. "It will be so very refreshing, don't you think so? There is a coolness on the water when the sun drops and the sun drops in these latitudes so very, very fast."

Mr. Moto was imperturbable and smiling and Wilson could not tell what Mr. Moto thought. He even had a moment's suspicion that Mr. Moto had deliberately left him alone with Eva Hitchings.

Kito had come from the cabin bringing a tray and glasses.

"Here's looking at you," Mr. Moto said. "It is so very nice the way you say it in America. But I do not know what it means."

"Neither do I," Wilson said, and he looked at Mr. Moto over the rim of his glass.

"But even so," said Mr. Moto, "the expression is very, very nice and the day is very, very nice like a painting upon silk. Do you know our Japanese artists? I think we have had some of the greatest painters in the world."

As though nothing else were on his mind, Mr. Moto seated himself and began dicoursing on the culture of Japan. He seemed lost in the subject, as he sat there talking, making nervous little gestures with his fingers, as if he were painting one of the pictures of which he spoke.

"Yes," Wilson heard him say, "they are beautiful; very, very beautiful."

He could not help thinking, as he sat there listening, that Mr. Moto was an amazing man. Mr. Moto was talking of pictures, while Wilson was sitting doggedly, trying to match his wits against Mr. Moto, trying to gauge in his own mind how much Mr. Moto knew. It was like a bridge game when one tried to place the cards in one's opponent's hands. How much did Mr. Moto know? He suspected a great deal, but how much did he know? Wilson could only conjecture, but he was quite sure that Mr. Moto did not know as much as he did. He was very sure, for instance, that Mr. Moto did not know that Mr. Chang had left Shanghai; and the knowledge was a card in Wilson's hand. Mr. Moto might have guessed everything but he needed knowledge still. He needed definite facts and he must not learn the facts.

"If you will excuse me, please," Mr. Moto was saying, "my nation's art is something which I can understand. To me it is reality. Now with your art it is different, please. I have been to so many of your great galleries in Europe. I have tried so hard to appreciate but always there is something which eludes me. So often your artists avoid the facts, the small details, as though they were not pleasant." Mr. Moto took a sip of his whisky and smiled. "Do you avoid the facts, Mr. Hitchings? Do you, Miss Hitchings?"

The suddenness of Mr. Moto's question took Wilson off his guard. He could almost believe that Mr. Moto had been guessing his thoughts while he had been talking.

"I try to deal with reality," Wilson Hitchings said, and Eva Hitchings did not answer.

"I am very, very glad," said Mr. Moto. "Thank you very much. Excuse me, but could I help you, Mr. Hitchings? We both think so very much. Might I ask what you are dealing with just now?"

Wilson tried to keep his own thoughts steady. When it came to matching his wits with Mr. Moto, he felt like an amateur boxer in the ring with a professional, completely aware of his lack of subtlety, and of his dullness of perception.

"Suppose you guess," he invited, "and I'll tell you if you are right."

"Thank you," said Mr. Moto. "That will be very amusing."

"I guess that you are worried, Mr. Hitchings. You are not the sort to be worried about yourself. You are worried about your Bank. I am so very, very sorry."

If Mr. Moto was not to guess too much, Wilson knew that he must tell the truth as nearly as was possible.

"Wouldn't you be worried, Mr. Moto," he inquired, "if you found that the Branch Manager of your family's banking house had mixed himself in a mess like this?"

"I should be very, very worried," Mr. Moto said. "It is very hard for you and I am very sorry. I wonder what you are going to do? Nothing, I hope that is rash, please—nothing that is foolish."

"No," said Wilson. "I am not going to do anything foolish, Mr. Moto. There is nothing I can do. Things are bad enough already. You were right when you told me to keep quietly out of this. The less I am seen in this, the better, Mr. Moto."

Mr. Moto nodded his head genially.

"Please," he said, "I am so very, very glad. So glad you see so clearly now. So glad you will do nothing foolish when you get on shore. You can see now how dangerous it is; and Miss Hitchings, she will do nothing, also?"

"Not if I can help it," Wilson said. "I hope Miss Hitchings will let me look after her."

"Please," said Mr. Moto. "I am so very, very glad. You see, everything is so very nearly finished. It has been difficult, since these men have not been very nice. I hope so much they will not trouble you after this evening. You will leave that to me, I hope. When I get ashore I wish to go completely unobserved. And now, Miss Hitchings, will you do me a favor, please?"

"What is it?" Eva asked. Wilson felt his heart give an unexpected leap. Mr. Moto had drawn a photograph from his pocket.

"Miss Hitchings, you see so many interesting people in that very interesting house of yours," Mr. Moto said. "Please, have you ever seen the man in this picture there? It would save so much trouble if you have seen him. It is the only thing of which I wish to be entirely sure."

Eva Hitchings was looking at the photograph, holding it carefully in both hands. Wilson wished to give her some signal but he did not dare. She frowned, studying the picture.

"I have seen a number of people like him," she said. "He seems very well dressed and dark. He is a rather good example of a certain type, but I don't think I have seen exactly that man before."

Mr. Moto sighed.

"I am sorry," he said, "so very, very sorry. I think he is the man who will be carrying the money. I think—but I must be sure. I must go to look, myself. And now, there is only one thing more."

"What is it?" asked Wilson Hitchings.

Mr. Moto stood up.

"When you get ashore," Mr. Moto said, "please, I beg you to do nothing. It would be very, very nice, I think, if you went quietly to your hotel and dined, but do not go near the Plantation. Neither of you, please. It will not be very nice out there tonight. They will be so very anxious to get this money on the boat. Remember, you must do nothing, Mr. Hitchings."

"Yes," said Wilson. "I'll remember."

"I am so glad," Mr. Moto said. "And now, if you will excuse me, I shall go forward to start the engine. No, please, do not bother, Mr. Hitchings. I shall need no help. Will you stand by the wheel, please? It will be growing dark in a very little while."

Mr. Moto moved away, forward, and Wilson looked at Eva Hitchings.

"Thanks," he said, "for not letting me down. Did you know the man in that picture, Eva?"

She nodded.

"Yes," she whispered. "He's the man, the one who takes the money."

"Well," said Wilson. "Moto mustn't see him. We've got to tell them, Eva. I hate it. But we've got to tell them."

# 12

THERE WAS no difficulty in getting the sampan back. The cool efficiency of Mr. Moto, which seemed to make him at home in any situation, made everything move perfectly without any sense of effort.

"Thank you so much for being so polite," Mr. Moto said. "Yes, I can do many, many things. I can mix drinks and wait on table, and I am a very good valet. I can navigate and manage small boats. I have studied at two foreign universities. I also know carpentry and surveying and five Chinese dialects. So very many things come in useful. Ah, there are the lights in line. You steer so very nicely, Mr. Hitchings."

"Thanks," said Wilson. "Yes, Mr. Moto, you are a useful man."

"It is so very nice to have you say so," Mr. Moto said. "It has been a pleasure to make your acquaintance. I think I should go back to the engines, please."

Everything ran smoothly except Wilson Hitchings' thoughts and those made him hate himelf because he had not been frank with Mr. Moto. He had not realized how much he had grown to like the man who was so different from himself in race and in tradition. He liked him for his courage. He liked him for his wit. And Mr. Moto trusted him—that was the worst of all. Eva Hitchings stood beside him near the wheel and her presence gave him an unexpected sense of security.

"I feel like Judas Iscariot," Wilson Hitchings said.

"Yes," she said. "I know the way you feel."

"But you understand me, don't you?" he asked.

He saw her face near his, white and shadowy in the dark.

"Do you care if I understand?" she asked.

"Yes," he said. "I do."

"I am glad of that," she answered.

He was convinced that he should not feel about her the way he did. It complicated matters and had nothing to do with actuality, but it made no difference.

"Eva," he whispered, "I am going to get you out of this. This isn't any place for you." She laughed very softly.

"You're awfully nice," she said. "It's curious, I have just been thinking that I might have to look after you."

He did not answer her because he heard Mr. Moto calling softly.

"Please, is everything all right?" Mr. Moto asked. "If you will give me the wheel, I know a dock where we can tie up. We should be alongside in a very few minutes. What a nice time we had."

"Yes," said Wilson. "Very nice. So interesting."

"So very interesting," Mr. Moto said. "Excuse me, there is one thing more I wish to ask. There is a man named Mr. Maddock. Did you see him this morning, Mr. Hitchings?"

The lights from the city rising up into the darkness of the hills came up from the harbor in a dim, faint light. Wilson hoped that the light would be faint enough so that Mr. Moto would not see him clearly.

"What makes you think I saw him?" Wilson asked.

"Please," said Mr. Moto. "I saw him this morning going to your hotel. Could you tell me what he wanted, please?"

"He came to sell me information," Wilson said. "He seemed very nervous. I didn't buy the information because I knew it already."

"Thank you," said Mr. Moto, "very much. I think you were very wise. He is not a very nice man but he is very, very capable. And now we shall be ashore in a few minutes. I can manage everything very nicely. I shall telephone you in the morning, Mr. Hitchings. Remember, keep away from the Plantation, please. You must not bother about anything. Kito will look after the men forward. Walk to the street and find an automobile and have a pleasant evening."

There was no one at the dock where they landed but Mr. Moto was very careful. He stood for a full minute examining the shadows made by the street lights.

"Good-by," whispered Mr. Moto, as he climbed up to the pier. "I must leave you now, please. It has been so very, very nice."

"Good-by," said Wilson. "Good luck, Mr. Moto."

The three of them walked together to the street which ran by the waterfront. A closed car was standing waiting at the curb and the driver was opening the door.

"Good-by," said Mr. Moto again. "I am so sorry I have so very much to do."

He stepped into the car, the door slammed, and the car moved off, while Wilson and Eva Hitchings stood staring after him.

"Now what do you think of that?" said Wilson. "He has it all arranged. We must get to the Plantation as quickly as we can. There won't be much time if he starts like that."

There was no trouble in finding a taxicab and a driver; and Wilson told the driver to hurry. As the car moved through the city, he felt as if he were at the Plantation already. He hardly noticed that Eva Hitchings was holding his hand.

"We've got to hurry," he said again.

"Yes, Wilson," she said. "We're hurrying."

"I suppose Wilkie was playing the stock market," he said. "That's the way these things always happen."

"Yes," said Eva Hitchings. "I'm afraid he was. You mustn't be too hard on him."

"I can't be," Wilson told her. "I wish to Heaven I could."

Her fingers tightened over his.

"What are you thinking about?" she asked. "I wish you wouldn't look so far away."

"I'm thinking about you," he answered. "And I wish very much I wasn't but I can't help it."

Although common sense told him it was incongruous, what he did seemed perfectly in keeping with the time and the place. Before he knew what he was doing, his arm was around her and her head was on his shoulder.

"Think about me some more," she suggested. "Maybe it will do you good. It might make you less responsible."

"Why do you like me?" Wilson asked.

"I don't know," she said.

"Well, it's the same here," Wilson said. "I don't know why I like you either. Eva, I want to tell you something. . . . "

It was true he felt less responsible. He did not seem to care much about Hitchings Brothers, or Mr. Maddock, or Mr. Chang, or Mr. Wilkie. He had an odd sense of being himself for the first time in his life. He did not lose that feeling until they were in the mountains, passing through the gateposts of the drive that was marked "Hitchings Plantation."

"Well," said Wilson, "we are coming home."

"Yes," she said. "I am coming home. It sems as though I had never been at home until just now."

# 13

Wilson recalled what Mr. Moto had said the night before. He had an accurate faculty for remembering conversations.

"The only thing I need to know now," Mr. Moto had said, "is how Mr. Chang's money disappears at Hitchings Plantation and reappears in Manchukuo. I only need to know who gets it and who brings it there. Then, a few simple words over the cable to suitable persons will do the rest."

It was ironical to think that such a short while ago Wilson had been in sympathy with Mr. Moto's efforts. That was before he knew that the Manager of Hitchings Brothers had involved himself in that fantastic scheme.

A few minutes before, Mr. Moto had shown him a photograph, hoping to get an answer. Clearly enough Mr. Moto was still looking for the man who had brought the money, and he had not found him yet. His search had brought him aboard the sampan, Wilson knew, and his search had not succeeded. Wilson could guess by then that Mr. Moto never did anything without a definite reason. There was a reason for his idle conversation as he sipped abstemiously at his whisky. Wilson had watched him in a dull fascination. Mr. Moto had been trying to find out something as he talked, his restless eyes darting from face to face. Mr. Moto had been hoping to learn what both of those two strangers thought. He was painting a picture in his mind, each line of it was pitilessly accurate. His manner had been enough to tell Wilson that the picture was nearly finished.

Although it was early in the evening, only shortly after nine, the lights of the house were on full blast, casting uncertain yellow patterns against the trees and bushes around it. Halfway up the drive Wilson told the car to stop and paid off the driver. Even at that distance from the house, he could hear the music from the front room. He could not tell why the atmosphere of the place set his nerves on edge, unless it was the contrast of the music and the lights against a certain half-lost dignity. It reminded him of an old estate in the East, turned into a roadhouse or into a private school, because of death or misfortune. There was the same sadness about Hitchings Plantation in the dark—the same muted speech of better days; and yet, there was an ugliness about it too. There was a rank, musty smell of vegetation and a feeling that unseen eyes were on them, as they walked toward the house.

"It might be better if we went in by a back door," Wilson said. "We don't want to make a scene in front."

He heard Eva Hitchings laugh.

"You're very silly sometimes," Eva said. "They probably know we are here already. There should be watchers all around the house." But her voice was very low, as though the silence depressed her. "They will be looking for Mr. Moto, don't you think?"

A moment later, Wilson saw that she was right, when a man stepped noiselessly from a clump of bamboo close by the road. There was enough light from the house by then to make him out fairly clearly.

"Why, howdy, pal," the man said. "Howdy, Miss Hitchings. Say, what the hell are you doing here? I thought you was out sailing." It was Mr. Maddock speaking. He stood in front of them as black as an undertaker, a hand in either pocket.

"We came back early, Mr. Maddock," Wilson said.

"Well, well," said Mr. Maddock. "That's interesting, pal."

"I am glad I met you," Wilson said. "Are you enjoying the evening, sir?"

"Yes," said Mr. Maddock. "It's nice I met you too, before some of the boys got rough with you. What the hell do you want here, pal?"

"Miss Hitchings lives here, doesn't she?" Wilson asked.

"Say what you want to say quick, pal," said Mr. Maddock urgently. "What's your game? Have you got the cops with you and the wagon?"

"Don't be nervous, Mr. Maddock," Wilson told him. "I'm in a hurry too. I'm in a hurry to see Mr. Wilkie. He's here, isn't he? And I'm in a hurry to see a Chinese gentleman called Mr. Chang. I take it he's here too."

Mr. Maddock made a half-audible sound in his throat.

"Wise guy, ain't you?" he said. "How the hell did you know that?"

"Never mind," said Wilson. It was plain that Mr. Maddock was startled. "I know so much that I'm frightened for you, Mr. Maddock. They've got to get that money on the boat just as quick as they can get it, see? Will you take me in to Wilkie, or do you want me to go alone?"

Then Eva Hitchings spoke. "You'd better hurry, Paul," she said. "He means it. He's worried about the Bank."

"Excuse me," Mr. Maddock said. "The big boy wouldn't miss

seeing you for anything. So you was worried about the Bank, was you? Excuse me, first I had better frisk you, pal. Reach up at the sky easy. No hard feelings, pal." His left hand fluttered over Wilson's pockets.

"Oh-oh," said Mr. Maddock. His hand had come upon the gunmetal revolver, and he balanced it on his palm. "Say," he said. "That's George's gun. What's the story, pal?"

"I took it away from him," Wilson said. "He was antisocial, Mr. Maddock."

"The hell you say," said Mr. Maddock.

"The hell I don't!" said Wilson. "George and the two sailors are tied up in their bunks and the boat is at the public dock. You had better get them untied quickly. You haven't got much time."

"You don't say?" said Mr. Maddock. "And where's that Jap boy, Kito?"

"I wouldn't trust him if I were you," Wilson answered. "I don't know where he is."

Mr. Maddock tapped Wilson's chest. "And you're looking for the big guy, are you?" he said. "All right, you're going to see him now, whether you like it or not. Step ahead of me, and you too, missy, through the garden to the office door. You know the way. Step lively. I knew there would be a blow-off. Didn't I say it was time to lam?"

Eva Hitchings walked first, and then Wilson and then Mr. Maddock. They walked around the house, over the path and by the overgrown garden, past the brightly lighted kitchen and then around the corner to an inconspicuous door with a window beside it. The shutters of the window were closed and the curtain was drawn, but Wilson could see a chink of light.

Someone was in the room behind the door. Mr. Maddock was knocking softly—one rap, then a pause and four short raps. The door opened a crack and he heard Mr. Maddock say: "It's okay. It's Maddock. Open up and be damn quick! This way, missy. This way, pal."

And Eva and Wilson Hitchings were standing in a small square room that was furnished like an office, and Mr. Maddock was shooting home a bolt on the door. The room was probably Eva's father's office, because the furniture was old and there were old photographs on the wall. Against the wall opposite where he was standing was a battered rolltop desk. There was a safe beside it with its door open and half a dozen assorted chairs that must have come from other parts of the house. But Wilson remembered the furnishings only afterward. The room was stifling hot and filled with cigarette smoke and bright with electric light. Mr. Wilkie was seated near the desk, with his coat off, staring at him.

In front of the desk, in ugly business clothes, wearing a heavy watch-chain, was a placid fat Chinese, and Wilson knew who he was. He was Mr. Chang, the man he had seen for an instant in his uncle's house and the man he had seen again in Joe's Place at Shanghai. Two other men were kneeling in front of the safe. They were evidently packing neat piles of bills into a black traveling bag that lay at Mr. Chang's feet. One of them was the half-caste croupier, and the other Wilson had also seen before. He had seen him in Shanghai; a lean, cadaverous man, with dead-black hair—thin, bony features and cool white skin. There was a Russian cigarette drooping from the corner of his mouth, just as Wilson had seen it last. His narrow eyes were on Wilson and his thin forehead was creased under his black hair. It was a face that was hard to forget, a wild, relentless face. There was an instant silence as Mr. Wilkie started from his chair.

"Maddock, you damn fool!" Mr. Wilkie said. "What do you mean by this?"

Mr. Chang raised his hand and allowed it to fall gently on his knee.

"Sit down, Mr. Wilkie!" he said. His voice was high and bell-like. His enunciation was perfect. "What is it, Mr. Maddock?" Mr. Maddock gave his head a jerk toward Wilson Hitchings.

"There's plenty, boss," said Mr. Maddock. "This guy has tied up the boat at the public dock and tied up George and them two Kanakas in it. Kito's lammed, that's what." The dark-haired man got slowly to his feet.

"So," he began in a strange, foreign voice, and he leaned toward Mr. Wilkie. "So, that's what comes of your foolishness. You said he was a fool. Do you still think that he's a fool?"

"Be quiet!" said Mr. Chang. "Wait a minute, please." He picked up a telephone on the desk and called a number, and then he was speaking in Chinese, softly, swiftly, while everyone watched him without speaking, until he set down the telephone.

"That will do," Mr. Chang said. "That will be attended to. Yes, I agree with you, Sergi. It was an asinine idea of Mr. Wilkie's, and one I should have prevented, should I have known it. Maddock, bring a chair for Miss Hitchings and a chair for the gentleman! So you found them walking here, did you, Maddock? You did very well to bring them. I see you remember me, Mr. Hitchings. It is so pleasant to see one of the family here. I heard from a Mr. Stanley, in Shanghai, that you were interested in our arrangements. I have always enjoyed your uncle's conversation, and I know you will be reasonable. You have evidently come here to say something. You find us rather occupied. We are arranging to ship this money—$200,000 worth—to our poor friends in Manchuria. If you have anything to say, may I ask you to say it quickly?"

Wilson nodded toward Mr. Wilkie, who had leaned back in his chair.

"I hope you can give me just a few minutes," he said, politely. "And then you'll understand why I'm here, I think. You will if you are a reasonable man."

Mr. Chang's moonlike face curled in an easy smile and he clasped his hands across his stomach.

"My dear young friend," he said. "I have always admired the Hitchings family. You will find me very reasonable. It is my hope that we will both be very reasonable tonight. I have come here with the simple purpose of being reasonable. Pay no attention to these fellows. You and I are businessmen. What do you wish to say?"

At another time the reasonableness of Mr. Chang might have been solid and reassuring, for Mr. Chang was like a solid businessman, and an admirably fat one, from the Chinese point of view. His impassivity gave the impression of conservative reliability. But there was a quality in all that solidness which Wilson Hitchings had never encountered before. There was something adamantine behind the pale-yellow corpulence of Mr. Chang, that was as cool and as hard as the jade which his people loved. Mr. Chang's cool and emotionless glance was disconcerting. Mr. Chang was like a capable poker player, who had drawn a very good hand and who was willing to back his hand to the limit. The impact of his personality was heavy in the room, so definite that there was no doubt that it was Mr. Chang who was giving orders. When Wilson looked at Mr. Wilkie the latter avoided his glance. Mr. Wilkie was looking hot and tired, no longer cool and dapper.

"Eva, my dear," Mr. Wilkie said, "I think I had better take you to some other part of the house. This is something which you do not need to understand—something between Mr. Chang and me and Mr. Hitchings."

Eva Hitchings stood up straight.

"I would rather stay, thank you," she answered. "I'm afraid I understand everything rather well. You have been lying to me, Uncle Joe. I don't know that I blame you, but you have been lying."

"My dear, " began Mr. Wilkie, "that is very inaccurate."

Mr. Chang raised a heavy blunt-fingered hand.

"That will do, if you please," he said. "I am negotiating this business, Mr. Wilkie. Miss Eva must stay with us, since she is involved. I hope she will find—pleasantly involved. No one should leave this room until we understand each other. Now, Mr. Hitchings, do not allow yourself to be interrupted, please," and Mr. Chang placed a hand on either knee and bent his head attentively forward.

Without being able to ascribe any reason for it, Wilson suddenly had a very definite wish that he was not there. Although he summoned up all his will power and self-control, he felt his confidence evaporating under Mr. Chang's cool scrutiny; because Mr. Chang was very sure of something, insolently sure of something, and Wilson did not know what. He only knew that he was caught in some combination as intricate and involved as a piece of Chinese carving.

"First, I want you to understand my reason for being here," Wilson said. "I want you to understand I am here entirely of my own free will, not because I approve of what you are doing but because I did not know until today that Mr. Wilkie had been extending the interests of Hitchings Brothers, without our advice or consent, Mr. Chang." He stopped and nodded at the money on the floor.

"Sergi," said Mr. Chang, "continue with the money. . . . That is very clearly put, Mr. Hitchings, I knew that you would be logical and reasonable. I was so sure of it that I wished to talk to you, until I found that Mr. Wilkie had been so impetuous as to send you out to sea. You are concerned—and naturally concerned, because you find Hitchings Brothers involved in a transaction which may hurt its reputation. You are quite right. Mr. Wilkie, as Manager, has been helping more than necessary in transferring funds. It does truly involve Hitchings Brothers but I have a very high opinion of your family. You are not here to speak about recriminations and right and wrong. We both have our own interests. I presume you are here to make a proposition. What is your proposition, Mr. Hitchings?"

Wilson Hitchings kept his eyes on Mr. Chang and tried to speak coolly but there was a tremor in his voice.

"You are correct, Mr. Chang," he said. "I have come here to warn you to get this money out of here as quickly as possible and to get yourself and your messenger out with it. I don't think you have got much time. There is a Japanese agent here, Mr. Chang. He's found out everything about your methods. There is only one thing he wants. He wants to identify the man who is handling the money."

Sergi paused with a handful of currency clasped between his fingers and stared at Wilson unblinkingly.

"Ah," he said, in a silky, gentle voice. "So he has got as far as that."

"Yes," said Wilson. "He has got as far as that. . . . I do not mind about you, Mr. Sergi, whoever you may be,—I remember that I saw you in Shanghai,—or about you either, Mr. Chang; but I do mind about Mr. Wilkie. I must stop Hitchings Brothers being identified with this. That's why I'm telling you to pack up quickly and get yourselves and the money on the boat."

Mr. Chang's blunt fingers closed on his knees and relaxed but his face was impassively intent.

"Your concern is quite natural," he said. "I had the intuition that we could cooperate with one another. I even suggested it to your uncle in Shanghai. I was sorry he refused, but perhaps he will understand the necessity now. You are speaking of a Mr. Moto, I presume? I have made several attempts to be rid of Mr. Moto. Where did you see this Mr. Moto today? I should like to know, because we have been looking for him."

Wilson Hitchings answered deliberately.

"Mr. Moto had concealed himself in Mr. Wilkie's boat," he said. "He was in a great hurry the last time I saw him. That is why I tell you that you haven't got much time."

Mr. Chang leaned forward; his eyes were stony and unblinking.

"So that is where he was," he said. "I am deeply obliged to you, Mr. Hitchings. You have been a very great help to a useful cause tonight. Go out quickly, Mr. Maddock. You have men enough, I think. When Mr. Moto comes, bring him here. I want to be sure of everything myself. I want no error this time. Be careful with him, Mr. Maddock."

Mr. Maddock grinned and his Adam's apple moved slowly up and down.

"You want to see him here," he said, "before he gets the works?"

"Exactly," said Mr. Chang. "No one has seemed to be able to give him what you call 'the works'—certainly not last night."

"Okay, boss," said Mr. Maddock. He walked noiselessly to the door and closed it softly behind him, and the room was silent for a moment.

"Chang," said the pale man named Sergi, looking up from the traveling bag, "you had better not. This is dangerous."

"Allow me to attend to this," said Mr. Chang gently. "It is the only way for business to continue. He would do the same to you."

Wilson Hitchings opened his mouth to speak and stopped. He felt the blood drumming hotly in his ears and he heard Eva Hitchings ask the question which he had meant to ask himself.

"What are you going to do with Mr. Moto?"

Mr. Chang leaned back in his chair with his hands still on his knees.

"We will consider that in a moment," he said. "Please do not worry. Mr. Maddock is very capable in such matters. He will unquestionably bring Mr. Moto here. No doubt Mr. Moto is in the shrubbery at this very minute. You look surprised? Surely you follow me, Mr. Hitchings?"

Wilson Hitchings cleared his throat. "No," he said, "I don't."

"Pierre," said Mr. Chang. "Place a chair for Mr. Hitchings and a chair for the young lady, please. Also one for Mr. Moto—to be ready when he arrives. You know, Mr. Hitchings, really I would prefer that you sat down. Your mind will be more tranquil sitting down. I wish you to realize that we must help each other. Consider me as your elder brother, Mr. Hitchings."

In spite of himself, Wilson felt all his concentration was on the face of Mr. Chang. He tried to draw his eyes away but he could not. "You must realize that we are partners," said Mr. Chang. "You and Miss Hitchings, Mr. Wilkie and I."

Wilson cleared his throat again. He felt the perspiration gathering clammily on his forehead.

"He's right, Hitchings," Mr. Wilkie said. "Now, think and be reasonable, Hitchings."

Something inside of Wilson was struggling against his self-control—something as close to panic as anything that he had ever known.

"What do you mean?" he asked hoarsely. "If you mean I am going to be a partner in a murder, you are mistaken, Mr. Chang."

"Wait!" Mr. Chang's voice was very gentle. "Control yourself. You are going too far ahead. Think of yourself, Mr. Hitchings. Relax and allow the current to guide you. You have done the only thing which is reasonable and possible tonight. You have done the only thing that can save your house and that is very admirable. Your business house is very close to ruin if any of this affair is exposed. You have seen that yourself. We are not speaking of murder. We are speaking of continuing a very lucrative and patriotic business."

"Go on!" said Wilson Hitchings, and he felt his heart beating in his throat.

"That is better," said Mr. Chang, soothingly. "You are thinking of your family now and of the honor of your house. You will go far in the Orient, Mr. Hitchings. It is a good family and a good house. They will both be safe in my hands and Mr. Wilkie's, Mr. Hitchings. I can promise you that and I do not break a promise."

Wilson Hitchings tried to think, but instead he found himself struggling against a will and a determination which was stronger than his own. He tried to speak casually but he knew that he made a very bad attempt.

"You are not quite clear," he said, with difficulty. "I am trying to follow you, but you are not quite clear."

Mr. Chang nodded brightly, almost sympathetically.

"I have an admiration for you, Mr. Hitchings," he said. "You are controlling yourself very well, and so is the young lady. She will be loyal to you and you will be loyal to your house. There are many painful matters which we must face upon the road of life. I was young once myself and I appreciate your qualms. Quite beyond our own intention, we become involved in difficulties, as you are involved tonight. Then a sensible man will go forward with the tide and I know that you are sensible. If this affair becomes public, it will mean ruin to your business. You must help us so that this will not happen. You think this is the last time we shall forward money in this manner, is it not so, Mr. Hitchings?"

"Yes," said Wilson. "Yes, I think so."

"But your reason, Mr. Hitchings," Mr. Chang continued smoothly, "will tell you that it is not so. This method of sending money is too valuable and too lucrative for us. We cannot give it up. We shall continue, because your house is so involved that it will allow us to continue." Mr. Chang paused and Mr. Wilkie spoke, confidently, like a man in a directors' meeting.

"There won't be any complications, Hitchings," he said. "There won't be a breath of scandal."

"Wait a moment," said Mr. Chang. "Wait a moment, please. I know the Hitchings family. They are cold and logical and Mr. Hitchings is an excellent representative. He is beginning to understand already. In a few minutes he will see that his own personal interest will be involved also—that we are partners already. I think perhaps you follow me now. I see your mind putting my words together, Mr. Hitchings. Sit quietly and think. Please do not move."

"I think you had better go on," Wilson Hitchings said. His mind was dealing with something so ugly and so sinister, and so far from his anticipations, that it took away his breath. Mr. Chang was nodding his head approvingly.

"Ah," he said. "You are a very promising young man. Anyone involved in a business transaction must be personally interested. That is why I have a surprise for you tonight. Be tranquil. Listen to me, please. Your logic must tell you that Mr. Moto must be eliminated. Tonight you and Miss Hitchings will be a party in that elimination indirectly. I see you did not expect it. Quiet, Mr. Hitchings! Think! Think of yourself and the Hitchings Bank. You have been a party to it already. Of your own free will, you told us to expect Mr. Moto, Mr. Hitchings."

Wilson Hitchings sat motionless but the words were like a blow across his face. The whole business was as clear as daylight and as ugly as his thoughts.

"That's a lie!" he stammered. He was ashamed of himself for stammering. "I hadn't the least idea—"

"Of course, it is a lie!" said Eva Hitchings. "You can't do a thing like that. Do you think I'll stay here and let you do it—do you think that?"

"Wait!" said Mr. Chang softly. "One little minute please! Think, I beg you. No matter what the result will be, you will be suspected, always. Think of your family, Mr. Hitchings. And what is this man to you? He is not your affair. He will be got rid of so no one can find him. You must rely on me. Think very carefully, please. The family, Mr. Hitchings—the family."

Then Wilson Hitchings was on his feet.

"Damn the family!" he said hoarsely. "Do you think we would soil our hands with a bunch of crooks like you?"

"Sergi," said Mr. Chang, gently. "Pierre . . . "

But Wilson scarcely heard him. He had darted toward the door and his hand was on the lock. He was wrenching at the door, when he heard Eva Hitchings scream; and then her scream was choked. Then a coat was over his head and he was tripped backward over the floor.

"Help!" Wilson shouted. "Murder!"

Even then he was shocked at the banality of his words. A knee was thrust into the pit of his stomach with all the weight of Mr. Chang behind it. He was gasping, choking for his breath. Someone had his shoulders and was pulling him to his feet.

"A chair, Sergi," Mr. Chang was saying. "Tie him to the chair. Adhesive tape for the mouth, please, but I shall let him get his breath."

The coat was jerked from his head and he was staring into Mr. Chang's cool eyes.

"First a handkerchief," said Mr. Chang, "and then the tape. Can you hear me, Mr. Hitchings? You will have been here, Mr. Hitchings, and you will not have said a word. I doubt if anyone will believe your story, about being bound and gagged. You are far too much involved—but you are not a fool. Your judgment will come back."

Wilson was still struggling for his breath and there was a mist before his eyes, but he could see the room plainly enough. Opposite him, Eva Hitchings was also being tied to a chair and the croupier tied a handkerchief over her mouth. Mr. Wilkie was leaning over her.

"Eva, my dear," Mr. Wilkie was saying, "I am very sorry for all this, but it will be over in a very little while."

Sergi was tossing the pile of bank notes again into the open bag, and Mr. Chang had seated himself before the desk.

"I am so sorry," Mr. Chang said. "I hope you will bear me no ill will, Mr. Hitchings. I think you will thank me in the end. You will come to realize that human life counts far less in the Orient. It may disturb you for a little while but in the end you will forget. When we get back to Shanghai, we shall have a talk about it, over a very good dinner. You will sympathize with my point of view. I am essentially a nationalist. I have no great love or respect for Japan, but Mr. Moto, himself, will understand everything perfectly. You need not have him on your conscience, Mr. Hitchings. No, you need fear nothing. All you need is a little time for quiet consideration. No one will harm you. It is out of the question, of course. Now, simply think of my speech in the nature of a farewell until I return in a few hours. I telephoned a while ago to have the sampan put in order. Sergi and I will leave with the money. There is a vessel outside waiting for us called the *Eastern Light.* So you knew? I supposed you did. We need not have any secrets any longer." He paused, and there was a rap on the door. One long—and four short raps.

"Let them in, Sergi," said Mr. Chang. "That will be Mr. Moto. We should have caught him in any event, Mr. Hitchings, so do not have it any too heavily on your conscience."

# 14

WILSON STARED at the door and felt deathly ill. Sergi had opened the door and stepped aside, revealing Mr. Moto, with his purple necktie awry and with a smudge of black earth on his cheek, walking carefully as though the ground were hot. The reason for his care was supplied by Mr. Maddock who came directly behind him, with the muzzle of a pistol pressed against Mr. Moto's back.

"Easy, pal," said Mr. Maddock. "The boss wants to see you, pal."

"Close the door, Sergi," said Mr. Chang. He paused and examined Mr. Moto, thoughtfully. "It is nice to see you, Mr. Moto," Mr. Chang said. "You have given us a great deal of trouble."

Mr. Moto bowed.

"Easy, pal," said Mr. Maddock. "Keep your hands still, pal."

"Excuse me," said Mr. Moto. His voice was as steady as ever. "I did not know you were here, Mr. Chang, though I suppose I should have guessed. Everything has been done so very, very well—except last night you were so clumsy."

"Thank you," said Mr. Chang, gently. "I felt that circumstances demanded my management."

The gold in Mr. Moto's teeth gleamed. He was looking at Sergi with the lively interest of a professional, who forgets personal discomfort and danger in a pursuit of knowledge. Sergi looked back at him, with a cigarette still drooping from the corner of his mouth.

"How do you do, Mr. Moto," Sergi said.

"How do you do," said Mr. Moto. "I am so very, very glad to know who it has been. It is so very, very nice to know that a skillful man has been working. I hope you have been well since Mongolia."

"Yes," said Sergi. "Thank you."

"I am so very, very glad," said Mr. Moto politely. "It is such an uncertain life. I have always respected your work so very, very much. Do you remember the code at the Naval Conference?"

The other man's face brightened and he smiled.

"Yes," he answered. "Naturally."

"You stole it so very, very nicely," Mr. Moto said. "I am so very glad to see Mr. Sergi, Mr. Chang. Now, I do not feel that I have been slow or stupid. He is so very, very clever." Mr. Moto drew his breath through his teeth. "And now I suppose," he inquired, "you are leaving for Harbin?"

"Yes," said Sergi, "in that general direction. I am a fur buyer for a London house."

"Ah, yes," said Mr. Moto. "How very, very nice. It would be so nice to know, even though it does no good."

"You are quite right," agreed Mr. Chang. "It will do no good, but of course, you understand why."

"Yes," said Mr. Moto. "Yes, of course. There is only one solution, naturally. Please do not think I am begging for any other." His glance had moved swiftly toward Wilson Hitchings. "So you did not take my advice," Mr. Moto said. "But then, I was very sure you would not, Mr. Hitchings. Please do not shake your head. All this is very natural, quite to be expected."

Mr. Chang placed his hands on his knees.

"Tie his wrists, Sergi," he said. "Gag him! You have made all the arrangements, Mr. Maddock?"

"Okay, boss," said Mr. Maddock.

"And they know where to bring him afterward?"

"Yes, boss," said Mr. Maddock. "It's all okay."

"Do you need any help, Mr. Maddock?" Mr. Chang inquired. "I should be glad to spare Pierre to help."

"Nix," said Mr. Maddock. "I can manage him okay."

"Very well," said Mr. Chang. "I think you had better start."

"Come on, pal," said Mr. Maddock.

"Good-by, Moto," said Sergi, smoothly. "I suppose it will be my turn some day."

Mr. Moto nodded. The door opened. Standing very straight and walking carefully, Mr. Moto stepped into the dark and Mr. Maddock followed him, noiselessly. Sergi bent down and locked the traveling bag. Mr. Wilkie sat staring at the floor. Everyone seemed to be waiting for something—including Mr. Chang, who had not moved from his chair. Wilson could hear Mr. Chang's breath, smooth and regular. Then Mr. Chang was studying him attentively.

"Listen to me," said Mr. Chang. "In a few minutes it will be over. I know you are not a fool, Mr. Hitchings. Listen to me carefully. You and Miss Hitchings will remain here for a few hours. Mr. Wilkie will stay to look after you. He will take every care of your comfort. I shall go to see that Sergi arrives properly at the *Eastern Light.* By the time I come back, I hope you will have had opportunity to think. I hope that you will be reasonable with so much to gain and so little to lose. I shall be surprised if you are not. I shall dislike making other plans. Pierre, you shall come with us to the dock. I shall want my raincoat. Are you ready, Sergi?"

Sergi nodded, and lighted a cigarette.

"Then we have nothing to do but wait for Mr. Maddock," said Chang. "What are you doing, Mr. Wilkie?"

"I am getting a drink, if you don't mind," Mr. Wilkie said. He opened a drawer of the desk, pulled out a bottle of whisky, drew out the cork and tilted the bottle to his lips.

Wilson waited for a sound outside. He strained his ears, but heard no sound.

"Don't be nervous, Mr. Wilkie," said Mr. Chang. "I shall be back soon enough. I shall manage everything correctly. You must not let these matters trouble you. There are a hundred other things to do, if our friends are not reasonable. Open the door, Sergi, Mr. Maddock is knocking."

Mr. Chang rose and straightened his coat, as Mr. Maddock stepped jauntily across the threshold.

"Everything went through properly?" Mr. Chang inquired.

Mr. Maddock shrugged his narrow shoulders.

"Hell," he said. "Why shouldn't it? You didn't hear no roughhouse, did you? He croaked easy without a sound. He's on his way to take a dive over the cliff by now."

"Very good," said Mr. Chang. "You are highly satisfactory, Maddock, and now you can go out with us on the boat. You first, Sergi. I shall see you later, Mr. Hitchings."

What amazed Wilson even then in that moment of incredulous revulsion was Mr. Chang's extreme casualness. He recalled that his uncle had once told him that a foreigner could never wholly comprehend the Eastern point of view. The actions of Mr. Chang and Mr. Moto must have been bound up in an etiquette of behavior that was admirably mixed with pride. He had seen Mr. Moto being conducted into the dark under Mr. Chang's directions, to be murdered in cold blood; yet the control of Mr. Moto and of Mr. Chang had been so perfect that there was no more emphasis on the whole affair than there might be in the exchange of ordinary social amenities. Mr. Chang had said that life was cheap, and Mr. Moto must have been in most emphatic agreement. The philosophy of those two men held something more than life. There was no doubt that manners were placed above it—manners that had placed them beyond the sickening horror which Wilson felt. He could have believed that they both would have considered his emotions uncivilized and barbaric. Mr. Chang, who had just indulged in murder, was leaving the room as calmly as a businessman might leave his office. Sergi had put on a dark hat and looked like an innocent traveling salesman. Mr. Maddock was noiseless and impersonal. He even took the trouble to lean over and pat Wilson's cheek almost affectionately, and he grinned when Wilson winced away from his cold touch.

"So long, pal," said Mr. Maddock, softly. "Seeing life, ain't you, pal?"

## 15

THEY WERE all gone. They were gone like abstract thought leaving only a memory. There was still the odor of cigarette smoke in the room. Wilson was still tied in his chair, sitting mutely, facing Eva Hitchings, but the atmosphere of the room was changing into the commonplace so that Mr. Chang seemed impossible.

Wilson allowed his glance to rest on Mr. Wilkie, and it was clear that Mr. Wilkie did not share the cool assurance of Mr. Chang. Mr. Wilkie had all the attributes of a gambler who is playing for stakes that are too high for his resources. He looked old. His face was moist and drawn and there was a tremor in his fingers. He picked up the whisky bottle and took another drink, breathed deeply and drew the back of his hand across his lips.

"You saw that?" said Mr. Wilkie, in a strained voice, and he seemed to be talking because he wanted to assure himself that he was not alone. "Eva, Eva, I am so sorry that you saw it; but listen to me, both of you. I don't like it any more than you do. You understand we are all caught in this now, don't you? You must do what he says. For Heaven's sake, do what he says!"

He seemed to expect an answer. He appeared to have forgotten that neither of them could speak.

"Listen, Hitchings," he said. "I honestly can feel for you. I am not entirely callous. I started in this because the firm's accounts got mixed; and then I could not stop. You will know why when you talk some more to that man Chang. It was my idea to have the money lost over the gaming table, and it wasn't a bad idea, but I am not a murderer any more than either of you two are. It is only because I am desperate, Hitchings.

"If you will be sensible, I promise both of you that everything will be all right. No one will ever hear a breath of this. I don't want it to come out any more than you. I am a sound man in the community and I am fond of you, Eva. I am devoted to you, even if you do not believe it.

"Please, Mr. Hitchings. Please, be reasonable. I don't know what will happen if you aren't. You've seen him; he won't stop at anything."

But Wilson Hitchings was not reasonable. He was struggling until his chair toppled and creaked.

"Don't do that!" said Mr. Wilkie. "That will do no good. You must not do that, Mr. Hitchings."

A sound at the door made Mr. Wilkie start. Someone was rapping—one long, and four short raps—and Mr. Wilkie's mouth dropped open.

"He's back," Mr. Wilkie whispered, and his face was as white as paper. "He's changed his mind. He's back. Tell him you'll do anything he says, Hitchings! Tell him! It's your only chance!"

Mr. Wilkie's hands were fumbling with the lock in uncertain trembling haste.

"Yes," he was saying. "All right. All right."

Someone from the outside pushed the door so suddenly that it checked his speech and threw Mr. Wilkie off his balance, so that he stepped backward.

Wilson heard Eva Hitchings make a sound which was half a sob and half a groan. A small man in a dark alpaca coat bounded into the room as though he had been thrown there, and he slammed the door shut with his right hand.

"You must not make a sound please, Mr. Wilkie," he was saying. "This is Moto speaking. Mr. Chang will not be here to help you. Not ever again, I think. Yes, I am back, I am not dead. Mr. Maddock and Pierre will manage Mr. Chang and Sergi on the boat. It will be worth it to them for what there is in the traveling bag—two hundred thousand dollars. Mr. Maddock was so quick to understand. He is so very fond of money. Do you understand me, Mr. Wilkie? Mr. Chang is so rich that he has paid to have himself eliminated, I think. It was entirely my own idea."

Mr. Moto spoke politely, without undue emotion. He stood in the center of the disordered little office without ever withdrawing his eyes from Mr. Wilkie, watching Mr. Wilkie as a doctor might watch a patient, or a snake might watch a bird.

"Mr. Wilkie." His speech was slower, but his voice was carefully modulated. "Please try to understand me. Please do not let panic make you do something which you may regret. I am not bluffing, as you say in your country, Mr. Wilkie. When I say that there is nothing for you to do, I tell the truth. It is all over for you, Mr. Wilkie, but do not be alarmed. You are no concern of mine. I shall not hurt even you if you see the truth." Mr. Moto paused, still watching Mr. Wilkie. And then there was a change of attitude. All at once, Mr. Moto was no longer alert. His gold-filled teeth glittered in a smile.

"I think you believe me," Mr. Moto said. "I am so happy that you believe me. It is so much better."

Then Mr. Wilkie found his voice.

"What . . . " he began. "How did you do it?"

"Thank you," Mr. Moto said. "I shall be so glad to tell you. I manage such affairs so often. It is not very difficult. Everyone likes money. This morning I contrived to speak with Mr. Maddock. Yes, there is always someone who likes money. I even thought to approach you, Mr. Wilkie, but excuse me, I knew you were nervous but you have none of Mr. Maddock's background and experience, and excuse me, not his courage. Mr. Maddock understood me perfectly as soon as I explained. How do you say it in your country? He was very glad to sell out for two hundred thousand dollars when he knew no questions would be asked. A part of the bargain was that Mr. Maddock should bring me here this evening. I wished to be sure who was the man carrying the money. The Russian carrier pigeon, as Mr. Maddock called him. The rest was very simple. Some of my own men seized the boat. Some former members of our Navy. There is enough fuel oil to take her into mid-Pacific. They have put a wireless aboard and I have arranged to have her met. Mr. Maddock will be landed safely in Japan together with his traveling bag. I tried so hard to keep my word, but I am so afraid that Mr. Chang and Sergi will not be there, because everything in the future will be much more simple without them. I was so glad to see Mr. Chang. I did not expect him here. I shall not bother to search you for a weapon, Mr. Wilkie, because I know you will not use it. Instead, if you have a knife in your pocket, I shall ask you to cut Miss Hitchings free and to rub her wrists carefully. I am afraid she has been tied too tight; and—will you permit me, Mr. Hitchings?"

Mr. Moto turned to Wilson Hitchings, without another glance at Mr. Wilkie, and with quick expert fingers removed the gag from Wilson's mouth. Wilson spoke with difficulty because his mouth was sore and swollen.

"It was the family," he said, chokingly. "I am sorry, Moto. I didn't think they would try to kill you." Mr. Moto was bending over Wilson's wrists.

"Please," said Mr. Moto cordially, "do not give it another thought. I should have done as you did in your place, Mr. Hitchings. I was sure that you would come here. I was so sure that you would be thinking of your family and the Bank."

"Damn the Bank!" said Wilson Hitchings. "Damn the family!"

"Please do not say that," said Mr. Moto, quickly. "Please. I counted on you to come here as quickly as possible. Your doing so has helped me very much. It has stopped them from suspecting anything, because of course you were sincere. May I rub your wrists, please, Mr. Hitchings? If I had not wished you to speak to Mr. Chang, I should have told you what I will tell you now. There will be no word from me about Hitchings Brothers, ever. Any more than there will be from Mr. Wilkie over there, if you do not lose your temper. I must depend on your discretion, please, as you must depend on mine. It is why I have been so frank. I have done so many things which are not nice and quite beyond your laws, although I hope that you are glad I did them, Mr. Hitchings."

Wilson nodded; his speech was growing clearer.

"If you ask me," Wilson said, "I think you did a fine job, Mr. Moto."

Wilson got to his feet. His legs were still numb, so that he staggered drunkenly across the room and knelt very clumsily beside Eva Hitchings. Then his arms were around her and her chestnut-colored head was on his shoulder.

"Eva," he said. "I have made an awful mess of this. I am sorry, Eva . . . "

"You needn't be sorry," he heard her answer faintly, "because I don't think you have at all."

"I said I would get you out of this," said Wilson. "Well, I am going to get you out."

She moved back her head and he saw that she was smiling. "And you said something else," said Eva. "I didn't think I would ever hear you say it. It was so sacrilegious. You said, 'Damn the family.'"

"Yes," said Wilson. "Damn the family. I have pulled them out of this hole. Mr. Wilkie, do you hear me? I am speaking to you now. You are lucky that Hitchings Brothers has a reputation. I can promise you that nothing will be said—nothing will be done, provided you will resign three months from now. Not because of this, but because you are inefficient. I understand you own Hitchings Plantation, Mr. Wilkie. You will sell it to me, first thing tomorrow morning, for exactly what you paid for it. I came here to close this place, and I am going to close it. I have promised to give it back to Eva and she is going to have it, but she's going to take that sign off the gate—and I'll tell you why, Mr. Wilkie. It will come off because she promised to marry me tonight. As long as she was silly enough to promise, I think that's the best way out for everybody. . . . Don't you, Mr. Moto?"

Mr. Moto raised his hand before his lips and drew in his breath with a sibilant hiss.

"I think that is nice," said Mr. Moto, "so very, very nice."

# MR. MOTO IS SO SORRY

# 1

THE POLICE official in his shoddy gray suit of European clothes looked up from his notebook and papers with expressionless dark eyes and sucked in his breath politely. Calvin Gates had been in Japan less than a week, but it had been time enough to learn a good deal about the Japanese. They were watching, always watching, hundreds of impassive faces with their dark, bright eyes.

They were watching him now as he sat at a small table in the dining saloon of the boat which was to carry him across to Fusan in Korea. The dining room stewards were watching. Outside, near the gangway, a pair of squat muscular porters in cotton, kimonolike jumpers were watching. Two khaki-clad officers, each with heavy spectacles and a heavy saber, seated at a near-by table, were watching. He took off his hat and laid it on the table and passed his hand over his closely cropped, sandy hair. His hand seemed large and awkward, his whole body needlessly heavy. The damp, oily smell of dock-water came through an open window and with it sounds of efficient hoistings and bangings and of strange voices speaking a tongue-twisting language.

"Excuse," said the policeman. "You are an American?"

Calvin Gates agreed. His passport was on the table. He had been questioned so often that he no longer felt uneasy.

"You are thirty-two years old," the policeman said. "What does your father do?"

"He's dead," said Calvin Gates.

"Oh," the policeman said, "I am so sorry for you. You are a student? What do you study, please?"

"Anthropology," said Calvin Gates. It was an inaccuracy, but it could not make much difference.

"Oh yes," the policeman said. "What is anthropology?"

"The science of man," said Calvin Gates.

"Oh yes," the policeman repeated, "the science of man. You do not write books? You will not write books about Japan? You are just traveling through Japan?"

The American rested his lean freckled hands on the table and they seemed to him almost barbarously strong. The policeman studied his face, which was also lean and freckled, waiting for his reply. Calvin Gates blinked his grayish eyes and sighed. Suddenly he felt tired and homesick and entirely out of place.

"I have to travel through as fast as I can," he said.

"Oh," said the policeman. "How long have you been in Japan?"

"Less than a week," Gates answered. "Just long enough to make the necessary arrangements to go to Mongolia."

Was the man being dull, Gates wondered, or was he simply being officious? He was busy scribbling notes in his book and occasionally drawing in a sibilant breath.

"You pass on to Mukden?" the policeman said. "You do not stop?"

"Only for train connections," Gates answered.

"Oh yes," said the policeman, "oh excuse."

"From Mukden to Shan-hai-kuan," the traveler continued amiably. "From there I proceed to Peiping, and from there to Kalgan."

"Oh yes," the policeman said. "What do you do in Mongolia?"

"I have explained a good many times," Gates answered wearily. "I am joining a scientific expedition."

"Oh yes," the policeman said, "a scientific expedition. Where is the scientific expedition in Mongolia?"

"Inner Mongolia," Gates repeated patiently. "I am joining what is known as the 'Gilbreth Expedition.' The other members left here two weeks ago. I shall be told where I am to find them when I reach Kalgan. You must have seen them when they went through here."

"Oh yes," said the policeman. "Please why did you not go with them?"

"Because I could not make arrangements to come earlier."

"Thank you." The policeman wrote carefully in his book. "You go to find something in Mongolia? What do you go to find?"

"Primitive man," Gates said.

"Oh," said the policeman, "primitive man. You go and catch a man?"

The American blinked his grayish eyes.

"The man we're going to catch is dead," he said.

"Oh," said the policeman, "you go to catch a dead man?"

"Yes," said Gates, "the man we hope to catch has been dead at least a million years."

The policeman wrote carefully in his book.

"Oh," he said, "dead one million years. Here are your papers, please. So sorry for you we cannot talk longer. There are two other passengers."

The policeman rose and bowed, leaving Calvin Gates to wonder, not for the first time, what it was all about. Everything he said would be in his dossier. Doubtless someone in some office would check over all his ambiguous remarks. His desire to join the Gilbreth Expedition had been explained at meticulous length, but repetition did not seem to matter. Calvin Gates rose, picked up his trench coat and turned to walk out of the little dining saloon. He was moving toward the door when a voice said: "Oh, excuse me."

A small man had risen from a corner table and was smiling and bowing. He was carefully dressed in a neatly tailored blue serge suit. His linen was stiffly starched. His jet black hair was brushed stiff like a Prussian officer's.

"Excuse me," the little man said again. He was holding out a visiting card, a simple bit of oblong card on which was printed "I. A. MOTO." The name meant absolutely nothing, but Calvin Gates was not surprised.

"Are you the police too?" he asked.

"Oh no," the other said and laughed. "But I am friends of Americans. I have been to America. Shall we sit down and have some whisky? It would be so very nice."

Calvin Gates was beyond being astonished, for other Japanese had been helpful before through no understandable motive.

"Thank you," he began. "It's getting late—"

"Oh no," said Mr. Moto, "please. Never too late for whisky in America. Ha! Ha! I admire America so much. I am so afraid that you are tired of our policemen."

Mr. Moto bowed and pulled back a chair and Calvin Gates sat down.

"So sorry," said Mr. Moto. "The policemen work so hard. Please, I have studied at college in America. I could not help but overhear. You are embarking on a scientific expedition for Mongolia? That will be very, very interesting and very, very nice. It is very lovely in Mongolia."

"Have you ever been there?" Calvin asked.

"Oh yes." Mr. Moto bobbed his head and smiled. "I have been to the region where you are going." Mr. Moto smiled again and clasped his delicate brown hands. "To Ghuru Nor."

Calvin Gates felt something jump inside him, and for the first time in many days he was uneasy. The little man was looking at him unblinkingly, still smiling.

"How do you know where I'm going?" he asked. "I never told the policeman that."

"Please," said Mr. Moto. "Excuse me, please. I have read of it in the Tokyo newspaper. I am so interested. You see—in your country I studied anthropology. You are Nordic, Mr. Gates, with a trace of Alpine. Nordics are so very nice."

Calvin Gates took off his hat. Uneasiness, and a sudden feeling of being hunted and a suspect returned to him, although, after all, there was no reason why he should consider himself a fugitive.

"Please," said Mr. Moto. "I am so very interested. Geologically speaking the Central Asian plateau may have been the cradle for the human race so very nicely. Geologically the Himalayas are so new. Before they were thrust up, the animals and flowers of the land about the Malay Archipelago extended over Central Asia, did they not? The woolly rhinoceros was there and also the anthropoids. Then the Himalayas cut off those poor monkeys. Am I not right? To live, these creatures had to come down from the trees. It is interesting to consider that they turned to men; very, very interesting. No doubt the ancestors of the Peiping Man are there. We have heard of bones in the deposits near Ghuru Nor. I am so very, very pleased that you are going, Mr. Gates."

"You certainly know all about it," Calvin Gates said. "Are you connected with some university?"

"Oh no," said Mr. Moto, "oh no, please." He smiled in the determined engaging manner of his race, displaying a row of uneven teeth, highly inlaid with gold. "There is only one thing which is—ha ha—so very funny."

Calvin Gates was unable to appreciate Mr. Moto's sociable merriment, nor could he tell whether its purpose was to put him at ease or not.

"Something's funny, is it?" he inquired.

"Yes," said Mr. Moto gleefully, "so funny. So sorry that I startle you perhaps."

"You don't startle me," said Calvin Gates.

There was an intense beady glint in the eyes of the small man opposite him, but his voice was smooth and genial.

"So glad I do not," said Mr. Moto. "Thank you. I have learned so many very lovely jokes in America. It is so funny that the primitive man, who lived so many years ago, should have selected such an interesting place to die. It is so funny that the drift where his bones rest at Ghuru Nor should be one of the most strategic points in the area between Russia and North China. So funny for the primitive man."

Mr. Moto laughed again and rubbed his delicate hands together. He was making such an obvious effort to be agreeable that Calvin's watchfulness relaxed.

"Are you an army officer?" Calvin asked him.

The beady look returned to Mr. Moto's eyes, and for a moment his smile was unnatural and fixed.

"No," he said, "not army—please. So nice to see Americans, and it is so very nice that you are going to Mongolia. Perhaps we can have a good talk tomorrow. I should like so very much to be of help. You may be lonely on the train tomorrow going through Korea, although there is your countrywoman going also on the train. She is on the boat now. Perhaps you know her?"

"A countrywoman?" Calvin Gates repeated.

"An American young lady," said Mr. Moto. "Yes. She is traveling with a Russian, who may be a courier, I think. See, the policeman is talking to them now."

Calvin Gates glanced across the room. A slight dark girl in a brown tweed traveling suit was sitting with the policeman. He could tell she was an American without knowing why. He knew it even before she spoke in a drawling voice, and it occurred to him disinterestedly that she would have been good-looking if she had paid attention to her clothes. As it was, she did not appear interested in looks. It was as though she considered them as something best concealed.

"Yes," she was saying, "Winnetka, Illinois; born in 1910. It's on the passport, isn't it? And my color's white as a rule. And my father's a manufacturer."

"Oh," said the policeman, "yes, he makes things?"

"What did you think he did," the girl asked, "walk a tightrope?"

Her voice dropped to a monotone again and Mr. Moto sighed.

"It does no good to get angry," he said. "The poor policeman works so hard. You do not know the young lady?"

"No." Calvin Gates shook his head. "There's a large population in America. I've never met them all."

"A tourist, I suppose," said Mr. Moto. "You are going to Mongolia alone?"

It might have been imagination, but it seemed that Mr. Moto was watching him with unnecessary attention.

"As far as I know," said Calvin Gates.

"Oh," said Mr. Moto. "We will have a nice talk in the morning."

Calvin Gates rose and bowed. It seemed to him that he was always bowing and smiling until his facial muscles were strained from polite grimaces. The girl's voice, with its midwestern articulation, had been the only thing in two days that had reminded him of home.

When he passed along a narrow passage toward his stateroom, a steward, a flat-faced, snub-nosed boy, bowed and hissed and opened his door and switched on the light. Calvin threw his hat and trench coat on the berth, seated himself on a small stool and took a notebook and pencil from his pocket.

"Second class to Shimonoseki," he wrote. "Mothers nursing babies. Old men taking off their clothes and scratching. Rice fields. Chatter, chatter. Rice wine. Soldiers. Clap clap of wooden shoes. Police. What does your grandfather do? Little boat. Mr. Moto, who knows anthropology. Fusan tomorrow, but must not take pictures."

He realized that his words would be unintelligible to most, but they would never be so to him. They would always bring back a hundred noises and faces and that sense of being an outlander in a train that ran through a country unbelievably like that country's pictures, with its tall blue hills, and bamboo, and tiny farms, with its concrete dams and its high tension wires and its factories, with its population half in kimonos and half in European clothes. It was a land of smiles and grimness, half toylike, half efficient.

He rose, took off his coat and glanced at his baggage. As soon as he did so he discovered that his brief case, which he had left beside his steamer trunk, had disappeared. He opened the door and shouted into the passageway.

"Boysan!" he shouted. The flat-faced room steward came running.

"Look here," Calvin Gates said, "where's the little bag, the one that was there?"

The flat brown face stared at him.

"Bag." Calvin Gates said to the boy. "Little bag, so big." The boy drew in his breath.

He spoke loudly, as one does when dealing with a foreigner, in the absurd hope that shouting might make the meaning clearer. Even while he spoke he knew that he was achieving nothing.

"Get someone who can speak English," Calvin Gates shouted. "All my notes—papers are in that bag."

At that same moment a door across the passageway opened, and Mr. Moto appeared, holding a small brown brief case in his hand, displaying his gold teeth and bowing.

"Oh," said Mr. Moto, "I am so very, very sorry. Can this be your bag? This ship boy was very stupid."

"Thanks," said Calvin Gates. "Thank you very much."

"Oh no," said Mr. Moto. "I am so glad to help. Good night until tomorrow."

"Good night," said Calvin Gates. He closed his door and sat down with his brief case across his knees. He was positive that he had seen the bag deposited in his own stateroom. He was positive that the bag had not been placed in Mr. Moto's room by mistake. Mr. Moto had been looking through his papers, but the papers were all there in the order he had left them—only a few personal letters, and nothing of any importance. He took out the last letter about Dr. Gilbreth, which had been written him by the Doctor's business representative in New York.

> Dear Cal:—
>
> You could have knocked me over with a feather when I got your letter asking how to find Gilbreth. He must have told you about the shooting in Mongolia. The office here will be in touch with him since we handle his accounts, but even a cable will take weeks sometimes to deliver. The best way to find him will be to go to the man in Kalgan who is seeing to his supplies and transportation. He is a part-German, part-Russian, who does trading in Mongolia by the name of Holtz. When you find him in Kalgan, he can probably get you out at a time when he is sending out supplies by motor.
>
> Gilbreth has an artist going out to join him, a good-looking girl with a temper. You may meet her on the

> way, as she only left last week. Gilbreth was no end pleased by the check your uncle sent. It made all the difference in his being able to go, and it was like the old gentleman not to want any acknowledgment. Bella made that clear enough when she brought in the check. When you see him, be sure to thank him for us. . . .

There was nothing which was important, but it was obvious that Mr. Moto had been seeking something. Now that he thought of it, all of Mr. Moto's conversation had been more adroit than any of the questions of the police. He could almost believe that Mr. Moto's gentle words had been probing into his past, that there was something odd about him which Mr. Moto had seen but which no one else had noticed. He unfolded his map of China and Japan, and stared at it as he had twenty times before, still only half convinced that he was doing what he set out to do. He could locate himself at the narrow strait which separated Japan from the mainland of Asia, and he could see the curve of the railroad which started at the port of Fusan, and wound up through the promontory of Korea, and thence through Manchuria to Mukden. It would take twenty-four hours to reach Mukden by train provided there was no delay, and that would not be half the journey. He must pass the night at Mukden and take another train westward through Manchuria to Shan-hai-kuan by the Great Wall of China. There he must change and on the following morning he would arrive at Peiping, only to change trains again. Then he must travel north for another day's journey before he reached Kalgan. He had no way of telling how far he must travel after that—somewhere to the north where there was no railroad—until he could find Dr. Gilbreth to tell him what he wanted.

Long after he had folded the map again, when he tried to go to sleep he could see the line of railroads and those unknown cities.

## 2

CALVIN GATES lay in his berth staring at the dark, while the steady beat of the engines, almost like the heart pulsations of a living organism, quivered rhythmically through the little ship. As he listened the whole vessel seemed alive, awake and conscious. There were knowing little creakings of the woodwork and strange premonitory shivers from the deck beneath. He knew that he would not sleep well that night, for it had been that way before, when his mind moved to vanished possibilities of what he might have said and what he might have done.

Finally he turned on the light and dressed. Then he put on his hat and coat and looked at his wrist watch. It was one o'clock in the morning and he knew that the ship would be well out on that body of water which divided Japan from the mainland.

The key to his cabin door lay on the washstand and he picked it up, drew back the bolt, and turned the heavy brass doorknob. Outside, the narrow passageway which ran between the passengers' cabins was brightly lighted and empty. He closed his door and locked it, and tried the lock carefully before he put the key in his pocket. The dining-room doors were closed and the flat-faced room steward was sleeping in a folding chair. He walked by, careful not to wake him, up the stairs to the boat deck.

The ship was moving over a cool, placid sea. Her lights made little yellow pools on the gently undulating waves. As far as his sight carried there were no shore lights and no lights of other ships. He had the small deck entirely to himself, and the loneliness gave him a sense of comfort, and a feeling of motion without his own volition. It was pleasant to know that he was moving.

He was moving away from it, moving away. He was thinking that Central Park would be misty in the haze of a sultry summer day, when some half-heard sound brought his attention back to the rail where he was leaning and back to the quiet deck, with the rhythmical sounds of the engine and the whirr of the ventilator fans. He was sure that he never consciously heard a sound, yet he knew that he was not alone—he knew before he turned.

"Good evening," a voice said. "It is such a very lovely evening."

"Oh," Calvin said, "good evening." A man had moved beside him with soft, almost noiseless steps; it was his acquaintance of the early evening, the fragile Japanese gentleman, Mr. I. A. Moto.

"Ha ha," said Mr. Moto with a forced laugh. It seemed to Calvin that the Japanese were always trying to laugh. "I find it hard to sleep on boats and trains. Ha ha, I am always wide awake."

"Yes," Calvin said politely, "I find it hard myself. I was thinking and I could not sleep."

"Oh," said Mr. Moto, "you were thinking?"

"Yes," said Calvin.

"Oh," said Mr. Moto, "you were thinking of New York?"

Mr. Moto's face was only a blur in the dark.

"How did you know I came from New York?" Calvin asked.

There was a sibilant hiss of politely indrawn breath from the blur of Mr. Moto's face.

"Excuse me, please," said Mr. Moto. "You have the New York voice. The young American lady on board comes from the Middle West. I like to think that I can always tell. New York is such a very lovely city. You like Tokyo? We are trying so hard to be like New York."

"I wonder why you do?" Calvin asked.

"Perhaps," said Mr. Moto, "we all admire your country so much, how it has reached out from such a little country and become so great."

"You're reaching out too, aren't you?" Calvin asked.

"Oh yes," said Mr. Moto. "We must live. We are such a little people."

"You've done a lot," said Calvin.

"It is so kind of you to say so," Mr. Moto said. "I hope so much you like Japan. We make so very many interesting things—so many small things which are so easy to carry. Our workmen are so very, very careful. Perhaps you have bought some small articles?"

The question was a part of that whole aimless conversation, which was so like his other conversations with other Japanese—the exploits of Japan, the antiquity of Japanese culture, and Japan's peculiar mission in the Orient—but something told Calvin that Mr. Moto was waiting, attentively waiting, for the answer to that trivial question.

"Why yes," said Calvin. "I've bought some small things, nothing much."

"I am so glad," said Mr. Moto. "Perhaps you have seen our silver work with the inlay of gunmetal cut right through the silver? It is so very nice. Perhaps you have bought a cigarette case of that work?"

"No," said Calvin, "I haven't."

"You do not smoke, perhaps," said Mr. Moto. "Those cases are so nice. There is an inlaid pattern of small birds flying through grasses. I am so very fond of it. Perhaps you have seen the pattern on silver? So very many little birds."

There was no doubt any longer that the talk was leading somewhere. Calvin understood that Mr. Moto was waiting patiently, not for an answer as much as for some change of voice. He knew he was not wrong when Mr. Moto spoke again.

"You have not seen the cases with the inlays of the little birds?"

"No," said Calvin.

"Ha ha," said Mr. Moto. "Excuse me, please. It is so very interesting that you are going to Mongolia. Ghuru Nor is very beautiful. Have you heard of the prince who lives there?"

"No," said Calvin. "Is there a prince?"

"Oh yes," said Mr. Moto brightly. "The men who are not priests wear pigtails. Such a very backward country. The prince's name is Wu Fang. That is his Chinese name, of course."

"Does he wear a pigtail too?" Calvin asked.

"Oh yes," said Mr. Moto. "He lives in a small palace and keeps camels. He has an army too. The Mongolians are very, very jolly."

"I'm glad to hear it," Calvin said.

"Oh yes," said Mr. Moto. "You will like it all so very, very much, that is if there is no trouble."

"Trouble?" Calvin repeated.

Mr. Moto laughed.

"Ha ha," said Mr. Moto. "I hope so very much that you will have no trouble."

"Well," said Calvin, "it's a complicated world. I think I'll go back and try to get some sleep."

"Yes," said Mr. Moto, "I shall go back too, I think. It has been so very pleasant. Thank you very much. You first, please, Mr. Gates."

When Calvin walked down the stairs to the passageway with Mr. Moto just behind him, he felt the bewilderment he had experienced before when he had come in contact with an Oriental mind. He was sure that the conversation had not been aimless, although it led nowhere. Something in Mr. Moto's interest was disturbing. Even Mr. Moto's footsteps behind him were disturbing. He took his key from his pocket to open his stateroom door and the key did not turn in the lock.

"Excuse me," said Mr. Moto, "is there something wrong?"

"It's the key," Calvin told him; "it doesn't seem to work."

"So sorry," Mr. Moto said. "The key does not work? How very, very funny."

But it did not seem to Calvin that it was very funny.

"Look here," he said, turning on Mr. Moto, "what's all this about?"

"I do not know," said Mr. Moto. "We will go and find the boy."

The boy was still asleep in his chair near the dining saloon. Mr. Moto spoke sharply and the boy's eyes opened.

"The boy will know how," said Mr. Moto. "Let the boy try the key, please. Thank you very much."

The boy turned the key. The lock clicked and he opened the stateroom door.

"Ha ha," said Mr. Moto. "It is all right now, I think."

"Thank you," said Calvin. "It's all right now."

"So very glad," Mr. Moto said. "Good night."

Calvin Gates shot the bolt of his stateroom door again and looked grimly at his trunk and bags beneath the berth. When he had first tried the door someone had been inside; and now whoever it was had gone; and Mr. Moto was looking for a cigarette case with a design of little birds upon it, lots of little birds.

Whatever it was that Mr. Moto wanted, it was no affair of his, and he was able to go to sleep. He was able to dream of pigtails and of places of which he had no knowledge, and through his dreams he could hear Mr. Moto's voice.

"So very nice," Mr. Moto was saying, "so very, very nice."

## 3

AT THE REAR of the train which left Fusan the next morning there was an observation car where Japanese businessmen and Japanese army officers sat and smoked and talked in sharp loud voices. The road for the most part followed river beds, back from which rose brownish hills and bluish mountains. There were green patches of farms near the river, but for the most part the country was bleak and rugged, and even the highest hills were bare of trees. That bareness gave the impression of a land which had been lived in for millenniums without much change. The Korean houses were like something from the Stone Age, round mud huts with curious mushroom-shaped thatch roofs. White-clad bearded men stood near them smoking pipes. White-robed farmers walked along the paths with their hands clasped behind them, wearing high black varnished hats perched airily above their heads.

It may have been because of the total unfamiliarity of the scene outside that Calvin experienced an increasing sensation of self-consciousness. He had not realized the extent of this malaise until he saw the girl whom he had seen on the boat the night before. She walked into the observation car, looked about her carelessly and selected one of the wicker chairs, lighted a cigarette and opened a book. Calvin Gates smiled and bowed, but she only nodded to him curtly as though to tell him that she did not need his company, and then he saw the reason. A shabbily dressed, youngish man entered the car a moment later and took the chair beside her.

The dress, the turn of the head, the smile, the familiarity with everything showed that he was not there for his own pleasure. The tilt of his head indicated his profession, and the way his fountain pen was clipped into his upper coat pocket suggest its constant use in keeping a petty cash account. All those small details gave him that cosmopolitan quality common to all guides and couriers. He might have been a native of half a dozen countries from Norway to the Balkans, but he certainly was not an American. The cut of his clothes and the sharp point of his nose and chin and the motions of his hands indicated some other origin, and his voice also showed it even though it was devoid of any accent, the facile voice of a man of many tongues.

"Everything is safe in the baggage car, Miss Dillaway," Calvin heard him say. "They will look over the baggage again at Antung."

The girl turned her head with a sort of impatient annoyance, and slapped a firm brown hand down on her open book.

"For goodness' sakes, Boris," she said, "isn't this all Japanese territory?"

As soon as he heard the name, Calvin Gates understood the face and voice. The man was a Russian.

"It's only a formality, Miss Dillaway," he explained, looking at her with patient, slightly protruding, bluish eyes. "Antung is on the border of Manchukuo, a separate state you understand."

"Rubbish," said Miss Dillaway. "It's Japanese, isn't it?"

Then a curious thing happened. As Miss Dillaway was speaking, the blond Russian had glanced toward the door of the observation car, and at that same moment Mr. Moto appeared, a somewhat startling sight.

Mr. Moto was dressed in black-and-white checked sport clothes, and his spindly legs glowed in green and red golf stockings. For a moment Calvin Gates was tempted to laugh, but the inclination left him when he saw the face of Miss Dillaway's companion.

The bluish eyes of that blond young man had grown more

protruding, and his hands had dropped slowly until they gripped the arms of his wicker chair.

"What's the matter with you, Boris?" Miss Dillaway was saying, "Are you sick?"

Her voice aroused the Russian from his reverie.

"Oh no," he said. "It is nothing, nothing."

"Well, don't look as though you'd seen a ghost," Miss Dillaway said. "You give me the creeps, and the Japanese are trouble enough."

"Please," Boris said hastily in low agitated tones. "They understand what you are saying."

"Well, let 'em understand," said Miss Dillaway. "I'm not doing any harm."

If Mr. Moto heard, he paid no attention. Without even bestowing a glance on them he moved toward Calvin Gates.

"So nice to see you," Mr. Moto said, "so very nice."

"Good morning," Calvin answered. "Are you going to play golf, Mr. Moto?"

"Ha ha," said Mr. Moto. "I wear these clothes so often traveling, because they do not get out of press. I used to press so many trousers in America."

"Did you?" Calvin asked him.

"Oh yes," said Mr. Moto, "yes." He raised his hand before his mouth and drew in his breath. "When I was studying in America. They will examine the baggage at Antung and the policeman must see your papers. I should be so very glad to help you, if you would not mind."

"Thank you," said Calvin. "Hello, look at that!"

The train had stopped on a siding while they were speaking, and another train was going by them.

"Yes," said Mr. Moto, "soldiers. A troop train, I suppose."

A long train rolled by them with black heads of small khaki-clad men peering from its windows and then flat cars loaded with artillery, car after car of guns and caisons.

"It looks like a war," Calvin said.

"No, not a war," said Mr. Moto. "They are just soldiers, new soldiers. I am so very afraid that we will be delayed by troop trains. We will be very many hours late before we reach Mukden—so many hours."

Calvin looked out of the window with a new interest.

"Those guns look like German seventy-sevens," he said.

Mr. Moto's head had turned toward him with a birdlike sort of quickness.

"Not exactly," Mr. Moto said. "You understand artillery?"

"Yes," Calvin said, "a little."

He was aware that Mr. Moto was favoring him with his full attention.

"You are not," Mr. Moto said, "an army officer yourself?"

"No," Calvin answered, "but I've done quite a lot of military reading. Sometimes I've thought of being a soldier."

"Oh," said Mr. Moto. "You are so fortunate not to be a soldier. The breech mechanism of our field-pieces is different from light German guns. So sorry we will be delayed to let the troops go by."

There were soldiers enough in Korea, but when the train rolled the next day through what had been Manchuria iron hats and khaki uniforms and field equipment became part of the landscape, and the landscape itself had changed. The land had assumed a level, peaceful aspect, reminding him somewhat of a prairie state at home. There were small farms and narrow roads as far as he could see, and in some way, though the sight was new, it all appeared familiar. The country had begun to resemble the scenes on the blue-and-white china plates which had been placed before him as a child. There were the same houses with the same sweeping curves to their eaves, the same willow trees drooping above them, the identical bridges across the streams. The same figures, half reassuring and half grotesque, bent over fields or plodded with poles on their shoulders. The oddest sights seemed to fit into a sort of decorous order, impervious to change, and life rose robustly out of the earth in earthen houses and villages surrounded by high walls. Life sank back into the earth again, to a past which was marked by the mounds of ancestral graves that dotted corners of nearly every field.

The train was moving through this new country when he had his first conversation with Miss Dillaway. She appeared in the observation car about eight o'clock the next morning and took a chair next his and drew a timetable out of her pocketbook.

"Hello," Miss Dillaway said. "It's a funny country, isn't it? It looks like a plate."

"I'm sorry you thought of that," Calvin Gates said. "I had thought that was an original idea with me."

Miss Dillaway glanced out the window and wrinkled her nose.

"There's nothing original about any of it," she said. "It's been going on for two thousand years. Have you ever been out here before?"

"No," said Calvin, "never."

"Neither have I," said Miss Dillaway, "and I'd like to see a gas tank and a factory chimney."

"Didn't you see enough in Japan?" Calvin asked her.

"Japan!" Miss Dillaway laughed shortly. "It isn't permanent. It's almost pathetic to see those poor people trying." She nodded toward the fields and farms out the window. "All this is going to swallow them up in two or three hundred years. Maybe they realize it even now. They look like little boys playing soldier, don't they? And don't tell me not to say it out loud. I'm tired of being told to be quiet."

The train had stopped at a station as she spoke, similar to all the other wayside stations they had been passing. It was built of gray brick, evidently designed by some European engineer, and behind it was a cluster of brown mud houses which made two slovenly lines along a muddy street. All around the station building was a wall of white sandbags. A corporal's guard armed with rifles had filed from the station and stood at attention.

"Look at them," said Miss Dillaway. "They've gobbled up Manchuria and they still have to hide behind sandbags. It's pathetic, isn't it?"

"They don't look pathetic to me," Calvin said. "They look as if they knew their business."

"It's pathetic just the same," said Miss Dillaway, "because they won't get anywhere. Are you going as far as Peiping?"

Calvin Gates nodded. "Farther than that," he said, and Miss Dillaway seemed pleased.

"Then we'd better stick together," she said; "that is, if you don't mind. Frankly this country and this train are giving me the creeps, and that Russian guide I had, he's leaving."

"Leaving?" Calvin said.

Miss Dillaway wrinkled her nose again as though some smell in the car offended her.

"You've seen him, haven't you?" she answered. "The Russian with the fountain pen, who's been following me around? I'm no good with languages and I'm apt to lose my temper. I asked them at the hotel for a courier and they dug up Boris. I guess I don't understand foreigners very well. He's faded out on me. He gave me notice just after we came into this car yesterday morning. Something must have happened."

"What happened?" Calvin Gates asked.

Miss Dillaway made a careless gesture.

"You know how foreigners are," she said. "Boris was as nice as pie and suddenly he froze up and said he was leaving me at Mukden. I can't understand foreigners. It isn't my business. I just want to get where I'm going." She looked at him frankly. "I guess you don't care where you're going, do you?"

"What makes you think that?" Calvin asked.

"I'm sorry," said Miss Dillaway. "I've just been watching you on the train, the way you've been watching me, and you just gave me the idea that you didn't care where you were going. Do you mind telling me where you're going?"

Her question did not seem out of place, and he knew that her interest was friendly.

"Farther than Peiping," Calvin said. "I've been wanting to talk for two days to anyone except the police. I'm going to a place called Ghuru Nor. I'm looking for an expedition that's being run by a Dr. Gilbreth." He stopped because Miss Dillaway looked startled.

"What's the matter?" Calvin asked.

"Look here," said Miss Dillaway. "You don't look like anybody Gilbreth would take. You don't mean he's taking you?"

"Why shouldn't he?" Calvin asked. "At any rate I'm going to find him."

"No reason," Miss Dillaway said. "I'm interested because I'm going there myself."

Miss Dillaway looked at him again carefully and impersonally.

"What's your line, Mr. Gates?"

Her calm examination embarrassed him.

"I haven't got any line," he said. "What's your line?"

"Artist," said Miss Dillaway. "Painting scale pictures of pots and pans and skulls and landscapes. I've been on a lot of these things, but never into Asia. If you're going because of curiosity you won't like it. It's always hot and the food is always bad and everybody's always quarreling. It sounds all right when you get home, but it's terrible when you're there. I wouldn't do it if I weren't paid for it. Why are you doing it?"

Calvin Gates felt his face grow red. She would be the girl who was mentioned in the letter, the good-looking girl with a temper.

"For personal reasons," he said.

"Sorry," said Miss Dillaway. "I didn't mean to step on your toes, Gates. Well, as long as we've met, we'd better try to get there. It's nearly lunchtime, isn't it? Would you like to buy me a drink before lunch? They have some things in the dining car."

"Thanks," said Calvin.

Miss Dillaway walked ahead of him, briskly, her head and shoulders very straight. She sat down at one of the tables in the dining car and nodded to the chair opposite.

"Boy," she called, "whisky-soda. Is that what you want, Gates? Two whisky-sodas. Well, here's looking at you, Gates! Good luck!"

Calvin raised his glass. "If you don't mind my saying so," he said, "you don't seem very pleased that I'm going to Ghuru Nor. Of course, I didn't expect any loud applause." Calvin paused and smiled at her. "But I have some good points, you know. I might be useful."

Miss Dillaway set down her glass.

"Forget it, Gates," she said. "This is business for me, and you're one of these people looking for adventure. You haven't been on as many of these things as I have. I've been in Persia and I've been bitten by fleas in the Mesopotamian Desert, and I've been in Central America, and the west coast of Africa. I go because I earn my pay, and I've seen lads who go for fun. They generally make trouble. They sit around the camp and just make trouble. There's nothing else for 'em to do. I don't mean it personally."

"I can carry your sketchbooks," Calvin said.

"Don't be silly," said Miss Dillaway. "As long as we're going, we've got to get acquainted. You're probably a nice boy. I hope you are."

"Thanks," said Calvin.

"Don't get touchy," said Miss Dillaway. "I never fight with anybody on expeditions." She raised her hand in front of her mouth and drew in her breath. "Who is that Japanese friend of yours? The one with the gold teeth and the golf stockings?"

"His name is Moto," said Calvin. "He picked me up on the boat."

"Well, he's tried to pick me up all day," Miss Dillaway said. "That's why I picked you up instead, Gates. Look, here comes Boris. He always hangs around when he thinks I'm going to take a drink."

She was right. The blond Russian was walking down the aisle, hesitating, smiling.

"Sit down, Boris," said Miss Dillaway. "This is Mr. Gates. What are you going to have, vodka?"

Boris clicked his heels together and shook hands.

"I am so happy to make your acquaintance, sir," he said. "Anything, my dear Miss Dillaway, anything at all."

"No use being polite," Miss Dillaway replied. "You guaranteed to see me through, and now you're walking out on me."

Boris sat down. There was a look of pained concern in his protuberant, bluish eyes.

"But I have explained," he said. "There was a message from my wife. I have told you and I have told you—she is ill and I must go back. Nothing short of the most serious news—"

"Forget it," said Miss Dillaway. "There's your vodka, Boris."

"Your very good health," Boris said. "Now that you have found a fellow countryman everything will be easy. The hotel porter will see you on the train at Mukden, and there will be a man to care for the baggage at the Shan-hai-kuan customs. I have really been superfluous, my dear Miss Dillaway. You manage all without me."

"All right," said Miss Dillaway. "You see me into the hotel at Mukden and you'll get your pay. We've been all over it, Boris."

But Boris was still deeply worried. His manner was ingratiating and contrite. His voice was placating and anxious.

"Just once again, Miss Dillaway," he said, "I am so sorry. I can take no pay from you for what I have done. Instead, if you please, I should like to make a peace offering." He put his hand in his inside pocket and cleared his throat. "I should like to give this to you as a peace offering. It is a silver cigarette case. Perhaps you saw them in Japan, with the dark metal inlay that goes all the way through it. Will you please accept it, Miss Dillaway?"

His speech was elaborate and formal, and Calvin Gates was also cynical enough to believe that the gesture was not made for nothing. The Russian had produced a small silver cigarette case such as a lady might carry in her bag, certainly of no great intrinsic value. He laid it almost timidly on the table in front of Miss Dillaway, where it rattled with the glasses in time to the vibration of the train. It was only when she picked it up that something flashed in Calvin Gates's memory. The cover was decorated by a design of reeds and birds, a number of little birds flying among grasses. As she held it, Mr. Moto's voice came through his memory, gentle, softly modulated.

"Very beautiful," Mr. Moto had said, "little birds, lots of little birds."

The Russian's forehead was moist and he spoke again with genuine feeling.

"It is not worthy of you," he said; "but I beg you to accept it, Miss Dillaway, and use it if you can, and I will take no pay."

Miss Dillaway picked up the case carelessly.

"Thanks," she said. "That's kind of you, Boris. You'll get your pay at Mukden. There's no use going through gestures about it."

"Please, my dear Miss Dillaway," the courier said. "I'm afraid you mistake the purpose of my little gift."

"Never mind," said Miss Dillaway, "thanks. Now run along, Boris. I want to talk to Mr. Gates. I'll see you in the hotel tonight at Mukden."

Boris rose and clicked his heels together and Miss Dillaway sighed.

"Putting me under obligations, isn't he?" she said. "I have a cigarette case already. It's a simple little game, isn't it?" And she opened her bag and dropped the cigarette case inside it. "Do you want one of my cigarettes? It's the same sort of case you see with a different design. What's the matter, Gates?"

"Nothing," said Calvin. "It's a pretty cigarette case."

"That isn't what you were thinking," Miss Dillaway said.

That was all that happened, an obscure incident in a long and tedious journey. There was nothing, when he thought of it later, that was peculiar, except that sight of little birds inlaid in black upon the silver.

When the train pulled into the shed at Mukden—hours late, as Mr. Moto had predicted—it had only been a tedious journey that had ended in a disorderly rush of porters. They arrived in the early evening and Calvin saw Boris through the coal smoke helping with Miss Dillaway's bags, and then, when Gates was moving away from the train indecisively, Mr. Moto stepped beside him.

"I should be so pleased to take you to the hotel," said Mr. Moto. "It is so confusing here at night."

"Thanks," said Calvin, "thank you very much."

"It is such a pleasure," said Mr. Moto. "It must be interesting here to a stranger."

Mr. Moto was right; even in the dark it was interesting. The air had a cold, nervous quality, and a thousand different sounds carried through it in the dark. It was a new, dark world, full of twinkling lights and voices, and it made him forget about the boat and train, as a traveler forgets such incidents almost as soon as they are over.

# 4

IN FRONT OF the station in the dark, while Mr. Moto signaled for a taxicab, it seemed to him that the place was full of violent memories of war and the rumors of war. He did not need daylight to know that he was at a crossroads, where tides of empire had met and ripped and swirled. The square outside the station, and the droshkies which were waiting beside the automobiles and rickshaws, showed that Russia had been there once. A beggar woman in blue rags came cringing up to them, holding out her hand. Mr. Moto spoke to her sternly and she went away.

"Not Chinese," Mr. Moto explained. "A Russian woman in Chinese clothes. Mukden is so nice. There are so very many points of interest. I hope so much that you can see them."

"I'm going on tomorrow," Calvin said.

"Oh," said Mr. Moto, "so sorry for you that you cannot see them. Here is the motor, please."

The sound of motor horns broke in on his voice, while he talked precisely about the unfortunate incident which had precipitated the crisis ending in the establishment of the Manchukuo state.

"You must understand," said Mr. Moto, "that the Chinese make everything so very difficult."

"Is that why you have soldiers at all the stations?" Calvin asked.

"Ha ha," said Mr. Moto, "yes, the soldiers at all the stations."

The hotel, like the droshkies, must have dated back to the Russian days. Once he was inside, except for the Japanese attendants, he might have been in a provincial French hotel. There was the same slow-moving lift, the same broad staircases and ornate woodwork.

Miss Dillaway was already at the desk. She waited for him while he was assigned a room.

"Well, I've paid Boris off," she said. "Will you have dinner with me? How about meeting down here in half an hour?"

Calvin glanced at Mr. Moto.

"Please," said Mr. Moto hastily, "I have so much to do tonight. The manager is a friend of mine." He waved at a gray-haired Japanese gentleman in a morning coat, who stood behind the desk. "I shall dine with the manager."

She was waiting for him half an hour later, her hair pulled tight back from her forehead, her face shining and guiltless of powder.

"Well," said Miss Dillaway. "I hope your room's better than mine. I always thought the Japanese were clean, but I don't think my room's clean. I wonder where Boris went."

"Isn't he here?" Calvin asked.

Miss Dillaway shook her head. She was still in her brown tweed suit and she made a small, lonely, uncompromising figure in the high-ceilinged, dingy dining room, like a girl in a boarding school, he thought.

"The food's bad, isn't it?" she said. "I wouldn't touch that salad if I were you, Gates. I don't know why that Russian still bothers me. I don't know whether I hurt his feelings, or what. Foreigners are touchy, aren't they? Look at your Japanese friend looking at us."

"Don't worry about the Russian," Calvin said.

"I only worry about him," Miss Dillaway answered, "because he always looked so worried. He was like the White Rabbit in *Alice in Wonderland*, always startled like a rabbit. The only thing I don't worry about is myself, I guess. I suppose I'll start bothering about you next."

"Why?" asked Calvin.

Miss Dillaway's eyes grew narrow, and she smiled at him.

"I don't know," she said. "Maybe it's this air. You act as though something was the matter with you."

"Perhaps you frighten me," Calvin said.

"Don't be silly, Gates," said Miss Dillaway. "I don't frighten you and you know it. The trouble is you don't get anywhere with me. That's it, isn't it? You've never seen anyone who could look out for herself probably. Well, I can, and that's why I'm going to get some rest. Good night, Gates."

Calvin rose and bowed.

"And don't get into trouble, Gates," Miss Dillaway said. "I want to see you on the train tomorrow. Where's my bag?"

Calvin handed it to her.

"I must be losing my wits," she said. "It's the first time I've let that bag out of my hand. Take care of yourself. Good night."

"I'm going up too," Calvin said. "I'll see you as far as your room."

Calvin opened the tall French window of his hotel room and stepped out on a small balcony in front of it and drew a deep breath of the night air. Down below him he could see the lights of automobiles and carriages, and he could hear the sounds of horns and the clatter of hoofs. Behind him his room was almost comfortable—a single wooden bed with his baggage piled in front of it, a green carpet, a bureau and a writing table, and cream-colored, painted walls, and a single electric light that hung suspended from the center of the room. Life had become a succession of similar rooms, varying in comfort and discomfort.

He stood at the window, thinking of Miss Dillaway, and his thoughts were puzzled and confused, for he could not tell whether he liked her or not; he had never seen anyone like her. She was as lonely as he was and as out of place in those surroundings. It would surely not have been difficult for her to have been friendly, and yet it seemed to him that each time she had started to be friendly she had stopped herself deliberately. She had been like someone who was playing a part, like someone trying to be something she was not. More than once she had actually tried to be unattractive, and her casual rudeness had a note which did not ring true. He was almost sure of that, for now and then when she was not thinking she had lost all mannerism. He had seen it happen once across the table that evening. Her lips had lost their habitual defiant twist and her face instead of looking harsh and sharp had grown delicate and sensitive. He had been surprised once by its beauty, a dark, patrician sort of beauty, and even her voice had changed; it was as though she had forgotten herself, because a moment later her face was sharp again. He had tried to reassure her; he had tried to make her see that there was no reason to be afraid of him.

"And she never lets her purse go," Calvin said to himself. "She's just the kind that wouldn't."

His wrist watch had a luminous dial. He looked at it when he awoke that night. It was twenty minutes before twelve and someone was tapping on his door, softly but insistently. The light switch was just above the table by his bed. When he pulled it, the light glowed dimly. A breeze swayed the curtains before his open window, and the sound outside his door continued, a furtive, gentle knocking. He got into his slippers and put on his trench coat.

"What's the matter out there?" he began, and then his eyes became accustomed to the dimly lighted hall, Miss Dillaway's former courier, the Russian named Boris, stood outside the door.

"Hello," Calvin said to him. "What do you want?"

He found himself growing indignant as he spoke. It was exactly as Miss Dillaway had said; the man was like the White Rabbit in

*Alice in Wonderland.* He was smiling placatingly; his forehead was moist with perspiration.

"I beg your pardon, sir," he said. "I wonder if I might come in."

"What's the matter with you?" began Calvin. He might have gone further, but something in the other's expression stopped him more than any explanation could have. The man in front of him was fighting against some sort of fear, and he was controlling that fear with a visible effort.

"I beg your pardon, sir," he said again. "I appreciate your irritation, quite. I shall only be a minute. It is just one matter that is important."

Calvin Gates felt a strange, tingling sensation at the base of his spine. It did not require any explanation for him to realize that there was something wrong. Some ugly, unseen thing was coming to him out of the dullness of that journey. Some implication was being conveyed by that stranger's anguish.

"Come inside," Calvin said. "What's the matter with you, Boris?"

Boris came inside and closed the door behind him.

"Thank you, sir," he said. "I shall only be a moment. I do not think there is any danger."

"Danger," said Calvin, "what danger?"

The Russian blinked his blue eyes and smiled.

"It is just a manner of speaking, sir," he said. "I—have been distressed by something—a little detail about Miss Dillaway."

"What about Miss Dillaway?" Calvin asked him. "What's the matter?"

"Nothing," said Boris, "nothing really. It is only a simple detail—but I fear I have not been gentlemanly. I gave her a cigarette case. If you are traveling with her, sir, it might be better if you took it. A friend of mine may ask for it. I promised it to him—and if you will give it—" His voice was very low, almost expressionless.

"Who?" Calvin said. "What are you talking about?"

Boris moistened his lips before he answered, and he seemed to find the answer difficult.

"That is all, sir," he said. "It was intended for a friend of mine. I did not think at the time." His voice trailed off almost into a whisper, and Calvin stared at him grimly.

"You're going to do some thinking now," he said. "You've run into the wrong person this time. You're going to tell me what this is about before you get out of here."

Boris moistened his lips again and shrugged his shoulders.

"It is nothing," he began. "I was foolish to speak of it, perhaps. But a friend of mine will ask for it. Miss Dillaway might not understand. She is so—determined. I do not want her to be hurt. You see—a friend of mine—"

He paused, seemingly searching for a word, and his mouth had fallen open. He was staring beyond Calvin Gates in the direction of the French window, just as a creaking sound and a fresh gust of air made Calvin turn in the direction of Boris's startled glance.

The window had been pushed open quickly, and a small and stocky man stepped from the balcony halfway into the room. When he thought of it afterward, Calvin Gates had only an indefinite impression of him—of a broad, flat-nosed face, tightly closed lips and steady dark eyes, and dark somber European clothes. It was not the face but the action that Calvin Gates recalled, and the action was completely smooth and steady, giving no impression of haste. The man was holding a pistol, leveling it with the almost gentle motion of an expert marksman. In that fraction of a second, while Calvin gazed unbelievingly, he could see that the weapon was equipped with a silencing device—he could even recognize the model. Then, before anyone moved or spoke, there was a single shot, which came with a sound not much louder than that of an airrifle. There was no word, nothing but the breeze from the open window and that sudden sound. The eyes of Boris grew wide and staring; his knees buckled beneath him. Calvin reached toward him instinctively, but Boris was a dead weight, sinking to the floor. He was sinking to the floor with a bullet hole drilled through the center of his forehead, just above his eyes, a perfect shot both merciful and merciless. He had died without a word. When Calvin Gates looked up the window and the balcony were empty. It had all been as perfect and as inevitable and as accurately rehearsed as a moment in the theater. It had been cold-blooded murder done by an expert in the art, and so completely done that there was nothing left but silence.

Calvin Gates had never seen a dead man, but no experience was necessary to make the signs familiar. The mark on the forehead with the few drops of blood that oozed from it made him stand paralyzed, incapable of consecutive thought.

The night breeze still waved the dingy window curtains and the room was so quiet that he could hear the curtains scrape against the panes and sashes. That gentle and insignificant noise reminded him that everything had been discreet. Whoever it was who had fired the shot must have been standing on the balcony listening by the window, and he must have moved from some other room which opened on that balcony. Whoever it was had desired secrecy and silence. Calvin Gates drew a deep breath and the color came back to his freckled face.

His thoughts went no further because of a sound outside the door of his room. There was a click and the knob was turning. At the same instant he realized that the door was no longer locked.

There was no time to make a move, if he had wished to make one, before Mr. Moto had opened the door and closed it softly behind him.

"Oh," Mr. Moto said very gently. "He is—liquidated?"

## 5

CALVIN STARED BACK without answering and there seemed to be no adequate answer. Mr. Moto had changed from his sport suit into a modest suit of black. He stood beside the closed door examining the dead man without a trace of surprise. Not a line of his delicate features moved, but his eyes were lively and very bright. Finally Mr. Moto drew in his breath with a soft, sibilant hiss.

"So sorry for you," Mr. Moto said, "so very, very sorry. You did not kill him I think." Calvin had intended to be impersonal and calm, but Mr. Moto's question broke down his resolution.

"No," Calvin said, "I guess you know I didn't."

"Please," Mr. Moto's voice was hardly more than a whisper. "Do not speak so loudly. I am so sorry for you, Mr. Gates. I could not help but hear the sound."

"What did you hear?" Calvin asked him. "You were listening, were you? Why? What are you sneaking around me for?"

Mr. Moto raised a fragile, coffee-colored hand.

"Please," he said. "It will be nice if you will please be reasonable. You were here in this room alone with this man who is now dead. I saw him enter, Mr. Gates."

"And what business was it of yours if he did?" Calvin said.

"Please," said Mr. Moto again. "It would be so very nice if you were calmer, Mr. Gates. Do not concern yourself with who I am, please. I must ask you to sit in that chair by the writing table, please."

Before he spoke, Calvin took a careful step toward him.

"You go to the devil," he said, "unless you're going to try to kill me first."

"No," said Mr. Moto, "no please. It would not help. It would be so very nice if you would sit down—in the chair by the writing table, please. Do you not think it would be very, very nice?"

Mr. Moto smiled as he asked the question. There was a moment's silence and Calvin drew his trench coat around him and scowled.

"All right," he said. "I'm sitting down."

"So sorry for you," Mr. Moto said. "If you will excuse me, please."

Mr. Moto was displaying the sprightly impersonality of an undertaker, and it was apparent that he had dealt with similar situations. All his movements were adroit and unhurried like those of a hunter who finally moves to the point where the game has fallen.

"So too bad," Mr. Moto said, "so very, very clumsy."

First he knelt beside the body and touched it delicately. Then his hands moved flutteringly through the dead man's pockets, but it was evident to Calvin that Mr. Moto did not find what he wanted.

"So too bad," he murmured again, "so very, very clumsy."

Finally he rose from his knees, dusted his trousers carefully, clasped his hands together and bowed.

"And now I must ask a favor," Mr. Moto said. "It would be so much nicer for me and for you if you will grant this favor. Do not be angry, please."

Calvin Gates understood at once that Mr. Moto was not asking a favor—he was making a definite request.

"What do you want?" Calvin repeated.

The answer was hesitant, but the hesitation was only make-believe; every intonation and every gesture of Mr. Moto's was coldly precise.

"So sorry," Mr. Moto said. "It is all such a very bad mistake. We are so happy to die for our Emperor—sometimes we do too much."

"What do you want?" Calvin repeated.

"That you will allow me to search your person," Mr. Moto said. "I shall do so with the greatest respect. It is simply a matter of passing my hands over the pockets of your coat and over your pajamas. Such a simple matter."

"Suppose I don't agree?" Calvin asked.

"Then," Mr. Moto said, "someone else would do it."

"You've been through all my baggage," Calvin said. "Isn't that enough?"

"I am so sorry," Mr. Moto said. "Nothing was taken. Will you please stand up?"

Calvin stood up and Mr. Moto's hands touched him gently.

"So kind of you," said Mr. Moto, "so very, very kind. I suppose you are thinking of so many things. You are wondering what we are going to do. If you will help, everything will be so nice."

"It would be a whole lot easier," Calvin said, "if you didn't talk about things being nice. There doesn't seem to be much for me to do, does there? A man comes in here, a stranger, and he's killed in front of me."

Mr. Moto lighted a cigarette and perched himself carefully on the edge of the bed.

"It was all so very clumsy," Mr. Moto said. "He should not have been killed. It was all such a very bad mistake." Mr. Moto smiled brightly. "The best we can do is to forget. Do you not think it would be nicer, Mr. Gates?"

"Forget?" repeated Calvin.

Mr. Moto nodded and smiled.

"It has all been so bad," he repeated. "So much better to say nothing about mistakes. Will you listen to me for a moment, please?"

Calvin did not answer and Mr. Moto continued as though he had hit upon a happy social stratagem.

"You must not mind so much about so little. You are on a journey, and I hope so much that you will have a very happy journey."

Mr. Moto paused. The words were charmingly soft, but Calvin could feel an insistence behind them which resembled a threat.

"Go ahead, Mr. Moto, I am not a fool," he answered.

"Oh no. You are not a fool, Mr. Gates," Mr. Moto agreed cordially. "Because you are not a fool, I make a suggestion, a humble, nice suggestion."

"Go ahead," said Calvin.

"If you agree," said Mr. Moto, "I shall speak to my friend, the manager. He is so very nice to tourists. He will give you another room and your baggage will be brought there. This will only be a little secret, and I hope so much that you will say nothing, particularly to that young lady, Miss Dillaway. She would be very much disturbed. I hope so much that you understand me. If you do not you will not have a happy journey."

"Is that a threat?" asked Calvin.

"Please," said Mr. Moto. "That is not a nice word. I am trying so very hard. It is not a threat, but a request, I am so afraid. I am so sorry for you. You are suspected by the police."

Calvin felt his face change color, while Mr. Moto sat there watching him.

"You better tell me what you mean," he said.

"Oh yes," said Mr. Moto, "I shall be so very glad. You are going to such a strange place, Mongolia. My country is so interested in Mongolia. You say you are a scientist. That is not so, Mr. Gates. Do not interrupt me, please. We have means of information. You did very badly at Yale University. You have been in businesses since, but not successful. You have won some prizes at shooting with the rifle and the revolver. It is so funny you should be traveling, please—There are so many funny people in Asia, Mr. Gates. So many are here to get away from their police."

Mr. Moto leaned forward slightly and his glance was fixed steadily on the other's face.

"I'm afraid you are a dangerous man, Mr. Gates, although I cannot be quite sure. I think perhaps that you might like to kill me. Do not try it, if you please."

Calvin Gates put his hands in the pockets of his trench coat.

"I might try if I had the chance," he said. "I don't like you, Mr. Moto."

"So sorry," Mr. Moto answered. "But you will listen please. I received a telegram about you tonight. The police in your country are looking for you, Mr. Gates."

Calvin Gates hesitated before he answered. He tried to keep his face composed and to hide whatever it was he felt, and he could understand at last the reason for all of Mr. Moto's interest. He was in something that was very close to danger.

"The police?" he said. "You must be crazy."

"No," said Mr. Moto. "So sorry to be rude. There are so many people in Asia wanted by the police. It will be so much nicer in Mongolia. There are no police in Mongolia."

Calvin passed his hand across his forehead.

"That can't be so," he said. "There must be something wrong somewhere. They wouldn't do that. He wouldn't. It was a family matter, Mr. Moto. I can explain it to you, if you want. There must be some mistake."

But Mr. Moto's face showed him that there was no mistake.

"Please," Mr. Moto said, "there is no reason to explain. You can help me, so very much. If you will travel quickly, everything will be so nice."

"What do they want me for?" Calvin asked.

Mr. Moto smiled and drew in his breath.

"For taking money," he said. "Excuse my rudeness, please. Someone has been taking a great deal of money from a gentleman in New York for several years. He says that it is you. I hope so much they are not right."

"For several years?" Calvin repeated, and his face felt moist and clammy. "It was only once—it wasn't for several years. It was my uncle—it was a family matter. He wouldn't—he couldn't have called in the police. He's too much of a man for that—"

Mr. Moto drew in his breath again.

"So sorry," he said. "But you do not want to go back. I think. Please, am I not right?"

For a moment Calvin's mind moved back sickeningly into the past.

"I never knew that she'd done it before," he said, and his freckled face looked ugly. "But it's like her, though, and it's like her to get out from under—that girl would lie her head off—"

He stopped, suddenly realizing that Mr. Moto was no friend of his.

"You're right," he said, "I don't want to go back. If I could, I wouldn't want to. It would kill him if he knew about it. I'm going ahead to see this through. I've got to get there to see this Gilbreth."

Mr. Moto rose from his seat on the bed and stood before Calvin. His manner had changed to a sort of businesslike precision, which took Calvin off his guard. He realized that in his agitation at the news he had said a good deal more than he intended.

"It is so much nicer," Mr. Moto said, "now that we understand each other. I think we will get along so very nicely, if you are careful, Mr. Gates."

Mr. Moto pointed a delicate finger at him and nodded solemnly.

"Believe me, you must be careful, please. I am so used to bad men, Mr. Gates. They do not frighten me, not very much. I should not enjoy it if you had your hands upon my throat. I was so very happy that you have no weapons in your baggage. You look so gentle, but I think that you are dangerous, and able to think."

Calvin Gates scowled at Mr. Moto, "So nice of you to say so," he answered, "but you're wrong. I'm a sentimental fool, or I wouldn't be here tonight."

Mr. Moto raised his hand in polite agreement.

"Oh yes," he said, "Nordics are never very logical. I am not asking what you have done, Mr. Gates. You are wanted by the police for taking money, but you are more than a thief I think. I do not ask about you, and you do not ask about me."

Calvin Gates's forehead was smoother.

"I don't ask about you," Calvin said, "because I don't give one continental damn."

"Thank you," said Mr. Moto, "so very much. I am glad that you say it clearly. Our authorities have been asked to detain you, but I think it can be arranged perhaps. So nice that I have influence."

"Detain me?" repeated Calvin Gates.

"Yes," said Mr. Moto, "yes."

"All right, you want me to keep still," Calvin told him. "Anything else, Mr. Moto? I'm ready to oblige, as long as I can keep on going."

Mr. Moto rubbed his hands together very softly.

"You will leave tomorrow on your journey as if nothing had happened," he said. "There is only one thing more. There is a cigarette case inlaid with little birds. It is not here."

Calvin Gates answered almost cordially.

"If that's what you want," he said, "I can get it for you. It might have been easier if you'd just asked for it before."

Mr. Moto shook his head very quickly.

"It is exactly what I do not want, please," he said. "I know where the little case is now, since you do not have it. You will do nothing and forget about it altogether. This is very important, please."

"All right," said Calvin Gates. "I don't know what your game is, but I'll forget it."

"I am so very glad," Mr. Moto said, "that you should understand. It is a very important game, please. I should not hesitate to go very, very far in it. I do not want anything disturbed. And now I shall show you to your room. It will be right across the hall, and I hope you will have a very pleasant night and such a very pleasant journey."

Calvin Gates stepped carefully past the dead man near the door.

"Well," he said, "I suppose I'll be seeing you again."

"I hope not," said Mr. Moto gently. "For your sake, Mr. Gates."

Calvin Gates hesitated. He knew so little that he could not tell how far to go; he only knew that he had been caught up in something entirely beyond his own control, and that he was not the only one who was caught. He was thinking of Miss Dillaway with her hair tied in an uncompromising knot, who made no effort to appear attractive.

"So you know who has that case?" he asked.

"Yes," said Mr. Moto, "I am so sure that I know now." He nodded toward the dead man. "Since he does not have it, and you have not. It was very important that the case should go where you are going. I wish so much for it to go there without trouble. It must. This was all such a bad mistake."

"It seems to me," said Calvin, "that it will be dangerous for Miss Dillaway."

Mr. Moto's expression gave no hint of agreement or disagreement.

"It will be dangerous for you if you should meddle," Mr. Moto said.

"Thanks," Calvin Gates answered, and he paused, and he and Mr. Moto looked at each other carefully. "I won't forget that, Moto."

"I am so glad," Mr. Moto breathed softly, "so glad you won't forget. I should be so sorry for you. May I show you your new room, please? It is right across the hall. I am so sorry, I shall be busy here tonight, so that we cannot have a pleasant talk."

The room where Mr. Moto took him was almost the same as the one he had left.

"Your bags will arrive in a few minutes," Mr. Moto said. "I am sorry I must leave you, I am so very busy."

## 6

WHEN MR. MOTO left him, Calvin opened the window and peered out into a dark courtyard; then he closed the window and stood with his ear close to the door listening to sounds from the room across the hall. He could hear a soft thud of footsteps, and he could hear Mr. Moto's voice speaking in an insistent undertone.

He had not been listening long before there was a knock at his door. Two men who were obviously not hotel attendants carried his trunk into the room. They gazed at him incuriously and set the trunk at the head of the bed, and returned a moment later with his brief case and his bag. One of them brought in his clothes, which he laid carefully on a chair. Calvin took a piece of money from his trouser pocket, but they looked at him blankly and shook their heads. He heard them hurry across the hall again, open a door and close it, and a moment later he opened his own door. The hallway stretched before him to right and left, absolutely empty, and Calvin closed his door noiselessly and smiled. He had been surprised at first that his room had not been watched, but now he was not surprised: the thing that he proposed to do was so obvious that only a fool would have attempted it, and Mr. Moto had said that he was not a fool.

He turned out the light and dressed quickly in the dark. Then he opened the door again and stepped out into the hall, holding his shoes in his hand. He dropped them noisily in front of his door and listened. There was a confused and gentle murmur of voices in the room across the hall. Standing in the hallway, Calvin Gates slammed his door shut, and ran on tiptoe down the hall. He had judged the distance he must travel and the chances he must take.

He darted along the corridor in his stocking feet past the well of the lift to the stairway. When he reached the angle of the stairs, he paused in its shelter and looked behind him. He had moved quickly and just quickly enough. Not a second after he had reached the stairs the door of the room he had first occupied opened and Mr. Moto's head appeared. Mr. Moto was looking across the hall toward the shoes. Calvin Gates could not help smiling at their guilelessness. Mr. Moto gazed at them before he closed the door again, and Calvin's smile grew broader.

"I guess," he murmured, "Mr. Moto has put me in bed for the night."

He waited for a few moments, but the hall was empty. Finally he stepped from the angle of the stairs and continued moving softly down the corridor. He had seen Miss Dillaway to her room that night, and he remembered the number. He knocked upon her door without any hesitation, because the noise was a chance that he was obliged to take and he had realized long ago that when one started it was always better to move ahead. He knocked three times, and when he paused he was relieved to hear the key in the lock. A moment later Miss Dillaway opened the door a crack. He could not see her, but he heard her voice—a voice that was soft and incredulous.

"What's the matter, Gates?" she asked. "What is it?"

Calvin pushed the door open and he was in her room before he answered.

"Don't make a noise," he whispered.

He had forgotten about propriety and she had only been an abstraction to him until he was in her room, but when he was there he felt a self-conscious embarrassment at his rudeness. He had broken in upon something which he was not meant to see, upon a different person from the girl he had known on the train and upon a sort of privacy that made him stare at her blankly. She had on a negligee of delicate pastel green. Her bare feet were thrust into green silk mules, and her hair fell over her back and shoulders in a dark, misty cloud that framed the delicate oval of her face. Even with the startled look in her wide brown eyes her face was beautiful. In that moment of surprise she was very young and entirely untouched by the world outside.

The bare ugliness of the room had been changed by her small possessions—a gold-backed comb and brush upon the bureau, and some books on a chair. Her small blue leather traveling clock was on the table. They were all small things, but all of them made her different and all of them told him that he should not be there. For a second she was breathless and confused, and he shared her confusion.

"What do you mean by coming in here?" she said breathlessly. "What do you mean by pushing the door open?"

"I'm sorry," said Calvin Gates. Her face was growing red and so was his. "I didn't mean to startle you. I haven't got much time."

Miss Dillaway bit her lower lip and pulled her green gown more tightly about her, a quick instinctive gesture which reminded him that he was staring at her.

"Gates," she said, "are you going to get out of here or shall I have to ring? I didn't think you'd act like this. You're like all the rest of them. I thought—"

"Don't," Calvin answered, "There isn't time. I came here to help you."

"Oh," she said, "that's one way of putting it."

"Don't," Calvin Gates repeated. "I do want to help you, Miss Dillaway. I'm afraid you're in trouble."

The confusion and the anger had left her face and her brown eyes grew wider.

"Go ahead," she answered. "What is it, Gates?" And Calvin told her bluntly because it was the only way to tell it.

"Your Russian has been murdered," he told her. "A political murder I think—by the police."

She walked toward him and rested her hand on his arm and her lips trembled. It was an ugly enough moment, but he was only conscious that she trusted him and that she had touched his arm.

"Murdered," she whispered. "How do you know that?"

"I know it," he answered, "because I saw him die."

She reached her hand toward him again, and he held it in his for a moment.

"It's going to be all right," he said.

Then she drew her hand away and it was exactly as though a door had closed between them, for her composure had come back—that same casual mask which he had seen on the train.

"I want you to listen," Calvin Gates went on. "I want you to try to trust me and do what I tell you. Do you think you can?"

"Yes," she said, "I think I can. I don't know you very well." And she smiled. It was a poor attempt at a smile. "Do you have to be so dramatic, Gates?"

Calvin Gates looked back at her soberly.

"I'm sorry," he began, "to have broken in here."

"Good heavens," said Miss Dillaway, "let's not go over that again. What are you staring at, Gates?"

"It's you," said Calvin Gates, "you're beautiful."

"Well, you needn't look so surprised," said Miss Dillaway. "You didn't come here to tell me that."

"No," he said, "I didn't. The Russian was killed on account of that cigarette case, the one he gave you, the one you put in your purse. They know you have it, Miss Dillaway. You must get rid of it at once."

She pushed her hair back from her forehead again.

"Why should he be killed on account of that?" she asked.

Calvin Gates shook his head. "You'll have to take my word for it," he said. "There isn't any time to find out why. I'm asking you to give me your purse with that cigarette case right away."

"But why?" she asked him. "Aren't you going to tell me why?"

"Not now," said Calvin Gates.

Miss Dillaway put her head to one side. "But why should I?" she asked.

"Because I'm asking you," Calvin said, "and I'm asking you to do it quickly, because you need help worse than you ever did in your life."

She stood there for a moment small and straight in her light green gown, like a painting in a gallery, and then she smiled.

"My knight," she said, "my knight in armor."

The effect of her remark on Calvin was not agreeable.

"I wish you wouldn't call me that," he said. "You can either give me your purse or not."

"I'm sorry, Gates," she said, and her voice was suddenly contrite. "I'm generally able to look out for myself, you know. Suppose I give you my purse, then what?"

"In half an hour I want you to ring your bell," Calvin told her. "Open your door and scream if you want to. Say a man broke into your room and snatched your purse. Say that you think he was a Russian. Make all the noise you like, I'll be there to help."

She looked at him and said nothing.

"Well," said Calvin Gates, "will you do it, or won't you?"

When she answered all her embarrassment had gone.

"I never thought I'd do a thing like this," she said, "do what I'm told without knowing why. I don't know anything about you. I don't know why I do it. Are you really going on that expedition, Gates? I'm all alone here. Are you really being honest?"

"I'm going to leave with you for Peiping tomorrow," Calvin told her.

Miss Dillaway put her hand under the pillow of her bed, and drew out her worn black leather handbag. Now that she was in her green gown the handbag looked incongruous.

"I'll take my money and my passport out," she said

"Please don't," said Calvin Gates. "That's what you are to make the row about, because your money and your passport are gone. Don't speak about the cigarette case until they ask you." He took the bag out of her hand.

"Remember," he said, "in half an hour."

Miss Dillaway nodded.

"I don't know anything about it," she said, "but I suppose I ought to thank you, Gates." There was an added touch of color in her cheeks and her eyes were bright. "Take care of yourself, will you, Gates? I don't want to miss you on the train tomorrow."

# 7

TAKE CARE of yourself, Gates.

Those casual words had an ironical sound when he stopped to think of them.

"Yes," his thoughts were whispering, "I don't much care what happens. I might as well go out this way as any other."

He was under no illusions, since Mr. Moto's implications, though gentle, had been precise. It was in Mr. Moto's power to make him disappear as completely as the man whom he had spoken to that night. He lay in his bed five minutes later, listening, occasionally looking at his watch, but there was no sound to indicate that the hotel was not asleep. It was up to Miss Dillaway to do the rest, and he wondered if she would. As it happened, she did it very well, better than he had hoped.

First he heard the lift moving and a pounding of steps on the stairs. Then he heard Miss Dillaway's voice in the hall.

"Doesn't anyone hear my bell?" she was calling. "Can't someone come up here? Help!"

Calvin Gates lay still and listened. Doors were opening and a murmur of voices grew louder, but Miss Dillaway's voice rose above them angrily.

"What sort of a place do you call this?" he heard Miss Dillaway saying. "He came into my room. He snatched my purse and ran. Isn't there anybody here who can understand English? Aren't you going to do anything?"

The murmur of voices continued as Calvin Gates got slowly out of bed and put on his trench coat and opened his door. At the far end of the long corridor half a dozen people had gathered. The gray-haired hotel manager was there, still in his frock coat, some hotel boys, and Mr. Moto, and some Japanese men in kimonos.

"Please, madam," the hotel manager was saying, "please be calm."

"Calm!" Miss Dillaway snapped at him. "He came right into my room. I want my passport and my letters of credit and my traveler's checks." Then she noticed Calvin Gates.

"Hello," she said, "it's time you woke up. You're an American, aren't you? Aren't you going to help me? Someone stole my purse."

"Your purse?" said Calvin Gates. "I'm sorry."

"Sorry!" Miss Dillaway said. "Everybody says he's sorry. Aren't you going to do something? You're a man, aren't you? I've lost my purse."

"Now wait a minute," said Calvin Gates, "I don't see how—" But Mr. Moto interrupted him.

"Please," said Mr. Moto, and he looked disturbed and puzzled. "Everyone is looking. When did it happen, please?"

"He was in here just three minutes ago," Miss Dillaway cried. "I began calling as soon as he ran out. He ran down the stairs—down there."

"Downstairs?" Mr. Moto said soothingly. "Make no doubt he will be found. Did you lock your door, please?"

"Don't ask idiotic questions," Miss Dillaway said. "Of course I locked my door. But any fool could pick a lock like that, and there wasn't any bolt. He woke me up when he was reaching under the pillow."

"Oh yes," said Mr. Moto. "So sorry to ask stupid questions. What did he look like, please?"

"Look like?" Miss Dillaway repeated. "I can't see in the dark."

"So silly of me," Mr. Moto murmured; "so you did not see." Before she could answer, he turned and looked at Calvin Gates.

"He wasn't tall, and he wasn't Japanese. He spoke to me," Miss Dillaway said.

"Ah, he spoke to you?" Mr. Moto brightened. "Oh? What did he tell you, please?"

"What do you think?" Miss Dillaway answered. "Do you think we talked about the weather? He told me he'd kill me if I cried out."

"Oh," said Mr. Moto, "so interesting. Thank you. Not a large man—and how did his voice sound, please?"

Miss Dillaway's answer was prompt and incisive.

"Like someone who has learned English out of a book," she said. "He wasn't English. His voice was in his throat. He might have been German, or Russian perhaps."

"Ah," said Mr. Moto, "Russian? Was there anything more, please?"

"Yes, one thing more." Calvin Gates drew in his breath, waiting for her to go on. "He had perfume on him."

Calvin Gates exhaled softly. Miss Dillaway had done better than he'd thought, Mr. Moto's eyes were bright and still and he rubbed his hands together gently.

"Thank you," he said. "What sort of perfume, please?"

"How should I know?" Miss Dillaway said. "It had musk in it, that's all."

"Ah," said Mr. Moto, "musk. Thank you so very much. I am so very, very grateful."

He paused. A voice was calling from the stairway—one of the hotel boys was running down the hall, calling something in Japanese. Mr. Moto smiled delightedly.

"Wait," said Mr. Moto. "So nice that you had patience. They have found your purse—on the stairs."

A moment later he was holding it out to her, bowing above it. There was an excited surge of Japanese voices.

"So glad," said Mr. Moto. "I hope so much it is yours."

"Yes," said Miss Dillaway, "of course it's mine. They found it on the stairs?"

Mr. Moto bowed again.

"Will you very kindly examine it, please?" he asked. "Yes. The thief must have been so frightened that he dropped it. I hope so much that everything is there."

Miss Dillaway was looking through the purse.

"Yes," she said, "everything. Why, he didn't even take my money! There's only one thing that's gone, and it doesn't matter."

"I am so very pleased." Mr. Moto drew in his breath and smiled, but it seemed to Calvin that his smile was hardly more than a courteous gesture. "What was it that did not matter?"

Miss Dillaway shrugged her shoulders.

"Just a silver cigarette case," she said. "It was given to me yesterday. I've still got one of my own. I guess I'm pretty lucky and thank you very much."

"You are so welcome," Mr. Moto said. "A silver cigarette case? What did it look like, please? We shall try so hard to find it."

"Really," said Miss Dillaway, "it doesn't amount to anything. I don't really care at all. It was Japanese work of silver inlaid with gunmetal. There were birds on it."

"Ah," said Mr. Moto, "lots of little birds? Please, you did not count them, did you?"

"Count them?" said Miss Dillaway. "Why under the sun should I count them?"

"No reason." Mr. Moto sighed. "Thank you so much."

"Thank you," said Miss Dillaway. "You've all been very kind."

"It has been such a great pleasure," said Mr. Moto. "I am sure you will not be disturbed again; so very, very sure."

"Is there anything more I can do, Miss Dillaway?" Calvin Gates asked her.

Miss Dillaway wrinkled her nose.

"More?" she answered. "I don't see that you've done anything except stand there."

Calvin Gates turned without answering and walked slowly down the hall, and Mr. Moto fell in step beside him.

"Mr. Gates," he said.

"Yes," Calvin answered.

Mr. Moto drew in his breath behind his hand.

"This is so very unfortunate. I am so very much ashamed. Everything has been so very clumsy. Now I must start all over again."

"I don't know what you're driving at," Calvin said. "I suppose someone stole that case."

"Yes," said Mr. Moto, "I think that I must kill myself if I do not find that case."

"Kill yourself?" Calvin Gates repeated.

Mr. Moto's gold teeth glittered in a polite impersonal smile.

"So sorry," he said. "A code of honor. You will say nothing about his, I hope so very much."

"I told you I wouldn't," said Calvin Gates. Mr. Moto drew a card from his pocket and wrote something on it.

"My address, please," he said. "If you hear about that case I should be so very glad if you would let me know. Have you traveled in England, Mr. Gates?"

"Yes," said Calvin Gates, "a little."

"Ha ha," said Mr. Moto, "exactly what I thought. That is where you learned to put your shoes outside your door? So very few Americans learn to put their shoes outside their doors at night. I hope that you will have such a very pleasant journey."

## 8

AT NOON the next day Calvin Gates walked across the lobby to the desk to pay his bill. He still did not know whether he had been clever or not the night before, but he knew that he had done a dangerous thing and for the first time in a long while he was not thinking about himself. He was learning that a determined urbanity was one of Japan's heaven-sent gifts and that all which was ugly or difficult was repressed by power of will. The night was lost in a sunny morning. Memory had banished in the winelike air that set Calvin Gates's nerves tingling in a staccato sort of rhythm, like the hoofbeats of the horses which drew those ancient Russian droshkies across the square outside.

The manager bowed and smiled and handed him his bill.

"Breakfast is included," the manager said. "The porter will take you to the train and find you seats. It is best to leave please in three quarters of an hour. I hope that you were comfortable last night?"

Calvin put his change carefully in his pocket. His brownish freckled face was as imperturbable as the face in front of him.

"A very comfortable night," he said. "You have such a nice hotel."

"So glad," the manager said, "thank you." And that was all.

Calvin Gates leaned an elbow on the hotel desk.

"And Mr. Moto," he inquired, "is he up this morning yet?"

"So sorry," the manager said. "Mr. Moto was up early. He is gone."

"Oh," said Calvin Gates, "he is busy, I suppose?"

"Yes," the manager in his frock coat seized eagerly upon the explanation. "He is busy."

All the past was lost in the imperturbable present. Calvin Gates was thinking that the Japanese had a good many impossible things to explain in the last few years, but that they always faced the facts with that same smile. They explained their adventure in Manchukuo in that same manner, and their infiltration beyond the Chinese Wall. Like Mr. Moto they were always very busy—always busy, a nervous, vital race.

There was a tramp of feet outside on the square, that indescribable sound of a body of men marching at route order, and he stepped to the hotel door to watch. A battalion of infantry was moving by in iron helmets, weighted down under complete field equipment, out perhaps for a practice march or possibly for something else. The new conquerors of Manchuria were moving across the square, squat, woodeny boys who were evidently an ordinary sight, to be accepted wearily as an old story by the people. First there had been the Manchus, then the Russians, and then the Old Marshal, and then the Japanese. He was still watching them when Miss Dillaway stepped out the door and stood beside him.

"Hello," she said. "Do you want to play soldier?" Her head was tilted toward him.

"Hello," he answered. "It looks as though there's going to be a war."

Miss Dillaway wrinkled her nose.

"Suppose you get down to earth," she said. "It isn't any of our business, is it? We've got half an hour before we leave for the station. Suppose you tell me exactly what happened last night."

"Not here," said Calvin Gates. "We're probably being watched."

"All right," said Miss Dillaway, "if you like to pretend that you're in a dime novel."

She did not bring up the subject again until they were on the train seated side by side.

"Now tell me about last night," she said.

Calvin Gates folded his hands across his knee. "The less you know about it the better," he answered. "It was true what I told you last night. He was killed."

Miss Dillaway gave a short, unmusical laugh.

"All right," she said. "Have it your own way. It might be better if you told me. Didn't I behave all right last night?"

"No one could have done better," said Calvin Gates.

She leaned nearer to him so that their shoulders touched.

"Where's that cigarette case?" she said.

"It doesn't matter," he said.

"Oh yes, it does," she answered. "You'd better tell me or I won't stop talking."

"It's in my pocket," Calvin said. She was startled. Her eyes were suddenly wide and incredulous.

"Don't say any more," said Calvin Gates.

Miss Dillaway's voice was low.

"You don't care much what happens to you, do you, Gates?" she said.

Calvin Gates smiled at her. "No," he answered, "not very much."

Miss Dillaway squared her shoulders.

"I knew there was something the matter with you the first time I saw you. What did you keep it for?"

"No good reason," he said. "He asked me to, that's all."

"Who ?"

"The Russian."

"Oh he did, did he?" said Miss Dillaway. "Well, why did you do what he asked you?"

Calvin Gates frowned and looked at the freckles on the back of his hands.

"Well," said Miss Dillaway, "you haven't answered, Gates."

He turned to her again as though he had forgotten her and her question.

"Frankly, it's a little hard to answer," he said. "but I suppose you ought to have some sort of explanation."

"Thank you," said Miss Dillaway, "that's very thoughtful of you, Gates."

He ignored her remark and looked straight ahead of him, speaking slowly.

"I'm not so worried about the Japanese," he said, "it's the others. There must be some others to whom this thing is very important. It's some form of a message of course. Those others may still think you have it. That's why I'm keeping it, Miss Dillaway. In case there is any trouble, it might be better to have it than not. Of course I may be wrong."

Miss Dillaway glanced at him sideways.

"So you're doing this for me. Is that true?" she said.

"Partly," he nodded slowly.

"Well, you needn't," said Miss Dillaway. "You'd better throw it out the window, Gates."

"Perhaps," said Calvin Gates, "but I'm not sure. They might not believe that we'd thrown it out the window. If they did believe, they might think that we understood about it. I think it's better keeping it, a great deal better."

"Don't you think," inquired Miss Dillaway, and her words were sweetly deliberate, "you are taking a good deal on yourself?"

"Perhaps," Calvin Gates agreed. "We're rather in the dark. Perhaps nothing will happen at all, but I think you need some help, Miss Dillaway."

"I haven't asked you for help, have I?" Miss Dillaway inquired.

"No," said Calvin Gates.

Miss Dillaway's color grew higher and she sat up straighter and clasped her hands tightly together. She looked sideways at him and started to speak and paused, and finally her voice had a curious note.

"You aren't doing this because you're attracted to me, are you Gates? You can't be, because you've hardly seen me."

He was surprised by the abruptness of her question and surprised because her assurance was gone, but he was startled by his own answer. He had intended to speak lightly and instead he was being serious.

"I saw you last night," he said.

She turned away from him and looked out the window.

"You can't be doing this just because you saw me with my hair down my back," Miss Dillaway said.

"I'm not sure," said Calvin Gates.

Miss Dillaway turned back from the window.

"Don't try to be gallant, Gates," she said. "That sort of thing is stuff and nonsense. Of course I wouldn't have asked that question if I'd even thought that you'd pretend to take it seriously."

"Why is it nonsense," Calvin asked her, "to look the way you did last night?"

He felt her shoulder beside his stiffen and her lips closed tight.

"It's nonsense," she said, "because it makes trouble. I have my work to do and I don't want to be bothered. I don't want to be bothered when I'm traveling by myself."

"So you put on a disguise," said Calvin Gates. "Is that what you mean?"

Miss Dillaway looked surprised. "It isn't what I mean exactly. I like to be judged for what I am, not for the way I look, and now you say because you saw me in a green kimono—It's rather silly, Gates."

"Is it?" Calvin asked her. "I don't see why."

"I'll tell you why," said Miss Dillaway. "Because you're a romanticist, Gates. You're a type which ought to be extinct—the knight errant type. Anyone in a green negligee would do. You don't care who's inside it. You only care for the idea."

"No," said Calvin Gates, "that isn't true."

Miss Dillaway's eyes sparkled. "Oh yes, it's true," she said. "Any lady in any wrapper. I wish you'd give me back that cigarette case, Gates. I can manage it just as well as you can. I don't even know who you are. Why should I be obliged to you?"

"I'm not asking you to be obliged," said Calvin Gates.

"Oh yes, you are," Miss Dillaway answered, "but you never even thought of it that way."

Calvin Gates stood up.

"Just the same I'm going to keep it," he said, "whether you like it or not. You're a funny person, Miss Dillaway. First I like you and then I don't. I may be a romanticist, but I'm not afraid of life."

She looked startled and then she smiled.

"No one ever said that to me before," she said. "I'm not afraid of life."

"You're running away from it," he told her. You're running away from it now."

"Then so are you," said Miss Dillaway tartly. "You're running away from something, at any rate. I don't understand you, Gates."

"It doesn't really matter," Calvin said.

The observation car was almost a copy of the one they had left the day before, and he sat in another of the wicker chairs staring out the window. The remarks he had made to Miss Dillaway afforded him no satisfaction. Instead he was obsessed by a lonely sense of his own futility. He was alone again in a world of Orientals, of Japanese army officers and Japanese businessmen. Outside the country had grown level and there were faint yellowish dust clouds on the horizon, and the same mud villages and blue-clad laborers.

It must have been an hour later when Miss Dillaway entered the car and seated herself in a vacant chair beside him.

"Hello," she said, "are you angry with me, Gates?"

"No," he told her.

"I'm glad you're not," Miss Dillaway said, "because I don't like it there alone. People keep watching me."

"Who?" he asked. "Anyone in particular?"

Miss Dillaway shook her head.

"No one in particular, just the train guard and the train boy. I'd rather be with you. You're better, Gates."

"It's kind of you to say so," he answered.

She wrinkled her nose and sniffed.

"I'm sorry if I've been disagreeable. It's just the way I am, I guess. we can't help being what we are."

"No," he answered, "I don't suppose we can."

"If I could, I'd change right away," she said.

"So would I," he answered.

"The trouble is we just have to keep being what we are unless something changes us. Do you suppose anything will ever change us, Gates?"

Calvin Gates smiled and forgot that they were in Manchuria.

"Probably for the worse," he said.

She laughed and held out her hand. "You're not so bad," she answered. "Let's go into the dining car and have a drink. I'll match you for who pays."

"No," he said, "I'll buy it."

"I'm not being ladylike, am I?" she said, "I told you we couldn't change. I'll match you, I can't help it, Gates."

Nevertheless Miss Dillaway had changed. She was no longer concealing her personality from him or trying to act a part and it must have been an effort for her to go as far as that. It pleased him, more than he thought was possible, that she had surrendered to some intuition and, without knowing who he was or what, had given him her friendship. It made him happy even though he knew that there would be only one ending. It would be better to tell her something about himself beforehand; it would be the only honorable way, since they were friends, but he hesitated.

"I know I'm disagreeable when I'm traveling, Gates," she said confidingly. "My temper always goes to pieces when I'm worried, and I say any amount of things that I'm sorry for afterwards. I'm frightened most of the time when I'm on these trips and I don't want anyone to know it. It's not as bad with you. I'm really having a nice time."

"So am I," said Calvin Gates, "the first time in a long while, and you're the only reason for it, Miss Dillaway."

"You'd better call me Dillaway," she said. "My first name is Sylvia, and I don't like it much. My friends all call me Dillaway. I may as well warn you, I'm as likely as not to snap your head off before we get to Peiping, and you'll probably want to choke me. You should have seen the way I tore into poor Boris. At the customs' shed." She stopped and caught her breath. "Aren't you going to tell me what happened to him, Gates? How did he—"

Calvin interrupted her and spoke quickly. If she had to know, and it would probably be better if she did, he wished to make that whole ugly affair casual and literal.

"He came to my room to ask me to take that cigarette case he gave you. He was shot while he was talking to me. A man came in and shot him from the balcony. It isn't pleasant, but I suppose you ought to know. Then Mr. Moto came and took the whole thing in hand."

"That little man?" she said.

"Yes, it had something to do with the police. What do you know about that Russian?"

"Nothing," she answered. "I asked for a courier at the hotel."

Calvin Gates nodded.

"What do you think he was doing?"

"Carrying a message," she answered promptly. "He was frightened in the train. What do you suppose that thing's about? Have you looked at it?"

"No," he said, "but I think he had told someone else that he had given it to you. He had all evening to make arrangements."

Calvin Gates folded his hands carefully, unfolded them again and laid them palm down upon each knee.

"I've been trying most of last night to figure it out. Granted that it is some sort of message, it's a very important one, or they wouldn't have killed the man who was carrying it. If it is a message, it is probably going to someone near where we are going, but after that I'm puzzled. Whoever sent the message certainly wanted it delivered."

"Well, that's obvious," Miss Dillaway said.

"The next point is not so obvious," he answered. "Moto wants it delivered too. In fact, he told me so."

"Now wait a minute," said Miss Dillaway. "This can't be right. If he wanted the message delivered why should they have killed Boris?"

Calvin Gates moved his shoulders uneasily and drummed his fingers on his knee.

"I gathered that it was a mistake," he explained slowly. "I don't think Mr. Moto liked it. He seemed to want to have things go smoothly. At any rate he told me so."

Miss Dillaway looked at him hard.

"It seems to me that he told you quite a good deal."

"Yes," Calvin Gates looked back at her. "He told me a good deal."

Miss Dillaway wrinkled her forehead.

"You're not being frank, Gates," she said. "Why should he have told you that much?"

Calvin Gates felt his fingers grip his knees tightly because the time had come. In another minute she would know that he was not a nice young man and certainly not a proper person for a friend. He was surprised how much he valued her friendship and how much he wanted her to think well of him, now that she would not and could not, because she was honest, devastatingly honest.

"Because Mr. Moto has something on me," he said. He spoke slowly because every word hurt him. "He thought he could make me let you carry that cigarette case for him. I think I fooled him last night. He doesn't know who's got it now."

She looked at him startled, exactly the way he thought that she would look.

"How could a little Japanese have anything on you?" she asked. "I don't see how it's possible."

Calvin spoke more slowly and his mouth was grim and straight.

"I may as well tell you I'm a notorious character, Miss Dillaway," he said. He tried to speak casually, but his voice was strained and discordant. "I am a fugitive from justice, Miss Dillaway." He saw her start and stare at him exactly as he knew she would and he went on grimly. If there was anything between them, it would be better to have it over.

"I like you well enough so that I'm blunt," he went on. "I found out last night that Mr. Moto knew everything about me. He's a Japanese agent. The whole nation seems to be alive with them. He threatened to turn me over to the authorities, if I said anything about last night and if I didn't let you carry that cigarette case. He's smart, but maybe I was smarter. You haven't got it now."

Her brown eyes had the same look that he had seen back at the hotel. He saw her clasp and unclasp her hands and when she spoke her voice was low and frightened.

"I generally know about people," she said. "I knew that something was the matter with you. What did you do back home, Gates?"

"I forged a check," he said. He had meant to keep his voice low, but instead it was harsh and bitter. He saw her start when he said it, but her eyes were still and deep.

"You did it on account of some girl," she said. "You did, Gates, didn't you?"

He stared out of the window before he answered. The train was moving rapidly across a level country which gave an impression of another age, with interminable cultivated fields, surrounding mud villages each behind a high mud wall. It was as though the clock had been turned back a thousand years, and there he was wretched in the present.

"Not exactly," he said slowly. "She was my first cousin and I always disliked her very much. It doesn't really matter. The point is I'm a forger. The point is I'm all washed up. Maybe it's just as well I told you. Forgers aren't popular with anyone, I guess. Keep your checkbook away from me, Miss Dillaway."

He leaned back in his wicker chair and stared straight ahead of him, uncomfortable at her silence, because her silence was worse than words. He was waiting for her to speak, bracing himself to hear what she might say. He saw her glance at him sideways.

"Do you still want to match me for a drink?" she said.

His face grew bright red underneath his tan and freckles. He had never known that he could be moved so deeply by anything that anyone could say to him.

"Do you mean you still want to talk to me?" he asked. "I haven't been joking, Dillaway."

Miss Dillaway wrinkled her nose.

"See if you've got a coin in your pocket," she said. "You've got clumsy hands for a forger, Gates." And that was all she said.

He put his hand in his pocket and drew out a Japanese coin with a hole through the middle of it.

"The trouble with it is," he said, "that it hasn't got any heads or tails."

Miss Dillaway laughed.

"You can't make heads or tails of anything in Japan," she answered, "that's why. I've got an American fifty-cent piece. Wait a minute."

She was opening her handbag and the train was slowing down beside one of those incongruous, half-European looking stations, built of neat gray brick with a gray tiled roof. Beyond it, perhaps half a mile away, he could see a town, larger than any they had passed, with somber gray brick walls and an arched gate with battlements on either side and with a curved roof structure above it. A line of two-wheeled carts drawn by chunky little horses moved into the town, and behind them came a row of donkeys laden with fagots. The train guard was drawn up on the station platform and their bayonets glittered in the summer sun, partly concealing a group of Chinese country people who stood behind them, watching incuriously. The train was slowing down and a food vendor with tea and rice and spaghetti was running beside it, calling in a plaintive singsong voice.

"It looks like a big town," said Calvin Gates, "I wonder what it is."

"It looks dirty," said Miss Dillaway. "Here's the fifty-cent piece, Gates. Look at the barbed wire and sandbags. You'd better call it, Gates. What do you want, heads or tails?"

"Heads," he said.

Miss Dillaway slapped the coin on the back of her hand.

"You lose, Gates," she said. "It's tails. Why look, what's happening now?"

The rear door of the observation car had opened and a young Japanese subaltern entered, followed by two soldiers with their rifles with bayonets at port. The officer was hardly out of his teens and his expression was eager and ambitious. He was holding a piece of paper in his hand which he consulted scrupulously, and finally looked at Calvin Gates. Calvin put his hand in his pocket and looked back at the officer.

"I'm afraid," he said, "Mr. Moto's guessed I've got that cigarette case."

Miss Dillaway pulled his sleeve.

"Then give it to me, Gates," she said.

Calvin Gates did not look at her, but continued to examine the officer.

"It's too late now," he answered. "I'm afraid we'd better say good-by, Miss Dillaway. You've been nice to me—much too nice."

The officer halted before Calvin Gates and spoke very slowly in English, accenting each syllable tonelessly and conscientiously, like a student who has learned the language from a phrase book.

"Good afternoon," the officer said. "Please, you come with me."

Calvin smiled, but the officer did not smile.

"Where?" Calvin asked.

The officer paused, laboring hard with the eccentricities of an unknown tongue.

"Arise off your sit, please," he said. "Go off the train with me at once."

Calvin Gates rose.

"Well," he said, "good-by, Miss Dillaway."

Miss Dillaway had risen also.

"If you're getting off this train," she said, "I'm getting off with you."

"No." Calvin Gate's tone was sharp. "You're doing no such thing. This is my party, and it wouldn't do you any good, but if you see Dr. Gilbreth up there, I wish you'd tell him that I forged that check."

"But Gates—" she clung tight to his arm—"what are they going to do with you?"

His expression was not entirely agreeable. He stood a head and shoulders above the little officer.

"It doesn't make a bit of difference," he said.

"But they don't even understand English," Miss Dillaway cried.

"It doesn't make any difference," Calvin Gates repeated. "Good-by, Miss Dillaway."

He walked toward the rear platform with the officer beside him and the soldiers just behind.

"Gates!" Miss Dillaway called after him, but he did not answer. In fact he only half heard her, for he seemed to have moved from the train already and from all that country.

# 9

OUT ON the station platform, warm in the late June sunlight, the crowd of chattering, blue-clad Chinese rustics moved hastily aside. He had a glimpse of rolls of bedding and dilapidated baggage, broad dull faces and dull staring eyes. The air was heavy with the odors of coal smoke, and of dough cakes, spaghetti and curiously varnished chickens that were exposed for sale.

"This way please," the officer said.

He was conducted into a bare and dirty room with a bench along one side of a wall, made greasy by others who had leaned against it waiting. Some soldiers sitting on the bench looked at him and looked away.

"Please," the lieutenant said, "you sit." And Calvin Gates sat down. At the end of the room, behind a plain wooden table, was seated a sallow, sickly-looking officer, whose eyes blinked from behind heavy lensed spectacles. In a sharp querulous voice he interrogated a tall, muscular Chinese peasant, clad in nothing but slippers and blue trousers. A Japanese guard whose head reached hardly above the shoulder of the Chinese stood beside him. Without knowing the language, Calvin Gates could understand what was happening by the intonation and by the repetition of syllables. The Chinese was denying something doggedly and stolidly as the officer pressed the question. The lieutenant who had brought Calvin in glanced toward the table and sat down.

"Will not take long," he said.

The voice of the officer suddenly grew sharper, and the guard standing on tiptoe struck the Chinese across the face. The lieutenant glanced sideways at Calvin Gates.

"Bad man," he said, "naughty man, a bandit."

Calvin could see the train through the open window, still waiting, and he wondered why it was delayed. He finally leaned his back against the wall where so many others had leaned before him and drew a travel folder from his pocket, a descriptive pamphlet of Mukden which he had found at the hotel. The lieutenant turned toward him quickly.

"I can read, can't I?" Calvin asked.

"Yes," the lieutenant said, "oh yes."

The writer of the pamphlet had been like the lieutenant, a student not wholly familiar with the English language, and thus the words and tenses of that folder progressed with a breathless, eager inaccuracy—MANCHURIAN INCIDENT AND NORTH BARRACKS. At 10:30 P.M. on the 18th of Sept. 1931, the Manchurian Incident was started by the insolent explosion of the railway track at Liutiso Kou between Mukden and Wen-kuan-tun stations of the South Manchurian Railway, which was executed by the Chinese regular soldiers. After the explosion the Chinese soldiers attempted to flee themselves in the direction of the North Barracks, but just then they were found by the Japanese railway guards under Lieutenant Kawamoto, who were patrolling the place on duty. Suddenly the both sides exchanged the bullets and the Japanese made a fierce pursuit after them. In the next moment, the Chinese forces of some three companies appeared from the thickly grown Kaolian field near the North Barracks, against which the Japanese opposed bravely and desperately, meantime despatching the urgent report to their commander. The skirmish developed speedily and the Japanese troop was compelled to make a violent attack upon the North Barracks where were stationed the brigade of Major-General Wang-icho, to lead the conditions favorable. After several hours of fierce battle, the barracks fell completely into the hand of the Japanese forces.

On the other hand, the Japanese regiment in Mukden rose in concert with the railway guards in the midnight of the same day and succeeded in occupying the walled town, East Barracks, Aerodrome, etc., fighting till 2:00 P.M. of the following day with the reinforcement of the other regiments stationed at Liao-yang and Hai-chang.

The North Barracks is opened to the public inspection, and can be reached in 20 minutes by motor car from S.M.R. Mukden Station.

The words of that short account contained an indirect significance, which revealed something of the spirit of Japan. They conveyed an inevitable sense of going somewhere and a sense of destiny. That incident had happened a good many years back but it had repeated itself since and would repeat itself again. In a small way Calvin felt its element before him in that ugly fly-brown room, illustrated by the heavy Chinese prisoner and the diminutive guard beside him.

The guard gave the prisoner a prod with the butt of his rifle, and the man walked away, beyond the imagination of Calvin Gates, impassively, without fear or anger, with a patient resignation and a poise beyond Calvin's understanding. The lieutenant looked after him complacently.

"Naughty man," he said. "Will be shot. Get off your sit please. The officer will see you."

The sallow Japanese behind the table drummed the tips of his fingers on the boards and spoke sharply in the same querulous, scolding tones. The lieutenant twitched at Calvin's sleeve and the two walked over to the table. That twitch on the sleeve, gentle though it had been, was almost a discourtesy. He knew that his resentment was not childish, because he was already learning something of the importance of personal dignity and something of that Oriental term, "face," which no European can entirely define.

"Take your hand off me," he said to the lieutenant. It was a small matter but he knew that the soldiers and the two officers in the room understood him. Although the lieutenant's face was blank, he understood. The officer behind the table rose from his chair and spoke again in Japanese. The lieutenant drew in his breath, bowed to Calvin Gates and spoke in his schoolbook English.

"Sorry," he said. "Excuse."

Not entirely to Calvin's surprise, but to his relief, the officer behind the table spoke in excellent English.

"Excuse him," he said. "You are Mr. Gates I think. I am the colonel here in command of the district. There was a telegram about you."

The colonel spoke in Japanese again and the lieutenant saluted and gave an order. There was a scuffling noise of feet which made Calvin Gates look behind him. The lieutenant and the soldiers were leaving the room. The colonel watched them go and did not speak until he and Gates were alone.

The light from the window glittered on the colonel's glasses and he stood stiffly behind the table.

"It is a telegram from a gentleman who knows you, a very important man who shares my political beliefs. His name is Mr. Moto."

"I thought it was," said Calvin Gates. "About a cigarette case, is it?"

There was no longer any doubt that Mr. Moto knew where the cigarette case was, and now Calvin knew that Mr. Moto had guessed even before he had left the hotel at Mukden. He remembered Mr. Moto's polite remark about the shoes outside the door; it was then that Mr. Moto had guessed.

"Yes," the colonel said. "He is asking to be sure if you have a cigarette case with little birds upon it."

"He is right," said Calvin Gates. "I suppose you want it, Colonel."

"Yes," the colonel said. "So sorry to trouble you, but I must see it."

Calvin reached in his inside pocket, but the colonel stopped him.

"Be careful," he said. "Step to the corner here in case someone is looking through the window. Now you may take it out. Thank you."

The colonel took the cigarette case in both hands and bowed. He turned it over carefully, opened it and closed it.

"Thank you," the colonel said suddenly. "Thank you so very much. You may take it back now, Mr. Gates."

"What—" said Calvin Gates. "You want me to take it back? What for? I don't want it."

Before he answered the colonel smiled at him as though they both knew something which had better not be expressed.

"Of course, " the colonel said. "That is what Mr. Moto has

directed. He only wished to be sure all was in order. I am so sure that you understand."

"Understand what?" Calvin asked him.

The colonel smiled again.

"Of course," the colonel said. "Mr. Moto has explained. It is an honor to meet a friend of Mr. Moto. They will bring some tea if you will join me, please. The other instructions will not take a moment."

Calvin Gates felt his thoughts move dizzily, but his instinct told him that it was better to show no astonishment.

"Here is the tea and a chair for you," the colonel said.

"This is so very important. Will you please sit down?"

Two soldiers had entered as the colonel was speaking, one carrying a chair and another a blue-and-white teapot.

"Mr. Moto is a very able man," he said.

"Yes," said Calvin, " a very able man."

"And he forgets nothing," the colonel said.

"No," said Calvin, "I don't believe he forgets anything."

"So you must listen," the colonel said, "as I speak for Mr. Moto." The colonel lowered his voice.

"There was a long telegram. Mr. Moto wanted you told that others know you have the case. I hope you understand."

"Oh," said Calvin Gates, "some others know, do they?"

"Yes," The colonel sipped his tea. "It is so unfortunate. Mr. Moto is afraid that they may try to get it. He asked that you be very careful. You must not let it be stolen. You are not to give it away until you reach Kalgan. A man there will ask for it. His name is Mr. Holtz. Mr. Moto is most anxious that Mr. Holtz should have it."

"He didn't say anything more?" asked Calvin Gates.

"Just one thing more," the colonel said. "He wanted me to say that the others understand you are Mr. Moto's friend, and that is dangerous."

The colonel sipped his tea and the light glittered on his glasses.

"He is sorry that it is so dangerous for you. Have you a weapon, Mr. Gates?"

Calvin Gates shook his head and the colonel opened the drawer of the table.

"You see," he said, "Mr. Moto thinks of everything." He reached in the drawer and drew out an automatic pistol. "There," the colonel said. "I hope so much that you will not have to use it, and here is an extra clip of cartridges. Mr. Moto thinks of everything, does he not?"

Calvin took the pistol in the palm of his hand, examined it for a moment and slipped it into his coat pocket.

"Yes," he said a little vaguely, "Mr. Moto thinks of everything. Look here, Colonel, you'd better take this cigarette case. I don't want it."

The colonel raised his cup delicately and sipped his tea before he answered.

"Mr. Moto was afraid of that," he said. "It will do no good to give the case away. The others know you have it. They will try to get it at any rate. Mr. Moto wants you to keep it now. It is the best way he knows of having it delivered."

"Suppose I refuse?" Calvin asked him. "I don't want to be mixed up in this."

"Please." The colonel raised his hand. "You are so involved already. I do not like to threaten. You do not want to go to a military prison. You might stay there very long."

"Oh," said Calvin, "that's it."

"Yes," the colonel answered. "I think that you had much rather get back upon the train. You see the train is waiting."

Calvin Gates glanced out the window. The train was waiting and the colonel was waiting also. Although his thoughts were undefined and clouded by uncertainty, he was beginning to understand what had happened, and the brain of Mr. Moto was behind it. For some reason of his own, ever since they had first met on the boat, Mr. Moto had been waiting while one thing led to another.

Calvin Gates folded his hands across his knee and he felt as he had before, like a slow-witted barbarian who was uncouthly trying to understand unknown complexites.

"Why does Mr. Moto want me to carry this thing?" he asked.

The colonel smiled as though he had explained everything, though he had not expected the abruptness of the question. He replaced his glasses carefully on the wide bridge of his nose and studied Calvin carefully through the lenses.

"There is no reason to explain," the colonel said. "Mr. Moto wishes this delivered to the right person, and he wishes no one to be suspicious. He is sure that you can do it."

The colonel smiled as though he had explained everything.

"He says he wants you to be comfortable and to have a happy journey."

Calvin Gates got to his feet and shook his head.

"He's wrong," he said. "I won't do it."

The colonel rose also.

"You are making a great mistake," he said. "Excuse me, please." He raised his voice and called something in his own language.

The soldier opened the door so quickly that Calvin was sure that he had been waiting for the order. He opened the door and stood aside, and Calvin heard a voice he recognized. It was the lieutenant speaking.

"You come in please," the lieutenant said; and Miss Dillaway was standing in the doorway. Her chin was high and her eyes were snapping angrily.

"Hello, Gates," she said. "What have they been doing to you? That soldier wouldn't let me come in."

The colonel spoke before Calvin Gates could answer.

"So sorry, madam," he said. "You must stay, I think."

Calvin Gates spoke quickly.

"Wait a minute," he said. "She has nothing to do with it."

"So sorry," the colonel said, "she must stay here too, unless, of course, you change your mind."

"What's he talking about?" asked Miss Dillaway.

Calvin Gates shrugged his shoulders.

"It's all right," he said. "I'll take it along—if that's the way it is."

The colonel smiled and bowed. "Thank you," he said, "that is so much better."

"And you haven't got anything more to tell me?" Calvin asked.

"No," said the colonel. He held out his hand. "Good-by. Nothing more to tell you, Mr. Gates."

As they crossed the station platform Miss Dillaway touched his arm.

"What happened?" she asked. "What have they been doing to you, Gates? What have we gotten into?"

Calvin Gates looked grimly at the train and pressed his lips together. There was no need to tell her about that scene in the station, no need that she should be alarmed.

"Just passport trouble," he said. "Just questions."

Miss Dillaway laughed shortly.

"Well," she said. "You didn't think I was going to go on without you, did you? I came out to get you. I'm glad it's only about a passport. I was afraid it was something else. If anything happens, I'm going to stop your being a hero, Gates." And then her smile died away as she glanced up at him; his face was set and hard.

"I hope to heaven you can," he said.

## 10

THE SUN moved with the hours of the afternoon in its arc across a warm blue sky where a few thin grayish clouds were floating. It moved deliberately with the hours until it was so low over the limitless rolling plain that the light became benign and soft and the horizon assumed a reddish hue that was reflected on the clouds, making them shell pink and purple. The waning light softened the harsh outlines and made the walled towns that they passed mysteriously remote in a sort of timeless loneliness and endowed the whole country with an exotic portentous beauty. The train moved through that level country as surely as though the hours were pulling it. The map showed him that they were nearing the venerable city of Shan-hai-kuan by the first gate in the Great Wall of China of which he had heard so much but knew so little. The motion of the train through that changing but changeless country was almost reassuring.

Miss Dillaway looked out the window, and her face made a sharp, incisive profile, as clear and even as the profile on a coin.

"I was born in Winnetka, Illinois," Miss Dillaway said suddenly, and she was evidently speaking her thoughts aloud. "I went to Chicago University and then I went to art school. I started as a commercial artist. I had to earn my living. I'm not bad at accurate work. You've never had to earn your living, have you, Gates?"

"What made you guess that?" Calvin asked her.

"Your attitude," she answered. "You just look that way. It might have saved you trouble if you'd had to earn your living. It gets you in closer touch with facts."

"I'll have to earn my living from now on," he said.

She leaned forward under some sudden impulse and rested her

hand for a moment on his knee, and that momentary contact startled him.

"What's the trouble at home?" she asked. "You'd better tell me, Gates."

"I'd rather not," he said, "if you don't mind."

It was no use. Whether he explained or not, in another day or two he would never see Miss Sylvia Dillaway again.

"All right," said Miss Dillaway. "If you don't want to talk, reach me down my sketching box, the big one on the rack there."

She sat with her sketching box on the opposite seat, counting tubes of oil paint, arranging and rearranging all the tools of her trade as if she had forgotten his existence.

She was like others he had known who could retire suddenly behind the walls of their own interests, leaving him alone. She had asked for his confidence, but he was sure that it would have done no good to have talked about himself. It was better to try to live in the present and to examine the utter strangeness of that present. When he looked out of the window there was nothing in the scene which reminded him of anything, no face or voice in the train which reminded him of anything.

In one sense that unfamiliarity was a relief, but in another it was not. He had to walk dumbly through a world he did not know, coping with a language which he did not understand, while he waited for some event to occur that he could not anticipate. Thoughtlessly, he put his hand into the side pocket of his coat and for a second what he felt there surprised him. He had almost forgotten the automatic pistol, and he still had not the remotest idea why it had been given him. Nevertheless he was glad that he had it.

Every now and then the train boy moved past him, a young uniformed Japanese, and once or twice a member of the train guard paced slowly down the aisle. Since he had boarded the train again after his interview at that station, it seemed to him that he had acquired an added importance and that there was some unspoken sort of understanding.

"Please," the train boy said slowly when it was growing dark, as though he had learned his words from a phrase book, "you get off train at Shan-hai-kuan and take sleeping train. Baggage goes to customs. Thank you please."

The sun was down and the world was gray and then it was black, and the train moved for a long while through a dark country where there was hardly ever a gleam of light. It was after nine in the evening before the train reached Shan-hai-kuan. Even if he had not known that the wall was there, it was plain that they had passed from a land of order to a land of noise and confusion. Whistles were blowing. Porters and station employees and food vendors ran beside the train, shouting and waving their arms. The whole train shed was a babble of high voices and laughter and escaping steam. Calvin Gates stared uncertainly through the smoky window.

"It looks as though everyone outside has gone crazy," he said.

Just as the train was coming to a stop and just as he had turned from the window, he saw a man of his own race thrust his way through the crowd and swing aboard. He had a glimpse of a red face and of a trench coat like his own, and then an instant later he saw the face again. A wiry, stocky European carrying a riding crop strode down the aisle toward them with a curious rolling gait. His face was ruddy from the out-of-doors, of a deep color that made his grayish eyes seem very light. He pushed past two Japanese businessmen who were starting for the door and caught sight of Calvin and Miss Dillaway.

"Hello, hello," he called. His voice was nasal and metallic and he jerked off his felt hat. "Is this by any chance Miss Dillaway?

"Yes, it is," Miss Dillaway answered. "How do you know my name?"

She must have been as surprised as Calvin Gates to hear her name called in that remote place. The stranger's hard red face crinkled into a smile and he pulled a letter from his pocket.

"That's fine," he said, "fine. So you're the little artist lady, are you? Here's a letter from Dr. Gilbreth explaining who I am. Read it any time. My name is Hamby, miss, Captain Sam Hamby, Dardanelles, Messines Ridge. Long time ago wasn't it? Professional soldier, miss, with the Cavalry of the Prince of Ghuru Nor. I was coming down from up there on business and Dr. Gilbreth asked me to pop over here and meet you. He thought it might be easier for you. There's a spot of mix-up over in Mongolia. Don't worry, things are always mixed up in China."

Miss Dillaway read the note which he handed her and gave the red-faced stranger a smile of quick relief.

"Well," she said, "that explains everything. It's awfully kind of you, Captain Hamby, and I won't say two greenhorns like us don't need help. This is Mr. Gates, who is going up there with me, Mr. Calvin Gates from New York."

The wrinkles around Captain Hamby's lips grew deeper, and

though he smiled his face grew watchful, and his eyes looked still and glassy. They reminded Calvin of the eyes of a sailor or a hunter that were accustomed to stare across great distances.

"Well, well," said Captain Hamby, "funny that Gilbreth never spoke of you. The word was that only Miss Dillaway was traveling up to Ghuru Nor."

There was something in the other's face that Calvin did not like, although he could not tell just why—something still and something watchful. His curiosity, though it was natural, aroused in Calvin a sudden resentment. Through the thoughtfulness of Dr. Gilbreth, Captain Hamby had come to take Miss Dillaway from him; and he had not wanted it just yet. It gave him a strange, unreasoning pang of jealousy which increased when he saw that Miss Dillaway looked happy and relieved.

"Dr. Gilbreth doesn't know I'm coming," Calvin said; "but I'm an old acquaintance of his. I can assure you that he won't object. I've come all the way from New York on a piece of business with him."

For a second Captain Hamby's eyes maintained that curious, glassy look, and then they twinkled and his smile grew broader.

"That's fine," said Captain Hamby, "fine. Any friend of Gilbreth's a friend of mine. Capital chap, the Doctor. The more the merrier, Gates. Just leave everything to me. By Jove, that's awkward." Captain Hamby paused and thrust his hands in his coat pockets. "I must have left my fags in my old kit bag and I'm perishing for a smoke. Neither of you two have a cigarette, have you?"

The question was casual enough, but there was nothing casual about Captain Hamby's light gray eyes. In the instant's hesitation that followed Calvin saw Miss Dillaway steal a sideways glance at him.

"You have a cigarette, haven't you, Gates?" she said.

Calvin produced a paper package from his pocket. A little line appeared between Captain Hamby's light eyebrows and disappeared again.

"Thanks," he said, "awfully. Deuced careless of me to forget my fags. Now you leave everything to me, I know the ropes here. I've got boys to handle the bags. We'll get through the customs before you can say knife. I'll get three compartments—Chinese sleeping train. Right? Not as good as a *wagon-lit,* but it's clean. Just leave everything to me."

Captain Hamby waved his hand toward the rear of the train in a broad, expansive gesture.

"Back there in Manchukuo—just you understand this—" his red

face wrinkled in a pantomime—"everything is dead serious; but over here—" the wrinkles curved into an exaggerated grin—"over here everything is funny, always something is funny in China. I ought to know. I've been here long enough. Just remember to keep smiling—smile, smile, smile."

Although the hard nasal voice and the pronunciation puzzled Calvin, he was beginning to comprehend that Captain Hamby was a part of that new country and as much in keeping with it as the native population. Captain Hamby was a type which Calvin had heard casually mentioned, but one which he had never seen—the Old China Hand. The analysis of Miss Dillaway went even further.

"Australian, aren't you, Captain Hamby?" she asked.

"You win, Miss Dillaway," Captain Hamby said. "Been around a bit, haven't you, to pick me out so easy? Just a noisy Aussie, and that's about the same as American, isn't it? We better pop off the train now. Just leave everything to me."

Captain Hamby jerked a window open with a quick heave of his broad shoulders and began shouting directions to the station platform in a curious mixture of English and Chinese.

"Here come the boys," he said. "The bags will be out in a minute. All you have to do is get on the other train and wait. I'll take you."

"We're certainly glad to see you," said Miss Dillaway.

"Righto," said Captain Hamby.

Two minutes later they were moving across the train shed with Captain Hamby just beside them, leading a line of four porters carrying their luggage. They were with a man who knew the ropes and who knew how to arrange everything in a way that was breezy and bullying and yet good-natured.

"Just jolly the Chinese," Captain Hamby said. "Every Chinese is a perfect gentleman. Over there—very grim; over here—comic opera."

With Captain Hamby no great effort seemed necessary. He exchanged a few sharp sentences with the Chinese Customs and then, before Calvin could even understand what formality had taken place, they were in three compartments of the Peiping train with all their baggage identified and stowed away. Captain Hamby pulled a handkerchief from his pocket, grinned and mopped his brow.

"Everything's shipshape now, eh what?" he said. "Miss Dillaway bunks there, you next, Gates, and me right beside you. I'll leave our connecting door open, Gates. And now how about a drink?

Always travel with whisky in China if you know what's good for you. I'll get the boy." He opened the door and hurried into the narrow passageway outside. "Boy," Calvin could hear him shouting, "boy!"

Miss Dillaway looked after him smilingly.

"Isn't he wonderful?" she said.

"He's been a help," said Calvin Gates, but her remark gave him another twinge of jealous resentment. Miss Dillaway wrinkled her nose.

"He was a help," she said, "and a lot of help you'd have been. Don't be such a snob, Gates."

"I'm not a snob," said Calvin. "I just wonder why he asked for a cigarette."

"Why shouldn't he ask for a cigarette?" she inquired.

"No reason," Calvin answered, "but he might have had some of his own."

Captain Hamby was back with the train boy before she had time to reply. The Captain was carrying a bottle of English whisky and the train boy followed with a tray and glasses and soda.

"You can get anything you like if you know how to get it," Captain Hamby said. "Soda, Miss Dillaway? I'll take mine neat. Chin chin!"

"Chin chin," said Miss Dillaway. They sat side by side on Calvin Gates's bunk, with the glasses on a wooden hinged table in front of them. The sleeping compartment was of plain varnished wood with a single dim yellow electric bulb, but, as Captain Hamby had said, it was reasonably clean. There was a sliding glass paneled door which communicated with the passageway outside. Other passengers stared through the panel curiously and Captain Hamby pulled the shade.

"You'll get used to that," he said. "White people are a traveling circus to the Chinese. They still think our knees bend backward upcountry and that we eat babies' eyes, but they're all right, always ready for a laugh. Just pack up your troubles in your old kit bag, and smile, boys, that's the style. What's the use of worrying? It never was worth while."

"Did you say there was some trouble up where you came from?" Calvin asked.

The Captain laughed and reached for the whisky bottle.

"There's a lot of talk going around in China, always talk," he said.

"What sort of talk?" asked Calvin Gates.

The Captain reached for one of Calvin's cigarettes and spoke with it dangling from his lips, so that its glowing end moved jerkily with his words.

"Out here," said Captain Hamby, "you'll find out there's always trouble. There's either some war lord in the provinces, or a disbanded army running wild, or the Japanese. This time it looks like the Japanese. They're setting out to start something. Out our way it's hard to get through the wall."

"What wall?" Calvin asked him.

The Captain's light gray eyes met with his with a calculating glance.

"Seems as though you're new here," the Captain said. "I'm referring to the real wall of China built before Christ. It isn't much more than a mound now but there's a gate in it outside of Kalgan, and then there comes Mongolia. It's hard to get through now. That's why Gilbreth sent me."

"Oh," said Calvin Gates, "I see. You mean the Japanese?"

Captain Hamby nodded and finished his drink.

"You can't be sure," he said and lowered his voice. "It looks as though they're pushing in again. First it was Manchuria and then it was Jehol, and then influence over Peiping. It looks like all North China this time. Another incident—of course you can never be sure. I've seen enough of this never to be sure. Someone might start shooting. Anyway, up where I live things aren't going right. Maybe I don't make myself clear."

Captain Hamby took off his felt hat and it changed him. His dark brown hair was very closely clipped and growing gray at the temples, but he looked neither young nor old. The wrinkles in his forehead and the crow's-feet about his eyes were made by wind and dust rather than by age.

"I'm sorry," he said. "I talk Chinese and Russian and Mongolian so much that I don't make myself clear in English. I come from Ghuru Nor. I'm commanding the Prince's Cavalry. The Prince is up-to-date, Prince Wu Fang at Ghuru Nor—that's his Chinese name. He's not bad, the Prince. It's a way to earn your living. Soldier of fortune—Captain Sam Hamby. Served under the Christian General and under the old marshal and the young marshal. Who wants another drink?"

Captain Hamby stared ahead of him at nothing. A whistle blew and the train had begun to move. Captain Hamby had spoken, he had explained himself perfectly, and his hard-bitten face and wiry body confirmed his speech. Miss Dillaway was looking at him with a respect that was annoying.

"You must have seen a lot," Miss Dillaway said.

"Beg pardon?" said Captain Hamby, and his glance traveled toward her out of nowhere. "Oh yes, a lot, and it's nice to see an English-speaking girl again. We're going to get on fine, Miss Dillaway. Well, we're off. I'm here to get you up to Ghuru Nor just as fast as we can go. No delaying, or the line to Kalgan may be cut. Old man Holtz will take us out from Kalgan."

The Captain blinked his pale gray eyes and continued to watch Miss Dillaway.

"Gilbreth was worried about you," he said. "The Prince received him and is interested. His Highness is an educated man. I was going down here at any rate on business for the Prince—purchases—firearms. Gilbreth is twenty miles away from the palace, digging in a hill—funny business, digging."

"The palace," said Miss Dillaway. "Is there a palace?"

"You'll see it," the Captain answered. "A real palace with white and orange yurts in front and courtyards and red and yellow lama priests and attendants with peacock plumes. You can paint some pretty pictures there. Yes, it's quite a palace, like the days of Ghengis Khan."

Captain Hamby paused again, but it semed to Calvin that his nasal unmusical voice still echoed above the rumbling of the train. He was not showing off now that he had spoken about himself. He had spoken and something of his past was with them on the train, turbulent and restive. Hearing, one could not help but wonder what had brought him there, but there was no doubt that everything he said was true.

"Don't blame you, if you don't believe me," Captain Hamby said. "When you see the antelope and the camels and the prayer flags blowing and the black men with their pigtails and their pointed boots, I'll guarantee you'll think you're dreaming. It hasn't changed since Marco Polo except the Prince has a radio and guns."

"What does he want them for?" Calvin asked.

The Captain laughed shortly.

"You don't know the Asiatic situation," he said, "or else you'd know that Ghuru Nor is an important place right now. Mongolia's made up of principalities, and each prince is an independent little monarch. In the old days they dined once a year at table with the

Emperor in Peking. The principality of Ghuru Nor has the old caravan route going through it, the shortest way to outer Mongolia and Russia, and the hills at Ghuru Nor are strategic. Either Russia or Japan wants them in case there is a war. I'll show you on the map tomorrow, except maps aren't worth much in Mongolia."

Miss Dillaway sat listening.

"Don't ask the Captain questions, Gates," she said. "I've never been there, Captain Hamby, but I guess it's about the same as any other place that's off the map. I've been in Persia and Mesopotamia and Central Africa. Is there typhus?"

"Yes," said Captain Hamby, "sometimes, Miss Dillaway."

"How's the water? Is there dysentery?"

"The water isn't bad," Captain Hamby said. "Not enough people to spoil it."

Miss Dillaway rose. "Well," she said, "I'm glad to hear it. I think I'll go to sleep. I'll see you in the morning, Captain."

Captain Hamby bowed.

"I knew you were all right just as soon as I saw you, Miss Dillaway," he said. "I guess I won't need to tell you anything, you know the ropes."

"Thanks," said Miss Dillaway. "I won't be any trouble."

The Captain sat down again when Miss Dillaway was gone and reached for the bottle.

"What a girl," he said. "What a girl."

"Yes," said Calvin Gates, "Miss Dillaway is very nice."

"That isn't what I meant," the Captain answered. "I meant she knows her way around. I meant she hasn't got any silly ideas, and what's more she's beautiful." Captain Hamby sighed and took a sip of his whisky. "Yes, beautiful, and no wrong ideas."

Calvin Gates did not answer.

Captain Hamby disappeared through the narrow communicating door into his own compartment and came back in his shirt sleeves.

"What's the use of worrying," he was humming, "it never was worth while. How about another drink?"

"I don't mind," said Calvin Gates. Captain Hamby jerked his thumb toward the rear of the train.

"Everything all right back there?"

"Where?" asked Calvin Gates.

"Manchukuo. Were the Japanese all right? No trouble with the police?" The Captain's voice became lower and more confidential. "Nothing you want to tell me? Nothing on your mind?"

Calvin Gates put his hands in his pockets.

"No," he answered. "Why should there be?"

The Captain's gray eyes watched him steadily.

"No reason," he said, "except the Japanese are pretty officious these days. They're crawling around like flies at Ghuru Nor, dropping in all the time. Funny little fellows, nervous, always nervous."

"Yes," said Calvin Gates, "they're nervous."

The Captain jerked his thumb toward the rear of the train again.

"You're sure everything was all right back there?"

"Yes," said Calvin, "everything was perfectly all right."

"That's fine," the Captain said, "that's fine. You look pretty fit, Gates—as though you could take care of yourself. Be sure to lock your door to the passage and I'll leave the one between us open. You're sure there's nothing you want to tell me?"

They looked at each other for a moment in silence; Captain Hamby smiled invitingly.

"Only to thank you for the whisky," Calvin said.

"That's fine." Captain Hamby's smile grew broader.

"That's the way it ought to be. Just keep your door locked, Gates."

When he was alone Calvin realized that he was as tired as a swimmer who had been battered by waves into an acquiescent sort of weariness. His thin freckled face showed the strain of the last twenty-four hours, but the strain was more than physical. First there had been Mr. Moto and now there was Captain Hamby, both appearing out of nowhere. Logical as the explanation may have been, he knew that Captain Hamby was not there only to help Miss Dillaway. The Captain was made for more important tasks, and there was no mistaking those last remarks.

It was strange to think that Captain Hamby was just the sort of man he should have liked and that he represented all the things that Calvin Gates had wished to be, and yet, in spite of it, Calvin did not like him. Hamby had been a soldier, for he had the stamp of the profession, which could never be described or entirely concealed. He had seen the world and had lived on danger and on change. Was he going on the same road as Captain Hamby, Calvin wondered?

The train swayed from side to side on the rough roadbed and the dark outside was like a door that shut him into his compartment while he was moving all the time farther from anything he knew. The compartment was a garish little place in the dim yellow electric light, without beauty or elaboration or extra comfort. The door leading to the Captain's sleeping place was closed. He pulled open his door to the passage and peered out into a dim smoky emptiness. When he closed the door again he found that there was no way to fasten it except by a sort of flat brass hook. He put the hook down carefully, glanced at Captain Hamby's closed door, and thrust his hand into the inside pocket of his coat. His fingers touched the cigarette case and he brought it out and laid it on his knee.

As far as he could see there was nothing extraordinary, either in its appearance or manufacture, that differed from dozens he had seen in jewelers' windows in Toyko. The work upon it, though delicate and beautiful, was not unusual in a land where minute skilled workmanship cost almost nothing. The silver had been cut straight through and black metal had been inlaid so that the design appeared both inside and outside the cover in a delicate silhouette. The result was a scene, familiar enough in Japanese and Chinese art, of small birds which rested, walked and flew among tufts of tall grasses, both black and delicate against the silver. He could see nothing more significant, look as he might inside and out, no sign of marks or scratching, and the metal was absolutely solid. The design was all that could mean anything. He remembered Mr. Moto's interest in the number of the birds, and now he counted six of them, three of them in the air, two perched upon the grasses, and one upon the ground.

He put the case back and reached into the side pocket of his coat. It was a thirty-eight caliber automatic which had been given him, of American make. He took out the clip and found that it was fully loaded, a dangerous thing to be carrying about in a land where he was a stranger. He finally took off his coat and rolled it up carefully, lay down on his berth and put the coat beneath his head. Then he switched off the light. The empty glasses on the little table rattled with the swaying of the car. The last thing he remembered was the rattling of the glasses.

It was also the first sound which came to his consciousness when he woke up, but he knew that such a harmless sound had not wakened him. He lay for a moment listening and then he slipped softly from his berth. The faint dusky light which filtered from the corridor outside showed him the compartment was empty. The train swayed and the glasses rattled and then there was another sound which came from the passageway outside—a dull metallic click. Someone was working quietly and expertly upon the lock of his door. Someone outside had thrust a knife blade through the crack and was lifting the brass catch, probably a simple enough matter for anyone who knew his business. His coat was still lying on the berth, and for a moment he thought of reaching for it before common sense stopped him and told him that the noise of a shot would arouse every passenger in the train. He stood hesitating, and then it was too late. The door was slid open gently, and the light in the passage revealed a squat, stocky figure which stood poised in the doorway for an instant. Then the figure moved and Calvin Gates moved also. The head of the intruder was turned away from him toward the empty berth when Calvin threw himself forward and landed square on the intruder's back. The impact threw the other off his balance and they both fell crashing against the table. At the same instant the man beneath him turned and Calvin could hear the sharp intake of his breath. A hand pulled at his collar and he saw that someone had turned on the light.

"Steady," he heard a voice saying, "steady." Someone was pulling at his shoulders and Calvin scrambled to his feet. His mind worked slowly and his ears were ringing. For a moment the whole place was hazy and then he saw a figure half sprawled across his berth. A hand was on his shoulder, shaking him, and it was Captain Hamby speaking.

"Steady," Captain Hamby said. "It's right as rain."

# 11

CALVIN GATES spoke with difficulty and his voice sounded like a stranger speaking.

"I must have struck my head," he said.

"Steady," said Captain Hamby. "You'll be better in a minute.

"Someone came in here," said Calvin Gates.

"Yes," said Captain Hamby, "somebody came in. I hit him when you grabbed him. Everything's all right."

Calvin Gates shook his head and the haze was lifting, leaving the whole scene clear. A stocky, heavy man in cheap dark clothes lay sprawled half upon the floor and half upon the berth. His face was like a yellowish stupid mask with the lips and eyes half open. It was a brutal, ugly face and suddenly Calvin remembered. It was the man who had stepped through his hotel window at Mukden. Captain Hamby in his shirt sleeves was bending over holding a short riding crop. Calvin Gates looked behind him; the door to the passageway was closed.

"Pack up your troubles in your old kit bag," Captain Hamby was humming. "Smile boys, that's the style."

"You say you hit him?" Calvin asked.

Captain Hamby looked around with no emotion in his pale gray eyes and held up his riding crop.

"Hit him with three pounds of lead," he said. "Didn't know you were awake until you grabbed him. Handsome-looking johnny, ain't he? *Ronin.*"

"What?" said Calvin Gates.

*"Ronin."* Hamby's gray eyes studied him impersonally. "That means strong-arm Japanese—the gunman type. Ugly-looking fellow, what?"

"Is he dead?" asked Calvin Gates.

"No," said Captain Hamby, "not quite. I hit him hard enough. Ugly fellow, isn't he? Not a nice chap to be dropping in at night." Captain Hamby laid his crop on the berth and rubbed his hands. "Help me open the window, Gates."

"What for?" Calvin asked.

Captain Hamby's red face wrinkled into a grin.

"Because we don't want trouble," he said. "You follow me, don't you, Gates?"

"But you can't do that," Calvin Gates began, and Captain Hamby stopped smiling.

"Stow it, Gates," he said. "You know what he came in here for. It was either him or you, Gates. Maybe you didn't notice this. Look down there on the floor."

Calvin Gates looked down. A pistol with a silencer was lying at his feet.

"You see," said Captain Hamby, "it was either him or you. It don't pay to be fussy sometimes, Gates. Open the window. You take his head, I'll take his feet."

Calvin Gates opened the window. His mouth felt dry and his hands were shaking.

"While you've a lucifer to light your fag," Captain Hamby hummed, "smile boys, that's the style. Keep smiling. Heave him, Gates."

Captain Hamby turned away from the window and rubbed his hands.

"Well," he said, "nothing more to think about. Feeling all right, Gates?"

"Yes," said Calvin, "better, thank you."

"That's fine," said Captain Hamby, "fine. You didn't do so badly either. But you take my advice. Don't you try to wrestle with 'em. Hit 'em on the head." The Captain put his own head to one side and smiled.

"Anything you want to tell me, Gates?"

It was more of a request than a question, and Calvin Gates was puzzled. He still did not like the Captain, even when he had every reason to be grateful. The Captain's cool gray eyes stared at him and beyond him without warmth or interest, and they left Calvin Gates under no illusions that he would have been the one to go out the window if it had suited Captain Hamby.

Calvin reached for his coat where it lay on the berth and put it on and put his hand in his pocket.

"Hamby," he said, "I'm going to ask you something. Just where do you fit in?"

Captain Hamby picked up his riding crop and balanced it in his hand.

"Now we're talking sense," he said. "White men ought to stick together in this country, and we're going to stick together. You've been looking at me sideways, haven't you? I don't mind telling you I came down here to meet a Russian whose first name was Boris, who was acting as a guide for a lady named Miss Dillaway. Boris was planning to hand me a little personal favor in the shape of a silver cigarette case. What happened to Boris, Gates?"

"He's dead," said Calvin Gates.

Captain Hamby played absent-mindedly with his riding crop.

"I guessed it," he said. "The Japs popped him off, I suppose. I guessed it when I didn't see him. It couldn't be—excuse me if I seem impertinent—it couldn't be that he gave you a silver cigarette case, Gates? That couldn't be why you had a caller tonight?"

Calvin Gates nodded without speaking.

"That's fine," said Captain Hamby, "fine. So the Japs are on your trail, eh? And you and I are in the same boat. That's fine. I guess we better have a little talk."

Captain Hamby seated himself on the edge of the berth and rested his riding crop across his knees while his short, stubby fingers caressed it abstractedly.

"I don't like to be impertinent," Captain Hamby continued. "I've learned tolerance from the Chinese, Gates. They are the most civilized, tolerant people in the world. Anything goes within limits. The last thing I am is nosy; but I answered your question, now you answer one. Where do you fit in?"

It would have been a reasonable question—if there had not been a sort of personal offense in the Captain's voice which was a challenge to his instinct. He experienced an unreasoning antipathy for the cold-blooded self-assurance of that compact red-faced man, and at the same time something warned him to be careful—that Captain Hamby would use him so far only as he might be useful. Suddenly, Calvin knew that it was not an accident but the deliberate action of part of his nature which had led him where he was. There was no use fooling him. He had been happy in those ugly hours back in Mukden, and he was almost happy now. In spite of the blow on his head his mind was working smoothly.

"All right," he said, "I'll tell you. It takes a while to tell."

"That's fine," said Captain Hamby, "fine. Sit down, Gates. Let's talk like pals."

Calvin Gates sat down beside the Captain with his hand still in his coat pocket.

"It's this way," he began. "That Russian who was with Miss Dillaway on the boat—I didn't know either of them then—and then there was a Japanese named Mr. Moto—"

It seemed to him that the wrinkles about the Captain's eyes grew deeper and that his whole expression grew more intent.

"You know him?" Calvin asked.

"Brother," said Captain Hamby, "I know everybody. And Boris saw him, did he? Go ahead."

Calvin went on, drawing on a concise and accurate memory. He told of Mukden; he left out almost nothing, except the incident of the automatic pistol. Captain Hamby fingered the riding crop across his knees and listened without comment. He listened as though the whole story were natural.

"What the use of worrying," he hummed softly, "it never was worth while . . . That was fine work, fine. So you have the cigarette case, Gates?"

"Yes," said Calvin Gates.

"That's fine," said Captain Hamby. "Now you can hand it over."

Calvin sat up straighter. There was no mistaking Captain Hamby's urgency and eagerness. A light in Captain Hamby's gray eyes sent a quiver up Calvin's spine. Captain Hamby had no further use for him. Once Captain Hamby had the cigarette case Calvin knew that he would never get to Ghuru Nor. He would be disposed of like an empty bottle. The cigarette case had become a passport, as long as he kept it in his pocket.

"Not just yet," Calvin said.

Captain Hamby's expression was quizzical; he shifted his feet and coughed.

"Just why not, Gates?" he asked.

"Because I don't like the way you look," Calvin answered. "I'm not going to be tossed out that window too. You can have that case when you get us safely up to Ghuru Nor."

The Captain leaned a trifle farther forward. "Is that a fact?" he began, and then he stopped, dead still. Calvin Gates had pulled the pistol from his pocket. Captain Hamby raised his eyebrows and gazed at it thoughtfully.

"While you've a lucifer to light your fag," he hummed, "smile, boys, that's the style . . . No reason for getting jumpy, Gates; my word, no reason at all. I was going to take you up to Ghuru Nor at any rate. There'll be fewer questions asked. Hand me over the case. I can keep it better—really."

"You'll get it when we get there," said Calvin Gates.

Captain Hamby shrugged his shoulders.

"Don't trust me, do you, Gates?" he asked.

"I trust you as long as I've got that case in my pocket," said Calvin Gates.

Captain Hamby's face wrinkled into a smile. "All right," he said, "all right. No hard feeling, Gates."

"No," said Calvin, "none at all."

"Mind you do what I tell you then," the Captain said. "We've got to travel quick."

"That's all right," said Calvin.

"That's fine," Captain Hamby said, "fine."

"Anything else you want to tell me?" asked Calvin Gates.

"No," said Captain Hamby, "nothing else, I think."

"Then perhaps you'll go where you belong," said Calvin Gates, "and if you'll excuse me I'm going to lock my door."

Captain Hamby rose from his seat on the edge of the berth, and Calvin followed his example.

"What's the use of worrying," Captain Hamby hummed. "No need to be jumpy, old man. I'll take care of you, never fear."

"I'm sure you will," Calvin answered.

"We'll get on fine when we understand each other."

The Captain's tone was placating and smooth. "So put away the sidearm, Gates, and how about shaking hands on it? We'll have to be pals, you know."

Captain Hamby held out his right hand. The gesture and his whole manner were suddenly disarming, but there was an involuntary contraction about the corners of his mouth. The shadow passed over the Captain's face and was gone, but Calvin Gates understood the expression as clearly as though the man had spoken. Calvin transferred his pistol from his right hand to his left and dropped it into his jacket pocket, but he did not take his hand away.

"Delighted to shake hands," he said.

The Captain's lips twitched slightly and then curved into his smile.

"No hard feeling, Gates," he said again. "We can take things as they come, can't we?"

"Absolutely," Calvin said.

"Fine," the Captain said. "We'll have a nice talk later on." There was no doubt that they understood each other. The Captain's manner had been almost perfect, but not quite. Calvin knew as sure as fate that the Captain had proposed to do something more than simply to shake his hand.

## 12

AT HALF-PAST eight the next morning Miss Dillaway knocked on his compartment door. She looked cheerfully neat and efficient. Outside the sun shone hot and brilliant out of a cloudless sky upon an unchanging landscape of mud villages and green fields. He could hear Captain Hamby moving about in his own quarters.

"While you've a lucifer to light your fag," Captain Hamby was singing, "smile, smile, smile."

Miss Dillaway was looking at him curiously.

"You don't seem very glad to see me," Miss Dillaway said. "What are you scowling at, Gates?"

"Smile, smile, smile," Calvin answered. "That song's getting on my nerves."

"Oh that's it, is it?" said Miss Dillaway. "It wouldn't hurt you to be like Captain Hamby. At any rate, he smiles."

The side of Calvin's head throbbed with a dull, constant pain, and that last remark of hers did not ease it. He felt that same unreasoning jealousy which he had experienced the night before. It seemed to him that she was through with him already.

"I wish we'd never laid eyes on him," Calvin said.

"You're being awfully silly, Gates," Miss Dillaway replied. "Why are you so rude to Captain Hamby?"

"What's so wonderful about him?" Calvin asked. "Do you like him because he sings?"

"Why Gates," said Miss Dillaway, "I don't particularly like him."

"Then why do you have to be so nice to him?" Calvin asked.

"Why, Gates," said Miss Dillaway, "why shouldn't we both be nice to him? He's helping us, isn't he?" There was a loud knock on the compartment door. It was Captain Hamby with his red face smooth and shining.

"Well, well," he said, "I'm not intruding, am I? I heard you talking. We'll be at Peiping inside an hour, right outside the walls. Sorry we have to go right through it, but we ought to connect with the train north with luck."

"What?" said Miss Dillaway, "aren't we going to stop?"

"Too bad, isn't it?" Captain Hamby smiled at her. "We better get north, I think. My job is to get you north." Miss Dillaway smiled back.

"Anything you say," she said, "but I'm sorry not to see Peiping."

"Don't you worry," Captain Hamby said, "You and I will see it some other time. Who wants a spot of breakfast?"

"I've had mine, thanks, " Miss Dillaway said.

"Well, I haven't. Come on, Gates." Captain Hamby slapped Calvin on the shoulder. "You'll do better with some coffee, what?"

They walked together to a greasy dining car full of cigarette smoke.

"Too bad we have to hurry through," Captain Hamby said. His

glance moved about the dining car as though he could see everything at once. "No need of telling Miss Dillaway about last night and no need to be so jumpy, Gates. You've figured me out wrong."

"I'm sorry if I did," Calvin said.

"Well, all I want is to have things smooth," said Captain Hamby. "Perhaps I was a bit put out last night, just a bit. We all have feelings, don't we, Gates? Yes, I was put out, but when I came to think it over I saw that you were right. It only means we're partners, don't it, Gates? So I'm going to lay the cards right down. Frank and open, that's my way. I'm nothing but an open book." The Captain's hard mouth creased into an ingratiating smile and he lighted a cigarette and allowed it to droop from his lower lip.

"It takes a bit of doing here to get along," he said. "I have a certain reputation, Gates. A lot of people when they want a job done think of Sam Hamby to do it. There'll be a spot of cash in this for you, Gates, if we deliver that cigarette case to the proper party. Three thousand dollars gold, not mex. I want you on our side."

Calvin Gates looked thoughtfully across the table.

"That's quite a lot of money," he said.

"And all for you," said Captain Hamby. "I want you on our side."

Captain Hamby's eyes narrowed and he exhaled a puff of cigarette smoke from the corner of his mouth.

"Out in this country the way things are today anything can happen, anything does happen. If a pink elephant walked in here now I wouldn't turn a hair. I would only say it's China. Great place for a fellow to get along these days, if the fellow has the guts. Opium smuggling, gun running, bribery, war lords, bandits, spies—they're all outside the window here. The sky's the limit these days."

"I begin to think you're right," Calvin Gates agreed.

"Righto," said Captain Hamby cordially.

He could not understand what Captain Hamby was talking about, but he listened as though he understood.

"Facts," Captain Hamby said, "I like facts—and you and I know 'em, I guess. Here's China. Up there is Russia. Down there is Japan. Japan isn't through with China. She started on China and she can't stop now. Her Government is committed to dominate China and we know she's ready for another move. There's only one thing that makes her wait."

"Russia?" Calvin asked him.

"Righto," said Captain Hamby. "Russia doesn't want it. You know that, but here's something you don't know. Russia's got an army now. Let Japan start and Russia is going to strike her in the side and it won't be on the Amur River either. My word, Gates, she's going to move into Mongolia, and the first position she will occupy will be the hills at Ghuru Nor. My word, no fooling, she's ready to do it, Gates."

"How do you know?" Calvin asked, but he was sure that Captain Hamby possessed some way of knowing. Hamby rubbed the side of his nose and smiled.

"No harm telling you," he said, "as long as you and I are traveling together, Ghuru Nor is only a day's march from Outer Mongolia, and that's the same as Russia. Russia will take that line of hills at Ghuru Nor and the road is clear to Kalgan. I know they're ready for it, because the Prince has been paid to let 'em in. The main thing is to get there before the Japs move in first. Do you get the picture now? Two divisions are up there waiting just one day's march off—waiting for the proper information. Well, there's where we come in."

"Where?" Calvin asked him, although he half knew where.

"No harm telling you," said Captain Hamby. "The Russian Intelligence is sending the message up to Ghuru Nor. It looks like the Japanese caught on, don't it? Cipher can be decoded. They were using another system. Well, they got Boris good and proper. It was a spot of luck he lighted onto you. Anything you want to say?"

Calvin Gates was silent for a moment, but he understood about the cigarette case now.

"If you looked at that cigarette case," he inquired, "could you tell what it meant? It's nothing but an ordinary commercial article."

Captain Hamby's reply was prompt and frank.

"No," he said, "I couldn't; but my word, they can read it where it's going. They'll be waiting for it at Kalgan."

Captain Hamby's glance darted about the dining car and rested on Calvin Gates. His face was cordial, but his glance was cool and distant.

"Surprises me that you don't ask something else," he said. "This Japanese johnny, Mr. Moto, where does he fit in? The police want one thing, and Mr. Moto wants something else. What about Mr. Moto, Gates? I need to find that out."

"I don't understand him," Calvin agreed, "not any more than you."

Captain Hamby's expression, though still agreeable, was less reassuring. He put another lump of sugar in his coffee and stirred it delicately; at the same time he began to hum a snatch of that refrain which seemed to have grafted itself like a disease upon his mind.

"Smile, smile, smile. . . . I don't like that coming from you after I've been on the up and up. You can't think I'm so woolly in the head that I don't know that Moto is one of the tidiest secret agents in Japan. I've seen Moto in Nanking and I've seen him in Shanghai, and wherever that little blighter goes, trouble comes right after him. Are you going to tell me about Mr. Moto, Gates?"

The Captain's expression was mocking but restrained. What this implied was so unexpected that Calvin Gates found it difficult to answer.

"Look here," he said, "I don't know what you're driving at. I'm going up to join the Gilbreth Expedition at Ghuru Nor. I've told you everything I know about Mr. Moto."

"Oh my," said Captain Hamby. "So you don't want to talk, eh? I'm giving you an out, Gates. I'm making you a proposition, don't you see?"

"No," said Calvin Gates, "I don't see"—and it was true. He had never been as completely nonplussed as he was when he studied Captain Hamby's face across the table.

"My word, it don't do any good to bluff," Captain Hamby said, and his voice was placating again. "We're white men, Gates, and we're the same sort of white men, looking out where our bread is buttered, aren't we? My word, you had me puzzled for a while when I saw you there in Shan-hai-kuan. That confused look on your face, it was all done so neat and tidy. My word, it was, until you spoke of Mr. Moto. And then I saw the gun—tourists don't carry guns." Captain Hamby spoke more softly and tapped his blunt forefinger on the table emphasizing every word. "Moto gave you that case. You're carrying it for him. It's time to sell out, Gates, or else you can let me in. What does Moto want? Are the Japs moving in to Ghuru Nor?"

The deliberate, unmusical tones of Captain Hamby's voice struck into Calvin's ears with an unpleasant physical sensation. At last he could understand completely what Captain Hamby meant. He might talk himself blue in the face and Hamby would not believe him. There was nothing for him to do but accept the situation.

"I don't know what Mr. Moto wants," he said.

"My word, fellow," said Captain Hamby, "don't you see your number's up? Come now, I don't know your history. Was it the army? I was cashiered myself. Or maybe it was larceny that got you here, taking somebody's money, what? When the Japanese get their hands on a white man it's always something like that. Tell it to your uncle, Gates. Some jam, eh what, and Mr. Moto comes along?"

"I don't know what he wants," said Calvin Gates. The dining room suddenly seemed insufferably hot. He pulled out a handkerchief and mopped his forehead.

"Got the wind up, have you, Gates?" Captain Hamby said. "Guessed it right, didn't I? Come now, what's Moto to you? I'm offering you three thousand gold to tell me what he wants."

Calvin Gates put his handkerchief back in his pocket. "I told you I don't know what he wants," he said.

Captain Hamby's lips pressed themselves tight together; his gray eyes had never looked colder.

"So that's the way it lies, is it, Gates? You won't play in with me?"

"I'll paddle my own canoe, thanks," said Calvin Gates.

"Oh!" Captain Hamby's face was ugly. "I'm not offering enough money, am I, Gates?"

Captain Hamby rested his chin on the palm of his hand, and the wrinkles deepened about the corners of his eyes.

"I don't make it out," he said. "You certainly have guts, Gates. I wonder if you know how much. It don't pay to run afoul of me, not ever. You're going to get what's coming to you just as sure as fate."

"Thanks for telling me," Calvin said. Captain Hamby pushed back his chair.

"Yes," he said, "you've got guts. We know where we stand, don't we, Gates? I hope you know what you're doing. We better go back and get off the train. What's the use of worrying, it never was worth while."

Captain Hamby walked out of the car in front of him, still humming his favorite tune.

"While you've a lucifer to light your fag," Captain Hamby was humming, "smile, boys, that's the style."

But Calvin knew that Captain Hamby was not smiling. He could not forget Captain Hamby's look as he had arisen from the table. The fact had been as hard and as competent as ever, but somehow it had been marked by indecision. The day was sweltering hot but Calvin Gates felt cold.

Miss Dillaway was in her compartment closing her bag.

"Here," said Captain Hamby, "let me lend a hand, Miss Dillaway."

Miss Dillaway smiled at him and it seemed to Calvin Gates that there was no reason to be so civil. He walked to his own compartment and sat there waiting. He still could not recover from his surprise at what Captain Hamby thought of him. Mr. Moto knew of him as a fugitive from justice and Captain Hamby considered him an employee of Japan.

"I must tell Dillaway," he murmured to himself. "Dillaway will think that's funny."

He sat by the window trying to think. Outside he could see a long gray city wall and he did not need to be told what wall it was. The train had reached Peiping.

The guidebook had told Calvin Gates a few facts, but it had been his experience that facts very seldom conveyed much useful information. The guidebook had informed him that the Peiping-Mukden line on which they were traveling arrived at the Chien Men East Station which lay inside the Chinese City and just south of the Tartar City Wall. Kalgan, where they were going, was reached by a different railroad, the Peiping-Suiyuan line, and it would be necessary to travel across the city to make the connection. He did not know the dramatic intricacies of the city of Peiping, where walls and gates divided the whole area into quarters like armed camps and where the houses themselves and parts of houses stood behind more walls, making Peiping the most private, remote and mysterious city in the world. He had not even heard, or if he had he could not understand the significance, of the Chinese City, the Tartar City, the Imperial City, and finally the Forbidden City in the center of it all, a vacant shell where the yellow tiled roofs, the pavilions and palaces of a dead empire shone behind high pink stuccoed walls.

The fact conveyed nothing until he got off the train, and then he saw the massive wall of slate-colored brick, a huge curtain of defense towering above the train shed—a last remnant of the barbaric magnificence of Peiping, when it had been the center of the greatest empire in the world.

He stood with his trench coat over his arm momentarily forgotten by everyone while the Chinese porters, their breaths heavy with garlic and their shaven heads and faces dripping with perspiration, piled the baggage out of the car and strapped it across their shoulders. Captain Hamby must have sent word ahead, because it was evident that they had been expected. A tall gaunt Chinese in a black silk robe had come running on slippered feet to the Captain the moment they were off the train, and Captain Hamby had moved a yard or so away with him, and now the Captain was talking volubly and earnestly in Chinese, occasionally moving his hand in a quick gesture. Calvin knew that he and Miss Dillaway formed a part of the conversation, for he saw that black solemn man glance towards them once or twice.

Again Calvin Gates had a helpless feeling. The startling brilliance of the sun, the round, well-fed faces of the khaki-clad Chinese police, the blue and black Chinese gowns, the chatter of the porters and hotel runners while the passengers descended in a steady stream and moved toward the station gate—all had a menacing aspect.

Those strange sights and the aching of his head and the bright sunlight must have made him stupid, for he did not realize that anything was wrong until Captain Hamby had left him standing on the station platform with Miss Dillaway. Then he saw that something had upset her. She had been happy enough that morning, but now her face was pale and drawn.

"Gates," she began, and stopped, and her voice as much as her face startled him. She was looking at him strangely, no longer as a friend might look, but curiously and with a sort of compassion. Something surely had happened in those last minutes on the train, but he could think of nothing which had been unusual.

"Dillaway," he said, "what is it?" And he took her by the arm, but she wrenched her arm away.

"Look here," said Calvin Gates. "What is it?"

"Don't touch me," she said. "Don't you ever dare to touch me. Captain Hamby's told me, Gates."

"What did he tell you?" Calvin stammered. "Look here, Dillaway, what's the matter?"

"Do you mean to stand here and ask me that?" Her voice was low and vibrant. "After what you've done?"

All he could do was stare at her in blank amazement. Her attack had been so sudden, and he had thought that they were friends. His surprise was changing into a sort of desperation. Now that it had gone so mysteriously, he valued that friendship.

"Dillaway," he stammered, "I haven't done anything to you. I hope to die if I've ever—"

She interrupted him in a low, choked voice.

"It makes me so ashamed," she said, "ashamed that I ever spoke to you. You haven't done anything? My God, Gates, but I've been an idiot about you! Captain Hamby's told me. Now do you understand?"

His own expression must have frightened her, because she drew back from him.

"Hamby?" Calvin said. "So he was talking to you when he fixed your bag, was he? Well, what did he say? I don't understand."

"Don't," said Miss Dillaway sharply. "That only makes it worse." And her voice trembled. "God knows why I'm giving you a chance. I suppose because I liked you. I suppose I should have known it myself, after seeing you with that Japanese at the hotel and after seeing you drinking tea with that other Japanese at the station. There isn't any doubt about it, Gates. It only makes it worse if you try to lie. You've used me as something to hide behind. You're working for the Japanese, Gates, and Captain Hamby knows it."

Her words were dazzlingly blinding as the sunlight.

"Dillaway—" said Calvin Gates, and he found that he was pleading with her. He was pleading and struggling against that suspicion in her mind because it was taking her away from him, and yet he could see the logic of the suspicion. He was struggling with fantastic shadows.

"Dillaway," he pleaded. "Won't you please listen, Dillaway? Don't look at me like that. Don't you know me well enough to know that I couldn't be mixed up in such a thing? I told you about Mr. Moto, Dillaway. I care about your good opinion more than anything. I'd rather die than have you think that I'd made use of you."

Miss Dillaway shook her head.

"I'm giving you your chance, Gates," she said. "You'd better give me that cigarette case and get away while you can. I'm not blaming you, but it's sort of a surprise. I thought I liked you, Gates."

An ugly look come over Calvin's face.

"Did Hamby suggest that?" he asked.

"No," she answered in that same tired voice. "I suggested it to him. I don't want you to be hurt, Gates."

Calvin felt his fingernails bite into the palms of his hands.

"That's kind of you," he said. "And you believe that black-leg and you don't believe me?"

"But what are you?" she answered. "Why should I believe you, Gates?"

He was calm again. Life had clamped upon him with an icy finality.

"Well," he said, "that's you. There's no reason why you should if you don't want to. You'd rather keep on with Captain Hamby than go along with me?"

"Dr. Gilbreth sent him," she said.

"All right," Calvin answered. "If you think Hamby's more honest than I am, go ahead, I'm through. Did he tell you whom he was working for? Probably not, because he's willing to work for anyone if he gets the money. I was going to make the best of his society on account of you. Lord knows what he'll do when he gets this, but here it is. Take your cigarette case and go along with Hamby, Dillaway. It may help you more than me right now—as long as you look at things this way." And he took the cigarette case from his pocket and put it in her hand. Miss Dillaway fumbled with her pocketbook, dropped the cigarette case inside it and closed it with a snap.

"Gates," she said, "I want you to know I'm not angry. I couldn't be angry with anyone like you, but I never want to see you again."

"Well," Calvin said, "that's plain enough." He turned on his heel and the station platform was unsteady beneath his feet, and he did not turn to look back. He did not care even to stop for his baggage. He was through.

"Here," Hamby called to him. "Where are you going, Gates?"

He was able to answer carelessly.

"Just to the end of the platform," he said, "I'm just going to stretch my legs."

He was going to stretch his legs a good long way, but he strolled along carelessly because Hamby was watching him. He felt better with every step he took.

"Well," he said to himself, "that's that."

He surrendered his ticket at the gate and walked quickly through the station. He was through with it, just as he had said.

# 13

HE REALIZED with a sense of shock how angry he had been only when he reached the sunlit square outside the station. The anger and the indignation which he felt had been like a touch of sun which had burned away his wits, leaving him standing pale and abstracted, like the survivor of some great disaster. Although she had sent him away, he knew that he should not have gone, but now everything they had both said seemed irreparable.

Then a single definite thought came into his mind. There had been another disaster which had brought him to that place. He must go ahead by himself to that other railroad station and take that other train. He had crossed the ocean to see a man named Dr. Gilbreth at a place called Ghuru Nor. Voices came to him through his thoughts, and brought his mind back to the present. Hands were twitching at his sleeves, and he saw that he stood before the station in the middle of a crowd of perspiring Chinese.

"Rickshaw," they were shouting at him, "rickshaw, marster?"

It was that insistent clamor that made him realize that he had no idea of where to go; but there was one person in the crowd who seemed to understand his desire. A large Chinese in a visor cap kicked his way through the ring of rickshaw coolies and touched Calvin's arm. His face was as round and benign as a harvest moon. He was wearing a shabby chauffeur's uniform.

"Taxicab," he said in a liquid, bell-like voice. "Nice taxicab. This way, marster."

"Yes," said Calvin.

"Quick all time," came the answer. "This way, marster."

Later Calvin remembered that he never said where he wished to go. Smilingly the driver pointed to a closed black automobile of an antiquated type.

"Nice car, marster," the Chinese said, "nice clean. Get in, marster," and he opened the door with one hand and supported Calvin's arm with the other.

Calvin's foot was on the running board, when a hand against his back sent him inside sprawling and the door of the car slammed shut. Something hard was prodded into Calvin's back.

"Get up on the sit," a voice said.

Still on his hands and knees, Calvin glanced sideways. The voice had told him already that a Japanese was speaking and there he was, a small man like the rest of his race, with a square jaw and a blunt nose. His dark eyes were narrow and ugly. He was jabbing a small blunt pistol repeatedly at Calvin's side, and he spoke slowly and distinctly.

"Get up on the sit. You come with me," he said.

Then Calvin understood what had happened; it was the cigarette case again, and they thought he had the case. He got up from his hands and knees and sat down and turned his head to look at his captor. There he was in shoddy European clothes like a million of his countrymen, and he evidently knew his business. He held the pistol close to Calvin's side.

"What are you going to do?" Calvin asked. It was a foolish question. The Japanese pushed his ribs with the pistol and spoke carefully with a pause between each word.

"You sit still," he said, "and shut up your damn mouth."

Calvin Gates leaned back and folded his hands across his knee with no further desire for conversation. Yet even in that stunned moment of his surprise he remembered thinking that the words with which he had been addressed were the first words of rudeness or insolence that he had heard from anyone of the Japanese or Chinese race. It was not a pleasant omen. It meant that he was as good as finished and no longer worth consideration. It would have been different if they had not thought that the cigarette case was in his pocket, and then he thought of something else. The same thing might happen to Miss Dillaway when they found it was not there. No matter what the provocation had been, he should not have left her. He moved uneasily and the pistol prodded back into his ribs.

His resentment and his pride disappeared when the pistol prodded into his ribs, but it was too late. Given the opportunity, his own strength was greater than that of the square-jawed man beside him; and the desire to use his strength almost overcame any prudence until the pressure on his side reminded him that he might as well have been tied hand and foot. He could see the thick neck of the Chinese chauffeur in the seat in front, and the car was already moving. It moved along a broad street past a pink stucco wall with yellow tiles on top. He had a glimpse of a moat with white marble bridges arching over it, and next they were threading their way through broad thoroughfares with blank gray walls and red doorways, past rickshaws whose occupants carried sunshades above their heads, past Chinese who stood on the corners cooling themselves with brightly colored fans, past old men carrying bird cages, past carts being drawn by sweating men. The ride was not a long one. The car finally swerved out of one of those broad streets into a narrow alley so suddenly that he was thrown against the man beside him. The Japanese struck him hard on the side of his face and jabbed the pistol into his ribs again.

"You sit still," he said.

Calvin spoke for the second time.

"I won't forget that," he answered, and the Japanese struck him again.

"You shut your mouth," he said.

They were in a narrow, unpaved alley with high, blank walls on either side of it, and the car had stopped in front of a broad red gate. They waited only for the driver to blow his horn before the gate swung open, allowing them to drive into a broad courtyard where they stopped again. The Chinese driver, still bland and smiling, opened the car door.

"Get out. You follow him," his captor said.

They were in a large dusty enclosure bounded by high walls with long narrow buildings erected against them, the roofs of which shimmered from the heat of the sun. The courtyard was paved with gray mud brick, and had been swept scrupulously clean. The cleanliness was what he remembered best, and the fresh red paint on the doors and the latticed windows. Calvin knew that he was in the outer courtyard of a large establishment which might have been a native hostelry or perhaps a palace, and the walls shut him in as securely as the entrance to a prison, away from any sort of help and away from any possibility of escape. He felt the pistol in the small of his back, as he followed the Chinese driver. The sound of their feet as they clattered on the gray stone tiles made him wonder if he would ever walk back that way alive and the chances of doing so seemed slight. A weight in his right-hand jacket pocket reminded him that he was still armed. Apparently no one had given the possibility of his carrying a weapon serious attention. Even so it did not help with a pistol leveled at his back.

He followed obediently to one of the buildings by the wall, halting while the driver opened a door and stood aside. A further prod of the pistol on his back was his order to walk ahead.

Whatever was going to happen to him would happen soon, and the thought caused him no great fear. His only desire was not to die unless the man behind him died with him. He knew it was not a proper thought for such a time, but it stopped him from being afraid.

He stepped over a high threshold into a room which seemed dark after the glare outside, until his eyes became accustomed to the light. Then he saw that it was a large, long room, one side of which was a bare wall, and that light came through four windows which faced the courtyard, a soft light that filtered through rice paper, which was pasted over the windows in place of glass. It showed the bare beams of the building above him supported by a line of smooth red columns, and the beams were carved and colored in blues and reds and gold. At one end of the room was what he took for a platform covered with matting, with a small teakwood table upon it. The only other furnishing was a long bench against the wall. His guard walked in directly behind him and the driver closed the door leaving them alone. In the silence which followed Calvin could hear a pattering of feet and voices in the courtyard.

"Stand up," the Japanese said. "Stand still." And he pointed his pistol at Calvin's head. Calvin leaned against one of the pillars and shrugged his shoulders. The man in front of him grinned at him.

"Funny aren't you?" Calvin said. There was no response, but the pistol was still pointed at his head.

He realized that it was meant to be amusing, and that he was not to be shot just yet. They were obviously waiting for someone and they did not have to wait long. It could not have been more than a minute before the door opened again, making a rectangle of bright sunlight, and a man in clean white linen stepped over the high threshold and slammed the door shut.

Though it was still hard for him to distinguish the features of one Asiatic from another, he was certain that the newcomer was also Japanese in spite of his being larger than most of his race. He was a broad-shouldered, muscular man of middle age, and the first Japanese that Calvin had seen who looked entirely at home in European clothes. His figure might have been that of a European in the white suit, but in spite of the civilian clothes he was, like Captain Hamby, a military man, with the soldier's posture and the soldier's brisk, decisive step. When the light struck the side of one of his high cheeks Calvin saw two scars. He had seen the same on the cheeks of Prussian officers, the scars from a German students' duel. They were deep enough to have affected the muscles in one corner of the mouth, so that one corner drooped down slightly while the other tilted up.

The man in white gave a sharp order and Calvin's guard drew back, still holding his pistol ready. He halted in front of Calvin and stood with his hands clasped behind his back and spoke in a sharp, businesslike voice in English that was slurred by a German accent.

"You're an American named Calvin Gates," he said.

It occurred to Calvin that there was no reason to be polite.

"And I take you for a Japanese educated in Germany," he answered. "You know my name, but I don't know yours."

The mouth of the man turned upward one corner, but the other corner remained immobile.

"Quite right," he said. "You are speaking to Major Ahara of the Japanese army."

"That's interesting," said Calvin Gates, "but it doesn't mean a thing to me."

The corner of the Major's mouth twisted upward for a second time.

"I have never liked Americans," he said. "I hope very soon we go to war with America. It will be so after we finish our business here."

"That's interesting," said Calvin Gates.

The Major looked at him with frank distaste.

"I dislike Americans very much," he said, "so I do not care to talk. I am informed you have a cigarette case with you."

"What of it?" said Calvin Gates.

The Major unclasped his hands from behind his back.

"You will give it to me at once," he said.

Calvin Gates still leaned against the red pillar. The guard was listening, interested. He had lowered his pistol, but he still held it in his hand.

"And then what?" Calvin said.

The Major's lips twitched.

"You and I both know then what, Mr. Gates," he answered.

"Very well," said Calvin Gates. "There's no use lying to you." And he put his right hand into his pocket. The Major took a step forward, holding out his hand.

"That is sensible of you," he said, "and if you answer questions freely you'll have an easier time. You will be made to talk at any rate."

"That's considerate of you, Major," Calvin said.

His hand had tightened over the pistol. It was out of his pocket and he fired at just the same instant. The single shot made a roaring sound. The guard had staggered backward against the wall. The Major was standing in front of him, and Calvin took a step backward.

"That wasn't so bright of you," Major," he said. "You Japanese are always so damn sure. Don't you ever search people when you catch them?"

The Major raised a hand to his head. He was no longer an army officer with a brisk military manner; his voice was quiet and subdued.

"Will you please to kill me now," he said. "The information was you were not armed. I wish you would kill me please before the rest come."

"Sensitive, aren't you?" said Calvin Gates. "Don't worry, you'll go when I go."

He paused a moment, listening. He could hear voices and footsteps in the courtyard and the sound of a motor horn, but no one came near the door. The man he had shot had sunk down to the bench, groaning softly and holding his hand against his side, but no one came near the door. Calvin grinned at the Major.

"It looks as though they thought that shot was meant for me," he said.

The Major's face twitched and he repeated his plea again.

"I wish you would kill me, please," he said.

Calvin Gates moved toward him.

"Proud, aren't you?" he said, and he shifted the pistol from his right hand to his left. "Kill yourself if you want to. I'd rather do it this way," and he struck the Major on the jaw. He saw the eyes glaze and the mouth fall open, and he struck again.

The Major was sinking to his knees and Calvin watched him. He had struck him twice with all his force, and the Major would be no trouble for a while.

Calvin Gates stood still and his face assumed an expression almost of stupid surprise as the consciousness of what he had done came over him. What amazed him most was that it had been so easy, and he had the same sort of astonishment that comes to an amateur at a gambling table after a series of successive winnings. In less than half a minute, for the first time in his life, he had fired upon a human being as coolly as though he were practicing a snap shot in a shooting gallery. Instead of hitting an abstract mark he had hit a human being and had inflicted what was probably a fatal wound. A moment later he had beaten a second individual into temporary insensibility, and it all had occurred almost as fast as thought.

He had never realized his own capacity until just then, and it had an ironic significance. Standing there in that strange place, the conviction came upon him that he was doing exactly what he had always wanted, for he had always longed to be in danger. For once in his life he had achieved what he wanted, and now that he had achieved it he was not greatly elated, for he suddenly understood that his whole life had been built for such a situation and that he was only useful in such surroundings.

Now that he was faced with the reality, it was not much to be proud of, for the thing which he had done was out of keeping with his sense of fitness and humanity. Yet now that he had done it, there was no time for drawing back. He would have to go on very quickly, if he were to avail himself even of the slender chance of getting out of that courtyard and into the street alive.

Even while he was thinking, another part of him began to act. He found himself stepping toward the doorway with an even, unhurried step. At the same time he was thinking that he could do all this more easily again if he came out alive; he would be better equipped to kill and less appalled at facing the prospect. He would be like Captain Hamby, given time; it was the only thing he was good for, to be like Captain Hamby.

He understood very clearly that he must open the door and walk out into the court. The casualness of his appearance might provoke a moment of uncertainty which might allow him time to reach the gate. If anyone attempted to stop him, he must shoot again without compunction, and he felt no great compunction; he was getting more like Hamby all the time.

The courtyard had been empty when he had crossed it, but now he could hear voices which were raised in some sort of altercation. Whatever might be happening outside, it was too late for him to stop. Putting his pistol back in his jacket pocket, but still holding his hand over it, Calvin opened the door and stepped out into the brilliant sunshine.

The instant that he was in the courtyard, however, the pistol was out again and ready in his hand, while the scene outside flashed accurately across his mind, at first with only the significance that comes to a marksman. Across the court standing by the door of another of those buildings built against the wall was a knot of Japanese. They had not even noticed his appearance, for all their attention was focused upon the center of the courtyard. The antiquated black car which had brought him still stood there empty, and beside it was a smaller, tan-colored vehicle with a driver in a khaki uniform at the wheel. Midway between that brown automobile and where he stood, three Japanese stood arguing excitedly. All these details flashed before him instantaneously, just as he stepped over the high Chinese threshold. The three in the center of the courtyard saw him at the same instant, and their voices stopped.

"Run," his mind was saying; "get over to the gate."

Then one of the three was walking toward him holding up his hand.

"Please," he was calling. "One moment, Mr. Gates." And Calvin recognized the voice, and the black-and-white golf suit and the golden smile. It was Mr. Moto, walking toward him blandly.

"So nice to see you, Mr. Gates," Mr. Motto spoke quickly. "So fortunate."

His speech ended in a quick sibilant hiss, and he assumed a queer fixed smile. "Will you please come with me now, or I am so afraid that we will both be killed?"

There was no doubt that it was Mr. Moto. His appearance in that checked suit was as preposterous as his words, but Mr. Moto took his clothes and his words entirely for granted.

"How did you get here?" Calvin asked him, still holding his pistol ready. Mr. Moto's reply was brisk and businesslike.

"No need for the pistol now, please," Mr. Moto said. "I came by airplane. I cannot understand. This is very terrible. They do not like me here. Army officers are so very, very cross. So many factions in Japan. Please follow me. Do not shoot unless I tell you."

In spite of the merry contour of his mouth, there was a nervous tremor in his fingers and his eyes blinked rapidly.

"You must not spoil everything," said Mr. Moto, "when I work so hard. I thought that I understood Americans. Sorry to be rude. Do not talk but follow me."

Mr. Moto spun quickly on his heel and began walking back toward the little brown car, and Calvin followed. The two Japanese stood near the automobile, wooden-faced, youngish men, both scowling sullenly.

"Get in," Mr. Moto said, and then he spoke volubly in Japanese. His words made a snapping sound like electric sparks. One of the young men snapped a sentence back and Mr. Moto drew a paper from his pocket and tapped it with his forefinger. Whatever was written upon it seemed conclusive, for without another word Mr. Moto also climbed into the car and gave an order to the driver. The engine started and the car rolled through the gate. Mr. Moto's breath whistled softly through his teeth.

"So glad," he said. "The army faction is so very hard to deal with. What happened please?"

"I shot a man," said Calvin Gates. He felt stupid and dull from the reaction. "They grabbed me at the station—I suppose it's that damned cigarette case."

He found himself staring at Mr. Moto, who nodded sympathetically.

"So sorry," Mr. Moto said. "Such a bad mistake for you to leave your friends. The military faction are so impetuous. Ha ha. Our soldiers are so brave, but so very, very rash. I came as soon as I had heard."

"You came from where?" said Calvin Gates.

"Please," said Mr. Moto, "it does not matter. We are going where it will be safer for us please. We will be like friends and have whisky like Americans. What happened please? I hope they were polite."

"They were going to kill me, and you know it," said Calvin Gates.

"Oh yes," said Mr. Moto, "they woud liquidate, of course, but I hope so much that they were polite. I should not wish to report rudeness. What happened, please?"

Mr. Moto listened and rubbed his hands together, and looked troubled.

"That is very serious," he said, "that they should have been so impolite. It makes me very, very angry. There is no reason to be impolite in a liquidation. I have seen so many where everything was nice."

Mr. Moto smiled as though he had hit upon a happier thought.

"But you shot the man who struck you, did you not? So much nicer for your honor. And the major with the scar upon his cheek. That is Major Ahara. Ha ha. He has tried to kill me in the political troubles, but he is a very lovely man. He always loved his flowers. Such very beautiful azaleas in his garden, Mr. Gates. I heard the first shot, but I did not hear the second. I hope so very, very much you shot him also. . . . You did not? I cannot understand. Americans are so very, very puzzling. So much kinder to have killed him than have struck him, Mr. Gates. Excuse me—so much more polite. You are so very, very puzzling, Mr. Gates."

"Why?" asked Calvin Gates, and he felt that his wits were leaving him.

"Because I am so afraid that now he must kill himself. You understand that he is in too much disgrace. So lucky for you that he did not search you, and so like some younger officers. It has to do with the more radical wing of our military party, Mr. Gates, and they are so much out of hand."

If most of what Mr. Moto had said was not entirely comprehensible, there was one thing of which Calvin was entirely convinced.

"I wish I had never set eyes on you," he said.

## 14

MR. MOTO raised his hand before his mouth and drew in his breath.

"So sorry," he said, "but excuse me, Mr. Gates, this was all so unnecessary. I had made such careful plans. I had tried to think about you and just what you would do. There was a lady on the train, such a very lovely lady, and yet you did not stay with her. I do not understand. You would have been safe with Captain Hamby."

Calvin Gates was startled.

"How did you know about Hamby?" he asked.

"Please," said Mr. Moto, "it does not matter. All that matters is that I am so very stupid. I was so sure that you would stay with Captain Hamby and the lady. I do not see, indeed I do not see. But surely you gave Captain Hamby the cigarette case with the little birds upon it?"

Calvin Gates shook his head, and Mr. Moto gave a start, but his face was inscrutable. All the complicated repressions of a complicated race made it difficult to read.

"I didn't trust him," said Calvin Gates.

Mr. Moto's hands rubbed against each other nervously.

"So very silly of me," he said. "I had never thought of that. When I heard that Captain Hamby had come to meet you, I thought there would not be the slightest doubt. You are so very difficult, Mr. Gates. You leave the lady, and now you have the cigarette case with you. I had not thought of that."

"I haven't got it," Calvin told him.

He had not believed that Mr. Moto could display such emotion.

Mr. Moto half rose from his seat and struck his hand on his forehead.

"Did they take it from you back there?" he almost shouted. "Quickly, Mr. Gates."

Mr. Moto's cheeks had grown greenish and sallow, and he seized Calvin by the lapel of his coat.

"No," said Calvin, "they didn't take it."

Mr. Moto groaned and muttered something in his own language.

"This is so very terrible," he groaned. "You did not throw it away?" and his fingers twitched at Calvin's coat lapel.

"No," Calvin said. "You needn't pull at me, Mr. Moto. I gave the thing back to Miss Dillaway. We had a quarrel and I got angry. I wish I'd never seen it or you, Mr. Moto. I'm worried about Miss Dillaway."

Mr. Moto sank back in his seat. The color had returned to his cheeks and he sighed deeply.

"Excuse my rudeness, please," he said. "I was so very startled. So Miss Dillaway has it then. But you spoke to Captain Hamby about that cigarette case? Surely you did that?"

Calvin moved his shoulders impatiently.

"Well," he said, "what's going to happen to her? I know that thing is dangerous for her, Moto. Of course I spoke to Hamby about it. He told me what it was—a code message going to the Russians. It's military information, and instead of trying to intercept it, you do everything to have it go through. Hamby knows about you, Moto, and he thinks I'm helping you. He offered me three thousand dollars if I would tell him what you wanted."

He had expected the news to be disturbing, but instead Moto gave a little jump in his seat and clapped his hands.

"Oh," said Mr. Moto, "that is so very nice. So exactly what I wished. I am so obliged to you, Mr. Gates. So very much obliged."

Calvin Gates scowled at him.

"What's going to happen to that message and what's going to happen to Miss Dillaway?" he asked. "Aren't you going to stop it?"

"Please," said Mr. Moto, "that is why I have worked so hard. I do not wish to stop it. It must not be disturbed. It is going to a man in Kalgan named Mr. Holtz, and now I think it will surely go there. It is so very nice."

"Moto," Calvin asked him, "are you a patriotic Japanese?"

Mr. Moto looked as though the question pained him.

"I should be so pleased to die for my emperor," he said. "This is all so very nice. You have done me such a service, Mr. Gates. The army will be angry at you, but I shall see that you are safe. So nice that Captain Hamby knows so much," and Mr. Moto smiled as though some secret joke of his own amused him.

"I've learned quite a lot on the train ride, Mr. Moto," Calvin said. "Do you know the Russians have two divisions they are going to move to this place called Ghuru Nor? Do you know that, and do you mean to say that you're not going to stop that message?"

Mr. Moto turned his head toward Calvin with a quick birdlike gesture and smiled and rubbed his hands.

"This does not concern you, Mr. Gates," he said. "Why are you so interested?"

"Because I want to know what's going to happen to Miss Dillaway," Calvin said. "She has that cigarette case."

"Then why did you not stay with her?" said Mr. Moto. "What was it that made you angry?"

Calvin scowled at the little man on the seat beside him and repressed a growing desire to shake him. His motives were entirely beyond him, but he could not help but admire Mr. Moto in a way.

"Hamby told her I was a Japanese spy," he said. "I've got a good deal to thank you for, Moto. He told her I was a Japanese spy, and she said I was making use of her."

Mr. Moto put his hand before his mouth and his shoulders began to shake.

"Excuse me," said Mr. Moto, "it is so rude to laugh. Things are so difficult, but they are so very funny. I have been using both of you I think. Ha ha, I am using everyone. And they caught you back there and they never knew you had such information. So sorry if I laugh, Mr. Gates. You will laugh too when you understand."

Mr. Moto rubbed his hand across his eyes.

"I've found you," Mr. Moto said, "in the offices of the Intelligence section of the staff of our Third Army. You had the information of Russia they are trying so hard to get. Excuse me, your position is so confusing."

Calvin Gates scowled back at him.

"To hell with your nonsense, Moto," he said. "Miss Dillaway's got that cigarette case. What's going to happen to her?"

Mr. Moto's face became dull and masklike.

"I hope so much that nothing bad will happen," he said. "It depends on Captain Hamby, I am so afraid. You do not understand me very well, but I am so obliged to you, Mr. Gates. I think I shall not need you any further. We will talk about your plans in just a minute. We are going to the house of a friend of mine, a very important Japanese friend. He is not there, but you will be so very welcome. We are arriving now, I think."

Calvin Gates had not noticed where they had been going. He had lost all sense of direction long ago and nearly all sense of time. He was moving in a sort of fantasy not relieved by Mr. Moto's conversation and Captain Hamby's remark that anything might happen was growing increasingly true. The car had stopped in another alley which was almost like the one they had left, before another red gate in another gray wall. The driver opened the door of the car. A gate keeper in a white livery stood waiting.

"Get out quickly please," said Mr. Moto. Calvin hesitated.

"Quickly," Mr. Moto said. "It is dangerous in the street." And Calvin got out quickly.

"It is my friend's house," Mr. Moto said. "You are so welcome."

They were in a courtyard and the gate had closed behind them. The courtyard was cool and shaded by a huge matting awning supported on bamboo poles. There was a pool in the center of the court surrounded by potted bushes. A Japanese servant in a white uniform stood before Mr. Moto bowing.

"This way please," Mr. Moto said. "It is nicer than where we were last, is it not? You will like it here so much."

They walked through a round gate in the wall into a second courtyard, and then through another red doorway into a room. The floor was covered with heavy carpets, the chairs and tables were black lacquer and there were pictures of Chinese landscapes upon the wall.

"A very simple room," Mr. Moto said. "My friend has such good taste. They will bring us some whisky in a moment. Ha ha, all Americans like whisky. Sit down, Mr. Gates. The chairs are so very comfortable."

Calvin seated himself beside a small lacquer table and looked about him. The room he saw was used as some sort of office. There was a great flat desk at one end with a telephone and books and papers. A table in the center of the room supported a large map tacked to a board, a military map with colored pins upon it. Mr. Moto smiled and rubbed his hands.

"My friend allows me to work here," he said.

A servant had appeared carrying a tray with bottles and glasses.

He placed them upon the table beside Calvin and bowed and smiled and hissed. A second servant followed holding a sheaf of papers which he handed to Mr. Moto. Mr. Moto took them quickly and hurried over to the desk.

"Please refresh yourself," he said. "Ask for what you wish. Excuse, I shall be busy for a little while."

Mr. Moto seated himself behind the desk and read each paper carefully. When he had finished, he placed them in a drawer and picked up the telephone.

"Please pour yourself whisky," he said. "Captain Hamby and Miss Dillaway are on the train for Kalgan. They have no trouble." Then he began speaking into the telephone, in Chinese or Japanese, Calvin could not tell.

He only realized that he was sitting there comfortably, sipping whisky and water, while Miss Dillaway was with Captain Hamby, going where he should have been going. Mr. Moto had said it was nice, but he knew it was not true. The game was not nice which Mr. Moto was playing, if it was not even safe to linger on the street, and it was not hard to see that the game was reaching some sort of crisis. Through the obscurity which surrounded that intrigue and through that ignorance of his, an American's ignorance of the geography and the affairs of the Far East, he was still able to gain a sense of forces taking shape. It was a game for high stakes, where China was involved, and war, and peace. Even as a stranger he could feel the shadow of Japan moving inexorably across the map of China. The shadow was already across Peiping, and moving farther. There was some sort of Japanese army control in Peiping already, and forces were advancing beneath the shadow. Russia was playing a part in it, and the Japanese factions of which Mr. Moto had spoken.

"*Arigato,*" Mr. Moto was saying over the telephone, "*arigato.*"

There was no doubt any longer that Mr. Moto was a very important man. He was balancing those forces as Calvin sat there watching, holding the strings of intrigue in his fingers, pulling this one and that, moving people here and there. He had used Calvin Gates and now he was using Captain Hamby. Before long there would be some sort of denouement when everything would evolve into sinister action. He would not have minded if Miss Dillaway had not been there.

"*Arigato,*" Mr. Moto was saying. He was speaking in a quick, authoritative voice.

"So very nice," Mr. Moto said. "Yes, Captain Hamby and Miss Dillaway are upon the train. You will be so glad to know that the major whom you struck has decided not to kill himself. He is in an airplane now on his way to Kalgan to find Captain Hamby. The young soldiers are so impetuous. So very many things are happening. It seems that your American Embassy is very much upset about your scientific expedition. There is some difficulty, the local prince is holding them. You are so very fortunate to be here, Mr. Gates. I must be leaving in a little while, but you must remain here quietly for a day or two and then you will be quite safe. Matters will be settled in one way or another in a day or two."

Calvin set his glass on the table and stood up.

"Where are you going?" he asked.

Mr. Moto had taken some papers from the drawer and they were rustling softly in his hand.

"So sorry," he said, "I must go north. I have just ordered a plane at the flying field. I must be at Kalgan when Captain Hamby arrives. It is so very important."

Calvin walked across the heavy carpet to the desk and leaned both hands upon it.

"Do you mean you're leaving me here as a prisoner?"

Mr. Moto raised his eyebrows.

"Please," he said, "as a guest not as a prisoner, please. It is only so that you will be safe. Recall, please, what happened to you just this morning, Mr. Gates."

"What's going to happen to Miss Dillaway?" Calvin asked him. "Is she going to be safe?"

Mr. Moto smiled. It was one of those determined smiles peculiar to his race, which had nothing to do with humor.

"Everything possible will be done," he said. "Of course, I cannot be sure."

Calvin Gates leaned his weight more firmly on the desk. Mr. Moto had been polite and almost cordial. He had spoken to him as a guest, but his hospitality did not conceal the truth that Mr. Moto might do anything with him that he chose.

"Please."

"Mr. Moto," Calvin said, "is there anything that might induce you to take me with you? I have to go up there.

Mr. Moto looked and blinked at him.

"You wish to go with me?" he said. "Please tell me why."

Calvin Gates hesitated. It had been difficult for him always to reveal himself to anyone, and before he could bring himself to speak, Mr. Moto continued.

"Excuse me," Mr. Moto said, "it is so necessary to be frank. I wonder why you want to go to Ghuru Nor, a very funny place for one like you to go. You said you were planning to join an expedition. It is not true."

"No," said Calvin, "it isn't true; I gave it as a reason. I've crossed the ocean to go there. There's a man named Dr. Gilbreth, and I have to see him."

"So interesting," Mr. Moto murmured. "Please tell me why."

Calvin's fingers grew white as they pressed against the desk.

"Do not be embarrassed," Mr. Moto said softly. "It will be nicer if you tell me why."

Calvin found that his voice was unsteady. He had given up nearly everything to keep secret what he was now telling. He had believed that he would die rather than speak of it, yet now he found himself speaking to a stranger of another race.

"You know something about it," he said, "because you told me I was wanted by the police. It surprised me very much. I don't know why it should have, except that one does not expect such a gesture from one's family. You said I was wanted for theft, but there's another word for it. It's forgery they want to see me about. I confessed to it before I went away. It's that scientific expedition, Mr. Moto. Dr. Gilbreth was given a forged check of ten thousand dollars. It was honored by the bank."

"Oh yes," said Mr. Moto softly, "yes. I do not understand—you forged the check?"

"I didn't." Calvin choked on his words and cleared his throat. "I took the blame. Someone else did. I'm afraid I'm not being clear."

"So sorry for you," said Mr. Moto. "Why must you see Dr. Gilbreth, please? To prove your innocence perhaps? Surely a communication could have reached him just as well."

Never in his life had he felt so wretched as when he stood there meeting Mr. Moto's glance. In some way his pride was hurt, not that he was ashamed. It was rather that his story had a ridiculous ring when it was put into words.

"He's the only one in the world who will know who forged it," Calvin said. "I've come out here to ask him not to tell. You believe me, don't you?"

"So sorry," said Mr. Moto. "People do such strange things. Will you finish please."

"Oh hell," said Calvin. Mr. Moto's quiet voice seemed to be pulling the words from him. "Maybe I was crazy, I don't know. A girl wrote that check. My uncle's daughter, if you want to know. She was crazy about this Dr. Gilbreth. She was sure to be caught with it. It's a family matter. I didn't do it for her, I did it for the old man. I knew he'd like it better that way. He's always looked out for me and I haven't been such a help. Wild, Mr. Moto, always wild. Never seemed able to settle down, that's the story, Mr. Moto, and you wouldn't have dragged it out of me if you'd cut me to pieces, except that I want to keep on traveling. I don't want to stay here, Mr. Moto."

He felt tired when he had finished, as though he had been through some violent physical effort. Yet he felt better when he had spoken, relieved because he had broken some repression inside his mind. It had not occurred to him before that there might be gentlemen in Japan with feelings like his own until Mr. Moto spoke again. Mr. Moto stood up, clasped his hands in front of him.

"So honored," Mr. Moto said, "so very deeply honored that you should have told me. Gentlemen do such very strange things, even in Japan. So honored, but still I do not understand."

"Understand what?" Calvin asked.

"Why you cannot wait," Mr. Moto said. "In three days—in four days I think, you might see Dr. Gilbreth much more easily."

Calvin Gates stammered and felt his face grow red.

"I can't leave Miss Dillaway up there," he said. "I don't know what's going to happen to her and you won't tell me. I can't leave her like that. I've got to go on. I've got to be starting now."

Mr. Moto placed the tips of his fingers together and hissed respectfully.

"I cannot understand," he said, "which it is you desire the most—to see Miss Dillaway or to see Dr. Gilbreth."

"Does it make any difference?" Calvin asked him.

"Please," said Mr. Moto, "excuse me. It would make a difference to yourself. You would be so much happier if you could make up your mind. It seems to me you are confused. You are willing to add difficulty for yourself because a lady is in difficulty—not a logical reason I am afraid—so much nicer if we know just what we want."

"Logical enough for me," said Calvin Gates.

Mr. Moto glanced up at the painted beams of the ceiling.

"So often," he said, "I have seen such gracious ladies disrupt political combinations." He sighed and still stared at the ceiling seemingly lost in memory. "Such a lovely girl in Washington—I was so much younger then. She sold me the navy plans of a submarine. The price was thirty thousand yen. When the blue prints came, they were of a tugboat. Such a lovely lady. Such a lovely lady in Tokyo. She took me to see the goldfish in her garden, and there were the assassins behind the little trees. Not her fault but theirs that I am still alive—they were such poor shots. I do not understand lovely ladies, but still I trust them sometimes. First you quarrel with Miss Dillaway and then you wish to find her. I have done the same thing myself, but not I like to think I have learned better. Excuse me, Mr. Gates, you must like Miss Dillaway so very, very much."

Mr. Moto's manner had grown friendly as he confided those details of an earlier life. Perhaps he was telling more about himself than he thought. Calvin saw him for the first time as a lonely sentimental man, moving in a garish world of intrigue and sudden death.

"Yes," he said, "I still trust them sometimes. I hope so very much that this is worth your while."

Mr. Moto's voice seemed to draw speech from Calvin Gates against his will.

"Suppose I do like her very much or suppose I don't," he said, "it would be the same thing. I should want to go away."

Mr. Moto's expression brightened.

"Oh," he said, "I understand so perfectly. It is a code of chivalry. Oh yes, we have a code in Japan, a very careful code. It makes us do so many things we do not have to do. It is why Major Ahara thought that he must kill himself." Mr. Moto sighed. "I am so very sorry that he decided not to kill himself." Mr. Moto's quick bright eyes moved again toward the ceiling. "He is such a very vigorous man, so powerful politically. He represents the extreme military clique and he wants so very much to get that cigarette case. I have been sent by the Government to estimate the situation here and with authority to investigate and direct a certain military operation, and now he is so cross with me because I am conservative."

Mr. Moto smiled deprecatingly and rustled the papers on his desk.

"So nice to have a little talk with you, Mr. Gates. So funny that I should be saying so much to a stranger. I suppose you wonder why."

"I don't believe you do anything without a reason," Calvin said, and Mr. Moto looked very pleased.

"Please," said Mr. Moto, "it was because you expressed a wish to go with me. You might be useful, but it is so necessary for you to understand that everything is so very serious. A human being counts for so very little. I hope you understand."

"I'll do anything you say," Calvin said, "as long as I go on. I don't care what happens after that."

"What happens after that," Mr. Moto repeated. "You mean—there will not be so very much for you after that? It is as though I offered you employment—oh excuse me, please."

A voice at the doorway had interrupted him. It was one of the white-clad Japanese servants, no longer obsequious and polite. The boy had been running and now he spoke with sharp intakes of breath, and the news, whatever it was, could not have been pleasant, for Mr. Moto walked hastily around the desk. He spoke sharply and the boy turned and darted out the door. Mr. Moto's eyes had a sharp beady glint and all expression had left his face.

"Well," Mr. Moto said. "This is not very nice."

"What's the matter?" Calvin asked.

Mr. Moto spoke rapidly, but his voice was still low and soft.

"There are soldiers in the courtyard," Mr. Moto said. "They are coming with the General of Intelligence."

Calvin's hand moved toward his coat pocket and Mr. Moto seized his arm.

"Please," he whispered, "be very careful please. I am so very uncertain—I am not sure whether they want you or whether it is to be a liquidation."

"A liquidation?" Calvin repeated after him.

"It may be that they decide to liquidate me." Mr. Moto's voice was softly insistent. "Sit down where you were, Mr. Gates, and pour yourself some whisky please. You have your pistol in your pocket? That is very nice. A man is coming in, a general. He will not bring soldiers in here with him yet. I shall talk to the general, but give me your attention. If I rub my hands together like this, will you be so kind as to shoot the general very quickly, please."

"Shoot the general?" Calvin repeated.

"Yes," said Mr. Moto, "please. If I rub my hands together—so. It may be so very necessary, and do not hesitate. Do not rise when he comes in. The general is so very nice. If I rub my hands together—so."

Calvin Gates sat down. Mr. Moto was calm enough, but Mr. Moto's calmness set Calvin's heart to beating crazily when he heard the precise click of boot heels on the pavement of the courtyard.

The general was a small man. He paused at the open door and the sun glinted on his spectacles and his belt and riding boots shone brightly. He was in khaki field uniform which fitted him so loosely that he looked more like a professor than a general, a very serious man whose narrow, receding chin and heavy lips were framed by a little black moustache.

He began speaking in a thin high voice as he stepped over the threshold and Mr. Moto advanced, bowing, with his hands clasped in front of him.

"So very nice to see you, my dear sir," Mr. Moto said, "so very, very nice."

Those English words answering the general's native speech puzzled Calvin Gates and they must have puzzled the general also.

"Please," Mr. Moto answered, "we will speak in English. This other gentleman does not understand Japanese, I am so very sorry, and your English, General, is so very, very good."

The general looked at Calvin Gates through his heavy spectacles.

"There is no reason for this," he said. "I came to have a private talk. Why have you brought this man here?"

"Excellency," said Mr. Moto, "this man is here for my own reasons, please."

The general turned toward Mr. Moto and frowned.

"This is not correct," he said. "He has insulted the army."

Mr. Moto clasped his hands together.

"So sorry for you, my dear sir," he answered. "You understand my position here. You have seen the orders please?"

The general's frown grew deeper. There was something venemous in the way he looked at Mr. Moto, as though he were repressing a thousand things which he wished to say and do. He drew in his breath with a sharp, sputtering sound and spoke again in Japanese. His words snapped like little whips and he struck his hands together, while Mr. Moto stood listening.

"So sorry," Mr. Moto answered in English. "So sorry for you, my dear General."

The general swallowed over a word and continued speaking. His narrow face had grown livid. Mr. Moto clasped his hands again.

"So sorry for you, my dear General," he said. "You cannot arrest this man because I have my reasons. So sorry for Major Ahara."

The general drew in his breath again and Mr. Moto pulled a paper from his inside coat pocket. There was a heavy seal upon the corner which Mr. Moto indicated respectfully.

"So sorry for you," said Mr. Moto softly. "I should be so very sad to report that you saw this and disobeyed. I have full control, my dear sir. There can be no doubt about it."

Mr. Moto replaced the paper but the sight of it had changed the general's tone. He appeared to be expostulating when he spoke again. He walked to the table that held the map and began pointing at the pins. Mr. Moto followed him and leaned above the map, but once while the general continued speaking, Mr. Moto glanced toward Calvin Gates and smiled.

"So sorry," Mr. Moto said. "Nothing must move. I understand so well that you are anxious, my dear General. The staff had full directions just last night. So sorry that no troops must move."

The general burst into another torrent of words and emphasized them by beating his fist on the table while Mr. Moto listened.

"So sorry," Mr. Moto said, "that we have different ways of thinking. I understand about the Russian dispositions. Yes. Nothing must move. My humblest regrets. So very sorry."

The general did not speak again. He backed away from the table and glared at Mr. Moto. Then he turned on his heel and walked toward the door. Mr. Moto bowed and stood at the doorway watching while the click of the general's boot heels grew fainter. When he turned back to Calvin his face was wreathed in one of those determined smiles which hid some other feeling.

"The army extremists are so very sensitive," Mr. Moto said. "First it was Major Ahara, and now it is the general. He feels so very much disgraced to have been corrected. I am so very much afraid that he may dispose of himself." Calvin repressed a desire to laugh, because a wild sort of humor was in the situation which combined that blood-thirsty politeness, that composure and petulance.

"If everybody wants to kill himself," Calvin said, "there won't be any army left."

"Yes," said Mr. Moto, "that is very, very true. So many of our most useful people have killed themselves for honor. You think it is funny, and yet you have indicated that you are so very glad to lose your good name."

"I hadn't thought of that," said Calvin Gates.

"Excuse me please," said Mr. Moto, "for calling it to your attention. I am so afraid it will be necessary for you to go with me now. I am so afraid I cannot leave you here, even if I wished. The general might forget himself. I must use you, Mr. Gates."

Mr. Moto's eyes were no longer opaque but deep and calculating. He walked back to the table with its map.

"We must leave here quickly," he said. "It will not be safe to stay much longer. There is a plane waiting at the flying field. May I ask you to glance at this map? It will interest you I think. Thank you so very much."

Calvin did not know whether to be surprised or alarmed at Mr. Moto's new confiding quality. As far as he could see Mr. Moto had entirely forgotten the confidential nature of his mission, and instead appeared anxious to tell everything, both anxious and insistent.

Calvin Gates stood looking over Mr. Moto's shoulder at a large military map, the legends of which were written in Japanese, but his ignorance of the characters did not prevent his knowing what it represented. Near the bottom of the sheet he could see the city of Peiping and the hard black curve of a railroad running north from it into a mountainous country. Farther north the mountains ceased and ended at a huge bare stretch. Mr. Moto tapped it with his finger.

"The Mongolian plateau," he said, "such a very interesting place, a rolling, treeless country. It is where the savage tribes once lived that used to conquer China. You observe that it is not so far from Peiping. The strip beyond the mountains where I place my finger is Inner Mongolia. Beyond it to the north is the republic of Outer Mongolia, which is a Russian puppet state. I hope so much you understand."

"Go ahead," said Calvin Gates.

"It is so very nice," Mr. Moto said, "that you are so very clever. You can see so well without my telling you that Inner Mongolia lies between what we call Outer Mongolia and North China. Now if you please, I must be very, very frank. It is essential for its economic future that the Japanese Empire should dominate North China."

"I have heard you were going to grab it," Calvin said. "Everyone knows that."

Mr. Moto looked surprised and pained.

"That is not a nice way of saying it," he said. "Excuse me, your own great country has taken territory. The British Empire has taken nearly half the globe. Why should not Japan? It is the manifest destiny of stronger nations. Nevertheless, we do not wish to grab. We only desire a partnership, a cordial co-operation, an understanding with the Chinese. We wish to advise and to help them, to develop their resources. I am sure that you are clever enough to understand."

Mr. Moto paused and sighed.

"It is very unfortunate that so many nationalistic elements of the Chinese are so difficult. We have tried so very hard to offer advice and co-operation. We have offered them our army to pacify the country, yet they grow difficult, particularly the American-educated Chinese. If I am rude, I am so sorry."

"They probably want to run their own country in their own way," said Calvin Gates.

"Yes," Mr. Moto agreed. "It is necessary now to convince them that they must co-operate. It is believed in highest quarters that there must be a show of force."

"You mean there's going to be a war?" Calvin asked.

"Please," said Mr. Moto, "hardly that. Nothing more than a military occupation. It is so unfortunate that the great powers do not understand."

Mr. Moto pointed at the map again.

"It would be so unfortunate, for instance, if Russia did not like it. As a result of such a demonstration, Russia might move into Inner Mongolia. It is so important to be sure. Look where I am pointing please. You see that line of hills; it is Ghuru Nor. If Russia decides to move, she will occupy them. Now look over here, please, farther to the right. Those little pins represent three divisions of our army on the Mongolian plateau. You heard the general speaking. He is so very anxious to move forward to occupy Ghuru Nor at once as a necessary protection before the demonstration starts."

"I don't blame him," said Calvin Gates.

"Thank you," said Mr. Moto. "You have the military mind. And now we come to the cigarette case, Mr. Gates. The Russian Intelligence have discovered the very day when we propose to make this demonstration. The date is conveyed by the little birds upon the case. Do you mind if I am very frank? There will be an incident the day after tomorrow, Mr. Gates."

Mr. Moto's gold teeth glittered. He appeared delighted at Calvin Gates's bewilderment.

"Then I'm damned if I understand," Calvin Gates blurted out. "You mean you're going to let the Russians get that message?"

Mr. Moto nodded in delighted agreement.

"Yes," he said, "oh yes, that is so exactly. I am so glad for you that you understand. It must have been so puzzling for you. I am so very anxious for a certain Russian official to get the message telling him the exact day and hour, and to be convinced that it is right. He must be certain that it is not a trap. So nice you understand."

Calvin Gates had heard of the subtleties of the Oriental mind, but he could not understand.

"You must have some reason," Calvin said.

"Yes," Mr. Moto said. "Yes, a reason. I am such a humble man, but I am so fortunate to have the confidence of some very great—some august individuals. I speak for a very august individual. You heard me address the general? You see those pins upon the map? The staff has given advancing orders for those little pins. The staff wished those little pins to be moving yesterday toward Ghuru Nor. I have used my authority yesterday to countermand that order. Those little pins cannot move until I tell them, I represent such a very august personage."

"Who's that," asked Calvin Gates, "the Emperor of Japan?"

Mr. Moto looked startled.

"Please," he answered, "I cannot permit you to use the word. I only said a very august personage."

"And you're sending that message in," said Calvin Gates, "and stopping your army from acting."

"Yes," said Mr. Moto. "Please, they cannot act unless I give the order. I want so much for you to understand."

"I don't blame the army for wanting to kill you," said Calvin Gates.

"So nice of you to see," said Mr. Moto. "I am not speaking for nothing. It concerns you so much. We are now in Peiping. In a very few minutes, we shall take a luncheon basket and go to the flying field. A plane will be waiting to take us north. You will observe the city just at the edge of those mountains. That is Kalgan, Mr. Gates. It is where the camel caravans used to start out into Mongolia. It is where Captain Hamby will arrive early this evening. I am so afraid that the army intelligence knows already that Captain Hamby and Miss Dillaway possess that cigarette case. We shall land at Kalgan, Mr. Gates. The field is no good, but we shall land. You follow me so far?"

"Yes," said Calvin Gates.

"Thank you," said Mr. Moto, "so very much. I was so very

pleased that Captain Hamby believes I am using you. That is why you are going with me, because I am using you again. I know where Captain Hamby will go at Kalgan."

"And you're going after him," Calvin interrupted.

"Please," said Mr. Moto, "wait. I am not going after Captain Hamby. You are, Mr. Gates. It is your regard for Miss Dillaway that brings you and also the Captain's offer of three thousand dollars. I am so sure Captain Hamby will appreciate. You are to tell to Captain Hamby all I have told you, and all about my humble self. He wants to know so very much. There is only one thing not to tell him—not what the cigarette case means, please."

"But I don't see what you're driving at," Calvin Gates began.

Mr. Moto's ingratiating smile disappeared.

"I do not ask you to see," he said. "I ask you to do what I say, please. If you do not, you will be so sorry. You have shot a Japanese subject, Mr. Gates."

Calvin Gates grew angry.

"You needn't threaten," he said. "If you want me to tell Hamby what I know about you, I'm glad to do it. But I'd look out for Captain Hamby."

"Thank you," said Mr. Moto, "so kind of you to tell me. It is time to be starting now I think. Please excuse if I was rude. So sorry."

Mr. Moto picked up a small brief case from the desk.

"You're sure you want me to tell Hamby everything?" said Calvin Gates.

"Yes," said Mr. Moto. "So sorry for you we cannot wait for lunch, but there will be sandwiches in the plane."

Calvin Gates was not thinking of food, he was thinking of Captain Hamby, and of Captain Hamby's endless song about the troubles in the old kit bag. Captain Sam Hamby could look out for himself, and Captain Hamby was not a man to be caught in any trap.

"So sorry for *you,* Mr. Moto," Calvin said.

## 15

MR. MOTO must have said exactly what he wanted, no more, no less, for his loquacity ceased abruptly and he no longer seemed anxious to discourse upon the economic aims of Japan or upon his nation's manifest destiny.

Nevertheless in the next half-hour Calvin Gates observed that Japan's manifest destiny had reached Peiping. The great northern capital of China, nominally under China's central Government, appeared already to be under Japanese control, and it was obvious even to a stranger that some understanding had been reached between Japanese and Chinese officials which was definite though obscure. The small brown automobile was waiting in the alley outside the house. It started off at high speed the moment he and Mr. Moto were inside and the Chinese policeman directing traffic at the street corners allowed the car to pass without a single interruption.

Out beyond the city walls the car drove to the center of a flying field without a question being asked, straight up to a small cabin plane with its engine already running. Two Chinese attendants who were standing near it hurried to open the doors. A Japanese pilot was waiting at the controls.

As soon as they were inside, and even before they were seated, the engine gave a roar and the plane taxied to the end of the field and turned into the wind. The increased acceleration of the engine made conversation difficult, but Calvin Gates shouted to Mr. Moto.

"You certainly have good service," he shouted.

Mr. Moto nodded and smiled, opened a cardboard box, took a sandwich from it, and passed it to Calvin Gates.

"Too much noise to talk," Mr. Moto called. "Look out the window, it is very nice." Then he took out a map from his brief case and handed it to Calvin. Just as the plane lifted from the ground Calvin looked at his wrist watch; it was half-past two in the afternoon. Mr. Moto had folded his hands and closed his eyes.

When Mr. Moto closed his eyes, he became an ordinary person, a slightly weary Japanese businessman, and nothing more. It was hard to imagine that such an insignificant individual should be engaged in an intrigue, which dealt with war and the rumors of war. He might have been the emissary of an august personage equipped with some portentous sort of authority, but now his mouth was half open, displaying his gold-filled teeth, and his small sharp face was in repose, while Calvin Gates was left, as he had been left before, to make anything he liked of everything which had happened.

Why was he aboard that plane, at all? He was there because he wished to meet a man named Gilbreth and the meeting would ruin him for good. He was there because a girl, whom he had met two days before, and who had no possible claim upon him, might be in difficulty.

If a stranger had come to him and had presented such a case, he would have doubted that stranger's sanity. Yet though he could see himself objectively, logic did nothing to alter the impulses within him which made him face life as though it were a game played by arbitrary and artificial rules. It did no good to realize that he was ruining himself by those rules, even when he could look quite clearly into the future. Before he was finished he would be turned into a shabby sort of adventurer who hung on the outskirts of a disordered world. He was on the road already, watching himself move deliberately along it.

He had the strange feeling of being a partially disembodied spirit, a feeling of being carried rather slowly through the air away from something which had been himself, away from any possible connection with his past or with tradition.

He could see the land below him in a new perspective, much as he saw himself. He had heard so much of the riches of China and of the density of its population that he was surprised by the barren ruggedness of the country. The city of Peiping was growing flat, resolving itself into the mystical plan of its early builders, with the yellow roofs of its Forbidden City and its Imperial lakes and gardens set like a jewel in the center of the streets and walls. From the distance, for the plane was climbing higher, the gates and temples and the Drum Tower and Bell Tower all took on the unity of the conception of a single mind. And then they were over a treeless, bare wilderness of mountains, which rose in successive steps away from the plain. He could see the roofs of temples and villages and palaces, a part of some ancient tradition which was as artificial as his own traditions. The country grew more melancholy and rugged, until he was conscious of nothing but a chaotic mass of mountains, which lay beneath them in misty waves almost like a sea, in dusky reds and purples and yellows. It seemed like a barren land hardly worth a struggle, but men had fought over it since the dawn of history.

Mr. Moto opened his eyes and sat up straight; then he touched Calvin's arm.

"Nankow Pass," Mr. Moto said. He spoke impersonally like a guide from Cook's. "A part of the Great Wall of China—very, very interesting."

The wall stretched beneath them over that hilly country like a snake, in an endless succession of curtains and watch-towers, the last and greatest defense between the capital and the barbarians of the North.

"The older wall is farther north," Mr. Moto said, "by Kalgan. Very, very interesting."

The bare, mountainous country beyond the wall glowed hotly in the clear, bright air, as they passed over it with the deceptive slowness of a plane at a high altitude and, beyond another range toward the horizon, he could see the beginnings of a country that was a yellowish, sandy green. He nudged Mr. Moto and pointed.

"Out here?" Mr. Moto said. "Mongolia. We should reach Kalgan in a few minutes now."

Mr. Moto was nearly right about the time. They had traversed, in hardly more than an hour, a country which had once taken a camel caravan a week to cover.

The plane was losing altitude, descending toward a broad, dusty valley with a rampart of purple hills beyond it. There was a drab-colored city in the valley continually growing clearer—a railroad station, narrow streets, gray-tiled roofs, and large areas enclosed by earthen walls.

"The old compounds," Mr. Moto said, "for the horses and the camels, when the caravans went to Urga. So very interesting." But Calvin was growing weary with unfamiliar sights. Mr. Moto touched his arm again, and pointed out of the window.

"Down there," he said, "is where Captain Hamby will stop when the train comes in—the compound of a company that does business with Mongolia. It is conducted by a gentleman whose name is Mr. Holtz."

Mr. Moto was pointing toward a walled enclosure that looked almost like a fortress. It was toylike from the distance, with figures of men and animals moving behind thick mud walls.

"The Captain stays there always," Mr. Moto said. "Yes—they will be waiting for the cigarette case—so very eager."

His voice was hardly audible because the change of pressure deafened Calvin Gates as the plane descended. They landed in a dusty field which could have been used only for emergencies, but an automobile was waiting for them on the bare brown ground and a dusty, tired-looking Japanese was waiting with it. He spoke to Mr. Moto excitedly while Calvin stood blinking stupidly in the glare of the afternoon sunlight.

"So very nice we got here so quickly," Mr. Moto said. "We shall have an opportunity for a little rest. We are going to the China Hotel, such a nice hotel. Get in the automobile, please."

Calvin did not try to see where they were going, for all sights and sounds had become monotonous and endowed with a peculiar similarity. The hotel consisted of a slatternly courtyard with cell-like rooms that opened off it. An old Chinese in a dirty black gown led them to two narrow, connecting cubicles, each with a bed, a chair and a basin of water, with flies from the courtyard buzzing through open windows.

"This is your room, please," Mr. Moto said. "You will want so much to rest I think. There is nothing to do till sundown, and it will not be nice if you go outside. Make yourself comfortable, please."

Mr. Moto and the Japanese who met them moved into the next room and Calvin Gates listened incuriously to their voices. The buzzing of the flies mingled drowsily with their talk, and the sound made Calvin Gates aware of his own weariness. As he lay down on the narrow bed he felt almost contented. At least he was where he had wished to go. He was very nearly on the edge of no man's land, where civilization as he had known it ended. The city and its walls bore the definite imprint of a Chinese culture but beyond the hills which encircled it he had seen the crumbling mound of China's ancient wall, and there were no more cities beyond that mound, only the yellowish green rolling country, where the plateau of Central Asia began, a space upon which no civilization either of the East or West had made a very permanent imprint. He was at the edge of that blank which Mr. Moto had shown him on the map, over which Japan and Russia both sought to gain control while they eyed each other like wrestlers waiting to come to grips.

It was dusk when he was awakened by a hand grasping his shoulder, and when he opened his eyes, he saw Mr. Moto standing over him.

"So very nice you slept," Mr. Moto said. "I am having tea and sandwiches sent in. It is time you were awake now, please. The train has come. Captain Hamby and Miss Dillaway have arrived."

Calvin Gates stood up, and saw that Mr. Moto's face looked thin and anxious in the dusk. His voice was as soft as ever, but Calvin could detect a vibration of excitement in it.

"You are prepared to do what I told you?" Mr. Moto said.

Calvin Gates looked back at him, but Mr. Moto's expression told him nothing.

"I promised you, didn't I?" he said.

Mr. Moto clasped his hands and bowed.

"It is so nice that I can believe you," he said. "You are like a man in a game of chess. You will just move forward, please."

"Go ahead," said Calvin Gates, "tell me what to do."

"First you will have tea and a sandwich," Mr. Moto said. "You must not be surprised at anything."

"Believe me," said Calvin fervently, "I won't be surprised at anything."

"So glad for you," Mr. Moto said. "There will be a boy waiting for you who will take you to Captain Hamby, please. Captain Hamby will be staying with this merchant who does business with Mongolia. He is Mr. Holtz, part German, part Russian, very fat. Please to remember the name."

"All right," said Calvin, "I'll remember."

"He lives in a place behind great walls," Mr. Moto said. "Matters are so unsettled here that businessmen must protect themselves. You are to go to the main gate; the guide will show you there. You are to beat upon the gate and shout for Captain Hamby. It will be very strange inside, but they will take you to Captain Hamby I think, and then you are to be very frank with Captain Hamby, please, just exactly as I told you, please."

Calvin Gates shrugged his shoulders impatiently.

"You'd better tell me exactly what you want," he said.

"So very glad to tell you," Mr. Moto answered steadily. "Captain Hamby must understand that you have been working for me and that you are finished, please. You have escaped from me. You have heard that he is staying with Mr. Holtz. You do not like me any more, but you have other reasons. You feel there is more money for you by telling him everything that you know about me. You are worried about Miss Dillaway. It will be nice to tell him that, and you must also tell him that white men must stick together. Excuse me, he will understand."

"White men must stick together," Calvin Gates repeated.

Mr. Moto's eyes never left his face.

"You are to tell him particularly that I have full powers over the army, please. It cannot move without me, and be sure to tell him this last. You have just left me at the China Hotel alone. Be sure to tell him that. Are you ready now? You do not look very happy, Mr. Gates."

A watchful look in Mr. Moto's eyes told Calvin Gates that his own expression must have changed, and it was more than an expression; it was a change within himself. He was not the same person who had started on those travels; he was not the same person with whom Mr. Moto had dealt a few hours before. Something had made him see himself entirely differently. Something made his thoughts move erratically, as though he had been awakened from a sleep which had been over him for years. He was very nearly at the end of his journey and yet he was at the parting of some road which lay inside himself.

"Why do you not answer please?" Mr. Moto was saying gently.

But Calvin Gates did not reply. He never knew what sort of person he had been all his life, until he saw himself in that minute's strange illumination; and he saw himself through the ruthless skill of Mr. Moto's mind. No other man had moved him as Mr. Moto had, like a chessman on a board. He had been a marionette that danced while someone pulled the strings; he had never been man enough to seize one of those strings with his own hand and snap it. He heard himself speaking in a thick hushed voice.

"To hell with it," Calvin said.

Mr. Moto's dark eyes grew intent and sharp.

"What?" Mr. Moto asked. "What have you said please?"

"To hell with it," said Calvin Gates. "I am tired of being pushed around."

He could see himself clearly for once. He had prided himself on living by a code and instead he had been moved by loyalty and circumstance, and he had never changed a circumstance. He had drifted aimlessly instead, without applying the independence of his mind to anything in life. He saw himself now in that dingy room with the painful clarity of truth, an ineffective romanticist, and it was Mr. Moto who made him see.

"You can't make me run errands for you." He was speaking, telling the truth to himself at last. "If I wanted to, I could lie and say 'yes,' but I won't lie. I'm not going to be a part of your ideas. I've been a part of somebody's ideas always, and I know where it's got me. By God, I've never given anything a thought. I've acted like someone in a copybook, taking everything that came, and I say to hell with minding your orders, Moto. I'm going out of here right, now, and—so sorry for you if you try to stop me."

"Mr. Gates," said Mr. Moto softly, "I am very much surprised."

"That doesn't bother me," said Calvin Gates. "To hell with you and your Oriental tricks and your majors and your generals, and to hell with Captain Hamby. I told you I would see Hamby, but I won't take your orders. I'm going to do what I want because it suits me not you. I'm going to do what I want for the first time in my life because I want it, and not because it's honorable or suitable."

"My dear Mr. Gates," said Mr. Moto gently, "I think I understand so well."

Calvin took a quick step toward him, but Mr. Moto did not move away.

"There is no need to be impetuous," Mr. Moto said, "because you have discovered something about yourself which was so very obvious. I am here alone, I am not armed. As long as you see Captain Hamby—"

"You heard me," Calvin interrupted him. "To hell with you and Hamby. I'll tell him what I think of you and what I think you're doing, and you can get out of my way right now."

Mr. Moto stood motionless for a moment and then he drew a soft sibilant breath and stepped aside.

"My dear Mr. Gates," he said, "I do not wish to stop you. Excuse me, I might try if I wished, but I am so very happy that you will do what you want. The boy is waiting outside to take you." Mr. Moto paused and smiled. "You see I can only hope that what you want is what I want—so difficult for me."

Calvin Gates scowled at him, but he could not tell whether he liked Mr. Moto or disliked him. He only knew that he understood himself. He was free for a little while at any rate of impulses and inhibitions which had always held him fast.

"I wouldn't be too sure," he said.

## 16

Mr. Moto sighed.

"It is so very interesting," Mr. Moto said, "to see how people change. I am so glad for you that you are changed, Mr. Gates. I am so happy to think that I may have helped you. Always judge what you want, please, Mr. Gates, before you think what you ought to do. Yes, always try to make events do what you wish them. So glad if I have made you understand. I should be so very honored to shake hands. I intend no trick, believe me, please."

"Why can't you be frank with me, Moto?" Calvin asked. "Well, never mind. I didn't think that you'd take things this way."

"So sorry that I cannot be frank," Mr. Moto answered. "But I should like so very much to be friendly. I think you are a nice man, Mr. Gates. I should be so honored to shake hands." And Calvin Gates shook hands with Mr. Moto. A Chinese boy in a plain gray gown was waiting outside the door.

"Follow me, please, master," he said softly, and Calvin followed him through the inn gate into a quiet, dusty street. It had grown cool now that the sun was down and the air was fresh and invigorating. The faint light which was still in the sky made all the buildings shadowy and large, and now the dusky strangeness of China, its sounds and smells, and all the ordinary resilience of its life surrounded him. They walked out of the narrow street into a broad, main thoroughfare with banners in Chinese characters strung above it, and with brightly lighted shops on either side, where cloth vendors chanted in singsong voices. Rickshaw bells rang at him warningly. He heard the tinny blare of a radio and the singing of caged birds. They crossed a small stream where women were washing clothes and then they turned from the shops into another narrow street which was lined again with shadowy walls. At the end of a ten minutes' walk his guide stopped at a corner and pointed toward a huge gate, across a narrow street.

"It is there," he said and then he slipped away leaving Calvin Gates gazing at a high mud wall which stretched into the shadows as far as he could see. There was nothing near him but those windowless walls, no light or sign of life, and the gate with a small door for pedestrians cut in one side was like the entrance to a fortress. It all was like some street in the Middle Ages when nearly every house was a stronghold prepared against attack.

He pulled at a string that hung near the door and he heard the deep, sonorous ringing of a bell, and, in answer, a wicket in the door slid open. The darkness in the street, for the light was waning rapidly, made it impossible for him to see anything of the face at the wicket except the glint of eyes. A voice called something to him, and Calvin called back loudly.

"Hamby," he called, "Captain Hamby!" And then he thought of

something else that might have significance and added: "Holtz. Ghuru Nor."

When he called to that unseen face at the wicket he had the feeling of shouting in space, a feeling that became a conviction when the opening was slid shut. He seized the rope again and pulled and pulled, and the insistent clatter of the bell chimed in with his anger at himself and at all the net of words and actions which had caught him. Before he knew what he was doing he found himself kicking at the door, and when his foot came in contact with the wood, the door opened inward so suddenly that he nearly lost his balance. He stumbled into a world which was entirely strange.

He was standing in a long, vaulted passage which opened into a dim, open space beyond, large enough to be the parade ground of a fort. The passage was lighted by torches set in brackets, like the torches of some castle gate. On either side of it was a room, carved out of the thick mud wall, and both the chambers glowed with a yellow, uncertain light. The place was reeking with the smell of burning oil from the torches and with the odors of sheep tallow and of rancid butter. In one of the rooms, some heavy men stripped to the waist were putting fuel under a huge caldron where a mutton stew was boiling. The room across the passage was filled with men sitting on their heels, eating with their fingers and chopsticks out of small round bowls. He had a confused glimpse in that flickering light of dark, greasy faces with high cheekbones and flat noses, of oily pigtails and greasy hats, of longsleeved robes and sashes, of silver amulets and of knives in silver scabbards, and of heavy boots with curved pointed toes. That first glimpse was like a picture out of focus, but it was enough to show him that he had stepped from an ancient, meticulous civilization into a barbarous world, that the gate through which he had passed had opened into Tartary and he was gazing at a group of Mongolians enjoying their evening meal.

He saw those sights only for an instant out of the corner of his eye because his immediate attention was given to two men in front of him. The first was a tall man in a long-sleeved robe with a silver knife in his belt and with heavy boots with up-turned toes, who stood grinning, showing a set of fine white teeth. The second man was more easy to comprehend; when one first saw him he might have seemed someone from a New York street on a hot summer night. He was a very fat German with a shaven head, in slippers, trousers and a shirt that was open at the neck. His heavy paunch shook comfortably when he moved. His small eyes peered through rolls of flesh that fell in heavy jowls around his jaw. His shaven head and his face were glowing with perspiration, and before he spoke he mopped his forehead with a blue bandanna handkerchief.

"Vell," he said. His voice was guttural and was small for his enormous weight. "I'm Holtz. Vat do you want yelling and kicking at the compound gate? Business hours is in the daytime. Vat do you want?"

"I want to speak to Hamby," Calvin Gates said, "Captain Sam Hamby. He came here when he got off the train." Mr. Holtz rubbed his handkerchief hard across his forehead and shouted something at the top of his lungs which made everyone stop talking.

"These Gott verdammt camel drivers," he said. "They will never shut up. You want to see Captain Hamby? Vy do you want to see Captain Hamby? Vat brought you here to see Captain Hamby?"

"I come from Mr. Moto," Calvin Gates said. "I want to see Hamby right away, it's important."

The fat man grunted and his eyes glittered above the pouches of flesh that nearly covered them. His corpulence had not made him good-natured. His mouth was small and his nose like a soft button dividing the expanse of his pinkish cheeks; but he was not good-natured. He spoke to the tall Mongol beside him in a voice which sounded like a high-pitched snarl. The Mongol turned and clattered away in his heavy boots with a horseman's swaying gait, and Mr. Holtz moved his half-concealed eyes back to Calvin.

"All right," he said, "I send to get him. To hell mit these Japanese. They crawl around like sand-fleas. It was bad enough before with war lords, and now come the Japanese." Mr. Holtz spat and grunted. "It gives me a pain in the belly," he added, "one big pain in the belly." Mr. Holtz was not a pre-possessing man, but at any rate Calvin could understand him. He was with one of his own sort again, who was devoid of Mr. Moto's subtlety.

"What is this place?" Calvin asked.

The small lips of Mr. Holtz opened slightly and he emitted a breathing, whistling sound. "It must be so," he said. "So it's your first time out here? You have that look. You are in the compound of Holtz and Company, the same which does business with Mongolia.

Ask 'em in Peiping who Holtz is. Ask 'em in Tientsin and Shanghai. Holtz buys everything, every damn thing in Central Asia—wool, antelope horn, wolf hide, Scythian bronze, gold dust, camels, horses, rugs. Holtz is loading camels next week with brick tea, leather goods and textiles. It's damn funny if you never heard of Holtz, my friend."

"It's new to me," said Calvin Gates.

"So," said Mr. Holtz, and it was difficult to decide whether he was genial or sneering.

"New to you, is it? Well, the caravan business is the oldest in the world. It's so antique that it was old when Marco Polo came across the routes. And it's new to you, is it? Well, so what! I think you got a lot to learn from Holtz and Company. Maybe you don't like what you learn when we do business? Huh?"

Mr. Holtz's eyes twinkled icily and his fingers twitched at hs waistband.

"It's interesting," said Calvin Gates politely, and Mr. Holtz exhaled another breath.

"So," he said imitating Calvin's voice. "It's interesting is it, to see a lot of Mongol camel drivers, lousy Mongol camel drivers, who haven't washed since they were born, swallowing their supper? Huh? Here is Excellency, Captain Hamby. Interesting? What?"

Captain Hamby walked into the archway from the dim space outside. He walked with a brisk, businesslike step, evidently completely at home, while the Mongol who had gone to fetch him rolled and clumped behind him. Captain Hamby was bareheaded and the light of the torches glinted from his hard gray eyes as he walked forward smiling.

"While you've a lucifer to light your fag," he was humming, "smile, boys, that's the style." And then his song stopped and he looked sharply first at Mr. Holtz and then at Calvin Gates.

"Well, well, well," said Captain Hamby, "only fancy this now. How'd you get here, Gates?"

"By plane," said Calvin Gates.

"Well, well, well," said Captain Hamby, "fancy that." He walked up to Calvin Gates still smiling at him. "And you came here to see me, did you, Gates? And you've met Mr. Holtz? You couldn't have done better. What can I do for you, Gates?"

"I'd like to speak to you," said Calvin Gates, "alone, for about five minutes."

Captain Hamby's face was hard and beaming. "That's fine," he said, "that's fine. A bit busy, but there's always time for a five minutes' chat. Mr. Holtz, this is my acquaintance, Mr. Gates—the one I was telling you about. Shake hands."

Mr. Holtz held out a heavy hand.

"Pleased to meet you, Mr. Gates," he said.

Mr. Holtz was fat but he was very strong. Before Calvin even suspected Mr. Holtz had snatched his hand and had jerked Calvin forward. The next instant Mr. Holtz's arms were around him tight, pressing him against his bulbous, perspiring body.

"Well," Mr. Holtz was saying, "nice to make your acquaintance, what?"

"All right, Holtz," Captain Hamby called.

The arms around Calvin Gates relaxed and Mr. Holtz stepped backwards. Captain Hamby was looking at them grinning. The pistol which had been in Calvin's side pocket was now in Captain Hamby's hand.

"No hard feelings, Gates," Captain Hamby said, "and don't blame Mr. Holtz. My word, he's just all heart. Just take it with a smile, Gates. So you want to have a talk with me?"

Calvin Gates looked from Mr. Holtz to Captain Hamby, and he took it with a smile.

"I'm not fool enough to start shooting here," he said. "I didn't come for that. I've just left Mr. Moto."

Captain Hamby's eyelids flickered. His short square figure was motionless.

"Moto sent you, did he?" he inquired.

"Yes," said Calvin Gates, "and I'm going to tell you why." He glanced around him and back at Captain Hamby's hard, expectant face. Captain Hamby was balancing the automatic in his hand.

"That's fine," he said. "You come along with me." And Captain Hamby put his arm through Calvin's.

"What's the use of worrying," Captain Hamby was humming, "it never was worth while. Tell 'em to wait till I get back, Holtz. Tell the Prince I won't be long."

They walked from under the archway into a huge compound. The last faint light of early evening still fell upon that open space, and the light was broken by the orange glow of torches and lanterns where men were working in the cool, evening air, packing articles into bales and boxes. The place was so unbelievable that Calvin Gates stopped to look. The whole center of the square was filled with camels, row upon row of camels sitting side by side with their long necks arched above their double humps.

"I never saw anything like that," said Calvin Gates.

"No?" Captain Hamby said. "You won't see anything like this a few years from now. It's one of Holtz's caravans, seven hundred of 'em. They're still working on the loads, baling up the brick tea and odds and ends. Holtz wants to get 'em moving off before there's any trouble. Funny-looking beggars, aren't they? Don't get near enough so they can get their teeth in you. A camel's bite can be deuced dangerous. The warehouses are over yonder. It's like loading up a freight train once they load those camels, and the beggars are in good condition too. Look at the humps, all good fat. They'll march six days without food or water; slow, but my word, they're useful where they're going—greatest sight in the world, Gates, something to remember if you come through this."

Calvin walked across the square beside Captain Hamby, as though he were a visitor being taken on a tour, past sweating groups of Chinese who wrapped up tea which had been pressed into large slabs for greater ease in transport, past heaps of embroidered, curved-toed riding boots, past bales of textiles and piles of copper utensils, past the open doors of warehouses stacked high with furs and wool.

"What do you mean by that last remark?" Calvin asked.

Captain Hamby had been humming, and now his humming stopped.

"My word," said Captain Hamby, "you put your neck out, didn't you? Walk on, we're in a hurry. The living quarters are over here."

Still arm and arm, they continued past the warehouses to a group of neat white buildings at the far corner of the compound, the door of one of which Captain Hamby pushed open. It was an office brightly lighted by a gasoline lantern, evidently where the business of Mr. Holtz was transacted. It was strange after the sights outside to be in a room with ledgers and tables and adding machines, and Captain Hamby must have understood Calvin's surprise.

"Holtz's office," he said. "It takes a bit of figuring to run this show." The hard light made the Captain's face jovially harsh. "Well," he said, "go on and talk. Now what's the game, Gates?"

Captain Hamby grew brisk and businesslike and everything

about him was genial except the cool glow in his eye. He stood with his hands on his hips, his feet wide apart.

Calvin Gates looked back at him and answered promptly.

"He brought me up here," he admitted, "but I've come here because I want to. I've come here to make you a proposition, Hamby."

Captain Hamby's eyes narrowed, but he still looked friendly.

"That's fine," he answered cordially. "So you thought over what I said on the train? Well, what's your propositon?"

It had seemed simple when he had thought of it, but now he was not so sure.

"A while ago," said Calvin Gates, "you offered me money to tell you what Mr. Moto wanted. I didn't know then, Hamby, but I know now. Is your proposition still open?"

Captain Hamby rubbed his hand softly on his coat.

"So you're tired of playing with the Japanese?" Captain Hamby said. "You figure there's more for you in it this way? Is that the picture, Gates?"

"That's the picture," Calvin answered. "I am going to get what I want out of this, Hamby, and you can give it to me and Mr. Moto can't."

It sounded brutally frank as he said it and it showed him how greatly he had changed. All his old compunctions had left him. Mr. Moto had used him and now he was using Mr. Moto. For the first time in his life he was changing circumstances to fit his own desires.

"My word," said Captain Hamby, "that's the sort of talk I like. What is it you want of me, Gates?"

"Nothing that ought to trouble you," Calvin said. "I want you to take me to Dr. Gilbreth. I've come a long way to see him. And I want you to promise that Miss Dillaway is put into Dr. Gilbreth's care. And I want you to arrange that I stay safe with you until this trouble's over. China and Japan won't be healthy for me after this. I'm coming over to your side, Hamby."

"Oh," said Captain Hamby, "I thought you didn't trust me, Gates."

"I don't," said Calvin, "about most things. But I see no reason why you shouldn't do this, because it isn't going to help you not to do it, and it isn't going to cause you trouble. There isn't any other place for me to go. Maybe I'll be useful to you, Hamby."

Captain Hamby nodded thoughtfully.

"You wouldn't lie to me, Gates?" he asked. "My word, if you're lying, you won't live."

Calvin shrugged his shoulders.

"I wouldn't be here if I were lying," he said, "and you know it."

Captain Hamby smiled brightly.

"You must want to see this Dr. Gilbreth a hell of a lot," he remarked. "What's the idea, Gates?"

"That's my business," Calvin answered.

Captain Hamby chuckled softly; he did not appear to be offended.

"Well, well," he said. "Don't be so touchy, Gates. You're talking the way I like a man to talk. Right in my own language. You tell me what Moto wants, and I'll know if it's the truth or not, no fear. And if it is the truth—" Captain Hamby grinned and held out his hand. "I'll do what you want, word of honor, Gates. You'll see Gilbreth, and Miss Dillaway will be put in Gilbreth's care, and you'll come up along with me, and everything is fine. I know how to keep a promise, Gates, no fear. Now what does Moto want? Shake hands."

Their hands met and Captain Hamby's grasp was firm and hard.

"No fear, Gates," Captain Hamby said.

"All right," said Calvin Gates, "I'm going to trust you, Hamby. Mr. Moto's after you."

Captain Hamby rubbed the palms of his hands carefully on the sides of his coat.

"Is that a fact?" he said.

"He wants to get you to the China Hotel," Calvin said. "He wanted me to make it clear to you that he's alone there, but I don't believe it. He's after something, Hamby. He's able to run the whole Japanese army if he wants. I've seen him give orders to a general."

Captain Hamby swung back and forth on his heels. "Smile," he hummed, "smile, smile." And Calvin felt his eyes move over him, examining his clothes and his hands and feet.

"I don't want to be a party to a murder," Calvin said. "Moto's strong on liquidation, Hamby."

Captain Hamby teetered from his toes to his heels and back.

"Damned considerate of you," Captain Hamby said. "My word, I'd never thought of that. Are you telling me he's out from Tokyo and that he's giving orders to the army? My word, I've seen him do that once before. Has he got papers on him? Tell me what you saw, Gates."

Calvin told him while Captain Hamby teetered on his heels and listened.

"My word," said Captain Hamby, "he's got full powers, has he?" He stopped and began humming his favorite tune. "What's the use of worrying," Captain Hamby hummed, "it never was worth while . . . My word, you're selling out too cheap. You're either a fool or a damned liar, Gates."

"You can take your choice," Calvin answered.

"I will," said Captain Hamby. "You'll get what you want if it's true. Just step along with me now. Just keep smiling." Captain Hamby linked his arm through Calvin's. "Don't get jumpy, Gates."

"Well," said Calvin, "where are we going?"

"My word," said Captain Hamby, "no need to be so curious. You've been so deuced interesting that I want you to meet more company. Mr. Holtz and the Prince are over yonder. What you have said may change things quite a bit. Now don't get jumpy, Gates."

"What Prince?" asked Calvin Gates.

They were walking toward a brightly lighted building not far from the one they had left and Captain Hamby's hand tightened on Calvin's arm.

"No end obliged to you," he said, "for telling me all this. Puts a fascinating new complexion on matters. What Prince? My dear esteemed patron, Prince Wu of Ghuru Nor. He just came in last night to meet me. You saw some of his laddies by the gate eating mutton. Jolly sort of fellow, the Prince, the sharpest trader I ever knew. Steady's the word for it. Take things as they come and smile."

"Where's Miss Dillaway?" asked Calvin Gates.

"She's all right," said Captain Hamby, "right as rain. Don't get jumpy, Gates."

## 17

SOMEONE IN front of the doorway called out sharply, and when the Captain answered a Mongol carrying a rifle stepped out from the shadows.

"The Prince's guard," said Captain Hamby, "one of my boys. Never seen better soldiers. Well, here's Holtzy's house. Does himself rather well. No need of knocking, not a bit of need."

The house was one of those uncompromising, English bungalows, the architectural qualities of which do not vary much, no matter in what part of the world one finds them. Captain Hamby led him into a broad living room furnished with a number of comfortable chairs. He had a glimpse of a table covered with magazines, and of a wall covered with photographs. The room and its furnishings, all so familiar and commonplace, made the people in it the more remarkable. Seated in an oak mission chair, beside a table with a lamp upon it, was a middle-aged man whose whole appearance marked him as an exalted person. His hair was done up tight in a grayish black queue. His cheekbones were high and his dark brown eyes were so narrow that they seemed to be creased in a smile when he was not smiling. His cheeks were gaunt and sunken and a long thin, grayish moustache curled delicately past the corners of a proud, thin mouth. There was no doubt that Calvin was looking at the prince of Ghuru Nor. He was in a gown of turquoise blue, and the pointed toes of his high boots curved upward. He sat erect with a hand resting on each knee, like an ancestral portrait from the Manchu dynasty. Behind his chair were two Mongols, each leaning on a rifle, and a third, a thin pockmarked young man, crouched on his heels at the Prince's right. Mr. Holtz, still in his shirt sleeves, was seated near by drinking a glass of beer, and at the other end of the room four or five more of the Prince's retinue were standing: shiny-faced, glossy-haired young men, leaning on their rifles; but these were not all.

A man in white, seated in a chair near the Prince, had turned to look when the door had opened, and Calvin Gates remembered his face. It was Major Ahara with the saber scars upon his cheek. Major Ahara's heavy mouth had fallen open, and he was starting to rise from his chair.

"Sit down, Major," Captain Hamby said. "Surprised to see this gentleman, aren't you? Your Excellency—this is the American of whom I told you."

The Prince's eyes moved toward Calvin Gates and he nodded.

"I speak English," he said very slowly. "It is all we here can speak together. You go to join Dr. Gilbreth—he did not speak of you."

The slow voice stopped, but not long enough to allow Calvin to answer.

"What is it you want?" the Prince said to Captain Hamby. "We have been waiting."

"Your Highness." The Captain spoke both respectfully and familiarly, like a trusted advisor. "The matter of the cigarette case, Your Highness—it is my advice not to sell it yet."

Major Ahara was leaning forward in his chair listening.

"This Japanese officer has made us a generous offer for it," the Captain went on, "but a situation has arisen. This American has come from Mr. Moto. We must be careful, Your Highness. Mr. Moto is above the army."

The blank expression of the Prince showed plainly that his command of English was not good. He did not understand, but the Japanese major understood, and something in the careful speech caused him to jump to his feet.

"That is not so," the Major cried. "Moto has nothing to do with this, nothing to do with the army!"

Captain Hamby turned on him quickly and spoke in his loud, unmusical voice.

"Sit down," he said. "You Japanese are all alike, always so damn clever. You came here to buy that cigarette case. You flew here from Peiping. We didn't ask you here. Sit down and keep still."

Captain Hamby turned towards Mr. Holtz, who had set his glass of beer upon the floor, and jerked his thumb toward Calvin Gates.

"Holtz, you've got sense," Captain Hamby said. "This man, Gates, Moto sent him. Moto—the one who was here before—and he's in the China Hotel. Well, I'm going out to find him. Moto's been sent direct from Tokyo to give the order to the army. My word he has—and we can't let this go."

Mr. Holtz pursed his lips.

"These Japanese," he said. "My dear friend, it is a trap—perhaps."

Captain Hamby grinned.

"It won't be a trap," he said, "if I bring a handful of my boys."

Mr. Holtz rubbed his hand across his mouth.

"You don't ever stop, my friend," he said, "when there's money."

"Righto," said Captain Hamby. "Too right." He whirled around to Calvin Gates. "He was alone, last you saw of him, wasn't he?"

"Yes," said Calvin Gates, "he was alone."

"My friend," said Mr. Holtz, "I should be careful. Why should our dear friend Mr. Gates be here with such a story?"

Captain Hamby grinned.

"Because Moto couldn't come here himself," he answered. "Bloodthirsty devils, the Japanese. Like as not Moto knows he'd be assassinated if he showed his nose in the street. It's their army and their conservatives fighting. Subtle little beggars, the Japanese, always doing things hind end before. He doesn't want Ahara to get that cigarette case. My word, Moto's got some scheme."

Major Ahara pulled himself out of his chair a second time.

"It has nothing to do with the present situation," Major Ahara said. "Mr. Moto is a very bad man, very dangerous. Remember, if you please, the Japanese army will control this country in a very little while. The Prince will do well to respect the Japanese army. It will be better for everyone. I am offering a price for that cigarette case—ten thousand dollars gold—and a further sum for immediate occupation of Ghuru Nor—"

Captain Hamby's grin grew broader. He was evidently enjoying the situation, and the blank expression of the Prince, the sly watchfulness of Mr. Holtz. He was reading something between the lines and Calvin was more sure than ever that Hamby was no fool.

"You're offering money because you couldn't get it any other way," Captain Hamby said. "My word, you tried."

The Major's face twisted with a sudden spasm of temper. Although he controlled his facial muscles, his eyes were glowing.

"It will be better for you to take my offer," he said. "There are other things that I may do."

"Is that a threat?" Captain Hamby asked.

"Yes," the Major said in his guttural English, "that is a threat."

Captain Hamby laughed.

"My word," he said, "you Japanese johnnies are getting insolent. You're talking to a white man, Major—to an army officer, and a damned sight better one than you'll ever be. I don't give sixpence halfpenny for your army. Maybe we'll sell you that cigarette case and maybe we won't. Sit down, Major. We haven't talked to Russia yet."

Major Ahara did not sit down.

"I shall leave here at once," he said.

"Oh no you won't," said Captain Hamby. "You'll sit down and take it easy, Major."

The Major glanced about the room, shrugged his shoulders and sat down, but his eyes never left Captain Hamby's face.

"You are making a very great mistake," he said. "You insult the Japanese army."

Captain Hamby did not appear impressed; neither did the Prince, who still sat with his clawlike hands resting on his turquoise knees, nor Mr. Holtz who had folded his hands across his stomach.

"To hell with the Japanese army," Captain Hamby said. "Two Russian army corps would whip you."

Mr. Holtz raised a hand and dropped it limply on his knee.

"My dear friend," he said, "there is no reason to be insulting. Major Ahara is a nice gentleman. He has offered as a sum of money, not much, but he may offer more, and you are keeping us all waiting. What is it that you wish to do?"

Captain Hamby stepped up to Mr. Holtz and leaned over his chair.

"We don't go ahead," said Captain Hamby slowly, "until I see Moto."

"My friend!" expostulated Mr. Holtz.

"Wait a minute," said Captain Hamby. "Listen to me." And he leaned forward and whispered.

The whisper made the heavy body of Mr. Holtz grow taut and his eyes move forward through the wrinkles in his face like a crab's.

"My friend," said Mr. Holtz, "I never thought of that. No, you never stop where there is money. You had better tell the Prince."

"I'll tell him," said Captain Hamby. "His Highness is a sporting gentleman."

Then Captain Hamby spoke to the Prince in a tongue which was neither Chinese nor Japanese and the Prince answered in sharp interrogation. Captain Hamby looked back at Mr. Holtz.

"I told you," he said, "His Highness was a sporting gentleman."

Mr. Holtz moved restlessly and the chair creaked beneath his weight.

"I do not like it, Captain Hamby. Why do you trust our dear friend, Mr. Gates? Why do you think he tells the truth?"

Until his name was mentioned, Calvin had not realized how absorbed he had been. He had been trying hard to piece together what was behind the words.

"I'll take a chance on his telling the truth," Captain Hamby said. "Moto's alone at the China Hotel, isn't that right, Gates?"

"I told you he was," said Calvin Gates, "and I told you it's a trap."

"That's fine," said Captain Hamby, "that's just fine. You wouldn't be fooling me, would you, Gates? I'm depending a lot on your word. I'm going up to the China Hotel, and if I'm not back here in an hour, you're going to be shot."

"What are you talking about?" said Calvin Gates.

Captain Hamby looked at him hard.

"If I'm not back here in an hour it will mean you haven't told the truth, and you're going to be shot. We haven't time to be gentle tonight."

Calvin Gates glanced across the room and met the Prince's smiling eyes.

"Are you trying to frighten me?" Calvin asked.

"My word no," said Captain Hamby, "I'm just giving you the facts. You're in the middle of a serious business conference. The Prince is trying to decide whether to sell out to Russia or Japan. If I don't come back you won't be alive to know it. Anything you want to say? It's a fair proposition, isn't it?"

"And suppose you do come back?" said Calvin Gates.

Captain Hamby laughed.

"That's the way to talk," he said. "I've always liked you, Gates. My word, if I come back, you won't lose. The Prince will give you a cut-in, and I'll let you out to see the fun and I'll keep my promise. You only have to wait an hour." The Prince had pushed himself out of his chair and was standing, a gaunt, oldish man in a silk gown, leaning an arm on the shoulder of the attendant who had crouched beside him.

"Easy," said Captain Hamby, "don't get jumpy, Gates. I don't want to see Mr. Moto. I want to bring him here alive, and I'll get him if you've been accurate. Anything you want to say?"

Calvin Gates did not answer. Major Ahara shouted something and two of the Prince's guard seized him by the shoulders and pushed him back into his chair. The Prince called out an order and two more of the oily-faced men walked toward Calvin Gates.

"Take it easy, Gates," said Captain Hamby. "They're only going to lock you up. Take it easy, Gates."

Hands were on his arms and he was being pushed towards the door.

"While you've a lucifer to light your fag," Captain Hamby was humming, "smile, smile, smile."

Captain Hamby's humming stopped and his voice made the two guards who were escorting Calvin pause curiously.

"Just one thing while I'm gone, Holtz," Captain Hamby said. "You'd better get General Shirov and test the wireless. Tell Shirov we've got two Japanese. We'll have to settle this tonight."

A hoarse cry from Major Ahara interrupted him.

"You will not dare to do this," the Major shouted. "I will not stay here to face a Russian. You gave your word that this would be confidential."

"Well, well," said Captain Hamby and he looked both surprised and hurt. "Haven't you Japanese ever broken your words? You're talking to Captain Sam Hamby, who is negotiating for Prince Wu of Ghuru Nor. The Prince knows that he has to sell out to the wrong party and have his land overrun by the other party's army. We're going to get this matter settled once for all, right here tonight. We don't want any mistakes."

"There will be no mistake," said Major Ahara earnestly. "When I leave here I can assure you that orders will be given to occupy Ghuru Nor."

"That's fine," said Captain Hamby, "fine—when you leave here."

If Major Ahara made any response, Calvin Gates did not hear it, because his guards led him out of doors. Both of his arms were gripped tight, but the guards were not rough. He walked silently between them across a corner of the compound toward one of the warehouses which were built against the wall.

He was thinking of what Captain Hamby had said—that anything could happen in China; and now he was sure of it. If he had not seen it he would not have believed it possible that Captain Hamby or anyone else would dare to make such an attempt. It had the effrontery of banditry and the skill of diplomacy. Captain Hamby and the Prince of Ghuru Nor had made the camel compound into a small armed camp with Mr. Holtz to help them, and now in that temporary security they were estimating with whom it might be safer to deal, with Russia or Japan. A feeble Mongol chieftain was balancing two great powers, one against the other, a dangerous enough game and Calvin admired the Captain's skill. Undoubtedly he had been negotiating with both those powers, and now he was holding that cigarette case before them, watching as they both reached towards it. Calvin would have enjoyed that game of wits if he were not involved in it, but the guards walking beside him and the aura of grease and smoke which came from them reminded him that he was not a spectator, but a hostage for Captain Hamby's safety. Although it would do no good to kill him, there was a primitive sort of justice about the idea which would appeal to the Prince of Ghuru Nor.

They were leading him toward the closed door of a warehouse where a sentry stood with a rifle. One of his guards spoke a word of explanation. Then the door was shoved open a crack and Calvin Gates was pushed into an empty barnlike room, lighted with a single horn lantern which hung from the rafters. As the door slammed shut behind him he had an impression of a dry, strong smell of wool and of half-cured hides. He blinked for a moment at the feeble yellow light before he realized that he was not alone, and then he saw that he had nearly reached the end of his journey. He blinked again and cleared his throat.

"Hello, Dillaway," he said.

## 18

MISS DILLAWAY had been sitting on a packing box, and now she was on her feet hurrying toward him.

"Calvin," she called, "Calvin Gates!"

He knew that she was glad to see him and she was not angry any more, but what surprised him was his own pleasure at seeing her. It was as though nothing else mattered. Something about her made his heart pound in his throat. She was not even pretending that she was not glad to see him. She had forgotten to be brisk and casual, just as she had forgotten once before.

"Hello, Dillaway," he said again. "I've come to get you out of this."

"Have you?" she answered. "You're the only one I know who'd be fool enough to try." But the edge had left her voice. At first he thought she was laughing at him, and then he saw she was not.

"I'm afraid," she said, "I've been so damned afraid."

"It's going to be all right," said Calvin. "We'll get out of here. Nobody's going to hurt you. It might be a whole lot worse."

"I've been so damned afraid," Miss Dillaway said, "and I don't like it, and I wouldn't admit it to anybody else but you, and I suppose you're pleased."

The old sharpness was returning to her voice, but still he felt contented, because it told him that he had brought her confidence. She had as good as admitted that there was something in those qualities of his which she had ridiculed.

"I'm awfully glad to see you," Calvin said. "I never knew I'd be so glad."

His remark sounded futile. He reached toward her and touched her shoulder.

"Dillaway," he began, "if we ever get out of this—"

She pushed his hand away, but she held it tight for a moment.

"If we ever get out of this, I'm going to keep an eye on you," she said. "You need some sort of a guardian. I've been hearing about you, Gates. Don't you see who's in here with us? Don't you see Dr. Gilbreth?"

He had not noticed anyone else since he had set eyes on her, but now he saw a short, stocky man standing near them in a rumpled gray suit.

"Hello, Gilbreth," he said, "what are you doing here?" He was scarcely surprised, because nothing any longer surprised him, but there was the man whom he had traveled halfway around the world to meet, and whose face had not been wholly out of his memory for a long time. Somehow he had expected it to be changed, but there it was exactly as it had been in the past, and not such a very distant past either. There was Dr. Gilbreth, the eminent scholar, the lecturer and explorer, staring at him and making the past the present. There was the same long nose, the same thin grayish hair, the same long, weak, and studious mouth, and Calvin Gates had his old sense of amazement as to what a girl who was young and good-looking could ever have seen in such a man. He certainly did not look well then. He was no longer a dinner guest, talking about his travels; he was dirty and haggard and his face was covered with a stubble of beard.

"What am I doing here?" he said. "I'm in a den of thieves, and so are you—in case you don't know it. The Prince—have you seen the Prince?—have you seen Captain Hamby? They're holding the whole expedition up for ransom. They've made me cable for funds. I'm going down with Hamby to the bank to draw them tomorrow morning. Don't ask me if there isn't anything else I can do. There isn't except to pay up and get out. There isn't any way to get help. There isn't anything. It isn't any joke, Gates. The Prince means business."

"I guess he does," said Calvin. "He seems like a very remarkable man."

"He means business," said Dr. Gilbreth. "I thought I knew how to handle the natives. Everything was quiet enough in Mongolia two years ago and now it's anarchy. What did they throw you in here for, Gates?"

Calvin Gates shrugged his shoulders.

"It's Captain Hamby's idea," he said. "It looks as though the American flag won't do much good tonight, but I'm grateful to Hamby just the same. I wanted to see you, Gilbreth, and he promised I would. He's kept that part of his promise."

Dr. Gilbreth looked surprised. He looked at Calvin Gates and looked away.

"I don't understand you," he said. "You're not serious when you say you came all this way to see me personally. Wouldn't a letter or a cable have done just as well?"

"I don't think so," Calvin Gates answered. He was reaching the point at last and with it the end of his journey. Yet now that it was time to speak he had his old desire to remain silent. "It's a delicate matter," he said. "It concerns our family. You can help us, Dr. Gilbreth."

Dr. Gilbreth looked puzzled. Calvin wondered if the Doctor understood. He was trying to think of some method of putting everything delicately, but he could think of none.

"You mean your family sent you out to see me?" Dr. Gilbreth asked. "I don't understand. There was absolutely nothing—"

"I don't blame you for being surprised," said Calvin Gates. "We're such a long way from where we started, aren't we? It's hard to think back that far. They didn't send me, I came out myself."

"But why?" said Dr. Gilbreth. "I don't understand why."

Calvin Gates hesitated, still trying to choose words.

"Please excuse me for being so slow," he said. "It's rather hard to talk about. I'd give a good deal if I didn't have to. When you were raising funds for your expedition out here, we were all interested, you remember." He paused. It was not necessary to go into the details, because there was no doubt that Dr. Gilbreth remembered a good deal more than had been mentioned.

"You can't do things like this without money," Dr. Gilbreth said.

"I know," Calvin Gates agreed. "I don't criticize you. I'm not blaming you—for being interesting."

Dr. Gilbreth looked embarrassed.

"Go ahead, Gates," he said. "I know you're talking about that check."

"How do you know," Calvin asked, "that I'm talking about a check? Have you heard anything about it?"

"Never mind," said Dr. Gilbreth. "I want to know what you're getting at."

"All right," said Calvin, and his own voice reflected the other's impatience. "My cousin, Bella Gates, gave you a check as a contribution to your funds. I wish it hadn't been so large, but it was, ten thousand dollars. She got it for you because you said you needed that money very badly."

"I wish I hadn't put the thing so strongly," Dr. Gilbreth said. "I never intended—"

"Never mind about that," said Calvin. "I'm not criticizing and there's no reason to come to personalities. I don't care what she said to you, or what you said to her. She gave you a check for your expedition which was signed by her father. He's my uncle, Dr. Gilbreth, and I think a great deal of him. I'd like you to remember that. That check was honored by the bank. It's no concern of yours at all." He paused again. He did not like to appeal to Dr. Gilbreth or to anybody else, and he went straight ahead, no longer trying to choose his words.

"On the first of the month when the vouchers came in, that check was found to be a forgery, and that's why I'm here. I announced that I had forged that check before I left." He paused again and cleared his throat. "It came as rather of a shock, and now it looks as though the bank has taken the matter out of the family's hands. The authorities are investigating. You're certain to be asked questions because you know more about the circumstances. It's a delicate matter. We think a good deal of the family and my uncle brought me up, and he's had to put up with a good deal from me. When you are questioned I want you to say that I am the only one who could have forged that check. I can give you all the details, but I want you to be positive."

He waited, but Dr. Gilbreth did not answer, and Calvin Gates continued.

"You told us you couldn't be reached by cable for three or four weeks at a time," he said, "and I hope you were correct. When I left to come here I thought this whole business would be a skeleton in the family closet and the least said the better. Something must have happened back home. It seems this isn't the first time that there's been a forgery. I only found out the other day that the police at home were looking for me. It made it all the more important that I should see you. I didn't think the old man would do anything like that. He must have lost his temper. You have been out of touch, haven't you? You haven't heard anything about it? I'm taking my medicine for this, and I want to be sure I take it. From everything I've seen, they don't bother much about forgers here."

Dr. Gilbreth was blankly silent. He started to speak and checked himself, and stared at Calvin Gates as though he had encountered an entirely new member of the human species.

"But you didn't," he said. "I know you didn't forge it and I know who did."

The time and the place made no difference now that he and Dr. Gilbreth were face to face. He was living again in a world which he was leaving forever, where nothing had mattered much but manners and security.

He was living through a good part of his past in the silence that followed. His mind moved through days and nights that were irrevocably gone before he answered.

"You're mistaken," said Calvin, "I did it," and then he added a remark which might have been inconsequential if both of them had not understood. "She was crazy about you, Gilbreth."

Dr. Gilbreth still looked at him as though he were an unknown type of human being excavated from the ruins of some vanished civilization.

"I don't understand you." Dr. Gilbreth's voice was embarrassed and incredulous. "I'm damned if I understand what you want. It's embarrassing to me. No matter how you look at it, there's going to be talk, but it had nothing to do with you. Do you mean to stand here seriously and tell me that you came out to this God-forsaken place in order to get me to help you to ruin yourself? There's no one alive who would do such a fool thing as that. I won't believe it. I can't believe it, Gates."

Miss Dillaway's voice chimed in suddenly.

"Well, I believe it," she said. "It's just the sort of thing he would do. It's just the sort of chance you'd jump at, isn't it, Gates?"

He had not intended anyone to hear that conversation. When all his motives were analyzed by an outside mind they appeared almost ludicrous, and besides it was a matter between himself and his own conscience. Now that he had spoken to Gilbreth, he had committed himself once and for all. He had been tempted not to, ever since he had seen Miss Dillaway, but he had spoken.

"This is something you don't know anything about," he said. "For once in my life I've finished something I started."

"Oh yes, I understand," said Miss Dillaway. "We were talking about you, Gates."

Dr. Gilbreth's face was still incredulous.

"But you haven't any motive for doing such a thing," he said. "You didn't even like her. You two hardly spoke."

"Does it make any difference?" Calvin answered. "That's entirely up to me. I did it for the old man, if you want to know. I don't amount to much back home, but I think a lot of him. It's better this way."

There was a silence, as though no one could find an answer, and the silence was so long that Calvin spoke again.

"I suppose you think I'm a fool," he said, "but it doesn't matter. After all, that's up to me. It's the first positive thing I've ever done. That's something."

He had said as little as possible, for it was a subject which did not bear discussion, and yet he had an uncomfortable feeling that he had said everything, and perhaps too much.

"You're not a fool," said Miss Dillaway. There was a catch in her voice like laughter, but she was not laughing. "And I wouldn't have you different. The only trouble is that you need someone to look out for you. You're just not a type that can walk around alone. And for once in your life you're too late. You'd better tell him, Gilbreth." Dr. Gilbreth hesitated.

"Go ahead," said Miss Dillaway, "tell him, Gilbreth."

"I was reached by cable a week ago," Dr. Gilbreth said. "I didn't know you were coming out here, and I'm glad I didn't know. I wired the facts in self-protection." Dr. Gilbreth shrugged his shoulders. "Maybe I'm not a gentleman. Maybe it's better not to be. And I got an answer back before the wires were cut. I've got it in my pocket. You can read it if you like."

He handed Calvin Gates a piece of paper on which a few words were scrawled in pencil.

Your communication explains situation here stop have taken measures stop rely on your discretion stop to save scandal have stated I signed check and bookkeeper lost record stop authorities accept this explanation stop communicate this my nephew worried about him stop should have consulted me first tell idiot return at once funds forwarded him at Shanghai Roger Gates.

As Calvin stared at the sheet of paper the whole affair assumed an artificial quality—as though it had all been done by someone else.

"I'm sorry," he said slowly, still staring at the paper. "It would have been better if he hadn't known."

"Would it?" said Dr. Gilbreth. "How do you know it would? At any rate, it's over now, and there's nothing you can do."

"Think of that," said Miss Dillaway. "Nothing you can do." He thought that she was laughing at him, but again she was not laughing.

Now that it was finished he could see his whole course of action objectively, as though someone else had taken it, and it seemed quixotic and absurd, like something he might have done when he was much younger. He could not even remember what there had been about it that had once stirred him so deeply. His impulse no longer had validity; instead he discovered something close to egotism in his ideas of family and honor.

"Dillaway," he said, "I think I'm getting tired of chivalry."

"Well," said Miss Dillaway, "it's time you were."

# 19

"ANYWAY," HE SAID, "I met you, Dillaway, and I'm going to get you out of this."

"There you go," said Miss Dillaway, "starting out again."

Calvin Gates stared about the bare, dimly lighted shed. He had half forgotten where they were, until she made the last remark.

"Don't worry," he said. "I'm through with that, and I'm through with being what I was."

Dr. Gilbreth had begun to pace up and down the shed.

"Haven't we talked enough about you?" he inquired. "What's going on out there? What are they trying to do?"

Calvin looked at his wrist watch without answering.

"What's the matter?" Miss Dillaway asked. "Have you got an appointment, Gates?"

"I may have," said Calvin Gates, "in about five minutes." He did not wish to enlarge upon the subject, and he did not wish to be asked questions. "So you gave Hamby the cigarette case? I wish we had it now."

"Well, you can have it if you like," she answered.

"Not here," he answered. "Don't say that. It isn't even funny—if I could get my hands on that case—"

"I mean it," she said. "I've got it if you want it. It's right here in my purse."

She opened her purse and handed him the cigarette case. There it was in silver and black with the same birds that he remembered.

"But why didn't he take it from you?" Calvin cried. He knew Captain Hamby well enough to know that he would not have hesitated.

"I thought it might be useful, that's why I kept it," she answered. "Captain Hamby isn't so clever."

"But how did you keep it?" Calvin said. "I don't understand."

"It isn't being very bright if you don't," Miss Dillaway retorted. "Don't you remember that I had a cigarette case of my own, which I bought in Tokyo, with the same type of inlay—that's the one I gave him. Why are you looking at it that way? It won't burn your fingers."

As he stood there staring at the piece of silver his hands began to tremble. It was so completely unexpected that he could not think consecutively. She stood looking at him with a grim sort of triumph and with her old air of superiority.

"I'm not such an idiot, you know, Gates," she said.

"I never said you were," he answered, "but I never thought of this."

"Well, try to think back," said Miss Dillaway. "It's simple enough. When Boris offered me that cigarette case on the train you heard me tell him I had a case of my own."

"Yes," said Calvin, "I remember."

He could remember quite clearly now that she mentioned it, but the very simplicity of what had happened made it the more surprising. He stared at the cigarette case and back at Miss Dillaway again.

"Don't you believe me?" she said impatiently. "There it is."

"But why didn't you give him this one," he asked, "when Hamby asked you?"

She gave her head a quick, impatient shake.

"Because I didn't like the way he asked for it, if you want to know," she answered. "He was so sure he was going to get it that he didn't even bother to be polite. He didn't even bother to be impolite, either. I suppose you think that women aren't much use, Gates. That's what most of you romanticists think. You needn't act as though you wished you had thought of it yourself. If you want it, there it is—a present. Aren't you going to thank me?"

"I'm sorry," he said. "I haven't got time. I'm sorry. I'm trying to think. I want to remember every detail on this case."

The whole thing was completely in keeping with her character.

She had always said that she could look out for herself, and she had come very close to doing it. It was as though he had drawn a card to fill a poker hand when the last of his money lay upon the table, and she had given him the card. She had given him a key to let them out of prison. It was better than the bargain he had made with Hamby. If that failed, the cigarette case was still in his hands.

"What do you think I'd better do with it?" he asked.

"I don't know," she said, "that's up to you. I can't do anything, can I, Gates?"

"Well, what's so queer about it?" Dr. Gilbreth said. "It's only a cigarette case, isn't it?" Dr. Gilbreth did not understand, and there was no necessity to explain. Calvin held the cigarette case, and looked at it, until each detail of the design was clear in his memory. Then he opened it and with a sudden wrench he tore the inlaid cover from its hinges.

"What are you doing?" he heard Miss Dillaway ask, but instead of answering he bent the silver cover between his hands. It was a delicate but unstable piece of silverwork. The brittle iron of the inlay snapped as he bent it and bits of it fell to the earth floor at his feet.

"Pick those pieces up," he said to Miss Dillaway. "Hide them somewhere, each one in a different place. Break them first. Bend them out of shape."

He bent the silver in his hands until it broke and then he bent the pieces and broke them again; finally he ground each piece beneath his heel into a shapeless mass. There was nothing left when he had finished.

"They can't put that together," Calvin said, "not if they work a week."

"But what are you doing it for?" Miss Dillaway asked.

"Because I want to get you out of this," Calvin answered. "And no matter what happens—we've got them now, I think."

"But I don't see—" she began, and Calvin Gates stopped her. He was listening to a sound outside.

"Wait," he whispered. "Don't speak, don't say anything."

There was a stir outside the door. It was Captain Hamby. Calvin could hear him humming.

"What's the use of worrying, it never was worth while."

The heavy door creaked open and he stepped inside the shed.

"Hello," said Captain Hamby. "Everybody comfortable? Now don't start complaining. You're all lucky so far."

"Look here, Hamby—" Dr. Gilbreth began.

"Now, now," said Captain Hamby, "that's enough from you, Doctor. You're a secondary problem. You're wanted at the house, Gates. Come along now, come along. My word, this is quite a night."

"So you're back, are you?" Calvin asked. "I suggest you let us all out, Hamby."

Captain Hamby laughed—the laugh of a man in excellent spirits. Whatever the Captain had done since Calvin had seen him last must have been both agreeable and successful.

"Let everyone out!" Captain Hamby made an exaggerated gesture of surprise. "Now, now, that don't come into the bargain, Gates. I'm surprised that you should suggest it, an accurate man like you. Maybe my mind's failing, but I don't recall of talking of letting Miss Dillaway out. I promised to put her under the care of Dr. Gilbreth. Well, she is under his care, isn't she? It isn't my fault if his care don't amount to much. It isn't my fault if he's in trouble with the Prince. Keep your shirt on, Gates."

"You're an Australian, aren't you?" Calvin said. "I forgot your family came out on a convict ship."

Captain Hamby bit his lip and then he smiled again.

"And who are you to talk?" he said. "I don't bite the hand that feeds me, Gates, and you turned up Moto good and proper. I'm not yellow dog taking Japanese pay. Stow it, Gates, don't move."

"That's a lie," Miss Dillaway called out. "He never did that and you know it."

"Never mind it, Dillaway," Calvin said. "There's nothing I'm ashamed of."

"Isn't there?" said Captain Hamby. "Well, that's fine. And there's nothing I'm ashamed of either, when I deal with a new chum like you. I don't know what your lay was, Gates, but it don't make much difference now. You stow it. I'm keeping all of my bargain that I can. I'd promised you you'd talk with Gilbreth, didn't I? You've got a sight more than you deserve, my boy."

Calvin measured the distance between himself and Captain Hamby and leaned forward. Captain Hamby put his hands in his coat pocket and took a quick step back.

"Get some sense in your head, old chum," Captain Hamby said, "and no more of your bloody insults either. If I finished you off right here, nobody would mind. Instead I'm doing what I can for you. Are you coming with me, or do you want me to call some of my boys to drag you?"

"Don't bother," said Calvin, "I'm coming."

Captain Hamby's irritation vanished.

"That's fine," he said. "I've got nothing against you personally, Gates, upon my word. I'll do all I can for you. Just smile, smile, smile. Step ahead of me, smartly now."

Captain Hamby hummed beneath his breath about the lucifer and the old kit bag, as he walked beside Calvin Gates across the compound with two attendants close behind him.

"Just take things as they come, Gates," said Captain Hamby soothingly. "My word, this is none of my doing, it's only your own tight corner, but I promised you'd see the fun. Yes, it's quite a night. It isn't always things work out this neatly. While you've got a lucifer to light your fag—"

"Who wants to see me?" Calvin asked.

"Just smile, smile, smile," Captain Hamby said. "A Russian gentleman wants to see you. My word, I'm sorry, Gates. He thinks you murdered a pal of his in that hotel in Mukden. The Prince is allowing him to dispose of you, but I'll do what I can. My word, Gates."

"Never mind your word," Calvin said.

"That's fine," said Captain Hamby, "that's the sporting way to take it. I'll see that Miss Dillaway and the Doctor get back to Ghuru Nor. Maybe they'll get home sometime if they're lucky. We can't suit everybody these days. You're seeing the beginning of a war. Just between friends, the Prince is near to selling out to Russia, Gates. Just keep smiling. Here we are."

Mr. Holtz opened the door of his bungalow.

"So," he said to Captain Hamby, "here you are."

Everything in Mr. Holtz's room was much as Calvin had left it. The Prince was back in his chair at one end of the room, beside the table with the lamp upon it. Only when Calvin was in the center of the room was he aware of a strained, hushed sort of expectancy, and then he saw the reason. Seated in a stiff-backed wooden chair near the Prince was Mr. Moto.

## 20

THERE WAS a gash on the side of Mr. Moto's head and his coat was torn, but his eyes were bright and steady. His eyes turned toward Calvin Gates and then back across the room where he had been gazing before, straight at Major Ahara.

"Well, well," said Captain Hamby, "there's your old friend, Mr. Moto, Gates. Anything you want to say to Mr. Moto?"

"No," Calvin answered, "except that I told him to look out for you."

"It is all right," said Mr. Moto gently. "Please believe I do not blame you, Mr. Gates. I am so afraid that there is so much trouble."

"Yes," said Captain Hamby, "so much trouble. Gates, here's the gentleman who wants a word with you—over by the table. His name is General Shirov."

A man at the table close to where the Prince was seated turned around in his chair. He was a pale, youngish man with a sharp, studious face. He was holding some papers in his hand, and in that moment as Calvin watched him he wondered if he had not seen the face before; then he realized what had given him the notion, for the man called General Shirov was like the Russian whom he had first seen on the train. He had the same cut to his clothes and the same high forehead and the same blue, slightly protuberant eyes. He laid his papers carefully on his knee, but he did not speak for a moment.

In the odd silence which followed everything in the room appeared to be motionless, so that each face was registered photographically on Calvin's mind. He saw the guards by the door and the strange, barbaric robes of the Prince's retinue, so completely out of place among the rather ugly modern furnishings. He and Captain Hamby were standing in the center of it all, for Mr. Holtz with a placid grunt had eased himself back into his chair again. On his left hand he could see Mr. Moto looking grayish white and shaken, and straight in front of him the Prince sat, his narrow eyes glittering, his lean hands upon his knees. Near him by the table was General Shirov, and farther to the right he could see Major Ahara. The saber cuts on the Major's face were livid and his lips moved soundlessly. When General Shirov spoke even his voice was like that of the Russian whom Calvin had first seen on the train, the facile international voice of the born linguist.

"There are some questions I wish to ask you," he said to Calvin Gates. "I have heard the answers, but I wish to hear them from yourself."

His voice had the impersonal courtesy of a magistrate in court.

"I am questioning you for personal reasons. I am General Shirov, sir, in charge of the Russian Intelligence in China. I wish to ask you about a certain silver cigarette case. It would be helpful if you answered voluntarily, for time is very pressing."

There was another silence, and the General looked at Calvin wearily, and Calvin looked back trying to discover what sort of man it was who was speaking. There was no way to discover, because he was cloaked in a careful, unobtrusive sort of anonymity that revealed no trace of character.

"Go ahead," said Calvin Gates, "I'll answer."

"Thank you," said General Shirov. "Do I understand you are an agent for some government?"

"No," said Calvin Gates.

The General's pale eyebrows lifted slightly.

"Do you intend to convey the idea," he asked, "that you became involved in this matter entirely through accident?"

"Yes," said Calvin Gates. The General's fingers caressed the papers on his knee. His eyes were blue and unblinking.

"A very serious matter to be involved in just by accident, do you not think?" he said.

"Yes," said Calvin Gates.

"Very serious and very peculiar," the General said. "You met a Russian upon the train, between Fusan and Mukden, whose name was Boris, who was acting as courier for a young American lady—will you describe him please?"

The nose, the mouth and the protuberant blue eyes were much the same.

"He looked like you," said Calvin Gates.

The General rustled the papers upon his knee.

"That is right," he said, "the gentleman was my brother. Now you may appreciate my interest. My brother approached the American lady upon the train and offered her a cigarette case. You saw her take it, and that same evening my brother called upon you in your room and asked you to take charge of that cigarette case. This seems extraordinary to me, sir. Did it not seem so to you? Why do you suppose he did such a thing?"

The General's blue eyes were cool and passionless.

"He didn't have time to tell me," Calvin Gates answered. "He was disturbed about something. I gathered that there was some danger connected with that cigarette case."

The General nodded and sighed.

"Yes," he said, "some danger, and I understand from Captain

Hamby, who is here beside you now, that my brother was killed in your room. For personal reasons I should like to know who killed him. You say you did not, sir."

"I didn't," said Calvin Gates, and suddenly his mouth felt dry and parched. He was a prisoner undergoing examination at a bar of justice, and he knew that there was no particular reason why he should be believed. "Why should I have wanted to kill him?" he added.

"I do not know," the General said. "I am trying to understand your motives, sir." The General raised his hand from his knee and pointed to Mr. Moto. "Did this man kill him?"

"No," said Calvin, "he did not. He came into the room just a moment afterwards. I think he was surprised." In the silence that followed, Major Ahara drew a deep sibilant breath and stared across the room toward Mr. Moto.

"We will leave that matter for the moment," the Russian said. "After this, you went to the lady's room and she gave you the cigarette case, and you kept it. Why did you do that?"

Calvin Gates hesitated because it was a hard enough question to answer.

"I took it because I thought she would be in danger," he said. "I kept it because I thought we would be in danger anyway, with or without that cigarette case." He looked at Mr. Moto and Mr. Moto stared back at him stonily. "I thought that she and I might be safer if I kept it."

"Yes," General Shirov said. "Were those the only reasons?"

"I guess not," Calvin answered. "I guess I wanted to see what was going to happen. It made me forget some things about myself."

"Oh," said General Shirov, "some things about yourself? And you wished to protect the lady? That is peculiar, sir. When Captain Hamby asked you for this cigarette case you did not give it to him. Why did you not?"

"Because I didn't trust him," Calvin said.

For the first time in that interview the General's wide blue eyes left Calvin's face and turned toward Captain Hamby.

"That is something which I can believe," he said. "Captain Hamby promised us delivery and I find a Japanese here dealing with him."

Captain Hamby's face wrinkled into a hard, bright smile. "The Major came here," he said. "I didn't ask him. I'm always willing to talk business, Shirov. My word, it's coming your way, isn't it?"

"It is coming my way," said General Shirov, "because I have confided in you the latest news from Moscow—that is the only reason. Otherwise I would be the one to be marched outside."

"Righto," said Captain Hamby genially. "We have to use the tools at hand, General. Now if you want to talk business with the Prince—"

"One moment," said General Shirov, "one moment, please. I wish to ask this man another question. I do not trust you, Captain Hamby, about this cigarette case. I have not seen it yet. Now sir, if you please . . . You did not give that silver case to Captain Hamby, you kept it because you wished to protect the lady, and yet you gave it back to her and left her in Peiping. How did that protect her?"

Calvin felt his face redden. Instead of being dignified, he had been foolish, and everything he had said sounded like a tissue of falsehood, although it had only been the truth.

"I quarreled with her," he answered, "but I came up here to find her."

General Shirov's face relaxed into a pale, thin smile.

"That will do I think," he said. "Who is paying you, Captain Hamby or the Japanese?"

Calvin shrugged his shoulders.

"No one's paying me," he answered. "You can believe what I said or not."

"Perhaps," said General Shirov, "when I see the cigarette case—"

Captain Hamby took a step forward and his eyes were bright and angry. The Prince leaned backward in his chair and spoke in his high, thin voice.

"General Shirov," he said, "Captain Hamby has it in his pocket. You shall make your offer. There is only one thing which I must know first. I am sorry that my English is so slow. I was taught by an Englishman. He was brought by my father from Peiping, but that was long ago. It is the only language that everyone can understand, you and the Japanese."

"Excellency," the General answered, "your English is very good. What is it that you want to know?"

The Prince looked about him with a serene, cool dignity. "Tonight I am thinking of my people. If I sell to you, Japan will be my enemy. How can I be sure that my people will be protected? That is what I wish to know. Will a strong Russian army move to Ghuru Nor?"

The Russian agent spoke eagerly.

"There can be no doubt of it, Your Excellency," he answered. "I was at the concentration point a week ago. They are only waiting for the message. If Japan begins further pressure on North China, three divisions will move at once into Ghuru Nor."

There was another of those strange silences. Calvin Gates could feel his pulses beating. Out of the corner of his eye he saw Mr. Moto moisten the corner of his lips and heard him sigh.

"Well, you'll never have a better chance," Captain Hamby said. "There's the man right in front of you who is giving the Japanese troops their orders. My word, he's your prisoner just as soon as you pay the money. You've seen the papers in your pocket, haven't you?"

The Russian took the papers from his knee and set them on the table.

"They would appear correct," he said. "But I do not understand how he allowed you to take him. There is something that is not right."

A sudden noise at the right of the room made Calvin turn. Major Ahara had leapt out of his chair before anyone could lay a hand upon him and in a single bound he had reached the center of the room.

"It is true that there is something that is not right," he said. "The man sitting there is a traitor to his country."

Mr. Moto moved uneasily in his chair.

"Please," he said, "please."

"Yes," said Major Ahara, "a traitor to your emperor. You meant that message to be delivered. You allowed yourself to be brought here with the orders on you. Answer me if that is not so. You cannot answer."

"Please," said Mr. Moto, "that will be enough."

"Yes," said Captain Hamby. "My word, it will. Windy little beggars, you Japanese," and he seized Major Ahara's shoulders.

At the same instant the Major struck at Captain Hamby's arm and the Captain staggered backward with a choking cry of amazement. The room was filled with a confused clamor that sounded like the yelping from a kennel. A dark-gowned man lunged at the Major and missed him. An instant later the Japanese had tripped up the guard by the door and snatched it open. Then he sprang outside with Captain Hamby just behind him. The report of a pistol sounded in the compound, and then a second shot. Mr.

Holtz pushed past the crowd at the door. The Prince called out a high, sharp order, but he had not risen from his chair.

At its call the noise in the room died down.

"Hamby," shouted Mr. Holtz, and Captain Hamby's voice answered cheerily from the dark outside:

"It's all right, Holtz, the beggar's through." And then Captain Hamby sauntered back deliberately through the open door as though he had just stepped out to get a breath of air.

"Smile," Captain Hamby was humming, "smile, smile."

"My friend," said Mr. Holtz, "was that necessary? I told you I wanted none of that in here."

Captain Hamby's face wrinkled in his most exasperating smile.

"Just a peaceful merchant, aren't you, Holtz?" he said. "You're in this the same as everybody else. My word, the beggar was running like a rabbit. We couldn't let him get away."

"But he would not have got away," said Mr. Holtz, and the flesh about his eyes had gathered into dangerous little wrinkles. "Did I not tell you this was to be done out beyond if it was necessary? An officer, a Japanese officer—it is dangerous."

"To hell with the Japanese officers," Captain Hamby said. "You heard what Shirov told us, didn't you? This country will be Russian next week."

"I am not sure," said Mr. Holtz. "We cannot yet be sure."

"My word," said Captain Hamby, "you heard Shirov. We've done business with Shirov. We're sure already."

Then in the pause that followed, Mr. Moto spoke, and the contrast of his voice coming so suddenly after Captain Hamby's unmusical speech made every word decisive.

"I am so sorry that you did that," Mr. Moto said. "He was a very good officer. We had differences of political opinion, but he was very nice. I am so very, very sorry."

"Sorry, are you?" Captain Hamby said. "You'd better be sorry for yourself."

Mr. Moto looked at the Prince and at the Russian agent and then at Captain Hamby. His gold fillings glittered in a polite, intelligent smile.

"You mean I shall be liquidated also?" Mr. Moto said.

"Clever little beggar, aren't you?" Captain Hamby said. "You let yourself in for it, didn't you?"

Mr. Moto folded his hands on his lap.

"Perhaps," he said, "and perhaps it is time to make myself clear. You will not liquidate me yet I think. I know so much of Mr. Holtz and so much of you all. I have such a very high opinion of General Shirov. You are all so very, very clever. I know so very well what you are thinking—that, when we are no longer useful, this young American gentleman and I will be eliminated. Do you mind if I explain myself?"

"It don't matter," said Captain Hamby. "We haven't got the time."

But Mr. Holtz interrupted.

"One little minute," he said. "I want to hear what he says."

"And so do I," said General Shirov. "I want to understand."

"Thank you, General Shirov," said Mr. Moto, "so very, very much. I know you may be puzzled to see me here. My poor compatriot, the Major, was so very, very right. I wished that you would receive the cigarette case with the message it conveyed. I hoped so much that your brother would bring it to you, but there was so much opposition on the part of my own countrymen, so embarrassing to me. I am so afraid that your brother was alarmed when he saw me on the train. I hoped so much that he would bring it safely. I am so sorry for his accident. He was such a clever man."

General Shirov looked at Mr. Moto distrustfully, as though there might be an infernal machine in Mr. Moto's pocket.

"So you wanted me to get that message," he said. "That is kind of you, but the reason is not clear."

Mr. Moto smiled a golden, confidential smile. "Excuse me," he said, "I know so well it sounds irregular. I am so afraid that you might suspect me. If I had not been afraid, I should have been in touch with you myself. You are such a very brilliant man, General Shirov, and we have known each other so long and so unhappily. I was afraid if I came here freely that you would draw away and I wanted so very much to see you face to face. So much simpler for us both. I did not wish you to be alarmed, General Shirov. That is why I arranged for Captain Hamby to capture me. It seemed the only way that we might meet face to face—so very naturally."

The Russian had a peculiar and intent expression. Mr. Moto might have been a page of very fine print that he was trying to read.

"You wished to see me," he said. "Why did you wish to see me?"

Mr. Moto's expression had grown serious.

"Please," he said. "I wish that matters might settle themselves in a happier way, but I am so very much afraid that one of us will not leave this place. We understand such affairs so very, very well. You are here for information and so am I. It is your desire to find out what action my country will take toward China. I could tell you now, but you would not believe. That is why I have arranged for you to receive a message from your own sources. I have arranged it against the advice and wishes of so very many people."

"Yes," said General Shirov, "and what do you desire?"

Mr. Moto sighed.

"My desire is so very, very simple," Mr. Moto said. "There have been so many debates about it. Will Russia intervene if we move farther into China? We have tested the situation at the Amur River, but we are still not sure. If ever your great country will act, it will do so when you receive this message. It will be like a train of powder set alight. You and I know the situation so very, very well. We have our own intelligence in Moscow. If your country will strike, it will do so now, without an ultimatum or a declaration. Such formalities are so very, very silly. The decision must be already made I think. Your army will advance immediately to take up positions at Ghuru Nor. If it does so, we may know that we may expect an intervention. I wish to see if it does so, and I have done more than that."

Mr. Moto paused and rubbed his hands, but Shirov did not answer.

"Yes," said Mr. Moto. "I have done more than that. I have incurred the enmity of many important persons. I am risking my own honor. I have allowed myself to be taken with military secrets in my possession. You have already read the orders on the table? There is not a Japanese unit within two hundred miles of Ghuru Nor. You have your chance this evening—one which will not come again—and I have given you this chance. It is so important to see whether your country takes action that I have seen fit to precipitate the opportunity. This, please, is my own responsibility. I wonder what will happen when you see the message? I will tell you what it will say."

Mr. Moto paused again and glanced about the room. Captain Hamby was frowning and the Prince sat motionless and Mr. Holtz had craned his thick neck forward. The peaceful look had left the Russian's eyes.

"Yes," said Mr. Moto, "I will tell you. The day after tomorrow there will be a series of incidents outside of Peiping which will lead to demands on five Chinese provinces. If your country intervenes, I think it will be now or never." Mr. Moto rubbed his hands together.

"I think we will find out tonight. The Prince will be so interested and so will Mr. Holtz. I know so much of Mr. Holtz."

Mr. Moto turned toward the fat man and smiled.

"Mr. Holtz has worked so hard for Russia, but he has so very many commercial interests that he must consider other matters. He has a wireless with a short-wave sending-set in the next room of this house."

Mr. Holtz gave a startled grunt and Mr. Moto smiled again.

"Do not let it alarm you, please," Mr. Moto said. "Our intelligence is very good. Mr. Holtz will send a message and will get an answer in a very little while, and General Shirov may listen. Mr. Holtz will tell us whether there will be a movement toward Ghuru Nor. He will want so much to know in order to decide what he must do in order to help himself. We shall all be so interested. You will be able to get the answer I think, Mr. Holtz."

"Yes," said Mr. Holtz, "since you know so much. They will send orders here at once if they start to move. It is—arranged."

"I thought so," Mr. Moto answered. "It is so very, very nice. We shall know the news so soon, and the Prince will be so relieved and Mr. Holtz will be so relieved. They will both know which side to take. And then—if definite action is taken I shall be so very happy to kill myself. On the other hand it will be so very different. If there is no move I am so afraid that General Shirov must kill himself. Yes, I think that we shall liquidate the situation. It is my own idea."

Mr. Moto glanced brightly about the room.

"It is so very nice that everything is so well arranged," he said. "Do not look so anxious, Mr. Gates. Personally, I do not think that Russia is going to move. I hope so much for your sake, Mr. Gates. I hope so much I have made myself clear. Thank you so much for allowing me to speak."

Captain Hamby swayed backwards on his heels.

"While you've a lucifer to light your fag," he hummed, and no one interrupted him. "Clever beggar aren't you, Mr. Moto? So darned bright."

"Thank you," said Mr. Moto, "so very, very much."

There was no doubt that Mr. Moto had made himself clear to everyone. Whether the rest of them believed or not, Calvin Gates believed him. He had seen enough and heard enough so that there could be no mistake, and now everything that Mr. Moto had said or done was intelligible. He had accomplished everything which he had set out to do, and now he sat with his hands folded in his lap.

"Perhaps," Mr. Moto said, "Mr. Holtz will open communications upon the wireless. There should be a message soon."

"My word," said Captain Hamby, "this is jolly good. Get the buzzer going, Holtz."

Without answering, Mr. Holtz walked to the far end of the room and opened the door and Calvin Gates had a glimpse of a table covered with electrical apparatus.

"Well," said Mr. Holtz, "everything is ready."

The Russian stood up and there was a note in his voice that had not been there before. Calvin felt the floor unsteady beneath him because he knew what was coming.

"Hamby," said Shirov, "hand me that cigarette case, please. It will tell if this is true."

"One minute." The Prince spoke softly. "What price will you pay me?"

The serious, intent expression left the Russian's face and changed into a thin, cool smile.

"We will discuss that later," he said. "Mr. Moto's presence makes bargaining unnecessary. The corn between the millstones should not ask for money, Excellency. Give me that cigarette case. Give it to me quickly."

"My word," said Captain Hamby, "that's no way to talk."

"You will be paid when this is over," said General Shirov. "The cigarette case please. We must see if this is true first."

"Now," said Captain Hamby, "that's no way to talk. Here it is, look at it for yourself."

He whipped a cigarette case from his inside pocket and handed it to General Shirov. The Russian snatched it out of Hamby's hand and stared hard at the cover. He did not speak immediately, but anyone who watched him could have told that something was wrong.

"My word," said Captain Hamby, "what's the matter?"

"What does this mean?" The Russian's voice was thick. "This is not the case."

"Not the case?" said Mr. Moto, and his face went chalky white.

The Prince was out of his chair. He had turned from a motionless Chinese portrait into a figure of the god of war. He shouted something in his own language and Hamby answered back.

"This is too much," General Shirov shouted.

"Wait a minute," said Captain Hamby, "wait," and he ran to the door.

"I think," said Mr. Moto, "that he has gone to get the young lady, and I do not think she has it. I think it is in this room."

"Where in this room?" Shirov asked.

"Please," said Mr. Moto, "do not excite yourself. I am as anxious as you, believe me." He glanced soberly at Calvin Gates. "I think the young gentleman there has it. So sorry, Mr. Gates."

## 21

THE PRINCE stared hard at Calvin Gates and barked out an order. It was the moment for which Calvin Gates had been waiting, but now that it had come he did not feel wholly adequate to meet it. The men with whom he had to contend were as desperate as he was and, compared with their experience, his was like a child's. He had never seen Mr. Moto so profoundly agitated. The Prince and the Russian agent were both so stirred that they could not conceal their feelings. Surprise, indignation and distrust sounded in their words and swept across their faces.

"It is not him," he heard Mr. Holtz call behind him. "It is that Hamby, he has got it."

One of the Prince's men grasped Calvin's shoulder.

"Take your hands off me," said Calvin Gates, and he felt more sure of himself now that he was speaking. "I haven't got that cigarette case, but I know where it is."

His announcement had a quieting effect and the quiet was reassuring. He stood there in the center of that drama, momentarily master of the situation, and he knew that he must make the most of it. But he paused before he spoke again, careful not to hurry, watching the faces in front of him.

"Ah," said General Shirov, "so you know where it is." The Prince walked forward with a quick stamp of his heavy boots and stopped in front of him—a fantastic figure in his peaked cap, his blue gown and his pigtail.

"You will tell us," the Prince said in his high, slow voice, "at once."

The narrow, dark eyes of the Prince were ugly, but with an effort Calvin Gates grinned back at him.

"Well," he asked "how much will you give me, Prince?"

"One moment," Mr. Moto spoke quickly. "If I may say a word to Mr. Gates, please. It will do no good to force him I am afraid. He is such a stubborn man, but he will be reasonable when I explain. It is not a time to be difficult, Mr. Gates. You must understand that we are in danger. The Prince is so very angry, and General Shirov is so very angry. It may appear a small matter, but I assure you the cigarette case is vitally important please. Its loss delays everything. Until General Shirov sees it, how can he believe what I have told him? How can the Prince understand his situation? No doubt you think you are gaining something by this delay, but excuse me you are not. If we do not find this article promptly, I am so afraid it will be so very unfortunate for you. I am sure you will be reasonable, Mr. Gates."

There was no mistaking Mr. Moto's deep anxiety.

"I assure you, Mr. Gates," Mr. Moto added, "that there is nothing subtle in what I say."

The whole situation was ironical, but he had learned a good deal from Mr. Moto's subtlety. For once he was able to match his own wits against Mr. Moto's, and to speak in the same polished phrases.

"There is only one trouble," he said. "It is that our points of view are different, Mr. Moto. I do not care about the Russo-Japanese situation. The only thing I care about is personal freedom and my neck."

"Of course," said Mr. Moto gently, "that is so very logical, Mr. Gates, but please, if you are stubborn, you will be made to tell and that will not be very nice. Here is Miss Dillaway I think. I am so sure that she will agree with me."

The door of the bungalow had opened and Captain Hamby, with a firm grasp on Miss Dillaway's arm, was pushing her into the room.

"There's no use arguing," he was saying. "You don't want to see Gates killed, do you?"

"I don't know what you're talking about," Miss Dillaway said. She looked very small and lonely, but if she was afraid she did not show it. Her answer was brisk and uncompromising. Her head was defiantly erect.

"Now," said Captain Hamby and he gave her a gentle shake, "that's no way to talk."

Although it was not the time or place for like or dislike, Calvin Gates did not like Captain Hamby's manner. Something had broken down the restraint he had put upon himself, and there may have been some unconsidered reason for his action. He may have realized that he was safe for the moment. He was beside them before he knew what he was doing, and before caution or judgment came into play he had his hands on Captain Hamby and Captain Hamby dropped her arm.

"Here," said Captain Hamby, "here." And Captain Hamby stepped backward and put his hand in his pocket.

"I wouldn't try that," said Calvin Gates. "I know where the cigarette case is, Hamby." And Mr. Holtz had stepped down between them before he had finished speaking. He thought that they would seize him, but no one in the room moved.

"You can leave Miss Dillaway alone," Calvin said. "You all want to know where the cigarette case is, don't you? Well, I'll tell you where it is. Miss Dillaway gave Captain Hamby her own cigarette case, and she gave the other one to me, back there in the shed where you locked us up. Do you want to know what I did when I got it? Would that interest you, Mr. Moto? Would you be interested, Mr. Shirov?"

Calvin walked back to the center of the room. Everyone was giving him full attention although he could not tell even then whether his plan was good or bad.

"I looked at the design very carefully. There were some little birds and grasses. I remember every detail of that design and I can describe it accurately. If you give me a pencil and a paper I can draw it. I wonder if you get my point. Do you understand me, General Shirov?"

The Russian did not answer immediately, but Mr. Moto's mind was quicker.

"Mr. Gates," Mr. Moto said, "you are a very clever man, so very, very clever. You have of course destroyed the cigarette case."

"Exactly," said Calvin Gates. "It's out there in the shed very badly crushed. You won't be able to put it together I'm afraid, but I have it in my mind. Would you like me to draw it for you? I shall do it right away if we come to an agreement. I shall have to take your word and Genral Shirov's that one of you will see Miss Dillaway, Dr. Gilbreth, and me safely out of here, and that you will promise not to interfere with us further."

The proposal was received in absolute silence, a silence that was broken by a short, ugly laugh from Captain Hamby.

"So that's your idea, is it?" Captain Hamby said. "Going to be an artist are you, Gates? Don't give it a single thought, gentlemen. You let me have Mr. Gates outside for fifteen minutes, and he'll be begging to draw that picture."

"I've thought of that," said Calvin Gates. "There's only one trouble; you'd never be sure whether the picture was right."

General Shirov stroked his pointed chin thoughtfully.

"You are asking a good deal, my dear sir," he said. "How may we be sure that is is right at any rate?"

Calvin Gates shrugged his shoulders. There was no way for them actually to be sure. Ironically enough they had arrived at a question of integrity and character.

"You'll have to take my word," he said, "just as I have to take your word. It may be a risky business, but it's the only way. I have something that you want and you'll have to take my word. You'll have to believe me when I say that I have no interest in deceiving you. Besides, you will be able to see if I am deceiving you soon enough by what I draw. I've only been in this country two weeks. You can do it this way, or try any other with me, but believe me no other way will work."

"You leave it to me," Captain Hamby began; but General Shirov stopped him.

"That will do, sir," he said. "There must be no further mistakes, there is no time for them. This must be arranged without force. Have you a passport, Mr. Gates? If I may see the visas—"

"I have," said Calvin Gates. "I never thought of that."

General Shirov squared his shoulders and there was a different light in his unblinking blue eyes when he turned toward Calvin Gates.

"Your proposition seems the easiest solution, sir," he said. "When you were telling me your history a little while ago I suspected that you had other interests. Now I think that I was wrong. The passport may be a forgery, but I think not. I shall accept your proposition. I am flattered that you are willing to take my word and I am pleased to give it. I am a different type of man from certain others in this room."

"I thought you were," said Calvin Gates. "Will you agree that none of these other people interfere with us?"

"That will be arranged quite easily I think," General Shirov replied. "I am sorry we are so pressed now, Mr. Gates. I shall hope to make your further acquaintance later. If you will step to the table I have a pencil and paper, and may I ask the lady to come with us also, since she has seen that cigarette case too?"

Mr. Moto placed his hand before his lips and drew in his breath.

"You are so very sensible, Mr. Gates," he said. "It is so wise of you to see that Comrade Shirov and I are the only ones who count. Comrade Shirov is such a very nice man. You may rely upon him absolutely and you may rely upon me. You may be quite safe in assuming that none of these other gentlemen will interfere. They would not dare in any case." His bright, quick glance moved to General Shirov and he sighed.

"Yes, he is so very nice, because he is a gentleman. We give our word and we keep our word. I am so very sorry that he and I should be in collision. So very sorry that we have not time to chat together. We would have so very many interesting things to talk about."

General Shirov's lips curled into a thin smile.

"Yes," he said, "we would have a good deal to talk about."

"There's only one more detail," said Calvin Gates.

Mr. Moto looked startled. "What is that?" he asked.

"Dr. Gilbreth's party, they must be brought out safely."

"Oh," said Mr. Moto, and he smiled at the Prince. "So they are having trouble—that is so like His Excellency. They shall be brought out safely."

The Prince spoke suddenly. "Are you saying that I shall receive no recompense?" he asked slowly, and Mr. Moto beamed back at him.

"I am so afraid," he said. "You should have sold while there was an offer. We must arrange terms later now."

The Prince raised his hand from his knee and pointed at Captain Hamby.

"It was that man who advised me," he said.

"So sorry for Captain Hamby," said Mr. Moto gently. "So sorry that he carried affairs so far. I am so afraid that he should not have brought me here."

"If you step this way please, Mr. Gates," said General Shirov, "this way please, madame."

"Do not hesitate, Mr. Gates," Mr. Moto said cordially. "Either Comrade Shirov or I will be in complete control. The Prince and Mr. Holtz and Mr. Hamby will do what one of us tells them. Ha ha, it is so very funny. I am so sorry that Comrade Shirov should be an enemy of my country, and such a dangerous man."

"So sorry for you, Mr. Moto," General Shirov replied. "Here are the pencil and paper, Mr. Gates."

Calvin sat by the table with the pencil in his hand, and Miss

Dillaway stood beside him, and General Shirov and Mr. Moto. He could feel the contagion of their interest as he glanced at the paper. He could hear Captain Hamby and Mr. Holtz arguing loudly at the other end of the room.

"You thought you was so smart, what?" Mr. Holtz was saying. "You thought you was so smart to catch that Japanese."

"Well," the Russian said, "we are waiting, Mr. Gates."

Then Miss Dillaway leaned forward and spoke suddenly.

"Give me that paper, Gates," she said. "you don't know how to draw, I do. There were birds in the grass. Tell me how to draw them." She took the pencil in her small brown hand and glanced at him sideways. "He can't do everything, you know," she added.

## 22

"THERE WERE five tufts of grass," said Calvin Gates. "The grass was very high, particularly the large tuft in the center." He closed his eyes in order to remember better. "There was one detail about the grass. All the blades were bending to the left as though the wind blew them."

"Like this?" Miss Dillaway asked.

"Five tufts and the grass bending to the left," General Shirov repeated. "That is how it should be. And now the birds? Were they big or little, Mr. Gates?"

"Small birds," said Calvin Gates. "They seemed to have no tails and their beaks were long like woodcock. Three were flying in a little group over by the right. One was on the ground by the left, two were perched in a grass tuft in the center."

"Like this?" said Miss Dillaway.

Calvin Gates studied the drawing carefully and no one spoke.

"No," said Calvin. "The three birds flying were facing toward the right. One was a little ahead of the other two."

General Shirov leaned forward and picked up the paper and examined it for a moment with his lips pressed tight together.

"Mr. Holtz," he said, "is the wireless ready?"

"Yes, all ready," said Mr. Holtz.

"One moment," said Mr. Moto, "one moment please. Everything is correct? I am so very glad. I am so pleased to rely on Mr. Holtz.

We must know at once whether action will be taken. How will you find out?"

Mr. Holtz pursed his small lips.

"I shall ask for instructions," he said. "I shall find out. Never fear. General Shirov understands me."

Mr. Moto rubbed his hands together.

"I am so very sure you will," Mr. Moto said. "It is such a pleasure to rely on Mr. Holtz, who is giving us shelter in his house. Mr. Holtz is a man of property, with so many business interests. Mr. Holtz must be on the strong side."

"That is right," said Mr. Holtz. "I shall find for you what they will do up there."

"So very nice," Mr. Moto said. "We shall know when you get your answer. So sorry, General Shirov, that one of us must go. You understand me, I am so very sure. If your army does not march, I am so afraid that no one here will have much use for you. The Prince understands so well. He will become either Russian or Japanese. He will seize either you or me. Does His Highness understand?"

"I understand," the Prince said slowly. "In the meantime I am hospitable to both you gentlemen."

General Shirov made a quick impatient gesture.

"We have had enough talk," he said. "Everyone understands. They are simply waiting for the message."

He turned and walked away with Mr. Holtz toward the communicating door at the far end of the room.

"Smile," Captain Hamby was humming. "Smile, smile, smile." But he was not smiling.

"General Shirov is so sure," said Mr. Moto gently. "It may be well to have someone there to watch. He will be so disappointed if the answer is not what he hopes. So sorry—but he might forget himself."

The Prince nodded his head at Captain Hamby without answering. Captain Hamby followed to the door of the room where the wireless instrument stood.

"My word," said Captain Hamby, "you think of everything, don't you? He won't get away. I'll see to that."

Calvin Gates stood up and peered down the length of the room. The door was half open and he could see Mr. Holtz's broad back as he bent over the instrument at the table.

"Such an interesting instrument the wireless," Mr. Moto said.

"Will you hand me that pencil on the table and another piece of paper, Mr. Gates? Thank you so very much. Ah, they are calling for the station."

The sharp dot and dash of a spark came across the room, petulantly through the silence.

"Yes," said Mr. Moto, "that is the proper call."

Miss Dillaway put her hand on Calvin's arm.

"What are they doing?" she whispered. "What's happening, Gates?"

"We're out of it," he answered, "so what do you care, Dillaway?"

"Don't be so mysterious," Miss Dillaway said. "I can be interested, can't I? It's a lot better than being locked in a shed with Dr. Gilbreth."

"You can be interested if you like," said Calvin Gates. "There's either going to be a war with Russia or there isn't going to be a war, and that old gentleman in blue is a prince who is waiting to see whether he will ally himself to Russia or Japan, and Mr. Moto has precipitated an incident. Then there's a man in the other room named Holtz who owns this place and sends camels over the desert. He is in the other room now, sending a wireless message, and a very high class Russian spy is in there with him. Mr. Moto and the Russian spy don't get on very well. Depending on the answer to the message, your friend, Captain Hamby, and the Prince will take either Mr. Moto or the spy into custody, and that will be the end of one or the other—that's the picture roughly, and you can be interested if you like, but personally I don't care a hand as long as we're out of it."

"You don't?" said Miss Dillaway. "What's gotten into you, Gates? I thought that this was just the sort of thing you liked."

"Maybe I did," said Calvin Gates, "but I'm tired of it now."

"I suppose you're tired of me too," Miss Dillaway said.

"No," said Calvin Gates, "frankly I'm not. You're more interesting, Dillaway."

"I'm glad to hear it," she answered, "because you won't see anything like this again if I have anything to do with it."

"Do you want to have anything to do with it?" Calvin asked her.

"I don't know that I should mind," she said, "if I understand you rightly. You're interesting sometimes, Gates, but you're not going to get me into a party like this again."

"Look here," said Calvin Gates. "You started this. You were given that cigarette case, I wasn't."

She looked up at him and smiled.

"You need a guardian, Gates," she said. "You can't think straight when you argue, but never mind, I like it. You might be worse."

"So might you," said Calvin Gates.

"I suppose you're disorderly around the house," she said.

"Yes," he said, "I am."

"You would be," said Miss Dillaway. "I suppose—"

Mr. Moto's voice brought him back to the present.

"Will you please not talk?" Mr. Moto said. "Although it is very interesting that Mr. Gates is so disorderly. They are sending the message and I am trying to listen, please."

## 23

THE SHARP snap of the wireless was traveling through the room, and Calvin stood there listening with his hand over the girl's beside him. There were a great many things that he wished to tell her that must wait for some other time. He felt a sense of companionship which he had never experienced with anyone else. He was thinking that they would get on well together, and that they knew more of each other than most people. They had gone a long way together. He remembered when he had seen her first on that small boat. They had gone a long way since that night, and now they were standing in a room heavy with the reek of the Prince's unwashed Mongols. It would be something to remember.

Mr. Moto was writing on the paper on his knee.

"That is very nice," he said. "Your picture was correct I think, although it conveyed more than I thought it would. It was a code message. Shirov has advised that everything is clear."

"Do you know their code?" Calvin asked him.

"A little," said Mr. Moto, "enough to read I think. It is sent in a peculiar manner. We have tried to send false messages, but it has been impossible."

Mr. Holtz came slowly into the room mopping his face on a handkerchief.

"We have sent it," he said. "There should be an answer very quickly. We have asked for it. How are you feeling, Mr. Moto?"

Mr. Moto sighed.

"Happy," said Mr. Moto, "very, very happy, Mr. Holtz. I feel that I have done my duty. We shall know the attitude of Russia in such a little while, and that is something, Mr. Holtz. Thank you. I am so obliged for your kind co-operation."

"You are a very cool man, my friend," said Mr. Holtz.

"Thank you," said Mr. Moto, "so very much. It is sometimes so necessary to be cool. There are some things so necessary to die for. It has been so difficult to arrange this evening."

"What's he saying?" Miss Dillaway asked. "Who's going to die?"

"I'll tell you later," said Calvin. "I'm tired of trying to be a hero, Dillaway. I couldn't compete with Mr. Moto even if I wanted."

"Thank you," said Mr. Moto, "so very, very much, but this is simply a business matter. So very sorry that Miss Dillaway should be disturbed by it. We all here know that it is a simple business matter. We have all witnessed similar occurrences, though perhaps not so interesting. Mr. Holtz, have you a cigarette please?"

Mr. Holtz grunted and handed him a box from the table and lighted the match himself.

"Yes, my friend," he said, "you are very cool. I would not be if I were in your place. Perhaps I am in better touch with Russia."

"Yes," said Mr. Moto, "perhaps. You are so very sensible, Mr. Holtz. Thank you very much."

"Holtz," called Captain Hamby, "come back here, Holtz, they're calling."

Mr. Moto flipped the ash from his cigarette. "That is very fast," he said. "I did not think that it would be so fast."

The Prince leaned forward in his chair and looked at Mr. Moto.

"I know so well what you are thinking, my dear Prince," Mr. Moto said. "It must be so very difficult for you. I know what you are thinking. It is not very nice for me, to have that answer come so fast. It indicates that they must have been waiting, and that everything has been arranged. No, it is not very nice. I am so very glad that you have arranged suitably for yourself, Mr. Gates. I am sure that you may rely on General Shirov. I am so sorry that Miss Dillaway should be disturbed."

Mr. Moto wrote a line on the paper on his knee and folded it.

"Mr. Gates," he said, "may I ask a favor please? I am so very afraid that things are going badly. I hope so much that you will leave China promptly. When you are in Tokyo would you call on the gentleman at this address? He is a very distinguished gentleman and he is so very nice. It may be that he will introduce you to an even more distinguished gentleman. Will you simply tell him please that I arranged the matter in spite of difficulty? He will understand so clearly what I mean. Tell him that I have been so happy to have been of service."

Calvin took the paper.

"I don't see what you mean," he said, and Mr. Moto drew in his breath politely.

"I am so afraid that you will see in just a minute," Mr. Moto said. "It is not nice that their reply should come so quickly. I am so afraid that it means that they are grasping the opportunity. The plan was to give every possibility to the Russian command. They have it and I am so araid that they are taking it. It was what we wished to know, whether or not they would act. I was so afraid that they are acting now."

There was a stir at the far end of the room and Mr. Moto started and turned his head. Calvin saw Captain Hamby standing tense and motionless, staring through the half-open door of the room where the wireless instrument was kept. And then there was the sound of a shot. Captain Hamby shrugged his shoulders and turned upon his heel.

"Smile boys," Captain Hamby was humming. "Smile boys, that's the style. Banzai for Japan!"

Mr. Moto had started up from his chair and Calvin Gates had put his arm around Miss Dillaway's shoulder. The sound of the shot had made him feel sick and weak, but he did not want her to know it. He held her close to him and whispered to her quickly.

"It's going to be all right, Dillaway," he whispered. "Don't let it bother you, Dillaway."

"I'm not," she answered him faintly, "I'm not bothered at all."

Mr. Holtz walked out of his wireless room, mopping his face, and the damp, heavy folds of his cheeks looked pale, like a moon in a cloudy sky.

"Shirov, he has shot himself," he said.

"Yes?" said Mr. Moto sharply, "yes?"

Mr. Holtz pursed his lips and thrust his handkerchief into his trousers' pocket.

"Those Russians," said Mr. Holtz. "I am finished with those Russians. There is always trouble up there, always difficulty. The GPU have arrested Shirov's chief and two generals, and what orders do we get? *There must be no incident to provoke Japan.* They will just stand and do nothing!"

Mr. Moto placed his hand elegantly before his lips.

"So interesting," he said, "so very, very interesting. I must have possession of the message if you please. It will mean so much. So sorry that Comrade Shirov should have been obliged to shoot himself, although it was so necessary. He was such a dangerous man, but he was very nice. He always tried so hard."

Mr. Moto paused and rubbed his hands together briskly.

"Everybody tries so hard, but ideas are so very, very different. I try so hard, and Mr. Holtz, he tries so hard, and so did poor Major Ahara. He tried so hard to have me eliminated several times. So very nice that everything is settled."

Mr. Moto turned about briskly and clasped his hands and bowed to the Prince.

"We shall be glad to draw an agreement, my dear Prince," he said, "paying you for permission for our troops to assist you in defending your territory. It will be so nice to co-operate with you, my dear Prince."

"I hope," said Mr. Holtz heavily, "that I may have a trade agreement."

Mr. Moto smiled genially at Mr. Holtz.

"Our trade commission will be so glad to co-operate," Mr. Moto said. "You will be so glad to agree to handle only Japanese products, I think. All that Japan wants of anyone, of China or anyone, is economic co-operation and a cordial understanding."

Captain Hamby grinned and his hard gray eyes twinkled.

"My word," said Captain Hamby, "that's all that anyone wants, just a cordial understanding."

Mr. Moto looked at Captain Hamby unsmilingly.

"One moment please," he said. "May I say one word to the Prince in private, just one little word?"

Mr. Moto walked to where the Prince was sitting and whispered in his ear, and the Prince blinked his narrow eyes, and touched the shoulder of the man beside him, and said something in a gentle undertone.

"Well," said Captain Hamby, "what's the secret? My word, we're all friends aren't we?"

"So nice," said Mr. Moto, "that we are all friends."

"Here," cried Captain Hamby, "what's all this?"

The two guards who were standing behind the Prince's chair had moved before he spoke and were pointing their rifles at him. There was a hoarse, monosyllabic order and two more guards leveled their rifles. Captain Hamby's hand moved toward his pocket, but he must have thought better of it, for he finally stood stock-still.

"Not here," said Mr. Moto, "it is disturbing to the lady. Would you be kind enough to lead Captain Hamby outside please. So sorry, Captain Hamby, that you should have killed an officer of the Japanese army. Major Ahara was so very nice. Please do not be alarmed, Miss Dillaway. If you will show the lady a chair, Mr. Gates, do you not think it would be very nice if we had a cup of tea? The Prince will be so glad to join us I think, and Mr. Holtz will be so glad to get it. I am somewhat exhausted, please, but everything is so very nice."

# RIGHT YOU ARE, MR. MOTO

# 1

JACK RHYCE had not expected to see the Russians in San Francisco. The word in Washington had been that Mr. Molotov and his delegation would have left the city several hours before Rhyce's arrival; but no one could have notified Jack Rhyce of the change of plans without creating undue attention. It had also been a mistake to make a reservation at the Mark Hopkins Hotel, but they had said categorically in Washington that the celebration of the tenth anniversary of the United Nations would be over. Instead, the Russians were just leaving the Mark Hopkins when Jack Rhyce arrived by taxi from the airport. There was hardly time for him to get his bags out before the driver was shooed away by a police escort, and there was nothing left for him to do but stand in the small crowd that was gathering.

"What's going on?" he asked the bellboy. The question was unnecessary because at the moment he asked he saw the limousines and the faces of the drivers.

"It's the Russians," the bellboy said.

"What?" Jack Rhyce asked. "The Russians aren't staying here, are they?"

"No, sir," the bellboy said, "but Mr. Molotov has been having a cocktail with Secretary Dulles."

"Well," Jack Rhyce said, "good for Mr. Molotov."

It would have looked conspicuous if he had moved backwards. It was better, in his opinion, to stand quietly and watch. The guards were coming out and grouping themselves around the leading limousine. At first glance the men seemed interchangeable with any of the people who protected top-flight Russians—heavy, stocky men with potatolike faces, and not a beauty in the bunch; but then they were not selected for show. Russian features were hard to classify, and he had been out of touch with the problem for quite a while, but he was sure two of them were officers high up in the NKVD. He could only hope that the recognition was not mutual; not that there would have been any great harm in it. After all, nothing could have been more natural than that he should be in San Francisco at this particular time. Still, he would have felt easier if he had not encountered the Russians just when he was on the point of flying to Japan. He knew that one should never underrate them, not even when they were being jolly good fellows in front of the Mark Hopkins Hotel.

"The one with the glasses is Mr. Molotov," the bellboy said.

Jack Rhyce had not seen Mr. Molotov for quite a while, but he was not likely to forget him, with or without glasses, since they had met twice on social occasions and had once exchanged amenities over caviar and vodka, at the end of the war, when Jack Rhyce had been traveling with one of the American missions. Mr. Molotov was in no hurry. He smiled happily as he walked toward the limousine. His expression was exactly the same as it had been in Moscow when he had slapped Jack Rhyce on the shoulder.

"Young man," Mr. Molotov had said, "let us touch glasses in token of a lasting friendship between our two countries."

"This is a great honor, sir," Jack Rhyce had answered.

"No, no," Mr. Molotov said. "You and I both are men."

"Yes, Excellency," Jack Rhyce said, "and all men are brothers."

He was younger in those days, with a lot to learn. He had made his last speech in Russian, when the Foreign Minister had been speaking in English, and Russian had not been necessary.

"Young man," Mr. Molotov had said, "you speak Russian not badly."

Jack Rhyce instantly realized that by showing off his Russian, simply because he was proud of being top of a language class, he had called attention to himself. His chief had spoken to him very roughly about it afterward, and the Chief had been absolutely right.

"Just get it through your head," the Chief had said, "that boys like you aren't supposed to be heard at all, and that you don't wear striped pants all the time. Never try to be conspicuous. Never."

It was good advice, and Jack Rhyce seldom needed to be told things twice.

There was no way for him to discover whether any of the Russian party recognized him now or not. He could only tell himself again that, even if they did, it should make no particular difference. Mr. Molotov, still beaming, waved to the crowd. Then the car door closed. The Russian party was gone as completely as though it had never been there. They had his dossier, of course, but they had him connected with Washington and Berlin. There was no reason whatsoever for them to believe that he was going to the Orient. Still, he wished that he had not seen the Russians.

Jack Rhyce had been a guest in so many hotels that he could instantly catch the atmosphere of any place in which he stopped and could immediately fit into its background. For God's sake, as the Chief had once told him, never chaffer too long at a hotel reception desk, and as rapidly as possible get up to your room, and never be seen hanging aimlessly around the lobby. Experience had taught Jack Rhyce that the Chief nearly always was absolutely right. Twice during the war he had been to the Mark Hopkins Hotel, but only to ascend in the elevator to that popular cocktail room known as the Top of the Mark. He had been with the paratroopers in those days, and he had never dreamed that anyone would select him for what he was now doing, but even then his memory had been excellent. Consequently, he had the general layout of the hotel straight, almost the instant he was inside the door.

"Would you please hand me my briefcase, son?" he asked the bellboy.

The way you handled a briefcase could make you look like a traveling salesman or a corporation lawyer. It was better at the moment, Jack Rhyce thought, to be placed as a corporation lawyer. He printed his name carefully in block letters on the registration card.

"The name is Rhyce," he said. "John O. Rhyce, from Washington, D.C. I don't suppose you have any letters waiting for me? Or telegrams or messages?" He spoke in a gentle, cultivated voice with an accent difficult to identify.

"No messages, Mr. Rhyce," the clerk said, "but we do have your reservation. It's lucky you didn't come a day earlier, what with all the goings on. I hope you saw Mr. Molotov. He must have been leaving just when you came in."

"Oh, yes," Jack Rhyce said. "He was pointed out to me."

"Front," the clerk said—"Room 515."

If Jack's guess was right, he would be in the middle of the corridor, and he always slept more soundly there than at either end. It was a pleasant, airy room which looked toward the Bay.

"Well, thanks, son." Jack Rhyce said. "That extra quarter is for showing me Mr. Molotov."

Until the bellboy left, he stood gazing admiringly at the view, but as soon as the door was closed he started on a tour of inspection which was as routine as a plane checkup. No transom; the door lock sound, and in good order; no balconies or closely adjoining windows; no air shaft in the bathroom. It was five o'clock in the afternoon, ample time in which to make a final appraisal of all his personal effects before he went to dinner.

First he examined his passport. Unlike several others that he had carried, it told his true history except for his occupation—height five feet eleven, hair light brown, eyes blue, no distinguishing marks or features. His place of birth was Lincoln, Nebraska, where as a matter of fact his mother and his elder sister still lived. His date of birth was January 13th, 1920. His occupation was educator. A good deal of thought had been given to his photograph, and the general result was useful, in that it only vaguely resembled him. There was no disguising his high broad forehead, or the arch of his eyebrows, or the firmness of his jaw, but if he changed his expression he could repudiate the whole document, if necessary.

Next, he turned to his briefcase. He had been taught and he understood the great importance of cover. The proper odds and ends and letters in a briefcase could be of the utmost value, and one of the rules of the game was that one never could be too careful with cover details.

The latest advices were that Japan was getting hot again and with a tensing in the Pacific area, there was bound to be increased interest in any strange American in one of several quarters. Thus he expected and hoped that someone would go through his personal effects, either during his stopover in Hawaii or directly after his arrival in Tokyo, and the sooner this happened the better, as far as he was concerned. The main point was to demonstrate as early in the game as possible that he was harmless, with absolutely nothing to conceal.

He put his briefcase on the writing table and drew out its contents, placing the items in a neat row. He was satisfied with the way everything looked. The letters had obviously been well handled, and the odds and ends beside the letters were the sort of things that would get into a briefcase by accident, and each added its bit to the owner's background. There was, for instance, a small box of deodorant powder which confirmed his new personality, since affable people who wished to please dreaded perspiration. The New Testament which was also in the briefcase he had felt was too obvious by itself, and he had compromised by adding a small volume of the sayings of Buddha, published by the Oxford University Press. Both these volumes were also well worn, with many cogent passages marked in his own writing. The letters indicating his family background gave him particular pleasure. He could not forget the work which had gone into the one from Omaha, Nebraska. Not only the words but the handwriting accurately revealed the writer's character.

> DEAR, DARLING BUNNY:
>
> I am so pleased and so proud that this wonderful chance has come to you after so many years of working so hard for other people. I know you don't know much about the Japanese, any more than I do. But we both know their hearts are in the right place. And your personality that inspires trust in everyone will get through to them, I know, in spite of all the barriers of race and creed. I would be worried about the Oriental women that you are going to meet over there if I did not have a mother's knowledge of a devoted son. I know you will be thinking of me as much as I of you. Send me a postcard every day, and happy landings.
>
> MUMSIE

Although Jack Rhyce admitted that the letter might seem exaggerated, at the same time people who skimmed through briefcases often required definite leads, and the Oedipus complex was universal. After all, there could be little sinister about a mother's boy.

The second letter was written in a girlish hand on the stationery of the Department of Sociology of Goucher College.

> DEAR JACKIE:
>
> I'm going to miss you terribly. But seriously, sweetie, I think it's a grand thing that you are going away to new countries for a while, to study how other people live—not that I want you to get interested in any girls there, or anything like that. But seriously, sweetie,

> although I don't like to be a "bore," I do think the time has come for you to make up your mind. In fact, the time has come for both of us. This doesn't mean that I don't love you dearly, sweetie, but a girl can't stay waiting all the time for any man, can she? And this has been going on ever since we met at your Senior Prom—remember? I know your mother is a darling, but, honestly, I don't feel that she need interfere with a happy marriage. I've been reading a lot about these problems lately, and all the authorities say that they can resolve themselves, but we all have to do our part. I simply can't do everything. And so as you wing your way over the ocean, I hope . . .

Jack Rhyce did not read the rest of it, because he was familiar with the contents. The letter had been composed, though not handwritten, by an elderly spinster who specialized in cover work, and who had no sense of humor. She was not even amused by the signature, "Loads of love, your HELENA."

"Why do you think that's funny?" she asked him. "That's exactly the sort of girl who would want to marry you if you had a mother like that."

Both letters showed signs of constant reading. For the past two weeks he had spent a half hour persuing them before going to sleep, and his fingerprints proved it.

Then there were the more formal letters of introduction to representatives of a completely genuine institution known as the Asian Friendship League in Japan, and all other countries where the League had branches. The beauty of it all was that there was nothing wrong with any of this part of the cover. The organization had been honestly conceived by public-spirited citizens, and, at least in its Washington headquarters, had no employees with subversive records.

Connecting him with the Asia Friendship League had been the Chief's idea. It happened that the Chief had known the man who had given the money to form the Asia Friendship League. He was a Texas oil millionaire named Gus Tremaine who had established a charitable trust for tax purposes, and in fact had not known that the Asia Friendship League existed until the Chief had informed him of it personally. The trust money, Mr. Tremaine had explained, was handled by a board, the meetings of which he seldom attended; but he was most co-operative after the Chief had talked to him, and he had called and written the chairman of the Asia Friendship League personally.

Jack Rhyce now had the letter written to him, as a result, on the League's letterhead:

ASIA FRIENDSHIP LEAGUE
NATIONAL HEADQUARTERS
WASHINGTON, D.C.

DEAR MR. RHYCE:

It is a real delight to hear from Mr. Gus Tremaine that he has commissioned you, on his behalf, to make a survey of our work in the Orient, and to write a general report for him. This is just the sort of thing we like, and we like it all the better when it shows Mr. Tremaine's interest. You must not be prejudiced by any idle gossip regarding the Institute of Pacific Relations, or anything like that. You will find that in our show we have all the cards on the table and nothing up our sleeves. The main ideal behind our organization, endorsed by all the fine people whose names you see on the left margin of this letter, is in one word—good will. In fact, we have only one ax to grind, if you call it an ax, and that is that a lot of people out in the Pacific area need a lot of help, but not handouts that smack of colonialism. Our concept is simply to help folks to help themselves.

However, I am, as it were, talking out of school. You'll understand our aims better after we have lunch and spend an afternoon together on any day you name next week. And on your travels, you'll find out, too, what a swell, alert team of truly dedicated folks we have in Tokyo, Seoul, Hong Kong, Saigon and Thailand.

Well, anticipating a word from you, and looking forward to being of any help to you in any way I can, in what I honestly predict will be for you a real eye-opening adventure—

Cordially yours,
CHAS. K. HARRINGTON

This letter also showed signs of repeated reading. It had interested Jack Rhyce from the beginning.

## 2

AS SOON as he had received the Harrington letter, Jack Rhyce had asked to see the Chief, who listened carefully while Jack read the letter aloud.

"Well," the Chief said, "what's so funny about it?"

"I didn't say it sounded funny," Jack Rhyce said. "I said I thought it sounded phony."

"I wish you wouldn't bother me about these details, Buster," the Chief said. "The whole department is working on this cover for you. We're giving it everything we've got, and then when we come up with something you merely say it's phony."

"I only mean," Jack Rhyce said, "I sort of get the idea that this whole Friendship League setup sounds a little too good to be true."

There was an appreciable pause, and it seemed to Jack that perhaps the Chief was reviewing the bidding. It was the Chief's open mind that had finally put him where he was, in spite of competition.

"Have you read their literature yet?" the Chief asked.

"No, sir," Jack Rhyce said.

"Well, read it," the Chief said, "before you make any snap judgments. Of course it sounds like a front organization, but as far as we can see, this one is harmless, although Bill Gibson has not reported on it yet. Anyway, Chas. K. Harrington is harmless, and everyone else in his executive suite. They ought to be. They are drawing higher salaries than you or me, and they have expense accounts besides. Frankly, I never thought of this outfit to cover you until I saw that the Tremaine Foundation had set it up. Gus and I were in the war together. He's a Texan. Do you like Texans?"

"Not always," Jack Rhyce said.

"Well, I think maybe you ought to meet him," the Chief said, and looked hard at Jack again and smiled in a frigid way.

"You see, Gus is like you, Buster. He just doesn't believe that the world is full of people who want to do good by spending other peoples' money. But you're going to understand it. You'd better start learning, because we're going to turn you into one of those people."

"Maybe I'm not the right type, sir," Jack Rhyce said.

"You're going to be," the Chief said. "You're going to be a mother's boy, and have a sweetheart. I think we'll have her in the sociology department at Goucher College. You'll only have about two weeks before you start, so throw yourself into it, Buster."

Naturally, he was most anxious to throw himself into it. He had only been told until then that Gibson, in Tokyo, had requested help, and that he had been selected, but he still did not know what his mission was, and he had been careful not to ask. Now, however, as he sat in the Chief's office, listening to the humming of the air-conditioner, and the sounds of the Washington traffic, he understood that the plans had solidified, and that his briefing was about to start.

"Do you know what I found out the other day?" the Chief asked him. "I discovered that the boys and girls in the office call me Dick Tracy. Why do you suppose they do that?"

"Well," Jack answered, "I'd say it was mainly out of affection, and not because they think you're a figure of fun, or a comic, or anything like that."

The Chief turned on another of his icy smiles.

"Right," he said, "comics aren't comics any more. When I was a kid I was supposed to laugh at the Hall-Room Boys and Mutt and Jeff and the Katzenjammer Kids, but that's all over now. Nothing is really funny any more, not even a good pratfall, because it may have international significance. Right?"

"If you say so," Jack Rhyce said, "but I don't follow you."

"Now don't get fresh, Buster," the Chief told him. "I admit that I am circuitous this morning. I'm sorry to harp on the remark you made about this Asia Friendship League letter. You said you thought it might be phony, but I'm afraid you think it's funny too. Please don't think it is, because I'd like to have you come back alive from Tokyo."

He paused, and a silence fell between them.

"Let's skip that last remark," the Chief said. "All I'm trying to say is that these people like this Chas. K. Harrington aren't funny. Often they're not even stupid. Please don't underrate them, Buster. Oh, sure, a lot of them are grotesque. Most of them are ignorant in many sectors, because they're usually narrow and dogmatic—but don't forget they can be dangerous. They do have a certain idealism, and a kind of selflessness. They have what Tennyson called 'an all-increasing purpose,' even if it's fuzzy-minded. Never underestimate the do-gooders, Buster. As a class, they've made us a hell of a lot of trouble in the last thirty years. Please never think of them as being funny."

When the Chief got started, he had an orator's ability to begin in a slow, haphazard manner, and then with no appreciable effort to pull everything together.

"Incidentally," he said, "I wonder if you have ever read *Heaven's My Destination* by Thornton Wilder. I don't suppose so, because it was written when you were in short pants, except that of course they weren't wearing them when you were a boy, were they? I wish you would read it before you go to sleep tonight, because his central character is a do-gooder. Some people thought he was funny, but he wasn't. You're giving me your full attention, aren't you? You see, your cover is a do-gooder and you've got to understand the species."

He stopped and gazed at Jack Rhyce, but of course Jack was giving him his full attention.

"The thing to keep clearly in mind is that this individual you're going to represent, whom I call a do-gooder for want of a better word, is a distinctly modern type. There was nothing like him in the days of the Roman Empire, and he can only survive today in a country rich enough to afford him. There have been plenty of philanthropists before, and socialists and revolutionists—Tom Paines, and John Donnes, and Karl Marxes, and Arnold von Winkelrieds, and Wilhelm Tell, and Spartacus, and lots of other active characters whose hearts have bled for the common man, but not the same way our modern hearts bleed. Do-goodism in its purest form is new in the world. Maybe it's our greatest hope, but it's also our biggest danger—seriously."

"You mean certain people and ideologies take advantage of it?" Jack asked.

"You're smart today, Buster," the Chief said. "The trouble is, we're an incorrigibly romantic nation who believe, like Little Orphan Annie, that Daddy Warbucks will always be just around the corner. Do-gooders are unrealistic and their older models weren't, basically. The older models thought things through, but we don't think. We feel. The same used to be true of you, but I trust you're getting over it."

"How do you mean—it used to be true with me?" Jack asked.

"Do you remember," the Chief asked, "that damn-fool remark you made to Molotov just before we yanked you out of the paratroopers, about all men being brothers? That's what I mean—it was do-goodism. I damn near sent you back to the army after that."

Jack Rhyce was startled. The truth was you never could tell what the Chief would remember.

"I agree with you, sir," he answered. "I hope I'm better now."

"But I don't want you to be better *now*," the Chief said. "I want you to be a do-gooder. I want you to throw yourself into it. Now you've shown me your letter. Here's another for you, Buster, and after you read it maybe you won't feel that Chas. K. Harrington's Asia Friendship one is so phony. Don't hurry with it. Take your time."

He opened the top drawer of his desk and pulled out a photostat of a letter dated a week before from Amarillo, Texas.

> DEAR MR. HARRINGTON (he read):
>
> Due to my business commitments here and there I've been kind of out of touch with your project, the Asia Friendship League, but I've heard a lot about the fine things you're doing out there, and I feel right gratified, to use a Texas phrase.
>
> Now just in order to keep myself up to date, I am commissioning a young friend of mine, for whom I can vouch in every way, because we've rode the range together, and eaten brains at the same barbecue, to make a survey for me of everything you're doing, so I can have the whole picture straight, right here at El Rancho Chico.
>
> The name is Jack Rhyce—a good real American, by the way, though I'm not anti-foreign or anti-anything, partner. Take him right in and shoot the works to him, and send him around the world to all those places which I hope to see myself someday, where they ride in sampans and leave their shirttails out.

You're going to like Jack, so just feel free to tell him anything, because, honestly, he's a prince. And here are a few facts. Jack graduated from Oberlin College in 1941. He has a fine religious background, but is at the same time a real he-man. For example, he played right tackle for Oberlin on the team that almost got to the Sugar Bowl or someplace, and also commenced interesting himself in civic and welfare projects. For instance, during summer vacations, he was counselor for the Y.M.C.A. boy's camp at Lincoln, Nebraska; and helped out in various recreational projects, including the organization of the Tiny Tim Football League, which proved very popular.

He tells me he thinks he would have gone into settlement work if it had not been for the war, but he was just as quick as a Texan to heed his country's call, serving in the paratroopers until wounded. After this he did desk work for various services in Washington, and since then has stayed in Government, not wearing striped pants, but traveling the world for projects like Point Four and things like that. Jack's got a lot of swell ideas, and you two are going to have a lot in common. He's at loose ends now, and I don't know anyone who will understand and appreciate what you're up to better than Jack.

Why is he at loose ends? Well, frankly, because I've been lucky enough to shanghai him out of Washington with the eventual plan of having him as a sort of legman for me out here at Amarillo. How was I able to shanghai him? Well, frankly, don't kid Jack about it, but Cupid has entered into the picture in the shape of a very lovely little trick who is working in the department of sociology at Goucher College, whose name is Helena Jacoby. What with his lovely mother, whom he's never let down since he was five, and this Cupid deal, Jack needs a little more dough. Well, that's the story, Harrington. You'll hear from him, and give him the red carpet treatment all the way to everywhere, and so *hasta mañana.*

GUS TREMAINE

The strength of the letter was that its main facts were provable by investigation. He had been to Oberlin. He had played right tackle. He had been a Y.M.C.A. camp director, and his parents did entertain strong religious convictions. He had been a paratrooper until the Chief had run into him at Walter Reed Hospital. Since the war he had served in Washington.

"How do you like it?" the Chief asked. "It ought to be good, because I spent two nights over it, personally."

Jack Rhyce handed back the copy. It was amazing how intricately the Chief's mind could work.

"It looks pretty good, sir," he said, "but it might help if you were to tell me just why you've selected me for this spot, and what I'm supposed to do when I get there—in Japan."

For a moment the Chief looked annoyed, but finally he nodded.

"Maybe you've got a point there, Buster," he said. "You know I never play fun and games with anyone intentionally, don't you? I think it's early to give you the breakdown, but maybe you've got a point."

He paused and tapped his desk with his pencil.

"All right," he said. "Question Number One: You're going out to the East because you're not known there. Europeans, and especially Americans, stand out like sore thumbs in the East. Everybody knows your income and your girl friend in the Orient. Even the rickshaw pullers know whether you are a spy or not. Orientals are experts about people, as you'll find out, and that's why we are working so hard on your cover, but it won't help indefinitely. They find out everything eventually."

"What about Sorge?" Jack Rhyce asked. "He lasted quite a while."

He was speaking of one of the greatest men in the profession—the German Sorge who, in the guise of a newspaper correspondent, ran the Russian spy ring, and for years had given Moscow accurate intelligence regarding all Japanese intentions. He had been a foreigner, alone in a highly suspicious country, who had been watched by a highly organized secret police, and yet it had been a long while before the Japanese caught up with him.

"Sorge," the Chief said. "Exactly. Sorge had a good cover. But the Japs got him in the end, and made him sing. He must have forgotten his pillbox. I want you to keep yours handy, Buster."

They were both silent for a few seconds. They were professionals, and there was no need to underline anything.

"All right," the Chief said. "Question Number Two: You're

going out to assist Gibson. You'll be under his orders." And then he lowered his voice. "Gibson's got the wind up, and he doesn't scare easy. He thinks the Commies are planning a political assassination, and anti-American demonstrations in Tokyo. This is serious when you consider the total political picture." The Chief pushed back his desk chair and stood up. You never realized how tall he was until he was on his feet. He selected another chair and drew it close to Jack.

"Gibson's vague. But you know as well as I do that he's damned intuitive. He says a new personality is running things." The Chief's voice dropped to a still lower note. "An American personality, Gibson thinks. He asked for you, particularly."

"Did he say what the personality is doing?" Jack Rhyce asked.

It was never a good idea to ask the Chief direct questions, and he was not surprised that the Chief was annoyed.

"Damn it," the Chief said, "Gibson was necessarily vague. That's the trouble with this cold war. It's all vague. It isn't a question of stealing the secret plans. It's organization and propaganda and sudden ugly incidents; and our side hasn't learned yet to organize or to understand what people want. All we know is what they ought to want, but maybe we're learning slowly."

The Chief described a circle in the air with his right hand.

"All we can do is to sketch this character," he said. "He's an organizer, a new mind in the apparatus. There's been a sudden marked change in Japan, according to Gibson's estimate. The neutralist intelligentsia are getting more neutralist. There's more anti-Americanism, more pro-Communism. The Communist choral groups are getting better. There's more and better Red literature in the bookshops. There are new ideas. For instance, there's a new labor union that sells clothes at 40 per cent below the retail price. It's the bread and circus idea, but somehow it's done on subtler lines. It's Gibson's notion that all this is only the prelude to large-scale disturbances. You'll have to see him to get it straight, or maybe you'll even have to see the character."

This piece of exposition impressed Jack Rhyce because it lacked the Chief's usual balance.

"Maybe I haven't quite followed you," Jack Rhyce said. "It seems to me everything you say sounds like the usual Moscow technique."

Certainly he and everyone else had seen enough of it. The undeviating quality of the Moscow manufactured procedure was its greatest strength, because there came a saturation point when simple-minded men accepted boredom. The Chief nodded slowly.

"I'm sorry if I gave you that impression," he said. "Actually yours was my own initial reaction, until I examined the orders to organizers and all that sort of thing. It's all gayer. It doesn't taste so much like castor oil. You'll find you almost enjoy it. When was the last time you were in Tokyo?"

"Eight years ago," Jack said, "and only for two days. Tokyo looked pretty well bombed out then."

"Well," the Chief said, "I was there six months ago, and really you wouldn't know the place now. The Japs have that resilience, or national will to live, or whatever you may call it. The whole town's built up and it's bigger, better, busier. And any fool can observe that its atmosphere is predominantly American. It used to be Germany before the war, but now in Japan the fashion is the U.S.A. Even the shop signs are in English in districts no American ever visits. Maybe they think America is good because we won the war. I wouldn't know. I wouldn't care. Of course Japanese culture never will be American, but oh, boy, they have the superficialities! You hardly see a kimono in Tokyo any more. You don't hear the sound of a geta on the sidewalk. Go to a ball game—and you might think you were back at home from the sounds the crowd makes. The girls all wear American dresses and the men are in business suits. Do you think I'm getting away from my point?"

"I know you couldn't do that, sir," Jack Rhyce said, and he was quite right, because in the next few words the Chief pulled everything together.

"They like everything American. That's the point," the Chief said. "They don't fall for anything Russian. And this new propaganda has an American touch. It has jazz and neon lights in it. It's damn clever. And I think Gibson's right—it's dangerous. Communist-made Americanism always is, because it can form the background of serious disturbances. Frankly, I wouldn't say that Japan is very firmly in the camp of the freedom-loving nations. Why should it be? Well, we lost China, and God help us if Japan goes Communist. We'll be in the grinders then; and frankly, Gibson thinks there's a hell of a better chance of its happening than there was six months ago. Something new has been added from America and things are accelerating."

Jack Rhyce knew that the Chief had not given all the details yet.

Certainly the Bureau's organization in Japan was not so ineffective that it had not turned up a few concrete facts.

"I hope you're going to tell me what's been dug up," Jack Rhyce said. "After all, I have personal reasons for being curious."

"Oh, yes," the Chief said, and he sat down behind the desk again. "I've made a few mental notes. Of course we have our contacts in the left-wing organizations, but as far as we can make out, none of our people has seen this individual. However, there is reason to believe that he has been to Japan several times. We think we know his cover name. It's Ben Bushman. There's a lot of talk about a Ben in all the recent intercepts. The man who is really masterminding things out there is a Russian named Skirov who comes over to Tokyo to meet Ben. Gibson thinks there's a meeting due pretty soon. I don't need to ask you if you know about this Skirov, do I?"

"I know who he is all right, sir," Jack Rhyce answered.

The Chief smiled faintly, indicating that they both understood that the question had been a joke. Skirov had been on the Moscow first team for a long while, and the latest evaluations had placed him close to the first ten in Moscow.

"Yes," the Chief said. "He's been improving in the last few years like rare old wine, and he's slippery as an eel, always behind the scenes. Am I right in remembering that you've seen Skirov once?"

Jack Rhyce shook his head.

"No," he answered, "I'm sorry, sir, I missed him if he was at any of those parties in Moscow, but I have him clear in my mind, just as everyone else around here has. I examined his photographs only last week."

"You mean in relation to the new Politburo setup?" the Chief asked.

"Yes, sir," Jack Rhyce said, "in that connection, and I can give you his description verbatim."

The Chief sighed and tapped his pencil on the desk.

"I suppose it's too much to think you'll run into Skirov over there," the Chief said, "but if you should you know what the orders are regarding Skirov, don't you?"

"Yes, sir," Jack Rhyce answered.

The Chief had stopped tapping his desk. The pencil was motionless.

"No matter what it costs," he said, "don't forget the sky's the limit if you contact Skirov. There's just a hope that this new one—this

Big Ben—may lead you to him, but I doubt it. Skirov never sticks his neck out. That's why your main mission is this Big Ben. I want him located and taped."

"There's no personal description of him yet, is there?" Jack Rhyce asked.

"Nothing that is definite," the Chief said. "He may be big, because he's referred to occasionally as Big Ben. Once the phrase, 'the Honorable Pale-eyed,' was found in words contiguous to Ben's. I wish the Japanese were as clever at giving nicknames to foreigners as the Chinese. . . . But I'm getting off the point. All we have about our boy are theories. It looks as though he were energetic, and therefore young. If he's young, he must have some sort of war record. I'd say he was college-educated. He must have been in the East for a while at one point, because our bet is that he has a smattering of Japanese and a little Chinese. This might put him in the preacher class, but I doubt it. He must have a vigorous, engaging personality, be quite a ball of fire in fact; but he isn't in our files. There's one thing more that I'm pretty sure of. It looks to me like a safe bet that Big Ben has been in show business."

"What makes you go for that one, sir?" Jack Rhyce asked.

"The Communist drama groups in Japan," the Chief said. "You know how the Communists have always used folk drama to make their little points. I saw a lot of their plays before the war, in China. Now, according to Gibson, these productions, which used to be excruciatingly dull, have been jazzed up. Pretty girls are singing blues, there's soft-shoe and tap dancing, and American-type strippers."

"He sounds like someone in the Hollywood crowd," Jack Rhyce said.

"It could be," the Chief answered. "Naturally we've given some thought along that line, but Hollywood is more of a generic term than a place. For my money, Ben has been around the live stage, specifically musical comedy. I rather think, since we haven't dug him up, that he was in some Little Theater group. Or maybe he was in one of those road companies that are always traveling around the country doing revivals of Sigmund Romberg or Victor Herbert. Well, there's your picture. We want to know who Ben is, and you're going to help Gibson find out."

"What do we do if we find him?" Jack asked.

The Chief laughed, one of his rare laughs.

"You know my motto," he said. "Always do it with velvet gloves—

when possible. I wouldn't want to hurt this Big Ben for the world, if it isn't necessary, but we don't want political assassination or anti-American demonstrations either. Anyway, Bill Gibson will give you the line to take. Of course, if you run into Skirov, that will change the picture, and Bill's got his orders, too, about Skirov. Also, if you stir things up, it may be that the whole Skirov apparatus will get ugly. Don't forget that one. Now, there's one thing more." The Chief looked at his watch again.

"What's that, sir?" Jack Rhyce asked.

"Beginning tomorrow I want you to take two weeks off to study that material, and I want you to go up to the Farm to do it, and every afternoon you're to have a workout with George and the boys. Right through the whole curriculum—everything."

"It isn't necessary," Jack said. "I know those things."

"It won't hurt to have a refresher course," the Chief said. "From now on you're a do-gooder. And do-gooders don't carry rods. I want you to be good if you have to rough it up with people. Really, Jack, I'm most anxious for you to come back to me alive."

## 3

ONE OF the troubles with working in the office was that you could have no real life of your own because you knew too much, and because the off moment might arise when you forgot what was classified or what was not. The only people with whom you could be at ease were those of a selected group from the office, and even with them you could not wholly relax. Nevertheless, you always had to appear to be normal, because in no respect could you seem peculiar or conspicuous. It was no wonder that Jack Rhyce sometimes laughed sourly when he read the advertisements in *True Detective* magazine; no wonder that most members of the group went on drunken sprees when they returned from various assignments. The Chief was always lenient about these lapses, as long as they were done at the Farm. The worst of it was, that sometimes you hardly knew who you were, after months in foreign parts, and yet you finally adjusted to anything.

The Chief had once told Jack Rhyce that he had only one handicap: he was too good-looking, too athletic and well-set-up to avoid attracting attention. But for once his athletic build, his guileless face, and his irrepressible interest in everything around him were all helpful to his cover. As he sat in his bedroom in the Mark Hopkins, Jack Rhyce has almost forgotten who he was. His mind, in the solitude of the Farm, had absorbed all the facts and details, both about himself and Big Ben. He had almost developed a genuine enthusiasm for the self-improving opportunity that this trip to the Far East would give him, and he had been able to communicate this enthusiasm to Mr. Chas. K. Harrington, in several of his interviews.

Of course he had still harbored the suspicion, after that talk with the Chief, that there must be something wrong about the Friendship League, and the Chief was amused when he heard about it.

"I don't think so, although we haven't got a final check," he said. "The thing that saves them is that they're too damned obvious. After the Institute of Pacific Relations investigations, any sensible Comrade would think that this is a trap; but give them a good looking-over, Buster."

He had not forgotten what the Chief had told him. As he sat in his locked hotel room there in San Francisco, checking over for the last time the contents of his briefcase, he had an unworldly feeling. None of his precautions seemed correct for anyone who was going to write a favorable report about a fine organization, and who was so fortunate as to have his expenses paid to a wonderful part of the world. He examined the last papers in the briefcase, down to the final odds and ends that had seemingly fallen there by mistake—those bits that gave more veracity than any letters could, and all revealed character: the paper of matches from an inexpensive hotel, and a very respectable one, in midtown New York; the theater-ticket stubs to the matinee of a play which had only one week left to run; the memorandum of telephone numbers—all of persons to whom Chas. K. Harrington had referred him, in case anyone should want to confirm. There was one thing that bothered him slightly in his final summing-up. The net result of that briefcase, he suddenly feared, was too neat, too virtuous, lacking any sign of human weakness, and most people did have frailties. Perhaps, although it had been carefully discussed in Washington, it had too many earmarks of obviousness and exaggeration. He sat for a moment thinking carefully of possible remedies, and suddenly he had it. He would go to a drugstore that very evening and get a paper-bound copy of the Kinsey Report of the sex life of the

American Female, and put a plain paper cover over it. It would take several hours to get the book authentically dog-eared, but the trouble might be worth it. No one who searched that briefcase would ever doubt his character again—not with the New Testament, Buddha and Kinsey all together. He was still congratulating himself on the idea when his room telephone rang.

There was no reason, as he thought it over later, why the jangling of the bell should have run through his nerves like an electric shock. It must have been that sight of the Russians that made him start at the sound, and also, as far as he could tell, the fact that no one knew that he was in San Francisco. He watched the telephone for a considerable time without lifting it, but the bell continued ringing. Whoever was calling the room must have been very sure that he was there. He finally picked up the instrument.

"Hello," he said, and he spoke in the mellifluous, accentless voice that he had spent such a long time cultivating.

He was startled when a girl's voice answered.

"Hello"—the voice had a slightly husky quality, and sounded very young, and at the same time seductive. "Is this Mr. John Rhyce?"

"Yes," he answered, and he timed the pause very carefully. "Yes, this is Mr. Rhyce."

The voice changed immediately into confidential happiness. The words tumbled over each other in what seemed to him a Midwestern manner.

"Gosh, I'm glad I contacted you, Mr. Rhyce. I was afraid you might have left your room, or something. This is Ruth—Ruth Bogart."

"Oh," he said. "Oh, yes"—and he tried to cudgel his brains. Having been in the profession for a considerable period, he was naturally good with names and faces; but he could not place any Ruth Bogart.

"Don't you know who I am?" she asked.

"Why, no," he said, and he laughed. "I don't, to be quite frank; but then perhaps I'm not the Mr. Rhyce you're looking for either. Rhyce is a common name, but mine is spelled with a *y*."

"Of course it's spelled with a *y*," she said. "Oh, dear, didn't Mr. Harrington tell you? I'm one of the Asia League girls, and we're going on the same plane tomorrow."

"Why, no," he said, "Mr. Harrington didn't tell me."

"Oh, dear," she said. "He promised he was going to. Have you inquired for wires and everything?"

"There wasn't any wire," he answered.

"Oh, dear," she said. "Charlie gets so absent-minded sometimes. Well, just the same, I'm Ruth Bogart."

There was a slight pause while his mind moved rapidly, since there were a number of possibilities in that call, and the most important one was that it might have originated with the Russians.

"Well, it's very kind of you to give me a ring," he said, "especially when you must have many acquaintances in the city, Miss Bogart."

"No," she said, "I haven't, and it's awfully lonely in a strange city, isn't it?" If it weren't for her American voice, and the implacable self-confidence of American women, he would have thought the approach was crude. "I'm stopping here at the Mark, too, and—maybe I'm butting in, but Charles—I mean Mr. Harrington—did suggest I call you. I was hoping if you weren't too busy or something, we might have dinner. There's a place here called Fisherman's Wharf, I understand, where they have divine sea food. My room is 312."

"Why, that sounds swell," Jack Rhyce said. "I could certainly do with some sea food. I'll be knocking on 312 in just a jiffy."

It was much better to see what was going on than not, and he especially liked the word "jiffy," for it had a suggestive Friendship League sound. He looked in the mirror above the bureau and straightened his coat. Then he bent down and tested the laces of his brown crepe-soled shoes. Finally he gave a parting glance at his briefcase. It was the oldest game in the world, to lure someone away so that his room could be searched, and a girl was conventionally the shill. He very much hoped he was correct in this suspicion, because the sooner he was placed the better. The only doubt he harbored was how dumb he ought to be. Should he put his briefcase in the upper drawer of the bureau, or should he simply leave it on the writing table? He compromised by tossing it carelessly on the bed, closed the room door noisily behind him, and walked down the corridor eagerly and merrily, just in case anyone should be watching. There was an old saying in the business that a lot of men had saved their lives by giving the impression that they were easily beguiled by women. There had been a girl in Istanbul once, and a very pretty one, too, but that was another story, and he had been sorry when he heard later that she had fallen from a hotel window and died of a broken neck.

One of the oldest tricks was also the ambush, the alluring call on the telephone, the welcoming inward opening of the door, and the blow on the base of the skull. He was still whistling when he stepped out of the elevator and walked down the corridor to Room 312. A great deal of thought had been given at the Farm to the right and wrong way of entering a strange room. He rose to the balls of his feet, rapped briskly on the door of Room 312 with his left hand, his right low at his side, shoulders forward, knees bent, but only slightly.

"Oh," a voice said. "Just a moment, please."

His memory of the Russians made him very careful. He moved closer to the door and touched the knob with his left hand in order to be fully prepared when it turned. As the door opened inward, Jack Rhyce moved with it, almost touching the panel with his left shoulder, knees still bent, right hand still slightly down. There was bound to come a moment when the situation would reveal itself, and when you had your opportunity to advance or retreat, as long as you were moving with the door. Jack Rhyce entered the room almost on tiptoe, knees still bent. It was a duplicate of his own, and the bathroom door was closed. A glance at the bed showed that someone must have been resting on it at almost the moment he had knocked. He also had a glimpse of two matched suitcases of canvas airplane luggage. Of course he saw all those things at the very same instant he saw the girl who stood by the door.

She was very pretty, which did not surprise him. He would have estimated her age at not over twenty-five, until a glance at her hands made him doubtful. Her height was five feet six, hair dark brown, eyes gray-green. Her face was longish with a mouth that showed character, although you could not tell much about a woman's mouth when touched with lipstick. She wore a green dress of heavy silk with a thin yellow stripe in it, and she held a red leather handbag.

"Why, Mr. Rhyce," she smiled, "I didn't know you'd come rushing down quite so rapidly."

He smiled back in the overcordial manner that anyone might use when meeting an attractive girl. She was using very little make-up. The color in her cheeks was natural, and she had only a touch of lipstick. He had grown adept, long ago, in spotting persons engaged in his line of work. There was something indescribable about them that could awaken his intuition—an overalertness, perhaps, or a general impression of strain—but her personality baffled him, and he could not reach an immediate conclusion.

"I guess I hurried down faster than was polite," he said, "because it was such a surprise, and a real pleasure too, to hear a friendly voice in 'Frisco. I hope I didn't sound rude, or anything like that, when you called me, because that was my last intention. I'm terribly sorry that Charlie didn't say anything about you, and a little surprised, too, because without wanting to be forward or anything, I don't see how anyone like you could possibly skip anyone's mind."

He could not help being pleased with the general tone of his speech, all of which reflected his new character.

"Why, Mr. Rhyce," she said, "what cute things you say."

Her looks, and then the word cute, were like a tag in the museum case, although the possibility remained that she, too, had a cover.

"Well, I can only say it is a real pleasure, making your acquaintance, Miss Bogart," Jack Rhyce said, "and it will be fun exploring San Francisco with you. I'm especially glad you mentioned Fisherman's Wharf, and after that we might visit Chinatown. I believe it is the largest Chinese district anywhere in the United States."

There was no doubt that his weeks of work were paying off, and Mr. Wilder's novel had been of great assistance.

"I think dinner would be lovely," she said, "but I'm afraid I'll have to beg off on Chinatown, although it sounds awfully romantic and all that; and anyway, you and I are going to see a lot of these Oriental people pretty quickly, aren't we? I'm a little woozy, because I've just flown in from Chicago, and we have an early start tomorrow."

There was no doubt that she was very pretty, and of course, like all American girls, she obviously knew it. In the elevator she opened her red leather bag and took out a gold compact—genuine, not an ordinary plated job. She looked at herself critically in the little mirror, standing with her back to the elevator boy. Jack Rhyce could not avoid a sympathetic interest because it was the correct technique for examining the elevator operator.

"Oh, I forgot to powder my nose," she said.

Her nose looked straight and determined. It did not need powder, and he told her so.

"Well, anyway," she said, "this is a very exciting hotel. Do you know who was here this afternoon? Mr. Molotov himself, who was calling on Mr. Dulles. I had the good fortune to have a glimpse of him just as he was getting into his car."

"Did you?" Jack Rhyce said heartily, "I had that good fortune, myself. I was just getting in from the airport."

They were by the front door then and the doorman was whistling for a taxi.

"I know," she said, and gave him a playful smile. "I saw you, and I did hope you would be you."

It disturbed him that he had not seen her.

"You were so busy looking at those Russians," she said, "that I thought you almost wanted to speak to them."

"Well," he said, "I guess I forgot to look for pretty girls, or anything, being so close to Molotov. He was quite a character, wasn't he?"

"I thought he was cute," she said. "I was surprised. I thought he was just an old Teddy bear, didn't you?"

"Well," Jack Rhyce said, "not exactly a Teddy bear."

He kept wishing he could place her, so that he could be more at ease. The business with the compact mirror still disturbed him. As he sat down beside her in the taxi, she took out her compact again, and Jack Rhyce's shoulders stiffened slightly because there was really no valid reason for doing so a second time. Then she snapped her bag shut, and put her hand over his, where it rested on the seat beside him. Jack Rhyce was startled because her gesture did not fit correctly with the picture at the moment.

"It is so romantic, isn't it?" she said, "to see the sun setting over the Golden Gate? I never thought I'd have the opportunity."

"Yes," Jack Rhyce said, "I agree with you. It is going to be a lovely sunset."

But he was no longer listening to his words or hers. Her fingers were pressing on the back of his hand, first long, and then short, the Continental Code.

*"Being followed,"* he read: *"Orange-and-black taxi."*

He was not disturbed by the news that she had given him, but on the contrary, rather relieved. What did disturb him was his inability to place the girl.

*"Okay,"* he signaled back. *"So what?"*

*"Have message from Chief,"* she signaled back.

There was a happy smile on his face, and he drew his hand away. There were plenty of people in the outfit whom he did not know, since the cardinal principle in conducting such an operation was to have an individual know as few others as possible. What bothered him was that he still could not be sure of her.

"Driver," he asked, "what is the best place for sea food at Fisherman's Wharf?"

"I will never recommend one over another," the driver said, "but a lot of newcomers here sort of go for Fisherman's Grotto, maybe on account of the name."

Jack Rhyce studied the back of the driver's head carefully, thinking that he had talked more than was necessary, but then taxi drivers were apt to be verbose. He turned to the girl beside him.

"That's quite a name—the Fisherman's Grotto," he said. "Do you think we'd better try it?"

"Why, yes," she said. "I think it would be lovely." She sounded very happy, just the way a girl should who is being taken to dine at a place like the Fisherman's Grotto. "I always love to dine in new places, don't you? And we have so much to talk about, so many notes to compare."

"Yes," Jack Rhyce said, "and I can't tell you how pleased I am that we will be traveling together."

"That's why they hurried things up back East—just so we could," she said. "Mr. Tremaine said that so long as you were going, I might as well go with you, since you've traveled so much and this is all a new experience for me. He's a lovely old man, isn't he? I mean Mr. Tremaine—just a regular old Teddy bear."

"I never thought of him in that category, exactly," Jack Rhyce answered.

"It seems to me," she said, "that you don't seem to think of anybody as Teddy bears."

"Well, frankly, no, I haven't—not for a good many years," Jack Rhyce said. "And maybe it's just as well."

"Oh, dear," she said, "I hope you're not going to be a dim-view artist. I didn't think you would be, from what I heard of you at Goucher."

"Where?" he asked.

"Why, Goucher College, of course," she said. "Helena and I are both in the Department of Sociology, and we room together. In fact, frequently we're mistaken for each other."

"Now that you mention it," Jack Rhyce said, "I can see you look like Helena."

"I've heard so much about you," she said, "that I almost called you Jackie. What's the latest news of your mother?"

There was no time to answer because the taxi had stopped at the Fisherman's Wharf. Jack Rhyce was out and beside the driver as quickly as he could manage it. An orange-and-black cab had stopped behind them, and a slender man in his sixties got out of it. It was a calm, still day, and close to sunset, but there was plenty of light. He noticed that the Fisherman's Wharf was well equipped with artificial illumination. It was not the sort of place to finger anyone. The elderly man from the orange-and-black cab lingered outside the Fisherman's Grotto, examining some abalone shells. Jack Rhyce pulled his thoughts together abruptly. Granted there was no immediate danger, he would have felt safer if he had not met the Russians. There still remained the possibility that he had been spotted standing in the crowd, and the present reaction still might be more than a routine checkup.

"Helena says you always call your mother 'Mumsie,'" the girl beside him said.

"Oh, yes," he said, and he laughed in an embarrassed way, "but it's only a holdover from childhood."

Her last few words filled him with relief because it would have been difficult, at least in his judgment, for anyone outside of the office to have strung so many facts so consistently together. He was reasonably sure by now that she was the girl at Goucher College who had handwritten the "Dear Jackie" letter. For a second his mind moved from immediate necessities long enough for him to wonder how the Chief had ever found her, but it was none of his business, and the Chief would never tell. Still, he needed to make a further check before he finally accepted her.

"Well," he said, "so here we are at the Fisherman's Grotto," and he smiled and nodded to the headwaiter. There was still a choice of tables because the hour was early.

"I believe it's the season for Dungeness crabs," he said to her, "and if you've never tried one, they are a most rewarding experience."

Her smile was exaggeratedly gay and provocative, and he was naturally quick about playing by ear. She was telling him, as clearly as though she were speaking, that they both should be absorbed in each other's words and glances, and oblivious to what went on around them.

"Why, I never heard of them, Jackie," she said. "That's what Helena calls you, isn't it? Jackie?"

"Let's not go on any more about Helena," he said. "She's quite a distance away—already."

"Oh, dear," she said, and her smile grew reproachful. "I'm afraid you're mad at Helena because of what she said about your mother. You can't blame her for being a little tiny bit jealous, can you?"

"Well, it does get me a little miffed," he said, "and after all, as I repeat, Helena isn't here."

"Well, I think you're being rather naughty, Jackie," she said. "Do you think I'd make a better mother substitute than Helena?"

"I have an idea you'll be much better," he said. "In fact, I'll be glad to experiment. And may I call you Ruth?"

"Why, yes," she said, "only I hope you don't think I'm being forward, or susceptible, or anything like that, because that isn't really the case at all. I just believe in being myself, Jack. Don't you?"

It was one of the worst conversations in which he had indulged since he was sixteen, but as he threw himself into the make-believe, the thing assumed a quality that was almost genuine, particularly in the boy-meets-girl scene. The bored look of the waiter as he handed the menu proved, at any rate, that the audience believed.

"I think this occasion calls for a Martini or something like that, don't you?" he asked.

"I don't know that I care for a Martini," she said, "and I don't know that it would be any too good for you, either, now that I'm a mother substitute." Their glances met, and they both smiled fatuously at her little joke. "But I would like a nice bottle of that lovely California wine that is made by those priests, or something."

He was somewhat embarrassed that she had been smarter than he. Admittedly, it was conceivable that you might not know what went into a cocktail, but he wanted to tell her that you could also doctor a bottle of wine just as easily. In the end it might not have looked well if neither of them had taken a drink.

"We'll have both Martinis and the wine," he said, in a big-brotherly, reproving voice.

The most harmless thing in the world, the Chief was accustomed to say in one of his best lectures on cover, was a young couple falling in love. It was clear from the way she looked at him that she, too, could have heard that lecture of the Chief's. If things went right, he decided, no one would be surprised, if, after dinner, they stood for a while gazing across the bay at the lights of Alcatraz and if he put his arm around her and whispered in her ear, or if she whispered back.

It was a problem to appear completely engrossed in her, and at the same time to examine the man two tables behind. He looked like a bank clerk about to reach retirement age, and he made no apparent effort to hear what they were saying, showing that his job, obviously, was only to keep them both in sight.

"You can't blame me for being surprised when you called," Rhyce said. "No one gave me the least inkling that you'd be coming along, too."

"I know," she said. "It was Mr. Tremaine. He's impulsive, the way, I suppose, all rich people are."

Jack Rhyce laughed in an embarrassed way.

"I hope this doesn't mean they're losing faith in me, or anything like that," he said.

"Oh, no," she answered quickly, "it was only that it suddenly occurred to Mr. Tremaine that your job might be bigger than he thought, and that you might need some help. A girl with a typewriter, and things like that, you know."

"Are you good with a typewriter?" he asked.

"Yes," she said, and she laughed. "Any sort of typewriter."

"I hope we'll only have to use a standard brand," he said.

They looked at each other exactly as though they were falling in love.

"I didn't know the job was getting bigger," he said. "I'm very glad you're coming."

"So am I," she said, "because I love to travel. You know, just after I graduated from secretarial school I worked for a while for a man named Mr. Jackson, in Washington. He used to joke and say I had an itching foot, and it's awfully hard for a girl to travel alone."

"Well, where did you go to after you worked for Mr. Jackson, if you had an itching foot?"

"Oh, I went to Europe as soon as I could," she said. "I had a divine time traveling around there, seeing monuments and things like that, but I was with an insurance firm in London, mostly."

"Who was your boss in London?" Jack Rhyce asked.

"His name was Mr. Billings. It was a pretty big company in London," she said, "and it was a group of lovely people. I love London, don't you?"

"Yes," he said, "the few glimpses I've had of it. From my point of view, London is a man's town."

"But a girl can have a good time in a man's town, sometimes," she said. "I love everything about London. I always feel at home when I can hear Big Ben."

Jack raised his wineglass carefully. It reflected the old man eating two tables behind him. He was not listening, but it was still better to go on with the double talk.

"I wonder how Big Ben's striking these days?" he said. "It seemed to me his timing was erratic the last time I was in London. You know, I've been told you can hear Big Ben right in Tokyo, over the BBC—that is, when Radio Moscow doesn't interfere. I wonder if we'll hear Big Ben when we get to Tokyo?"

"I think we will," she said, "almost right away."

"Well," he said, "we'll have to remember to tune in."

She had told him almost everything, but she was still talking brightly, as though she were completely unconscious of it.

"I love to be in strange places and see strange people, don't you?" she asked.

"Yes," he answered. "Strange faces always fascinate me, too. I often play a little game with myself wondering who people are, and what they're thinking about; but maybe it's a bad habit and a waste of time."

"You can't ever tell though, can you?" she said. "Now there's a little old man, all sort of worn and threadbare just directly behind you, two tables away, and he keeps looking at us now and then, as if he were lonely. I wonder what he's been doing all his life."

Jack Rhyce laughed as though she had said something highly amusing.

"Whatever he'd done, he's kept alive," he said.

"They say, don't they," she said, "that San Francisco is the gateway to the Orient? And it's true, isn't it? Because I see there's an Oriental here. I can't tell whether he's Chinese or Japanese. Can you?"

"Where?" Jack Rhyce asked, and without intending it, his voice had an edge to it.

"Over there near that case with the queer fish on ice," she said.

A young Japanese, whom he had not noticed, had entered the Fisherman's Grotto.

"Oh," he said, "yes. I'd put him down for Japanese, and Nisei from his build. It's funny. I didn't see him come in."

She laughed again as though he said something highly amusing.

"Well," she said, "maybe we'd better go back to the hotel before we get into any trouble, because I didn't see him come in either."

"The only trouble we'll have here is to get the attention of the waiter," Jack Rhyce said. It was safe, in his opinion, to discount the Japanese.

The old man behind them must have paid his check already, because he rose when Jack Rhyce signaled to the waiter, sauntered slowly out of the restaurant—pausing, just as he passed their table, to light a thin black cigar, and to glance down at his wrist watch. The waiter arrived with the check just as the stranger went out the door. Jack Rhyce had a bill ready.

"Thanks," he said, "and keep the change."

He pushed back his chair. Miss Bogart raised her eyebrows. The lights were on outside and there was still daylight in the sky. Their shadow called a taxicab. The tension that had built up inside Jack Rhyce subsided slowly.

"He was a dear old man, wasn't he?" Ruth Bogart said. "I wonder where he's going now?"

"Home," Jack Rhyce said. "He's finished work, I think," and he linked his arm through hers affectionately, partly for relief, and partly because of cover. "The whole thing was only a check on our baggage," he told her softly.

This could be the only possible explanation of the shadow's actions. His glance at the watch and the lighting of the cigar confirmed the theory. They were only to be watched for a definite time, so that a warning could be given, in case they returned too soon—and now the time was up. He could light a cigar now.

"I think there's light enough," he said, "if you should care to look at Alcatraz through the telescope."

"That would be lovely," she said—and then she giggled—"as long as we don't get any nearer."

"That's one place where we probably won't end up," he said. Then, when he put a coin in the slot of the telescope, he added in a lower voice, "We can talk at the hotel. I think we're in the clear now."

"Why, it's fascinating," she said. "Hurry and take a look, before we have to spend another dime."

He had been careless, because he thought they were in the clear. Otherwise, he would not have kept his attention so long on Alcatraz. Consequently, when he heard a step behind him, he almost whirled around in a guilty way, instead of turning slowly.

"Sir," a voice said before he saw the speaker, "I beg your pardon, but would you like to see Chinatown?"

It was the young Japanese from the restaurant, the one whom he had thought might be American.

"No, thanks," Jack Rhyce said, "not tonight."

The Japanese, he saw, was at most in his early twenties. His neat, dark suit, his shirt open at the neck, and his hair done in a crew cut, gave him the appearance of a college student.

"There are many interesting things to see in Chinatown," the boy said. He was not persistent, but he was still there.

"I know," Jack Rhyce said, "but not tonight, thanks."

He had not seriously thought until then that there might be something wrong with the picture. The young man's hands were at his sides. There was no indication of a forward motion, and nothing in the face, or eyes, or shoulders, or in the set of the feet indicated trouble. Nevertheless, the Japanese had not moved.

"Excuse me, sir?" he said. "Would you mind if I ask you another question?"

"Why no, not at all," Jack Rhyce answered heartily. "Go ahead and ask it, son."

After all, he was a liberal-minded educator who liked kids. He smiled encouragingly at the Japanese.

"I was so near enough your table at the Fisherman's Grotto, sir," the young man said, "that I overheard some words you said to the young lady." He smiled back at Jack Rhyce. His face looked thin, sensitive, and handsome. "It was only accident—I did not mean to be intrusive."

Jack Rhyce laughed like a good-natured schoolteacher. After all, he had nothing to conceal, but, even so, he felt a slight tingling at the base of his skull.

"Why, that's all right son," he said, "perfectly all right. There's nothing I should mind having you overhear at all. The lady and I are strangers from the East, eating a fish dinner. What was it that we said that interested you?"

Jack Rhyce watched the young man move his fingers slowly across his palms before he spoke.

"Well, you see, I'm Japanese, sir," he said.

"Why, of course you are," Jack Rhyce said heartily, "and I can see that you're American, too. My guess is you were born right here in California. A lovely state, California."

"That is so, sir," the boy answered. "I was born here, and I'm a graduate of Cal. Tech."

"Well, well," Jack Rhyce said, "congratulations. That's a great school, isn't it Ruth—Cal. Tech.?"

"Yes, indeed it is," Ruth Bogart said. "One of my classmates at Goucher married a very cute boy from Cal. Tech. who majored in physics. I can't remember his name right now, but it will come to me in a minute."

"I was interested in what you were saying at the table," the boy said, "because I have relatives in Japan. May I introduce myself? My name is Nichi Naguchi. They called me Nick at college."

"Well, well," Jack Rhyce said. "This is a real pleasure, Nick. My name's Jack Rhyce, and this is Miss Bogart."

"I do wish we had time for you to show us Chinatown," Ruth Bogart said.

It was hard to tell whether or not the meeting was offbeat. After all, people were more breezy and friendly on the West Coast than the East.

"Well, don't hold back on us, Nick," Jack Rhyce said. "What was it you heard us say that caught your attention? Come on and tell us."

"Well, sir," the young Japanese said, "might I ask if you and Miss Bogart are going to Japan? You were saying you hoped to hear Big Ben strike in Tokyo, over the BBC."

The tingling at the base of his skull grew more pronounced. Now that Big Ben had been mentioned, he could not disregard the coincidence.

"Why certainly you can ask," Jack Rhyce said. "We haven't any secrets, Nick. Why sure, we're flying out that way tomorrow morning. Miss Bogart and I happen to be working for an organization in which we both take great pride—the Asia Friendship League—and I certainly hope that some of the things we're going to do may be of some assistance to your relatives there in Tokyo."

He watched for some revealing sign, however small, but the boy only looked reassured, and began to speak more eagerly.

"Since you have been so kind as to tell me," the boy said, "may I ask if you will not need a guide when you get to Tokyo? The Japanese language is difficult for Americans sometimes." He was overeager and laughed nervously. It was the first time that his Cal. Tech. veneer was gone. "I know a very good guide. He is my uncle. His English is very good. He is also fond of Americans, is very educated, knows all about Japan, all sights—everything. He can answer all questions, because he knows everything about Japan."

Jack Rhyce listened, balancing every word, but he could catch no undertone.

"Well, that's quite a recommendation, that he knows everything," he said, and he laughed before he finished. "Do you suppose he knows Big Ben?"

It was dangerous, but now and then you had to play a card.

There was nothing he could see in the boy's face, except uncomprehension.

"Big Ben?" the boy repeated.

Jack Rhyce laughed again, very heartily indeed.

"Didn't you get it, Nick?" he said. "The clock that you heard us talking about, you know, the one that strikes."

He still could read nothing in the boy's face.

"Oh, yes," the boy said, "I forgot. I am very sorry. If you would like, I can give you my uncle's address. I can write it on a card."

"Why, sure, Nick," Jack Rhyce said. "Jot it down and I'll look him up if I should ever need a guide."

"Thank you," the Japanese boy said. "Thank you very much."

"Not at all, Nick," Jack Rhyce said. "The pleasure is all ours, and I'll certainly give your uncle a buzz if I need him. Well, thanks, and so long."

"Good-by, sir," the boy said, "and good-by, Miss Bogart, and good luck, and a very happy trip."

They were alone, with their backs to Alcatraz. The wharf was more crowded now. No one among the parked cars or in the arcade seemed to take any interest in them, but it was safer to register an impression, in case there was anybody there who cared, and still to be very happy about what they were beginning to discover in each other.

"Well," he said, "that was quite a little human experience, wasn't it?" He put the card carefully in his wallet. "Everybody has always told me that San Francisco is a friendly city."

"Nichi Naguchi," she said. "They have funny names, don't they? But he was sort of shy and sweet. It was cute of him, wasn't it—thinking of his uncle? We should have asked him his address, so we could send him a picture card when we get to Tokyo. Oh, dear, that was stupid of me, not to think of it."

"It's all right," he told her. "I was just about to ask him myself, when I saw he had written his uncle's name on one of his own cards. His address is there, and everything."

"That was sweet and sort of sensitive of him, I think. Don't you?" she said. "Well, I'm glad we didn't ask him, because it might have looked too inquisitive. I don't like inquisitive people, do you?"

"No," he said. "They rub me the wrong way, somehow. This has been a lovely experience, getting to know you, Ruth."

"The same is true on my side, too," she said. "The more I know you, the better I think I'm going to like you, Jack. Let's stroll around and look at the fishing boats and things, before we go back to the hotel. Always get as much as you can out of any place you go to, has always been a motto of mine."

Undoubtedly she was as anxious to get back to the hotel as he, but it was never wise to hurry.

The elevator boy who took them to the third floor only looked bored when Jack got out with her.

"I'll just see you to your door," he said, "and see you're not locked out or anything."

"It isn't really necessary, Jack," she said, "but it's sweet of you to think of it."

When she took her room key from her handbag, he snatched it from her playfully, and there was even a merry, gentle little scuffle in the corridor, just in case anyone might be interested.

"Now really, Jack," she said, "now please try to behave."

When he turned the key in the door he was still laughing softly, and he approved of the way she covered him and watched the hall, and she kept the correct distance behind him when he entered the darkened room. The second the door was closed behind them he pointed to the closed bathroom door. She nodded, opened it, turned on the light, and pulled open the closet door afterwards.

"Okay," she whispered. "My God, I'm tired of being a Major Barbara!"

"Just a minute," he said gently, "just a minute before you get so frank." He took a pencil from his pocket and offered it to her. "Would you mind writing a few words on the back of this envelope?"

"Oh, so that's it?" she said.

"Yes, that's it," he answered, and his hand closed over her wrist. "I'll take your handbag while you're writing. It might get in your way."

They eyed each other for a moment.

"You don't miss any tricks, do you?" she said.

"I try not to," he answered. "Hurry, please."

"What do you want me to write?" she asked.

"Anything, as long as you write it," he told her. "Write 'I'll do my best to be a good co-operative girl if I go with you on this trip.'"

There was no hesitation when she wrote, but she did not write the words that he suggested. Instead, when she handed him back the envelope he read: *I don't like people who have to be so careful, and as I said, it has been a boring evening.*

Her writing was the same as the Helena letter that was in his briefcase.

"I'm sorry," he said, "if you think I'm disagreeable, but I had to make up my mind about you. Let's check on the luggage now."

He pointed to her matched suitcases. They were lying one on top of the other, with a small envelope briefcase on top. She unzipped the briefcase while he sat on the edge of the bed watching her, aware for the first time that he was feeling tired. All of her gaucheness was gone. Even before she looked up and nodded, he knew that the baggage had been searched.

"Good job?" he whispered.

She nodded back, smiling, and held up both her thumbs.

"It must have been a woman or a ribbon clerk," she whispered. "They folded the nylons back beautifully."

"Briefcase contents?" he whispered.

"All through everything," she whispered. "They had it out all over the writing table."

"Careless of them," he said.

"Clever of me," she whispered, "for being dainty and using lots of dusting powder. See where they brushed it off?"

He looked over her shoulder at the glass top of the writing table.

"Gloves," he said. "They dusted with them before they put them on."

"Smart as a whip, aren't you, Buster?" she said.

"You bet," he said, "right on the ball. What makes you call me Buster?"

"The Chief," she said. "He calls you that."

"Right," he said. "Now—what's the word?"

"Gibson asked for both of us. Big Ben's coming over. It's definite, he's from the States."

They both stopped and listened. Another guest was walking down the corridor with jaunty, heavy footsteps, and just as the steps passed, they heard a man's voice singing softly:

*For every day is ladies' day with me.*
*I'm quite at their disposal all the while!*

The song was from *The Red Mill*—an old song, and slightly incongruous for that reason, but then the comedy had been revived recently. They were both silent until the steps and the voice died away.

"Any identification?" he asked.

She shook her head.

"Nothing new. The Chief still likes show business."

"Well," he whispered, "things don't look too bad for us, now they've gone through the bags."

"Yes," she said, "I know, but what about that Jap?"

"I know," he said. "I'd like to get a check on him, but I think it's wiser not to signal Washington. Don't you?"

They looked at each other, and nodded. From now on, any communication with the Bureau might ruin everything.

"Well," he said, "I guess that's that. I wish I'd met you earlier before I took on this cover. I hate to be such a pratfall all day long."

"Oh, well," she said, "it won't be as bad as all that. Breakfast downstairs at 7:30, what? Good night, Buster."

"Good night," he said, and he put his hands on her shoulders. "Don't worry. We'll get through all right."

"Hell," she said, "I've given up worrying long ago. Haven't you noticed that?"

## 4

BY THE time he left Honolulu for Tokyo, Jack Rhyce was positive that he and Ruth Bogart were in the clear. It was inevitable, after a number of years' experience, that one should develop intuition. There was a sense of malaise—similar, he sometimes thought, to what psychiatrists called 'free guilt'—when you were being watched. You could not put your finger on any one thing, but finally you could learn to depend implicitly upon that feeling of imbalance. There had been none of that feeling in the airport at San Francisco, and none in Honolulu. When he showed Ruth Bogart the feather cloaks in the Bishop Museum, and the old mission house that had been transported in sections in ships around Cape Horn, he felt that he was exactly what he was supposed to be.

When the pictures of the early missionaries gazed at him sternly, he was able to gaze right back, and the question hardly crossed his mind as to what the Chief would have said about the missionaries. He was exactly what he should have been, and so was Ruth Bogart. He could even forget that they were boringly obvious. He was even able to take a surfboard out at Waikiki, in a perfectly carefree manner. He had learned a little of the trick of it while he had been stationed at Honolulu, during the last war, and it all served as part of the cover. He could be as expert as possible because he was a muscular do-gooder, full of good will toward the world. He was beginning to experience that wonderful feeling of complete creative success that came with perfect cover. There was confidence in such a feeling, but never overconfidence, only a thorough understanding of the cover itself, and a conviction that it had finally blended with his own personality.

On the afternoon when they boarded the plane for Tokyo, and began flying into the setting sun, nothing changed his mood, and he had always been highly sensitive to airports. The passengers on the plane were interesting, but not outstanding; a Hawaiian-Japanese couple, a Dutch businessman, two British businessmen, and then thirty members of a world tour group, all of whom could only have been exactly what they were. The project, as he learned from the world cruise director in the course of the trip, had been started by a travel agency which had founded an organization named the World Wide Club. Members of this organization, it seemed, paid their dues into a general account for several years, until at last the total sum had become large enough to pay a liberal down deposit on a round-the-world trip—and that was not all, either. During the years (as the director, who was a retired chemistry professor, told Jack Rhyce) in which the fund had been building up, there had been bi-weekly study groups, so that everybody by now knew quite a lot about the places to which they were going. Jack fell into the spirit of their trip at once, and told the cruise director that it was one of the greatest ideas he had ever heard of, and one that ought to spread to every city of the country.

"You know," he said, "the thought has just occurred to me, that we might incorporate this very travel idea into the organization which I happen to represent—the Asia Friendship League. One of our basic problems is to stimulate an interchange of travelers. Don't you think it is a great idea, Ruth?"

Of course she thought it was a great idea, and except for the Dutchman and the Englishmen, they all became a congenial group, flying across the Pacific at nineteen thousand feet. There were very few cocktails served, except to the Dutchman and the Englishmen, but still they began singing songs, and Jack Rhyce threw himself into the spirit of it, and he did have a good baritone. As far as he could remember later, they broke away from cover only once; it was Ruth Bogart's fault, not his. When it had grown dark, and dinner was over, and the merriment had died down, he took the sayings of Buddha from his briefcase.

"This fellow Buddha," he said, "has quite a lot to say. Some of it's a little difficult, due to his antiquity and his foreign way of life, but a lot of it fits right in with today. Would you like me to read you a little of it, Ruth?"

"Oh, shut up," she said, "and let me go to sleep."

"Why, of course," he said. "it was very thoughtless of me, chatting along this way, but I've been stimulated by this travel group and everything. Shall I ring to get you a pillow, Ruth? I know it is a tiring trip, with all this change of time and the plane vibration."

"Oh, shut up," she said again, and on the whole he could not blame her. They were silent for half an hour.

"Jack," she said. "I'm sorry."

"Oh, that's all right," he told her. "Everybody gets tired sometimes."

"Damn it, I'm not tired," she said. "It isn't weariness, it's schizophrenia. When we set down at Wake, can't we get away for twenty minutes and be ourselves?"

"Why yes," he said. "I think that would be a wonderful idea, but it will be dark at Wake—just before dawn."

"All right," she said, "in the dark then. In fact, it would look better if we did. We're supposed to be in love, aren't we? At least the idea is for us to give that impression."

"Yes," he said, "and you've been wonderful about it."

"Oh, shut up," she said, "and let me go to sleep."

She was still asleep hours later when the plane was letting down. He put his hand on her arm to awaken her, and she gave a start and looked around her for a moment, as though she did not know where she was or who she was. He knew exactly how she felt, because he had experienced the same confusion more than once himself. And this was dangerous, particularly on the beginning of a trip.

"Wake," he said, "in about thirty minutes."

"All right," she said. "I've got it now. I was having a bad dream, and I thought you were someone else."

"Just take it easy," he told her. "There's no reason for any bad dreams."

His guess about the time of arrival at Wake was approximately correct, because the announcement came over the loud speaker a few minutes later.

They would be on the ground at Wake Island in half an hour. It would still be dark. There would be a change of crew, and an hour or two hours on the ground. Transportation would be furnished, so that passengers could go to the resthouse, which was only a short distance from the field, for early morning refreshment. He had not touched at Wake when he had been to Japan eight years ago, but had been on other islands like it—atolls that were pinpoints on lonely seas. Even in the dark, when he stepped out of the plane, he could almost swear that he had been on Wake before. The lights on the field, the activity around the hangars were exactly the same as on other islands, and there was also the same warm humidity, and the sticky smell of salt in the air. They had been given a leaflet describing Wake, and even a map of the island, but he really did not need it. There was the field with the familiar cluster of buildings around it, the tarred streets, the Nissen huts, the army shacks, and then the lagoon. There was no check-up on the passengers, and there was no reason at all why he and Ruth Bogart should not walk to the resthouse or anywhere on that small island.

"God," she said, "it's lonely."

"Yes," he said, "it's lonely all right." But he was surprised that she should be impressed by it, because nothing was more lonely than the existence of anyone who was in the business, and she must have guessed what he was thinking.

"I mean, this is a different sort of loneliness," she said. "I'm used to being lonely in the middle of everything, but this is being lonely in the middle of nowhere."

Except for the field, the personnel at Wake was still asleep. They walked alone up a road illuminated only by dim electric lights, with ugly shadows of buildings on either side.

"We may as well take a look at the lagoon," he said. "It's later than I thought. It's getting light." It was true that the outlines of the buildings were growing more distinct. There was no reason why they could not be themselves for a moment.

"That crowd in the plane," he said—"did you think any of them seemed offbeat?"

"No," she said. "I had some ideas about the thin Englishman, but I'll clear him now."

"He'll do," he said. "I think we're still in the clear."

"Yes," she said. "I think so. You're still not worried about that Jap in San Francisco?"

"No," he said. "Not seriously, not after Honolulu."

"You don't think he was trying to tell us something, do you?"

"I've thought of that," he said, "but it doesn't seem to hold water. Let's forget him temporarily."

"I wish I could forget him and everything else. Do you ever feel that way?"

"Oh, yes," he answered, "lots of times."

"The hell of it is," she said, "that after a while you don't know what's what. You don't know what you are, because you can't be anything."

"Yes," he said, "I know what you mean. Maybe chameleons feel that way—not the kind you buy at circuses, but really good chameleons."

"We might have a nice time together, mightn't we," she said, "if we weren't all mixed up in this?"

"We might," he said, "but I'm not sure I would know how. I'm too much of a chameleon now. I might turn green and yellow and not know I was doing it."

"How long have you been in?" she asked.

"Long enough to forget what it's like outside," he said. "About ten years."

"Well," she said, "you don't act it altogether. Of course, I'm newer than that."

"Yes," he said, "of course. What were you doing outside?"

"College," she said, "majoring in Romance Languages. I met the Chief at a cocktail party in New York. Let's skip it, shall we?"

"Yes," he said, "let's skip it, but I hope your name isn't Ruth."

"Well, it is," she said, "and it's too bad you don't like it, and now let's both sign off. You're right. It's getting lighter."

"Yes, he said. "The lagoon's over there, I think. The Chief gave you a briefing, didn't he, about Big Ben?"

"Yes, I've got the whole story," she told him.

They walked for a while without speaking, through the moist, hot dark. He could see the outlines of a dilapidated portable house, on the right, quite clear against the lightening sky; but ahead there seemed to be nothing, and of course there would be nothing except white coral sand and water. In a few minutes now, there would be a glow of sunrise, and there would be a few magic minutes that always came to atolls, when the colors of sand and sea would be unbelievably beautiful.

"It seems queer to me," he said, "that they haven't picked him out by now, if he is a big man, once connected with show business. I never know anyone in show business who doesn't try to push into the front row, and I never knew one who could keep his mouth shut for long."

"Why, what's the matter?" she asked him. "Don't you like the theater?"

"I used to," he answered, "but I get nervous when I go now. The actors are all so obviously what they are. That's what I mean about our boy. He ought to be obvious, too."

He was glad they had gone for a walk. The sky in the east was growing brighter, and in a few minutes it would be sunrise. He felt almost happy, walking with his partner. In the distance he could hear the explosion of a motor warming up, and the noise of the island generating plant, and then he heard another sound, nearer, but some distance away. She must have heard it too, because she put her hand on his arm, and they both stood still, listening.

"Someone singing," she said.

"Yes," he answered, "over by that house, I think."

"San Francisco," she said. "You remember, don't you?"

Of course he remembered. She was referring to the footsteps outside the hotel door in San Francisco, and that snatch of outmoded song, and now in the dark a man was singing another song from *The Red Mill.* The singer's voice was excellent. It sounded carefree and happy, and full of the joy of living.

" . . . *In old New York!*" The words came carelessly and incongruously through the darkness. "*The peach-crop's always fine!*"

They stood motionless on the road, listening. Of course, it was only the time and place, he was thinking, that emphasized the coincidence, but nevertheless it was the sort of thing that could not have happened once in a thousand times. It was the kind of long shot that might possibly have a meaning, and you never could tell exactly how things were balanced. He could tell himself it was only Wake Island, but still there was the coincidence.

"It comes from over by the lagoon," he told the girl beside him.

"Let's move over that way." The song was coming from ahead and slightly to the right of them, and it continued as they walked.

*They're sweet and fair and on the square!*
*The maids of Manhattan for mine!*

Then the song was gone, but it had been just ahead of them, and there was light enough to see the lagoon, by now.

"From *The Red Mill,*" Jack Rhyce said, in a loud and hearty voice. "It sounds like home, doesn't it? Do you remember the rest of it, Ruth dear?"

"Why, no, Jack," she said, "of course I don't. Not that old song. Do you?"

"Why, Ruth dear, you can't fool me on old songs. It goes like this: *You cannot see in gay Paree, in London or in Cork! The queens you'll meet on any street in old New York.*"

He had not sung it badly, and it was not a bad idea—in fact, it was the exact thing he might have done, considering. It seemed very natural when he heard a voice call back.

"Hey, let's do it again, whoever you are. *In old New York! In old New York! . . .* "

The east was growing pink, but it was still not full day, so that shapes did not have the same definition that they would a few minutes later. A man in khaki swimming trunks was walking toward them. His yellow hair was dripping sea-water, and he had a towel over his right shoulder. At first, Jack Rhyce thought that the early light gave an extra illusion of size, but a second later he saw that the man was very large—two inches taller than he, he guessed, and a good twenty pounds heavier. He was beautifully built, too, tall and blond, heavy sandy eyebrows, greenish eyes, and a large mobile mouth.

There was occasionally a time when you could be sure of something, beyond any reasonable doubt. You never could tell when or how the sureness would strike, but such a moment of utter conviction was with him now. He felt his heart beat with a quick savage triumph that extended to his fingertips. It was one of those moments that made all drudgery worthwhile. He knew that he must be right. He knew that he could not be wrong. It was just as though someone were whispering in his ear, "There he is, there he is." It could not be anybody else. He knew as sure as fate that he was looking at Big Ben.

Nevertheless, even in that moment of revelation, he contrived to keep his balance because his training had been good. He knew that the one thing that would save the picture was to maintain the mood of the moment, which was one of joy of life and friendliness. Cover was the main thing, his common sense was saying, always cover. He found himself joining in the song without a quaver, just gay, always gay, and he put his arm around Ruth Bogart to emphasize this genial spirit.

*The peach-crop's always fine!*

He was singing. "Come on, Ruth . . . "

*They're sweet and fair and on the square!*
*The maids of Manhattan for mine!*

He paused to catch his breath, and the big man in the khaki swimming trunks raised his hand like an orchestra leader.

"Now we're hitting it," he said. "Come on, let's give it the works. Let's go. You take the lead, I'll follow. You know I'd pretty well forgotten those last two lines."

"Well, it's nice to meet another Red Miller," Jack Rhyce answered, "especially on a rock like this. All right, here we go. Come on and join in with us, Ruth. . . . "

*You cannot see in gay Paree, in London or in Cork!*
*The queens you'll meet on any street in old New York.*

If you had to be a damn fool, it was usually advisable to be one all the way down the line, and it required no intuition to tell him that it was important to be a damn fool now. He knew as sure as fate that he was talking to Big Ben, although he still had to prove it, and his main hope was that Big Ben did not have intuition, too—at least not so early in the morning. In the waxing light the man's size was more impressive than it had been before. In spite of all Jack Rhyce had learned at the Farm, he was not sure how things would come out if they reached a showdown in the next few seconds—but of course there was not going to be a showdown.

"Say, that was good," the big man said. And as far as Jack Rhyce could see, his smile was friendly, and his eyes showed no glint of suspicion. "You're not joining this flying installation here, are you?"

"No," Jack Rhyce said, and he laughed. "If you'll excuse my insulting such a lovely piece of real estate—Thank goodness, no.

We're just passengers from the resthouse, only out for a stroll, and heading west in about an hour."

The big man draped his towel more carefully around his shoulders.

"Oh," he said, "you mean flight Five-zero-one."

"Yes, I think that's the number," Jack Rhyce said. "It's sort of confusing, all this air travel. We were just saying, a few minutes ago, we didn't really know where we were. We *are* on Flight Five-oh-one, aren't we, Ruth?"

"Yes," Ruth said. "Don't be so vague, Jack. Of course it's Five Hundred and One."

Even the clumsy use of numerals could help with cover. They were just tourists indulging in a happy wayside adventure. The big man shook his head slowly.

"That's too bad," he said. "I'd hoped you were on some crew, or something, so we could think up some more old songs. You've got to think up something when you lay off on this rock. Let's see. There's a world tour group, isn't there, on this Flight Five-zero-one? There was something about it, seems to me, at Operations."

His voice was gentle and lazy, with a drawl that might have belonged either to the Tidewater country, or to the Southwest. Jack Rhyce did not attribute it to Texas, as he listened, and he was interested in more than the voice. Big Ben in trying to place them had overstepped, because it was doubtful whether a world tour group would be mentioned in Operations.

"That's right," Jack said, "there is a world tour group aboard, but we don't happen to be in the party. Miss Bogart and I are being employed by the Asia Friendship League, not that I suppose you would hear of it if you're working on an airline."

The big man shook his head vaguely in a way that expressed genuine regret.

"Well, it's too bad you're not staying on," he said, "because you both look like nice folks to get to know, and we might have gone swimming and fishing. We airline folk get lonely even though we move around. And now, as it is, we're just ships that pass in the night."

"That's a very nice way of putting it," Jack Rhyce said, "but it's a pleasure even to have made such a short acquaintance. I suppose we really ought to be getting back to that resthouse."

"Maybe so," the big man said, "but it's been a treat for me, too. Well, so long folks, and don't let those Japs give you wooden nickels."

"Well, so long," Jack Rhyce said, "and many happy landings."

They turned and walked back toward the airstrip. For a while he felt that the big man was watching them, but only for a very short time.

"Turn and wave to him," he said to Ruth Bogart.

"He's gone," she said. "He must be living in one of the huts back there."

"Well," he said, "that's that, at least for the moment."

"Do you think what I think?" she asked.

"I'm glad great minds think alike," he said. "It's lovely that we have so much in common."

"Oh, shut up," she said. "Do you think he is the same man that was singing in the hall?"

"Yes," he said, "I think so."

"Do you think he knew that we were in that room?"

Jack Rhyce sighed. You couldn't think of everything.

"That's a sixty-four-dollar question," he said, "but I shouldn't be surprised if we knew the answer someday."

No matter how you met a given situation, it was impossible to do everything right. There were other things he might have done at Wake Island, but he did his best to follow the maxims of the business, one of which was to disturb nothing unless it was absolutely necessary. Besides, he was only acting on a hunch. He had no way of proving it; yet if his hunch was right, they had him. Even if it had been wise, there was no necessity to ask questions at the moment. The man was obviously an airline employee. Now that he had appeared at Wake Island, he was as safe as a book in the reference library. Only a few discreet inquiries would be necessary to obtain his full life history, and all his life connections. The main question was how the inquiries should be made. As he said to Ruth Bogart, there was only one sixty-four-dollar question. *Did their man know who they were?* If so it would be best to break out of cover at once and communicate with Washington. Although hindsight was always clearer than foresight, Jack Rhyce could never convince himself that he had not moved properly at Wake. After all, he was under Gibson's orders, and he was only ten hours to Tokyo, but doubts still plagued him even after the plane had taken off.

"I might go up forward and have a chat with the crew," he said, "in a purely social way."

"I wouldn't, if I were you, Jack," she told him. "It could get back to Wake that you were asking."

Of course she was perfectly right, and besides, there had been no sign of recognition at that meeting, no uneasiness or tenseness that he had been able to detect.

"I didn't notice anything, either," she said, "except that I didn't quite believe that drawl."

"Yes," he said, "but I'm not sure."

"Did you notice his hands?" she asked.

It was an unnecessary question because he had not taken his eyes off them for more than a few seconds. There was nothing harder to disguise, or more revealing, than hands.

"The way he kept his fingers half-closed—they frightened me," she said.

He did not want to tell her that he had been thinking several times what he could possibly do if Big Ben were once to get him by the throat.

"He looked very able," he said, "very first-class."

He was not thinking of the hands when he made that estimate, but of the wide forehead, the greenish eyes, the careless-looking good-natured mouth, and the general ease of motion which showed that mind and body moved contentedly together.

"Well," he said, and he took the sayings of Buddha from his briefcase, "let's wait until we see Gibson." All they could very well do was to wait.

# 5

THE FIRST time Jack Rhyce had seen the islands of Japan from the air was when he had flown over Tokyo as an Intelligence observer on a B-29 bombing mission. They had come in from the sea on that occasion, on much the same line of approach that they were making now.

"We are now approaching the coast of Japan," the steward said over the loud speaker. "The sacred mountain of Fujiyama is visible off the left wing."

No one could say that the Japanese were not realists. Their representations of Fujiyama on block-print textiles and on porcelains were exactly like that cinder-coned volcano. All the beauties and the difficulties of Japan were starkly obvious as one approached the coast by air. The sharp folds of the mountains showed why only a fifth of the land was suitable for agriculture. He could see the bright green of the rice paddies, now that the plane was letting down, and he could also distinguish the lighter green of bamboo and the darker shades of giant fir trees. The fishing boats off the coast added a last touch to the broad picture of the Japanese struggle for existence. You could understand a great deal about Japanese character the moment you saw the coast, especially its elements of persistence and tenacity.

Japan's army was gone, and its navy, but not, as the Chief had said back in Washington, its national will to live. In Jack Rhyce's second visit to Japan, his brief trip during the Occupation, the Japanese in defeat had seemed more bewildering to him than they ever had before. They displayed a disturbing absence of rancor, a good-natured acceptance of reality, almost a polite regret for any inconveniences they might have caused. There was a relief from tension which he could understand, but much of the new attitude was so far removed from other behavior patterns he had know as to be unsusceptible of analysis. It was all very well to quote, as Intelligence officers did in those days, the old Japanese motto about the supple bamboo bending with the typhoon and never breaking. He was sure that this was an oversimplification. He had kept looking for something inscrutable in Japanese behavior, but he could find very little that answered the definition. They had been picking up the Tokyo wreckage as though nothing devastating had happened, smiling cheerfully in the depth of their misfortunes. After all, there had been too many earthquakes, too many tidal waves, not to have had a deep influence on the national point of view.

On this, his third arrival, he was not surprised to find that the new air terminal, shining with glass and plastic, was much handsomer than any in New York. The immigration official hardly glanced at him as he stamped the passport, and the customs examination was only a formality.

"Well," Rhyce said to Ruth Bogart, "that's that."

The time, he saw, had changed again. It was quarter to twelve o'clock.

"I wish you wouldn't keep making that remark," she said. "Maybe that and that will add up to something else someday."

Her face looked drawn, which was not surprising, because pursuing the sun across the Pacific was always a tiring process.

"We may as well get a taxi to the hotel," he said, "and not wait for the limousine. Nobody around here seems interested in us."

"I hope you're right," she said. "I don't want to go into an act right now. My God, I'm tired."

He wished that he was feeling more alert himself because it was hard to trust decisions made under the strain of fatigue. He noticed that the main concourse at the airport was not crowded, except for the smallish group that had come to meet the plane, hotel and travel agents, and friends of the passengers. The faces, as he examined them swiftly, were Japanese, but there was none of the Gilbert and Sullivan quality that a stranger might have expected. The women were dressed in the same style that one might see in New York. The men, bareheaded, wore neat dark business suits, proving once again that the Japanese were, superficially at least, the most adaptable people in the world. Only a few generations, he was thinking, lay between the grotesque shadows of the double-sworded Samurai, who had once roamed the streets of Tokyo as symbols of total feudalism, and this entirely Western scene. The changes in that brief span were impossible for even a vivid imagination to encompass and they had ended in an adequate acquisition of all the skills of Western culture. Perhaps Japan's main ineffectiveness lay in the too rapid merging of past with present, but then there had been no time for a gradual change. It was no wonder that there was something bizarre even in the self-conscious drabness of that group waiting at the airport. No Western observer that Jack Rhyce had ever heard of, and no Japanese either as far as his reading went, had been able to rationalize all the conflicts of the Japanese spirit.

These thoughts all came to him hurriedly and added up to a sort of bafflement, as he faced the crowd.

"Taxicab?" he said to the porter.

The porter, dressed in coveralls with the airline's name stitched across it, smiled, shook his head.

"Limousine," he said. "All people go in big limousine. Will stop at all hotels."

"No, no," Jack Rhyce answered slowly. "The lady and me—taxicab."

He was just as tired as Ruth Bogart. He did not want to be in a crowded car, and he was so anxious to make his point that he was not aware that anyone had been watching until a small, middle-aged Japanese, dressed in a business suit of an unpleasant purplish blue color and wearing very yellow tan shoes, stepped toward him.

"Excuse me, sir," he said. His hair was grayish and close-clipped, and he bowed in the manner of an older generation. "Do I speak to Mr. Rhyce?"

Jack Rhyce had honestly thought until that moment that they were in the clear. He wished that his mind were moving faster, and that everything did not have the blurred quality that was so frequently the outgrowth of fatigue. The main thing, he told himself, was not to appear too careful.

"Why, yes," he said, "I'm Mr. Rhyce."

The Japanese smiled again, and Jack Rhyce saw that both his upper incisor teeth were gold-covered.

"I am so very glad, sir. May I introduce myself?" His voice was high, and slightly monotonous. He gave a nervous deprecating laugh, and his hands moved with astonishing rapidity as he snatched a wallet from inside his purplish blue coat and whipped a name card out of it.

"Please," he said, holding out the card.

"Why, thanks," Jack Rhyce said as he took the card, "thanks a lot."

The thing to do was to take it slowly and clumsily. It was of great importance to exhibit no alertness or suspicion.

"I. A. MOTO," he said, reading aloud from the card. "Well, well, let's see—that name rings a bell somewhere." He did not want to overdo the slowness, but at the same time he did not wish to appear too bright; finally he allowed himself to break into a relieved smile. "Yes, I've got it now." He pulled out his own wallet and thumbed eagerly through papers and memoranda until he produced the card he had been given at Fisherman's Wharf.

"Yes, it's the same name," he said. "Moto. Yes, I've got it now. Your nephew gave me your name in San Francisco. Well, this is a real surprise." He turned to Ruth Bogart, smiling with fatuous enthusiasm. "You remember that nice Japanese boy on Fisherman's Wharf, don't you, Ruth dear, who told us about his uncle who might show us around the city?"

"Why, yes," Ruth Bogart said, and her face also grew radiant with delight. "Why, he must have sent over a cable. What a lovely thing of him to do."

It was quite a little scene, and Mr. Moto was laughing in courteous sympathy.

"Yes," he said, "my nephew. He sent a cable. Yes."

"Well," Jack Rhyce said. "It's a pleasure to meet you, Mr. Moto, and it's a mighty nice surprise to find you here, just when I was trying to tell the porter that I wanted a private taxicab to take us to the Imperial Hotel."

"Oh, yes," Mr. Moto said, "Teikoku Hotel."

"What's that one again?" Jack Rhyce asked.

"Teikoku," Mr. Moto said, "Japanese word for Imperial. We can get a taxicab downstairs. This way, please." And he spoke swiftly and eloquently to the porter.

"This is all mighty kind of you, Mr.—er—Moto," Jack Rhyce said. "This young lady and I are pretty tired. If you could just get us a taxi and tell the driver Imperial Hotel—then suppose you come around later and call my room at, say, six o'clock, and maybe we can talk over what you can show us in Tokyo. I'll be a little bit more on the ball by then."

"On the what?" Mr. Moto asked.

"On the ball," Jack Rhyce said, laughing at the small joke. "It's the American way of saying more wide-awake."

Mr. Moto looked delighted.

"On the ball," he said. "Oh, yes. Thank you so very much, and good-by until then. I will call at six o'clock, and we will both be more on the ball."

He laughed; Jack Rhyce and Ruth Bogart joined him.

They were silent in the taxi for the first few moments. There was no way of being sure about the driver's English. She put her hand over his and her fingers pressed quickly.

"Picked us up again."

"Yes," he signaled back, and at the same time he spoke aloud.

"Ruth, dear," he said, "it seems to me your face is on just a tiny bit crooked."

"Oh, Jack," she said, "why didn't you tell me sooner?" and she snatched her compact out of her handbag, and a moment later gave the signal of negative. No one was following, but then, why should there have been? They were going to the Imperial Hotel and the driver had been selected.

"Wasn't it nice of him to meet us, Jack?" she said.

"Yes," he answered, "it was very polite, wasn't it? I think it will be interesting to see more of him, don't you?"

"Yes," she said, "maybe. Well, I can't believe we're here, can you, Jack? So this is Tokyo. I must say it isn't so romantic as I thought it was going to be."

She was right. Tokyo was not a romantic city. It lay sprawling over a large area, divided by a muddy river and canals—a dusty, smoky city that sweltered in the summer and shivered in the winter. Except for the areas contiguous to the Imperial Palace, all the districts of that immense city were jumbled together planlessly like a deck of cards thrown on a table, so that dwellings, shops, temples and factories were shuffled into an indiscriminate confusion. There were districts, but there were no street names except for those that had been set up by the American Army of Occupation. He remembered a bright paragraph that had been written about Tokyo in a prewar guidebook. It was fortunate, the book had said, that most of the dwellings in Tokyo were of fragile frame construction, with paper windows, because they caught fire so easily in the winter, thus making better city planning possible when they were rebuilt. There had been ample opportunity to rebuild Tokyo. The great earthquake of 1923 almost razed the city, and during the war incendiary bombing had achieved virtually the same result—in fact, the modern business district in the vicinity of the Palace was about all that had withstood the bombing. Yet now there was hardly a sign of war. Tokyo was rebuilt again, in the same disorder as before, and with the same flimsiness and impermanence. The shops were back again, wide open to the street, displaying dried fish, vegetables, bolts of cloth, earthen and enamelware and banners in Japanese characters waved above them. You could buy anything in Tokyo, from raw tuna fish to a whole gamut of Western-style goods in the great department stores along the Ginza. Tokyo was itself again, but, as the Chief had said, there was a new veneer. There were signs advertising American toothpaste and American cosmetics, and the streets were as full of motor traffic as any American city, with driving that was even more aggressive. The variety of the vehicles on those teeming streets was a living and rather disturbing illustration of the efforts of the East to adjust itself to competition with the West.

Once when he was in Chungking, during the war, Jack Rhyce recalled having had a long conversation with a well-informed Chinese. It had taken place during an air raid, from which they had not bothered to seek shelter, and the words of his Oxford-educated acquaintance had been punctuated by the thudding of Japanese bombs. Industrialization, the Chinese had said, was not the private property of the Western world, but only a trick which the East could learn as easily as not, and perhaps this was so. Perhaps all learning, in the final analysis, was only a trick. Certainly the Japanese had learned industrialization, and they were still learning how to adapt it to their peculiar needs. The vehicles there in Tokyo were like illustrations for the Darwinian origin of species, and all the manufacturing nations in the world were represented in the picture. Japanese and English cycles, motor bikes, scooter bikes, pedicabs, small, three-wheeled private cars, larger three-wheeled trucks, heavy-duty Japanese trucks, small shiny Japanese cars that competed with the German Volkswagen, American light cars, American heavy cars, French and English and Italian motors—everything was there to answer any need, including rickshaws and hand-pushed barrows. Somehow this variety against the façades of the shops with their indecipherable signs managed to assume a monotony which he associated with the outskirts of any large city. But the Chief had been right. Where had the kimonos gone? And where were the wooden clogs called getas? There had been an effort everywhere to lift the face of Tokyo. There were strange echoes of New York, Chicago, and Hollywood. The American moving pictures and the GI's might have inspired the ball parks, beer halls and dance halls. But from the street, at any rate, there was no way of seeing behind the entrance doors, and the sliding windows, sanded or papered, of the wooden Japanese dwellings and inns along the main thoroughfare. There was only a suspicion, among all that modernity, of something older and more conventional, only an occasional, fleeting glimpse through a gateway of a dwarfed tree, or a pool or a rock garden. Nevertheless, as sure as fate, most of old Japan still lay behind those perishable façades, and it would remain at least for the foreseeable future.

"It's dreadfully noisy and crowded, isn't it?" Ruth Bogart said.

He remembered that she had never been there before, and that the noise and crowded feeling inspired by an Eastern city was different from the West. There was more patience and adroitness and discipline because populations were denser and living space was smaller. Tokyo gave a sense of teeming millions that one never experienced in London or New York, but Jack Rhyce knew that there was a peculiar peace behind those façades. Once they had reached home, all the Japanese women, in their New York cotton dresses and their high-heeled shoes, and all the Japanese schoolgirls, in their navy-blue skirts, and white middy blouses, and all the men in their business suits and all the Boy Scouts would move magically into another kind of life.

The shoes would be left outside. There would be straw matting underfoot. European clothes would be hung away, and there would be kimonos—no chairs, no beds; and still, perhaps, wooden blocks for pillows. There would be cushions beside low tables, a charcoal brazier and tea, and *sushi* made of raw fish and rice, and a porcelain jar of hot sake surrounded by minute cups. There would be the family tub for the hot bath, and now that it was summer, an open window would afford a glimpse of a tiny garden court, with goldfish in a lily pool. This picture would vary with poverty or wealth, but everywhere in Tokyo the pattern would be the same. The old conventions still lay just behind the modern curtain and behind the barrier of language. Every stranger, in his own way, was conscious of that older life. It must have been hard to live two lives at once, as people always did in Tokyo.

"Are you sure we're going the right way?" she asked.

Of course he was sure. It was true that he had scarcely been in Japan, but as soon as he had been briefed on his present assignment, he had spent so many hours on the Tokyo material that he could have found his way to any point in the city, without asking directions.

"We'll be there before long," he said. "You'll see the Imperial Palace grounds and the moat to your right in just a minute."

"You do know a lot of fascinating facts," she said. "I would have boned up on this, too, but I didn't know I was coming."

"It's going to be a great experience for you," he said. "We're reaching the handsomest part of Tokyo now. It might almost be Cleveland or Toledo, except for the Palace."

The Palace and the moat and the modern office buildings that stood opposite, across the broad avenue, gave a vivid illustration of the colossal effort Japan had made to compete in a dangerous and changing world, and spoke very eloquently of the cultural cleavage that had torn Japan for a century. There was no place in Tokyo where the pictures of old and new Japan appeared in more accurate focus. The Palace grounds of Japan's Emperor were guarded by a moat and behind it by a grim, sloping, dry masonry wall of black lava rock. At the wall's summit, through the artificially contorted outlines of pine trees, were the curving tiled roofs of ancient guardhouses. The area had been the citadel of the old Tokugawa fortress, before the Emperor had moved there, after Perry's visit to Japan. The walls and moat were at least a thousand years old, and the etiquette and spiritual qualities that they protected were vastly older. A part of the Palace had been destroyed by bombs, but the Emperor was still residing among the trees and gardens. Across the street the skyscraper buildings of banks and insurance companies, and the modern Nikatsu Hotel, made a dramatic contrast. Most of them were of a prewar vintage, and most of them had successfully survived the bombings. It was true, as he told Ruth Bogart, that when you saw them, you had the whole story of Japan, if you could manage to read it.

"Out there in the park by the Palace gates," he said, "is where the people gather in times of grief and mourning. They say that there were thousands of them on the day of the surrender."

He thought that he could still feel echoes of that time as they passed the Palace walls. The Emperor had addressed his people over the radio that day, the first time that his voice had ever been heard by the general public, and it was ironical that it had been difficult for many of his subjects to understand him because he spoke in the dialect of the old Court of Japan. It was a time, he said, when all must bear the unbearable; Japan had surrendered, and the subjects of Japan were asked to welcome their former enemies. And they had done so. They had put large signs on the airstrips reading WELCOME, U.S.A. It was still not difficult to imagine the park, filled with thousands of mourning Japanese, prostrate, beating their heads on the ground. Hundreds had disemboweled themselves before the walls that day, as a loyal gesture to the Emperor.

"You see," Jack Rhyce said, "they are very loyal. That's the main thing to remember about the Japanese. Loyalty is the essence of their religion, although they might not put it that way."

"How do you know so much about them," she asked, "if you've been here so little?"

"By reading," he said. "And in the war we took a prisoner now and then." But this was no time to talk about himself; they were driving up to the Imperial Hotel.

He heard her exclaim when she saw that low structure of yellowish volcanic stone, with its strange windows and angles. Although the hotel was designed by an American, it must have once represented the quintessence of Japanese aspirations. He had always thought it was one of the oddest buildings in the world, and he still thought so. While he went to register at the desk, he left Ruth Bogart standing by the baggage, staring bemused at the rough stone corridors and angles. The building had been completed in 1922, and, as a guidebook once put it, it was a maze of "terraces, logias, porte-cochères, turrets, inner gardens, glassed-in corridors and roof gardens . . . the salient architectural features of the exterior have been reproduced in the interior, where there are columns, ledges, winding tile stairs and templelike effects."

He could not tell whether he was surprised or relieved when he found that their rooms on the third floor of the front wing had a connecting door. Gibson had made the arrangements, and the connecting door might possibly have been an attempt at humor, except that Jack Rhyce knew that Gibson seldom made jokes. Three Japanese boys walked ahead of them, carrying their luggage. He was almost sure that he had seen at least one of them when he had been at the Imperial during the Occupation. The hotel had seemed old and tired then. Now he knew that it would never be young again, because it represented a Japanese dream that was lost, a fantastic, disturbing dream of misplaced grandeur and conflicting taste. He wondered, as he often had before, whether its famous architect, Mr. Frank Lloyd Wright, or some Japanese contractor had approved the final plans. He was inclined to settle for the contractor, because everything was too small and weirdly compact for Western taste. There was a Lilliputian quality about the rooms and everything inside them. The writing tables were too low, the wardrobes below normal height, and the walls of volcanic stone made everything look crowded.

"You can take either room you like," he said. "I don't really see much difference."

"Neither do I," she said. "I'll take this one." And then he saw that she had noticed the connecting door. He did not wish to discuss it then, while he was busy giving orders about the baggage.

"I'd go to sleep if I were you," he said. "Knock on the door if you want anything."

Before he decided on any course of action, he had to make a routine examination of his room. The draperies, the carpet, and the bed covering were all worn, and gave him again a melancholy feeling of creeping age. The bathtub was also too small. He had to bend his knees to reach the washbasin. He went carefully through the wardrobe and every drawer, looked behind the mirror and over every inch of the wall. He finally took off his coat and shoes and opened the door for a glance at the corridor, but there was no one there. The ubiquitous servants that he had remembered in the Occupation—the smiling maids in obis and getas, and the boys in white uniforms—had disappeared somewhere into the past. On the whole he approved of the selection of the rooms. They each looked over the fantastic porte-cochère and the hotel driveway, were all thick, so that it would be possible to talk freely if voices were kept low and all the locks were sound.

He knew the number he was to call, but he did not give it to the operator.

"I want to speak to Mr. William Gibson," he said, and he spelled the name out slowly, "at the Osaka Importing Company. If he asks who's calling, say it is Mr. John Rhyce," and he spelled the name carefully again, and put down the telephone.

It was half past one in the afternoon, but he did not feel hungry because of all the elapsed hours of the ocean flight. The sun of late June shone hot and strong on the lotus pool in front of the porte-cochère, and he stood at the room's small window looking at the pink and yellow lotus flowers while he waited for his call. He did not turn when he heard the door connecting the two rooms open, because he knew the sound of her step by then.

"Is everything all right in your place?" he asked.

"Yes," she said. "Everything's okay. So you knew this door was unlocked?"

"Yes," he said, "and the latch has been oiled, I think. Gibson must have wanted it that way."

"Well, let's keep it open for a while," she said. "It's awfully far away from everything here, isn't it? Do you like the way things are going?"

"No," he said, "not with that Jap meeting us at the plane. He looked to me as though he were in the business. When he reached into his pocket to take his wallet out, I almost thought he was going for a rod. You don't move that way without training. You just don't."

"So you're feeling jumpy, too, are you?"

"It's the trip," he answered. "I'll feel clearer just as soon as I get a little shut-eye. I'm just contacting Gibson. They ought to call back any minute now. How would you like some tea?"

She shook her head.

"How about a drink? I've a flask of bourbon in my bag."

"You sure it won't take the razor edge off your mind?" she said.

"It isn't kind to kid me," he said, and he pulled a flask from the bottom of his bag. Just then the telephone rang.

"Here," he said, "mix two stiff ones while I'm talking."

# 6

THERE WAS no mistaking the harsh quality of Bill Gibson's voice. Jack Rhyce was tired, but he had to go into an act again.

"Say, Bill," he said, "guess who this is? Jack Rhyce."

"Why, *Jack,*" Bill Gibson answered. There was no one who could throw himself into a game better than Bill. "Where did you ever drop from, you old buzzard, and what are you doing in Tokyo?"

"I thought you'd be surprised," Jack Rhyce said. "I'm over here to write a report for the Asia Friendship League. And who do you think I've got with me, to help out? Ruth Bogart. You remember Ruth, don't you? She's right up in the room here now, mixing us both a good stiff drink of bourbon. Why don't you drop everything, and come on up, Bill?"

"There's nothing, I'd rather do in the world," Bill Gibson said, "but right at the minute things are pretty busy in the office."

"Oh, now Bill," Jack Rhyce said, "can't you let things drop for just half an hour? It's been a long time no see, and—"

Bill Gibson's laugh interrupted him. It had just the right warmth, and the proper tolerant affection.

"Oh, all right," he said, "all right. You always did have a bad influence on me, Jack. Sure, I'll break away. What's your room number?"

Now that the point of urgency was made, the conversation was as good as over, but Bill Gibson's final remark struck Jack Rhyce as disconcerting.

"Leave your door unlocked," he said, "and save me some of that bourbon."

Ruth Bogart was standing close beside him, and Gibson's voice was loud enough so that she must have heard the conversation.

"Are you sure that was Gibson on the wire?" she asked.

He was sure it was Gibson's voice and he told her so. Besides there had been enough material in that conversation, innocuous though it had seemed, to afford a double-check.

"Why did he ask to leave the door unlocked?" she asked.

"I guess because he wants to get in in a hurry," he said. "Did you hear him say that things were pretty busy at the office?"

"Maybe I'm not going to have a nap after all," she said.

"It could be possible," he told her, "but how about that drink?"

The worst thing in the world for anyone in the business was to develop any dependence on alcohol, but he was sure that the whisky was good for both of them, under the circumstances. It was one of those few opportunities afforded them to be natural. They sat smiling at each other when they were not watching the unlocked door to the hall.

"Here's looking at you," she said. "I'd really like to have a hot bath and go to sleep."

"In a miniature tub?" he asked.

"Anything at all," she said. "Jack, are you carrying a rod?"

"Absolutely not," he said. "Are you?"

"I have one of those fountain pens," she said, "in my handbag."

"Well, never mind it now," he said. "I suppose you've been told that you're a very pretty girl."

"Yes," she said, and she looked prettier when she answered. "I've been told, but I'm glad you brought the subject up. And now do you mind if I make a remark about you, as long as we're being personal?"

"Why, no," he said, "anything at all."

But she hesitated before she answered, and the bright, efficient gaze left her face, making her look almost sad.

"I keep wondering what sort of a person you really are. I mean, what you're like when you're being yourself, what your tastes are, what you want most and everything like that."

He felt depressed after she had finished speaking. He could think of a number of things he had lost in the course of time. Besides, he had to tell the truth, and the truth was something that had been bothering him lately.

"You know," he said "I'm really beginning to forget what I used to be. That's the trouble with this business, isn't it?"

"Yes," she said. "It's beginning to be the same way with me. I keep forgetting. I wish we could have met on the outside. Have you ever thought of getting out of all of this?"

"I have thought along those lines," he said. "The trouble is, I don't know whether you ever can get outside, after you've been inside. Inside leaves a mark on you, and gives you disagreeable habits. I wouldn't know what I could do outside to earn my living any more. I was planning to be a lawyer before the war came—but that's all too late now."

"You could be a trustee," she said, "out front, in a bank with a marble floor. You wouldn't look half bad in a Brooks Brothers suit."

"Yes," he said, "or I could be a football coach; I used to play football. Or I could teach languages on the side, or maybe judo. I can drive a car pretty well—but I wouldn't want to do any of those things. If I ever were to get outside—"

He stopped because he had learned long ago that talking about one's self never added up to much.

"Go ahead," she said. "What would you do if you ever got outside?"

When he took another swallow of whisky, he felt more like himself than he had since Honolulu.

"Frankly, I wouldn't want to do anything immediately," he said. "I'd like to get a canoe and some canned goods and a tent. I'd paddle up through the lakes in Ontario until I got about a hundred miles from anywhere, and then I'd pitch the tent. And when I wasn't asleep I'd sit in the sun, doing absolutely nothing, just realizing that nobody could find me. But the main thing would be doing absolutely nothing—"

Just then the door opened. His mind was jerked from northern Ontario, and he realized he never should have been thinking of it. He was not surprised at the manner in which Bill Gibson entered the room, having seen Bill Gibson move fast before, on several occasions, although he had never understood how it could be done with excess weight and a sagging waistline. Bill Gibson was in a hurry, just as Jack Rhyce had said he might be. But even in a hurry, Bill Gibson looked the part he had played for years in Tokyo—a middle-aged American businessman who drank too much before lunch, who fell asleep at the club bridge table in the evening, who talked too much, and who had amorous proclivities which he could never suppress when he should. He was wearing a washable business suit. His jowls were heavy, with a blackish tinge, no matter how clean-shaven he might be. His black hair was brushed back in a pompadour, and he wore horn-rimmed spectacles. Although he had been in a hurry, he was not out of breath, and he had moved so silently that there had been no sound until the door opened.

"Hi," he said gently, and he nodded to Ruth. "Lock that door now, kid. I'm sorry to barge in this way, but I've had a hunch for the last few days that I'm hot as a pistol, and I don't want to be seen coming up here. There's no better place to play cops and robbers than the Imperial Hotel." He spoke easily and confidently, as he always did. "I'll take my weight off my feet and have a drink," he said, sitting down on the edge of the bed. "These rooms are all right to talk in. I've used them before. Well, what's the damn emergency, Buster? I thought I was to call you, and not you me."

Jack Rhyce nodded. He realized that he was being rebuked, and he knew Bill Gibson well enough to see that the situation was tense.

"That's right," he said. "I took the liberty, Bill. It's about Big Ben."

"All right," Bill Gibson said, "go ahead, and make it snappy if you don't mind."

"It's just a hunch," Jack Rhyce said, "but I have a feeling we've seen Big Ben."

He started with San Francisco and with the steps outside the door, and the singing of the tune, and then the other tune at Wake just as light was coming in the sky. He knew Bill Gibson well enough to make an interpolation.

"I've never been psychic," he said. "I never could tip tables, or write messages on a Ouija board, but when I heard that voice, it linked right up with that song in the hall. It wouldn't have given me a jolt if it had not been from the same show. The song in San Francisco was 'Every Day Is Ladies' Day with Me,' and it was 'The Streets of New York' on Wake, but they're both out of *The Red Mill.*"

"Did you sneak up on him?" Bill Gibson asked.

"I didn't want to try, on that terrain," Jack Rhyce said. "No, we just stood there, and I sang the same song back."

Bill Gibson took a generous drink of his bourbon.

"If I'm seen here it won't hurt to have the smell of American hooch on my breath," he said. "Well, describe him."

"He was in khaki trunks, old army-issue," Jack Rhyce said. "Hair was wet, yellow to ginger-colored after his dip in the lagoon. Bushy eyebrows; wide forehead; big mobile mouth, and talking with a drawl, more Tidewater than Texas; and he was damn big, and a beautiful build—all big, especially his hands."

"Bigger than you?" Bill Gibson asked.

"Yes," Jack Rhyce said, "some. I'd hate to tangle with him. He has beautiful co-ordination."

"How did he react?" Bill Gibson asked.

"Friendly. Maybe a little too God-awful friendly. He thought maybe Ruth and I were new airline personnel, and then he asked if we were passengers on a world cruise. He indicated he had read about the world cruise group on Operations teletype. That's the one wrong move he made. I don't think the fact would come through Operations. My hunch would be that he picked it up in San Francisco the night he was singing 'Every Day Is Ladies' Day with Me.'"

Bill Gibson took another swallow of his whisky.

"Ruth dear," he said, "would you look out the window in a nice careful way and see if there's an old beat-up Chevrolet out there—dark green, '51 model? Coupé, left front fender pretty well mashed in, a big dent on the left-hand door, and the door missing a handle. Let me know if you see it, will you, dear? . . . So your hunch is he's on a plane crew—what?"

Jack Rhyce nodded.

"And I'll bet he's only a few hours out of here right now," he said.

"There isn't any Chevrolet outside yet," Ruth said.

"Well, thanks, sweetie," Bill Gibson said. "Keep on looking, will you? That Chevvy's been like Mary's little lamb to me the last few days. . . . Did you check up on him at Wake?"

"No," Jack Rhyce said. "It was a big temptation, but it might have been a giveaway, and you'll have to be careful how you handle it here—not that I want to give advice, Bill. He looked very impressive to me—an able, thoughtful character."

Bill Gibson whistled softly.

"Maybe you've got something, Buster," he said. "It's the first good lead on him I've seen for quite a while. I hadn't been thinking much about plane crews."

"If you don't mind," Jack said, "if you've got the time I'd like to add a little more."

"All the time in the world," Bill Gibson said, "so long as that Chevvy isn't there. Keep looking, will you, darling? And I can do with another drink."

Sometimes it was hard for Jack Rhyce to realize that Bill Gibson's mind and techniques were among the best in the office. While Bill listened, he took off his horn-rimmed glasses, and his face looked bloated without them, and his eyes rheumy and dull, but he was not missing anything. He was listening to the encounter with the Russians, about the old bank clerk at the table, and then about the Japanese who mentioned the words Big Ben.

"Cripes, Jack," he said, "this thing is closing in."

"And that isn't all," Jack Rhyce said. "There was this other one at the airport."

"Let's see his card." Bill Gibson held out his hand. "Come on, Buster."

He held the card and squinted at it, and put back his glasses.

"It's a phony, as far as I know," he said. "Moto isn't a Japanese name, it's only a suffix to a name, like Yamamoto, or Mikimoto, who puts pearls in the oysters—and maybe there'll be some Mikimoto pearls for you, Ruth dear, if you happen to see that Chevrolet." He finished his drink in a single gulp. "Well, well, kids," he said, "it looks as if we're going to get some action pretty quick out of this one. Would you guess this Moto boy was in touch with Wake?"

"I couldn't guess," Jack said, "but the thought has crossed my mind, Bill."

Bill Gibson cleared his throat and looked at the empty glass on the floor beside him.

"No," he said, "no, I won't have another, thanks. Well, this has been very interesting to me, kids, because it ties up with some other stuff that's just come in. We have a few people ourselves who get around, you know. Big Ben is around, all right. I've a hell of a lot of things I've got to do, and I can't brief you now. It could spill everything if I were seen up here, but we've got to get together somewhere. Now here's what I want—"

He stood up. It was amazing how quickly he could pull himself off the bed, fat abdomen, jowls and everything.

"Now get this." He looked very much like a sales manager addressing a convention, or a coach, exhorting a team between the halves. "I want you two to take all tomorrow to get your cover sweetened with this Asia Friendship League. I also want you two to make damn fools of yourselves about each other. I'm glad to see you have the connecting door open already—not because I believe in sex, but because, under the circumstances, sex is the safest thing for you. That's why, the day after tomorrow, you're going on a shack-up job to a resort hotel up in the mountains. It's a real off-the-record honeymoon retreat, and no one will notice you, if you just keep interested in each other. I'll be up there Saturday night. You'll see me at the bar at six o'clock, but don't pay any attention to me. Go to the big dance that night and have a good time. My room will be in a cottage called Chrysanthemum Rest. It's near the ballroom. At ten o'clock, leave the ballroom as if you were going out in the dark to smooch. There'll be so much noise and music, no one will hear us talking, or care, but I don't want us to be seen together in Tokyo. I'm too damn hot. Have you got it, Jack?"

Jack was aware again that his mind was not working as accurately as it should. Bill Gibson had asked if he had got it, and the truth was that he had been getting too much in the last few hours. Granted that he had been trained until most of his actions were instinctive, a craving for rest was beginning to keep his mind from facts.

"Well, Bill," he said, "you've handed me quite a lot since you've been here."

"I've been concise," Bill Gibson answered, "but I'm in a hell of a hurry, Jack."

"This hotel," Jack Rhyce said. He was trying to get things into order, but if he could not get some rest, as sure as fate he would slip up on something, and once you made a slip, with circumstances the way they looked you seldom were given a chance to recover. "Where is it, and how do I get there?"

"In Miyanoshita, up in the mountains. Here's the name."

Bill Gibson scribbled the name on the back page of a notebook, and tore out the page. "The army used it during the Occupation. Officers and their wives spend the weekends there, and unattached young men and their Japanese and other girl friends. It's a peculiar place, like Japan, torn between two worlds, but comfortable and friendly."

"All right," Jack Rhyce said, "but if everything's so hot, why don't you give us the whole fill-in for everything right now?"

"There's not time," Bill Gibson said. "I mustn't be identified with you. But I'll tell you this, it's dangerous as hell. It's confirmed today. They are planning a political assassination—"

He did not complete his sentence because Ruth Bogart standing by the window, interrupted him.

"A Chevrolet with a dented fender is driving up," she said.

Bill Gibson was on his feet in an instant, and again it was surprising how quickly he could move.

"All right," he said. "Persistent bastards, aren't they? Let me know what whoever gets out looks like, but tell me later. Good luck. You've got everything?"

"Yes, Bill," Jack said. "We'll be seeing you."

"Right," Bill Gibson said. "Don't get in touch with me again, and remember: *safety in sex.*"

He was gone, so quietly that the closing of the room door hardly made a sound. The incongruity of some of the things Bill Gibson had said only occurred to Jack Rhyce later. One obeyed orders and there was no reasoning why in the business. There was no time to discuss whether he or Ruth Bogart liked the situation in which they had been ordered to participate. You were never yourself in the business, and you did what you were told.

Ruth Bogart was speaking to him from her place by the window.

"Only one man in the Chevrolet," she said. "He's parked, and getting out. Man, thirty-five or six, sun glasses, brown hair, balding at temples. Height five feet ten. Weight maybe one seventy. Pale face, professorial type. Aloha shirt with goldfish on it. Trousers white silk. Shoes, white buckskin trimmed with brown leather. He's entering the hotel. He seems American and harmless-looking."

Jack Rhyce did not move to the window to confirm because it seemed like a professional and accurate description.

"Right," he said. "You'd better go and lie down for a bit, Ruth, and order up something to eat if you want it."

"I don't want anything to eat now," she said, "but hadn't we better talk things over? Bill Gibson looked upset."

"You take a nap first," he answered. "I'm afraid we're going to have a lot of time to talk things over."

"Afraid?" she repeated after him, and he could not help thinking that she looked the way she might have on the outside, but it was not the time or place to let one's mind wander.

"Forget it," he said. "I didn't mean it personally."

"All right," she said, "I'll forget it. God, you really are a pro."

She was obviously not saying it in a complimentary way, and for a second her words gave him an accurate and devastating picture of himself, but one he could excuse.

"Yes," he said, "I'm a pro. We all have to be, don't we? Now go and lie down."

"Yes," she said, and she smiled at him although a smile was not necessary. "I'm a pro, too, a poor, tired pro."

She kicked off her shoes, and it seemed to him that their heels were too high for efficiency. Then she tossed herself inelegantly on the bed, indicating there was not much reason for reticences when you were in the business.

"I'll draw your curtains," he said.

"Thanks," she said, "and move my handbag near me, will you? Thanks, Jack."

He believed that she was already alseep when he closed the door to the adjoining room, and he envied her because instinct told him that one of them must stay awake until there was some assurance that things were moving in a settled groove; the Chevrolet outside was curious and disturbing. He stood by the window looking at it—

an inconspicuous American car, one of thousands of its vintage, and one which must have had several owners. It was exactly the sort of car he would have picked if he had wanted to tail someone. He was still gazing out of the window, and wondering whether it would be wiser to stray down and take a closer look when someone knocked loudly on the door.

His reaction of annoyance was a measure of his fatigue. The necessity for being alert again was difficult to face, but it was an absolute necessity because he could not imagine who would disturb him, and the knock had been too loud for hotel servants. It was no time to be careless, and also no time to be furtive. He walked to the door promptly and opened it, seemingly carelessly, but with a few technical precautions. He was too tired for further shocks, but he had to face another. Standing outside in the rather narrow corridor was the man whom Ruth Bogart had described—in the Aloha shirt with the goldfish on it.

He had taken off his sun glasses, but there was no mistaking the shirt, or the trousers of heavy Shantung silk, or the white buckskin shoes trimmed with tan, or the closely clipped brown hair, receding at the temples. Ruth Bogart had said he had a professional look, and she had been correct. He had the look which Jack Rhyce had begun to associate with hundreds of individuals sent out by the government to work on helpful commissions and projects—the eager and at the same time self-satisfied expression of someone who knew he knew the answers.

"Hello," the man in the Aloha shirt said, and he had a warm hail-fellow voice that fitted his professional expression. "You're Mr. Rhyce, aren't you? They said downstairs that you were still in your room."

Jack knew that the face of the man in the Aloha shirt was important and he catalogued it immediately—darkish, intellectual, brown eyes, high cheekbones, longish nose, pointed jaw, thin-lipped mouth, good teeth. These observations took only an instant as Jack Rhyce returned the other's smile.

"Well," he said, "the name is Rhyce, and I'm here all right, just off the plane."

"Well, it's a real pleasure to welcome you to Tokyo, Jack Rhyce," the man in the Aloha shirt said. "My name's Harry Pender, running the shop here for Asia Friendship, replacing Jules Blake, who was called home last week. Chas. Harrington wired you were coming in today. Seriously, it's fine to have you aboard."

Seriously, it was difficult to lapse into the cover again, and to give the proper illusion of delight when all sorts of thoughts and questions were moving in the background.

"Well, Harry Pender," Jack Rhyce said, "this is mighty kind of you to look me up so promptly. I was on the point of lying down and taking a little snooze. That plane trip has, frankly, left me a bit woozy, but come on in. You've woken me up already."

It was true that Harry Pender had woken him up. There were certain thoughts that demanded strict attention. Pender was undoubtedly the man in the Chevrolet, and why was it he had not called on the house telephone? How long had he been outside in the hall? Then, on top of those questions, Jack Rhyce had another thought. The Chief had made a mistake for once. If the Chevrolet with the battered fender had been following Bill Gibson, how about the Asia Friendship League? For a fraction of a second Jack Rhyce wished that the Chief were there to know that it was not harmless.

"I won't take a minute of your time," Mr. Harry Pender said. "Of course you're not oriented to Japan yet. No one ever is. I should have met you at the airport, but frankly, we're going to have a conference of Japanese writers tomorrow, and I've been unusually busy as a consequence, and also, all the office cars were in use. All that was left was our old Chevvy, and I've had to use it all morning, buzzing around."

"Meeting planes is always a problem," Jack Rhyce said. "You mustn't have me on your mind at all. I'm just here to look things over and do this report, you know. I can hardly wait to see the office tomorrow, and I'd like to sit in on that writers' conference."

Mr. Pender nodded enthusiastically. "Chas. Harrington indicated that you'd be right in here pitching," he said, "and the whole place is open to you, Jack Rhyce. Nothing up our sleeves or anything like that." He laughed heartily. "And I don't know any way in which you can get the spirit of what we're up to here more than by sitting in at the table with some of our Japanese writers. They're lovable people, the Japanese—I mean, when you get to know them."

"How do you mean—lovable?" Jack Rhyce asked.

"You'll see," Mr. Pender said. "You'll see. You'll get their spirit, given time. They're basically only a bunch of mixed-up kids, but lovable at heart. You'll see."

Jack Rhyce nodded in a respectful, sympathetic manner.

"I suppose I'm somewhat prejudiced in my point of view about the Japanese," he said. "You see, I was in the Pacific during the war."

For one mad moment he could not recollect whether or not his war service had been mentioned in that first letter to Mr. Harrington of the Asia Friendship League, but he was sure that it had been when Mr. Pender made a grave gesture of agreement.

"I know," Mr. Pender said. "I know the superb record that you made with the paratroopers in Burma. I wish I might have been with you, but I had to serve in a more sheltered branch myself, due to being in the Four F category—the U.S.O."

"Oh," Jack Rhyce said, "so you were in the U.S.O.?"

It was only because he was very tired. He could have kicked himself the moment he had said it. The U.S.O. and Big Ben might come together somewhere and he never should have betrayed interest. He almost thought there was a sharpening in Mr. Pender's brown eyes, but it might very well have been his imagination.

"It used to hurt at times," Mr. Pender said, "not to be able to be up forward with you boys, but then we did our best in our small way. I was in a singing troupe."

"That must have been fun," Jack Rhyce said, "and believe me, I'd like to have been able to change places with you at some points. I always did like singing. What sort of songs did you do?"

"Oh," Mr. Pender said, "we had a name. We called our group the Song Caravan, and they were a fine dedicated bunch in it—you know, boys and gals with a smattering of semiprofessional experience from the summer theaters and whatnot, lots of whom finally joined more active branches of the service. We sang all the popular numbers. We would just ask the crowd to holler for a number and we'd sing it. You might have seen us out in the Pacific if you hadn't been in Burma. We did get to Chungking once. Were you ever in Chungking?"

"Oh, yes," Jack Rhyce said, "once or twice, but only very briefly. Quite a place—Chungking."

"It was," Mr. Pender said. "It always seemed to me a very fascinating page of social history—Chungking; we must have a good long talk about it sometime, but it's all water over the dam now. We mustn't forget that we are entering into a new era of reconstruction and not destruction. I know you are going to agree with me—the Japanese basically are nothing but a bunch of mixed-up kids—but lovable." His glance traveled about the room with a casualness which could have been overelaborate. "Oh, by the way, the young lady who was coming over to assist you—is there anything I can do for her? What is her name? It's gone out of my head."

"Bogart," Jack Rhyce said, "Ruth Bogart. She's asleep, I think."

"I certainly don't blame her," Mr. Pender said. "But bring her over to the office tomorrow morning. The more the merrier. We'll only have the one day—until Monday—because we close things over the weekends, but we'll think up some program for you over Saturday and Sunday."

"Why, thanks," Jack Rhyce said, and to his surprise he felt genuinely self-conscious. "As a matter of fact," he paused and cleared his throat, "I'd sort of promised to take Miss Bogart to that hotel up in the hills where they have the hot springs at—where is it—Miyanoshita. You see, this is her first glimpse of Japan."

"Oh," Mr. Pender said, "I forgot to ask—were you here during the Occupation?"

"Only passing through for a day or two," Jack Rhyce said, and far from appearing watchful, Mr. Pender looked relaxed and tolerantly genial.

"We're going to have a lot of things to talk about, you and me," he said, "and I know you're going to like our bunch out here, and everything we're doing. And now, before I go, is there anything you want?"

"Well, no," Jack Rhyce said, "except maybe a little sleep, but thanks a lot for asking."

"Yes, sir," Mr. Pender said. "You and I are going to have a lot of fun together. I can feel it in my bones." He held out his hand again. His muscle tone was excellent. "Well, so long. How about up at the office at half past nine sharp tomorrow? You have the address, haven't you?"

"Oh, yes," Jack Rhyce said, "and thanks again a whole lot for dropping in."

After Mr. Pender had left, Jack Rhyce stood unobtrusively by his window watching the parked Chevrolet. In two and a half minutes Mr. Pender had reached it—approximately the time it should have taken him to walk down the staircases of the Imperial, across the lobby and out of its front door. Jack turned from the window and very gently opened the door of Ruth's room. She was wide awake, her head propped up on the pillow.

"I'm sorry if we've kept you awake," he said. "It was the man in the Aloha shirt."

She smiled at him, and again she looked very much as she might have on the outside.

"You didn't keep me awake," she said. "I went down and took a look at the car."

"That was a very good girl," he said, "provided you got away with it."

"I think I did," she said. "I'm pretty good with cars. There was nothing except a rod in the glove compartment."

"Oh," Jack Rhyce said. "What kind?"

"Beretta," she said, "all loaded."

"Oh," he said, "Beretta."

It was interesting that anyone in Mr. Pender's position should have been carrying an Italian officer's pistol. Pender had brown eyes but he did not look like an Italian.

"And now," she said, "go away and let me sleep, and you'd better, too. I think things are going to be quiet for a while."

They did not mention Mr. Pender again, but there was no need at the moment. They both had their own ideas about him—the same idea.

It was exasperating to discover the desire for sleep had left him, much as he needed it. He draped his coat over one of the small chairs, stretched out on his bed and tried to relax. The street sounds of Tokyo were nearly indistinguishable, now, from those of a European city, but he could not rid himself from watchful tension or from the intuitions which no one could help developing in the business. He was full of the old malaise that told him that a net was closing. The elderly man in San Francisco and the Nisei Japanese boy were parts of it, and so was the middle-aged Japanese named Moto who had picked him up at the airport. You developed a seventh sense for spotting opposite numbers; he would have bet his last dollar that Mr. Moto was in the business, except for the clumsy use of a name that, as Bill Gibson had pointed out, was not a name at all. It was so obvious that it might have been a signal, but there was no way of being sure. And then Pender was another strand of the net. If he had not said that he was a former U.S.O. entertainer, the Beretta in the car was indicative, and besides, there was the fact that Bill Gibson was on the run. The net was closing on Bill Gibson, and Bill knew it, but it might be, Jack Rhyce thought, that he and Ruth Bogart were still out of it. He was almost positive that Mr. Pender had accepted them.

Mr. Moto was due to call at six. There would be a chance then to evaluate and handle him, and until six there was nothing to do but rest. Then suddenly he realized he had forgotten something, and immediately he pushed open the adjoining door. Ruth Bogart was asleep. The hardness which he had occasionally noticed on her face was gone. The tenseness about her mouth had relaxed. Although her eyes were closed, she had a half-cheerful, half-expectant look. She was a very pretty girl now that she was sleep, the way she would have looked on the outside, and he was sure that her dreams had taken her there. He was sorry to bring her back into the business.

"Sorry," he said, "Just one thing, Ruth."

You could tell that she had been at the girl's branch of the Farm from the way she awakened. A second before she had been on the outside; now her right hand had moved toward her handbag, but it was only a half-conscious gesture.

"Okay," she said softly. "What?"

"This Moto character who's calling at six," he said. "I think he'll ring the house telephone and not barge up like Pender. I'll leave our door open. The bell will wake you. Get up and close the door but listen, and keep that fountain pen handy. It might just be we'll have to use it. Do you follow me, Ruth?"

"Yes," she said. "I'd have covered you anyway, Buster. Now go and relax or you'll be fidgety when he comes, and leave the door wide open. Don't be so delicate. I need company."

He could not tell whether she was being friendly or not, when she called him Buster; but he felt a twinge of annoyance because he had never liked the name, and also the mere fact that he was annoyed worried him. He would not have given the matter any thought if he had not been tired.

# 7

HE STILL could not sleep when he lay down again. The truth had begun to dawn on him that he was not physically the man he had been, that his old resilience and iron were wearing thin, and that he would have been better even three years earlier. Everyone in the business burned out eventually. Either their physical reflexes slowed up first, or their ability to keep concentrated on a single line. He knew it was the worst possible time to put his thoughts on a personal basis. It had been the girl's face that looked so young and happy in its sleep that had disturbed him. He began thinking, just when he should not have, of the outside. If he had stayed on the outside he would undoubtedly be married by now. He would have been in the law. He would have had a home and children, and he would have been a decent man—warm-hearted and genuine—not a suspicious, machine-tooled robot who had been through too much, a man who had played under so many covers that it was becoming impossible to guess what he could have been.

Of course there had always been people like himself who could not easily adjust to civil life after having faced the violences of war. There had been wonderful moments and triumphs. There was always the satisfaction of knowing that in ten years he had made a place for himself in a highly exacting profession, but in the end, what was there of real value? Very little, except what might lie in a set of disconnected memories, very little of which to be proud. And what was he in the end? He was a spy, or a secret agent, if you cared for a politer word, trained to live a life of lying and of subterfuge; trained to submerge his individuality into something he was not—to be a sneak, and if necessary a betrayer; trained to run from danger and let his best friend get it, if it helped the business; to kill or be killed inconspicuously; to die with his mouth shut, in the dark. There was only one loyalty—loyalty to the business. It was, by outside standards, a contemptible profession, and in the end, everybody in the business paid, because deceit was the same as erosion of character.

Why had he not gotten out of it, before it was too late? He raised himself on his elbow. The whisky flask was in his bag and the glasses were on the table. He could even see the traces of Ruth Bogart's lipstick on her glass. She should have been more careful. He sat up, with his eyes still on the bag, but then he leaned back again. Drinking was always dangerous in the business—it was far safer to indulge in bitter thoughts. It was too late for him to leave the business now. He remembered what she had called him a while ago—a pro; and you could not get from the inside to the outside once you were a pro. He wished to heaven he could sleep as she did. It meant that she still could get out of the business; he hoped she would. He resolved to tell her so, if they came out of this safe.

He must have been thinking of what he would say to her just as he fell asleep.

He was convinced that he was not the man he had been once, when the telephone awakened him. He heard Ruth Bogart close the adjoining door before he was on his feet. First he had not been able to sleep. Then he had slept too heavily, and like Ruth Bogart, he must have been on the outside, too, in his dreams. It was something that should never happen in the field.

"Hello," he said. "Jack Rhyce speaking."

At any rate, he was back under his cover again, hearty voice and everything. The time on his wrist watch was six to the dot. He was feeling very hungry, and also rested. He was on the beam again.

"Please." It was undoubtedly Mr. Moto speaking. There was the slow, gentle modulation he remembered, and also the monotony of speech that even excellent Japanese linguists sometimes found hard to escape. "I hope I did not awaken you, Mr. Rhyce."

"Oh, it's you, is it?" Jack Rhyce said. "Do I sound sleepy?"

There was a nervous laugh that went with conventional politeness.

"Just a little in your voice, Mr. Rhyce."

He had to admit that the man downstairs was a damned smart Jap, and when they were, it was hard to find anything smarter.

"Well, you win, as a matter of fact," Jack Rhyce said. "I have been having a little shut-eye. But come on right up, you've got the room number, haven't you?"

"The room number? Oh, yes."

It was a needless question. Of course he had the number. There was time for Jack Rhyce to tie his shoes, and put on his seersucker coat. As he did so he realized he had not unpacked anything. He hastily opened his Valpak and pulled some clothes out, because he did not want to give the impression that he might leave at any moment. Then he left the door to the hall half open because a locked door might be conspicuous, and then his heart gave a startled jump. He had completely forgotten the three glasses on the table, but as he moved toward them he saw that only two were there, one with the lipstick smears, and another. Ruth Bogart must have been in when he was asleep, and he felt very much ashamed. He should have thought of the two glasses himself—one of them with lipstick.

The tap on the door was gentle and discreet. Jack Rhyce was accustomed to Japanese manners, and he had listened for many wearisome hours to lectures by social anthropologists on Japanese psychology, but from his own experience in the cruder arena of combat intelligence, he doubted the correctness of many of the lecturers' conclusions. The background and the thought process of Japan were so different from his own that he had always avoided a confident appraisal. When Mr. Moto knocked, Jack felt a species of nervousness. He knew too much about Japan, yet he must not show it. Japanese were always sensitive.

"Well, well," Jack Rhyce said, "step right in. You're right on the dot, I see." He spoke loudly and deliberately, as one should to a foreigner.

Mr. Moto's features were finely chiseled. His hands were slender and graceful. In native dress, he would have been a fine figure of a trusted Samurai, and it was very possible that his family had held that feudal rank. But the hideous, purplish-blue business suit, aggressively pressed and arrogantly neat, ruined his romantic picture, and so did the very light tan shoes. Mr. Moto was more a figure of low comedy than a representative of old Japan. Then a startling idea came to Jack Rhyce—that he and Mr. Moto might both be impersonating clumsy people. If you took it one way, the hissing intake of Mr. Moto's breath had a Weber and Fields quality that was too loud and too comic. The same was true of his speech, yet Jack Rhyce could not definitely tell.

"So nice of you to receive me," Mr. Moto said. "You have enjoyed your sleep, I hope."

"Yes, sir," Jack Rhyce said. "I had a real nice shut-eye, thanks, and I feel very much better for it, Mr.—excuse me. I forget your name."

"Moto," Mr. Moto said. He laughed again, but there was no way of telling whether or not his politeness was deliberately overdrawn.

"Moto," Jack Rhyce said. If they were playing a Mr. Japan and Mr. America game, both of them knew their business. "I've got that straight now, and I hope you'll excuse it, Mr. Moto. Japanese names are tough for me to remember, and I suppose my name is hard for you—Rhyce."

"Oh, no," Mr. Moto said. "R is easy in Japan. We have trouble when we pronounce your letter rell. See—I cannot say it. Ha-ha-ha."

It was hard for Jack Rhyce to decide whether or not Mr. Moto was having deliberate trouble with his *l's*. It was true that the *l* sound was difficult for Japanese to accomplish, although good linguists could manage it. In the Pacific during the War, Jack Rhyce remembered, there had been a sea area christened "Alligator Lipstick." The term had been invented because the area was frequently mentioned by voice over the air and "Alligator Lipstick" was a jawbreaker for the average Japanese. It seemed to Jack Rhyce that sometimes Mr. Moto was having no trouble with his *l's* at all.

"That is comical, when you come to think of it," Jack Rhyce said, "but it takes all kinds to make a world, doesn't it? You know, I'm kind of hungry after that plane ride. I wonder if we could get some bacon and shirred eggs and tea. Maybe you can make the room boy understand in Japanese better than I can in English. Ha-ha-ha."

As he spoke he felt sorry for Ruth Bogart listening at the connecting door, and he added, "A whole flock of bacon and eggs and tea."

"Oh, yes," Mr. Moto said. "I shall call up room service. Everything is up to date at the Imperiar Hote-ru. Excuse me when I cannot say the *l*."

There was no breaking the law of averages. Sooner or later there would be a slip of the tongue, or else a careless gesture might become a chain reaction that ruined everything. Mr. Moto had slipped, and Jack Rhyce was sure that he was unaware of it. Mr. Moto had surmounted that stumbling block of the Japanese tongue by pronouncing the letter *l* with a subconscious fluency, indicating that he could speak a better brand of English than he was using. When he picked up the hotel telephone and asked for room service in Japanese, his accent was crisp and educated. There was something in the careless way in which he handled the instrument that was not Japanese, or English, or German, and certainly not Russian. His posture was very good, as he stood speaking into the receiver, showing that he had done his tour of military duty—the army, Jack Rhyce guessed, rather than navy; and if it was the army, he might have been in the fanatical wing that started the war. His face showed no passion or arrogance, but it was hard to classify Japanese features. When Mr. Moto gave the order, he asked for bacon and eggs and coffee—not tea; and Jack Rhyce was certain he had mentioned tea. He could not suppress a quiet satisfaction as he sat and listened to Mr. Moto's Japanese. He felt rested, and Mr. Moto had lost a trick in pronouncing the letter *l*.

"Everything will be right up," Mr. Moto said. "Chop-chop, as they say in China. Ha-ha."

"That's mighty kind of you," Jack Rhyce said. "This language barrier is a pretty tough thing, isn't it? Sit down, won't you, please? And I do hope the food does come up chop-chop, as you say. I could certainly do with a cup of coffee."

You were bound to fall flat on your face at one time or another. He could have bitten off his tongue the moment he mentioned coffee, but already it was too late. There was nothing to do but go ahead, without showing a trace of embarrassment.

"You know you've come at just the right time, Mr. Moto," he said. "I'm here to do a piece of work for an organization known as the Asia Friendship League, something in the nature of a report, and the more I think of it, the more sure I am that I'll need somebody like you to show me around."

Mr. Moto's glance had turned toward the glasses on the table; Jack Rhyce had a feeling that tension had relaxed when Mr. Moto saw them. There might have been some truth in that phrase of Bill Gibson's—safety in sex. You could discount a good deal of potential menace in a man if you saw a glass with lipstick smears in his bedroom.

"The Asia Friendship League," Mr. Moto said. "How very, very nice. The United States is such a kind nation, after the war, to do such nice things for Japan. The Asia Friendship League is known to me, and Mr. Pender, its new head, is such a good, nice man."

"So you know Mr. Pender?" Jack Rhyce said. "Well, that's fine. I've already had a warm and really constructive talk with him. He's going to show me around the shop tomorrow, and so I'm afraid I'll be pretty much engaged tomorrow. By the way, how about a little drink, Mr. Moto? Oh-oh . . . I've got to rinse the glasses."

"Oh, no," Mr. Moto said, "not for me. But you—prease, you help yourself."

Jack Rhyce took his flask from his open kit-bag and poured himself another drink.

"I suppose the tap water's all right in Tokyo?" he asked.

"Oh, yes," Mr. Moto said. "You see, the American Army has been here."

"Oh, yes," Jack Rhyce said. "Well, as I was saying, I'm going to be busy tomorrow, but Saturday and Sunday I shall need a little rest and relaxation. You know—maybe you've got a saying in Japan like ours in the States—all work and no play makes Jack a dull boy? And the nice thing about that little maxim is, my first name happens to be Jack."

Jack Rhyce smiled fatuously and sipped his drink. He was almost sure that Mr. Moto was smiling sympathetically.

"There are lots of amusements in Tokyo and its vicinity," Mr.

Moto said. "I would be so preased to show geisha girls or anything, Mr. Rhyce."

Jack Rhyce laughed easily.

"That would be swell sometime later," he said. "But this Saturday and Sunday I was thinking of taking a spin into the country. You see, I was here in the Occupation for a day or two, and the army had taken over a hotel up in the mountains. I've got the name of the place written down. It's in Mio—Mio—"

"Oh," Mr. Moto said, "Miyanoshita. Very nice."

Jack Rhyce took another sip from his drink, and gave Mr. Moto a man-to-man look.

"Well, I thought if you could rent me a good car, and a driver, I might go up there, and well—you know, take a girl along."

Mr. Moto nodded and tactfully drew in his breath.

"Oh, yes," he said. "I can drive myself. I can get a good car for you, and very nice girl."

"That's it," Jack Rhyce said. "That's the spirit, Mr. Moto. I had a hunch, right when I saw you at the airport, that you'd be broad-minded. A man has to have fun sometime, doesn't he?"

"Oh, yes," Mr. Moto said. "Oh, yes. If you wish, I can find four or five girls and you can make a choice."

"Well, that's fine," Jack Rhyce said, "but you supply the car, and I'll supply the young lady. Be around here at nine o'clock on Saturday morning."

"Oh, yes," Mr. Moto said, "and we can see Kamakura—many interesting things. The Daibutsu Buddha—very big and very old, and Eno-shima—very rovery, very many things."

There was a knock on the door. It was a waiter with bacon and eggs and coffee. Mr. Moto rose and bowed. The bow was old-fashioned, belonging more to the older than the new generation. "Nine, Saturday," he said. "Big, fine American car. Everything first-crass. You will be satisfied, I am sure, and thank you very much. Good night then, Mr. Rhyce."

It had been a long while since Jack Rhyce had been so unsure of his cover work. He could not tell exactly what anything was about, except that there had been that atmosphere of tenseness, and a combat of minds. That slip of his still worried him. There was no need to exaggerate its potential danger. His expression must have disturbed Ruth Bogart when he called her to come in.

"What went wrong?" she asked. "You sounded so terrific, you almost made me feel sick to my stomach."

Jack Rhyce pointed to the table and the tray.

"Sit down and eat it," he said. "I'll order up some more from room service." He stopped and imitated Mr. Moto's voice. "Everything is up to date in the Imperiar Hote-ru."

"But what is worrying you?" she asked.

"The coffee," he answered, and he told her.

"Well, it's over now," she said. "I didn't know you knew a word of Japanese. You said you'd hardly ever been in Japan."

There was nothing to do, and time stretched ahead of them uninterruptedly until the next morning. There was actually no reason why he should not talk about himself, or why they should not be reasonable human beings for a while.

"Frankly," he said. "I did live in Japan from the age zero to five. Japanese servants are devoted to kids, and I was speaking the language all the time. My father was a missionary, and the moral of that story is always to look out for missionaries' sons."

"You're too conscientious for me to have to look out for you," she said. "Why didn't you lose that Japanese when you went back to the States?"

He had not talked about the outside to anyone for several years. It was an unfamiliar and rather agreeable experience, to be sitting there in Tokyo, thinking of the outside.

"My father wanted me to keep it up," he said, "and he made me for quite a while. You see—don't laugh—he wanted me to be a missionary, too. It's peculiar what parents want their children to be, isn't it? The language came right back to me in the war at language school."

He stopped and passed the flask to her.

"We may as well finish this," he said, "and you heard what our friend told us—tap water's good in Tokyo. And thanks for doing that about the glasses. Thanks a lot."

"Don't mention it," she said. "You can't be a mastermind all the time, you know. Did he notice?"

"Oh, yes," he said, "he noticed. You wait until you see more of him. I'm afraid he's very smart."

"Afraid?" she repeated.

"That's right," he said. "I don't know where he fits in—not to mention this man Pender in the Chevrolet." He had forgotten that she did not know about Harry Pender.

"We're still in the clear with him, I think," he said, "or he wouldn't have told about the U.S.O. singing caravan. But we're running into something."

Her manner changed as she listened. All the outlines of her face had hardened. Her eyes were still very pretty, but they had hardened, too.

"Yes," she said, "we're walking into something, but let's not take it too big, if you know what I mean."

"I wish I could place the Jap," he said. "It's what I tell you I can't make out where he fits."

"All right," she said. "We'll find out. We're walking into it, but don't take it too big."

"There's the second time you've said that. Just what do you mean?" he asked.

She thought for a moment before she answered, and the hardness had not left her face.

"I suppose I'll have to be personal," she said. "We're teamed up on this, and we've got to stick together, and you're running the show, of course. I don't know as much as you do, but I've seen enough to like the way you work. There's only one thing about you that makes me nervous."

From the way that he reacted he knew that his nerves were still edgy, and he found it difficult to keep annoyance out of his voice.

"I'm sorry if I make you nervous," he told her. "Go ahead and tell me why."

"Because, as I was saying, you're too damned conscientious, Jack," she told him. "You try to think of everything, and no one can. Why not try to just think of one or two things tonight, and put the rest out of your head? It will be back in the morning."

"All right," he said. "Name the one or two things."

"Well, I'll name one," she answered. "How about thinking about me for a while? I wish you wouldn't take me as another responsibility. I'm really not as bad as that. Remember about the glasses?"

When she smiled at him his nerves were not on edge any longer.

"I mean," she said, "let's try to be friends as well as business associates. I think it would help the cover if we found out a little more about each other—what we really are, I mean, and not what we're pretending to be. We can pick that up again tomorrow."

"That's true," he said. "We don't know much about each other, do we? And maybe you're right. Maybe it wouldn't be a bad idea."

"Then go ahead and be yourself," she said. "Say anything, but for heaven's sake let's be ourselves. For instance, say something about Japan that isn't a free lecture. Just go ahead and say something."

Her mood, it struck him, was the same as his had been before he had fallen asleep. He understood exactly what she meant, and it saddened him that it was an effort to do what she asked. Instinctive caution was all around him. He had been in the business too long.

"Well," he said, "I suppose childhood is an impressionable age. Even if you can't remember the details, they are all back in your mind somewhere. I haven't been back to Japan since I was five, except for a few days in the Occupation, but it's all familiar. I can feel at home in it because I used to go to the mission school. I used to play with the gardener's boy." He paused and cleared his throat. "Is that the conversational line you wanted?"

"Yes," she said, "it is, and it's the first time you've been natural since I've seen you. Now I know quite a lot about you, but you don't know anything about me."

"No," he said, "but you don't have to tell me, Ruth."

"But aren't you curious about me?" she asked. "Guess what I was outside? Aren't you curious enough to guess?"

He was surprised that she asked the question because girls in the business seldom cared to talk about their pasts. It was a safe bet they all had them, and rather lurid ones, or they would not have been in the business. There was always some tragedy of love, or a broken home, or some hate or some frustration that was requited by the business. As his glance met hers, and as she raised her eyebrows slightly, he honestly preferred to take her as she was, without knowing any more.

"Why, yes," he said, "I could make an educated guess about you, but I don't know that you'd like it."

Her glance met his again, and then shifted.

"You're such a damn pro—aren't you?" she asked—"you know everything."

He was sorry to detect an undertone of antagonism in what she said. Antagonism, or clash of personality, would seriously interfere with their working smoothly together. He knew that she must be tired by the trip, and by Bill Gibson's hurried call, and by the Japanese; the appearance of Mr. Pender in the dented Chevrolet did not help to soothe one's nerves. The truth was that neither of them did know anything about the other, and in his opinion it was better that way, when working with a woman in the business. It was better to keep things on an impersonal basis, if possible, and not to quarrel or be unkind; but the strain of the day had told on him, too. Otherwise, he would not have been led further into the conversation.

"I'm sorry if I've displeased you," he said. "I've got a lot on my mind, you know. Of course I don't know everything, but maybe I've been around more than you have, and I've been acquainted with a lot of girls in the business—some good and some not. I know how they look and how they act, and I've often had to check their backgrounds. Naturally I can make an educated guess about you. Naturally I've made one to myself already."

He was sorry to notice that her face had flushed.

"So you think I'm just another tramp," she said. "Is that what you're trying to tell me?"

"No," he said, "I'm not trying to tell you anything. There's no cause for you to lose your temper, Ruth."

"I'm not losing my temper," she answered. He knew this was not true. "But I do think if two people are going to work together they understand each other better if they know something about each other, and if they're friends and not acquaintances. Suppose you tell me what you think you know about me, and I'll tell you if you're right."

"Why don't we keep what we think about each other to ourselves?" he said. "It might save a lot of trouble, but if you want it your way, I'll go along."

There was no use antagonizing her just when work was starting, but she had challenged his professional pride.

"If you stay in this racket," he said, "as long as I've been in it, you'll naturally learn to notice things about people, and not let them get on your nerves. You'll get further if you just sit quietly and look. All right, if you want the professor to give you an analysis—in the first place, you're not in the tramp class, and you never will be. You're too well bred. You have too much background and character to be a tramp."

"That's nice to know," she answered. "Go ahead, what else?"

He was no longer reluctant to go ahead. He had finally become interested in his ideas. If he had any gifts, his best had always been analysis of people.

"Now most girls in your position," he said, "always tell the same story. All of them are always born of wealthy parents, usually living on Southern plantations. Then along came a business failure, or else they married an undesirable man. The undesirable man is usually correct—but in your case the rest of it is true. You come from an excellent background. You were brought up in a large American city, but I can't tell which, from your accent. Upper-class accents are reasonably interchangeable."

"Go ahead," she said. "What else?"

"You never spent all the year in the city." He had forgotten Tokyo. He was always interested in blocking out a character. "You spent a lot of your time, while you were growing up, in the country—a riding country, but not the West. You schooled and jumped horses once."

There was a flicker of interest in her glance.

"What made you make that guess?" she asked.

"Your posture," he said, "but mainly your hands. You have beautiful hands, but they are strong above the average. They are riding hands."

"All right," she said. "You hit that one. Go ahead."

"All right," he said, "if you'll excuse my being personal. One or two things you said on this trip make me think you've been used to attention, and expect a good deal from people. You should, because you're exceedingly good-looking."

"Why, thanks," she said.

"I'm a man," he answered. "It's obvious; but I don't think I've been influenced by it."

"And, believe me, I haven't tried to influence you," she said. "And don't worry. I won't. So you think I was spoiled, do you? All right, I was, by the family and the servants."

"I'd also guess that you're an only child," he said. "That's only an educated guess. I'd say your father had great personal charm. Drinkers do, and I'm afraid he was a drunk. I've noticed how your expression changes every time I pick up my glass. You loved him and he disappointed you—so you were disillusioned by the father image. He died, I imagine, while you were away at a fashionable boarding school. Your mother married again, and you were on the loose with an independent income—a bright, popular girl. You went to college, and I'll bet it was nearer to Bryn Mawr than Goucher. You fell in love, and the boy friend left you flat. He wasn't killed in Korea or anything. He left you flat."

"What makes you say that?" she asked.

"From the way you act with a man," he said. "You don't trust men. Then you met the Chief. The Chief's good at spotting material, and he found that you were a natural at the business. You were rattling around loose, just the way I was when the Chief found me, and that's about all."

When he had finished he knew he had been very close to being right, from the cool, suspicious way in which she looked at him.

"Just how did you happen to see my file?" she asked. "I thought those things were confidential."

He shook his head slowly.

"No file," he said. "I've only found out about you by minding my own business, watching you. You asked for it."

She was looking at him with a new respect. At least her antagonism had gone. Suddenly she smiled at him, and he knew that they were friends.

"You make me feel naked," she said, "or like the tattooed woman in the circus. I didn't know I had everything written on me in fine print. Actually, in case you want to know, we owned a place in Virginia. In fact, I own it still."

"Now, listen," he said, "you don't have to tell me anything more about yourself. It doesn't help the general situation, and we shouldn't be talking like this. It's too dangerous, Ruth."

She shook her head in an exasperated way.

"You're always damn careful, aren't you?" she said. "How do you mean—too dangerous?"

"When you get talking this way you get interested," he said. "It's dangerous to get interested, or like anyone too much in the business, Ruth. You might have to ditch me, or I might have to ditch you tomorrow. You know that."

His hand rested on her shoulder, and she had not moved away, and he was right that it was dangerous.

"Well, thank heaven you have a human side," she said. "And I'm glad we've talked this way, and to hell with the business until tomorrow." She brushed his hand off and stood up. "Look, we haven't had anything to eat. Call for a room waiter since everything's so modern at the Imperial Hotel, and these eggs are cold, and everything. And I have another flask in my suitcase. After all, you're supposed to be crazy about me, Jack."

He was right that the whole thing was dangerous. He knew all the rules about women and emotional involvement. He knew that he was at least coming very close to breaking several of them, but he had never realized that the prospect could be so pleasant. For a moment or two, at any rate, he felt he was himself again, exactly as he had been on the outside. It was a transient sensation, but at the same time, it was a revelation, because he had never believed that clocks turned back.

"Let's save your flask for some other time," he said. "I'm having a good time without it. In fact—"

He stopped because his training was back with him.

"In fact, what?" she asked.

That twinge of caution was gone when he looked at her. He knew he was saying what a great many others had said before him, and yet he did not care.

"Maybe it won't hurt if we took a little time off," he said.

## 8

A GREAT deal of the business was very dull, but that ensuing Friday was one of the most irksome that Jack Rhyce could remember. His hours with the Asia Friendship League had a fatuous quality that demanded every bit of his patience in order to fall into the mood of the dedicated people in the Friendship office, and still not miss a trick. He could not tell, in the space of a day, exactly how dedicated all of them were. He could get only a general picture in his mind, yet he was reasonably sure that most of them had honest intentions and felt that they were engaged in a great work. His thoughts went back a dozen times that day to the briefing the Chief had given him in Washington, on the great American strength and weakness—the persistent belief that good will and good fellowship could conquer everything.

He wished that he could make up his mind as to whether or not Mr. Harry Pender honestly shared this viewpoint, but he had to set down the whole Pender problem as unfinished business. Mr. Pender made himself so hospitable and charming that no time was left for analysis. Besides, it was a time to be very, very careful, until he had told Bill Gibson his ideas. It was a time to be naïve and to convey emphatically the utter harmlessness of himself and Ruth Bogart. It was a time to be enthusiastic but dumb, in an open-handed way. It was also a time to show by a series of skillful shadings a picture of growing attachment between himself and Miss Bogart—one of those half-furtive, half-fleeting romances between two well-meaning people that burgeoned more rapidly in the Orient than anywhere else. All these details had kept Jack Rhyce very busy.

"Of course this is only a very quick fill-in," Mr. Pender kept saying. "You can't really start getting your teeth into anything until Monday, Jack."

Inevitably they had reached a first-name basis in a very few minutes.

"I can't wait to get the bit in my teeth, Harry," Jack Rhyce said, "and possibly to be of some help with the wonderful things you are doing here. I had no idea that you had such an inspiring picture to show me, or such lovely and artistic offices."

"You just wait," Harry Pender said. "These are only temporary quarters."

Temporary or not, the Asia Friendship League occupied, already, half the floor of a postwar office building in the neighborhood of the Ginza. Mr. Pender, as the head of the Japan branch, had a truly beautiful office overlooking a large section of the city, furnished with new Japanese furniture that had been adapted to the European fashion. The furniture had been designed right in the Friendship League; desks, chairs, coffee tables and everything were made by Japanese craftsmen, with authentic Japanese spirit, but also were suited to both Easterners and Westerners. A lot of leading Japanese artists and merchants had been consulted, and had been generous with their help, Mr. Pender explained, and the result had surely been worth the hours of conferences. All you had to do was to look at the lovely Oriental woods, turned out along chaste, modernistic lines, to realize that here the Friendship League had made an important good-will contribution. Its furniture was already on display in a number of Tokyo department stores; several exporters were expressing practical interest. In fact, it might very well start a new vogue, Mr. Pender said, and this was just a small example of what the Asia Friendship League was up to. The League's motto might in one word be termed Interest. Mr. Pender did not mean financial interest, but an honest interest in the other fellow out here in the East. Well, this interest was now flowing in all sorts of directions. There was a group in the office, for example, studying the new Japanese films. Then there was the sports group. And this afternoon, as Mr. Pender had said, there would be a panel discussion on writing in the conference auditorium. One of the Foundation's own girls, Miss Kettleback, was going to deliver a lecture to some young Japanese writers on the American novel. It was amazing, Mr. Pender said, how eager these intellectuals were for American culture. Just wait—the auditorium hall would be filled half an hour before the lecture started.

There was not really time, Mr. Pender said, to give a full runover of all the projects, but there was one which was a particular pet of his—the Friendly Pen Pals. Up to this point Jack Rhyce had listened brightly, but now his interest quickened.

"What's that again, Harry?" he asked.

"Well, it's an idea that is purely my own," Mr. Pender said, "and I hope you'll play it up big in your report, Jack. You've heard of Pen Pals in the States and Europe? Well, it just came over me—why not do it here? Why not get a lot of these Japanese kids in school and the universities to swap ideas and news with their own age groups back home? It would seem to me to be the very essence of the cultural interchange we're looking for, and it's working already. You'd be surprised."

Mr. Harry Pender was watching him expectantly when he finished, seemingly waiting for pleased surprise as the idea dawned, and Jack Rhyce nodded slowly. He was beginning to wonder how he had overlooked Mr. Pender in his research back in the states. The data might be in his notes at the hotel, but he could not remember the name or description, and he could not see how the Chief had overlooked him either. The idea of Pen Pals was original, and could form the basis of an excellent message center.

"There's only one thing I don't get," Jack Rhyce said. "I don't exactly see how they write to each other without a common language."

"That's right, Jack. That's the difficulty," Mr. Pender said. "I began playing around with that problem just as soon as I took over the center here, and then it came over me, just a week or two ago—why not set up a translation post right here in the League—just an informal unscrambling of the Tower of Babel, and translate the kids' letters? It's not so tough as you'd think. You'd be surprised at the number of Japanese around who can read or write English—and there's unemployment for a lot of intelligentsia. The translation center kills two birds with one stone. We have two big rooms now. Would you like to see them?"

Mr. Pender pushed back his chair, but Jack Rhyce shook his head. It was better not to be overcurious, and, besides, Bill Gibson knew the ground. Bill could never have missed the Friendship League for a moment, or this new man who was running it, and Bill would give the orders.

"Thanks, Harry," Jack Rhyce said. "I would be fascinated to see this project next week because I can begin to see already what a real thought there is behind it. But right now, how about some more on the organization's setup, before I go after the details?"

Mr. Pender nodded. "I think you're very wise, Jack," he said. "Take the whole thing slowly. You'll be able to get your teeth into everything beginning Monday. Of course, our basic trouble as I see it is getting personnel out here who are imbued with the right ideas in the social sense . . ."

Harry Pender was a good, fast talker when he discussed the problem of personnel. As Jack Rhyce listened, occasionally nodding in agreement when a cogent point was made, he constantly made mental notes of Mr. Pender's facial expressions and mannerisms. The type was familiar, the intellectual, professorial features, the pale skin, the brown eyes, the receding hair line. There was a fine photographic collection back in Washington of all known people in the business, and Jack Rhyce racked his memory for photographs of the Pender type, but he could make no identification. The trouble with the business recently was that new faces and new talents were continually appearing, and the photograph files were getting a year or two behind the contemporary parade.

He glanced across the office at Ruth Bogart.

"You're getting full notes on this, aren't you, Ruth?" he asked.

"Oh, yes," she said. "It's really fascinating, Mr. Pender."

His one anxiety was not to make a mistake, which might disturb the picture. That was one of the hardest things to learn—to keep things quiet.

It was late in the afternoon when entirely by accident Jack Rhyce picked up another piece of information that interested him. They had made a tour of the offices while Mr. Pender poured forth facts. The man, Jack Rhyce was thinking, must have been at some time the recipient of a Ph.D. degree, and he must have worked as an instructor, presumably in sociology in some college in the States; there was a depth and charm to his voice that fitted well with the U.S.O. Song Caravan.

"You see," Mr. Pender was saying, "this job here is a real challenge to me, Jack. I don't know why Chas. Harrington thought I was suitable for it. There I was, just running our settlement house on Pnompenh not six weeks ago—and along came the news that the League board had selected me for Tokyo. It's a big jump from a little settlement house in a one-horse town to a place like this."

"Pnompenh," Jack Rhyce said slowly, "I don't think I've ever heard of Pnompenh."

It was not true, what he had said, but this was not a time to be bright.

"I don't blame you," Mr. Pender said. "It's in Cambodia, and not many people get there now; but the Cambodians are very lovable people."

It was also an excellent place from which to communicate with China, but it was never wise to appear too interested. Jack Rhyce glanced unobtrusively at his wrist watch.

"This has been a very full and fascinating day, Harry," he said, "and I can't be too grateful to you for giving us all this time. But now maybe Ruth and I had better leave you and call things off until Monday, or else we'll lose perspective. We can get a taxi, can't we?"

"Oh, don't do that," Mr. Pender said. "Why don't we all go to a real Japanese restaurant for supper, and see night life in Tokyo?"

Jack Rhyce glanced at Ruth Bogart and shook his head.

"Let's make it sometime next week," he said. "I think Ruth's still tired from the trip. Aren't you, Ruth?"

"Well, yes," she said, "I am a little, Jack."

"I'll just take her for a walk along the Ginza," Jack Rhyce said. "I can find my way all right, thanks, Harry. I'm curious to see the Ginza. It was quite a shambles back in '47."

Mr. Pender smiled at them as they moved toward his office door.

"You won't recognize it now," he said. "It's everything it used to be, and more so. Well—" his smile grew broader and more tolerant— "have fun, kids, but come back to school on Monday."

The offices of the Friendship League had been air-conditioned, so that the heat on the street outside made one catch one's breath.

"That office and that damned Aloha shirt," she said.

"It was a fresh one since yesterday," he told her. "The fish were red yesterday. They were blue today. Did you notice?"

"Oh, yes," she said. "I'm a dumb girl, but I noticed quite a lot besides the fish."

"How much else?" he asked.

"Enough to know we'd better be careful," she told him.

"That's why we're walking down the Ginza," he said. "If anyone's tailing us . . . I agree, we'll have to be damn careful."

Every large city in the world was bound to have a characteristic street or square, and Jack Rhyce had seen enough of these to make intelligent comparisons. It seemed to him that the Ginza was the most vital of them all; it best expressed the *Geist*—he had to use a German word—of the people who had made it, although it was not a beautiful street, any more than Broadway was beautiful. The only civic decoration connected with it were the willows on either side of the thoroughfare that were peculiar to the Ginza district. He did not know what they symbolized. Perhaps they were supposed to illustrate the old saying of the supple tree bending before the wind, and perhaps they delivered a quiet, reassuring message of patience and of waiting to the crowds that thronged past them. It was a tawdry street, but very gay, with all the resilience and adaptability of its sidewalk trees. There were huge department stores, and smaller shops filled with garish, highly colored Japanese goods. There were motion picture houses displaying the latest Hollywood films as well as Japanese-made pictures. There were beer halls, cabarets and billboards, jewelry and cultured pearls. There was something for everyone on the Ginza. Though many of its shops had the impermanent construction which he associated with a Western mining town, the whole combination was a tribute to the indomitable spirit of a people anxious to be in the front rank of what was perhaps erroneously known as progress. The startling vigor of Japan was reflected in the burgeoning of manufactured articles that ran from celluloid and plastic toys up to vacuum cleaners and electric refrigerators. And where was Japan going to sell this glittering and sometimes meretricious output? This was one of the world's new, restive questions, and the world's future might be hanging on the answer. The motion picture houses, the beer halls and the cabarets with their beckoning invitations in English also showed the versatility of Japan. It was too early for the neon signs, but once they were turned on, the Ginza would be another Broadway, a center of national aspirations. Actually it was more significant than New York's Broadway of the present, because Broadway was tired, worldly-wise and cynical, whereas the Ginza was full of naïve, unfaltering hope. Now and then you could believe that you were on Broadway except for the Japanese features and the voices speaking a strange tongue, and the Japanese characters above the shops.

"It's a little spooky here, isn't it?" Ruth Bogart said.

"How do you mean?" he asked. "There aren't spooks around at four in the afternoon."

"I mean, it's half home, and half not," Ruth Bogart said. "I wonder whether the Japanese feel any more at home here than we do."

It was one of those interesting thoughts that could never be answered, and it showed that she was not anybody's fool. The truth was, he was thinking, he was growing too interested in her reactions, but it was pleasant to turn his attention to her after a difficult day.

"The beer halls are air-conditioned," he said. "Would you like to go in and have some beer and listen to some jazz?"

"No, thanks," she answered. "Let's walk. It's hot as hell, but I like to see the show. It isn't like Piccadilly, is it?"

"No," he said, "it isn't like anywhere else. Would you like some raw fish and rice? There must be some good *sushi* places down the side streets."

"Not raw fish," she said, "and don't try to be an informative guide using words for local color. To hell with the *sushi* places. Let's just walk along."

"I could show you quite a lot if I wanted to use the language," he said.

"I'd say we're seeing enough the way it is," she said. "I wouldn't say we had a tail on us. Would you?"

"No," he said. "I wouldn't. Between us we should have spotted one by now."

She smiled at him, and he smiled back because he shared her temporary relief.

"Then let's go back to the hotel and have a drink in the bar," she said. "And you can make eyes at me in front of the bar boys and the barflies, just to build the cover, darling—just to build the cover. They have an air-conditioned bar at the hotel. Did you know it?"

"We'll go there pretty soon," he said, "but there's one place I'd like to take you first. It's quite a distance, but we can get a taxi!"

"Oh, no," she said, "not any more sights today. I never did like sights."

"It won't take long," he told her, "and perhaps we can pick up some ideas."

Along the Ginza it was simple enough to find a taxi driver who could speak a little English.

"Street with all the bookstores," Jack Rhyce said. He took a paper from his pocket and pretended to read the name of the district from it, with a clumsy pronunciation.

"Bookstores?" she said, as soon as the cab had started on its way. "For heaven's sake, why bookstores?"

"You'll be surprised," he said, "at how many people are reading in Japan."

There were districts in every city where dealers in new and secondhand books congregated, but few were larger than the book street in Tokyo. The bookshops extended for block after block, and, like Ginza, they offered a little bit of everything. The wide-open doorways leading to the brightly lighted interiors displayed stacks of new paper-backed editions, translations from all over the world, the classical literature of Japan, and current fiction. Also older works were displayed in the show windows—books of art, court ceremonial and religious writings—but the books in English were more provocative than any. There was, for instance, in one shop window, a handsome set of leather volumes on the birds of northern Britain, published some years before Perry had anchored off Japan; an early set of the Waverley novels; a handsome edition of Emerson's essays; a book on navigation dated 1810; and *The Parent's Assistant* by Maria Edgeworth. These timeworn volumes each had its untold and unknown story of its ending in an Oriental bookstall. You could not help wondering who had first brought them to Japan. Had they been owned once by someone in the British Embassy, or by an American missionary, or had they come from the library of a once rich Japanese, impoverished by the war? No one would ever know the answer anymore than one could guess who would eventually read them. The past, the present and the future were all implicit in the bookstores.

Most of them were filled with customers, many of whom were reading as much of a volume as possible in the hope of getting the gist of it before they had to buy, but no one disturbed the furtive readers. No one interrupted Ruth Bogart or Jack Rhyce either, as they moved from shop to shop. The displays of periodicals were what interested him most, particularly the large numbers that dealt with Russia and Red China. These—some in Russian, some in English, some in Japanese—were crude but effective projections of American formats. Except for some scurrilous pictures of Uncle Sam and heavily armed gentlemen with dollar signs on their waistcoats who whipped starving workers into factories, everyone was happy in the pictures. Fat Chinese peasants were smilingly learning to read. Farmers were proudly operating tractors. Soldiers carrying the Freedom Flag of the Hammer and Sickle gave candy to little children.

"You see," he said, "how it rounds out the picture of the day?"

"Yes, naturally I see," she said, taking his arm and pressing it urgently. "But let's go. We shouldn't have come here."

"Why not?" he asked her. "What's the hurry?"

"Buy some cheap American magazine," she said, "and get out of here."

He did not ask her again what the matter was until they stood on the curb waving to a taxi.

"We're in the clear," he said. "There was nothing queer in any of those shops."

She shook her head impatiently.

"No," she said, "but we are. We were the only foreigners and everyone remembers foreigners. Where would you keep a lookout for new operators? Put yourself in their position, Jack."

He felt deeply mortified that he had not thought of her point himself. Too many small mistakes too often added up to something fatal, and there was no way of knowing how great a margin of error they possessed. A taxi had halted.

"There are some people looking at us," she said.

"What sort?" he asked.

"I don't know," she answered. "Little men."

"But, darling," he said, and he laughed loudly. Then he put his arm through hers and took her hand. At least he could leave the impression of love and dalliance if anyone was watching. "This country is full of little men. Insufficient food in infancy—and the large intestine of a Japanese is two feet longer than that of his opposite number in Europe. Did you know that?"

"No," she said. "How fascinating!" But she leaned against him and laughed up at him applaudingly.

When they were in the taxicab he put his arm around her. As Bill Gibson had said, there was safety in sex. They had only been two people in love looking for a copy of *Hollywood True Romances.*

"Oh, Jack," she said, and she giggled.

The taxi driver, if anyone asked him, would remember.

"Honey," he said, "I'll get you a nice cool drink in that nice cool bar. Frankly, I can't wait."

But she had been right. He had been a fool to be examining Red literature in Tokyo.

The bar of the Imperial Hotel was aggressively modern and so over-air-conditioned that Jack Rhyce felt for a moment that they were locked inside a refrigerator. They sat next to a sealed plate-glass window that looked out on a small Japanese garden containing a marble bust of an elderly man in the top half of a frock coat. Nearly all the tables were filled, some with prosperous Japanese businessmen, but most with rather weary-looking Europeans who appeared as peculiarly assorted as the English books they had seen exposed for sale. People were looking at them with the friendly curiosity with which foreigners in the Orient regard new strangers. There was nothing professional about anyone there, nothing technically disturbing. It was becoming easier and easier to appear conspicuously interested in Ruth Bogart.

"What would you like, sweet?" he asked, when the bar boy came to the table.

"Scotch on the rocks, darling," she said.

They gazed at each other fatuously for a while after the bar boy left, and then they both begun to laugh, and it was the first time in several weeks that he had been genuinely amused.

"Did you know, sweet," he said, "that rats are very adaptable creatures?"

"Why no, darling," she answered, "but what makes you think of rats?"

"The extreme coldness of this room," he said. "Once when I was crossing the ocean, the ship's captain asked me to a cocktail party. Have you ever been to a ship's captain's cocktail party?"

"Yes, darling," she said. "That's one reason why I travel by air."

"Well, this was a very nice ship's captain," Jack Rhyce said, "and he told an anecdote about a rat. It seems that this rat was locked up by mistake in the ship's refrigerator. He stayed there for four weeks and he didn't freeze to death. When they caught him he had a coat as heavy as mink. That's why I say rats are adaptable."

"Is there any moral to that story?" she asked.

"No," he said, "no. It's just an off-the-record story."

"Well," she said, "it's the first off-the-record story you've ever told to date."

"Yes," he said, "that's so. I'm afraid you're a bad influence on me."

"I hope I am," she said. "I really do, and I hope you'll tell some more."

He realized that he was happy, and happiness was such a rare sensation that he was suspicious of it, but the more he examined his mood, the more certain he was that it was genuine. He could discover no particular reason for it, and he did not particularly care. He only knew that it was something that made the whole day worth while.

"You know," he said, "I think you're a pretty clever girl."

"Why, thanks a lot," she said. "Coming from you, I must be."

The mood had not left him yet. He could even enjoy looking at the bust of the old man in the garden.

"In fact, maybe you are smarter than I am," he said. "You were right about those bookstores."

"I like to have you wrong sometimes," she said. "It shows that maybe you are human."

"Why, thanks a lot," he said, "but believe me, it's better not to be."

She smiled at him, ironically, but very pleasantly.

"You remind me of a poem of Whittier's," she said.

"What poem?" he asked.

"About the boy and the girl at the schoolhouse," she said. "'*I'm sorry that I spelt the word: I hate to go above you, because,'–the brown eyes lower fell,–'Because, you see, I love you!*'"

"Yes," he said, "but I don't like what comes later. *Dear girl! the grasses on her grave Have forty years been growing.*"

"I don't like that either," she said, "and I wish you hadn't brought it up."

But even so, nothing changed his mood.

"You know," he said, "I don't see why we shouldn't have a nice time going there tomorrow."

When she smiled at him again, it was exactly as though they were on the outside.

"Please," she said, "please let's, Jack."

## 9

JACK RHYCE glanced at his wrist watch as they stood beneath the porte-cochère of the Imperial Hotel. The time was 9:05 exactly. They had brought box luncheons, and they could make a leisurely trip, spending the whole day if they liked. Mr. Moto had done very well with the car. It was a vintage Buick limousine, with the chauffeur's seat separated by glass from the owner's.

"Thirty thousand yen to keep for week end," Mr. Moto said. "Me, automobile, and glass for privacy, everything. It is not too expensive, I hope."

"Oh, no," Jack Rhyce said, "not for this once. Everything's just swell, and here are some yens on account—just so you'll know I've got them, Mr. Moto."

He laughed heartily, and Mr. Moto laughed back. There was one good thing about the business. Money was never an obstacle, and nobody audited expense accounts if you happened to get home. Their suitcases were locked in the trunk behind. Everything was ready.

"All right," he said, "let's go"—and he smiled at Ruth Bogart affectionately for the benefit of the doorman. "That is, if you've remembered everything, sweet?"

"Silly," she said. "Of course I've remembered everything."

The mood of the afternoon before was still with him, and he felt no sensation of tenseness or discomfort. He was sure that they were not being watched or followed, and that they were still in the clear.

"By the way," he said, rolling down the glass partition, "we might stop for a few minutes at the Memorial Temple—the one for the soldiers, I mean. Miss Bogart might like to see it."

She looked at him questioningly, but he was sure that he was right about the temple. His asking to go there established them as sightseers, and for some reason the Japanese felt no resentment at Americans visiting the shrine of their war dead. The pine-shaded area of the temple's grounds stood in one of Tokyo's heavily populated districts, making a sharp contrast with the surging traffic on the street outside.

"Wait, please," Jack Rhyce said to Mr. Moto. "We won't be long"—and Mr. Moto smiled.

In plan, the temple was typical of all the shrines of Japan dedicated to the Shinto sect, which was more of a national loyalty than a religion. The arched stone-lined causeway leading to the red-lacquer pavilions, and also the smaller paths that diverged beneath the dark pines, had undoubtedly been adapted, like so much Japanese culture, from early Chinese religious structures; but time had added dignity to this adaptation until Japanese shrines possessed an austere beauty entirely their own. There was a Spartan simplicity in the repression of design, as well as in the repression of the people, mostly elderly, who moved about the grounds, stopping now and then before a pavilion, clapping their hands and bowing their heads in prayer. The ashes of soldiers who had died for the Emperor were preserved there, and where there were not ashes there were names.

"I come here," he said, "because I'm responsible for several of these names."

There was no necessity, he realized, to have given her this explanation.

"How many?" she asked.

"I don't know," he answered. "Twenty-thirty. More, perhaps. You can't always tell everything that a machine gun or a hand grenade does. And you see, most of them preferred to die."

They walked back to the car in silence, and he hoped he had taught her something about Japan that was both important and unfathomable. It was hard to realize that all the city streets had been torn by war, and that every person walking on them had lost some near relation, because the signs of war had almost disappeared, both from Tokyo and the faces of its people. It was valuable to understand that nothing was forgotten.

Even during the journey, Jack Rhyce knew that he would never forget the motor rides to Miyanoshita. It was one of those unrelated lapses that come into one's life when least expected, a sudden unalloyed period of beauty that became something more than memory. It was dangerous to feel as he was beginning to about the girl in the car beside him, but as he looked back over that long day he could not experience a single qualm of regret. Actually there had been no need for any, because there was nothing that he or she could have done about anything until they made contact with Bill Gibson at the hotel that night. There was no necessity to think or plan, and no immediate harm in being beguiled; and besides, all they did was part of the cover.

It was part of the cover to be conscious of her nearness and to hope that the car would soon take another curve so that she would lean against him. It was as though they were both on the outside, that day, and it was more of a fact than an illusion. It was a part of his business to know perfumes. The first instant he had met her he knew that she used Guerlain's and he had identified the variety, but there was nothing technical about the Guerlain any longer. He had immediately recognized her as beautiful, but now everything about her was subjective, not objective any longer, just as it might have been on the outside. The way a draft of air blew a wisp of hair across her forehead was beautiful, and so was the austere perfection of her profile when softened by a smile, and so were the quick gestures of her strong but delicate hands. A pair of white gloves lay across her lap, but she did not wear them, and she wore no rings, no jewelry at all except a plain gold clip.

"It's just as though we were on the outside," he said.

"Yes," she answered, "and please let's keep it that way." And she did not move away when he took her hand.

In a way that ride to Miyanoshita had everything. Later he could unroll it in his memory as one did a Chinese scroll painting, which should be seen in parts and never all at once.

Their ride took them past the area of heavy industry that surrounded Yokohama, then along the sea and finally into the country. Except for the heavy traffic on the roads, the disruptions of the machine age were gone once they reached the country. The thatched farmhouses, the jade-green of the rice plants reflected in the shallow water of the checkerboard squares of the paddies, the bamboo windbreaks, the farmers in their huge straw hats meticulously tending each rice shoot, the jagged mountains in the background were part of an eternal picture of a way of life that could survive all change. Yes, the ride had everything. There was the immense Daibutsu Buddha and the island of Enoshima, with its crowded inns and its shops of seashell ornaments, the scene of the most masterly satire yet written on Japan. *The Honorable Picnic.* This was a book which had been banned before the war, but was now on sale everywhere. Had the war taught the Japanese to laugh at themselves? Like all those questions, there was no definite answer, except that the humor of Japan was as detailed and specialized as its ornamental ivories.

Nothing that Ruth Bogart said or did was discordant. She had great adaptability, but Jack Rhyce was also sure that they both honestly liked the same things and were impressed by the same details. There were two incidents that day that were more vivid than the rest. The first was the sight of two wounded soldiers, on the path leading to one of the shrines at Kamakura. Each had an artificial hand, and each an artificial leg. They were dressed in well-washed khaki without insignia. When he stopped and gave them a fifty-yen note, they came to attention and saluted, and he had returned their salute before he recollected that he was in civilian clothes. They had spotted him as a soldier, too, and for a second all three of them must have been moving into the past. Now that the war was over, there was a lack of resentment impossible for a Westerner to understand.

Then there was the fortuneteller who had his concession just beyond the alms-seeking soldiers, an emaciated elderly man who smiled and beckoned the moment Jack Rhyce and Ruth Bogart betrayed interest. On a stand near him was a miniature red-lacquer temple with three small black-and-yellow birds Perched in front of it—goldfinches, Jack Rhyce believed. He had never been good about birds. But, going back to his early childhood, he remembered tame birds looking just like them that would sing and fly and return to their cage at a whistle. The fortuneteller was clearly used to Americans, because he whipped out from his pocket a typewritten explanation.

"Give any bird a fifty-yen folded note," Jack read. "Bird will drop it in the cash box, fly to temple door, ring bell, enter temple, get fortune on folded paper and bring back same."

"It might be worth fifty yen," Jack said.

"Yes," she said, "but let me pay for it. I want it to be my fortune." She handed the old man a folded note. He held it in front of one of the birds, and just as the explanation said, the bird took it in its beak and dropped it in a tiny money chest.

"Come on, Joe," the old man chanted, "come on, Chollie, go on, Joe."

The birds and their owner repeated a pattern that Jack Rhyce had seen in nearly every city in the world. That act of fortunetelling must have dated back to temple necromancy, but here the words were new. They had an unfamiliar ring beneath the hot Japanese sky, telling their tale of lonely American soldiers on leave, back at home now, or dead perhaps in Korea.

"Come on, Chollie, come on, Joe."

The tiny black and yellow bird cocked its head and its beady eye was remarkably intelligent. It fluttered from its perch to a tiny ladder that led to the temple porch. It pushed a small bell smartly with its beak, and the bell tinkled with a miniature clarity that completely rounded out the illusion. Then the bird disappeared inside the toy temple and emerged carrying a folded bit of paper.

Then the bird fluttered back to its perch, and Ruth Bogart took the paper from its beak.

"Don't be afraid to read it," Jack Rhyce said. "They only have good fortunes here."

He had meant to speak lightly, but he was disturbed by her intent look.

"Yes, I know it's rigged," she said, "but I want it to be true."

The strip of paper resembled one of those fortunes that one used to find as a child inside a snapper at a birthday party. She glanced at the words and handed it to him.

"Once you were unhappy," he read, "but you are very happy now."

"That's true, you know," she said. "Absolutely true."

"Well," he told her, "you wanted it to be."

"I don't have to want it. It's here," she said. "And you're happy too, aren't you? I mean for just now?"

"Oh, yes," he said, "I'm happy."

She laughed. She was watching the outlines of the rock pines against the cloudless sky.

"I was afraid you were going to say you were too happy," she said. "I love it when you're not careful, and you haven't been all day."

"If you want to know," he told her, "it's pleasant for a change."

"There's only one catch about it," she said. "It says I'm happy now but it doesn't say how long, and I want it to be long-term. Would you like it long-term?"

She had said she liked it when he was not too careful—and he was not careful then. With her standing close beside him in that place, so far removed from anything that was familiar to either of them, it would have been impossible for him to measure everything he said, and he would have hated himself afterwards if he had done so.

"Yes," he said. "You couldn't possibly know how much I want it that way."

That was all that either of them said, and it was all that was necessary. They both knew that the moment would be transient, but a weight was lifted from him. He felt a grateful relief that he was alive, but this relief had nothing to do with any of the cruder gratitudes for survival that he had experienced more recently. As it happened, neither of them had time to embroider on what they had said, because he heard a footstep behind them before she did, and he was back from the outside to the inside, turning slowly and accurately on his heel. Nothing was ever gained by appearing startled or suspicious.

He did not know that Mr. Moto had followed them until then, nor was there any sure way of telling how long Mr. Moto had been behind them or what he might have heard—not that what they might have said would have affected any situation. There was nothing harder, Jack Rhyce was thinking, than to tread softly on a graveled walk, and only that single footstep had attracted his attention.

"Oh, hello," Jack Rhyce said. "Have we been staying here too long?"

"Oh, no,"Mr. Moto said, "but there is still a great distance to go, and many things to see."

"All right," Jack said. He put a slight edge to his words because he wanted to make it clear that he had not approved of that gentle approach. "Go on back to the car. We'll be with you in a minute." When Mr. Moto moved away, Jack Rhyce waited deliberately until the purple suit and tan shoes were a hundred yards in front of them.

"Have you noticed one queer thing about him today?" Ruth Bogart asked.

"I've noticed several," Jack Rhyce said. "Which one did you notice?"

"He said he was a guide," she said, "but all day long he hasn't tried to explain one single thing to us. Did you ever see a guide like that?"

"That's right," he said, "but he's an A-1 driver. He has to be, with all the crazy driving on these roads."

It was one of the few moments when they were both inside that day.

"You're right about his being in the business," she said.

"He was once, anyway," he answered.

"Do you think he knows what we are?" she asked.

"Let's not worry right now," he said. "We'll know better when we see Bill tonight. Let's still try to be happy. I enjoy making the effort, as long as you do, too."

They had been in no hurry, and there were long, cool shadows across the road as they began to climb into the hills. The trees of the carefully tended forests that had replaced the rice farms in the landscape were the ginkgo, the feathery cryptomeria, trees that looked out of place when in a Western land, but fitted perfectly into the Japanese landscape. They would be at the hotel at half-past six.

There were hot springs at the hotel, and a swimming pool, he told her. The rooms were very comfortable, and the food and service were very good.

"But I'd rather stay at a Japanese inn," he said. "I'll take you to one sometime."

"I'd like it," she said, but he knew she was thinking of something else. "Jack?"

"Yes," he said.

"Jack, will you promise me something?"

"Promise what?" he asked.

"Don't be so cagey," she said. "If we get out of this, let's try to live on the outside. And promise me you'll get out of the business if I don't come back."

"Listen," he said, "have you got a hunch about something, Ruth?"

"No," she said, "no. But I'd like to have you promise before it gets you, Jack."

"Let's talk about it later," he said, "but I'm glad you like me that much."

"Yes, I like you that much," she said.

It must have been at that moment that the peacefulness of the day ended. It was time to drop a curtain on the day and think about the evening, and it was time to heed the warning of common sense. He looked through the plate glass at the back of Mr. Moto's head. The man's age, he was thinking again, was about fifty, but his reflexes were still excellent, and his driving on the switch-back turns of the mountainous road superb. Actually Jack Rhyce had not bothered to see whether the car was wired for sound, because nothing they had said was of any importance except those last speeches, but even a microphone would hardly have carried above the outside noises of the traffic on the heavily traveled road. He heard her laugh beside him.

"Don't worry," she said. "The car's all clean."

If she said so, she was correct, and it was not necessary to ask how she knew, or how she had made the opportunity to find out.

## 10

THE TOWN was on a slope of the winding road that led to Lake Hakone and, farther, toward the sacred Mount Fuji. The hot springs and the scenery had made it a resort for a great many years, patronized by the old nobility and wealthy people from Tokyo, many of whom had owned houses there; and the Japanese inns were excellent. The hotel to which they drove had been designed as a concession to European tastes, long before the war; time, plus the imagination of its proprietors, had given it an exotic Eurasian charm. Its grounds on the mountain slope were watered by rills from natural springs that made a continued merry sound of running water. The season was too late for the azaleas and some of the exotic blooms, but the hotel gardens were still very beautiful. The Japanese had ancient ways with plants and flowers which were different from those of other gardeners. They lavished a watchful care and patience on every shrub and even on the surrounding trees, so that everything, even if seemingly wild, was actually in order, even down to the arrangements of wind- and waterworn rocks.

The spirit conveyed by the hotel was agreeable. It had frankly been designed as a place for a happy holiday, and it had brought peace and happiness to many travelers. There were highly European swimming pools and tennis courts, but the public rooms, stiff with formal furniture, reminded him that even the most adaptable Japanese had trouble in selecting suitable assortments of Western chairs, tables and carpets. Yet in spite of a cleavage in taste that was hard to bridge, on the whole the hotel had succeeded; the reason for its success might have been its rambling informality, growing from a profusion of halls, staircases, outside galleries and connecting ells that had happy names in English with an Oriental lilt—Plum Blossom Cottage. Cozy Nook. The Peach Bloom.

Due to the crowded weekend, the parking spaces along the driveway were already filled with the cars of United States naval and air force personnel, and bellboys clad in white ducks were very busy with the luggage. The day was still warm but the air was cooler and fresher than it had been in Tokyo. Mr. Moto was speaking authoritatively to the Japanese concierge, and Jack Rhyce was contented to hear him say that his passengers were good people who would appreciate attention.

"I will take the car," Mr. Moto said, "but I will call later for orders and to see if all is right."

"You don't have to until tomorrow," Jack Rhyce told him. "It's been a very fine day, and thanks a lot."

The sunlight had grown softer and the shadows longer. He did not need to consult his wrist watch to know it was somewhat before six, but there was still plenty of time before dark to stroll about the grounds and to locate the cottage called Chrysanthemum Rest, where Bill Gibson would be staying. Nevertheless, he was afraid it would take more time than was available to be as familiar as he would wish to be with the halls and connecting passages of the rambling buildings.

"It's a mixed-up place, isn't it?" Ruth Bogart said, as they followed the boy with their bags. Being built on the side of a hill, the hotel had several levels. they were passing through an arcade, lined with display cases of silks, lacquer, ivories and porcelains, and occasionally they encountered a direction arrow pointing to HOT BATHS, MAIN BAR and DINING ROOM.

"Yes," he said, "this would be quite a place to play cops and robbers in, wouldn't it?"

He was ashamed of his lack of caution the instant he said it, but it was not such a bad estimate of the situation. There were many places where you could lose yourself, and too many exits and entrances for one ever to be at ease.

As Bill Gibson had said, a room had been reserved for them, very comfortable, as the clerk anxiously pointed out, with a bath, in a quiet section of the hotel known as Cozy Nook. Jack Rhyce did not know exactly what had been said or through whom the reservation had been made, but he found the solicitude of the clerk disturbing. Still, he only had to tell himself that nobody knew his business better than Bill Gibson in order to set his own mind at rest. When they followed the boy with their luggage along further passageways to the uper level of the hotel, he realized that in spite of years of practice in many places, the ground plan of this building was too much for him, and he greatly disliked the sensation of not being oriented. In consequence, his first task, he told himself, would be to get entrances and exits straight. Also the friendly smiles of the desk clerks had brought home to him again the necessity for cover, since the management seemed to be so clearly aware that he and Ruth Bogart had arrived for an off-the-record weekend. Although this could not have struck the hotel staff as unusual for two Americans, it was of the utmost importance to keep up the illusion. And now, facing the prospect, Jack Rhyce encountered in himself an embarrassment that made him very formal, especially when the boy opened the door to a spacious double bedroom. There was a 10 percent service charge, about which Japanese hotel employees were far more conscientious than their European counterparts, but still he gave a liberal tip and spoke enthusiastically as the boy backed out, bowing.

"This is a nice room, isn't it, dear?" he asked. "I think perhaps I'd better take the bed by the doorway, don't you?"

It did not help his sense of uneasiness to find that she was laughing at him.

"And if you want to bathe or anything," he said, "I'll go out for a half an hour and stroll around. The hot water comes directly from a hot spring, I believe, in case you'd like to know."

"Listen," she said, "you've traveled around considerably, haven't you? Haven't you ever been alone in a hotel bedroom with a girl before?"

"Well, yes," he said, "occasionally, now you ask me, but not exactly in this way, Ruth."

"Well," she said, "I don't see such a great difference and don't take it so seriously, for heaven's sake, even if your father was a missionary. I'm going to take a bath, and you'd better, too. Do you snore, darling?"

"No," he told her, and he lowered his voice, "you ought to know I don't; not in this business, Ruth."

She tossed her suitcase on the bed next to the wall and snapped it open. The easy way that she moved her luggage showed that she was much stronger than she looked.

"For heaven's sake," she said, but she lowered her voice just as carefully as he had, "the more we forget the business while we're in here, the better. Darling, aren't you going to give me a kiss or anything, after you've brought me all this way?"

She raised her voice when she asked that last question and looked at him meaningly.

"Why, dear," he said, "I've been waiting for this for hours."

"Oh, darling," she said, and then she whispered, "there's someone in the hall outside. We have the privacy of goldfish in this room."

His first instinct was to tiptoe to the door and snatch it open, but she held him and shook her head.

"No, no," she whispered, "maybe it isn't anything, but we'd better act damned silly. I think this place is spooky, Jack."

She was right about the room. There was a transom above the door and he especially disliked transoms. Two windows at the foot of the twin beds, both of them open now, looked over the carefully tended grounds at the rear of the hotel. The third window in the bathroom with ground glass obviously opened on the corridor, and now that the bathroom door was open, a sound of footsteps made a rhythmic beat along the corridor's jute carpet. They were the staccato steps of an Oriental, one of the hotel boys, he was very certain. Nevertheless, he quickly closed the bathroom door.

"Thanks," he said. "I seem to be losing my grip, what with one thing and another."

It was a mistake, he realized immediately, to have said such a thing out loud. He believed in holding a positive thought; as soon as one became overworried and overanxious, accidents frequently occurred. He stepped to the open window, examined the shades and curtains and then made a thorough inventory of the bedroom, which would have been unusually attractive under other circumstances. The Japanese prints on the wall seemed surprisingly good, although he was not a connoisseur of that sort of thing: pictures of strange bent-kneed men with staffs and heavy burdens on their backs, climbing mountains, crossing narrow-arched bridges, or laboring on farmsteads. The curtains that could be drawn before the windows were of heavy cotton, green and yellow with the bamboo motif so favored by Japanese textile designers. The twin beds with comfortable box-spring mattresses were in simple European taste, matching the large mirrored bureau and the taller dresser. Each was covered with a yellowish green spread of raw silk, and the walls had a matching greenish tint. Whoever had decorated the room had good taste. But there was one disturbing feature. The lock on the door was an old and clumsy contraption which any well trained operator could pick in a matter of seconds. The bathroom was commodious, and the tub, made out of marble slabs, gave it an old-fashioned charm.

Ruth Bogart had turned on the bathtub taps and the noise of the running water made a cheerful sound.

"I suppose we'll have to look nice but informal," she said, "if we're going to that dance." She was taking out clothing from her neatly packed bag. "I'll wear my light green silk."

"Better put on the dark green or a dark blue if you have it," he told her. "Remember, we are going to go outside."

"Right, I forgot," she said. "I wonder whether Gibson's got here yet."

"That's his problem," he told her. "I'm going out to walk around while you take your bath."

"You don't have to, you know," she said, "and I wish you'd put on something else besides that seersucker suit."

"I'll put on my blue one tonight," he said, "but haven't you noticed that everyone who does kind things for backward peoples customarily wears a seersucker suit?"

"Oh, dear," she said, and she smiled at him. "I wish we were really staying here and that there could be just two people in this room instead of four. I'm sick of split personalities."

She was still unpacking and hanging things in the bedroom closet as though they were going to stay there for an indefinite period. Her confident unpacking and the running water in the bath contrived to make a new bond in their relationship. The voices from the hotel guests came gaily through the open windows from the grounds outside. People were calling to each other at the swimming pool; army and navy mothers called to their children, and single men far away from home talked to their sweethearts. It was a tolerant hotel, a long way from anywhere, both moral and amoral, but agreeably enough the voices all sounded happy. Up by the swimming pool someone was singing, and then in the distance someone began whistling a tune that made Jack look at Ruth Bogart.

Both their faces had assumed their old watchful look because it was the tune they had last heard before the break of day at Wake Island.

*You cannot see in gay Paree, in London or in Cork!*
*The queens you'll meet on any street in old New York.*

"Well, well," he said softly, "our old favorite, isn't it?"

There was no reason, his common sense told him, to be unduly startled. The melodies from *The Red Mill* were always cropping up on modern records, and they were good, despite the lapse of time.

"It's no favorite of mine," she said. "I told you this place was spooky."

There was no one outside whom he recognized—only a stream of tennis players and of bathers coming down from the pool to dress for dinner.

"Well," he said, "go ahead and take your bath. I'd better go down there and see what I can see."

She shook her head emphatically.

"I'm not going to stay here alone," she said. "I'll go right down with you, and go dirty. That damn song. Frankly, it makes me frightened."

They walked around the grounds for a while, arm in arm, hanging on each other's words, laughing at each other's jests. They walked up the hill to the swimming pool, which was almost deserted now that the sun was low. They observed the empty tennis courts and the hotel greenhouses with their potted azaleas and their cyclamen and fuchsias. They stood in the shade of a giant cryptomeria which must have been at least four hundred years old. They wandered heedlessly past Chrysanthemum Rest—a small cottage, which sure enough was not much more than a hundred and fifty feet away from the ballroom ell. Bill Gibson could not have picked a better place for a private conversation because, as he had said, the noise of the orchestra would drown out anything else. Then they stopped at the fish pond and watched children feeding bread crumbs to the giant goldfish.

"You know," she said, "I wouldn't mind being a fish myself, right now. No wonder they live a hundred years."

"Don't wish that, sweet," he said loudly enough so that everyone could hear, because there was safety in sex. "Just compromise and be a mermaid."

"All right, if you say so," she answered, "you old seadog, you."

He gave an involuntary shudder at her remark, but still, the cover was not so bad as he thought it was going to be.

"Just don't overplay," he whispered to her amorously.

"All right," she said, "you old seadog, you." And then she laughed.

There was reassurance in her laughter; it meant that, like him, she had noticed nothing out of the ordinary. All they saw were happy people, young, carefree, many of them handsome, all concerned only with each other. It was very much like another musical comedy song—"Love is Sweeping the Country"—at that kindly hotel at sunset.

"Hold my hand," she said. "It looks better, and now maybe we'd better go up and get ready for dinner."

"Let's go to that place called the Main Bar," he said. "We haven't seen it, and there may be something new there."

The Main Bar was on the hotel's lower level. The inspiration for its decoration must have been derived from foreign influence close to the turn of the century, because it had the earmarks of another happier age, and its spiritual quality, if such a thing could be attributed to a bar, was remarkable close to the music of Victor

Herbert. Its dark woodwork was like the Old New York where the peach crop was always fine. Its comfortable chairs and tables were not crowded too closely together. The bar itself, with its magnificent array of glass, was almost as long and hospitable as the now mythical bar in Shanghai that was once believed to be the longest bar in the world. The only concession to a changing world lay in the new bar stools, those importations from the French *bistro* that had reached America at the end of Prohibition. A dozen happy couples, now that the dinner hour was approaching, were taking over the tables in groups of fours and twos, and several unaccompanied men were seated at the bar. Still, the room was large enough so that it gave a quiet, half-empty impression; the voices of its patrons were partially absorbed by its spaciousness.

"It's awfully Gothic, isn't it?" she said. "Like a church."

"I'm not carried away by the resemblance," he told her. He beckoned to a waiter. "Would you like a gin and tonic, dear?"

They had selected a table in a far corner from which the whole room was visible. He was already giving the people a mental screening even while he was thinking that he was tired of this sort of watchful analysis.

"Scotch and water," she answered, "and I hope we can get bathed and ready for dinner pretty soon. Everybody here looks very cool and comfortable, and though you're smarter than I am, I can't locate any types."

"Don't try too hard. Don't forget we're in love," he said. He leaned back and sipped his drink. She was right that there was no one who showed interesting signs. If it had not been for that tune, he would have believed that the place was wholly antiseptic, and of course Bill Gibson must have thought so, too, or he would not have named it as a contact point.

"That's right," she said. "I've got to keep remembering. You look handsomer tonight than you did yesterday, but you could do with a clean shirt, and I'd like it, at any rate, if you could get your seersucker suit pressed."

"Oh, don't say that," he told her. "It makes me look informal, feeble and good-natured. Nobody cares what happens to a man in a seersucker suit."

"I care at the moment," she said, "if only because I don't want to be left alone in this rat-race. Oh, Jack! Look across the room."

His glance followed hers to the entrance by the bar.

"Well, well," he said; "now things are looking up."

He had to admit that he felt as Livingstone and Stanley must have when they encountered each other in the interior of Africa. At least things were moving according to plan, because Bill Gibson had entered the room, and there was no mistaking what Bill was. He was a tired, middle-aged American exporter from Tokyo out for a good time over the weekend. He was obviously having one, and he must have had a good time at the hotel on previous occasions because he waved to a group at one table and sat down with a couple at another, putting his arm playfully around the girl's waist.

"Where's Dorothy?" they heard him say. "Why didn't you bring Dorothy?"

No one in the business was more consummate than Bill Gibson. In fact, his appearance gave Jack Rhyce a slight spasm of professional envy. Bill's loud Aloha shirt was art. The paunchy roll of his walk and the slump of his shoulders were beautiful. He sauntered in an aimless way about the room, just as a lonely man with a few drinks should. He walked close by the table where Jack and Ruth Bogart sat, and Jack was exasperated by the obviousness of the contact. Bill was his senior in the business, but that was no reason to treat his junior like an amateur with such a clumsy check-in. For a second Jack thought he might be given some sort of signal, but nothing in Bill's expression changed as he passed the table, no warning gesture, no signal of anxiety. The truth was that Bill Gibson could not have noticed anything off color either, or he would not have moved so carelessly. His face was flushed as though he had been in the sun by the swimming pool. His jowls had their old purplish tinge, his eyes their deceptive glazed expression. He passed their table and ambled to the bar, hoisted himself on one of the stools; Jack heard him calling happily:

"Another Scotch and soda, and make it a double this time, Boy-san."

"Listen," Ruth Bogart said, "school's out now, isn't it? Can't we please go up and get a bath?"

"You go ahead," Jack Rhyce said. "Maybe I ought to stick around here a few minutes."

"No," she answered. "All those corridors . . . I won't go up there alone."

"Now, listen," he began, "I don't think there's a cough in a carload here." And then he checked himself, and his voice dropped to a whisper. "Fasten your seat belt," he whispered, "and for God's sake let's be natural. Boy!" He raised his voice and waved to the bar waiter. "Two more, please. You'll have another, won't you, dear?"

"Oh," she said, "yes, if you'd honestly like me to get tight, darling."

## 11

SHE WAS a good girl, back in the act again. She had glanced for only a fraction of a second at the doorway to the bar, but the instant had been long enough for her to see what he had seen. There was no mistaking the sandy hair, the bushy eyebrows, the clear-eyed glance, the easy walk, the lazily swinging arms, and the characteristic half bend of the fingers of the man who had just entered. Once you had seen Big Ben, you could not miss him. He was wearing khaki trousers, army issue, and he, too, wore an Aloha shirt, and even in that moment of impact Jack Rhyce made a mental note that the shirt had a fish design similar to the shirt of Mr. Harry Pender at the Asia Friendship League.

"The fish," she whispered.

"Yes," he answered. "For God's sake let's be 'natural.' . . . You look awfully sweet tonight, honey."

After all, there were plenty of fish designs on plenty of Aloha shirts, but still there was the coincidence. He saw Bill Gibson at the bar tossing off his double Scotch and soda. Bill had the description and Bill never missed anything. He must have seen, of course; he and Jack Rhyce must both have shared the same surprise and consternation, and also the same exalted sense you always had when the game was getting hot—because anything might happen now, anything, or nothing. It was unsafe to rely on intuition, and just as unsafe to discount it absolutely, but things had gone beyond the intuitive stage in Jack Rhyce's reasoning. The coincidences had gone so far that there was scarcely a reasonable doubt any longer that the man was Big Ben. His appearance at the hotel at just this time confirmed the fact. Bill Gibson's mind must have been moving in the same channels, but he continued drinking his whisky without a glance at the doorway. After all, there was nothing else to do. There was only one question hanging in the air, unanswered by the voices around them: *How much did Big Ben know?* Did he know who Bill Gibson was? Did he know who they were? There was no immediate answer to those questions, but very soon there was bound to be one.

There was bound to be because, as Big Ben stood by the door, their glances met, and Jack saw that he had recognized them. He could feel it in the nerves of his neck before his reason confirmed the fact. The light was on Big Ben and as far as Jack could see there was no blankness or surprise. The face was mobile. Honest pleasure rippled over it. The corners of the wide, expressive mouth turned upward, yet that was not all. Big Ben waved to them from across the room. Jack Rhyce waved back and beckoned, at the same time lifting his gin and tonic glass.

"Darling," he said loudly, "just look who's coming over! Ships that pass in the night, darling!" And then he lowered his voice, "Don't forget, for God's sake, that we're in love."

Big Ben sauntered toward them. Jack did not like to think that the physical sensation he experienced was one of fear; in fact, he was fairly convinced that it was not. It was rather a state of intense warning and watchfulness that set all his perceptions at concert pitch, with the result that he had seldom experienced such complete awareness. It might have been his mood, which Ruth Bogart had detected when she had told him once not to take it too big, but he was not unsure of himself. There was nothing easier to detect than overanxiety or overinquisitiveness, but he knew that he would not overplay. All that bothered him was the perennial pitfall of an unconsidered word or gesture; there was nothing which could prevent this contingency except hoping for the best. He pushed back his chair and stood up, smiling.

"Well, hello, troops," Big Ben said.

"Why, hello yourself," Jack Rhyce said. "If it isn't our sweet swinger from Wake. Remember, Ruth? *In old New York! In old New York!*"

He was even able to put the lilt of the tune in his voice.

"I certainly do remember," Ruth Bogart said. She smiled in just the right way, invitingly, but at the same time not seekingly. "It was terribly romantic out there before dawn, and you had such a lovely voice."

"Gee, thanks," Big Ben said. "It was quite a surprise to me to hear the *boy friend* . . . " He underlined the words with gentle humor, and smiled tolerantly at them.

"Oh, now," Jack Rhyce said, "come. What an implication! We were just out for a stroll at Wake, weren't we, Ruth?"

" . . . to hear the boy friend," Big Ben repeated with a chuckle, "answer right back from nowhere—it almost made me jump out of my swim trunks."

"We certainly owe you a drink if I did that," Jack said. "Take a chair and take the weight off your feet, and give your order to the waiter. It ought to be a double or a triple for a boy as big as you."

"Aw, come on," Big Ben said, and his hands relaxed on the table in front of him and he smiled at them both. "You're not such a peewee yourself, fella. I'll bet you played football in your time."

"Is that so?" Jack said. "Well, you win. Mr. Holmes, I played right half for Oberlin. Where did you play?"

"Oh, shucks," Big Ben said. "I was never in the big team like that. I only played for a jerk-water Southern Baptist college."

His words trailed off apologetically, and then he gave his order to the waiter.

"You savvy what's called Bloody Mary, Boy-san? Vodka and tomato juice, nice and cold and big. Sorry, folks, if I'm unconventional, but you see, this is my playtime."

Jack had never watched or listened more carefully, but he could detect no flaw. The Baptist college explained that Southern accent; there was no uneasiness anywhere. He could assume very safely now that he and Ruth were accepted for what they appeared to be and that they were in the clear. He was so sure of this that he had to fight down a rising sense of elation, because they were in an advantageous position as long as the position lasted.

"Seriously," Jack Rhyce said, "this is a real pleasure, meeting you. I suppose we ought to introduce ourselves. My name's Rhyce—Jack Rhyce, and this is Ruth Bogart. We're just traveling through—out here to make a survey for one of these foundations."

"Oh, yes," Big Ben said. "Seems you mentioned the name of it back there at Wake. Seems to me it had the name of Friendship in it."

"You really have some memory," Jack Rhyce said, "and it's mighty flattering that we made such an impression on you during our brief visit. The name's the Asia Friendship League."

"That's it," Big Ben said. "Say, it's a pleasure to meet you two nice people again, Jack Rhyce and Ruth Bogart. My name's Ben Bushman. Just old Flight Engineer Bushman, at the present time. Our crew lays over at Tokyo about ten days out of every month, and

Bushman comes up here for ease and relaxation." He chuckled happily. "Just the way Jack Rhyce and Ruth Bogart have come up to study Asia Friendship. Am I right, or am I right?"

"Well now, I don't exactly know how to answer that one," Jack Rhyce said. He laughed self-consciously, and so did Ruth Bogart.

"But you must admit it is a friendly place here, Mr. Bushman," she said, and smiled at him dazzlingly.

"Now, now, honey," Big Ben said, "let's cut out the Bushman part. You call me Ben, and just remember I'm tolerant as hell, and I don't blame Jack here, for one minute, but any time if two isn't company and there isn't a crowd, just kind of look around for me, will you? We might sing some old songs, or something. I'm nuts for old songs."

"Why, that will be splendid, Ben," Ruth Bogart said. "Jack loves old songs, too, and he has a lovely voice, if I do say so . . . but if he gets preachy or tiresome, I'll know where to turn, and two will still be company, won't it, Ben?"

"Oh, now, Ruth," Jack Rhyce said. He wished that her flirtatiousness did not sound so genuine, but she was right as far as the business went. "I'm not as bad as all that, am I? But she's right, Ben. I do like a jam session sometimes."

"Well, maybe we can have one tonight," Big Ben said. "There's always a few groups here who like to sing, later in the evening. Just drop down here into the bar sometime later, say eleven—that is, if you haven't something better to do."

He smiled in a very friendly way.

"Oh, come," Jack Rhyce said, "you mustn't kid us, Ben."

Big Ben slapped him affectionately on the shoulder and stood up.

"I'm not kidding you, boy," he said, "I'm envying you. Well, see you later, I hope. And now I've got to be gittin'."

"What's your hurry?" Jack said. "Have another drink. Don't go."

Big Ben shook his head.

"Thanks," he said, "but I want to get cleaned up for this dancing party, and maybe I can find a girl myself. You two make me lonely. Well, I'll see you later, troops."

Jack Rhyce heard Ruth Bogart sigh. He drew a deep breath himself, but his abnormal consciousness of life and motion was still with him as he watched Big Ben. The man's walk was lazily loose-jointed, but at the same time perfectly coordinated. It was the gait of the highly proficient all-round athlete who could move from an eight-oar shell to the tennis courts, the boxing ring, the baseball diamond, or the football field with no need for conscious adjustment. You could not help admiring him because he was aesthetically magnificent. He sauntered past the bar without stopping, shoulders carelessly squared and arms swinging easily. If Bill Gibson had not seen him come in, Bill had surely seen him by now. Jack's first instinct was to deliver some sort of warning, but this would have been superfluous, and besides it had become more important than ever that neither he nor Ruth Bogart should be connected with Bill Gibson. Things were moving so fast that everything at any moment might pour itself into a barrel and go over Niagara Falls.

"It was all so natural, wasn't it?" she said, and her words echoed exactly what he had been thinking.

That conversation with Big Ben had been so frank and real, so entirely in keeping with the guises they had assumed, and so banal and dull, that he could nearly believe that it had been true, but actually it had been interwoven with threads of truth. Football at Oberlin, song fests because both of them honestly loved to sing, and even his growing interest in Ruth Bogart had all contributed to honesty. That piece about the Southern Baptist college was especially appealing. It was the one bit of really tangible revelation that had come through to him; its hidden tones had been touching in their frankness. It had all been small-time, Big Ben said, and Jack Rhyce could recall a lingering note of sadness. The Baptist college must have been true, just as there must have been some sort of social frustration there similar to what everyone faced in one's adolescent years, and to which most people had learned to adjust. There had been something in that unknown Southern Baptist college that Big Ben could not handle yet, although later he had traveled to more sophisticated fields. Jack Rhyce could see the place in his imagination. Small institutions for higher learning were apt to have a dreary similarity in the South. He could imagine a quadrangle of decrepit dormitories, a chapel in bad repair, a lecture hall, a tiny library with its carefully culled collection of deserving books, a football field with its goal posts and bare bleachers, and long-needled pines covering a flat sandy country in the background. It all could have fitted into the composition of a Benton picture. The pinch of poverty would be over it, but at the same time lines of social demarcation would be etched more strongly by the poverty, making them far harsher than any differentiations existing in the North. Distinction would be more than just the other side of the tracks in such a place; there was a quality in Big Ben's voice and gait that told its own story. *White trash* was the name for it, that unhappy phrase which was applied to people living in the clearings behind the pine-grown old fields, who had not solved for generations any of their economic problems. No matter what he had done at football, no matter about his singing town or in a great city. As he put the theoretical story to voice, Big Ben had been white trash once; and it was not hard to project imagination further, and see him in a mill gether. Jack Rhyce believed that the Chief in Washington had been right, if not about the missionary, at least about the religious background. Big Ben's father might very possibly have been one of those itinerant preachers. The contagion of pulpit inflection still remained in Big Ben's voice. It was a hymn-singing voice which Jack Rhyce could readily identify, since in many ways he and Big Ben had sprung from a common background, sharing many of the same repressions and simplicities. A minister's son could spot a minister's son. The saying was not wholly a joke.

He felt her hand on his arm, shaking him insistently.

"Darling, you've got to talk to me," she said—"that is, if we're going to keep sitting in this damn place, or else if you keep sitting like a wooden Indian everybody will begin to think we've had a fight. What have you been thinking about, Jack?"

"You ought to know," he said, "about You-Know-Who, and you needn't have given him such a big glad eye."

"You-Know-Whom, you mean," she said. "At least you don't know everything, do you, Fearless Fosdick?"

"Maybe Fosdick knows a little about You-Know-Whom," he said.

"And maybe Miss Fosdick does, too," she answered, "and Miss Fosdick knows she can make him in about five minutes, if necessary. Maybe we should have registered as Mr. and Mrs. Fosdick. Do you think he was poor white trash, Jack?"

The mere fact that their minds had reached the same place independently gave his theory added substance.

"Yes," he said, "I shouldn't wonder. I didn't know you knew the South."

"There were Southern girls in boarding school," she said. "My roommate was a Southern girl—deep South, very deep. People like him are apt to go off the track somewhere. I ought to know, because I've been off myself. Were you ever off it?"

"I was on two drops into Burma during the war," he said. "There weren't any tracks at all there. I'm sort of used to being off the rails."

They were leaning toward each other, ostensibly absorbed in each other's words, and they had waited long enough in the bar. They both had known, without saying so, that they should not leave the place directly on Big Ben's heels. Jack signaled to a waiter, and paid the check.

"Well," she said, "thank goodness. Does this mean we can bathe and change? Or have you got some other thought?"

The double bedroom, as she had said, afforded all the privacy of a goldfish bowl.

"Anyway," he said, "we may be able to talk with your bath water running."

"And we can talk with me splashing in it," she said. "You don't have to look, but I'm going to have a bath."

They were another eager, happy couple when they left the bar, as they walked hand in hand following the signs along the hotel corridor that pointed to the ell called Cozy Nook.

"You know, darling," he told her, "I was just thinking of another one of those *Red Mill* songs. Ben might just as well have sung it at Wake."

"Oh, sing it now, dear," she said, "softly, just for me."

He drew her closer to him. They made a very pretty abstraction, flushed with their drinks from the Main Bar, on their way to Cozy Nook.

*Not that you are fair, dear,*
*Not that you are true,*
*Not your golden hair, dear,*
*Not your eyes of blue.*

He stopped and laughed.

"It doesn't fit, does it?" he said. "Your hair is too dark, dear, and your eyes are grayish green."

"Never mind," she said. "I approve of the general scheme. Go ahead and finish it."

As a matter of fact, when he finished it he approved of the general scheme himself.

*When we ask the reason,*
*Words are all too few!*
*So I know I love you, dear,*
*Because you're you.*

"I wish to goodness," she said, and her voice had a catch in it, "that I could be me again, or I, or whatever damn way you want to have it."

It was the old lament again, and there was no solution to it, or certainly not then. Besides, there was not time to discuss it then because they had reached their room door, and he was pulling the clumsy outmoded key from his coat pocket.

"Why, say," he said in the bemused tone that one should use after a session with the girl or one's choice at the Main Bar, "it's unlocked. I thought I'd locked it. Didn't you think I had, honey?"

"Why, yes, darling," she answered. "I kind of thought so." And then she giggled. "But I did have other things on my mind."

"Well, it all goes to show," he said, "that I'm losing my memory in my old age."

They both laughed like two college freshmen. Then they hastily opened the door, using the standard Farm precautions.

Mr. Moto was standing in the center of the room. The dust had been brushed from his light tan oxfords, his purplish-blue suit had been freshly pressed. Jack Rhyce was not entirely surprised to see him, but he hoped that he acted surprised. The illusion was helped when Ruth Bogart suppressed a startled scream that sounded technically genuine.

"Well, how the hell did you get in here?" Jack Rhyce asked, assuming the correct badgering tone of an honest American dealing with a wily Oriental.

"So sorry," Mr. Moto said, and Jack Rhyce was interested to see that his hands shook with artificial agitation. "The door was unlocked. So sorry."

The door had not been unlocked, and it was a safe assumption that Mr. Moto knew he knew it. The only solution for the problem was to become more confused, to raise one's voice a hectoring octave higher.

"And if the door was unlocked—so what?" Jack Rhyce said. "Does that mean you should walk inside?"

"Excuse," Mr. Moto said, and his hands fluttered placatingly, "but the door was wide open. More better, I thought, to wait for your return. Then things would not be stolen. Such old-fashioned doors in this hotel."

"That's funny," Jack Rhyce said in a more reasonable tone. "I thought I'd locked that door, but you never can tell, can you? Anyway, it doesn't look as if anybody had got into the suitcases, and you had your handbag down at the bar with you, didn't you, sweet?"

"Yes," Ruth Bogart said. "My gold clip would have been the only thing that really mattered anyway. I think it was very thoughtful of Mr. Moto to wait here for us."

He wished to heaven that he could place Mr. Moto who was becoming an annoyingly loose end to the problem.

"Of course I'm grateful to Mr. Moto too, sweet," he said. "I was only sort of startled at first, seeing him there, that's all. Excuse it, Mr. Moto. What did you want to see me for?"

Mr. Moto bobbed his head and rubbed his hands together. Once more Jack Rhyce had the impression of a character that was too Japanese to be true.

"First, may I ask you if all is right here, and proper?" Mr. Moto asked.

It did not alleviate Jack Rhyce's frustration when Ruth Bogart giggled softly at the word "proper." He even wondered whether Mr. Moto had used it intentionally, but then "proper" was a favorite Oriental word with many shades of meaning.

"Everything is swell, thanks," he answered.

"And your wishes for tomorrow?" Mr. Moto asked. "So many things to see. Might I suggest a picnic and a ride toward the base of Mount Fuji? And Lake Hakone is so very beautiful. But this means start early."

If it wasn't one problem, it was another. In the light of recent events, he should have rented a car and driven it himself, so that it would have been parked outside the hotel at all hours, if they needed to get away, but now his mobility was controlled by the Japanese in front of him. Bill Gibson, he was thinking, would not approve of what he had done about the car.

"I tell you what," he said. "You be waiting outside with the car at seven o'clock tomorrow morning, and then we'll decide what we want to do."

"Seven o'clock," Mr. Moto repeated, and Jack Rhyce could not tell whether it was a repetition or a question. It was a ridiculously early hour, out of keeping with a peaceful weekend, but it might be that they would badly need the car.

"Maybe it's a little early," Jack said, "but I was thinking we might climb some of the mountains." He smiled at Ruth Bogart affectionately. "You want to see as much of everything as you can, don't you, dear—that is, if you're not too sleepy in the morning?"

"Jack," she said, "I honestly don't know how I'll feel in the morning."

Jack Rhyce smiled at her patiently.

"Of course, dear, if you don't feel like it in the morning," he said, "we can change everything. But it won't hurt to have him here early, just in case, now will it?"

"All right," she said, "as long as it's just in case."

"Well, that's settled," Jack Rhyce said, smiling in a man-to-man way at Mr. Moto. "Let's make it eight, and thanks, and forgive anything I said about your being in the room. I'll see the door's locked next time."

## 12

HE STOOD close to the closed door listening to the sound of Mr. Moto's footsteps retreating down the hall in a clumsy, noisy rhythm wholly different from the soft step on the gravel by the temple. The footsteps indicated as plainly as words that Mr. Moto knew he would be listening. Ruth Bogart crossed the room, making a quick noiseless check of the suitcases. She shook her head as a signal that nothing had been disturbed. He moved to the window and peered out. The afterglow had left the sky, and the electric lights had been turned on along the paths of the hotel grounds. He drew the curtains carefully.

"Turn on the water in the tub," he whispered.

"Oh, Jack," she called as she turned the water on, "hasn't it been a wonderful day, darling?"

It was not the right adjective to describe it, and besides, the day was only just beginning. She moved close to him and rested her head on his shoulder, and he was glad to put his arms around her. He had seldom felt so grateful for companionship.

"My God," she said, "it's really started now."

"Yes," he said, "it's moving. what do you know about Skirov?"

"Skirov . . . " she repeated vaguely.

He could not blame her much when her whole mind must have been on the present.

"Yes," he said. "Skirov, the Russian who's running the Communist show here—the masterminder whom our boy makes contact with. The Chief briefed you on him, didn't he?"

"Oh, yes," she said. "I'm sorry, Jack. I was thinking about the Jap and the big goon down in the bar and everything. Yes, Skirov. I saw him in Vienna once—Cossack descent, I think."

"You saw him?" Jack Rhyce said. "Then you can tell me if I have his description straight. Middle forties, five feet five, one hundred twelve, thin, agile, delicate hands and feet, Mongoloid features."

"Yes," she said, "that's him."

Jack Rhyce lowered his voice, not because he was afraid of being overheard, but because he dreaded that his idea might not be right.

"All right," he said, "what about this Moto? Is he Skirov playing a Jap?"

He was conscious of his anxiety while he waited for her reaction. It had been one of those swift inspirations which he had learned to suspect, but if he were right, they might be able to end the show that evening, because they would have worked out the whole scheme of the apparatus. It would be Gibson's job to make the ultimate decision regarding Skirov, but from their point of view, the mission would be accomplished. The prospect of completing a mission always had its alluring side; he had never before been so desperately anxious to end one, not so much because of himself as because of her.

She was still considering his question. Her forehead was wrinkled and she gazed straight ahead of her. He was aware both of her nearness and her beauty, which annoyed him because his mind should have been concentrated on abstractions.

Finally she looked up at him, not enthusiastically, but with respect.

"I guess I was wrong in thinking that big, handsome boys like you are dumb," she said. "I like your thought. I wish I could buy it all."

He had already developed the thought further, while she was speaking.

"Maybe it's more reasonable than it sounds at first," he said. "Take it this way." He began to speak in a whisper, in spite of the running water. "They looked us over in San Francisco. They've got us down as innocent bystanders. They think we're absolutely pure."

"Yes," she said. "I check with that. I think we're clear to date. I had that feeling in the bar."

"Right," he said, and his enthusiasm rose. "Then what could be better than using us as a cover? Wouldn't you do it if you were on their side of the fence? Skirov and Big Ben want to meet. They know we're greenhorns. What's better than having Skirov as a Japanese chauffeur? That explains his being in the room—just to make a final check." He stopped and laughed quietly.

"What's so funny?" she asked.

"The two contacts," he said. "Us doing the same thing—coming up here for a meeting. It's like a convention in Atlantic City, isn't it?"

"Yes," she said, but she did not look amused. "It's funny if true. The trouble is, it's too good to be true. Life isn't made that way. It's too damned easy, darling."

Her criticism confirmed his own inner dread. She was right, that life never ran that way, and nothing ever came easy in the business.

"Besides, Jack," she said, "he simply isn't Skirov."

"You don't know Japs as well as I do," he answered. "This one's like something on the stage."

"I've got eyes too, dear," she said. "Perhaps he's trying to hide his rank or education, but I know he isn't Skirov."

"Well, if he isn't," Jack Rhyce asked, "who is he?"

She shook her head slowly, and her expression reminded him of the Whittier's poem about the schoolhouse.

"It's too bad—because it fits—but he just isn't," she said. "He's in the business, all right; I can spot that as well as you can—but he isn't Moscow-trained. You know he isn't, darling. You know how that Moscow school sticks out all over them. You can spot them a mile away, as easily as you can a German Volkswagen. Skirov is a Moscow boy. This one just isn't."

Jack Rhyce sighed.

"All right," he said. "But I still want Bill Gibson's reaction. Since you can spot them—what about Big Ben? Was he on the Moscow squad?"

"Yes," she said.

"I don't agree," he said. "But what makes you think so?"

"You'd have noticed it in the bar," she said, "if you hadn't been concentrating on the dialogue, darling. That Paul Robeson, Old Man River manner, that lift-that-bale, we'll-all-land-in-jail manner. It's late Moscow. It's still being taught there by their prewar American imports. They must have rather a quaint American section."

"I've got to watch him some more," Jack said. "He doesn't look much like it to me. He looks as American as all get-out."

He wanted to go on and tell her about his reconstruction of Big Ben's college days, but it would have to wait until later.

"Of course he's as American as all get-out," she said. "A lot of very American Americans have gone to Moscow. Jack Reed went and he's in the Red Square now, if they haven't moved him. Now unzip my dress, will you? I'm going to have that bath, but I'll leave the door open, if you have any more ideas."

He had a number of ideas as he sat in an easy chair near the window and listened to her splashing in the tub, but he had learned long ago that it was folly to spread ideas around. No one should ever know more than necessary in the business; the less you knew the less you could tell if they caught you. It occurred to him that he should not even have told her his idea about Skirov. His having done so went to show that he was talking too much, and besides he might be obliged to revise all his thinking after his meeting with Bill Gibson. Bill would have the whole story straight, while he and Ruth Bogart were still only on the fringes of it. Nevertheless, he was already getting his general shape and structure so clearly that a question of policy was beginning to arise. Should the apparatus be smashed, or should it be left alone in the hope of locating Skirov? But Bill Gibson, not he, would make the ultimate decision. The main thing was to get the picture straight.

"He wished that he did not have to see Bill Gibson that night, now that the dangers of the meeting had measurably increased with Big Ben on the scene. However, the importance of an immediate meeting had increased correspondingly, but now the contact must be made more carefully than ever. The room was growing dark. He rose and switched on the light that stood on the small table separating the twin beds.

"Jack," she called, "are you all right?"

"Yes," he said. "I'm fine."

"I thought you were going to tell me some new ideas."

"You know that's bad technique, to tell too much," he said; "and you know the reason, Ruth."

"Yes," she said, "I know."

She was out of the bathroom, brushing her hair by the mirror with quick, brisk, almost savage strokes. She was wearing an oldish cotton print robe.

"I'll buy you a kimono tomorrow," he said. "You'd look well in a kimono, green and blue."

"Thanks," she said, "I'm sorry about the thing I have on. I didn't know there was going to be a bedroom scene. I've started your bath for you."

"Thanks," he said. He began taking things from his suitcase, putting his brushes and toilet articles on the tall dresser, laying his blue suit carefully over the foot of the bed and his dark black shoes with their composition soles on the floor beneath it. Both he and she were neat as pins, as you were bound to be in the business.

"I was thinking about tonight," he said.

"Were you?" she said. "Well, you aren't the only one."

They looked at each other thoughtfully for a second.

"You know you're right about that goon," he said. "From the way he looked at you I think maybe you could take Big Ben—if you keep on encouraging him."

"Yes, I know I can," she answered.

"But at the same time it makes me mad," he said. "But maybe it's a good thing for tonight."

"Why for tonight?" she asked.

He hesitated before he answered, and she must have guessed what was running through his mind. Nevertheless, it was part of the business.

"I want Ben's mind to be off things for about an hour. You do it and I'll see Gibson," he said. "It's necesary to box that boy off. He mustn't worry where I am, and only be glad I'm not where he is. It's the best way of handling things, don't you think?"

Her face grew stiff and wooden. She did not answer.

"What is it, Ruth?" he asked. He spoke more gently. "Are you afraid of him?"

"No, I don't think so," she said, "but I hated that mental undressing way he looked at me, and you'd have to be mighty convincing with a man like that."

It was the business, it was what she was there for, and they both knew it, but still he felt his face redden.

"I didn't mean anything serious," he said. "Just a walk downtown or a ride up the mountain in his car."

The set expression left her face and she smiled.

"It's nice to know you're human occasionally," she said. "I'm glad the proposition doesn't appeal to you personally, but I don't think it would be a good one, anyway. It's too damned obvious, Jack, and he's a very smart man."

"Yes, he's smart," Jack said.

"It's just the thing we'd be expected to do," she said. "Don't you see it would tell him right away that there was something wrong with us? You've got to be jealous and difficult. It would look better if I simply let him know he was attractive to me—and made him want to get me away from you."

She moved closer to him and put her hands on his shoulders.

"Now listen, Ruth," he said, "I'm ashamed I made that proposition, but it was business, Ruth."

"Never mind the proposition, Jack," she told him, her grip on his shoulders tightening. "Just get it through your head that I want to stay with you tonight. I don't want to see you get a shiv in your back."

"If anybody's watching," he said, "it's going to be harder for two to get up to that cottage than one."

"Jack," she said, and she moved closer to him, "please—all right, I'm frightened. I'm scared as hell. All right, he's scared me, on your account more than mine, Jack. I promise I won't let you down."

He bent over and kissed her. Even as he did so he knew that under any circumstances he was being very foolish.

"All right," he said, "but put on a dark dress, and let's go down to dinner."

"Darling," she said again, "I won't let you down. You'd be surprised. I'm wonderful in the dark."

Jack Rhyce had often thought that any ballroom anywhere in the world was interchangeable with any other. There was every reason why this should be so, since the ballroom and the dances derived from it were a part of Western civilization that should have interested Spengler. If you thought of it in purely historical terms, the decline of the West—and he believed that in many ways the West was declining—could be interestingly illustrated by ballrooms and modern music. The time and place that night made thoughts like those more natural then usual because the ballroom of the hotel was an incongruity, like its native orchestra. The jazz and the people had no evolutionary place in the Japanese starlit night.

They were only there as part of the flotsam on the wave of history. At almost any time the European dancers might be whisked away, but the dance convention would be left behind because of its social, sensual and selective attributes. In fact, with the leisure of the machine age, how could people get on without dancing? They are no longer physically tired, and the imponderables of life are heavier, and with them grows the need to escape reality.

A great many couples were escaping in their different ways on the hotel dance floor at shortly before ten o'clock that night. They whirled with fancy steps that they had learned on other dance floors. No one noticed the elaborate Japanese paper decorations on the high ceiling. They were all following the uninspired rhythms of the Japanese orchestra, which did its best, in costume and manner, to follow the American tradition. The music was mediocre, and most of it dated, but everyone who danced lost part of his or her individuality in the pervading sound. The girls, both European and Japanese, were pretty. The men seemed to find it harder to surrender themselves to the pleasures of the evening. Their faces, as they danced looked less forgetful and more careworn than their partners'. Tall windows on both sides of the room opened directly on the hotel grounds so that the dancing was almost in the open air, but even so the orchestra sounded surprisingly loud. Its members, though small men, were eager, conscientious and vigorous.

She was a light and beautiful dancer, much better than he, but they were both of them good enough, in that rather pedestrian company, to be disturbingly outstanding. Their steps had a professional exactness, and they both looked well—she in her dark green and he in his conservatively cut blue suit. He was aware that they were attracting approving attention, which was something he could have dispensed with that night.

"Don't do anything fancy," he told her. "Just dance in a mediocre way. You're too good-looking as it is."

"That's what I thought about you when I saw you first," she said. "You're too good-looking for the business. You look like the answer to a maiden's prayer in this crowd."

"Do you see him anywhere?" he asked.

She smiled and shook her head.

"I wish he were here so we could keep an eye on him," he said. "We've been dancing about half an hour, haven't we?"

"Yes," she said. "Don't you like it?"

"I would under other circumstances," he told her, "but Bill's going to get nervous pretty soon. I wonder where he is."

"Bill?" she asked.

"No, no," he said. "The Big Boy. I gathered he was going to the dance tonight from the way he was talking in the bar."

He felt her shiver, and she shook her head.

"I wish you'd get him off your mind," she said, "or at least look as though you were having a good time so people won't wonder what we're going to do when we go outside. Hold me closer. Don't forget, we're supposed to be in love."

It was another half hour before he saw Big Ben. He had stepped in from the grounds outside. Instead of his Aloha shirt and khaki trousers, he wore a charcoal flannel suit, black shoes and a dark tie. He appeared very young to Jack Rhyce in that formal attire with his unruly sandy hair, his heavy eyebrows; only his eyes gave his age away. Eyes and hands were something that nobody ever could disguise.

"Good," Jack said. "There he is, coming in from outside."

"He felt her shiver again.

"Is he looking for us?" she asked.

"Yes," he said, "I think so."

"If he cuts in," she said, "cut back soon. Please, Jack."

"All right," he said, "but don't discourage him. It won't hurt to have him fall for you."

Big Ben smiled pleasantly while his glance roved over the dancers. Jack Rhyce noticed that he pulled his coat straight, although it had not been disarranged. Then Big Ben took a handkerchief and passed it lightly over his forehead, though he had not been dancing, and then made a gesture with his hands as though he were ridding them of imaginary dust.

"He sees us now," she said. "He's coming over."

"All right," Jack Rhyce said, "and when he cuts in, smile."

"Big Ben was moving toward them through the dancers, a head taller than most of the men. A second later he slapped Jack Rhyce on the shoulder. It was a friendly, good-natured slap.

"Hello, Oberlin," he said.

"Why, hello," Jack Rhyce answered, "Alabama Baptist U."

Big Ben's laugh was infectious.

"Your guessing cap's on crooked, boy," he said. "Not Alabama, Mississippi."

"Oh, come now," Jack Rhyce said, "your accent isn't thick enough. Let's make it Carolina."

"Okay," Big Ben said. "Carolina Baptist. And now may I relieve you of your lovely burden, Oberlin, just for a little while?"

"You mean you want to dance with my girl?" Jack Rhyce asked him. "All right, but just remember—only for a little while."

"Oh, now," Ruth Bogart said, "don't pretend to act so jealous, Jack. I'd love to dance with Ben just as long as he wants." She sighed, giving Big Ben another of her dazzling smiles. "Maybe I need a change . . . "

Jack Rhyce walked to an open doorway and watched them. Like many large men, Big Ben danced very well, even to the nervous jiggling beat of the orchestra.

"Hold me closer," she had said. "Don't forget that we are supposed to be in love."

You had to be able to estimate degrees of physical attraction, and to observe and capitalize on the onslaughts of desire, if you wanted to be successful in the business. It was a sordid matter, standing there watching Ruth Bogart and the big man dancing. He was ashamed of playing a part in that ugly scene, but it was business. Seeing them dance was like watching the merging of two different worlds, a world of grace, gentility and refinement with another of ruthless, dynamic force. It occurred to him that Big Ben might never before have had the experience of dancing with anyone like Ruth Bogart. she had never looked more delicate or more a perfect product of gentle upbringing than when Big Ben held her in his arms. He saw her lips move in some smiling remark. He saw Big Ben answer, and he did not care to guess what they had said.

In the beginning he had entertained a technical fear, which she had expressed in their room upstairs, that her approach might have been too obvious. It had been necessary for her to move fast but, at the same time, Big Ben was a clever man. There was always the question, in such encounters, as to the exact moment when intellectual objectiveness could be discounted. He realized, as soon as he saw them dancing, that Ruth Bogart must have considered this matter also. There was that saying that the desire of woman is to be desired, and a woman could instinctively estimate a man's desire. Rapid though the interplay had been, and obvious as it had seemed to Jack Rhyce as an observer, from what he could see as he stood watching Ruth Bogart had been right about Big Ben. They were a handsome couple on the dance floor. He was certain now that she was something new in his experience. It was certain that he would not forget. Those things did not take long when certain instincts were in the balance.

In its essence, jazz was not happy music. It was restless and lacking in order, reflecting very accurately the spirit of the era which had brought it into being. The world was unhappy and Jack Rhyce was in a better position than most of his contemporaries to know because it had been his business in many places to observe and deal with violence. All his generation had been born and nurtured in an age of discontent, but he was not able to explain the reason for it, unless that a system or a way of life was approaching dissolution. Logically there were less reasons for unhappiness today in any part of the world than there had been fifty years before. The cleavage between wealth and poverty had been greater then, and the voice of social conscience had only been a whisper. Communication and industrial advance had been negligible compared with the present, and so had public health and expectancy of life; yet back in that harder day the world had been much happier. There had been security then in that everyone knew what to expect. There had been strength and order, which perhaps were the attributes that mankind most desired. What was it that had palsied the hand of the political system which had ruled the world at the time of Rudyard Kipling, in as benign and enlightened a manner as many poltical thinkers were attempting to rule it now? What was it that had opened the Pandora box and the floodgates of discontent? What was it that had allowed minorities to give such a loud voice to their grievances that they could upset the lives of persons ten thousand miles away? And what was the basis of the nationalism that made all nations truculent? Why, in fact, was it that individuals all over the world were disturbed, overpopulating the mental institutions, rebelling against conventions, filling the streets with juvenile delinquents? Why was it that no firm hand could any longer quell a social riot? He knew it had been different once, before his time, and he knew that the answer to these questions lay in what was known as the phenomenon of change.

The same questions must have arisen when the Roman Empire was falling. They had been asked also in the briefer and turbulent dynasties of China, and in eighteenth-century France. Volumes had been written about the course of the disease, but its cause was still in doubt. There was no doubt at all, however, regarding the ultimate result, and in the world as he saw it, both in the East and in the West, the result was just around the corner, eager and waiting. Anarchy might rule for a while in North Africa, Egypt or Persia might upset the near East balance. Neutralism might reign in India, but still the result was just around the corner, just what it always had been—the ruthless oppression of absolute rule. It was now called "the dictatorship of the proletariat," but its end was the old dictatorship. The proletariat, with their agitators and their discontented, would be whipped back to their places, and order would be restored more merciless than the order of the Pax Romana or Britannica. And again there would be discontent, simply because man was a discontented being. The cycle would go on.

He realized that it was not the time or place to think of such things, but at least these thoughts made him a part of the stream of history. He and his generation were children of discontent. The drives of discontent had put him where he was, watching the dancers, and at the same time looking at the dark hotel grounds in order to memorize the shadowy places and the plan of the lighted paths. It was curious to think that the same drives which had placed him there had acted in such a different way upon Big Ben, who was still dancing with Ruth Bogart. Given different childhoods and different backgrounds, he and Big Ben might easily have swapped places. Tolerance was one of the troubles of the present. You knew, or you thought you knew, so much about human motivation that, in the end, you could not blame anyone for anything. And in the end rules and laws lost meaning. Perhaps it was this universal tolerance that was weakening the hand of order.

He looked into the night again. The cottage called Chrysanthemum Rest was completely visible. Though its shades and curtains were drawn, he could see that its rooms were lighted, as was the path that led straight toward it from one of the hotel verandas. But if one were to follow another path up toward the greenhouses, there would be shadow and concealment. He could not plan the full approach from where he stood. He would have to improvise after he had started. A glance at his wrist watch told him it was time—10:20 already. Ruth Bogart had been right in believing that it would look better if they walked out into the shadowy grounds together, and it was time to start now. He moved across the room to where she was dancing with Big Ben.

"Okay, Baptist," Jack said, "time for the praying colonels to go the showers—the half is over."

"Aw, gee, coach," Big Ben said, "nobody's even blown the whistle. Well, thanks a lot, honey. And how about us all meeting in the bar in a while? I'm going there right now to drown my frustrations, honey."

Ruth Bogart giggled appreciatively.

"I don't know whether Jack has frustrations or not," she said, "but whatever he does have, he always seems to be all for the drowning process. We'll be there whether I like it or not, won't we, darling?"

"Oh, come on," Jack said. He put his arm playfully around her. "You're going to have ginger ale, sweet. We'll see you down there, Ben."

"We'll dance a few minutes first," Ruth said, "and then I want to go out and get a breath of fresh air. It's awfully hot in here."

Big Ben laughed uproariously.

"And I bet you're getting a headache, too," he said. "How come? You didn't want fresh air when I asked you three minutes ago, honey? Well, no hard feelings. So long, troops."

They danced for a minute or two without speaking.

"He's gone all right," Jack said, "and he hasn't gone outside, either."

"That's so," she said. "I think you're right. I don't believe he's on to us at all."

"What makes you say that?" Jack asked her.

"Oh," she said. "Girls can tell about those things. If you want to know—from the way he tried to make me. It was an all-out and very clumsy effort, darling."

"It could be that we're barking up the wrong tree," Jack Rhyce said. "It could be that he's just a lonely soul on an airship. The world is full of them these days."

"It could be," she said. "But there was one queer thing about him."

"What?" he asked.

"He hadn't been dancing, had he?" she said. "But he was all in a glow, wringing wet with perspiration, darling. Did you notice him dust his hands and wipe his forehead when he came in. Whatever he was doing, he was exercising."

"Maybe he was playing Tarzan in the trees," Jack Rhyce said.

"His hands are so damned big," she said, "and his palms were sweating."

"Well, he's gone now," Jack Rhyce said. "Let's go out and look at the moon."

"Oh, Jack," she said, and the music had stopped so that everyone around could hear her, "who told you that there was a moon?"

## 13

THEY WALKED outside and toward the greenhouses, laughing and talking softly, only one of a number of other couples who were wandering about the grounds. While they walked they examined Chrysanthemum Rest from all angles. There was a clump of bamboo by its door, which was the only cover near it. Still talking softly, they examined the taller fir trees near the greenhouse. Jack was as sure as a fallible human being could be that he had missed nothing, having reconnoitered too many places not to be intensely aware of atmosphere. He had been able to tell for a long while, from his own physical reactions, whether or not a place was being watched. There was always a sort of tenseness in the air and an awareness of other people. He could swear that Chrysanthemum Rest was clear. They sat for a while close together on a bench in the shadow of an old cryptomeria, two lovers in case anyone should notice.

"Does it look all right to you?" he asked.

"Yes," she said. "There's only one offbeat thing. We've been out here for fifteen minutes, and have you noticed, no one's moved inside the house? Not a shadow against the curtains—nothing. perhaps he isn't there."

"He's being still," Jack said, "because he wants it to look as if he weren't there. Bill's a smart operator. Anything else?"

"No," she said. "I don't think we're being watched."

All that was left was the unavoidable danger that someone, by sheer inadvertence, might notice them entering Chrysanthemum Rest, a calculated risk which the bamboo thicket by the door would minimize. If they walked affectionately past the cottage, the thicket would conceal them from anyone standing higher up from the hill, and its shadow would partially protect them from anyone who would be looking from the hotel windows. Of course the door would be unlocked. There would only be the crucial second when they crossed the threshold. Nevertheless, he delayed for a while, with his attention glued on the Chrysanthemum cottage. It was a white frame building of European style, similar to the cottage annexes that surrounded summer hotels at home. It stood peacefully at the foot of the slope of lawn that led from the tree under which they sat. He wished he could be sure that Big Ben was in the bar. He even thought of making a check, but his feeling that the cottage was not under observation made him dismiss the idea.

"Come on. Let's go," he said. "We'll know a lot more after we've talked to Bill."

The brass of the dance orchestra blared across the lawn, interspersed with its drummer's beat. They were only a couple returning to the dance as they walked to Chrysanthemum Rest. His arm tightened around her waist as they reached the bamboo thicket.

"Follow me quick," he whispered.

They were inside the house in a twinkling, because they were both trained operators; the door was closed behind them without a sound and without a fingerprint on its knob, either. The place, as he had observed, was fully lighted. They were in a small entrance hall furnished with a European umbrella stand and a row of wooden pegs for coats and hats. A single open door showed a lighted room, comfortably furnished with wicker easy chairs and a couch. There was a Chinese rug on the floor and gay Japanese prints decorated the walls. The room, to Jack Rhyce's surprise, was empty; so they stood for a moment, breaths held, listening. He could detect no sound except the blare of the dance music. He raised hs eyebrows and gestured to Ruth Bogart. She understood his signal and they moved along the wall so that their shadows would not show on the drawn curtains. It never paid to hurry.

Later, he never could recall what it was that made him sure that something was wrong at Chrysanthemum Rest.

"Bill," he whispered. What with the noise of the music, he might have spoken aloud, but in any case he already had the conviction that he would not be answered.

The bedroom door was also open. The lights were on there, too. He tiptoed to the doorway with Ruth Bogart just behind him. Bill Gibson, in a clean pair of shantung silk pajamas, lay beneath the covers of his bed, eyes closed, head resting on his pillow, his clothes neatly folded on a chair at the end of the room. A glass, a half-empty bottle of whisky and a pill bottle stood under the lamp on the bedside table. His restful posture gave every indication that he was sound asleep, but he was not breathing. Bill Gibson was stone dead.

"Okay," Jack Rhyce whispered to her. He felt in his pocket a drew on a pair of gloves. "Better go through his suitcase, Ruth. Look for anything. Anything." But even as he spoke he knew there would not be anything they wanted.

While she moved noiselessly about the room, he stood still for a minute gazing at the body of Bill Gibson, trying to estimate the strengths and weaknesses of this new situation in much the same way a bridge player might assess the possibilities in dummy when the cards were on the board. Now that Bill Gibson was dead, a whole new line of action was required. He was still in the grip of shock, but he was able to see at once that he was looking at a professional, almost a classic job of elimination. If Bill Gibson had been breathing, Jack Rhyce himself would have thought that it was an overdose of sleeping pills, and after all, suicide due to strain or melancholia had always been a factor in the business. The only trouble was that they had come too early. Bill Gibson should have been discovered in the morning for the job to have been perfect, and doubtless that had been the intention. This was an encouraging thought for Jack Rhyce, in that it showed as plain as print that no one knew that Bill Gibson was there for a meeting. It meant as clearly as a certified document that he and Ruth Bogart were not suspected yet.

There was another plain fact. The decision must have been made some time previously that Bill Gibson should be put out of the way, since the whole job was one that had obviously required meticulous planning. It also betrayed an anxiety to keep things quiet which was completely understandable to anyone in the business, where violent ways of taking out a man, no matter how carefully worked, always offered embarrassing complications. On the other hand, the danger of complication at Chrysanthemum Rest was very small indeed. Success only required that the body be discovered in the morning. Without his being familiar with Japanese medical procedure, Jack Rhyce did not believe that a doctor called in the morning would make more than a perfunctory examination with the evidence before him; no doubt if a more thorough examination should be made this contingency would have been provided for. He picked up the pill bottle, which still held three yellow capsules, a very pretty touch in itself when added to a glimpse of the cork which had fallen to the floor. A drunken man had accidentally taken an overdose of sleeping pills. From the color of the capsules, and without reading the label he could guess that the drug was one of the better-known barbiturates of American manufacture, and he could guess from a minute abrasion at the corner of Bill Gibson's mouth that a lethal dose was safely in the stomach. There were several ways to make reluctant people swallow.

Jack Rhyce set down the pill bottle and sniffed off Bill Gibson's lips. There was the requisite odor of whisky to explain the half-empty whisky bottle on the table. The whisky had been applied overliberally to the lips, but no one would have noticed in the morning. Profesionally it was a job which had only one unavoidable drawback, and even this presupposed the presence of another professional, which indicated again that he and Ruth Bogart were not suspected yet. Like every killing in the business, this one had its signature, and this was ridiculously easy to decipher once you knew it was a killing. The job presupposed enormous and expert strength. It had required someone who could take care of Bill Gibson as gently and effortlessly as a nurse might handle a baby, and Bill Gibson was no weakling. He touched Bill Gibson's hand softly. The body was still warm. He slipped his hand under the head. The mark of a hypodermic was barely visible in the hair at the base of the neck. If one had not known exactly where to look, the mark could easily have gone unnoticed. He lowered the head very gently because it was all a very private matter in which he and his opposite numbers shared the same anxiety to keep it quiet, to keep it clean, to keep it above suspicion.

Ruth Bogart was looking at him from across the room and he nodded slowly in answer to her unspoken question.

"Yes," he said, "Ben was here all right. I wish I could have the privilege of polishing off that son-of-a-bitch. I always thought a lot of Bill."

"Yes, so did I," she said.

But when you were gone you were gone, in the business. His attention turned to the neatly folded clothes. Even the shoes by the chair were in meticulous alignment. The bedclothes were carelessly disarranged just as a man who was drunk might have moved them. The folded clothes were an error, or still better, an oversight. Bill Gibson must have folded them himself. He must have planned to meet them in pajamas and a dressing gown. Jack Rhyce peered into the bathroom. A burgundy silk dressing gown was hung from a hook on the bathroom door. He examined the back and sleeves. There was a slight tear at the right elbow, and the silk was scuffed and a few tiny hairs of woolen lint were mingled with the fabric. It was the blue piling from a carpet, and the Chinese carpet in the living room was blue.

Ruth Bogart had finished with Bill Gibson's baggage and with the contents of his pockets. She shook her head when he nodded to her—but then, Bill Gibson would have been careful to have nothing on him except cover identification.

"Where did it happen?" she asked.

"The living room," he said. "He must have grabbed Bill right by the front door. I'd like to polish off that son-of-a-bitch."

He walked gingerly to the living room and she followed him. Of course there had been a struggle. How was it she had put it—that Big Ben had been all of a glow, and he hadn't been dancing? Yet the signs had been eliminated, and nothing had been broken. However, the impersonal orderliness of the room told its own story of rearrangement. He could reconstruct what had happened as though it were going on now before his eyes—Big Ben in a noiseless bound, towering over Bill Gibson, the jolt in the solar plexus that knocked out the wind. Strangulation was not necessary if you knew the trick. Big Ben's arms wrapped around the smaller man's gasping body . . . the fighting for breath . . . the expert hands lowering the struggling man to the floor . . . The sleeping pills with the suitable label would have been in Big Ben's pocket.

"When you danced with him," he said to Ruth Bogart, "was there anything in his coat?"

"I think so," she said.

It would have been the hypodermic, but this would not have been bulky. The piling of the carpet was scuffed and trampled near the door—not markedly so, but still the evidence was there once you guessed the story.

"They don't know about us yet," he said, "or they wouldn't have pulled it this way, do you think?"

"I think you're right," she said. "You're pretty smart sometimes, Jack."

"Okay," he said. "We'd better get out of here, and brace yourself. There's one thing more that's going to be tough tonight."

"How do you mean? What else?" she asked, and for the first time since they had entered Chrysanthemum Rest he saw that her nerves were shaken.

"We've got to keep in the clear," he said. "We've got to go and meet that bastard in the bar."

"Oh, no," she said, "not that."

"Oh, yes," he said. "Just that, and we'd better be in the mood for it, too, because he's a smart Joe, dear. Muss yourself up a little. Kiss me. Put some lipstick on my cheek. He's got to know we've been out in the garden making love."

No matter what happened in the business you had to go on with the show. When they got theirs, you let them go, and the show had to go on, if only because you knew you had to get yours sometime in some sordid corner or some cellar or some prison, and you would try to take it without a prayer for mercy, if you were in the business. You learned how to dish it out and to take it, too, if you were in the business. The scene which had taken place in Chrysanthemum Rest was still in Jack Rhyce's mind when they left the small detached building. His arm was around her, and they stopped and kissed shamelessly directly underneath a light on the path to the hotel. After all, the hour—which was just past eleven now—was growing late enough so that inhibitions should be breaking if boys were to be boys and girls girls. But even then he realized that their abandon had a quality that was partially genuine.

"Darling," he said loudly, "you're adorable." She giggled. She was very good at that girlish giggle which must have been a vestige of the outside.

"Darling," she said, "not again. Not *here.* Everyone will see us."

She said it exactly as though they were not intending that any even remotely interested parties should see them. At some points there were lighter moments in the business. But their words and actions were only a shadow on his deeper thoughts. He did not have ice water in his veins any more than she, and he had not recovered from the impact of that pseudo-quiet death in Chrysanthemum Rest. His creative projections into Big Ben's character all added to the acuteness of his upset. In his imagination he could hear Big Ben's voice behind his own and hers, and the gentle drawl had a nauseating quality in his memory. He could hear Big Ben speaking as he pinned Bill Gibson down, gasping and helpless. The voice would be kind, since in the end personal animosity ought never to obtrude itself in the business, and if your emotions got the better of you it was time to resign and be a salesman of fancy motor cars. Jack Rhyce knew that the scene in Chrysanthemum Rest was playing on his emotions, which was not right. He could hear Big Ben's voice in his imagination.

"You're goin' out in a minute, friend," he could hear Big Ben saying. "You might as well go out easy and not fight, mightn't you, since you're goin' out anyway, friend? Easy's better than hard, isn't it? And I've got no hard feelings. I'll help you if you go out easy, and I'll be right with you, friend. Now swallow these pills. They won't hurt nobody. Just get them down or I have to make you. Swallow them, and then there'll be the needle, and you and I know that it won't hurt at all. Don't make me be rough, Mac, because it won't gain you anything. I know that poison kit you folks carry. In case you're curious, it's what you call Shot Number Two."

The soft imaginary voice of Big Ben mingled with the music from the ballroom, and Jack Rhyce knew it was time to pull himself together.

"I'm against alcohol as a crutch on general principles," he said, "but I think you and I could do with two good doubles in that bar right now, don't you?"

"I agree with you for once, darling," she said. He felt her shiver, and he shook her in a rough playful way.

"For God's sake pull yourself together," he said. "The show's on the road."

"All right," she said. "So it's on the road, and stop being a space cadet."

He straightened his blue coat and felt his belt. He might not be carrying a weapon but, given the showdown, a properly fixed belt was a good substitute. His was fixed. He wished that he could slash his belt across Big Ben's face just once. Twice would be better—twice and Big Ben's closest relative wouldn't know him.

## 14

THE ATMOSPHERE in the Main Bar had changed since he and Ruth Bogart had been there last, for the better as far as hotel receipts were concerned. There was no doubt any longer, if there ever had been previously, that the patrons—aside from their Japanese girl friends, who were trying to enter into the fun as vigorously as Madame Butterfly had in another generation—realized that they were far away from home. Their loneliness plus the dancing and the drinks had begun drawing them together, so that an alcoholic affection, plus an undercurrent of companionship in misery formed the motif for the now crowded bar. The flyers, the officers of the ground forces, the Navy personnel, the American civilians in and out of government jobs, and even a few Europeanized Japanese had begun to realize that they were all members of the Legion of the Lost Ones. No one had as yet started to sing "Gentlemen Rankers" or "The Road to Mandalay," but several men by the bar were already drunk, and an American girl was doing a dramatic recitation in a corner to which no one in her party listened. A sea of smoke and spilled drinks and voices washed like a wave over Jack Rhyce and Ruth Bogart.

"All right, honey," he said, "we're tight and full of fun, and we've got to check in here, honey, in a big way, and this is our night off. Why, lookit—there's Big Ben, just where he said he'd be." He leaned down until her hair brushed his cheek. "Just remember, he doesn't know who we are," he whispered. "Just hold that thought, sweet, and give me another kiss. It's better that I'm all lipsticked up tonight."

It was common sense aside from anything else. There could never be anything sinister about a man if he was smeared with lipstick, and what was it Bill Gibson had said? There was safety in sex. Perhaps if Bill had practiced that maxim himself he would not have been a corpse in Chrysanthemum Rest.

"Oh, Jack," Ruth Bogart said, and her voice had the shrill note that fitted with that happy evening, "look at Ben. He's got a man with a squeeze box with him. Aren't you glad we haven't gone to bed yet, darling?"

It gave him an unpleasant twinge to observe the number of amused faces that turned toward them after Ruth Bogart had asked her last question. Naturally she did not need to tell him to look at Big Ben. Big Ben stood in the middle of a noisy group near the center of the room, and sure enough, a man with an accordion was with him. He had learned the tricks of holding attention that could only have been derived from the theater. In fact, at the moment Big Ben might have been master of ceremonies in a night club, and perhaps he had held such a position once.

"Jack," she whispered, "he's changed his shirt."

She did not have to tell him. He had been wearing a white shirt when he had cut in on them on the dance floor, but now his shirt was blue.

"That's right," Jack said. "He's been having a busy evening, sweet. Wave to him. He's seen us now."

"Hi, Ben," she called.

"Why, sweetness," Big Ben called, and he shook his finger at her. "Say, whatever have you been doing to Oberlin? Honest, I couldn't guess."

Ruth glanced at Jack's face. She gave a stifled scream.

"Oh, Jack," she said, "I'm sorry. They told me in the States that it wouldn't come off, darling."

Jack Rhyce grinned self-consciously at Big Ben and the boys and girls around him, then he pulled out a pocket handkerchief, wiped his cheeks and lips, and shook his head.

"I guess the trouble is, dear, this isn't the States. Maybe nothing's kiss-proof in Japan."

It was a pretty good line, considering, and the laugh that greeted it confirmed this impression. A man with lipstick on him couldn't help but be a nice guy, especially in a bar.

The effort he was making made Jack Rhyce afraid that he might be overdoing things, until he saw there was no sharpness in Big Ben's glance.

"Say, boy," Big Ben said, "come on over here. Let's do a song number for the crowd. This fellow can really sing, folks."

"Oh, now," Jack said. "I might break my larynx."

Now that they knew he had a comic streak everything he said was funny. Ruth Bogart gave him a playful push.

"Oh, go ahead, Jack," she said. "You can sing just as well as he can."

There is nothing harder in the world than to give a convincing imitation of being drunk. Jack Rhyce was wise enough not to try.

"Well, let me have a double Scotch first," he said, "so I can halfway catch up with things."

Big Ben gave a hearty whoop of laughter. Jack Rhyce tossed off the drink when it was handed to him in three quick swallows. He did not need to ask for another because someone immediately thrust a second into his hand, but those two quick slugs had surprisingly little effect. They only served to make everything more hideously grotesque, at the same time bringing the faces around him into clearer definition. Big Ben was holding a half-empty highball glass in exactly the expert way that an abstemious person handles a drink at a cocktail party. You could always pick a drinker from a nondrinker from the way he held his glass. Big

Ben, in spite of all his noice, was cold sober, but his sobriety had been hard to detect because his spirits and elation were not normal. Elation was exactly the word, the sort that came after emergence from danger. The truth was that Big Ben was happy, and also he must have felt completely safe. Like Jack Rhyce, he must have examined the hotel guests and must have concluded that there was not a cough in a carload.

"Well, I do feel better now," Jack said.

Big Ben patted his shoulder affectionately; in return Jack Rhyce gave him an affectionate punch on the chest—just two big boys roughhousing. There was no softness in Big Ben's midsection, as he had observed already at Wake. He was more of a wrestler than a boxer, but these were not the right thoughts for the moment, when even a thought could be detected if it influenced attitude.

"Say," Big Ben said, and his voice had a wheedling note in it, "now you've got yourself lubricated up, how about a little harmonizing? Ted here can play almost anything on a squeeze box. How about a piece from *The Red Mill?* How about 'Every Day Is Ladies' Day with me'? Huh, Jack?"

"Oh, say," Jack Rhyce said, "why that old chestnut?"

"Aw, come on," Big Ben said. "It's got real melody. It's a swell song."

"Why is it you have this yen for *The Red Mill,*" Jack Rhyce asked, "when it was written before you and I were born, Ben?"

Big Ben drew his hand across his eyes.

"I know," he said. "It don't sound reasonable, does it. Yet it's a kind of a theme song with me. Will you sing it with me if I tell you why?"

His invitation, which included the group around them again, had a professional tone. He was a born master of ceremonies, and in the relief he must have been feeling, he might have dropped his guard.

"Why, sure," Jack said, "If it's a good yarn."

"Aw, shucks," Big Ben said, "it isn't much of a one—just kid stuff. You know how it is when you're a kid, how things kind of happen so you don't forget." His voice was eager and appealing. "It was senior year in this Baptist college down South. . . . It's a kind of corny yarn, now I think of it. . . . There was this banker in town—the local rich guy, and he had this pretty daughter with golden hair. Well, my folks were poor, in the missionary business actually, and I was sort of shy back then. For two years I used to walk past her house most every night, without daring to knock on the door, and then comes Senior year. That autumn when I'd sort of built up my ego by playing football, why I walked up the front stoop and rang the bell, and there she was all alone, and she asked me to come inside. Well, I was shy, but she asked me if I liked hearing music on the phonograph. It was one of those kind you wind with a crank, and there were lots of records belonging to the old man that went a long ways back. Well, we played them for a while, and then she put on this *Red Mill* record, and held my hand, and then—well, we kinda got to loving each other with that old *Red Mill* playing. then her old man came in, and he kicked me the hell out, and I never saw her again, but that's how I remember *The Red Mill.*" Big Ben's voice grew softer. "And I haven't forgot that old aristocratic bastard, either."

He had completely held his audience, and there were sympathetic murmurs applauding his tale of young frustration. The pride and sensitiveness that had run all through the incident had revealed themselves only in the last sentence. Something had happened then, something more than was told, of course, but *The Red Mill* was its monument to a new beginning, and the music of early youth was always the best music.

Big Ben shrugged his shoulders. "Then after that, before the war, I was with a sort of musical caravan, and what should happen—there was *The Red Mill.* Anyway, it kind of stays with me."

"That's quite a story, Ben," Jack Rhyce said, and he meant it. He had learned a lot from the story.

"Well," Big Ben said, "let's make a quick switch. Stand up here, fella. Let's show 'em. Strike up the band. 'Every Day Is Ladies' Day with Me.'"

Bill Gibson was dead at Chrysanthemum Rest. Their arms were draped over each other's shoulders as they sang, and Jack knew the words better than Big Ben.

> *And my pleasure it is double if they come to me in trouble,*
> *For I always find a way to make them smile, the little darlings!*

Applause came from all over the bar when they had finished. Show business was written all over Big Ben when he took in the applause.

"Say, Jack," he said, "if we only had straw hats and canes, we could soft-shoe it, couldn't we?"

If you played the game you had to play it through.

"We don't need hats and canes," Jack Rhyce said.

"Why, we don't sure enough," Big Ben said. "Come on. Strike up the band."

It wasn't a bad show either. Jack Rhyce had to admit that they both had an unusual gift of comic interpolation. In fact there was one moment when he was almost tempted to join in the laughter of the crowd as he watched Big Ben slip deliberately and recover himself. Actually his impulse to laugh died when he saw Ruth Bogart's expression as she watched them. Then an instant later he picked out the face of Mr. Moto. Mr. Moto was standing near the street entrance of the bar. Jack Rhyce remembered being ashamed of Mr. Moto's seeing him making a deliberate fool of himself, but then there was no reason why Mr. Moto should not have been there since he had been given the evening off. After all, enough was enough. Jack Rhyce was never surer of the truth of that aphorism than when the dance was over. He looked once toward the spot where Mr. Moto had been standing, but the Japanese was gone and Jack Rhyce could hardly blame him.

"Well, folks," Jack Rhyce said, "it's been nice seeing you. Come on, Ruth. Let's say good night."

They had done what was necessary. They had showed up in the bar and the clock showed it was ten minutes to twelve. He could tell from the tight grip of her hand when they walked toward the Cozy Nook ell that her nervous resistance was wearing thin.

"Jack," she said, as they closed the door of their room. They had not spent much time there, but the edges of unfamiliarity had been rounded off already, and they were both through with cover for the moment.

"Just a minute before you say anything," he told her, removing his coat and tie. "Just let me wash the touch of that goon off me first. I'm sorry, Ruth."

"You needn't be sorry," she said. "Nobody could have done better than you did, Jack."

She was standing just where he had left her when he came back rubbing his face and shoulders with a bath towel.

"Darling," she said, "you've washed the lipstick off and now you won't have anything to remember me by. Please unzip the back of my dress. I don't know why people always sell unzippable dresses."

"Maybe they do it to get girls into trouble," he said.

"Jack," she said, "don't you think it would look better if we turned out the lights?"

"How do you mean," she asked, "look better?"

"More conventional," she said, "more what's expected of us. We don't know who's watching or listening."

"Just get it into your head," he said, "no one's watching or listening. We're out of this as of now."

"But it won't be long," she said. "And it would be better if you did turn out the lights. I must look like hell."

"Oh, no, you don't at all," he said.

"Well, I feel like hell," she answered.

"All right," he told her, "I don't blame you. So do I. We haven't exactly been playing charades tonight."

He turned out the lights, except the one in the bathroom, but he could still see her standing there.

"We used to play charades at home," she said. "Did you ever play them?"

"If it's just the same with you," he said, "let's not get reminiscing. Why, yes, I used to play charades with the banker's daughter, dear, until the banker threw me out."

"Jack," she said, "wasn't it God-awful?"

"Yes," he said.

"Jack," she said, "I don't know anything about Bill Gibson's setup here, do you?"

"No," he answered, "and we won't now Bill's dead."

"Jack," she said, "what are we going to do?"

It was the question he had been asking himself for quite a while, because he was left with nothing, now that Bill Gibson was dead—no contacts, unless he communicated with home, and that was far too dangerous under the circumstances.

"I don't know," he said, "but maybe we'll think of something in the morning."

"Is that the best you can do?" she asked. "Come here. Come closer. I want to ask you something."

If only because they were in the same predicament, they were close enough already.

"I haven't got any bright answers," he said. "I couldn't win any giveaway show tonight."

"Why did they kill Bill?" she whispered.

"Because he knew something they didn't want passed on," he

said. "You know that. That's always why we kill people in this racket."

"But what did he know?" she asked.

"He didn't tell us," he said, "but we've got to try to find out, come morning."

"Jack," she said, "wasn't it awful?"

He felt her arms steal around his neck, and she buried her face against his shoulder.

"Go ahead and cry if it does you any good," he said. "I don't blame you, Ruth."

"I'm not going to cry," she said, "but I'm glad you're here, Jack."

"I wish you weren't," he said.

"Oh, Jack," she said, "I don't think that's very polite, considering everything."

"I mean it's too damn dangerous here," he said. "Let's face it. I mean I love you, Ruth—and I'm not pretending."

"Well," she said. "I'd almost given up hoping that you'd ever say it."

"Well, I have," he told her. "But it's a damn fool thing for anyone like me to say."

He was right about that last statement. It was bad for business to fall in love, especially with anyone like her, but he had said it, and there they were, alone together with their secrets, miles away from any help except what they could give each other. Miles away from anything that made for common sense. . . .

Hindsight was always simpler than foresight. Later it was easy enough to tell himself that no one should rely on convictions that had no solid foundation of fact—except that his belief that they were in the clear did have its own foundation: he could always return to the indisputable point that Bill Gibson would not have been killed in the way he had if anyone had suspected who Jack Rhyce and Ruth Bogart were. As a matter of fact, time was to prove that Rhyce had been right in these assumptions. But still he should have allowed for the unexpected. He should have been more alert, after finding the Japanese in his room, and particularly after the incident of the footstep on the temple path. The trouble was, there had been so much on his mind, that he had finally yielded to the temptation of blacking out the whole problem for a few hours that night, which had been inexcusable. You always paid for such a thing as that in some coin or other, but he never dreamed that he would pay so soon. In fact, he did not even bother to do anything about the lock on the bedroom door, because he was so sure that they would be undisturbed.

The hour when he was awakened must have been shortly after two. The two double whiskies he had drunk may have made him sleep more soundly than usual, but he doubted it. The truth was that the callers were such expert operators that even if he had propped a chair beneath the doorknob they could have handled it without waking him. He had often heard older men in the bureau, including the Chief, say that prewar Japanese agents were tops in the field. They loved intricacies, and if they knew what they wanted, their patience was inordinate.

Actually the first he knew of anything wrong was when they switched on the ceiling lights. It was the light rather than the click of the switch that had aroused him. In the instant his sight was adjusting to the light, he was on his feet. In fact, before he could see clearly, he heard someone speaking just in front of him.

"Please, Mr. Rhyce, no noise, please."

Then everything was cleared. Mr. Moto and two other stocky Japanese in blue serge suits were in the bedroom. Operator was written all them.

Ruth Bogart, in her twin bed next the wall, reached for her handbag, but the man nearest to her knocked it from her hand.

"Quiet, please," Mr. Moto said. All the previous awkwardness had gone from his voice. His English had become impeccable, and his accent was highly educated. "Get dressed, please, Mr. Rhyce. The man here will hand you your clothes." Mr. Moto smiled politely. "He was a valet once for a member of your cabinet in Washington—before the war, of course."

The loquaciousness disturbed Jack Rhyce because it indicated that Mr. Moto's belief that he held the cards. So far no one had pulled a gun, which also meant that the situation was in hand. Jack Rhyce wished he was not barefoot in pajamas, and he also wished that he could keep down his rising anger.

"I'll give you and your chumps just ten seconds to clear out of here," he said, "or else by God I'll throw you out, right through the window."

The three Japanese were a crowd, but given luck, Jack Rhyce believed that he might do it.

Mr. Moto raised his hand in a placating gesture.

"Please," he said, "make no disturbance, Mr. Rhyce, or I shall be obliged to call for the police."

"How's that again," Jack Rhyce said, "you little yellow bastard?"

"Please do not be insulting," Mr. Moto said, "though I can understand how you feel at the moment, Mr. Rhyce. I mentioned the police."

"Oh," Jack Rhyce said, "so you're a cop, are you?"

Mr. Moto looked grave and shook his head. "Not what you call a cop," he said. "I am just what you are, Mr. Rhyce, and you and I do not want cops, do we? I only want a quiet talk with you. It would be a pity if I were to call the police."

"Go ahead and do it," Jack Rhyce said, "and I'll use the same word to you again. Go ahead and do it, you impertinent little yellow bastard. Call in your police."

He had made the Japanese angry, which was perhaps a useless luxury.

"I do not understand," Mr. Moto said. "You must be an intelligent man to have been sent here, Mr. Rhyce, and your work was very good last evening—but not the police, Mr. Rhyce. I should have to tell you and the lady here had murdered Mr. Gibson. I think you would help me rather than have me do that, Mr. Rhyce."

Then Jack Rhyce realized that he was in grave difficulty, and the expressions of the two assistants confirmed the fact.

"Well, well," he said, "so that's the picture, is it? All right, tell your goddamn valet to hand me my pants and a clean white shirt. From the way he looks I'll bet he stole the plans for the wrong battleship, even if he could find his way around Washington." There was no change in the three foreign faces watching him. He grinned at Ruth Bogart. "Anyway," he said, "the house detectives haven't got us, Ruth."

While he pulled on his trousers over his pajamas, Mr. Moto rubbed his hands together softly.

"Now that is better," he said. "I understand how a sudden intrusion can be upsetting."

The first surprise was leaving Jack Rhyce. Although he still needed time, the directions were growing clearer. He pointed to his shoes and socks, and where they were handed to him he sat on the edge of his bed and stole another glance at Ruth Bogart. The whiteness of her face showed that they both were beginning to see where the Japanese were fitting in.

"Oh, yes," Mr. Moto said. "Please, may I repeat, you did it very well? So neat with the pills, so nice with the needle—so nice to be a big strong man, Mr. Rhyce. No reason to tell the police. Your chief and my chief would prefer it otherwise, don't you think?"

Jack Rhyce pulled a clean shirt over his head, tightened his belt carefully, took the tie that was handed him and knotted it deliberately, Mr. Moto had not moved his glance from him, nor would Jack have done so either, if he had been in Mr. Moto's place.

"Not the belt, please," Mr. Moto said, "Mr. Rhyce. I should rather hear Big Ben strike only over the BBC."

He heard Ruth Bogart draw in her breath, and her mind must have gone, as his hand, to Fisherman's Wharf in San Francisco.

"So that's the way the ball bounces," Jack Rhyce said. "You've got me down for Big Ben?"

"Yes," Mr. Moto said. "Your coat, please, Mr. Rhyce."

Jack Rhyce snatched the coat from the blue-suited man.

"I'll put that on myself," he said.

He had a sudden unreasoning fear that if he were helped they might pinion his arms behind him.

"We will leave quietly," Mr. Moto said. "I never like to do more than is necessary. That is why Miss Bogart will stay here. She will understand that it will do no good to make trouble. I shall drive her back to Tokyo myself in the morning."

Ruth Bogart cleared her throat.

"You don't know what you're doing," she began.

It was not the time to break security; indeed it was still a question whether they would have been believed if they had attempted to explain.

Jack Rhyce smiled at her and shook his head.

"I don't really think there's much you can do, Ruth," he said, "the way the ball is bouncing."

"But, Jack," she said, "they're going to—"

"Let's not be mind readers," he said.

Mr. Moto rubbed his hands together again.

"It is so true," he said, "what you say about the ball bouncing. One day it is you. One day it is me. The young lady is not important, Mr. Rhyce. I can give you my assurance that I will see her off for home, myself, from the airport tomorrow." He picked up her handbag and tossed it to one of the men. "I shall give it back also tomorrow."

"Okay," Jack Rhyce said. "Do you mind if I ask you one question?"

"If it is short," Mr. Moto answered. "The sooner we leave the better, Mr. Rhyce."

Jack Rhyce nodded toward the curtained windows.

"What makes you think I killed that man down there?"

"Because he knew too much about something you know, too, Mr. Rhyce," Mr. Moto said. "We're going where we can have a quiet talk, and I think you will tell us what he knew before we are finished, Mr. Rhyce. Moscow does not know all the tricks."

"You ought to know I'm not a graduate from there," Jack Rhyce said. "Well, as long as I have your word about Miss Bogart—"

"I repeat," Mr. Moto said, "never do anything unnecessary. Why should she come to harm? Are you ready now, Mr. Rhyce?"

"Jack—" Ruth Bogart began. Her voice was dangerously loud.

It was not a time for handsome speeches, and besides, everything was strictly business.

"Don't, Ruth," he said—"but it's been nice to have known you. Come on, let's go."

He still was not recovered from surprise, but he began to see that there were several reasons why they should have mistaken him for Big Ben. Everything, he knew, was very dangerous.

They walked in a compact, softly stepping group down a flight of stairs and out into the night.

"By the way," Jack Rhyce said, "what time is it?"

Mr. Moto turned his head quickly.

"Why?" he asked. "Have you an appointment, Mr. Rhyce?"

Jack Rhyce did not answer. It was dark and very still. The hotel and the small town around it seemed sound asleep. The car that had brought them there was parked on the drive.

"You will sit in the front with me, please," Mr. Moto said. "The men will be in the back. One of them will have you covered. He is a good man with a pistol."

Jack got into the car without speaking. Mr. Moto took the wheel. The place where they went was not far from the hotel. It was a substantially built Japanese house surrounded by a high wall. The car stopped at the entrace door.

"You will step out quietly, please," Mr. Moto said.

Jack Rhyce gave way to a purely professional piece of exasperation.

"Tell that goon of yours to take his hands off me," he said. "I can still get out of a car."

A light burning above the doorway showed the raised platform where one sat to remove one's shoes, but there was no neat row of shoes such as one might have seen if the house had been occupied. Its dark windows and the unkempt condition of the shrubbery indicated that it had stood vacant for some time and had been opened only for this special occasion. Mr. Moto gave an order and one of the men opened the front door, at the same time switching on the lights in the entrance hall.

"The man will not touch you," Mr. Moto said. "Walk just behind me into the house, please. It belongs to a Baron. An American general had it as a resthouse during the Occupation. Many of its rooms are European."

Jack Rhyce was not interested in the ownership or the architecture of the house, nor did he have time to think of the incongruity of what had happened to him. The dark night, the strangeness, and the belief that time might be running short were things that one thought of later. There was a distance of about six paces of gravel driveway between the car and the lighted hallway of the house. Mr. Moto walked a pace ahead of him, not bothering to look back, which showed that he trusted the man who was walking a pace behind, but the man behind was overanxious. He was too close, as Jack could tell from the sound of his steps, and if you held a gun at someone's back, one of the first principles was to keep a decent interval.

If one debated on whether or not to take a chance, one always ended with indecision. In the last analysis it was the contempt in Mr. Moto's tone that made Jack take the chance, in spite of the obvious risks involved. He whirled on the ball of his right foot, and he was correct that the man in the blue suit was too close. Jack Rhyce had his wrist in his left hand and the barrel of the pistol to the ground in the split second before he brought his fist across to the jaw with all the momentum of his body behind it. The pistol exploded at the same moment. Then the hand that held it relaxed, and Jack Rhyce had the weapon—from its size and weight, another one of those Berettas. Mr. Moto turned with the light of the door behind him. Jack Rhyce spoke before anything went further.

"Shall we leave it the way it is?" he said. "I told you I didn't want that man crowding me—and tell the other one to stop."

The other blue suit was back in the doorway, and Mr. Moto gave a curt order.

"I am so sorry he annoyed you," Mr. Moto said. "Yes, he was very clumsy."

"Not clumsy," Jack said, "just overanxious. Let's not you and me get overanxious. I'll get you anyway before you and the other one get me."

They stood completely motionless for seconds that seemed to Jack Rhyce to last for a long while.

"Yes," Mr. Moto said. "Yes, and what do you suggest?"

"You tell that friend of yours behind you," Jack Rhyce said, "to come over here and help his friend. He's coming to, now. I don't like being treated this way, Mr. Moto."

Mr. Moto was silhouetted by the light behind him so that it was impossible to see his face, and now one could gauge his reaction only from his voice."

"Yes," Mr. Moto said, "yes?"

The rising inflection of the last word turned it into a question.

"You tell your two people to keep out of the way," Jack Rhyce said, "and I'll go into that house with you. I want to talk to you as much as you want to talk to me. I'm not Big Ben, and I didn't kill Gibson. Frankly, he was my boss."

The light from the doorway was on his face, and he still could see only the shadow of Mr. Moto, but part of the tension was gone. The disarming of the guard had done it, and there was doubt in Mr. Moto's voice.

"You say you are not Big Ben?"

"You're damned well right I'm not," Jack answered. "I'm on the American team, the same as Gibson. He came up here to meet me. He was dead by the time we got there, and I want to know what he knew as much as you do. Maybe we can do some business if we go inside."

He heard Mr. Moto sigh softly. "You may put the pistol of the clumsy man in your pocket, Mr. Rhyce," Mr. Moto said. "If you gave it to him now he would kill himself for shame, but I am grateful to him for his clumsiness. You would of course have shot it out with me if you had been Big Ben."

"Yes," Jack Rhyce said, and he sighed, too, now that the tension was easing. "That's exactly the point I've been trying to make, and I had to move damn fast to make it. Here, take the gun, I don't need it any more. I never did like the balance of these Italian rods." He tossed the pistol on the driveway.

"Thank you," Mr. Moto said. "I am very mortified that I should be so mistaken. Excuse me, please."

"That's all right," Jack Rhyce said. "I've been sort of trying to explain you myself the last two days. It's too bad we didn't know sooner we were after the same boy."

"It was so very stupid of me," Mr. Moto said again. "I was so stupid, I think, because I have tried too hard, and thought too hard. So you were after Big Ben, too?"

"Yes," Jack Rhyce said, and everything was easy now, and relaxed. "That's why I was sent over from the States for. Gibson was worried and wanted help."

## 15

EITHER TELL the whole truth or none at all was an almost infallible business maxim. Under present circumstances, even though the position of the Japanese was still equivocal, the only solution was frankness. At least they were after the same thing. At least they were all in the business.

The man on the ground groaned and struggled to his hands and knees. Jack put his hands beneath his arms and pulled him to his feet. After all, there were times when one could afford to be cordial.

"Out like a light, weren't you, Mac?" Jack Rhyce said, and slapped him affectionately on the back. "Never mind. We're all pals now. Your gun's right over there."

Mr. Moto laughed in a completely genuine way.

"His English is not good. Tell him in Japanese."

"I apologize for your discomfort," Jack Rhyce said in Japanese. "So it was the tea and the coffee back there at the hotel that gave me away on the language, was it?"

Mr. Moto laughed again, and both the men in blue serge smiled. Everything could change very quickly in Japan.

"Oh, no," Mr. Moto said. "Earlier, Mr. Rhyce."

"Earlier?" Jack Rhyce repeated.

"Mr. Moto nodded.

"In Burma, Mr. Rhyce," Mr. Moto said. "We had your name on file. Japanese linguist, born in Japan. I even had a glimpse of you once in Myitkyina." Mr. Moto laughed heartily. "I did not speak because I was moving the other way, but I remembered you when I saw you at the airport, Mr. Rhyce." Everyone laughed heartily. After all, the war was over.

"The word always was that you people had good Intelligence," Jack Rhyce said, "but I didn't know you were working so hard at it now."

"Oh, not so hard," Mr. Moto said, "with shortness of funds and the misfortunes. Poor Japan. We would not have made a mistake such as I have made tonight, before the war. The machinery was not bad before the war."

"Still, there was the German, Sorge," Jack Rhyce said.

"Oh, yes, Sorge," Mr. Moto said. "Such a nice man, Sorge. So intelligent; but don't forget, please, we caught Sorge. And did you Americans catch Dr. Fuchs? And the British who always boast so much about their Intelligence—did they stop Burgess or MacLean? So hard, so very difficult to manage everything."

It was a relief to talk naturally, without being under the necessity of cover. That Mr. Moto spoke so frankly indicated more than professional courtesy. It showed a colleague's respect.

"It's a tough life all right," Jack Rhyce said. "It's beginning to get me down these days."

"Get you down?" Mr. Moto said. "I wish so much I could visit your great country more often. I cannot keep up with the idiom now. Before everything was so unhappy, I was over once a year at least, New York, Washington, or Honolulu. Even when my duties were in Paris and London I endeavored to spend a week or two of observation in New York. Ha-ha. . . . In old New York the peach-crop's always fine, isn't it, Mr. Rhyce?"

"I wish I knew where you picked that one up," Jack Rhyce said.

"A song from *The Red Mill* was sung in the third floor corridor of the Mark Hopkins Hotel in San Francisco," Mr. Moto answered, "the evening before you left, Mr. Rhyce?"

"You haven't got such a bad setup, have you?" Jack Rhyce said. "So the Japanese schoolboy tailed me from Fisherman's Wharf, but you Japs get things twisted, I was up on that floor, all right, but I didn't sing the song."

Mr. Moto sighed.

"So sorry I have been so very stupid," he said. "He was so sure that you were Mr. Ben that when he gave the signal, I came myself to meet you at the airport instead of sending someone else. I mention it only so that you will give me some excuse. But why do we stand out here?"

"That's easy," Jack Rhyce answered. "Because you haven't asked me in."

Mr. Moto drew in his breath in a loud, deprecating way.

"Oh!" he said. "The work has got me down, too, as you put it, so that I have lost my manners. This house is only loaned for a purpose for which I am so glad is now not necessary, by a very kind Japanese nobleman. So really little money now that individuals contribute. Poor Japan. He would be honored to know that you have been his guest. Come in, please, and my associates will warm us some sake. Do not be concerned about them. It is only they and me here, and unpleasantnesses are entirely over. Please to enter, Mr. Rhyce, and no need to take off shoes. This part of the Baron's residence is European."

The lights were on in the hall and also in a large room to the right. It was one of those newer houses. Jack Rhyce could see, that wealthier Japanese had built in the prosperous years that had preceded the war—a house half-European, half-Japanese, that had the schizophrenic quality of as much in present-day Japan. No Japanese, as far as Jack Rhyce knew, ever wishfully inhabited his Western rooms except for reasons of hospitality; and Jack Rhyce did not blame them, because the European section of such houses was usually as ugly and uncomfortable as its Japanese counterpart was beautiful. The house he entered now was no exception. The furnishings of the entrance hall gave forth a musty odor, from age and disuse; but they had been elaborate once, designed to impress, and perhaps please, the European guest, and also to display the owner's close acquaintance with Western living. The hall carpet was crimson, sprinkled with fleur-de-lis; the wallpaper artificial Cordovan leather; the mirror bad Victorian; and the chairs golden oak, upholstered with red plush.

Mr. Moto must have read the thoughts that ran through Jack's mind.

"We used to try so hard," Mr. Rhyce," he said. "Poor Japan. The chairs are equally hideous in the parlor, but Americans like chairs."

Several table lamps that were lighted in the cluttered, over-decorated parlor revealed oil paintings of English cattle, encased in immense gold frames, two pieces of artificial tapestry, tapestry-covered Jacobean chairs and upholstered easy chairs of a turn-of-the-century design. There was also a European fireplace with a coal grate, in which Jack Rhyce noticed a coal fire glowing in spite of the hot night. The coffee table had been cleared of its cigarette boxes and impedimenta; on it were knotted strings and leather thongs and a pair of handcuffs.

"Well, well," Jack Rhyce said, "so you were fixing to have a singing school."

Mr. Moto laughed boisterously.

"Ha-ha," he said, "so nice a way you have of saying funny things, Mr. Rhyce." He called an order in angry Japanese. "Take these away and bring the sake and cigarettes. Please sit down, Mr. Rhyce."

Jack Rhyce sat down in one of the easy chairs. The sake had come at almost the moment that Mr. Moto had called, in a jar with a glaze that looked like celadon.

"Beautiful," Jack Rhyce said, nodding to the jar.

"You appreciate it?" Mr. Moto asked. "I am so pleased. It has been in the Baron's family for many hundred years. The Baron would be pleased to present it to you, I think."

"What makes you think so?" Jack asked. "Maybe he's anti-American."

"Oh, no," Mr. Moto said. "He is my cousin. You enjoy the wine?"

He was grateful for the wine from the fragile thimble of a cup that one of the men offered him.

"These two boys you have with you," Jack Rhyce said, "look as though they had been in the Imperial Marines—very tough, I mean."

"So nice of you to notice," Mr. Moto said. "I hope you like the wine."

"I do," Jack Rhyce said. "It's nice and hot. I only wish it were a Texas jigger."

"A Texas jigger?" Mr. Moto said, and he burst into appropriate laughter when Jack Rhyce explained the phrase.

"Please tell the Marines in Japanese. They will appreciate about the jigger. One of them will stand beside you, ready to fill the cup."

Even into that European room there had crept an atmosphere of Oriental hospitality, politeness and good manners.

"To happy peace between the United States and poor Japan," Mr. Moto said. "Very foolish men made the war. Ha-ha. Nearly all of them are dead."

Jack Rhyce drank a second thimbleful of wine and held out his cup for more.

"Judging from my short stay here," he said, "it looks to me as though Japan is going to make out pretty well."

"You think?" Mr. Moto said. "There are so many dangers, but I am glad you think. It is very lovely to talk to an intelligent American agent who is engaged in my own line of work. Poor Japan. We had such a very lovely Intelligence system before the war."

"We heard you were starting work again," Jack Rhyce said. "Frankly, I didn't know it would be so good."

"Oh, thank you," Mr. Moto said, "but only in such a small way now. So little money. Let me see. There was once such nice men in your Intelligence in Washington. Do you remember Colonel Bryson? He was such a lovely man. I was so sorry he broke his neck in Vienna. Then there was Mr. Makepeace. They used to call him Tommy. What has become of him, I wonder?"

Obviously Mr. Moto was checking on Jack Rhyce's background, and Jack Rhyce was relieved that he could come up with an answer.

"He was in Prague six years ago," Jack Rhyce said, "but since then Mr. Makepeace has not been heard from."

"So too bad," Mr. Moto said. "Well, ha-ha, you cannot blame poor Japan for Mr. Makepeace. So too bad so many lovely people cannot live forever."

"That's quite a thought," Jack Rhyce said, "but we don't, you know."

The social amenities were nearly over. Mr. Moto waved to one of the attendants for a match and lighted a cigarette.

"And you?" he asked, pointing to the box.

"Thanks," Jack Rhyce said. "I don't use them."

"So right of you," Mr. Moto said. "So very, very right. I was taught that when I first entered the Intelligence. In the late twenties, it was. My Chief, dear old Mr. Naguna, never smoked cigarettes, for they left untidy traces. Dear old Mr. Naguna. Some more wine, Mr. Rhyce?"

"Thanks, I could do with a little more," Jack Rhyce said.

Mr. Moto gestured to one of the men.

"He is stupid," he said. "I told him to stay near you, Mr. Rhyce, but in his simple brain he was thinking that you must have had enough, just as in his simple brain he thought you would not turn on him as you did outside, because he had a weapon directed at your back. Poor Japan. We never can understand how you Westerners can drink so much and not lose your wits. Confidentially, that is why the German Sorge puzzled our Mr. Naguna for several years. It did not seem possible that Mr. Sorge could be brilliant, with his drinking. He was like a figure in a Kabuki play."

"I told you I could do with a drink," Jack Rhyce said. "I didn't mean a teaspoonful at a time."

Mr. Moto laughed. The Japanese sooner or later laughed too much.

"Mr. Rhyce, I like you so very much," he said, "because you are so—doctrinaire, as the French say, about cigarettes and everything. That turn on the left foot, out of doors, was very beautiful. I could admire it even when I did not know what might follow. But I did know that the move was not Russian—at least not what the procedure was in Moscow before the war, Mr. Rhyce."

"Thanks," Jack Rhyce said. "They'll be pleased to know that, back home."

"Mr. Moto drew in on his cigarette and passed his hands over his closely cropped, graying hair.

"When I see someone like you, so bright and young, in the profession, there is some excuse for my mistakes," he said. "I have never been familiar with Western features, but it would be my fallible opinion that you have a kind face, Mr. Rhyce. Please, I hope you will treat my errors kindly. I did not have the benefit of records because ours were destroyed in the bombing, and such as remained, which we did not burn ourselves, were taken over by your General McArthur. Such a very nice man—but poor Japan. Therefore, I can only rely on memory—but you were in Japan until the age of five. You were in Japanese language school in Colorado, because one of my own young men taught you and reported you as far above the average. Please do not make a mental note. Your Counterintelligence found him out. Then you were in combat Intelligence in Burma. Reports that came later said that your conduct with our people was most correct. Then there is an alert in my echelon, just as there must have been in yours. Elements in the Politburo were moving in. Poor Japan. So many people, so poor. So much discontent. The intellectuals so *après guerre.* Orders to look for a new personality. An American on file. The name on the intercept—Big Ben. Popular. Entertainment organizer, like someone on your stage, perhaps, or one of your motion picture entertainers who loved Russia. Look out for this American—Big Ben, with the singing voice and with the weakness for singing a song from that old entertainment called *Red Mill.* I heard it in New York when a very small boy, when my father was in the consulate in New York."

"That sure dates you," Jack Rhyce said. "That show opened in 1906 in old New York."

"Yes," Mr. Moto said. "But they still had the tune in 1912. Imagine my joy to hear of you from San Francisco. So pleased when I saw you at the airport. So pleased about the Friendship League which we have watched with interest. So pleased about your weekend excursion, just where Mr. Gibson was going. So pleased when you and the pretty Miss Bogart entered Chrysanthemum Rest—and then to find you are American Intelligence is difficult. My mind, I know, you too made up. I should have kept an open mind, but you will admit that everything did fit."

Mr. Moto paused. He had, after all, made his point.

"Don't blame yourself too much," Jack Rhyce said. "Anyway, you're not Russian. I've been worried about that from the first time you picked me up."

"Not Russian," Mr. Moto shook his head. "Nationalist Japan Party, Mr. Rhyce. Fascist, perhaps, but pro-Emperor, anti-Communist. So much trouble—poor Japan. But when the typhoon ceases, back will spring the bamboo."

An earnestness in Mr. Moto's words made Jack Rhyce realize that he might be hearing a true explanation of the Japanese mood and the Japanese aspirations.

"Are Nationalists anti-American these days?" he asked.

Mr. Moto shook his head vigorously.

"Not now," he said. "Not enlightened ones. The United States is so very useful. Later perhaps, but not now. So silly to shoot Santa Claus, as your politicians used to say when I was in Washington. You see, I'm being very frank, Mr. Rhyce."

"I'd say you give every appearance of being," Jack Rhyce said. But from his experience, frankness in the Western sense of the word did not exist in the Orient. The difficulties among most people always lay in a misconception of each other's values. There was always an ultimate shift of meaning—even between Americans and Englishmen, who thought as nearly alike as any two nations.

"I am being frank," Mr. Moto said, "because I hope so much that we will be temporary partners, Mr. Rhyce. There are groups here on the Left, and on the Right, too, so anxious to arouse feeling against America. And the plain Japanese man can change so quickly."

Mr. Moto paused, and while Jack Rhyce waited for him to continue, he had a moment to speculate on Mr. Moto's background. He came from the old aristocracy. He must have been educated abroad, probably in an Eastern American university. There had been all sorts of strains and cleavages in his mental upbringing, but there could never have been any wavering in loyalty. He stood for Old Japan.

"The Left Wing has been growing very dangerously lately," Mr. Moto said. "That is the trouble with fanatics. One should always multiply their danger by ten or twenty, I believe. At the moment we are as anxious as you are to uphold American prestige, and I am willing to pool information if you are, Mr. Rhyce."

Jack appeared to hesitate, even though the man seated opposite must have known already that he had no choice. With Bill Gibson dead, he did not know the organization, and things were closing in so rapidly that the only possible hope of achieving success was to rely on outside chance.

"I don't see why we shouldn't do business," he said slowly, "and maybe I know a few things you don't." He paused again. It was better to start slowly. "I have no briefing from Mr. Gibson, you understand. That was to have occurred up here. He only told me that he was being followed, and intimated that he was in danger. He didn't want us to be seen together."

"So right," Mr. Moto said. "Yes, so very right."

He did not blame Mr. Moto for looking discouraged. It was time to hurry on and show that he had some value.

"Still Mr. Gibson sent us back a few facts," Jack Rhyce went on. "This man, Big Ben, has been meeting a Russian agent named Skirov at intervals. Do you know this Skirov?"

Mr. Moto's features sharpened.

"Not prewar," he said, " an *après guerre* Russian, very well trained and very dangerous, Mr. Rhyce, I'm sorry we have not seen him, but I believe he had been in Japan."

"We rate him above this Big Ben," Jack Rhyce said. "Skirov has a very high priority back in our office."

"He is very well trained," Mr. Moto said, "a man of great potentials. We have tried very hard to find him."

"This Big Ben might lead him to us," Jack Rhyce said.

"Yes," Mr. Moto answered. "Why are you smiling, Mr. Rhyce?"

"About this Skirov," Jack Rhyce said. "I've never seen him, but we have a photograph and an accurate description. It might amuse you to know that when I found you up there in our room I had a hunch for a few minutes that you might be Skirov."

Mr. Moto smiled politely, but Jack Rhyce thought that he was startled.

"So funny how often people confuse things when they get fixed ideas," Mr. Moto said. "That was my difficulty with you, Mr. Rhyce. I had such very fixed ideas. What other information did Mr. Gibson send back home?"

"This meeting between Skirov and Big Ben," Jack Rhyce said, "Bill Gibson believed that there was one coming up, and there was something so important about it that he was upset. He had learned something new, but he did not have time to tell me in Tokyo, and he can't tell us now."

Mr. Moto lighted another cigarette. "I think I will have another cup of wine," he said. "Perhaps I know somewhat more than you about what was troubling Mr. Gibson. I am sorry, of course, that you do not know your apparatus here. It is a deep disappointment to me. I was hoping we could have profitable exchange of facts."

"You mean you won't tell me any more because you don't think I know anything worth while? Is that it?" Jack Rhyce asked.

"Yes," Mr. Moto said, "so sorry, Mr. Rhyce."

Jack Rhyce allowed a few moments to elapse before he spoke. It was clearer than ever to him that he could achieve nothing unless he had co-operation. There was still a risk, but it was a necessary one.

"Okay," he said. "Suppose I told you I've found Big Ben. Suppose I could say that I could finger him for you . . . then would you tell me what you think was on my boss's mind?" He had not anticipated the full effect of what he said. The Japanese gave a violent start before he could conceal his excitement.

"How very nice," Mr. Moto said. "You mean he's here in Japan now? I am so anxious for your answer, Mr. Rhyce."

Jack paused again. Now that they each had something that the other wanted he was certain that they could do business.

"You tell me what Big Ben and this Skirov are going to do," he said, "and I'll tell you who this Big Ben is. Is it a deal?"

"Oh, yes," Mr. Moto said, and there was no doubt that they would do business. "This Russian Skirov, do you know him?"

"I know all about him," Jack Rhyce said.

"Oh, yes," Mr. Moto said. "You were in Moscow in 1946, and you speak Russian very nicely, do you not? You made a remark to Mr. Molotov in 1946. You said all men are brothers."

Jack Rhyce winced at Mr. Moto's words. It was growing clearer every minute why Mr. Moto should have confused him with Big Ben.

"Just how the hell did you know that?" he asked.

Mr. Moto's hand fluttered to the lapel of his coat, and his fingers moved softly over the cloth.

"From a Chinese friend," he said. "We still have a few contacts. We have to know what is happening, as best we can. Poor Japan."

Jack Rhyce still spoke deliberately. The value of time was different in the East from what it was in the West, and it was never wise to be overeager.

"I'm not so sorry for poor Japan as I was before I met you," he said. "What is it that's so important about this Skirov meeting?"

A slight shifting of Mr. Moto's glance showed that he did not know all the answers either.

"We are still trying to discover," Mr. Moto said. "As you know yourself, it is hard to break the Communist security. The date is three days off. I'm so afraid that Mr. Gibson knew, or he would be still living. Our present information is that they are planning some coup that would have serious political repercussions that would adversely affect your country, I am afraid."

Jack Rhyce took his delicate porcelain wine cup from the table. He sipped the warm wine very slowly.

"You mean some sort of revolution?" he asked.

He knew that the question was not so preposterous as it sounded, because in the past there had been political upheavals in Japan, as sudden and violent as the island earthquakes.

"No," Mr. Moto said, "not Communist revolution. The picture is not yet set for that, but something that will cause popular disturbance, something that we think would be anti-American." He paused and laughed in the apologetic way of his countrymen when they were about to impart bad news. "I think there will be political murder, Mr. Rhyce, and afterwards public demonstrations."

There was sense in everything that was said. Political assassination, like public suicide, had often been an instrument of Japanese policy. One only had to turn the clock back as far as 1936 to recall the killings by the army clique.

"Who's going to get murdered?" Jack Rhyce asked.

"We hope to find out," Mr. Moto said. "It would be a murder, if I may venture to guess, that would be ascribed to United States imperialism; one of a liberal politician; but we do not know whom. But we do think we know the date—three days from now."

Bill Gibson must have known the date as well. Jack Rhyce was trying to put together again the details of that hurried call on the day of their arrival, the battered Chevrolet with the Beretta in the glove compartment, and to connect them with his visit to the Asia Friendship League.

"Do you know a man named Mr. Harry Pender," Jack Rhyce said, "who is heading the Asia Friendship League now? He was transferred recently from Cambodia, I think."

Mr. Moto raised his eyebrows.

"I know," he said. "You spent the day with Mr. Pender before you drove here, Mr. Rhyce."

"That's right," Jack Rhyce said. "Have you any information on him?"

"He is a very naughty man," Mr. Moto said. "His alias is Harry Wise. Hank is his cover name in the apparatus. Does that mean anything to you, Mr. Rhyce?"

Jack Rhyce nodded. The truth was that the name meant quite a lot.

"Washington must know him," Mr. Moto said, "if even our little Bureau knows him. What is it you say in the United States? They have been moving their first teams in here, in the last two weeks. But now I wish to hear from you. Where is Big Ben, Mr. Rhyce?"

"Haven't you guessed?" Jack Rhyce said. "You said I was singing that *Red Mill* song in the bar. He was right there with me, and you saw us do that dance together.

Mr. Moto was on his feet before Jack Rhyce had finished.

"Back at the hotel?" he spoke almost in a whisper. "Describe him, please."

"Flight engineer on an American airline. You saw us dancing side by side," Jack Rhyce said. "Six feet four. Weight about two-thirty, sandy hair, bushy eyebrows. Expression affable. In theater business, I think, and loves to sing. Favorite tune, *The Red Mill.*"

"Mr. Moto slapped his hand against his forehead. "Oh, dear me," he said. "Oh, yes, I saw you."

"Well, that's the thumbnail sketch, " Jack Rhyce said. "Does he ring any bell with you, Mr. Moto.

"Oh, dear me," Mr. Moto said. "Excuse me, I'm so sorry, Mr.

Rhyce. This is very serious. I've been so very stupid. We must leave here right away."

"Well," Jack Rhyce said, "I'm glad it rings a bell with you."

"Ha-ha," Mr. Moto said, "yes, it rings a bell. Yes, I shall recognize him. Mr. Rhyce, because he was the one who fingered you, as they say in the United States."

"How's that again?" Jack Rhyce asked, and he was also on his feet.

"Ha-ha!" Mr. Moto said. "It would be funny if I were not so ashamed. He said he was United States Intelligence, last night, after you sang the song, and he was so very, very nice. He told me you were Big Ben, Mr. Rhyce."

Momentarily Jack Rhyce must have looked as surprised as Mr. Moto had, but he regained hs composure immediately.

"But when you saw us both together," he said, "and when he spoke to you afterwards, it must at least have crossed your mind, didn't it, that *he* could have been Big Ben? He answered the description too, didn't he?"

Mr. Moto eyes him solemnly and nodded in slow agreement.

"Yes," he said. "Oh, yes, it crossed my mind. I can make no good excuse for my very great carelessness, except that I was so sure of you already; but I might say one thing more—if you will excuse it, Mr. Rhyce."

"I'll excuse it; I'm still curious," Jack Rhyce said.

Mr. Moto hesitated as though he did not like what he was about to say.

"Excuse me, please," he said. "When in the bar I only felt the more sure I was right in selecting you. You were so much more intelligent, so much more of a trained agent, Mr. Rhyce, so much more dangerous—while he, if you will excuse me, was so immature, so harmless, so like so many of your government officials, Mr. Rhyce, I believed there was no doubt, but please believe I was astute enough to recognize my error when you took my man's gun away. You would have begun shooting, not have waited to talk, if you had been Big Ben."

Jack Rhyce laughed shortly. There was no time to continue with post-mortems.

"That shows he's smarter than I am," he said.

Never to underestimate the methods of an adversary was a motto of the business. Never to think with pain of what he had done to you, but to try immediately to figure what you could do to him in return. The best way to achieve this last result was to put yourself in his place, and to think like him and not like yourself. Although everyone was fallible, Jack Rhyce could not believe that he had been wrong in more basic ideas. Big Ben's move had been inordinately clever, but it was not the time to dwell on the measure of his cleverness. It was time to put oneself inside Big Ben's mind to see why he had done it, and to estimate what he had won and lost.

Had he learned through some fluke who the couple in Cozy Nook were, and had he taken that method to knock them out of the game? This was still unbelievable in Jack Rhyce's judgment. The nature of the murder disputed the possibility and so did all of Big Ben's subsequent behavior. Life had made Jack Rhyce enough of a cynic so that he was positive that he could detect sincerity. Big Ben had shown no professional interest in them while they had been in the bar, but something had occurred later to cause a change, and Jack Rhyce believed he knew exactly what the circumstance had been. Mr. Moto must have entered the bar while they were singing, and Big Ben's glance must have picked out the face in the crowd and instantly have identified it. Mr. Moto had been the one who spelled danger, and the improvisation that Big Ben had conceived, though brilliant, also had a touch of desperation in it. It was the red herring across the trail, the smoke screen that permitted escape. The idea must have come to Big Ben while each was following the other in the ludicrous soft-shoe dance.

The truth was that the sight of Mr. Moto must have come to Big Ben as a stunning shock. He knew who Mr. Moto was. He also must have known that the Japanese were on the lookout for him and had doubtless obtained some sort of description. In fact, Big Ben's mind probably had moved further. He must have suspected that Mr. Moto had come to the hotel to make contact with Bill Gibson, the American agent. While they were still doing that soft-shoe dance Big Ben must have been fairly certain that Mr. Moto would visit Chrysanthemum Rest, if he had not done so already. Mr. Moto, as a secret agent, would know that it was murder. Already, in fact, Mr. Moto might be looking for the murderer. It was no wonder that Big Ben had been obliged to move quickly.

"I think we'd better leave," Mr. Moto said. "You can continue thinking while we're moving, Mr. Rhyce."

"All right," Jack Rhyce said; "but let's get our lines straight first.

You saw us go into that cottage. You were watching us all evening. Right?"

"Yes," Mr. Moto said, "watching carefully."

"Then you went into the cottage yourself," Jack Rhyce said. "Right?"

"Yes," Mr. Moto said, "so very right."

"When did you get to the bar?"

"When you and he were dancing," Mr. Moto said.

"And after I left, what happened?"

"He walked over to me," Mr. Moto said. "He asked me if I were looking for Big Ben."

"So he knew who you were," Jack Rhyce said. "He'll be halfway to Tokyo by now. He was frightened when he saw you or he wouldn't have thought so fast. Frightened people are the ones who think the fastest. Have you ever noticed that?"

"Yes," Mr. Moto said. "I am thinking you are unusually intelligent, Mr. Rhyce."

"Thanks," Jack Rhyce said, "but let's remember one thing more. He was startled when he saw you. That means he hadn't see you earlier. Do you agree?"

A shadow of doubt crossed Mr. Moto's face, and he shook his head.

"I don't agree," he said. "It might also be he knew I was following you all the time. Both you and he are such very clever men."

It occurred to Jack that ironically enough both their lines of thinking were academically correct, even though one must be right and the other wrong.

"I think you presuppose too much," Jack Rhyce said. "He's good, but everyone has failings. Don't forget, he had a lot on his mind last night. I don't believe he saw you until you were in the bar, because of one thing my thoughts keep coming back to."

"You are interesting," Mr. Moto said. "To what do your thoughts go back?"

"If he had known that Miss Bogart and I were up there to meet Bill Gibson, he wouldn't have killed him that way. Don't forget he knew who you were. If he had seen you tailing us he would have made some guesses as to who we were, too. He didn't know. He saw you the first time in the bar."

Mr. Moto nodded, and at least he looked half-convinced.

"He's going to be tougher to catch now, because he knows you're after him," Jack Rhyce said. "I suggest that we drive straight back in the morning, and I'll see Pender first thing Monday, just as though nothing had happened. The name is Ben Bushman. You can check on him at the hotel and you can find his airline, but you had better let me try Pender."

"Yes," Mr. Moto said. "And what is it that Mr. Gibson knew that makes him dead tonight? Fortunately we have people working. I hope in another day to have the full details."

"And you'll let me know?" Jack Rhyce said.

"Yes," Mr. Moto said, "with pleasure, Mr. Rhyce."

"I'll appreciate it," Jack Rhyce said. "I know you've got a lot to keep you busy, but maybe you wouldn't mind walking back with me until you can point out the hotel."

"Yes," Mr. Moto said, "we should be moving before it grows too light. There is only one thing more I have to say. If you'll excuse me, there may be much trouble."

"Yes," Jack Rhyce answered. "We'll have to be ready for it."

Mr. Moto hesitated. He seemed to be considering the happiest way of phrasing an embarrassing suggestion.

"Then it might be just as well," Mr. Moto said, and his words were measured, "if you did not tell Miss Bogart what we have been saying."

"I agree with you," Jack Rhyce said. "She won't be useful here any longer. Suppose we send her home on Monday?"

Mr. Moto nodded.

"With so much pleasure," he said. "She is a very lovely lady. And now we should start back."

It was still dark outside when they passed through the gate to the road, but a refreshing coolness in the air told the hour almost as accurately as a watch. In half an hour the sky would begin to lighten and the stars would disappear.

## 16

"A VERY lovely dawn," Mr. Moto said. "In a few moments I shall let you proceed alone. A lovely time for a walk if one has difficulty with sleeping. That is what I should say to the hall-boy if you should see him. Say it in Japanese. He will be so interested to see you returning. He also is in what you call the business, Mr. Rhyce."

The hotel was dark, except for the lights in the corridors and along the drive. A path with steps to break the steepest portion of its ascent led, through a garden of ponds and tiny cascades bordered with dwarf pines and maple, to the upper terrace. He walked up the path carelessly, as though he had been out for a stroll because of inability to sleep. The terrace with its chairs and wicker tables was dark, except for a light shining over the ell marked Cozy Nook. He was halfway across the terrace when he saw Ruth Bogart, and he knew she had been standing in a shadow watching as he walked up the drive.

"Jack," she whispered, but he was only a hotel guest again.

"Why, sweetness," he said, "were you out looking for me? I only went out for a little stroll. I thought you were sound asleep."

She tapped her foot petulantly.

"I wish you'd told me, dear," she answered. "It did make me frightened to wake up all alone, and I couldn't find you. Are you all right?"

"Oh, yes, dear," Jack Rhyce said, "and I'm pretty sleepy now. It's only that I do wake up in the middle of the night sometimes, and I don't believe in these sleeping pills after what I've read about them. Instead, I go out for a walk."

"But where have you been?" she said. "I couldn't find you anywhere."

"Oh, just down the road a piece," he said. "It's lovely country here, and such a clear starlit night."

"You honestly should have told me," she said. "It was mean of you to make me frightened, dear."

"I'm sorry," he said. "But let's forget about it now, and sneak upstairs to old Cozy Nook, or else people will think we've had a quarrel or something."

"We really will have a quarrel," she said, "if you walk out on me again."

They had said enough to explain themselves to anyone who might have been listening, and now they walked carefully up the stairs of the Cozy Nook ell without another word until they were back inside their room. From the way she clung to him he knew she had been afraid for him. It all went to show how unwise it was for two people in the business to become emotionally involved. Instead of planning objectively, his concern for her threatened to throw other factors out of balance, but there was nothing he could do about it, except to feel more convinced than ever that she must be kept free from involvement. It was no place for her, and the Chief should never have sent her out. Although they were talking in whispers, they might as well have been speaking out loud.

"What's the matter, Jack?" she asked.

It was a woman's question. They always knew when something was the matter.

"It's all right," he answered. "There wasn't any trouble."

"You made them believe you?" she asked.

"Oh, yes," he answered.

"Did you have to tell them who we were?"

"Oh, I had to tell them this and that," he said.

"But exactly what did you tell them?"

"Oh, this and that," he answered.

"Jack," she said, "did you find out what Bill Gibson knew?"

"No," he answered, "not exactly."

"Jack," she whispered, "you're not being fair. Why aren't you telling me the truth?"

"You ought to know why," he answered. "Because from now on it's safer to keep you in the dark."

"I don't care whether it's safe or not," she said. "I want to stay in this with you."

It was bad soap opera, but although he was intellectually aware of it, he was moved by her wish. That was the trouble with being emotionally involved.

"Thanks," he answered, "but the thing's moved far enough so that you're not necessary on the job here any more. I want you to be back in Washington ready to meet me at the airport when I get there. It would be common sense even if I had not lost my head about you, Ruth."

Yet he could not be sure that he was right. If he had not cared about her, it was possible that he might have still thought of her as useful. Anyone as attractive as she, and as good an operator, always did have uses.

"This shouldn't have happened with you and me," he said. "It was all a great mistake—professionally speaking, Ruth."

"I don't know," she said, "and I don't care. Anyway, I'm not going back. You're going to want me around when you know what I know."

"It's got to be awfully good," he said.

"It is," she answered. "I know how to get Big Ben, and it's got to be me, and nobody else. You were right. He's fallen for me, flat on his face. Now what do you think of that?"

In the realm of Intelligence the first rule was never to underestimate any individual, but as events developed, another rule crept in—never to overestimate him, either. Everyone had his weaknesses. *The Red Mill* was a weakness, and in Intelligence a woman always—or almost always—made her appearance eventually. That was the reason for the Mata Haris. They were always there for some useful, though seldom proper, purpose. They were the ones who finally caught the best ones out. At any time any man might become a fool about a woman.

"You mean you've seen our boy again?" he asked.

It was dark, and they were whispering, but still she was able to giggle in that annoying way that she used so well as cover.

"Am I going home on the first plane out?" she asked.

"Go ahead," he answered, "and tell me about our boy."

"My boy," she answered. "And he's pretty cute in some ways, too—wistful. You're not mad at me, are you? It was all done in a business way, and you've been pretty businesslike yourself."

"I've had to be," he said. "I'm not able to move from one thing to another indefinitely."

She giggled noiselessly again.

"That's why you need a girl along," she said. "You must be awful in a man's world, Jack, thinking clearly and cutting down everybody by the numbers."

"Go ahead and tell me about our boy—I mean your boy," he said.

"Well, he was kind of sweet," she answered. "You see it was this way. After you left with those people I didn't know exactly what to do. I know you told me to stay right here, but I couldn't help being upset, considering. We shouldn't let our emotions get involved, should we?"

"No," he said, "we shouldn't."

"Anyway," she said, "I felt I had to do something, and so I went downstairs, and outdoors and out to the driveway, and who do you think I saw?"

"All right," he said. "You got out on the driveway and you saw Big Ben. What was he doing?"

"He had come out of the hotel with one of those big army Valpaks," she said. "He was putting it in the back of a car."

"It was a dark green Chevrolet coupé with a dented fender, wasn't it?" he asked.

"Yes," she said. "Naturally."

"They haven't got much of a car pool, have they?" he said. "But then, they didn't know that we'd spotted it. Was he in a hurry?"

"No, he was perfectly natural," she said. "That's one thing you can say about him. He's always natural. I didn't think we ought to let him go away like that, so I walked out into the driveway and said hello."

"Was he surprised? How did he act?" he asked.

"Natural," she said. "He didn't seem surprised at all. He said, 'Why, hi, there. Are you out looking for the boy friend?' And I said, 'Yes. A sort of funny thing happened. A Japanese knocked on the door awhile ago and asked him to step out for a minute, and he hasn't come back, and I'm wondering where he is.'"

If he had planned it he couldn't have given her better lines. She had said all the right things, and she knew her business.

"He laughed," she went on. "He said, 'It was only a little joke I played, honey, and I'm hell on jokes. He'll be coming back all right. Why, I was just coming up to knock on your door myself, as soon as I'd stowed this bag.'"

Putting oneself inside Big Ben's mind, it was barely possible that he had been amused by the collegiate quality of the episode. Big men were more apt to be practical jokers than smaller ones. It was just as serious to overestimate as to underestimate.

"I asked him if he honestly meant that he had got you out of the way on purpose," she said, "and he said, 'It was just a kind of gag. But I'm crazy about you, honey, and what you need is a real man, honey, and not one of these do-gooders who talks like a greeting-card salesman.' How do you like that one, darling?"

"I don't like it," he answered, "but it was the way I've tried to talk. What did you tell him then?"

"What did you expect?" she asked. "I said I was beginning to like him too, and I said that you were always so prim and proper, and that I liked people with a real sense of humor. I said I wished he wasn't checking out and leaving so soon. I had to say something, didn't I, Jack? That's what I'm here for, isn't it?"

"Yes," he said, "I guess you're right about that one, Ruth."

"You see," she said, "he liked me. In fact, he liked me so much that he forgot one or two things. It was important to play up to him, wasn't it?"

"Yes," he said. "How did you play up?"

"Oh, not so very much," she said. "But never mind it, Jack. Only, when he held me in his arms I kept thinking of Bill Gibson, and wondering where you were. It was damned unpleasant, Jack. And if you want to know, I'm tired of sex tonight."

It helped him only a little to tell himself that of course she had to do what she had done, and that he had to view the whole business as objectively useful.

"For just a second I thought he was going to take his bag out of that Chevrolet and stay," she said. "But he didn't."

"Not even when you asked him?" he asked her.

"Right," she said, "not even when I asked him. And if I may say so, I sounded awfully good. He honestly did want to stay, but there was something that made him know he had to go in a hurry. He kept saying, 'Gosh, I wish it wasn't fixed so that I had to leave here.'" She gave a perfect imitation of his accent.

"Yes," Jack Rhyce said, "but anyway, he went."

"But not immediately," she said. "He kept saying, 'Gee, I'm crazy about you, honey.' He seemed to be trying to make up his mind about something."

"All right," Jack Rhyce said. "And then he made up his mind?"

"Yes," she said, "he made it up. He said, 'Honey, this mustn't be good-by. Call me as soon as you get to the city.' Then he wrote down a telephone number and gave it to me. If he wasn't there I was to leave my name and he'd call me back."

After all, when you were in the business you had to give it everything you had.

"Good going," he said. "I can use that number."

"Oh, no, you can't," she said, "because I've torn it up already. Besides, he'll know my voice. When you want him, I'm the only one who can talk to him, Jack—and I guess you want him, don't you?"

"Yes," he said, "I'm going to want him all right."

"Then you've got to keep me around," she said, "and now let's stop being so businesslike, Jack. God, I wish we were both on the outside."

They were a long way from the outside, but the desire for escape and humdrum security formed a tantalizing vision that had an unattainable quality.

"I'm going to talk to you about being on the outside when we get home," he said.

"Let's talk about it now," she said. "We could have a cabin by a lake like the people in that book who took to the woods. I'm a pretty good cook, and you could fish or make snowshoes or whatever they do in the woods."

"Yes," he said, "but we'd better talk about it sometime later, not now."

As a matter of fact, you wouldn't have to do much of anything," she said. "I have a pretty good income. You'd be surprised. We could travel and see the pyramids or the Taj, or we could go into the Mau Mau region."

"No," he said, "I'd rather buy a farm."

"A dairy farm," she said. "You could put on white overalls and a jumper every time you milked a cow."

"I can milk a cow, as a matter of fact," he said.

"I wish I could talk you into traveling," she said. "Only think what it would be like if you and I went to London, and if we didn't have to check in anywhere, and didn't have to be startled when we saw one of those damned familiar faces—if we could just be ourselves, having a quiet breakfast and reading the papers, without having to watch for anything, without a single damned compulsion."

"Without having to talk to anyone," he said. "Without having to find out anything, even the time of day."

"Without having to look over our shoulders once," she said.

"Without a switch-blade in your handbag, dear," he said; "without a pill, or anything."

"That reminds me, what happened to my handbag, Jack?"

Her question broke the illusion. They never should have indulged themselves with talk about the outside, or with the immature wishes that such talk engendered.

"Moto has it," he said. "He'll bring it in the morning. Look. It's getting light already. We're going to pull out of here first thing after breakfast."

"Going where?" she said.

"Back to Tokyo," he said.

"Doing what?"

"Doing just what we did before," he said. "The Friendship League. Mr. Harry Pender, all that sort of thing."

"Aren't you going to tell me anything?" she asked.

"No," he said. "What you don't know won't hurt you."

"You've found out something, haven't you?" she asked.

"Never mind," he said. "What you don't know won't hurt you, Ruth."

"Is it as tough as all that?"

"Never mind," he said.

"I don't," she said, "as long as it means you like me."

"That's the trouble," he said. "I like you."

"I won't be any trouble, Jack," she said. "I'll promise you I won't."

"I know you won't," he said.

"Then let's talk about the outside some more," she said. "There are all sorts of things I'd like to tell you—about when I was a girl at school, about parties, about all sorts of things. Jack, it's time we got to know each other in an outside way."

"I know," he said. "Later—there isn't time right now."

There was never time to think about yourself when you were in the business. Externals kept crowding in, each offering its own insistent problem. He wished to heaven he could keep her out of it, but it was too late now, after what she had told him. You had to move forward. You never could move back, and outside it was daylight, and the first birds were singing. Bill Gibson was dead in Chrysanthemum Rest—an overdose of sleeping pills—but still the show had to go on. He would have known better what to do if he had only known what Bill Gibson had been prepared to tell him. Yet even without the knowledge the picture was growing clearer. Time was all that was needed. He wished that he did not have the feeling that time was running out.

## 17

JACK RHYCE knew a great many stories about the business; and all of them, when one delved beneath their surfaces, had one thing in common—a universal element of simplicity. After all, the framework of an apparatus could not be complex, if only because too many links and convolutions threatened confusion, and Communist techniques ordinarily left their own dreary signatures. Consequently, later, whenever Jack Rhyce reviewed his procedures in Japan he was not surprised to find how little there was about them that was bizarre or even interesting. A series of coincidences had given him a lucky break, although the break had been complicated by the killing. There was also the mistake in identity that had arisen between himself and the Japanese element in the picture, which fortunately had been rectified. Aside from these complexities, the picture was like any one of dozens of others that kept repeating themselves in various parts of the world. Any trained agent, Jack Rhyce knew well, could have achieved the final results that he did. As soon as he had made contact with the Japanese, the lines all began to untangle. It was only the old story of infiltration and cover. As soon as he had spotted Mr. Pender and the Pen Pal room in the Asia Friendship office, most of the rest began to be routine. There was only one unknown element that made him apprehensive, and this lay in Mr. Moto's remarks about political assassination. The balance of everything in the Orient was precarious. It was his duty to learn more, especially if it would have anti-American repercussions. The Japanese had their own network of agents and, as Mr. Moto had said, they doubtless would turn up facts. However, there was every reason for him to do some thinking of his own.

After they returned to the Imperial Hotel on Sunday afternoon, he left Ruth Bogart in her room. The less she knew, the better off she was. He told her to sit quietly and to read a good book, but not to leave the room in case he telephoned. He and Mr. Moto left the hotel together in the Buick. He was the foreigner again who needed a guide, and if anyone was listening, they had only heard him ask to be taken to the Mei-ji Museum. They talked while Mr. Moto drove expertly through the traffic. Although the ride was a short one, they were able to say a good deal by the time they had parked the car in front of the conventional European building that housed the pictures illustrating the reign of Japan's greatest Emperor. The hour was late enough so that the place was closed, but under the circumstances, it was all the better.

"I know the guardians," Mr. Moto said. "They will put on the lights, and while I telephone you may enjoy the pictures. I think I can do everything from here very safely."

It was only a question of Moto's getting the latest news, which was the province of the Japanese, not that of Rhyce, and so Jack walked alone up the great marble staircase to the two great galleries. Granted that the pictures themselves had little individual artistic merit, together they made a panorama that illustrated one of the most dramatic life spans in history. The Emperor Mei-ji had been born and had spent his childhood and youth in a feudal Japan, insulated from the world. The Emperor had been a figurehead in those days, under the rule of the great Tokugawa lords. The early scenes of his birth and coronation showed the rituals of a country which had hardly changed since its cultural contacts with the Tang dynasty in China. It was the appearance of the American Navy in the early 1850's that had finally awakened the nation's latent instinct for survival. There were the pictures of the Emperor arriving in Tokyo to establish his rule in the Tokugawa fortress, scenes of war and incipient rebellion, and the strangely touching painting of the Emperor's mission departing on foreign ships to study the civilization and customs of the West. There was the Emperor drilling his troops in the European manner; there was the war with China, the war with Russia, the European costumes and uniforms, the Europeanized Japanese Navy, the annexation of Korea; and finally the crowd at the moat by the black wall of the Tokyo fortress lamenting the Emperor's death in 1912. If the current of time had run more swiftly since that year, nothing, not even the atom bomb at Hiroshima, had presented a greater succession of contrast; for in the Emperor's lifetime, a nation with smaller resources, more backward and seemingly less adaptable than China, had become a modern state and a world power, and its future was still implicit in the pictures. He must have examined these for more than half an hour before Mr. Moto joined him.

"You understand them, do you not?" Mr. Moto said. "They are our Bayeaux tapestry. Poor Japan."

He had not thought of comparing the pictures with the tapestry of the Norman ships embarking their horses and their chain-mailed soldiers, with their steel helmets and nose protectors, for the battle of Britain, but it was not a bad comparison. Under the rule of the Emperor, Japan had gone through many crises as great as Hastings, and the story was not over yet.

"Skirov is believed to be here, but cannot be traced," Mr. Moto said. "There is much activity. Large quantities of banners have been made already saying 'Down with American Imperialism' and 'Avenge the People's Martyr.' Communists are always so well organized for demonstrations."

In view of what he had seen in other parts of the world, the news was normal and not surprising. The Rosenbergs not so long ago had been the people's martyrs.

"We will have more definite news by tomorrow, I hope," Mr. Moto said. "Some of our best people are working tonight. I shall be out myself. I should also tell you that they have found the lodging of your Mr. Ben, but he has not returned."

"Miss Bogart can get him if necessary," Jack Rhyce said.

Mr. Moto shook his head slowly. "It will not be necessary," he said, "if he is not hiding."

"You can reach me at the hotel tonight," Jack Rhyce said, "and tomorrow at ten-thirty I will be there at the Friendship League, talking to Mr. Pender."

They did not speak as they walked down the marble staircase. After all, the business was routine, and the only question to be answered concerned the reason for the meeting of Skirov and Big Ben.

"I'll drive you to the hotel," Mr. Moto said. "It will look better."

They did not speak again until they were in the Buick, but both of them were thinking.

"Is it only your idea, or is it straight information," Jack Rhyce asked, "that there is going to be a killing?"

"There are the signs," Mr. Moto said. "Our people have seen them. 'Avenge the People's Martyrs.' They are meant to be out on the streets, Mr. Rhyce. They are not being made for nothing."

He had cultivated a deep respect for Communist agitation. Although the art was as old as revolution itself, Communist discipline had streamlined old processes until a mob could now be organized for any purpose as neatly as a billboard artist could paint a picture.

"Will it be a large demonstration?" he asked.

Mr. Moto nodded.

"Simultaneous outbreaks in different quarters. The street fighters are being given special training. It will be ugly, I am very much afraid, but not on the largest scale. It will be another step forward for Russia. Poor Japan."

"It's funny, isn't it," Jack Rhyce said, "to know that riots are being planned, without knowing what's going to set them off?"

"Yes," Mr. Moto said. "These people understand my country." He cleared his throat in a nervous way. "You do not, perhaps, remember the army officers' uprising in 1936 which cost the lives of so many very nice people in the government? A very unpleasant time. Ha-ha. so many of us were so busy. A great deal can be accomplished by assassination."

"Depending on whom you assassinate," Jack Rhyce said.

"Exactly," Mr. Moto said. "I am afraid they will pick out someone very good."

"From the slogans on the banners," Jack Rhyce said, "it sounds as though they were going to take out a left-wing Liberal."

"Yes," Mr. Moto said; "yes, I think."

"Can you name some prospects?" Jack Rhyce asked.

"Oh, yes," Mr. Moto said, "there are several possibilities. Eight, perhaps ten I have considered. I wish so very much your Mr. Gibson were alive. Are you sure you only know him and no one else in his apparatus?"

"I told you once I didn't," Jack Rhyce said. "Don't you trust me?"

"Oh, please," Mr. Moto drew in his breath carefully. "Yes, as much as you trust me, I'm very much afraid."

"I'm working with you," Jack Rhyce said. "As long as we both want the same thing we can keep our cards facing up."

"I am not anti-American," Mr. Moto said. "I hope so very much that you are not anti-Japanese, Mr. Rhyce."

"Not at the minute," Jack Rhyce said. "I'm anti-Communist right now."

Mr. Moto drew in his breath again very carefully.

"Americans are so very nice, but sentimental sometimes. May I ask you what you intend to do about this Big Ben?"

"It depends on what he's up to," Jack Rhyce answered.

Mr. Moto cleared his throat and sucked in another breath.

"Would you object," Mr. Moto asked, "if any people were to question him?"

"Not if it's necessary," Jack Rhyce said, "but I'd rather have him followed. He can lead us to what we want just as easily that way as by our going to work on him."

"Ha-ha," Mr. Moto said. "Americans are always so very sentimental when they are not using flame-throwers and napalm. Ha-ha. Excuse me. If we cannot trace him tonight, I am very much afraid we should use Miss Bogart to find him."

"All right," Jack Rhyce said. "You can use your own judgment. Maybe we shouldn't leave him loose too long."

"Thank you," Mr. Moto said. "I am so very pleased that you trust me a little, Mr. Rhyce."

"Oh, I do," Jack Rhyce said, "maybe quite a little."

There was not much more to say.

"From now on," Mr. Moto said, "there will be a car and driver in your name, outside of your hotel. He will take you to me at any hour, I am so sorry that I am so busy."

"Are you sure you wouldn't like me to go out with you and help?" Jack Rhyce asked.

"So very sure," Mr. Moto answered quickly. "You would only be conspicuous, Mr. Rhyce. And please take care of Miss Bogart. She may be so very useful tomorrow. You understand?"

Jack Rhyce nodded. It was easy enough to understand when everything was lapsing into ordinary routine. Emotion had no value in the business. He and Mr. Moto and Big Ben were all expendable pieces on the squares of Intelligence. Jack Rhyce was glad to discover that his momentary desire for vengeance on Big Ben had almost evaporated. As matters had turned out, Big Ben was common property now, and after hearing Mr. Moto speak it was difficult to be under much illusion regarding Big Ben's future. The net was around him, and a European was too conspicuous in the Orient to hide for very long. The number of Big Ben was nearly up. Ben was paying the price of stupidity. That was the only way Jack could assess Ben's having given the telephone number to Ruth Bogart.

She was sitting quietly in her room when he returned, and the adjoining door was open.

"Is everything all right?" he asked.

"Yes," she answered. "Everything's very dull. Have they picked up Big Ben?"

"No, not yet," he told her.

She smiled at him.

"Isn't it lucky that I'm here?" she said. "Do you want me to try that number?"

"No," he said, "not yet."

"Then suppose I put on an evening dress and we go out for dinner," she said.

"Only in the hotel," he answered. "I don't want us to be buzzing around too much right now."

He arrived at the Asia Friendship League offices at half-past ten next morning to find that Mr. Harry Pender was already seated in his private office wearing a fresh Aloha shirt. The light from the window glinted cheerfully on his spectacles as he waved a welcoming hand.

"Come in, Jack," he said. "Come in. Are you ready to pick my brains?"

"I'm all set and raring to go, Harry," Jack Rhyce said, "if you honestly have time to give me some more fill-in on the League picture."

"Why, all the time in the world, Jack," Mr. Pender said. "Sit down. Have a cigarette?"

"No thanks, I never use them, Harry," Jack Rhyce said, and he seated himself in a comfortable modernistic chair.

He was embarrassed that he had not placed Harry Pender until Mr. Moto had explained him, but after all, he had only seen the face in a group photograph, and never in the flesh. Very little doubt remained with Jack Rhyce now. The man before him was certainly the individual who was known as Harry Wise and who had recently been placed on the doubtful list at the office, a former American college instructor who had been holding a Communist card since late 1930's, but with no definite record of activity. He looked older than his photograph as Jack recalled it, and since he had not been heard from, he must have been behind the Curtain for some time. Conceivably he had been one of the Americans in Chinese prison camps who had been mentioned by American war prisoners; conceivably he had been one of the Europeans who had been mentioned in connection with the germ warfare accusations. It was a pity to be so far away from source material.

"It sure is nice to see you safe back from that place," Harry Pender said. "I see in the Japan *Times* that one of our fellow countrymen took too many sleeping pills up there. I hope it didn't spoil your fun."

"Oh, there was a little mix-up with the Japanese authorities," Jack Rhyce said, "but it didn't amount to anything. You see, we left yesterday morning and drove around seeing the sights. I sort of wanted to get oriented a little—you know, get the feel of the country."

"That's a very wise thing to do," Harry Pender said. "A first impression has a lot of value. You know what people say—either spend ten days or ten years. By the way, where's our girl friend? Ruth Bogart, I mean."

"She's back at the hotel," Jack Rhyce answered. The question had indicated an unnecessary curiosity. "She wasn't feeling so well this morning, a little Japanese stomach, but nothing serious."

"Too bad," Mr. Pender said. "I hope you've given her something for it. Do you want me to send one of my girls over?"

"Oh, no," Jack answered. "She's going to be all right. I just told her to take it easy. Well, let's get down to business. I hope I told you emphatically enough the other day, Harry, how impressed I was with your whole layout here, and all the fine things you're doing. I want to read up on all the social studies you're making, every one of them."

Harry Pender took off his horn-rimmed spectacles and held them between his thumb and middle finger.

"Don't read too much, Jack," he said, "or you won't see the forest for the trees."

"I know exactly what you mean, Harry," Jack Rhyce said. "But gosh, I've got to begin somewhere. Everything can't be as smooth sailing as it looks around here, Harry. You must have some pretty big policy problems."

Mr. Pender allowed his glasses to swing like a pendulum between his fingers. He raised his eyebrows inquiringly.

"I mean, for instance," Jack Rhyce said, " problems of personnel. You were mentioning this on Friday, I think."

"Oh," Harry Pender said, "of course every office has its turnover. It takes time making selections, but on the whole, we have a fine team all the way down the line."

"Oh, I never meant to say you didn't," Jack said quickly. "I was just wondering, well, whether you had any trouble with Communists or anything like that." He had intended to bring out the subject with flat-footed innocence, and from the tolerant way Mr. Pender laughed, he was rather sure he had.

"Excuse me for laughing, Jack," Harry Pender said, "but that question of yours is completely characteristic of the point of view that everyone brings here from the States. Rumors become grossly exaggerated. Why, there's hardly a Communist in Japan, in the sinister sense of the word—but you will find varieties of liberals. From my observation, democracy has a permanent foothold in Japan."

"Well, it's mighty nice to hear you say so, Harry," Jack Rhyce said. "It's the sort of reaction I hope to fit in my report. I'm glad, too, if there's a healthy liberal party here. I hope they're interested in putting social welfare on a sensible scientific basis."

He watched the horn-rimmed spectacles moving in a slow, thoughtful arc, and he was happy to notice that Mr. Pender was giving him his smiling, friendly approval.

"You'll find liberalism here in the best sense of the word," he said, "and the leaders are highly dedicated people. I want you to get to know some, Jack, I want you to get this Communism bias thoroughly washed out of your hair."

"It's curious," Jack Rhyce said, "how distance distorts facts. Back in the States we hardly hear about Japanese Progressives, let alone learning their names. Who are some of them, Harry?"

He hoped that his interest appeared fatuously genuine. Mr. Pender's thoughtful eyes were fixed on him, but he could not detect a glint of suspicion or any diminution in the current rapport between them.

"I think we can help you there," Mr. Pender said, "because the League is just doing a pamphlet on the subject, with thumbnail biographies of eight or ten of the top-flight liberal politicians.

There's Hata, for instance, and there's Iwara, and Yamashita and Nichiwara. I'll be delighted to show you the copy we're preparing."

"Gosh, Harry," Jack Rhyce said, "I'd sure like to see it. Who's the best of them, would you say?"

"Oh," Harry Pender said, and as far as Jack Rhyce could see, he was taking the question casually, "everyone of them has quite a following, but Hata is head and shoulders above the rest. Noshimura Hata. I'll see that you meet him sometime."

"Can you arrange it?" Jack Rhyce asked. "It would be a real pleasure if you could, provided he lives around here."

"He does, as a matter of fact," Harry Pender said, "in an attractive house with a beautiful garden. His collection of dwarf trees is very widely known."

"I didn't know liberal intellectuals had large homes and gardens," Jack said.

"Hata is an educated liberal," Harry Pender answered. The swing of the spectacles in his fingers accelerated slightly. "An Oxford graduate, a member of a wealthy family, and a philanthropist."

"Oh," Jack Rhyce said, "then he can speak English, can't he?"

Granted that he had picked up the information he had wanted, had the cost been too great? Perhaps he should not have pursued the subject so long after the name of Noshimura Hata had been mentioned, and yet there had been the danger of dropping the thing too suddenly.

His attention was now riveted on the swinging glasses in the right hand of Mr. Pender. There was no doubt that the motion had been accelerated, and there was always betrayal in unconscious gesture. Instinct was delivering its message to Jack Rhyce, telling him that a crucial stage had been reached, the outcome of which depended on the next few words. It was time to drop all show of interest, to move on to something else.

"All you say," Jack Rhyce said, "goes to prove that preconceived opinions are always off the beam, aren't they? I had no idea that the Japanese would be so enthusisatic about sports, for instance. Now, if you've got the time, I'd love to hear whether you're dovetailing a good sports program in with your other projects."

"Sports had a leading priority with us," Harry Pender answered. "Nothing pulls people together so much as meeting on a playing field. In fact, I should put sports ahead of any other cultural interchange when it comes to the promotion of good will . . . "

At least they were away from liberalism, and embarked on a sea of verbiage which, to keep the cover right, ought to demand most of the morning for a crossing. It was necessary to sit there for an hour or more mouthing idealistic platitudes, being, as the Chief would say, a do-gooder in every sense of the word. Talking with Harry Pender was both real and unreal. It was ironic to think that they were each talking only for the other's benefit. Did Mr. Pender believe he was impressing him? And did his own artificial guilelessness seem real to Mr. Pender? He only knew that they both were artists, each concealing any impatience or boredom he may have felt while they discussed the Asia Friendship League.

It was quarter of twelve when he ventured to push back his chair.

"Harry," he said, "it's been swell of you to give me so much of your time. I have as many ideas packed in my mind as I have reading matter in my briefcase now. I guess I'd better take the rest of the day just sitting in the hotel room boning up on the material."

"It's been a good morning for me, too, Jack," Mr. Pender answered. "How about a bite of lunch before you start reading reports? Not more than five minutes away from here is the best beef sukiyaki restaurant in the world."

Jack Rhyce picked up his briefcase and endeavored to straighten out the wrinkles in his seersucker coat.

"There's nothing I'd like better, Harry. And please give me a raincheck on that offer," he said. "But right now I'd honestly better go back to the hotel and see how Ruth is. How would lunch tomorrow be, instead? Because I'll be right back here tomorrow morning, making a nuisance of myself with another batch of questions."

She was in her room, reading Terry's *Japanese Empire.* She looked up inquiringly when he came in.

"Has anything happened here?" he asked.

"Yes," she said. "One thing, Big Ben telephoned."

He tried to forget about her as a person, when she told that news. Nothing must interfere with the business, and she must have felt the same way, from the excitement in her eyes.

"What did he want?" he asked.

"He wanted to make a date for five this afternoon," she said. "I told him I wasn't sure that I could get away. I said I'd call him back at three."

"That's my girl," Jack Rhyce said. "I think the time has come to pick him up, Ruth. It's a good thing you're along, all right."

"Thank you, sir," she answered. "How did you get on with Pender?"

"I wish I knew," he said. "He worries me a little. He's in the business all right. I think I'd better see the Japs again, right off. I'll be back in about an hour."

"Aren't you going to cut me in on anything?" she asked.

"Only about Big Ben," he said. "Don't ask for any more."

"I won't," she told him; "but, Jack—be careful. Don't be too sure of yourself."

Frankly, he wished he felt more assured.

He had not been under the hotel porte-cochère for half a minute before the car and the driver that Mr. Moto had indicated the day before appeared. The meeting place was the back room of a curio shop. Mr. Moto, still in his blue suit, sat at a table with a telephone in front of him, drinking a cup of tea.

"No more news than yesterday," he said. "So sorry."

"I'm sorry, too," Jack answered.

"And how is Mr. Pender? Did you see him?" Mr. Moto asked.

Jack Rhyce nodded. "You were right about him," he said. "We have his photograph, but he looks ten years older. He knows a lot about liberal politicians. I've been doing some thinking this morning."

"I am so glad to hear it," Mr. Moto said, "and I hope so much that you will tell me the results."

"We don't seem to know what's going to happen, do we?" Jack Rhyce said. "You only know that they're making plans for an organized demonstration, and you guess that there's going to be a political killing. We had the same word in Washington. But it's only a guess, isn't it?"

"That is true," Mr. Moto said. "Our people are working, but they have come on nothing new."

"Then I think we'd better pick up Big Ben," Jack Rhyce said. "I'm sorry, I hate to break up an apparatus."

"No one has seen him," he said. "He is hiding very carefully."

It was time to tell the news, and time to lay the lines.

"Not so carefully," he said. "I think maybe we're overrating our boy. He called up Miss Bogart this morning. He wants to make a date with her for this afternoon. She said she wasn't sure that she could do it. She'll call him back at three."

Mr. Moto stared at the teacup, and his forehead wrinkled and he shook his head.

"I do not like it," he said. "It does not sound correct."

"Meaning it doesn't sound like the first team?" Jack said.

Mr. Moto's gold teeth flashed when he answered.

"I am so glad you use the expression," he said. "I wish that Miss Bogart would give us the telephone number. We could have traced it by this time."

"I told you she wouldn't," Jack Rhyce said, "and I decided not to put further pressure on her. The fact is she may be highly useful in picking up Big Ben, and she was sent over here to be useful. She'll call him any time we want."

"She does not want to leave you," Mr. Moto said. "That is very proper, Mr. Rhyce, but I do not like it. I do not like it."

"I agree," Jack Rhyce said. "A lot of angles in this situation worry me. You can trace the number when she calls him. We may need it if anything goes wrong, but I don't believe much in tracing numbers."

"May I ask why?" Mr. Moto said.

"Because it's too obvious," Jack Rhyce said. "They always use a public telephone in some public place—a bar or a railroad station."

"If we knew the telephone," Mr. Moto said, "we could be watching and take him when he makes the call."

"Yes," Jack Rhyce said, "but I don't think our chances would be good. He's a professional—he would be on the lookout for strangers. We're safer to let Miss Bogart call him. It's better not to be too busy when we're closing in."

Mr. Moto was silent for a moment. Then he nodded slowly.

"I think I am inclined to agree with you, Mr. Rhyce," Mr. Moto said. "I realize that Miss Bogart is a very intelligent girl who has had training in handling these matters. I shall call on you at the hotel at a quarter before three."

"And I'll go along with you later," Jack Rhyce said. "Trace the call, then, if you want, but let's catch him where he's waiting for Miss Bogart. It will be safer and surer that way. And I want to be along when you pick him up—just out of interest, Mr. Moto."

## 18

JACK RHYCE had played a part in several similar actions in America and Europe, the details of which seldom varied. Find your man and keep him at a given spot. Get the group distributed. Have the car ready. Close in simultaneously from all sides. This was the one maneuver that required expert coordination and experience. If properly executed, there would hardly be a ripple of a struggle. Often pedestrians ten feet away did not notice the group around the victim, trussed and pinioned in the approved style, being half pushed, half carried to the waiting car. Even if things did not move quite as planned, a well-placed blow at the back of the skull could solve the difficulty. Big Ben was a big man, but he could be handled, given the proper group. Jack Rhyce was certain that there would be no trouble if he were in the party.

"Oh," Mr. Moto said, "you do not trust us, Mr. Rhyce? You will think differently, I am sure, when you see my people. Poor men. They are not well paid, but they are as neat as your FBI."

The obviousness of the operation was a sufficient explanation as to why Mr. Moto did not like it, since the use of a woman to lure a man was among the most shopworn in the sordid bags of tricks which everyone knew backwards in the business. Yet it was a trick that worked the most frequently of them all. Jack only had to remind himself that he too had fallen in love with Ruth Bogart freely to accept the motives of Big Ben. The repugnance that he felt at having to use her in this venerable trick only convinced him further of Big Ben's infatuation and, besides, he had seen them on the dance floor.

By the time he and Mr. Moto reached the hotel, the preliminary preparations were all in hand: the equipment immediately necessary was packed in Mr. Moto's briefcase. When Ruth Bogart saw the briefcase she smiled a thin, Mona Lisa smile, Jack had never seen her looking prettier. The excitement and the exacting demands which would be made of her in the next few minutes had added to the delicacy of her features and the luster of her hair. Even her voice had a new seductive quality.

"So you boys need me, do you?" she said. "All right, rig up the telephone."

When Mr. Moto took out of his briefcase and methodically arranged the instruments, Jack watched him with approval. There were right and wrong procedures in wire tapping, and Mr. Moto knew all the proper ones.

"I suggest that we both listen, Mr. Rhyce," he said as he handed Jack Rhyce a pair of earphones of Japanese manufacture. The Japanese were able to make anything.

"Are you sure this won't be too big a load?" Jack Rhyce asked.

"Don't be silly, Jack," Ruth Bogart said. "He knows his stuff." She smiled her brightest smile. "I couldn't have set this up better myself, and now it is three o'clock, I think. Perhaps—if you are ready—I'd better make the call?"

"No," Jack Rhyce said. "Let him wonder. Let him sweat it out for ten minutes."

He never forgot the interval of waiting, or how happy Ruth Bogart looked.

"Jack," she said, "you're glad I'm along now, aren't you?"

"Yes," he answered, "at the moment, Ruth."

"It's nice to know I'm useful, under the proper circumstances," she said. "Maybe that's all any woman wants."

They did not speak for another minute or two, and then Mr. Moto broke the silence.

"Excuse the question," Mr. Moto said. "Do you carry a blackjack with you, Mr. Rhyce?"

"Funny you should ask that," Jack Rhyce answered, "because I was thinking of it myself. No, I haven't one with me."

Mr. Moto reached inside his briefcase.

"If you will permit, it will be a pleasure to present you with this one," he said. "It may be useful, and ha-ha, it will be easier for you to reach him, if needed."

Jack balanced the instrument expertly in his hand before he slipped it into his back pocket.

"Thanks," he said. "I'll do my best to be neat and clean if necessary."

"I'm sure," Mr. Moto said. "So very sure you will be. And now perhaps Miss Bogart should make the call. Let us not have the gentleman too discouraged."

They sat silent while Ruth Bogart gave the number, and there followed, of course, a moment of suspense until they heard the answering voice. The connection was very clear. There was no doubt in the world that it was Big Ben.

"Gosh, honey," he said, and his voice was plaintive, "I've been settin' here. I mighty near thought it was a brush-off."

"Oh, Ben," she said, "I'm sorry, but I couldn't call until I was alone."

"You mean he's back with you?" Big Ben asked. "Why honey, I kind of got the idea he might have left you for good back there in the mountains. When did he come back?"

"He said he wasn't able to sleep," Ruth Bogart answered. "He just said he went out with some Japanese friends and drank some sake."

"And he's hanging around you now, is he?"

"Ben, don't be that way," she said. "I told you I was tired of him, and he's gone now."

"Well, don't forget you're my girl now, honey. How about say around six tonight?"

She first glanced questioningly at Mr. Moto.

"Why that would be lovely, Ben," she then said. "Will you call for me at the hotel?"

There was a silence on the other end of the wire.

"Why, honey," he said. "I had some trouble there, last time I was in Tokyo, and the folks there maybe don't like me too much. How about going down to the Ginza and meeting me outside the Cimaroon beer hall? It's a GI place, honey, with good food and singing and everything. I'll be waiting by the front entrance, come six o'clock."

"But, Ben, dear, I don't know this town."

"I'm going to see personally that you're going to know it and love it before you're through, honey," he said. "It's no trouble to get there. Just you tell the hotel doorman. Any taxi driver can take you to the Cimaroon."

"Well, then you be right outside," she said. "It's spooky alone in a place where you don't know the language or anything. Are you sure you'll be there, Ben dear?"

"Sure as hell isn't freezing. Just you don't worry. Take a cab," he said.

"All right," she said, "but it makes me a little frightened, Ben."

"Aw, now," he said, "there's nothing to be scared of, honey. Wear something cute and fluffy. I only wish it was six already. Don't forget—the Cimaroon. You got it, honey?"

They all had it—the Cimaroon—and the conversation was over, and they each sat for a moment in a questioning sort of silence.

"How did I do?" she asked.

Jack had been analyzing every pause and change of tone in the speeches. A voice over the telephone without features or personalities to support it was a disembodied thing. Although he had no doubt that the voice belonged to Big Ben, there was a doubt as to whether it had been wholly credulous. In the end, everyone speaking on the telephone always assumed a new and peculiar personality. Even Ruth Bogart's voice had exhibited strain, and the same had been true with Big Ben, but there had been so little deviation that he could safely attribute it to the medium of communication.

"You did fine, I think," he said. "Don't you think so, Moto?"

Mr. Moto was dismantling the wire-tapping device.

"It is not for me to analyze the European mind, but on the whole he gave me the impression that he wanted so very greatly to see Miss Bogart."

Mr. Moto snapped his briefcase shut.

"The Cimaroon is a beer hall and night club, frequented by American soldiers and sailors, a suitable place for him to select," he said. "It should not be difficult to take him quickly if he is waiting on the sidewalk. I must be leaving now to make arrangements. The car and driver will be waiting to take you there, Mr. Rhyce. May I ask you to arrive in front of the Cimaroon at half-past five?"

"Let's make it 5:15, if it's all the same with you," Jack said. "Those Joes have second thoughts, and get careful and early sometimes. Once I had to do a snatch in Paris—one of the first I ever was mixed with—but never mind it now."

"Thank you," Mr. Moto said. "I quite agree with 5:15."

"And what about me?" Ruth Bogart asked. "Am I going with you, or not?"

"Certainly not," Jack Rhyce said quickly. "There won't be any need, Ruth."

"If he doesn't see me, he may not show," she said. "I've known it to happen, Jack."

As things stood then it seemed safe to discount that possibility. Jack was actually experiencing a feeling which was almost one of peace. As far as he could see, the Japan assignment was drawing to a close. If the ending was not wholly satisfactory, it was effective, and with the way things were going, they could not beat about the bush forever. His main mission had been Big Ben. He took the blackjack from his hip pocket, tossed it in the air and caught it, with the same carelessness he would have caught a baseball on the outside. It was very nicely constructed. The Japanese were always good at detail.

"No, it won't be necessary," Ruth," he said. "You'll only be in the way if there's any kind of hassle. He's a big boy, and he may muss things up."

"I think Mr. Rhyce is correct," Mr. Moto said. "I am most grateful to you, Miss Bogart, and it would be so nice if I could pay you my respects when this is over. Perhaps a Japanese supper tonight; but—ha-ha—not at the Cimaroon, and just with me and Mr. Rhyce. But—ha-ha—not with Mr. Ben. At 5:15, then, Mr. Rhyce, and thank you very much."

The feeling that everything was over still persisted after Moto had gone. It resembled the easing of tensions he had experienced before when a job was almost finished, and everything was in the groove. But this time elation was added to his relief, which he tried to check because he always distrusted elation. Finally his conscience troubled him with a nagging suspicion that he was ending things too quickly, not following them as far as he might to an ultimate conclusion. It was true that he was hedging his bets, but it was better to hedge than lose, and they were winning enough. At least they were crippling the apparatus by taking out Big Ben.

"You know, I feel pretty good on the whole," he said to her. "When we get him, we can move the hell out of here and head for home."

Her expression had brightened, too.

"It can't be soon enough for me," she said. "And why can't we start being ourselves when we get on that plane?"

"I don't see why we can't from there on in," he answered.

"What do you mean?" she asked. "From there on in?"

"A lot of things," he said, "and we ought to be able to start discussing them as soon as I get back here."

"Do you mean you still love me?" she asked.

"It's unprofessional, but I do," he said, "and a lot of other things. Come to think of it, I wouldn't have missed any of this."

"Even being unprofessional?" she asked.

"Yes," he said, "even being unprofessional."

"Jack," she said, "what's going to happen to him?"

"He's not our problem," he said. "The Japs will take him over. But it's the best we could do under the circumstances, Ruth." He turned and strode across the room and back. "We might have gone further into this if Bill Gibson hadn't died, but I think it's time now to stop this show, I really do."

"It's sticky, letting the Japs take him," she said. "I wish you and I weren't in it."

"We're in it all right," he said.

"You're too nice for it," she said, "and maybe I am, too."

"I wouldn't be surprised," he told her, "but let's put our minds on pulling out of here tomorrow, Ruth."

The interval before his departure for the Cimaroon always remained in his memory as a domestic sort of scene.

"I don't suppose we'd better inquire about plane reservations yet," he said. "No reason for anyone to know that we're checking out, but if you want something to do while I'm out you might start packing your suitcases. There might be space on something tomorrow."

"Jack," she said, "don't you think you ought to wear something heavier and darker than that seersucker coat?"

"Oh, I don't think so," he answered. "This won't be night work, and it's awfully hot outside."

"I wish you were carrying a gun," she said, "just in case. Wouldn't you like to borrow my fountain pen gadget? It doesn't look as though I'm going to need it."

"I can do fine with this jack," he said. He was feeling almost jovial now that everything was set. "I'm really pretty good at controlling one of these."

"I think you ought not to wear crepe-soled shoes," she said. "You might slip in them. I don't know whether you ever knew Bobby Burke, who used to work in Paris. He slipped making a swing at Oscar Ertz—you know, the Czech—just outside the Gare du Nord. He skidded on the pavement and had a shiv in him before he could recover."

"These shoes are skid-proof," he told her. "No, I never did know Bob, but I've heard plenty about him. Ought I to be jealous?"

"Darling," she said, "I never knew about you, dear, and you never knew about me. You won't ever need to be jealous. Now let me take a look at you. You look awfully handsome."

"So do you," he said. It was time to be going, but he did not want to leave her.

"Jack," she said, "if you do hit him, follow through. Let him have it all. He's an awfully big man, you know. Now you'd better kiss me good-by. I don't want you to be late."

"Don't forget Moto's coming to take us out to dinner when we get back," he said. "I wish we were going alone. We haven't had much fun here, what with one thing and another."

"Oh," she said, "there'll be lots of other times. Take care, Jack, please take care."

He remembered those last words most distinctly. In fact, they echoed in his memory all the way out of the hotel. He had a final glimpse of her before he closed the door. She was standing smiling, very straight and neat, and looking very happy.

The taste of the American GI was responsible for most of the innovations along the Ginza, and it was worth remembering that they reflected the immaturities of youth—naturally enough, since the age average was low in the American armed forces. Thus it was not wholly fair to be overcritical of the garish beer halls and night clubs, as full of gay plastic color and light as the jukeboxes at home, for they filled very adequately an intense demand for release. In fact, Jack Rhyce thought the Cimaroon offered everything that he would have wanted when he was an undergraduate at Oberlin—air-conditioning, cold beer on draught, an enormous gaudy bar, a jazz orchestra, a Japanese torch singer, and dozens of tables with pretty, smiling Japanese hostesses. He half wished he were back in the army. It had been different in the paratroops in Burma.

Although it was only 5:15, the Cimaroon was already full. The brash notes of the orchestra, the high voice of the singer, and the chatter of the patrons over their drinks rose to such an intensity that his transient wish that he were a boy again vanished. Instead, it occurred to him that the noise would be an excellent background for a shot, and it could easily be minutes before anyone would know just what had happened. You had to consider seriously such contingencies in a place like the Cimaroon, as well as check the entrances and exits. These were limited, as far as he could observe, to a wide entrance on the street, and to two doors in back leading to service quarters. He stopped making these mental notes only when he reminded himself that he was not running the party and that instead he was in the guise of a foreign attaché.

Mr. Moto was waiting at a wall table, facing the door—a conventional position under the circumstances. He waved a welcome to Jack Rhyce in an exaggeratedly European manner.

"Beer, of course?" Mr. Moto said. "It is so cool and comfortable here."

It was cool but noisy, and Jack had a feeling that the Cimaroon did not belong in Japan or anywhere else. He took only a sip or two of beer because he disapproved of drinking before any such event as the one they were approaching.

"Everyone is posted," Mr. Moto said. "Ha-ha, we will use the same Buick in which I drove you."

"Have you looked for him all through this bulding?" Jack asked.

"Oh, yes," Mr. Moto said. "No sign. Are you thinking of something, Mr. Rhyce?"

"I'm just wondering whether he will be hiding until he sees her," Jack Rhyce said. "Maybe we were wrong in not having her drive up."

Mr. Moto thought for a few moments.

"I very much approve your thoroughness, Mr. Rhyce," he said. "It is too late. We might call her, from the manager's office."

"The office was a cubbyhole of a room, only a few paces from where they were sitting, and it was startlingly silent, once they had closed the door. She answered almost immediately.

"Ruth, we've got a second thought," he said. "Maybe you'd better take a taxi and come here at six o'clock. Get out and stand by the main entrance.

"Okay," she said. "It's nice that great minds think alike sometimes. I'll be there."

He felt a momentary qualm as they returned to the table, simply because he disliked revising a plan on such short notice. It showed once again that he was not sure of himself when it came to Ruth Bogart; and besides, any revision always presented a new set of factors. Yet he had not the slightest premonition that he had made an error until it was six o'clock. It was six and there was no sign of any American girl, let alone Ruth Bogart, outside the Cimaroon.

"There is traffic," Mr. Moto said. "She may have misjudged the time. Do not let it upset you for five more minutes, Mr. Rhyce."

He had not meant to show his feelings, nor had he thought he would, for he had believed that experience had made him immune to sudden reverses—but he had not felt a shock of helpless panic for years comparable to what he experienced then. Everyone went wrong sometime, he said to himself, and this was it for him.

"I'd better telephone and see if she's left," he said.

"When he reached the manager's office and gave the number he noticed that his hands shook. It did no good to tell himself that he must quiet down. He had never in his life wished for anything so vehemently as that he might hear her voice answer, but there was no answer. She had gone. Outside the office he was startled at the sight of his own face, reflected from one of the wall mirrors.

"I think they've double-crossed us," he said.

Mr. Moto looked very grave, and glanced at his wrist watch.

"If so, I share your feelings," he said. "But wait, We gain nothing by hurrying, Mr. Rhyce. Remember that you yourself made her wait ten minutes, only not to appear too prompt. She may be doing this, too—and please remember just one thing more."

"What's that" Jack Rhyce answered.

"I am to blame as much as you are Mr. Rhyce. And—what is it they say in America? The show must go on in any case, Mr. Rhyce?"

He did not like the appraising look in Mr. Moto's eyes. After all, he was representing the Intelligence of his country.

"Damn it," he said. "Don't you tell me how to behave."

"That is better," Mr. Moto said. "I know I would not need to remind you, Mr. Rhyce."

Jack Rhyce stood up.

"I'm going now," he said.

"Where, please?" Mr. Moto asked.

He restrained his impatience. After all, he represented the Service.

"Back to the hotel," he said. "It's the place to start from, isn't it?"

He still did not like the inquisitive, measuring look in Mr. Moto's eyes. The Japanese was waiting to see how he would behave.

"Yes, that will be the proper procedure," Mr. Moto said. "I shall go with you. They have won this game. He was brighter than we thought him."

It was accepted practice on any battlefield to draw opponents to one spot, and then to strike in another. There were four of them in the car, two Japanese in front and he and Mr. Moto behind. They sat in rigid silence until they were slowed by the traffic at the Shinbashi station.

"I'm so very sorry," Mr. Moto said.

The remark jangled against the raw edges of Jack's nerves. The Japanese were always expressing sorrow which they did not mean.

"To hell with it," he said.

"I did not mean so sorry for you," Mr. Moto said, "as much as so sorry we both were mistaken. I am not being personal, Mr. Rhyce."

"Do you think they got her in the room or outside?" Mr. Rhyce asked.

"It would be the room, I think," Mr. Moto answered. "It would have been worked carefully."

He was relieved by that opinion because, if true, his asking her to join them was not responsible for what had happened. The car turned in the drive of the Imperial Hotel, and the lotus pool and the low building looked as ugly as his thoughts.

"Let us not appear too worried," Mr. Moto said. "I shall ask a question or two and join you in your room. I think we had better set up the telephone again."

"Why the telephone?" Jack Rhyce asked.

Mr. Moto gave him another inquiring look.

"Because they will be making contact with you," he said, "allowing only time for your return from the Cimaroon. Why else would they have caught her, Mr. Rhyce?"

What had come over him, he wondered, not to have thought of it before? He should at least have conceived of the possibility and have taken suitable precautions. Instead, he had been drawn off as easily as though he had been the third team. What had happened that had made them able to outguess him? At some point something had occurred to give away the show. It might have been something that night in the place called the Main Bar, or it might have been something that morning in the office of Mr. Harry Pender. Some detail had gone wrong somewhere, and now it was futile to guess what it might have been. Play as safe as possible all across the board was another maxim of the business, and he had disobeyed it by not having her room guarded.

He had certainly acted like the third team. Neither his mind nor hers had been on their work. They had been thinking about the outside.

He never forgot the appearance of her room. What engraved it so vividly on his memory was that everything was exactly as he had anticipated. The lock of the door had been forced by someone who had examined the lock before, with an instrument that had made it give immediately. The only sign of struggle was an overturned suitcase that had fallen from the bed to the floor. Her handbag was gone from the table. They must have taken it with them when they left, but they had not bothered with any further search. Even with her gone, her personality was left. There was the faint scent of the Guerlain perfume she used, and the bottle was still on her dressing table beside her gold-backed comb and brush. He picked up the brush and gazed at the initials on the back, R. B. She had started packing, just as he had suggested, and her dresses and her lingerie that had fallen from the overturned suitcase still showed signs of careful folding. Mr. Moto came in while he was holding one of her dresses. Jack Rhyce laid it down gently.

"They were not seen to leave," Mr. Moto said; "but then, no one was watching. We should have thought of this and taken measures, but the conversation on the telephone sounded so very true. I am so sorry. I am also very much ashamed."

"You and me both," Jack Rhyce said. "Sorry and ashamed. What are you doing now?"

Mr. Moto, having adjusted the broken lock so that the door would close, had opened his briefcase.

"The telephone," he said. "We must both listen, I think."

"I don't see why you're so damn sure they'll call," Jack said.

"Please, it is inevitable," Mr. Moto answered. "They would not have taken her otherwise. They will call quickly before you go elsewhere. I have already taken steps to have the call traced, but I fear it will not help. They are so very clever. Excuse. They know you are in love with her, Mr. Rhyce."

The words came out brutally in the ravaged room, and Jack felt his face grow brick-red, but he knew he had no right to be angry. His rights to be particular about anything had gone because of his stupidity.

"It was a mistake," he said. "We both knew we were damn fools—not that it does any good."

"Please, I am not criticizing," Mr. Moto said. "It may be a mistake, but sometimes one cannot help them, Mr. Rhyce."

"Unless it is necessary," Jack Rhyce said, "I'd just as soon not bring this subject up again."

It was infuriating to have something which should have belonged only to him and her tossed out in the open to be used as a point in a game. Mr. Moto's manner was considerate; his voice silkily smooth when he answered.

I do not wish to offend," he said. "I only speak because I think you should be ready. I think they will be prepared to make you an interesting proposal, Mr. Rhyce."

Jack gave a start. He had been staring at the overturned suitcase, and his thoughts had wandered from what Mr. Moto was saying.

"What sort?" he asked.

"I do not know," Mr. Moto said. "So much of our work is always in the dark, but I think you have come close to finding something that worries them, Mr. Rhyce."

It was true about working in the dark. Even when a hand was half-played you never could be wholly sure where the other cards lay, but already Mr. Moto's words had aroused a suspicion in Jack Rhyce that gripped him with icy fingers. Bill Gibson's cynical statement about safety in sex flashed across his memory. He cleared his throat.

"Do you think they're going to propose a swap?" he asked.

When Mr. Moto answered, his voice was soft and measured.

"Yes, Mr. Rhyce," he said. "I believe they will offer to bring Miss Bogart safely back if you will agree to leave here. You see, I think they are afraid you know too much."

Jack Rhyce felt a spasm in the pit of his stomach and his heart was beating faster, but still he could notice that Mr. Moto was watching him very carefully. He was even able to resent the detached critical manner and the air of academic curiosity. Mr. Moto was weighing him in an Oriental, not a European, balance.

"You will have to make a decision as to whether to leave or whether to stay," he said; "and I am so very much afraid I cannot help you, Mr. Rhyce."

Of course he had to make up his mind, and he had the training to do it.

"Damn you"—he said, and the sound of his voice warned him that he must compose himself—"you don't have to help me."

Mr. Moto was still watching him very carefully.

"So sorry for you, Mr. Rhyce," he said. "Will you have a cigarette?"

"No, thanks," Jack Rhyce said. "I told you I didn't smoke."

"Oh, I remember. Excuse, please," Mr. Moto said. "When I was a younger man I, too, was abstemious, in that and in other regards—"

Jack felt his face redden again. He took a quick stride across the room.

"That's about all I'm going to take from you," he said.

Mr. Moto watched him without moving a muscle.

"You do not allow me to finish," he said. "I was about to add that, even so, one cannot give up everything."

Just then the telephone rang. The small bell had a laughing, mocking sound, and he was not prepared for the sound because he had not been wholly convinced that they would call. Mr. Moto slipped the earphones over his head.

"Answer quickly, please," he whispered. "Seem to be anxious, please."

When Jack picked up the telephone he was steadier. He even felt a spasm of annoyance that Mr. Moto should tell him how to act. He had had it bad before—as bad as the small man who was listening had ever had.

"Hello," he said. His voice was even and agreeable. He had learned long ago to give nothing away by voice. He was playing the old game of wits, and the fact that the telephone had rung at all confirmed Mr. Moto's assertion that he had something they wanted.

"Hello." He recognized the voice on the other end of the line immediately. "That's you, isn't it, Jack?"

"Indeed it is," he said.

His response was affable and easy. He had control of himself again.

"This is Harry Pender, Jack. You recognize my voice, don't you?"

"Well, well, Harry," Jack Rhyce said. "It's nice of you to give me a ring. I sure do recognize your voice. I'd know it anywhere."

"Okay, Jack," Harry Pender said, "then let's cut out the monkey business. You and I won't have to do our clowning from now on in."

"Thanks," Jack Rhyce said. "That's a big relief. Okay. What's on your mind?"

"We've got Ruth Bogart here. I thought you'd like to know."

Though he had anticipated it, he found it hard to control himself, and the instant while he struggled for calmness could not have been lost on Mr. Pender.

"Thanks for letting me know," he said. "I was beginning to be worried about her."

There was a good-natured laugh on the other end of the wire.

"We thought you might be. Well, take it easy, Jack. She's right here, and we wish you were, too. And she's happy and comfortable as of now, Jack. I'll let you speak to her in a minute."

"Why, thanks," Jack Rhyce said, "thanks a lot."

He heard Harry Pender laugh again.

"You know who I am, don't you, Jack? I mean you've got me taped by now?"

"Yes," Jack Rhyce said, "I've got a pretty good working idea, but I'm quite a ways away from the files."

Harry Pender's laugh had a corroding effect. He was too brisk and too excited, obviously on edge.

"I may as well admit," he said, "that I was pretty dumb regarding you. All of us were. In fact, we never got wise to you until just before lunchtime today. Nice going and congratulations, Jack."

At least it bolstered his ego to know that he had seen right in believing that he had been in the clear over the week end.

"Thanks for the compliment," he said. "Anybody in our line of work appreciates a kind word, Harry."

"No reason why we shouldn't all be friends in this thing, Jack,"

Harry Pender said, "even if we are on different sides of the fence. That's the thought I want you to hold for the next minute or two if you can manage, Jack. As I was saying, we have been sort of dumb around here, but you haven't operated in the East much, have you?"

"Why, no, Harry," Jack Rhyce answered. "This is my first time out here on a job, in case the fact is useful."

"Well, that's what threw me, Jack," Harry Pender said. "And you did look damn good for what you were, and the boys had cleared you in 'Frisco. When we heard you'd been looking at the bookshops, I admit, I should have taken the news more seriously, instead of discounting it. Maybe you'd still be fooling me, if it hadn't been for a very nice guy who just blew in here, by the name of Skirov. Remember him, Jack?"

"The name's familiar," Jack Rhyce said, "but I can't say that I remember him exactly. I don't think I ever saw him, but I'm sure I'd recognize him."

"Well, he remembers you, boy," Harry Pender said. "He saw you in Moscow back in '46. He was a waiter at one of those big parties, and passed you caviar. Just as soon as I described you he clicked. You were talking to Molotov back in '46. You were saying all men are brothers."

Jack exchanged a glance with Mr. Moto. The Chief had said it was a damn fool thing to say, and the Chief had been, as usual, correct. Never try to be conspicuous, the Chief had said.

"Now we're on the subject," Jack Rhyce said, "I was kind of slow in locating you myself, although I had you down for a phony the first time you came in. It's nice to know that Skirov's safe in town, and thank you for the information, because we're interested in Skirov."

A pause followed and Jack Rhyce, who had never listened harder, was conscious of faint sounds of others listening on the far end of the line.

"You've been real busy during your stay here, haven't you, Jack?" Harry Pender said.

"Yes," Jack Rhyce said, "busy as a bird dog."

"And dogs have their day. Ever hear that one, Jack?"

He fought down the frustration that was growing on him, and spoke with patience.

"Let's cut out the hamming, Harry," he said, "and get down to the point."

"All right, Jack," Harry Pender spoke soothingly. "We're busy here, too, as you may have gathered—busy enough so we didn't want Bill Gibson around, and we don't want you, either, Jack. Do you get my drift?"

"I get some vague idea," Jack said. "Is it a threat or a promise, Harry?"

There was another silence on the line, longer than the one that proceeded it.

"It's neither, Jack," he heard Harry Pender answer. "It's a firm offer that we're making."

His eyes encountered Mr. Moto's half-inquisitive, half-blank stare. He felt as though a cord were being drawn tight about his head. Anybody in the business could have told what was coming."

"Well," he said, "go ahead and make it. I've got an open mind."

He had been standing all that time. Now he would have reached for a chair and sat down if the Japanese had not been watching.

"I thought you'd have an open mind, Jack." Harry Pender said, and his voice was placatingly gentle. "That's why I'm going to such trouble to have this little chat—because now that we've pooled our notes here, we know you've a real reputation. Skirov, for instance, knows about that job you pulled at Istanbul, and that other one in Athens. We know you're a pro, Jack, and not someone off an analytic couch."

"Go ahead," Jack said. "It could be, if I'm a pro, that I'm tracing this call, Harry."

"It could be," Harry Pender said, "but it takes time, and we're moving out of here when I hang up."

"Then let's cut out the hamming," Jack Rhyce said. "I'm waiting for that offer, Harry."

It came in mild, insinuating tones.

"You're fond of Ruth, here, aren't you, Jack? You wouldn't want to have her taken to the mainland, for instance, or go through any kind of drill? She wouldn't be much fun to see afterwards, would she? And you know, they do keep alive—surprisingly often—don't you, Jack?"

Jack Rhyce tried to laugh. It would have been shameful if he had betrayed his pain.

"I understand your build-up. Why don't you get to the point?" he said.

"Don't get mad," Harry Pender said. "The point is, we're busy here, and we don't want you monkeying around. We want you the hell out of here. How does that one sound, Jack?"

He felt his heart beat faster. Mr. Moto had been right. They thought he might know something that was dangerous.

"If you want it straight, Harry," he said. "I don't like this town much, or the folks in it, including you."

"Now you're talking," Harry Pender said. "I had an idea we could get together, Jack. You'd like to have Ruth Bogart back at the hotel tonight, safe and sound, wouldn't you, and you know what I mean by safe and sound, don't you? If not, there's a pal of yours named Big Ben here who might explain it. Would you like to talk with Ben, Jack?"

He could hear Big Ben singing at the other end of the wire. He was singing "Every Day Is Ladies' Day with Me." Jack Rhyce put his hand to his forehead. His face had grown damp, but he kept his voice steady.

"Let's cut out the technique," he said. "Consider you've scared hell out of me. Yes, I'd like Ruth back safe and sound. So what's the proposition?"

"It's easy." Harry Pender's voice was as warm and as enthusiastic as a radio announcer's advertising a commercial. "Half an hour from now Ruth here will be knocking at your door. There's a night flight leaving for Honolulu at eleven, and we have two tickets for you free. Merely pack your bags, and shut up and go to the airport. How do you like that, Jack?"

"It sounds wonderful," he said, and he noticed that there was genuine relief in Harry Pender's voice. He was thankful that, under the circumstances, he could still put two and two together.

"I thought you'd get the point, Jack," Harry Pender said. "There's nothing like being reasonable."

"That's right," Jack answered carefully. "And how do I know we'll ever get to the airport, Harry?"

"You've got to trust us for that, Jack," Harry Pender said, "Just the way we're going to trust you. Give me your word—you communicate with no one from the minute you set down that telephone, and Ruth here will be back with you in half an hour, with a nice boy from our office to expedite your passage. And you have my word, you'll get that plane, Jack. How does it sound to you? Would you like to speak to Ruth?"

"Yes, I'd like to speak to her," he said. There was a pause, and he was glad that it was not a long one. He was trying to think of some palliation—some way out. Then he heard her voice, and it was excruciating agony to hear it. Her voice was faint and level.

"Hello, Jack."

"Ruth," he asked, "are you all right?"

"I'm all right, Jack," she said, "but don't do it. Don't—" Her voice was choked off in a stifled gasp that ended in a scream.

Mr. Moto was watching him, and Mr. Moto's expression had changed when their glances met. Jack could not tell whether the expression was one of sympathy or surprise. He only knew that his own expression had revealed his pain. It was over in an instant because Harry Pender's voice was back on the wire.

"Sorry for the interruption," he said. "Will you take the proposition, or won't you?"

"Suppose I don't?" Jack Rhyce said.

"We'll handle you anyway," Harry Pender said. "Give us twenty minutes and Ruth will tell us what you know. Won't you, Ruth?"

Jack Rhyce felt a new wave of nausea sweep over him, and he set down the telephone. There was one thing certain—she did not know enough. He sank down in a chair, drew out a handkerchief and mopped his forehead. Then the telephone rang again.

"Let it ring," he said. "To hell with it. Let it ring." For a moment he felt as though he were going to be sick to his stomach. For a moment he could not speak.

"Take those goddam earphones off," he said. "Excuse me. I'll be all right in a minute." He felt his shoulders move convulsively and he hid his face in his hands for a second.

"Excuse me," he said.

"That is quite all right," Mr. Moto said. "Would you like a little whisky, Mr. Rhyce?"

Jack Rhyce shook his head.

"You didn't think I'd do it, did you?" Jack Rhyce said.

"No, I did not," Mr. Moto said. "You are a very nice man. But please be easier in your mind, for you did what you should have, Mr. Rhyce."

"How in hell can I be easy in my mind," he said, "when we should have put a guard here?"

Mr. Moto raised his hand and let it fall abruptly to his side.

"It is something that we'll regret always—you more than I, I am so very much afraid," he said. "But in life we cannot relive regrets."

"That's right," Jack said. "Excuse me again, I'm all right now."

He was far from all right. He knew that he would never be the man he had been a hour or so before. There was certain things that could haunt one always—things that time itself could never solve. But he had to go on with it. He had to keep moving straight ahead, and all he could do was to try to make what was happening to Ruth Bogart to some extent worth while.

His training had not left him. He had learned long ago not to forget words or pauses on a a telephone.

"Pender said a boy from the office, didn't he?" Jack Rhyce said. "That was a slip, I think."

"I'm not quite sure that I follow you," Mr. Moto answered.

Jack Rhyce was not impatient. He actually did not care whether Mr. Moto followed him. His mind was moving forward to another fact.

"We know right from the horse's mouth that Skirov is in town," he said. It was Skirov who would be calling the plays, now that he was in town. It was necessary to give thought to this other personality. "That's another mistake of Pender's. Maybe we can connect with him now. Anyway, there's no use hanging around here any longer."

"No," Mr. Moto answered. "We must go to where the call came from. They will have gone, but there may be traces."

"I wouldn't do that," Jack said. At least his mind was moving forward again out of the nightmare of self-incrimination that had entangled it. Mr. Moto's statement was still true, that they would not have attempted what they had if they had not been afraid that he knew something, and Harry Pender had said himself that they had not guessed his identity until just before lunch. He remembered the accelerated swing of the glasses in Mr. Pender's hand that morning when he had pursued the subject of liberal politicians, and he recalled the exact point in their conversation when the swing had changed.

All that Intelligence finally consisted of was finding facts, evaluating them and fitting them together until they formed a larger fact. A lot of it was choice and chance. You often could not tell whether you were right until the very end, and there were many times when you had to leave the path of painfully accumulated evidence to play a hunch. All he had left was a hunch—not a good one, but one which at least could fit the circumstances as he knew them. He was prepared to play it because it was all that was left, and it was better to move than to do nothing.

"I wouldn't go chasing down that call," he said again, "and if you do, I won't go with you. Did you ever hear of a man named Noshimura Hata?"

"Oh, yes," Mr. Moto said. "I know Mr. Hata."

"He's a very important liberal, isn't he?" Jack Rhyce asked.

"Yes," Mr. Moto said. "Where did you hear of him, please?"

"In Mr. Pender's office, this morning," Jack Rhyce said. "Pender said he was head and shoulders above any other politician in the liberal party, and afterwards I think he was sorry that he had said it."

Mr. Moto's gold teeth gleamed, but he was not smiling.

"So—" Mr. Moto said, "so—"

"It's only a guess," Jack Rhyce said, "but maybe it's worth a gamble. I can only tell you what I think."

"Yes," Mr. Moto said. "Thank you, and tell me what you think."

"I think they were going to kill this Mr. Hata tomorrow—but now I think they will do it tonight, now that I didn't take their offer. I'd get him out of his house, if I were you. I'd be delighted to wait there for whoever is coming to do the job, and I'll bet it will be Big Ben."

Mr. Moto was on his feet.

"I think that is a very nice suggestion, Mr. Rhyce," he said, "and I think you are a very nice man. Let me have the telephone. We must arrange to move at once."

"It's only a guess, you know," Jack Rhyce said.

"Yes, but one must always guess," Mr. Moto answered. "I shall be there with you, Mr. Rhyce, to wait for whoever may be coming."

Jack Rhyce had a friendlier feeling for Mr. Moto than any he had previously experienced.

"I don't know whether you are a very nice man or not," he said, "but anyway, you're willing to take a chance."

"Thank you so very much," Mr. Moto said. "And now if you will move, please, I shall use the telephone, Mr. Rhyce."

Mr. Moto spoke Japanese. His voice was not strident like that of most men in authority; instead it was gentle, musical and melodious. Jack Rhyce stood for a moment listening. It was a matter of logistics, men, motors and distance. As he listened, his own anguish, which had been dulled for the last few minutes, returned to him again. He could control it now, but he knew that it would be with him always. He walked to the overturned suitcase and replaced the tumbled-out clothing very carefully in an order of which he hoped she would have approved. He walked to the dressing table, picked up the comb and brush and perfume bottle, and put all three in the suitcases. He touched his lips to the back of the brush, and he did not care in the least whether Mr. Moto saw him or not. He closed the suitcase and snapped the lock, and, as he did so, he knew in his heart that he was doing all he ever could for Ruth Bogart.

## 19

HE MUST have been on fifty similar cases since he had been connected with the business, although in this one the setting was more interesting than in many. Again it was the old matter of waiting. Again, it was the trap or ambush or whatever technical name you might choose to give it. But this time, from the very beginning, there had been a feeling of promise in the air. Since so much of Intelligence consisted of moving tentatively into the unknown and never knowing exactly when you would finally collide with a stone wall or step upon the deadfall, it was never wise to leave premonition out of any calculation. Again and again in his professional career Jack Rhyce had experienced the gambler's conviction that the right numbers were coming up, and if you had it, it was surprisingly apt to be correct. You could call it nonsense, or fourth dimension, but it was there—whatever name you gave it. He knew as sure as fate that things were going to work that night. If you sacrificed enough, he sometimes thought, you were bound to get something in return, and the only thing that we wanted just then was to see the job through, and meet Big Ben in the process. He had paid down enough for the privilege. For the rest of his natural life he had given up peace of mind. Even though she had told him to go ahead—and her voice and her scream would echo in his memory always—he would wonder whether duty had been worth it. Even afterwards his ingenuity would work on belated plans that might have saved her and still have achieved what they were there for. Undoubtedly, given time, he would figure out a way.

The actual plan for assassination was conventional and safe. As it turned out later, the prognosis was correct that it would look like an American job. A stolen American army car was in the picture, and the only thing that gave Jack Rhyce a shock was that wallet subsequently discovered on the premises—purported to be his, with excellently forged identity papers considering the short space of time allowed for their preparation. They had said that they would handle him, and they had meant it either way.

The house and grounds stood in one of Tokyo's most comfortable and desirable districts on land not far from the palace grounds themselves. In the old days the great Tokugawa fortress had been surrounded by concentric ramparts. Beyond these had been a further ring of houses occupied by the Shoguns' most trusted retainers. Further back the houses of the minor officials had stood, including the land of the Hata family which had been subdivided toward the end of the last century. The house of Mr. Noshimura Hata still occupied part of it. Actually, as it happened, Jack Rhyce never set eyes on the liberal politician, because Mr. Hata had been carried to a safer spot before Mr. Moto and he made their appearance. So also had the servants, who had been replaced by operators. The operation had run with a smoothness that had impresed Jack Rhyce professionally.

The lights were on by the gate in the small front garden, and the larger garden with the lawn in back was also lighted by stone lanterns.

"It is fortunate," Mr. Moto said, "that Mr. Hata likes to leave many of his ground lights on at night. He is afraid of burglars, which is amusing I think, when he is such a very liberal man."

After what had happened earlier, rigorous precautions were taken in case the house was watched; a schedule had been made of the household routine. This had all taken time, but it was worth it. It was half-past eight o'clock once they were inside the house, and Mr. Hata's retiring hour was ten.

"First he walks through the garden," Mr. Moto said, "Having put on the kimono and recited Buddhist prayers. I shall be Mr. Hata, and you may watch me from the house. We must all be very careful, but I do not think the killing will be in the garden."

The austere charm of that house formed a violent contrast to Jack Rhyce's thoughts. The sparseness of its furnishings, the bare space of its walls, gave a balanced beauty to its interior that was a rebuke to the overcluttered houses back at home. Space had a more eloquent appeal in an overcrowded country like Japan. It was prized more than material possessions, and Jack Rhyce had never been more conscious of its beauty than he had been when he stood on the resilient floor matting in the sleeping room of Mr. Hata's house. It was a room intended solely for rest. Aside from the bedding prepared for the night and a black lacquer head rest, there were no other furnishings except a low table and a scroll painting of flowers in a niche sunk into the inside wall with an arrangement of flowers beneath it. The outer wall was formed entirely of sliding glass panels that opened on Mr. Hata's garden, and on that warm evening the panels had been pushed back so that the garden with its stone lanterns was a projection of the room itself. Although his thoughts were still in turmoil, Jack Rhyce was not immune to the garden's beauty. He was vaguely aware of a way of life different from his own, more serene and more peaceful, and one deriving pleasure from a few small things rather than from ostentatious masses of larger ones. The garden from the standpoint of area was a very small affair, but assiduous art gave the illusion of its being a Japanese countryside. The lawn was a plain, the carefully twisted and trained pines and the small deciduous trees that bordered it became in imagination wind-swept forests. The eccentrically eroded stones that had been placed in relationship to each other only after hours of study were mountains and wild country. The miniature chain of ponds magnified themselves to lakes. While watching this miniature achievement, one could think with sorrow how fast the world was changing, and how a little time might be left, tomorrow, even in Japan, for a garden like Mr. Hata's. The garden spelled peace, but it did not give him peace of mind that night.

Nevertheless, he had not been outwardly restless. The business had taught him long ago the patience of a fisherman or a hunter, who could be alerted at any second—but there was more to it than that. Patience in the business demanded an endurance that raised the watcher beyond self, to a realm where personal consideration meant nothing. It resembled an artist's dedication, although it could hardly be said that the business was an art. He had not been restless, because of training; but his thoughts were beyond control. He was back again looking at the suitcase that had tumbled on the floor. He tortured himself again with what might have been if she had not been left alone, with how she had looked on that long drive to the mountains, with what she had said when they were alone at Wake, and finally with the knowledge that everything was ended and all contact had been cut forever. He could not think what was happening to her now, or speculate on whether she was alive or dead. It was best to know that it was absolutely ended.

He was waiting in a corner of the sleeping room when Mr. Moto stepped through the paneled windows from the garden.

"Is it time to turn off the garden lights?" Jack Rhyce asked.

"Yes," Mr. Moto said, "as soon as I have seen arrangements are understood, the house will go to sleep. We may still be a long while waiting."

It was impossible to know how long they would wait, but by then they both must have believed they would not draw a blank. There was a feeling in the air, a telepathic sense of something already moving.

"When the garden lights go out," Mr. Moto said, "I shall ask you to step outside, Mr. Rhyce, and stand by the corner of the house. I shall rest on the bed. The windows will be open. I think he will approach through the garden and attempt to enter by the windows. When he is near enough you may move on him, Mr. Rhyce, but please let us be patient and wait until he is near, for we do not wish shooting. There are so many questions in a neighborhood whenever shots are fired."

It was Mr. Moto's party and not his.

"Don't worry. I haven't got a gun," Jack Rhyce said, "only the jack you gave me."

"It is so much better," Mr. Moto said. "There are others here who will take the further steps if necessary. If he enters this garden or this house, I do not think he will get away from us."

"That's fine with me," Jack Rhyce said. "I want him out as much as you do."

Both his tone and his wish showed him that he had traveled a long way in the last few hours. He had never waited avidly wanting to kill before. The desire was neither practical nor professional in a field where personal wishes should never have intruded.

"So glad you agree," Mr. Moto said. "He will plan to use a knife, I think. Perhaps you would like one also, Mr. Rhyce?"

"It is not necessary," Jack Rhyce said. He had a tingling feeling of anticipation which was premature when there might still be a long period of waiting. "He won't cut me. There's only one thing I want."

"Yes?" Mr. Moto said. "What is that, Mr. Rhyce?"

"I want you to let me handle him. I want him to know I'm here."

"It will be a pleasure," Mr. Moto said, "if he comes through the garden and not through the house, when he will be my responsibility, Mr. Rhyce."

"Even so," Jack Rhyce said, "I'd like him to know I'm here."

"I can understand your viewpoint, Mr. Rhyce," Mr. Moto said. "I hope so very much that he will know we both are here, but there can be no chances."

"We won't miss any," Jack Rhyce said.

He had learned how to take cover as skillfully as any jungle fighter in Japan. When the lights were out he blended into the shadows by the angle of the house so completely that he was a part of the shrubbery. The night was warm as a Burmese rain forest, but drier, and the glow of the city's lights was reflected in the sky. The grounds and the house were peacefully silent in spite of the monotones of the great city that rose all round them. The noises of the Orient were more eccentric and more staccato than those of the West, shriller voices, shriller music, shriller laughter. Still, it was possible to attune the ear to closer sounds. A stirring of the bushes near the driveway revealed the presence of one of the guards and Jack Rhyce could hear a whisper of breeze in the pine trees.

The approach was made with such care and deliberation that Jack Rhyce had heard the first sound fully ten minutes before Big Ben slipped through the bushes at the far end of the garden and began his walk across the lawn toward the bedroom ell. He moved unhurriedly with a noiseless, deliberate confidence which showed he was wholly familiar with the house and grounds. Once he was on the lawn the background of the trees and shrubbery combined with the lights reflected in the sky made him stand out clearly. He wore a seersucker suit, almost identical with the one Jack Rhyce had worn earlier in the evening. He paused to listen as he drew near the house. He would have been an easy target for a pistol with a silencer, Jack Rhyce was thinking, and he was glad that the idea had not crossed Mr. Moto's mind. He wanted Big Ben to know that he was there. Ben was drawing nearer, lazily, gracefully. When he was a few yards from the house he reached in his pocket, drew out a knife and switched open the blade carelessly. Jack Rhyce coughed gently, but loudly enough to hold the other momentarily motionless. Then before Big Ben could move, he was on top of him, and his blackjack had struck the knife out of the hand holding it. Big Ben took a step backward; he must have known in that second that he could not get away. Jack Rhyce spoke softly, as though there were actually sleepers in the house.

"It's me, Ben. It's Jack." He could not see the expression on Big Ben's face, but the laugh was all that was necessary.

"Hello, you gum-shoe bastard," he said. "That girl of yours was pretty good, but she didn't last for long."

The words, and not the time or place, robbed Jack Rhyce of his judgment. He had told himself long ago that it would be unsafe to close with Big Ben, yet that was what he did; and before he could get a wrestling hold, Ben had him by the throat. The feel of the hands was what cleared Jack Rhyce's head even before the thought flashed through him that his neck would be broken in seconds. He was in luck to be close enough to bring up his knee before Big Ben moved clear, but he had to strike again before the hold relaxed. There was a vicious moment when they rolled together on the ground. Before Jack was able to get a full swing to the jaw, he could feel Ben's thumbs groping for his eyes. He rolled free and was on his feet while Big Ben was still on hands and knees. He delivered a kick with all his force to the side of the bleeding head, and Big Ben rolled over on his face.

Ruth Bogart had been right about the crepe-soled shoes. Hard leather, lumberman's boots, would have been better. Then he felt arms, holding him, and he heard Mr. Moto speak.

"That is enough, Mr. Rhyce," he said. "You can leave him to the others now, I think. It would be so much nicer, as you Americans say, if you were not killing, Mr. Rhyce. Perhaps you would feel unhappy about it later. Americans are such sentimental people."

He felt his breath coming in gasps that made it hard for him to be able to speak.

"He's not half dead," he said.

"No," Mr. Moto answered, "but I do not think we need worry about the ultimate result. My men are very conscientious, and I am afraid you will have to wash, and rearrange your clothing. You did very well indeed, but I was glad I had a knife with which to strike him in the back. He was so very strong. Let us go. We are not required here any longer, Mr. Rhyce."

Jack Rhyce's first impression was one of shame, that he had not been capable of finishing Big Ben without Mr. Moto's intervention; but as far as he was concerned, the thing was over. It was something that never would be repeated, and now he had to move on to something else. Again there was nothing but a hunch to work on, but again he had the gambler's instinct. Besides, there was always some return if you paid a price.

"All right," he said. "That's one down. Now let's go and get this Skirov, or I'll go myself if you're not interested."

It was too dark to observe facial expression, but he heard the sharp intake of Mr. Moto's breath.

"I shall be very pleased to accompany you," he said. "But where is Skirov?"

Although it was only a hunch, it was still based on a line of reasoning. Skirov, who always kept in the background, would be in a quiet place where he would not be likely to be under surveillance. He would not be at any headquarters. He would be in communication, but removed from the center of trouble.

"It's only a guess," Jack Rhyce said, "but it's an educated one. I believe he's in Mr. Pender's office in the Asia Friendship League. Anyway, it may be worth trying."

"And what makes you think that?" Mr. Moto asked.

"Do you remember Pender on the telephone?" Jack Rhyce answered. "He was too damned elated on that telephone. He was talking about a boy from the office seeing us off for the airport. I think he made a slip when he used the word 'office.'"

He heard Mr. Moto laugh. He was beginning to understand the various meanings of Japanese laughter.

"It would be a pleasure to try," Mr. Moto said. "I think, Mr. Rhyce, that you are a very clever man."

## 20

"So he fell out the window?" the Chief asked.

"Yes, sir," Jack Rhyce answered. "Eight stories, from Mr. Pender's office in the Asia Friendship League."

"You're sure he was Skirov?" the Chief asked.

"Yes, sir," Jack Rhyce said. "There was time to take photographs and fingerprints before he fell out the window. This Japanese—this Mr. Moto—checked them with his records. I have them with me, sir."

"Moto," the Chief said. "That's not a name. It is a suffix."

"Yes," Jack Rhyce answered. "That's what Bill Gibson told me."

He was having difficulty adjusting himself to the results of plane travel. Less than forty-eight hours previously he had been in

Tokyo, and now he still had the feeling experienced by other air passengers, that some part of him had been left behind, and this illusion was sharper than it had ever been before. Certainly, after other trips, the Chief's office had seemed like home, or if not home, a threshold to rest and safety; but now it extended no such welcome.

"Oh, yes, Gibson," the Chief said. "That's a tough one. It's no fun sitting here on this job, hearing that people you've raised and been fond of are gone. It's no fun because you can't do anything except send out more. Maybe you'll face it yourself sometime. I'm not going to hold down this desk forever, Buster."

He was still such a long way from home that it had almost skipped his mind that the Chief sometimes called him Buster. At another time, the open hint that the Chief had given him that he might be in the line would have awakened a thrill of pleasure, and his conscience told him that it should right now.

"I don't think Bill had a hard time, sir," he said. "I'm afraid it was different for Miss Bogart."

The Chief picked up a pencil and tapped its eraser end softly on his desk.

"I've often wished this business were not coeducational," he said, "but then the score more than makes the trip pay off. We can scratch Skirov and this Big Ben character, but what's your evidence on Pender?"

"The word of this Mr. Moto," Jack Rhyce said; "and there was a piece in the paper before I left that Mr. Pender was struck and run over by a truck in Tokyo."

"It's a queer thing," the Chief said. "I used to be something of a specialist on the prewar Orient, but I never heard of this Moto. Of course, they're devious over there."

"You might have missed him because he was abroad, sir," Jack Rhyce said. "If you want my suggestion, I would inquire from State. From what he said, he would have been some sort of embassy attaché. And I have another line on him. He said his cousin is a Baron who owns a semi-European house in Miyanoshita—that is, if he was being straight. I can fill out the description and get it in the works."

"Yes," the Chief said. "We ought to get a line on him. It's hard to understand why Bill Gibson didn't know him."

"I have a hunch that maybe this Moto is like you, sir," Jack Rhyce said, "from one or two things he let go."

"If it's all the same with you," the Chief said, "I'd rather not be like a Jap. I don't forget the war."

"I didn't mean it that way, sir," Jack Rhyce said. "But now you've brought the matter up, I'd rather be like Mr. Moto than most of them. I only intended to suggest that he's behind the scenes like you in some dummy office. I don't believe he steps out front often. He's getting on, you know, for the rough stuff, Chief."

"That's right," the Chief said. "I'm getting on, myself. As I said, I won't be warming this chair indefinitely. It is only a question of whom I pull out from the rough stuff, as you call it, to occupy it. But let's stay with one thing at a time. I'd like to get a little more of the feel of this Moto, Jack. I'd almost like to hop a plane and go over and take a look at him."

"I think you'd find it hard to come up with him, sir," Jack Rhyce said. "I don't think he'd have appeared at all if he hadn't set me down for this Big Ben. One thing else about him—he's as slick as a whistle with a shiv, and I ought to know."

He felt no enthusiasm for what he was saying, still, he was no longer being two things at once, as he sat there in the Chief's office. He was not a do-gooder any more, enamored of an enthusiastic American girl, whose profile he could not forget, whose hands were both strong and delicate, whose loyalty and humor were both impeccable. He was out from cover, and far from safety in sex.

"He sounds like a right guy," the Chief said.

"If I were guessing, I'd say he's from the nobility, sir," Jack Rhyce said, "or in the very high officer class. He might have been something in the Imperial household, educated in America, the East coast, I should say. But I'll get it all down on my report and put it in the works."

"Quick with a shiv," the Chief said. "It always amuses me, this talk about stabbing someone in the back. It's ten to one you hit a rib, and when someone's moving around anatomy doesn't count."

"As a matter of fact, sir," Jack Rhyce said, "the knife was one of those small samurai blades. I think it was partly in a rib because it was still in the back at the time I left."

"Well," the Chief said, "that's enough for a quick runover. Are there any other loose ends that we ought to tie up?"

"That's all, sir," Jack Rhyce said, "except for disposing of Miss Bogart's personal effects. I brought them with my luggage, and they're outside now."

"I'll attend to them," the Chief said. "That's one of the tough things about where I sit, Jack."

"By the way, sir," Jack Rhyce said, "I suppose Ruth Bogart is a cover name?"

"The Ruth's real, the Bogart isn't," the Chief said. "If I were you, I'd only be inquisitive when you're asked to be, Buster."

He appreciated the Chief's reproof, but also he resented it.

"When you've been in the business ten years, sir," he said, "and trained on the Farm, and have all your personality knocked out of you on the road, even so sometimes you can't help being personally interested if you have to throw in with someone for a while. Occasionally, in spite of finishing school, you can't help being human, sir."

The Chief picked up his pencil again, but he did not tap it on the desk. From where he sat, he had frequently had to deal with temperament. He understood better than most psychiatrists the inevitable results of long repressions.

"I forgot to remark, you're looking tired, Jack. I know you've had it rough," he said, "but I know you, and it's nothing that a couple of weeks off and some sleep won't fix."

His diagnosis could have been correct some weeks ago, but it was not right intrinsically any longer. Something had happened that was new and different from the moment Jack Rhyce had seen the empty room in the Imperial Hotel in Tokyo, yet he had not known exactly what had happened until the Chief rebuked his inquisitiveness.

"Even if I rest up," he said, "I'm afraid I'll still stay human, chief. I won't be the old smooth-running machine again."

The Chief smiled at him tolerantly.

"Listen, Buster," he said, "you're in no shape to analyze yourself right now. What you need is a shot in the arm and sleep. The Doc's in from the Farm today. He'll take you home and sit with you until you cork off. Never mind putting anything in the works until tomorrow afternoon. I know enough to get the framework started."

"Very well, sir," Jack Rhyce said, and he pushed back his chair.

"That's better," the Chief said. "That's my boy. Anything else on your mind before you go?"

"Only one thing else, sir," Jack Rhyce said. "If I can't know her name, I'd appreciate it if you could see your way clear to give me a photograph.

The Chief raised his eyebrows rebukingly and let his pencil drop to the desk, and the minute disorderly sound it made was an adequate measure of his surprise.

"So that's the way it was?" he said. "I wouldn't have thought it of you, Jack. I'm sorry for you, son."

Jack Rhyce was glad that the thing was in the open for once, and it would only be for once.

"That's the way it was," he said. "We fell in love like a couple of kids. We both knew it was a damn fool thing to do, but it didn't spoil the operation, Chief."

"She wouldn't have wanted it to," the Chief said. "She was a very good girl, Jack."

"She wanted me to go ahead," he said. "She told me to, over the telephone. Anyway, we couldn't have found her in time."

"You didn't tell me she spoke to you," the Chief said.

"I left it out," Jack answered. "Maybe I should have this time. It's something that belongs to her and me. As I was saying, sometimes you can't help being human, Chief."

He was talking too much, and he despised self-pity. He wanted the interview to finish.

"I'll tell you all about her someday," the Chief said, "but I don't believe now is quite the time."

"Thanks," Jack Rhyce answered, "if it's just the same to you, I'd rather not know any more about her, except what belonged to us. I admit it wasn't very much."

He stood up. He had not intended to speak his full mind, at that particular interview, but that brief talk about her had crystallized his thoughts.

"As I say, it wasn't much," he said. "We both knew we were being foolish, and we didn't have many opportunities to talk, but we both decided that we'd go back to the outside when we came home. She isn't here, but I'm going, anyway, sir."

"Now, wait a minute—" the Chief began—"this is all on the spur of the moment. Is it anything I said that made you come up with this?"

"No, sir," Jack Rhyce answered, "nothing you said, but I'm going to hand in my resignation, sir."

"Now, Jack," the Chief said, "you can't do that. You're the best man in the office. You're in line to follow me here. I as good as told you, didn't I? You'd be like a fish out of water, on the outside. You can't do this, Jack."

He was aware that what the Chief said was true. He had intended to talk it over and think it over, but instead it was done already.

"I've got reasons, sir," he said.

"All right," the Chief said. "Just name the reasons."

Jack Rhyce squared his shoulders and pulled his thoughts together.

"Things happen sometimes," he said, "that you can't put into words, sir. After what happened over there, even if I stayed on the job, I could never be the man I used to be. I felt it coming over me in Tokyo. Being with her made me too human, Chief, and when you get too human you get fallible, and when you get to thinking about the outside you get forgetful—part of you is on one side and part of you is on the other. Part of me's back there. I've lost something, and I'll never get it back."

The Chief was also on his feet. "You're talking off the top of your head," he said, "and everything you say is specious, Jack."

"You may be right, sir," Jack Rhyce said. "It isn't so much what I say as what I feel. And besides, she wanted me on the outside. She asked me to promise."

"Jack," the Chief said, "give yourself a chance before you start crossing Rubicons. You're going through what everyone in the outfit goes through periodically. I've seen it and heard it all. Sure, something chips off you every time you go through anything, but you're the kind it only makes sharper, Jack. I'm willing to make you a bet: in a week or so you'll want to stay in the business on acount of her, and not leave it because of her. You've got too much Moxie to take a step like that. Now don't interrupt me."

Jack Rhyce had cleared his throat but he had no intention of interrupting.

"I just want two promises from you," the Chief said. "Don't say anything to anyone about this talk, and promise me you won't make a decision until you've had that shot in the arm and two weeks away somewhere."

"All right," Jack said, "if that's the way you want it."

At any rate, he had said exactly what was on his mind, and he believed that he was right in everything he had stated, and he felt closer to her, now that he had spoken, than he had since he had gone. He knew as sure as fate that he was not coming back.